Craig Price was the kind of man that women loathe, despise, fear . . . and yet are attracted to as though by a magnet.

He horse-traded and gambled, mostly with a rigged deck. He bought companies, milked them, and threw them away. He met some attractive women—and he threw them away too . . .

Craig Price boasted that he'd known at least a hundred women intimately. At one time, in one place, he might, he bragged, have been capable of marrying any or all of them.

Also by Robert Ruark

SOMETHING OF VALUE
UHURU
THE HONEY BADGER
USE ENOUGH GUN

and published by Corgi Books

Robert Ruark

Poor No More

CORGI BOOKS
A DIVISION OF TRANSWORLD PUBLISHERS LTD

POOR NO MORE

A CORGI BOOK 0 552 08713 0

Originally published in Great Britain
by Hamish Hamilton Ltd.

PRINTING HISTORY
Hamish Hamilton edition published 1959
Corgi edition published 1962
Corgi edition reissued 1964
Corgi edition reprinted 1964
Corgi edition reprinted 1965
Corgi edition reprinted 1967
Corgi edition reprinted 1968
Corgi edition reprinted 1969
Corgi edition reprinted 1970
Corgi edition reissued 1971
Corgi edition reprinted 1972
Corgi edition reprinted 1974
Corgi edition reprinted 1975
Corgi edition reprinted 1976
Corgi edition reprinted 1977

*It is customary to say that the characters
in this book bear no resemblance
to anyone living or dead. This would
certainly be a lie, but working out just
who is who is bound to be difficult.*

This book is set in 9pt Times Roman

Corgi Books are published by Transworld Publishers Ltd,
Century House, 61–63 Uxbridge Road,
Ealing, London, W.5.
Made and printed in Great Britain by
C. Nicholls & Company Ltd
The Philips Park Press, Manchester

THIS BOOK
IS FOR
POLLY AND
BENTON WEBB

PROLOGUE

YOUNG Sam Price stepped out of a patch of grey-dusty, dry-scraggly mesquite. He was carrying a dead jack-rabbit, held swinging by the ears. He was a gangling little boy, touching eleven years old, and he was beginning to sprout up in awkward angles, like wind-tossed corn stalks. His patched buckskin breeches exposed a length of bramble-scratched ankle. His feet, in home-made *huaraches*, were dirty, and too big for the rest of him. A lock of red hair fell limply over his pale eyebrows and freckled forehead. His eyes were a washed denim blue, and a recession of chin gave him a rabbity look, providing an odd sort of kinship with the jack-rabbit he carried. Young Sam Price hurried across a stretch of sunbaked, drought-cracked clay, and stopped short as he saw a strange dun horse hitched to the post in front of a square adobe house roofed with rough red tiles. The house was whitewashed, but the slopped-on 'wash was beginning to scab, giving the 'dobe shack a leprous look.

Sam Price stopped to inspect the dun horse, which was sway-backed, spavined, with a ewe-neck and an ugly Roman nose. Washboard ribs showed through the dust-stifined hide. The worn cheap saddle was deeply scored by brush-marks. Sam Price looked at the horse with grave suspicion, as at a stranger come unbidden.

He walked past the horse and was met by his mother at the front door. Ada Price's hands were folded underneath a washed-out blue-checked gingham apron. Her mouth drew a thin line over toothless gums, and her faded pink hair was skinned tightly back in a bun. There were still faint signs of a former prettiness, and the resemblance between mother and son was striking.

'Who belongs to the horse, Ma?'

Ada Price looked angrily at the depleted animal.

'Hurry up and skin out that jack,' she said. 'It's a mercy you trapped it. We'll at least have eatin'-meat for supper. Your pa's back.'

'But that ain't the horse he left with . . .'

'I know it. Now run along and skin that jack and wash up for supper.'

'He didn't find it again *this* time, Ma?'

7

The woman's pale eyes were bitter.

'You *seen* the horse,' she said.

'Yes, ma'am,' the boy said and went round behind the house. As he started to shuck the hide from the jack-rabbit, he said softly aloud to himself. 'Maybe next time he'll find it, or if he don't *I* will. Jim Bowie knowed it was there, and a lot of other people knowed it was there. Old Coronado had it, all right. Pa nearly 'bout found it hisself.'

He gutted the rabbit and rinsed it at the pump stand. Then he washed his hands, picked up the cleaned carcass, and went into the house to meet his father. A lean yellow hound worried the rabbit's head, hide and guts that the boy had left on the ground.

Sam Price's father was sitting in a mottled cowhide chair drinking mescal out of a tin cup. He was a big man, spare, with an enormous black beard covering most of his face. He was wearing filthy buckskin, much patched by clumsy fingers. The nose was craggy, but the mouth surrounding a corncob pipe was strangely weak and soft, almost a woman's mouth.

'Howdy, boy,' Nate Price said. 'What's that you got there?'

'Supper,' Sam Price said, handing the red wet carcass to his mother. 'You keepin' all right, Pa?'

'Tolable,' Nate Price said. 'Had a little Injun trouble and some short rations, is all.'

'Ain't no good me askin' how you made out. I seen the horse.'

'Yes, you seen the horse all right. But it's *there*, and I know it's *there*, and as soon as I make another stake I'll go after it again.'

'Can I go with you next time, Pa?'

'Mebbe so, mebbe not. Who'd look after your ma?'

Ada Price laughed mirthlessly as she dropped chunks of floured rabbit into a grease-spitting iron spider.

'The same as always,' she said. 'Your ma.'

The father and son looked at each other swiftly, as if caught together in a guilty secret.

BOOK ONE

BOOK ONE

1

OLD Sam Price owned the only strip of private concrete walk in the town. It was fifty feet long, and stretched across the front of his house and side yard. The square, two-storey house behind the sidewalk sat proud and yellow on the best corner in town, sheltered by a grove of moss-bearded live oaks. The sun-reflecting, crushed-oyster shell street which spread past its veranda travelled two long cheerful blocks down to the waterfront.

A wide side yard reached out to a similar house, but white, in which lived Miss Effie, the sister of Sam Price's wife, Miss Caroline. Miss Effie was married to a Captain Tommy Dunbar. The families were not on the warmest speaking terms and so Miss Caroline had erected a rose garden as a barrier between Miss Effie and herself. The Yellow Eclipses, Red Radiances, Sutter's Gold and Blanche Mallerins made a formidably thorny barrier between the sisters.

Sam Price's hard-pine house was classic of its time. The front room constituted the parlour, which bore the stiff aspect of a room in which only the preacher on his monthly visit could expect to be comfortable. A large stove wearing the trademark *Kalamazoo* provided heat, and the furniture was of the plush-prickly horsehair type which does not invite a visitor to tarry. The pictures were mostly of small fat children being protected by large shaggy dogs.

The other rooms accepted casual warmth from fireplaces. The only comfortable downstairs room was the kitchen which reached futilely towards the dining-room via a sort of pantry in which the family generally took its meals. The kitchen, which owned a large wood-burning stove, gave on to the back-porch, which contained a pump-shelf and granite-ware wash-basin in which it was customary to wash your hands before meals. A soiled roller-towel was fixed to the outer wall of the kitchen. As a modern addition the porch also contained a toilet in which Miss Caroline kept the Cubeb cigarettes which were supposed to relieve the asthma which afflicted her, and made her more tempery.

Two steps away was a closet in which bad little boys were sometimes locked for their sins, and the punishment was made less unbearable by reason that Sam Price kept his arsenal of shotguns and rifles there.

Over to the right was the sitting-room—a dingy little cubicle which held one comfortable chair, one un-cheerful fireplace and a hand-cranked big-horned gramophone on which the old man played his favourite music. The music consisted of such lugubrious ballads as 'The Wreck of the Old Ninety-Seven', 'Birmingham Jail' and the 'Sinking of the *Titanic*'.

In the side yard to the right of the house there was an enormous waxy-flowered magnolia tree in which lived a succession of mocking-birds, who kept the night nervously vibrant with their scattered silver coins of song. Behind, a large Smyrna fig-tree dropped its burst purple fruits at precisely the same time the glossy-green June bugs came to eat them. In back, Miss Caroline cherished an arbour which produced the only Malaga grapes in the community, and which were very highly regarded by a profusion of scarlet tanagers, sparrows, blue jays and cat birds.

Underneath the house there was a sanctuary for small boys such as young Craig Price, old Sam's grandson, who could always find something new and different to do under the house on rainy days.

The house sat primly on ventilated brick stilts, which gave small headroom for young Craig to inspect his grandmother's old and mouldered side-saddle that had long since been retired to pasture underneath the house. Old hunting tents to be kept safe against the wet, and such interesting accumulations as oars, cast-nets and row-boats, old books and magazines, all lived amicably with the rustling rats under Sam Price's house.

Across the oak grove to the left was the small cottage in which Craig's grandmother had been born. To the right down the street Craig's Aunt Jane, Uncle Dunbar and his Great-Uncle Walker were to be found. A bit farther along was the boarding house run by his Cousin Kate.

New Truro was a compact town stretched tautly along the river. Two prim drug stores faced each other on the main street: two sloven grocery stores faced each other on the same street. There was one wooden-benched moving picture theatre, which showed the current William S. Hart horse epics and offered piano accompaniment to the sub-titles.

On the jetsamed shore there were, successively, the salt-weathered pilot dock, the wind-tortured pilot house, the shabby, reeking shrimp dock and the austere fuelling dock, with a chaste tarry cord-and-bronze-filled marine chandlery and the convivial cedar bench making a breeze-swept oasis next the awkward semi-hotel which sold *Virginia Dare* as wine of the country. Apart from a filling station and another seedier filling station which peddled illegal corn whisky, in the dark of the moon, there was very little else in the cedared town but a sandy-floored school which offered sparse education only six months a year. A church and a large oak-grove called The Grove abutted on the baseball diamond where the pick-up town team played every Sunday. There was one pool-room with warped cues, and a very small post office in which every resident had a lock-box, and the aseptically virginal postmistress knew everything about everybody.

This was a town of ribald sea wind and salty warmth, of drowsy summer smells, where the nearest quail called sweetly five hundred yards from the centre of the village, and the harsh wings of ducks whistled low on the cold cloudy mornings over the crouching marshes where the red-shouldered blackbirds sang when the sun shredded the mists. This was a tiny town which hummed to the sounds of the cicadas in the oak trees, where Spanish moss bearded the oaks and outside, in the swamps, the cypress; where bullbats wheeled in the milky summer dusk and the jaunty jays screamed profanely from the pecan trees. This was a town where Craig's second cousin presided over a tiny railroad station, where the W.B. and S. train which made a thirty-mile trip once a day except on week-ends was called 'The Willing But Slow'.

This, then, was the town where Craig Price spent all his summers, and as many week-ends and holidays as he could manage in the spring, autumn and winter. But for the intervention of school, plus his parents, he would have spent all his time there, for this was the town to delight the heart of a small boy.

Old Sam Price sat in his wicker rocking-chair. He was a man of seventy-some years, he wasn't quite sure, but he would say, dod-limb it, he felt as bad as any man in his seventies could possibly feel, even when Miss Caroline wasn't nagging at him. Sam Price had straggled down the path of his life with two violent aversions—more latterly his wife, and always sustained labour. He had generally avoided labour, except in scrofulous patches, but Miss Caroline lingered on to fret him for his sins.

The old man's once-red beard was now nearly all white, stained yellow around the lips from nicotine. His coat-front was drifted with tobacco ash. His nose was long and pointed sharply over his pipe. He wore soft-sided Congress gaiters, and lace-up long drawers that peeped out the back of his pants. At this moment he was playing 'Old Zip Coon' on a home-made fiddle, spitting reflectively into the fire, and assuaging his aches, from time to time, with a solid swig of white corn whisky from a two-quart jar. The room in which he sat was thick with a mingled odour of dirty old man, whisky, dogs, tobacco juice and burning logs. Sam Price looked, as he sawed at his home-made fiddle, rather like a mussy old dog who had been taught a new trick.

Presently he put his violin down, took another drink, and turned to a small boy who was sitting on the floor by the chairside, patting a grossly obese cocker spaniel bitch and two setters, one blue-black, one spotted in liver-and-white. The boy and the dogs were all of a cluster, like puppies sleeping. Sam Price smiled at the boy.

'A man can't turn around in his own room for boys and dogs', he said. 'What are you plaguing me for now?'

13

'Tell some more about the olden days,' the boy said.

'Not until you pay me for it in the usual coin,' Sam Price said. 'Go fetch some more firewood. It's chilly in here for old bones.'

'Yessir,' the boy replied and unscrambled himself from the dogs. He was a fattish boy of about ten, with bright, steady brown eyes, brown, cowlicked hair, and strong square shoulders. He was wearing knickers and a flannel shirt and short hunting boots.

As he went down the hall, his grandmother poked her head out of the kitchen. It was a fat, unpleasantly white face, with a pursy mouth and a negligible nose. She wore, as always, black bombazine, and smelled musty, like a funeral.

'Where are you going *now*, Craig, hunting *again*?' in a petulant tone that implied he might be going out to rob a bank.

'No, ma'am,' Craig Price said. 'Just to get some wood for Grandpa.'

'Pity he can't fetch his own firewood,' she sniffed. 'He ain't too weak to walk down to Niggertown for whisky.'

'Yessum. I mean no ma'am,' the boy said, and scuttled down the stairs. He returned shortly with his arms cradling a stack of wood which obscured his chin. He dumped the short logs into the wood basket, and tossed two sticks on the fire. Greedy fingers of flame seized the fat pine.

'Now,' he said, 'tell me some more about Coronado's treasure, please, Grandpa.'

The old man sighed.

'I musta told you about the lost San Saba mines a hundred times,' he said. 'I spent more time telling it than I did looking for it.'

He paused to touch a match to the pipe.

'It was my pa that was sick with the real gold fever, like everybody else in them days in the South-west. Everybody had the lost-gold itch. I went along with him a few times, but I couldn't see no future in it. Ma died of the galloping consumption while we were off in sagebrush dodging Injuns, and it kind of curdled me on gold-hunting. But it never soured Pa. All his life he was like a man possessed. Every time he could raise a stake he would saddle up and go off looking. He was flat solid convinced that the gold was there—there was an awful lot of evidence that it was stashed away somewhere by the old Spanish conquistadores. Two, three people came mighty nigh to finding it. I reckon Jim Bowie come the closest.

'Some say Bowie actually had seen the lost San Saba—that some Lipan Apache Injun he'd befriended showed it to him, and that he was planning to dig out the treasure when the Mexican war started, and the secret died with him at the Alamo.'

'Was he really the kind of man everybody said?' Craig Price asked. 'Everything I've read about him makes him stand about ten foot tall.'

'I dunno. He was killed by the Santa Anna boys before I was born. But by all accounts he was a regular boar coon. He must of been a considerable feller to have all those stories grow up around him. Either him or his brother Rezin is supposed to have invented the Bowie knife, and evidently Jim killed a power of people with it. They say that when the Mexicans attacked the Alamo, and Bowie was laying sick to death, before they finally killed him there was dead Mexicans stacked up like cordwood all around his bed.'

'I wisht I'd lived back in those days,' the boy said. 'Jim Bowie, lassoing alligators and wild cattle and fighting duels and looking for gold. Lafitte and the pirates and all like that. It must have been mighty exciting.'

'I guess it seems so when you hear about it or read about it, because a lot of lies get told as time passes. I wouldn't be surprised, if you could check real close, you might find a few inaccuracies in the Bible. All I can remember about the good old days is that we were powerful short on plumbing and I can't remember ever going to bed with a full gut when I was your age. Pa had gold in his eyes and gold in his heart, but he never seemed to have no silver in his pocket. Me and Ma lived mainly off jack-rabbits and corn-meal when Pa was off looking for treasure. Then Ma died, and when Pa went off into the bush again, he just never showed up no more. I don't know whether a Mexican or a Injun dry-gulched him, or a rattlesnake bit him, or what. For all I know he might have found the San Saba. Or almost. A passel of people died looking for it, when it seemed, from maps and landmarks, that the treasure was just over the hill. But don't you think for a minute that the rich-readin' stuff you've foundered yourself on is the pure-T gospel. Your hero Billy the Kid was just a dirty little gunman and I don't imagine the likes of Dan Boone and Bigfoot Wallace were over-clean in their personal habits. Your pirate, Lafitte, was just another seagoing highwayman.'

'Tell about how you left Texas and came East,' the boy said. The old man took another drink, wiped his moustache, and fired up his pipe again before he answered.

'Well, after Pa died, I made a couple more expeditions with some other crazy boys, but we never had the right sort of maps and information about the Llanos, and we mighty nigh starved to death. It seemed to me to be damn' foolishness to waste a life chasing rainbows like Pa did. So one day I figured I didn't want to be a hard-scrabble farmer or run a little bad-luck cattle-spread, and oil hadn't come to view in them days, so I forked a horse—actually you might say I stole it—and rode over to Galveston. I sold the horse, and hung around the docks, doing any sort of work I could find, and one night when I was about twenty years old, I was drinking tequila with some other bums in a cheap bar,

15

and got talking with a fellow. We had some more drinks and some more talk and then we had some more drinks and then an argument about nothing and the first thing you knew we were at it, hammer-and-tongs. After an hour or so of us punching each other to pieces, the man sort of grinned through what was left of his face, and said: "Let's call this a draw, and have another drink." I surmised he had a point, and when we washed off the blood and had some more tequila, he said he was bosun on a sailing ship, and that they were short-handed.

' "It's a rough ship, and a hungry ship, but any man your size," he said—I was lean but ropy in them days—"any man your size that'll put up the kind of fight you just give me ought to make a good sailor. Come on down to the ship and we'll see the mate and sign you on as an ordinary seaman."

'Well, hell, son, I didn't have no family nor neither no prospects, and I was sick and tired of West Texas and wild goose-chases after hid-out treasure, so I collected my possibles—one hickory shirt and an extra pair of pants—and went for a sailor. This bosun turned out to be real nice fellow, his name was Joe Something, I disremember, and bimebye I went AB. I stuck on her, and visited a passel of strange places. One time, off Takoradi in West Africa, the third mate died of the fever and my friend Joe went mate and I went bosun. For four or five years I had me quite a time.' The old man's eyes lit reminiscently.

'I'll go to sea, some day when I get big,' Craig Price said. 'Tell me some more about it.'

'Not now,' Sam Price said. 'I'm feeling tired and awful poorly. Suppose you up anchor and take that fleet of hounds out of here and go see if you can shoot me a quail for my supper. I got kind of a hankering for one.'

Craig Price roused the dogs and went out the door. The old man leaned back in his chair and said: 'Don't forget your knife, Jim Bowie. There's a mess of *ho*-stile Apaches between here and Foxtown.'

The boy grinned: 'I ain't invented the Bowie knife yet, I'm too little. I'll take on the Apaches barehanded.'

He went to his room and took down a little 20-gauge shotgun from its rack, while the setters went wild at the sight of the gun. He left the house, and headed through an orchard in the direction of a field in which, he was certain, there would be a covey of quail. As the dogs fanned out ahead of him, he thought, sadly: *Grandpa's going to die soon, and then I'll be all alone.*

At the moment young Craig whistled the dogs to heel, he was Buffalo Bill, and he was going out to shoot a few hundred buffalo to feed the Irish labourers who built the Union Pacific towards the West. He would have preferred to have been Jim Bridger, the scout, but Grandpa Sam's desire for a quail for his supper seemed more of a business-like victualling job than scouting against the

Crows or Blackfeet. This was purely a meat hunt. The Injuns would have to wait another day.

He walked steadily over a sandy rise, where crepe myrtle competed with the oaks, until he hit a ford. He paused to drink where the shallow creek water burbled—not so much because he was thirsty, but because he loved the bitter taste of the brown leaf-dyed water. In any case a man never knew how long he'd be without water if he was going off to shoot a couple hundred buffaloes to feed the hungry Irish railroad hands.

On the other side of the ford, the great prairies began—long stretches of yellow broom grass dotted by sparkleberry bushes, chinquapin trees, scrub pine and gallberry bushes. On these prairies there was sure to be buffalo—buffalo weighing less than six ounces, buffalo which rose with a blood-chilling roar, and which were called quail by the natives.

The dogs ranged out ahead, aiming for a sawdust pile that seemed to have a peculiar attraction for quail, and Buffalo Bill shaded his eyes in the approved fashion, seeking a hostile Sioux here, looking for buffalo sign there. He found it; a neat circle mashed down in the grass and white-dotted with yesterday's quail droppings. At the same time he found the roosting place, his trusty scouts announced the presence of provender. Frank, the blue-black one, was pointing, and Sandy, the live-and-white one, was, for a change, backstanding.

Buffalo Bill's heart leaped rapidly upward and stuck in his throat. He checked his Sharps rifle, which was in reality a 20-dollar scattergun, product of the American Arms Co. He walked up behind his scouts, who were showing signs of nervousness, and commanded them to flush the buffalo. The scouts jumped into the middle of the covey, the birds exploded like separately detonated bombs, and Buffalo Bill missed with both barrels. His trusty scouts looked at him with ill-disguised contempt.

Buffalo Bill inspected his courage, and also regarded himself without admiration.

'If they'd of been Injuns,' he said, 'instead of buffalo, they'd of had my hair. As it is I figure I been tromped down in a stampede, and all the Irish railroad hands will starve to death unless I improve on the singles.'

The dogs were ranging forward now, towards where the scattered quail had pitched in the broom grass. Buffalo Bill followed, and suddenly observed that Frank, his most trusty scout, was frozen so fast he appeared to be a stump. Buffalo Bill walked up behind Frank, and two birds roared up from under the dog's nose. Buffalo Bill fired twice, and committed what could only be described as a snappy double. He reloaded swiftly, and as he closed the gun, another bird got up behind him. He whirled and dropped it in a cloud of feathers. Buffalo Bill smirked, his

17

confidence regained, and the Irish railroad hands were fed for another day.

The dogs retrieved, and Buffalo Bill changed character. Once again he was young Craig Price, carrying the meat home to Grandpa. He called the dogs, and shaped a course for home, swerving slightly to pause in Foxtown, where the coloured folk lived. He wanted to stop off at Irey Ivin's store to buy a nickel's worth of Brown Dogs, a local delicacy made of burnt sugar and peanuts.

Foxtown, called by most Niggertown, was a jolly village outside of New Truro. It was peopled entirely by Negroes, who lived in grey-planked, tarpaper-roofed one- and two-room shacks, most of which were owned by white landlords. Rent for the better houses was as much as two dollars a month, but the rent was nearly always in arrears. On most, the front stoop was aslant, and the steps rotting or rotted. In every back yard there was an iron pot, big enough to scald a hog or hold the washing. There was an invariable chinaberry tree in front, under which fat black babies, seldom wearing more than a flour-sacking shift, rolled and tumbled with lean tomcats and indeterminate dogs, usually yellow, sharp-faced, with upcurled tails. The yards were grassless, the sand clean-swept. The pervading odour was of fried fish, invaded sharply by the sulphurous smell of outdoor privies. The women mostly collected in the back yard, when they were not heading shrimp at the shrimp factory. The men squatted in clumps around the doorsteps, laughing uproariously at small humour, playing mumblepeg and broadly relating their amorous exploits. A voice:

'I 'uz to de co'thouse when dey try de preacher for dee-voce. Co'thouse jampack, white folks too. Preacher wife, Iovary, she stan' up strong befo' de judge an' say: "When I marry de Revent, I give him *my solemn breach of promise* I be true. De Revent know I love him. But dat one night he come home wid a rose in he coat, smellin' lak monkey rum, I know he be untrue. And it was Community Sunday, too."'

'De judge, he say: "*What kind of Sunday*?"'

'Iovary, she rear back and say: "Judge, for God's sake, ain't you never hear of Community Sunday?"''

(Laughter, in deep bass voices.)

'Den Iovary she *say* she say: "Revent, I *knows* it was Sister Lizzie Swain give you dat rose."'

'And den *twenty-five* gals stan' right up in co't and holler: "*Dat a lie*!"''

(More deep bass laughter and sounds of palms smacking dungareed legs.)

Among the women, Aunt Melissy Simmons was holding court. Aunt Melissy was a waspish plum-black women, the unchallenged

18

social leader and high priestess of the corps of young gals who headed shrimp in the shrimp factory.

'I has to leave de shrimp house to go to co't, because seem lak everybody I know suin' me. Right now, Mista Jack Robinson he got *five* sewages agin me already. I tell dem woman: "Y'all woman behave 'til I gits back. I don' want no hair-pullin' and knife-stickin 'bout some wuthless man. Y'all behave, yeddy, or I snatch you bal'-headed." So I goes to co't, and when I gits back, you never see sich a commotion in all yo' born days. Dey is hair-pullin' and kickin' and scratchin' and hollerin' fit to wake de dead. One little gal, she ain't hardly ten year old, she still keep cryin' when de fuss die down. I see what wrong, and I say:

' "Who spit dat gob hot spit in dat chile eye? Step forward." Big sassy yaller gal step forward, an' I plain snatch her bal'-headed. Den we has peace when I comes back from de nex' sewage.'

(Applause, and high-pitched laughter.)

'Don' pay monkey round wid Melissy, she boun' to snatch you bal'-headed.'

'Yas, Lawd.'

'I see her take a stick one time to her man, beat him 'til he cry lak a chile.'

'Gal, you speaks true.'

'Melissy, she sho' a holy terror when her temper rise.'

'Dat she is, praise be.'

'She fierce lak a tagger-cat. She mean as a snake when somebody cross her path.'

'A—*men.*'

Melissy beamed.

As Craig approached the store, a little girl named Dessie was swinging under an oak tree. As she gained momentum, Craig said laughing: 'Dessie, I can see your tail.'

Swinging ever higher, Dessie replied with dignity. 'Mista Craig, you keep talkin' bad-mouth like that, I gon' tell Mista Cholly Figgles on you.' Mr. Charles Phillips was chief of police.

Then Dessie giggled and swung even higher, her honour appeased, her tail still exposed.

Craig proceeded, and stopped again to pass a word with another friend, a comfortably ample lady named Snoree. She was sitting on the sagging porch of her home, rocking and attending to a recent infant. A young piebald goat emerged from under the house and fixed Craig with a baleful yellow stare.

'Hidy, Mista Craig,' Snoree said. 'Looks lak us done found another one.'

'Howdy, Snoree,' Craig replied. 'What you gonna call this one?'

'I thinkin' of callin' it Blushie Mae, 'cause I so shamed of bein'

19

so careless.' She laughed richly at her wit. 'From now on, *any*-thing enter *me* gone be food.'

'How many children you got now, Snoree?' Craig paused to perform the amenities.

'I reckon I got about eight head.'

'What you need, Snoree, is a good husband to look after you.'

'Mista Craig,' Snoree said with great conviction, 'after Blushie Mae, I just ain't *studyin'* mens.'

She turned and spoke sharply to somebody behind her in the house.

'Woodrow,' she snapped. 'Go blow yo' nose on dat dishrag. Anything I does *despise* is nastiness. I bids you good day, Mista Craig. I gots to feed dis chile.' She opened her dress and more or less flung an enormous breast at Blushie Mae, who seized it with tiny pink-palmed brown hands and butted at it like a calf.

Craig was never happier than when he was in Foxtown, unless it was when he was playing Buffalo Bill behind the bird-dogs. He knew, of course, every Negro in the village. He generally managed to slip out from under Miss Caroline's vulture-like surveillance when the moon was full and a big revival was on. He stopped now to say 'howdy' to an enormous mountain of a man, his water-melon lips split in a smile over blue gums.

'Hey, Buddy Roadie,' he said. 'How's the family makin' out? What kind of quail we got this year on your place?'

'Mista Craig, I swears fo' God and three other 'sponsible witness, I dunno what we's got de mostest of, younguns or quail-buhds. Seem lak us keep finin' chillun us didn't know us had, and de price fatback powerful high. De quail eatin' up all de fiel' peas, and it be nice did you come wid yo' gun an' thin 'em out some, yeddy? Be nice did you see a possom on de way, because us still got some sweet taters in de hill, sore hankerin' for possum. How de old gentleman, poorly?'

'Poorly, but he's curin' it his way.'

'Speakin' of curin' it, it jus' happen I out lookin' round de place an' I done come on a whisky still. I don't know *who* so *bad* he make licker on my place, so I do what de law say, confiserate de evidence. You tell de Cap'n I be around to press a little call wid some de evidence. Look lak' pretty good evidence. Been dere since last spring. I *think*.'

'I'll tell him, Buddy Roadie. And I'll be down next week to help you with the quail.'

'Dat powerful neighbourly, Mista Craig. Does you see a squirrel or two, even if you doesn't see no possum, remember de pecan season comin' on and dem squirrel powerful rough on a money crop. I see you later when I comes 'round wid de evidence.'

Life among the Negro quotient of the town was wonderful to Craig. It was based on a friendly non-intrusion of privacy but was compounded of mutual enjoyment. Craig had been reared, earlier on, by a magnificent African, a former slave called Mammy by Craig and Aunt Laura by the *Bokra*, the white folkses. Mammy died when she was about ninety, and she never weighed more in pounds than her ultimate age. Her husband, Uncle Cornelius, was a white-headed, coal-black gentleman with the fierce features of a Roman noble. They raised Craig polite.

'If you can't keep up wid de bell cow,' Mammy would say, after some social scandal among the whites, 'you's got to gallop wid de gang.' And, 'I had a little dog and his name was Dash. I'd rudder be a nigger dan po' white trash.'

Uncle Cornelius would say: 'Remember, Mista Craig, you's born gentle, and you's got to live up to de mark. Both yo' grandpas is gentlemen. See you follows in dey foots, or I take a stick to yo' hide. Gentlemen is gentle to everybody, white or black. Not like dese po' *Bokra*, think dey own de earth because dey trash and shamed, got to shove other people around because dey shamed.'

And Mammy would run out her lip and say, with an eloquent African sniff, after some parental reprimand had forced her Baby to tears, 'Trouble wid dese young married folk, dey doesn't know a *good* chile when dey sees one.'

And Aunt Lily, Craig's mother's old nurse, would say: 'You little and you fat, but I switched yo' Ma when she a big gal ripe for weddin', and I wear you out right now does you get uppity.'

When Craig went to visit the antiseptically clean little house of Mammy and Uncle Cornelius, he was served alone at table, while his mentors stood primly in attendance. Later, after they had eaten—and Craig had retired formally to the living-room—the social niceties had been fulfilled, and he entered into a rich life among the coloured folk. He rode the horse-drays with the draymen. He fished with the black fishermen who sang original African toting-chants as they hauled the purse-seines on the pogey boats. He swam naked in the Yellow Hole with his black picanin companions, with whom he also hunted rabbits and coons and possums, following the fretful yapping of the mangy feisty curs who fancied themselves hounds.

The possum hunts always ended up in somebody's shack, breeze-wayed open from end to end, wall-papered with the Sunday funny-papers, always quivering to the blast of a pine-knot fire. The hunter home from the hills was rewarded with possum and sweet taters, a little dipper of scuppernong wine, cold cornbread and hard ham. Or there would be the remnants of fried rabbit, cold, or a re-heated dish of squirrel-head stew. When the coffee came around, somebody got out a banjo or a home-made guitar composed of a cigar-box with steel-wire strings. Somebody would kick up the fire and throw another knot or two aboard, and the harmony would begin. 'Nobody Knows De Trouble I Sees',

21

and 'Go Down, Moses, Into Egyp' Lan'', were deeply ingrained into the boy's subconsciousness. He would sometimes come awake at night, with the moon high, with the entire throaty refrain throbbing in his head.

2

NEW TRURO was a town in which, Cousin Gertie Gurthrie always said, the white folks were either struttin' like a peacock or bent like a hoop. Like most tiny towns, especially waterfront towns, it was filled with characters, and the people spoke a salty piece. In twentieth-century America, the English-descended residents still used a variable dialect embracing words from most of the shires of England, plus a flavourful corruption which was purely local.

The characters, white and black, were considerably larger than life. There was Hook, who was such a talented thief that a friend once remarked that when he was reading in bed, Hook slipped in and stole the lamp so fast the friend kept right on reading.

There was the Widder, who spoke a fancy brand of rhetoric that was almost poesy. Young Craig, being indoctrinated by the Widder's snaggle-toothed brother, Perce, in the arts of game-poaching and gentle profanity, used to sit for hours and listen to the Widder talk. She was a skinny dark woman who looked rather like a peahen, and it was supposed that from time to time she had a man in her life since Husband passed to his reward.

The Widder would say:

'He took fatal sick, and I always knew that apolexy was heditary.'

Or, when confronted by a certain-short-necked man with a decidedly piggish face:

'Every time I see that man I feel like lookin' for the barbecue sauce.'

The Widder would say that she was just crazy about stationary things you could move all around; that everywhere she turned somebody offered her a hardichoke; and that the new mama and papa were so fretted about germs that when anybody was around they completely oscillated the baby.

Cousin Mamie had a colourful turn of phrase as well. She would say:

'Twig him, still in the stid, stiff as a weddin' jessie,' of which the translation was: 'Look at him, still in bed, drunk as a goat.' Cousin Mamie had her own argot. To be amorous was to be 'ando.' Something beautiful, such as flowers, was 'ambitty.' Her version of a hen-party playing bridge was 'roosterin'. She referred to the nose-tilted groups as 'woodpecker society', and a 'philly-loo bird' was a fowl that didn't care where he was going, so he flew backward to see where he'd been. Or, as variation, he stuck his bill in the ground and whistled with his tail. One lady she knew had a behind like a country pump shelf.

There was the Italian shrimp merchant, who never quite mastered New Truro talk, but who made a valiant stab at it. Angelo would say: 'I am highly delightful to be here.' When confronted with a comely lass who cast down her eyes and simpered at a compliment, Angelo would say: 'What would be the use of me trying to flatten you?' And he always said: 'Thank you very so much.' When he got rich, he took up backhorse riding.

Angelo became increasingly prosperous, and built a large house. He informed a Miss Birdie Mae White, a lady of acerbic tongue, that the new house included a kitchenette in the kitchen, and she asked him waspishly if he also owned a raincoat and a slicker. Miss Birdie Mae once was asked if a receptacle in front of the house was the mailbox, and she replied: 'Christ, no, it's the hen's nest. They get nervous on the ground on account of foxes.'

Uncle Cuffy, a coloured gentleman, was possessed of the ability to talk coarse and fine, a complete change-over from basso profundo to high tenor. They said he came to Uncle Jimmy's store one time and said, basso: 'I want a bar of soap,' and then, tenor: 'And a pound of lard.'

Uncle Jimmy was a man of short temper. He replied: 'Hold on, goddamit, I can't wait on but one man at a time.'

It was a town of special humour. A medical doctor had started the semblance of a hospital—this was the doctor who had the pickled Siamese twins in a jar under his house, as Craig discovered to his delicious horror one day—and the coloured folk were beginning to turn away from simple, home-grown obstetrics, to hospital care for baby-growing. The lone interns were irreverent sorts, so a whole dynasty of flamboyantly named children began.

One set of girl twins were named Syphyllys and Gonoreah. There was a Thyroid Jones and a Hysterectomy Smith. There was an Embolism Evans, a Stricture Sutton, and one lady-child with no surname who was simply listed as Vagina.

New Truro was a town where a coloured lady once remarked, to her swain who was parked in a T-Model Ford:

'Bubber, why doesn't you give me no excuse to get out and walk?'

It was a town where a white lawyer, cross-examining a witness, asked: 'If you had of begun running from a certain stake, and had of ran so many feet, where would you of went?'

It was a town in which, during a bastardy trial, the Judge inquired of a young, but unmarried, mother: 'Is it true you had an illegitimate child for the Reverent King?'

'Yassuh, Judge, but I is only sixteen years old.'

23

Her mama, large and sweating and righteous, popped up indignantly.

'Yas, Judge, and she was fas' asleep, and he weighed over three hundred pounds, and wore a size twenty collar.'

'Guilty!' the Judge roared, 'of assault with intent to kill!'

That was the town as Craig knew it in the city limits. Outside the city limits it was quite a different town.

Apart from his coloured friends, and a few shiftless hairy white adults who treated him as a grown man, joshed him roughly and taught him to hunt and fish, Craig Price was a solitary boy. He took very little interest in community sport. He was clumsy at baseball, and ran too slow to be very good at football. He roved the woods, winter and summer, and he spent a great deal of time in a small *bateau* Great-Uncle Tommy made him. Everywhere he went, hunting or fishing, he took a book—any sort of book. He had never been actually taught to read—at least not by the C-A-T-*cat* D-O-G-*dog* method. But he was reading, photographing the page, before he touched four. He lived inside the books, and fought for the privilege, because reading was regarded as sissy by athletic louts who were his age-mates. When he was called 'Sissy', and 'Fatty', he fought; although he wept from rage and often vomited after the battle, he fought with a blind desire to kill his tormentors. One day, when he was six and in kindergarten, his principal tormentor jeered at him as he sat during the play period on the flat roof of the re-done garage in which the children received gold stars for good behaviour. Craig was reading *Ivanhoe*, and was lost to the noisy scuffling of the baby athletes below him. One child, big and muscular for his seven years, looked up and said: 'Come on down off that roof and play football.'

'I don't want to. I'm reading.' Craig placed a finger in the book to keep his place.

'You're yellow. Old Sissy Price. That's why he's so fat.' This aside to the swarm of sadistic children who always flock to a bear-baiting.

'I am *not* yellow. I'm reading, and I don't want to play.'

'Cowardy-cat, cowardy-cat. Fatty Price is a sissy.' The young mob started a chant.

'I'll bet you're afraid to jump off that roof,' his chief tormentor said. 'I dare you. I double-dare you to jump.'

Craig closed his book, and dog-eared the page.

'All right,' he said, 'I'll jump.' He put the book under his arm.

He jumped, ten feet straight down, and landed with both booted feet in the upturned face of his enemy, breaking his nose and knocking out several teeth. There was a tremendous explosion in the kindergarten. Fathers and mothers were sent for, and Craig was withdrawn from early education by popular request. His mother put him to bed for a week as punishment, which delighted him. He completed *Ivanhoe* and relaxed with *Robin Hood*. He had nearly finished *Treasure Island* when he grudgingly returned to freedom. That, at the age of six, when the other kids were painfully ploughing through *The Little Red Hen*.

He fought almost daily in early grammar school, as he was baited at recess or foot-padded on his way home. Always, stomach-griping pangs of fear preceded the first punch, and often he was beaten. When an enemy had him down, and was pummelling away, some lout would pant: 'Holler nuff, and I'll let you up!' Weeping and cursing with all the fluency he had learned from the waterfront and his adult friends, Craig used knees and elbows or, if possible, a stick or a rock, but he never hollered 'Nuff!' Before he was ten, his associates gave up tormenting him and left him alone.

'Oh, hell,' they said. 'Leave him be. Let him read if he wants to. If you mess with him you'll just have to fight him, and he don't fight clean. It's too much trouble,' and went back to playing football, while Craig wandered off into the wood or on to the water with a gun or a fishpole, but always a book.

The boy lived completely inside himself. To himself he was not fat little Craig, or Sissy Price, or even the boy whose early accumulation of broad knowledge made him so bored with childish school instruction that his grades were terrible—until one perceptive teacher decided to skip him over a grade and watch the results. He sprang from first to third grade, and made straight A's. He lost interest in the fourth grade, so they shoved him into the sixth and he made straight A's. At that time the progressive examinations and IQ tests were coming into vogue, and for three straight years Craig easily won the title of being the brightest child in his state.

Craig, alone in the autumn woods with his dogs, or fishing the chill frothy September surf, was not Craig at all. In his very early youth, he 'played like' he was Robin Hood or Jim Hawkins or Daniel Boone or even Tarzan of the Apes, who fascinated him to the point where he built a Tarzan house in a big wild cherry tree and even slept in it.

But gradually 'play like' became baby sport, and the first inner feeling of future importance began to form. Unconsciously, a sense of difference illuminated him. (Translated from thought, it would have been something like: 'I am Craig Price and I am different from these other people and some day I will travel to far places and do great things because I am Craig Price and I am different. I am lean and strong and handsome and some day everybody will be sorry that they weren't nicer to me when I come home in my big Pierce-Arrow with a beautiful woman by my side. Mysterious Craig Price, that nobody knows what he does, but he has the eagle look and he must be making plenty money and I'll bet he ain't even married to that beautiful foreign woman with all the real pearls and diamonds.')

Alone in his woods and fields, Mysterious Craig Price, aged ten and already in the seventh grade, thought of himself as The Chief, The Chief of What he wasn't quite sure. But certainly Mysterious Craig Price, The Chief, needed tremendous secrecy for his treasure of bullion and stolen gems, so he began to dig caves. He had an interlocking series of caves that covered acres, and were linked by secret passages that not even Injun Joe could trap him in.

At ten, he was steeping himself in any book that touched on distant places. When he took his fishing gear, his rod and cast-net, and unshipped the oars to head for Money Key, where pirate gold was supposedly buried, he was Columbus standing stoutly out to sea, or Balboa a-prowl for the Pacific. As he strode his pitching mental quarter-deck, staring sternly towards the vast unknown lands, he knew that scanty rations, weavilly biscuits and salt horse would not move his rascally crew of gutter-sweepings to mutiny. Not so long as The Captain strode his bridge, a belaying pin close to hand, a cutlass by his side and two pistols stuck into his belt. He'd shoot them down like dogs, and carve his way to the ringleaders, whom he would keel-haul, make to walk the plank, flog through the fleet and hang from the yard-arm. Pirates worried him not. He was too old a hand for that, and had not he himself been a pirate off Barbados?

It is possible that in Craig's mind he had badly scrambled history with fiction, and Rafael Sabatini was running ahead of Cortez' conquest of Mexico in terms of time and space. But this was of no importance to the man who had sunk the Spanish Armada single-handed and who had sailed the dark rivers of Malaya, standing off pirate junks with a shower of grapeshot, or who had pursued the slave trade in the South Pacific, confounding the screaming cannibals with dynamite sticks, lit by the glowing coal of the cigar he clenched in his teeth.

At this point Jack London took over, and Craig shipped his oars and dropped the hook near a sand-bar. He fished into his jacket and produced a ten-cent cigar which he had . . . er . . . acquired. He lit it, clenched it in his teeth, and looked sternly about for war canoes to repel. He puffed rapidly, to keep the coal glowing, but no howling mob of Solomon Islanders appeared. Only a seagull squawked indignantly at him, too far out of range for dynamite. Presently, the master of the teakwood blackbirder began to turn slightly green, and then bowed his head to loo'ard and threw up.

After Captain Ahab recovered from his retchings, he found by some miracle that he was actually Craig Price, aged ten, who was going fishing for Moby Dick. First he would gather some clams, which he did by wading barefoot in the mud and feeling for them

26

with his toes. If possible he would locate some softshell crabs, and tong up a few bushel of somebody else's oysters. This came under the head of free-booting on the high seas. Then he would head for a barnacly old wreck he knew, where sheepshead and Moorish stonecrab were sure to lurk, so he laid in a supply of sand-fiddler crabs as bait for the sheepshead. He would need shrimp, and possibly, small mullet for his other baits, so he wet his cast-net, shook it free of water, spread it between hand and teeth until it swirled like a dancer's skirt, and cast it until it hovered like a huge butterfly over a small school of skipping shrimp. They were just right for bait—small, grey-yellow—as they kicked and bucked on the deck when he untucked the lead-weighted hem of his net. Another cast provided a double-dozen tiny mullet, and the master of the good ship *Arabella* was ready for business.

But it booted a man badly to sail the Spanish Main on an empty stomach, so Captain Blood knocked a dozen or so of the fresh-caught clams on the gunwale, and gorged himself on the fresh, cold, salty clams, whose colour, inside the purple shells, was that of yellow cling-peaches. No man to stint himself at the trencher, he robbed an oyster bed, swished the oysters clean with his tongs, and ate a dozen or so. He opened them simply by bashing the thin lips with the back of his knife, and then sliding the blade in to cut the muscle and free the dripping, briny oyster-maidens from their prison-castle of shell. Fortified, he picked up his oars and headed for the wreck.

He rowed down a winding channel and noticed that the wild goats were grazing the marshes on the outer stretches of long, narrow, sea-oated sand-dunes which linked arms against the threatening force of the ocean. The goats always pleased him, as the wild marsh ponies farther down East pleased him. They gave him a pleasant sense of security, such as Robinson Crusoe might have had when he first observed wild goats on his island. If all else failed, if a man were to be marooned, there were fish in the sea and animals on the land. Goat might taste rank, especially the old billies, but they would at least sustain life and provide clothes for the marooné. An old white billy lifted his bearded chin and stared insolently at Craig.

'*Baa*,' he said, following the *baa* with a succession of flatulent-sounding snorts.

'*Baa* yourself,' Craig answered. 'If I had a gun I'd shoot you. Go play with the nannies and mind your own damn' business.'

'*Poot, poot, poot, BAAaaaa!*' The old william turned and stalked slowly away to attend to his patriarchal duties with the flock. His beard blew in the breeze, and he switched his tail insolently.

Craig bent to his oars, and in a few minutes achieved the wreck, where he slung his hook in an eddy that formed around the rusted, barnacle-crusted remains of a shrimp boat. There was a deep

27

hole, he knew from experience, just where his boat would settle when the tide swung her into the rip. He baited a light rod with a shrimp, and fixed a sand fiddler on to a hand-line, which he rigged into a limber forked stick stuck into one of the thole-pin holes. He rigged yet another hand-line in the same fashion, but baited a large grapple hook with a slab of semi-rotten meat. The Master of the Seas was now prepared for anything—sea-trout or blackfish or even pompano on the rod, sheapshead on the sand-fiddler, stone crab on the foul meat. If everything got going at once, he reflected, as he paid out the hand-lines and then cast line from his rod, he'd likely need three hands. *Like Grandpa says about the Model T—it needs a monkey to drive it: one hand on the wheel, one hand on the throttle, two feet on the pedals and a tail to keep the door shut.*

It was a lovely day for adventure. The sun burned as through a glass, reflecting glare from the deep blue skies only slightly tufted with white cloud. A breeze stirred the marsh grasses, which were busy with bird life. A bittern's hoarse '*thunk*' sounded in the distance. A big fish hawk circled high, waiting for his dinner to appear. Small hawks prospected low over the marshes, keenly seeking mice or marsh rats or little black marsh rabbits. White-and-blue herons sat haughtily on old salted-grey snags of long-dead trees. A gallinule tiptoed daintily down a narrow avenue of fetid mud next the marsh, and sandpipers reared their saucy behinds in the air as they tripped over the sand-bars. Away off in the distant wood, Craig knew that his pet bald eagle was sitting high in the rigging of a lightning-blasted tree—waiting, just waiting for that old osprey to seize on to a fish big enough to make it worth the eagle's stealing time. The grasses bent under the weight of the carolling red-winged blackbirds, and moistly over all was the smell Craig loved best—the perfume of sea and sand and marsh and stinking mud, all warmed by the sun into a delicious hellbroth.

The rod bent nearly double now, at the same time that the sand-fiddler-baited hand-line jumped off its outrigger. Craig fought the rod with both hands, and paid out the hand-line with his great and second toe, letting the line slide from its wet coils under his feet. He reeled in his rod-line as rapidly as possible, and reached down to hook a two-pound sea trout under the gills with the crooked fingers of his left hand, while he held the rod taut and high with the right. He yanked the fish into the boat, jammed the rod against the gunwhale with his right knee, and left the lovely speckled trout to flop while he began to tug gently on the taught hand-line. Bringing in the line with his right hand, he coiled the dripping line neatly with his left, and then, using two hands, drew alongside a sheepshead, firmly hooked in its nasty, pursy little mouth. Sheepsheads always reminded Craig of Miss Caroline. He got a gill-hold, and hauled the fish into the boat.

It was a good one, and would weigh three, maybe four pounds. Two big fish, flopping in the boat, made a fine sight. Just as Craig was admiring himself, the other hand-line jerked loose from its limber stick and presently, tugging very gently so as not to disillusion the rock crab, he was able to slip a net under a Moorish crab, black, yellow-spotted, with claws as big as grapefruit on a body not much bigger than a small orange. This was fine. Grandpa Sam purely loved those big ol' rock crabs, but you had to be careful, for those big, black-topped, yellow-undersided claws would clamp down on you like a steel trap. Craig picked up the crab, grabbing him behind the armpits so that the biting edges snapped harmlessly, and tossed him into a towsack which was hung, bag-body in the water, but neck and mouth bound tight against the boat's stern, and then dropped the flopping fish in after the crab. *Man alive*, Craig said to himself, *I am really off to a roaring start*!

He fished the ebb until noon, and filled his crocus-sack with trout and croakers, perch and Virginia mullet, a few small skipjack blues and another half-dozen big crabs. Then he stowed his gear, unshipped his oars, and rowed half a mile to Money Key, where a few small palmettos grew and the pirate treasure maybe was. Here he would swim naked, then cook himself a little lunch, and sort of laze around with Huckleberry Finn until the tide rose to speed him on his way home. Rowing a boat against the ebb was no fun, even if you did have horny-calloused hands from being a galley-slave.

After his swim, without bothering to put on any clothes—the sun would soon dry him so that he could scrape the salt off his carcass with his fingers—he gathered a few sticks of dry brined driftwood and built himself a small fire. He reached into the locker in the sternsheets of the beached boat, and brought out a small iron spider, a half-loaf of bread, a tin cup full of lard, a can containing a mixture of salt and pepper, a handful of flour twisted into a piece of slick brown mottled butcher paper, a small percolator, a square box of coffee, a paper cornucopia of sugar, an apple and two bananas. There was a thermos of drinking water in the shade under the thwarts, and Craig Price, Captain-Admiral of the Ocean Sea, was ready for chow. As all good Captain Admirals should, he would dine alone in stern splendour.

He had already fed sumptuously off oysters and clams, as he proceeded to the main course, mentally resolving to keel-haul the cook if he spoiled the meal. He gutted a small trout and a couple of perch, scaled them, rolled them in pepper-and-salted flour, and when the lard began to sizzle in the skillet, popped them in the pan. At the same time he laid two thick slices of bread alongside the fish and started his coffee boiling in the small fire. The fish turned crisply golden in the grease, as did the bread, and the coffee began to chuckle merrily in the percolator. Craig went back to his pantry and produced a tin plate, which he scoured hurriedly with sand and rinsed in the salt water, and then withdrew his fried fish and his grease-soggy-toasted bread from the spider and laid them in the plate. The screw-top of the thermos was his coffee-cup, and the Captain-Admiral of the Ocean Sea was now ready to dine. The white delicate fish came off the bones in delicious long flakes, and he dunked his bread in the grease that remained in the skillet. No, reflected the Captain-Admiral, he would *not* keel-haul the cook. That was a hell of a good cook. He finished the fish and bread down to the last moist bit, and drank another cup of coffee. He ate an apple and a banana and settled down for a nap under a palmetto. He would clean his cookery-gear when he woke, and then it would be time to go home.

When he woke, a feeling of tremendous calm and well-being possessed him. He set about washing up and stowing his gear properly, ship-shape and Bristol fashion, and as he moved about, barefoot, a sudden searing pain attacked his right foot, just under the ball of his great toe. He took the foot in his hand, and saw a blurred blue object deep under the opaque skin of the ball of his foot. He sat down hurriedly, and saw that he had stepped on a rusty nail, embedded in an old piece of flotsam planking. It had broken off as it entered his foot, and a good half of the nail was firmly wedged under the callus. He looked vaguely about him, biting his lips against the pain, and resolved that a man who was a man had to do what he had to do. Surgery at sea was painful, at best, but terribly necessary, as witness Cap'n Ahab when Moby Dick bit his leg off.

There were still some coals left in the fire. Craig got out his knife and whetted it against the oilstone he carried in his tackle-box. Then he placed the blade in the coals and left it until it was searing hot. He wished he had a bullet to bite, but lacking a bullet, he took a four-ounce pyramid sinker from the tackle-box and bit on it as he explored with the hot knife-blade the foreign presence in his foot. Using the tip of the knife, he dug in and around the rusty nail, and prised it out. Blood flowed, and he was slightly sick with the pain, but he cut a strip off his shirt-tail and bound the wound tightly. He would sneak some iodine when he got home, and not mention a word to Miss Caroline about his heroism. He limped, wounded, blood spreading under the jury-rigged bandage, and prepared to shove off.

The wounded Captain-Admiral sent his imaginary hands aloft to set the sails, while Craig Price bent to his oars with a right good will. He owned a feeling of accomplishment that Balboa must have felt when he first saw the Pacific. He had made his landfall, victualled his ship, and had quelled a mutiny before it started. It mattered very little that he was the entire rowing machinery of a slave-galley, for the *Sea Hawk* would be along any moment to rescue him. Surgery at sea was part of a sailor's pay.

The wind had risen, and saucy little droplets of the brash wavelets bounced off his sunburned nose. He smelt of fish scales and grease and marsh mud, but it was a blithesome craft, with a jaunty skipper, who arrived half-dead from fatigue-cum-sore-foot in an unknown port in the Far Caribees. He dragged the *Santa Maria* up on the beach, turned her over, and shouldered his oars, his fishing rod, his sack of fish, his hoard of golden oysters and platinum clams, and limped home, salty, sunburned and happy.

As he entered the house via the back porch, Miss Caroline met him on the stoop with a disapproving stare.

'Where have you been all day?' she asked.

'Fishin',' he replied. 'I got a lot of fish and some crabs and some clams and oysters and . . .'

'Clean the fish and then wash up. You're late for supper,' she said. Then, glaring suspiciously:

'What's the matter with your foot?'

'I cut it on a piece of glass,' said the Captain-Admiral of the Ocean Sea. What could a woman know of far places and a man with the look of eagles in his eyes, a man who could cut off his own leg without a whimper? But tomorrow he would tell Grandpa Sam, and Grandpa Sam wouldn't say: 'Wash up, you're late for supper,' to a man who had just discovered a new trade route to the Indies, and who had bitten a bullet as he sawed at his own flesh.

3

THE condition of going to Hell, and just how long eternity was apt to be, began to bother Craig Price when he was about nine years old, and it took him nearly a year to get over a daily visitation of sickening black gloom. His preoccupation with Hell and Eternity came at about the same time as The Dream. The Dream was never very clear, but it seemed that he was whirling in space, like a star, not doing very much but just fiddling around, minding his own business, when all of a sudden, something happened, and he knew that he was going to spin in ever-widening circles all the years there were to come, millions and billions and trillions of years, and he awoke sweating and wide-eyed, damply stricken with panicked relief.

Hell-consciousness possibly began first with the eerie gloom of a late-afternoon swamp, where he was waiting for a deer and listening to the mourning of the doves and all the little secret jungle noises that can be heard in a Carolina swamp when the evening starts to cool and the air is lambently still, the black branch water sinister, and the little coloured boys start to whistle through the forest as they drive the cow home. There is nothing sadder than a swamp, with its noises you will never identify, its dark mystery pent behind the cypress knees, its hint of veiled menace all around.

Hell-consciousness continued with the discovery of a drowned Negro, wedged into a marsh off Battery Island, a bloated purple corpse half-eaten by fishes. Hell continued with a bit of mischief involving the inspection of an above-ground tomb, with a glass aperture at the head of the concrete crypt so that the Widow Bell, a trifle touched in the head, might come daily to look at the Departed Bell. The tomb was not too far from school, and some of the more daring pupils made an occasional pilgrimage to see how much more the old gentleman's knotted beard had grown in his rotting skull. And, naturally, broke the glass window, the better to observe the maggots at work. Craig went along on a dare, despite all he'd heard about the weird diseases you could contract by associating with dead people at close hand. He was in a Ben Hur phase then, and knew that you could catch such things as leprosy merely by sending your dirty clothes to the wrong washer-woman. What you might possibly acquire from a corpse whose glass frontispiece had been battered in by vandals surpassed all macabre imagination, and at that time the wonderfully horrible moving picture, *Frankenstein*, had not yet been perpetrated. The ethical aspects of defiling the dead only vaguely troubled him.

Hell weighed very heavily on Craig's mind. He went to Sunday School, and had Hell heaved at his head. He sneaked out to camp meetings, white and black, and Hell was foremost in the exhortations. If you were bad, you caught Hell. If you got mad at somebody, you told them to go to Hell. Hell was Forever, and Forever was considerably longer than the last week before school let out, and Hell was certainly something you would collect if you were naughty and told lies and cussed and especially did anything nasty about little girls.

Eunice was advanced for her age, being about eleven in human-computed time, and as old as original sin in her own unrealized knowledge. It was a rainy day and Craig was playing under the house with a cousin, whittling out boats, when Eunice, who lived across the street, crawled under the house and announced, after proper social formalities, that she had discovered the secret of life.

'I know where babies come from,' Eunice said. 'What's that you're doing?'

'Makin' a boat,' Craig replied. 'What's that you said about babies?'

'I know where they come from,' Eunice tossed her head, and lifted her chin. 'I bet you don't, smarty.'

'The doctor brings 'em.' Craig said.

'He does *not*,' Eunice replied loftily. 'You have to call the doctor to get them out of the mama.'

'They come out of the *mama*? How do they get there?' Craig stopped whittling.

'The papas put them *in* the mama. Where you pee from. And they come out of the belly-button.'

'How can a baby come out of a *belly-button*? It's no bigger than a nickel. That's silly.'

'It is *not* silly. The papa takes his thing and puts it in where you pee and a baby grows inside the mama and when it's ready to be born they call the doctor and they take the baby out of the belly-button.'

'It must hurt a lot.'

'Oh, it hurts terrible—something awful. I heard Aunt Jo telling about when she had Jimmy. It hurt something dreadful. She said she never wanted to see another man as long as she lived, that's what she said.'

Eunice giggled, and cast down her eyes.

'If you'll show me yours, I'll show you mine,' she said. 'Let's make a baby. I don't care if it hurts. I don't care a bit.'

'Well, all right,' Craig said, and began to unbutton his pants.

The whole thing seemed a most mystifying feat of engineering to Craig, who had often inspected his navel and pondered its practicality, but Eunice was adamant on her theory that something miraculous happened to the mama after the papa put the basic ingredients of the baby inside her, and the mama opened up like the Red Sea when the Israelites were fleeing from old Pharaoh.

It seemed, at the time, a pretty dull pastime, but Craig came down with a sense of guilt that rode him like a hag. For several days, even weeks, they practised planting babies under the house, but no baby ever popped out of Eunice's navel. Another vestal named Lola was drafted, but while Lola was co-operative after she had received a candy-bar and Craig's best taw-marble, she failed to produce any navel-babies too, even though they had summoned a lusty child named Roy to aid in the scientific investigation.

Apart from the fact that girls and boys were indisputably dissimilar in construction, nothing else was proved. Except that everybody was going to Hell, and girls seemed to be constructed more neatly than boys. It was finally decided that somewhere, somehow, the formula for baby-production had gone wrong.

This happened on the day that Miss Caroline, looking for something mislaid under the house, stumbled on to the laboratory and put the scientists to flight with considerable malediction and a stout thrashing for Craig, using a limber lath to impress her point that Craig was going to Hell for his sins, which appeared to be a purely scientific effort to produce a baby from a navel.

Grandpa Sam was heard to snicker under his hand as Miss Caroline held forth on the wickedness of children, and said she didn't know what the world was coming to.

'This never happened to you when you were a little girl, Callie?' The old man was speaking gently. 'It happened to me, even as far away as Texas.' When the fumes cleared, Miss Caroline left Grandpa Sam severely alone for a week. The old man appeared younger as a result of being put in Coventry.

This was a delicate time of birds and bees and the pollination of flowers. Craig's mother received a full report from Miss Caroline about the biological experiments conducted under the house, and being a woman of inflexible mind and high purpose, Craig's mother got out some medical books that were relict of the days when her brother studied medicine, and shocked the little boy into a fresh expectation of Hell. She showed him pictures about the horrors of childbirth, drew diagrams, and assured him that even an illegal kiss could result in the most awful diseases. She stressed gonorrhoea for lunch, and served syphilis with the chicken dinner. Craig learned about buboes and chancres and breech presentations, and at ten was fully qualified to midwife a child. He shuddered in horror at the idea that procreation was so badly arranged, and took an active dislike to his mother for being so dirty-minded as to have had him. This dislike increased when, rummaging around the closet off his mother-and-father's bedroom, he encountered a hunting-boot filled to the brim with what then were called Merry Widows—*Agnes, Mabel* and *Becky* —contraceptives which came in a round tin box, which created great laughter when seen tossed, empty, by the side of the road.

All of a sudden, Craig knew what happened behind the locked doors after the roast-beef or chicken-and-dumpling dinner on Sunday afternoon, and he knew, with great disillusionment, that if he were headed for Hell for being bad, he wasn't going to be lonely.

4

CRAIG PRICE'S father was named Richard. He was slim, fox-nosed, and once had owned a thick suit of wavy brown hair which was now thinning. He stammered slightly in speech, but sang a lusty bass in the church choir. He was head book-keeper for a large feed-and-grain store, and he had proceeded to this eminence from a start as office-boy at a salary of four dollars a week. His secret desire was to be an artist, and he drew occasional pictures for the daily paper, after he completed a correspondence course in cartooning. He worked for a country-born businessman who wrote worthless cheques on Friday, and covered them with the expected incoming receipts on Monday. Richard Price had been the more-or-less hard money support of his father, Sam Price, and his mother, Miss Caroline, since he was fourteen years old, when his schooling stopped and he went to the big river town of Kensington to make his way in the world.

Richard Price worked hard and prospered. At one time he made as much salary as 125 dollars a week. He was encouraged to draw against prospect and was paying on a big brick house in the suburbs, and was also paying on two cars, a cow, a horse, and an outside man to tend the chickens and mow the lawn. He was a mild, agreeable but frail fellow, who was known as 'a good provider'. He was a member of the Country Club, but for some reason had been repeatedly denied entry into the Yacht Club. He smoked furiously, but never drank. This was attributable to the fact that he had got drunk on Christmas Eve of his twenty-first year, and had not regained consciousness until the 26th of December. But he was always the life of the party, and his slight stammer made his jokes seem more humorous than they actually were. His quartet was in high demand at most of the social events in Kensington.

He married, at twenty-four, a large, handsome, stubborn woman named Lilian, who came from New Truro as well. She had been the girl who rode astride when ladies rode side-saddle, who disliked all aspects of being a girl, and who had an inflexible will. She was the elder daughter of a family of two daughters and a son. She was ever resentful of the son, who became a doctor, and she had always wanted to become a doctor. She cowed her younger sister completely. She also completely dominated her husband. She had fierce physical energy, and a passion for up-lifting works and community service. Young Craig's first acute appraisal of his mother came when she gave away most of his toys and a majority of his clothes to one of the worthless poor-white mill-hand families she was always seeking out to help, whether they wanted it or not. His next appraisal resulted from her fierce attempt to educate him clinically in the business of sex and its liabilities, stressing its potential for both illegal procrea-tion and horrid disease. Although Craig resembled his mother physically to an almost ludicrous point, he was his father com-pletely in temperament.

Mother Lilian was the ogre in the house. She administered the punishment and prescribed the penalties, such as castor oil for eating green peaches or a stick laid across the behind for telling a lie. Father Richard never punished, never scolded. Only once did he correct Craig for some minor sin. He was commanded by his wife to beat the boy. He beat the boy, with a *turkey-feather duster*, and Craig wept, although his mother's punishments left him stony, proudly tearless.

In his very early childhood, Craig acquired a *bête noire* in the form of a lusty young ruffian named Darrell. Darrell lay in wait for Craig, outside the white picket fence, and would promptly set upon him the second the gate closed and Craig was in No Man's Land. Darrell, older than the five-year-old Craig, would start to belabour the boy, and the boy would weep and try to run away, with Darrell panting fire in flank-speed pursuit behind him. One day, as Craig made the safety of the gate, and clanged it shut, his mother met him with a stick. She beat him unmercifully.

'Every time you run from that boy,' she said, 'I intend to wear you out so bad you'll be glad to run back to him.'

Lilian's mother witnessed the beating, and protested violently.

'Shut your mouth, Mama,' Lilian said. 'Now, Craig,' she turned to the sobbing child. 'You go back out there and fight that little bastard.' The little bastard was at the time leaning over the fence, hugely enjoying what seemed to him a double triumph.

'I'm scared, I'm *scared*,' Craig sobbed. 'I try to hold his arms and he keeps hitting me in the face! I don't *want* to fight him!'

Craig's mother swiped him viciously again across the behind.

'You go fight him, or I'll keep this up all day!' she said.

'Lilian, you can't do this to your boy!' Grandmother was weeping now.

'Shut up, Mama,' said Lilian, and brandished her stave. 'Will you fight him, or will I beat you again?'

Craig looked at his two enemies, one jeering, one coldly implacable.

'I'll fight him,' he sobbed. 'Don't hit me any more!'

He raced for the gate, flung it open, and hurled himself on the jeering Darrell. His small fat fists were flails, and he sobbed and kicked and once bit his opponent on the neck. The opponent, surprised, lost his balance and fell, with Craig on top. When they finally managed to prise Craig off the fallen enemy, Craig had Darrell by the ears and was pounding his head up and down on the pavement. Craig was still weeping, but now it was Darrell running away, bawling at the fullest extent of his lungs.

Craig's mother broke her stick across her knee and went into the house without a word. After that Craig regarded his mother with guarded hostility, but he never ran away again. He walked with a slight swagger, and Darrell gave him ample sea-way.

Craig vaguely saw his father as a mild, woman-belaboured man. Miss Caroline nagged him on one side of the fence, and Lilian was always at hand to tell him what he did wrong on the other side. Old Sam Price had quit work of any substantial nature when he was in his middle thirties, and thereafter lived sketchily off political appointments while Miss Caroline ran a boarding house. When young Richard began to make enough money to contribute to the family funds, Sam Price gave up political appointments (register of deeds, town clerk) and settled down to play his fiddle, drink whisky and make ship models. He had a small pension from a completely unheroic participation in the War Between the States.

Craig's earliest memory of Miss Caroline as against his father was an oft-repeated scene around the fourth of every month. Miss Caroline, dressed as always in her musty-smelling bombazine, would be waiting for her son when he came home at night from the office.

'Did my money come today, Rosebud?'

'No, Mama. But it'll be here tomorrow or the next day.'

Miss Caroline would pout.

'I don't know why a Government can't get the pension money to a veteran's wife on time.'

'But Mama'—Richard made one feeble attempt at a joke, and thereafter abandoned it—'Papa fought on the wrong side. The Yankees *did* win it.'

'I don't believe a word of it,' Miss Caroline would say. 'I want my money. I want it now. You write somebody in Washington and tell them to send me my money.'

An occasional paying guest and what Richard added to the pension, kept the old folks fairly stylish in the mortgaged house in New Truro. Craig spent the summer, the holidays, and as many week-ends as he could manage with the old people. The rest of the time he spent with his family in the big brick house on the outskirts of Kensington.

Craig's father worked prodigiously. He took a law course at night, in addition to the art course. He strove mightily to become a certified public accountant, with the idea of going, some day, in business for himself. He put in fourteen hours a day, save Sundays, at the grain-and-feed store. While he was working, Lilian Price was off in the Ford raising funds for hospitals, selling insurance, healing the sick or ministering to the economic needs of the mill-hands. (She raised some money, once, for one indigent family of free-breeding morons, and they bought a second-hand car and had their pictures taken in front of it.)

So, in Kensington, Craig was largely free of parental supervision. Neither his mother nor father returned to the house until supper time, so between school and afternoons in the woods, he lived largely alone. As he grew older, he came to resent any interest his parents showed in his doings, and guarded his private life savagely. He kept himself as purposefully apart as an orphan. Only in Grandpa Sam did he confide, sensing that he was a confederate of the old man in a quiet rebellion.

'Why did you quit work so young?' he asked Sam Price one day. 'I mean, other people work until they're old.'

'I didn't see no dignity in labour,' the bearded old man said. 'I couldn't see the difference between being poor-poor and rich-poor. So I quit. The secret of long life is not to work yourself to

37

death. The only thing I got against poverty is that nobody ever really gets used to it enough to like it. But your grandma and your daddy are both hell-bent to work, and I figured two fanatics out of three are enough for any family.'

'Grandpa,' the boy asked seriously, 'What was Great-Grandma like, with Great-Grandpa always off chasing after buried treasure? What kind of life did she have?'

'I often wondered, later on,' the old man said, tugging at his beard. 'It couldn't of been much of a life. Pa was always off in the mesquite on them wild-goose chases. We never had much more'n a side of bacon and some salt and eggs in the house.

'We hard-scrabbled a little poozlybit of farm when the droughts and the floods let us, and we had a certain amount of skinny credit at a little store twenty miles away. If we had a horse handy, I used to ride in and pick up some molasses and such truck as that, but as I recollect, we lived on poke salad, jack-rabbits and dandelion greens more'n we lived off store vittles. Tell the truth, I don't know much about my family. I never saw much of Pa, and Ma was poorly a lot of the time, and she never had much to say. She kind of had the fun of life burned out of her. She taught me to cipher and read, and made me keep fairly clean, but I never found out what she thought or what sort of person she was like, or might have been like. I reckon she was kind of relieved when she died. She didn't take no pleasure in hardly nothing, not even if there'd been more pleasure for her to take. Certain sure she didn't pleasure herself none with Pa.'

'Was there anything you did as a little boy that you had fun out of? I mean, like I go huntin' and fishin'? What did you play? Did you have anybody to play with, or any games to play?'

The old man's eyes hooded briefly. He reached for his jug and took a drink before he answered.

'From the day I was born until after Ma died and Pa disappeared,' he said, and wiped the moisture from his moustache, 'I can't recollect I ever had one goddam minute of what you'd call fun until I went to Galveston and shipped out as a sailor on that ship I told you about. They talk about the wonderful days of childhood but it seems to me mine was all of a blank, and the only thing that marked it was when Pa left and when Pa came back. It was just like you were living in a world all by yourself. Ma was there, but she was powerful shadowy. I don't believe I ever seen her to laugh.'

'Well, you must have done *something* to fill in the time,' Craig said. 'What did you do all day?'

'I set some traps, but trapping things ain't any fun. You keep thinking about the poor critter in the trap, turning and twisting and chawing away at its own legs, and then you got to hit it on the skull to put it out of its misery, which ain't any fun, either. It reminded me kind of sad about the life of most people, although

38

I didn't know it then. I would of hunted, but we never had money for cartridges to waste on the kind of game that was handy. The only gun we had in the house for protection against the occasional Indian or thieving Mexican was an old cock-hammer ten-gauge shotgun. When Pa went off, he always taken the rifle. There wasn't no other people within fifteen, twenty mile, so there wasn't no other kids to play with. I hoed the garden and vowed that some day I'd go to China, even if I had to dig straight down. I went there, too.'

'What was it like? Were the Chinese people like us? Do they really eat dead rats? What was it *like*?'

'Disappointin',' the old man said. 'Too many sad people. Far as I know they didn't eat no rats. I think I'm tired of talking. Suppose you go find something to do.'

'Yes, Grandpa. But *Grandpa*, when you came here on the ship, why did you get off and stop going to sea? Why did you pick this place, of all the places?'

'I'll be good and goddamned if I know,' Sam Price said with sudden vehemence. 'For the last forty years I'd just as leave been in hell with my back broke. Now go find something to do, and don't bother me no more!'

'Yessir,' Craig said, wondering what he would find to do. *He's as lonely as me, he thought, maybe more. At least I got three dogs and a boat and a gun.*

He decided he would go and pick some blackberries, and maybe, if he was lucky, he'd see a rattlesnake.

5

IT was 1929, and the banks busted, and most folks followed the banks. It was 1929, and the wholesale groceries, having been gradually absorbed by the huge chain stores, went bankrupt. It was 1929, and Richard Price, Craig's father, had a nervous breakdown that further fruited into pneumonia and tuberculosis. It was 1929, and Sam Price died of cancer, and Caroline Price died of a heart attack. Old Sam's house in New Truro was sold up for taxes, and Richard Price lost his big square brick house in Kensington for the simple inability to pay. Craig Price's mother, Lilian, caught adult measles, which left her with an incurable heart weakness. And Craig Price, then a chubby sophomore in high school, failed to make the Hi-Y Club, largely because of a shy unsociability that approached surliness.

The events blurred in the boy's mind. Catastrophe piled on catastrophe, until catastrophe became almost meaningless. Mills closed, banks sent their respected presidents to jail for embezzlement, small stores filed bankruptcy petitions, and a few people, hopelessly strangled by financial entanglement, mustered up sufficient courage to shoot themselves, even in such a small metropolis as Kensington. The economic downfall of the Nation struck the South with special impact, because this was feudal society in which nearly everyone, except the poor folks, played Mr. Micawber and persisted in expecting that Something Would Turn Up. The dream was over, but nobody cared to wake up.

In one noble house on Front Street, the stiff-necked owners burnt ancient fine furniture during a harsh winter. Possibly they would not have sold the furniture, out of pride, even had there been a buyer. Richard Price, after two years' absence from his big brick house in the suburbs, moved back in as a tenant because nobody else could afford to buy it. He built a partition in the back hall, and converted the upstairs into separate apartments, which were rented to school-teachers and nurses. Craig was beginning to smoke cigarettes, and to take an active interest in girls. Suddenly thirteen-year-old Craig Price sped to a knowledge of sex which his mother had not been able to impart from her score of glossily graphic books and more vocally graphic lectures. The girls upstairs had frequent visitors. At puberty, it occurred to Craig that the laughter and the later departures were not entirely of a cultural nature, especially when he blundered upstairs one afternoon on some aimless errand and encountered one of the paying guests buck-naked in the presence of the family dentist, who was equally unhampered by garment. His scientific experiment with Eunice suddenly reformed in his mind, and he realized in one searing flash that the business of baby-production was not without its pleasurable diversion. The naked lady, decently clad once more, cornered him next day.

'Craig,' she said, 'I know you were upstairs yesterday. I'll give you a dollar not to tell your mother what you saw.'

'Keep your goddam dollar,' he said. 'I won't tell her anyway. But I *saw* you, and you *know* I saw you. I saw you naked in my house. You're a bad woman.'

'Not a *bad* woman, Craig. Just a woman. You'll understand when you get older.'

'I don't have to get older to understand,' Craig said. 'I don't ever want to see you again.' Craig didn't know it, but he was incipiently in love, and had received his first wound.

The formerly naked lady shrugged.

'All right, little boy,' she said. 'Go and tattle to your mother.' Shortly thereafter, she moved out. Craig never mentioned the matter to Lilian.

Seen through Craig's retrospective eyes, the years before he graduated from high school comprised almost pure fantasy. One year, when his mother was selling insurance—not life insurance, but the other kind, fire and theft, because his father was selling

40

life insurance—he was left almost completely alone for most of his waking hours. This was still in the rooming-house stage, as opposed to several other stages, such as when they later moved to a small house out of town so that Mother Lilian could run the kitchen in a suburban hotel. Late in the afternoon, several merry gentlemen, obviously quite drunk, rapped on the back door which led to the upstairs apartments, and Craig answered.

'What's a little boy like you doing here in a place like this?' one of the soberer of the merry gentlemen asked.

'I live here,' Craig said. 'What do you want?'

The most-nearly-sober gentleman looked at his less sober companions.

'But the manicurist in the hotel said that this was a . . .' He broke it off sharply, as he saw the boy's expression.

'Come on, gents,' he said. 'Let's go. There's been a mistake somewhere. Sorry son. Be seein' you.'

Craig heard a roar of a motor as the wheels spun in the back yard. Then, a voice from upstairs:

'Who was that, just left?'

'It's me, Craig. Some men came knocking on the door. They must of got the wrong house. They went away.'

The voice from upstairs said, in a lower tone, to somebody else. 'Goddammit, there goes dinner. Betsy called from the hotel and she . . .' The shrill voice dwindled to an angry buzz.

Shortly the phone rang, a taxi arrived, and two of the paying guests bustled out of the house.

It was almost impossible for the boy Craig to comprehend what was going on during the years from 1929 to 1931, while he completed his high school years, fell in love, was spurned, and lost his confidence in kissing games. He had seen his family go from two big cars to one ramshackle Ford, without emotion. Sam had died finally of the cancer which possessed him, leaving Craig with a sense almost of relief that it was over. Miss Caroline's passing bothered him not at all. He didn't truly understand the failures of the banks, and the bankruptcy of his father's firm was past his knowledge, since the firm continued, but under a new management, and without his father. Food appeared on the table at regular intervals, no matter where the family lived. He was warm in winter, well clothed, and did tolerably well in high school, and did not object to riding a bicycle three miles a day to get there. But it was always a blur, the actual events that knuckled themselves into the floury whole. And the events were always staccato.

One day he came back from high school and was not met, as usual, by the dogs. He whistled, and no dogs answered, to leap against him and give him the daily wet slap of eager tongue across the face. He went to look for his gun, and it was missing from its rack. Desperately he walked the fields, and searched the woods.

When his father arrived that night, Craig was panic-stricken.

'Somebody's stolen the dogs and my gun!' he cried. 'I've looked everywhere, and . . .'

Richard Price's face was grey and deeply bitten by lines around the mouth.

'You may as well know,' he said. 'I had to sell the dogs. I got a good offer, and I had to make a turn. The man that wanted the dogs wanted a gun, too. He'll sell everything back to me if I can raise the money when the bird-season's finished.'

'You won't raise the money,' Craig said. 'You always say you will but you won't. What *right* have you got to sell my dogs and my gun?'

'I'm your *father*,' Richard Price said very gently. 'And I sold my own gun some time back.'

Father and son looked at each other, and both turned away. Thereafter there was very little more to say.

With Grandpa Sam the parting had been different. The old man came back from his last trip North, where he had been taking radium treatments for an indisputable cancer which strangled him like an evilly flourishing weed. His skin was translucently waxen, and he was in unremitting pain. He managed a sickly grin when he got off the train, and as soon as he arrived at his son's now-rented house in Kensington, he called Craig aside.

'Let's you and me walk down to the cowlot,' he said, 'and get away from the strangers.'

The cow had gone from the cowlot—sold—and the pony had gone—sold—and the billygoat had gone, but the quail still whistled sweetly to each other, and the hollow croak of the raincrows could be heard in the patch of forest which braced the cowlot from behind. The cornstalks were sere and liver-spotted on the yellowed shucks, and a rabbit started, sat, and leisurely ran as the old man and the boy walked along the path, time-trodden through the cornfield. Sam Price grunted from his pain, but walked the last hundred yards to the Jimson weed-choked cowlot and sat down on a split-rail fence.

'Ain't no need for me to tell you I'm going to die,' he said. 'And the sooner the better. I'm rotten with this thing. It's spread from my mouth up, and from my neck down. Even the doctors quit fooling me, up at Hopkins.'

'But Grandpa, why? They must be able to do something, they got to be able to do something!'

'Nope, they can't do a dodlimbed thing. And anyhow, everybody's got to do it sometime—even you, my boy. One way's as good as the other when it comes time. In a way I'm glad. I never amounted to nothin', and what's more I didn't seem to care. I ploughed through seventy-odd years like a field-hand who don't care if the crop makes or don't make.'

The old man stopped for a moment, as pain knifed at him and slashed his face.

'Look here, son,' he said. 'I don't owe life nothing, and life don't owe me nothing. I ain't been any worse than the usual feller, and no better. Maybe I was born in the wrong time and place. But one thing I want you to promise me. Don't go through your life with this hook-worm philosophy I always had—just settin' and lettin' it pass. Grab it and use it and kick the crap right out of it, and don't never, ever, let it run *you*. You treat life like it was your enemy. Beat it on the head and knock it around until it hollers. Make it work *for* you, because you going to be dead a long, long time.

'Your daddy is just like me. He ain't got the guts to stand up and fight what he don't like. He's too agreeable. Don't you agree with nothing or nobody that don't please you. Kick 'em in the balls first and argue later. The Bible says turn the other cheek, but if you're smart you'll turn it away from the slap and kick 'em in the balls. Clean fighters never wound up nowhere except hung on crosses and otherwise dead. You twist anything hard enough and it'll come around to your way of thinking and doing.'

'But, Grandpa,' Craig said, 'you always been the quietest, easiest . . .'

The old man nodded.

'That's been my main trouble. I never even had guts enough to stick to sea-goin'. I never had the guts to stick to nothing, because I was so goddamned easy and nice. I never even worked much because somebody else would work for me. I should'a been one of those bad poets or somebody with a banjo the kings hired to keep them amused. I'll be dead in a month and I can't look back to a single thing I like, except maybe the promise of you. You got enough of that butt-headed mother of yours in you to ram down a wall if it gets in your way. It's a thing we lack on my side of the fence—meanness. You got to be mean to make it, especially now, when the whole damned world is turning upside, assbackwards, down. This world ain't no place for nice people. This is for dogs eating dogs, and the biggest son-of-a-bitch wins. Help me up, son, and let me lean on you a little. I need some bed.'

'Grandpa,' Craig said, shucking off Sam Price's shoes, after the old man had fortified himself with a slug of whisky. 'Did you mean *all* that, down at the cowlot? Didn't you get nothing at all out of all the years you've lived?'

Tears started in the faded, weary old eyes. Sam Price tottered spread-legged over to the bed and Craig pulled his pants off as he lay on top of the blankets. He lay there, beard stiffly erect, in his lace-up-the-back long drawers. Craig drew the blankets gently from underneath him and snugged them under the beard.

'Yep,' Sam Price said weakly. 'There was a whore-lady once, in

New Orleans, who seemed to think I was a right nice feller, and she cooked me some red beans and rice and didn't charge me nothing at all for the beans and rice nor nothing else. I heard some mighty pretty music in New Orleans, too, and one time when I was sea-goin', I put into Sydney Harbour in Australia on a nice clear day and looked at what a world might of been if people handled it right. I saw some palm-trees off the beach at Mombasa, in Africa. And I saw you, when you was first born, red and ugly and full of hair, with your nose broke, and I said to myself that is going to be the boy I started out to be. You better be that boy or I'll come back and ha'nt you. Turn out the light, son. I'm plumb wore-down.'

Craig snapped off the lights, and tiptoed out. He could hear his grandpa cursing fearfully in his pain, the curses intermingling with the laboured breathing and the snores.

6

LILIAN PRICE drove her son to college, a distance of 150 miles, in the Model-A Ford. Craig Price was nearly sixteen years old, and was wearing brown knickerbockers and white tennis shoes. In his pocket was an old, heavy-gold, hunting-case watch, the only legacy that old Sam Price left. His cow-licked brown hair fell over his right eye, and he had not quite lost his baby fat. But he smoked cigarettes with an air of bravado, and he had tasted his first real drink of whisky that summer, at the beach. He had fallen in love three times that summer, with girls named Mary, Fuzzy, and Helen. He had thrown up from the whisky, and had been regarded as a child by girls named Mary, Fuzzy, and Helen. His sacred love, Jane, nearly ten years older, had married an elderly gentleman who was at least thirty-five years old. Since he had been unsuccessful with three profane loves and one sacred love, Craig Price was off women permanently. Girls, he reckoned, were no damned good, and that included his mother, Lilian, who was saying as she deposited the boy in front of the Administration Building:

'You're on your own, now, son. The tuition is paid for the first quarter, and you've got fifty dollars cash money. We'll have to figure out something for next quarter. Maybe your daddy can make a turn. But I have to go back to Kensington. You take care of yourself, hear?'

The kiss was succinct, as one shakes hands politely with a stranger. Mother Lilian wheeled the Ford around on the loose gravel, and went away to—what? Craig looked after the depart-ing car with a feeling of relief. There would be, now, no more lectures on the horrors of sex. He felt himself born again, free at last, with his one jazzy college suit of long pants for Sundays only, his one other pair of shoes, his Blue-blacked Speller that old Sam Price had bought him, his gold watch, his half-dozen shirts and a sweater, his razor for the already-heavy beard, and his tragic emotional past behind him. He sighed deeply and looked around him at The University.

The University sat on a high plateau in the centre of the State, and it was the oldest State University in America. It was located in a place called Chapel Hill, North Carolina, stretched somewhere between Durham, where Duke University is, and Greensboro, where all the pretty girls were.

Chapel Hill was lovely in this September as Craig Price received his dormitory assignment from the Administration Building and lugged his scanty traps to a dormitory named Aycock. The trees were turning, but the enormous sward of grass was still green. The mellowed stone and brick buildings and the sharp-white of the fraternity houses, with their Doric and Corinthian colonnades, dominated a town which owned one main street and was dedicated simply to education and its by-products. Mr. Botts, the bootlegger, had not yet been discovered by Craig, Russ Columbo had not yet shot himself in an accident, and Mr. Crosby was just beginning to give 'When the Blue of the Night Meets the Gold of the Day' a real thrashing on a radio programme which professed to sell a cigar in which human saliva was not a principal ingredient. 'Love for Sale' had just been banned from the air as indecent, and Nancy Carroll was the prettiest thing in show business. It was the fall of 1931, when nobody in the world seemed to have any money.

At the time, Craig Price had not heard of anybody currently famous except Bing Crosby, Red Grange, Babe Ruth, and Russ Columbo. He knew the son and daughter of the former President of the University, Harry Chase, because they had summered in his precinct, but the new president, Frank Graham, was as unknown to Craig as Einstein. All Craig Price knew was that he was at a strange stage in his life called College, and that his mother had left in a gravelling flurry of wheels, his grandpa was dead, and his father was broke.

And that he, Craig Price, Captain-Admiral of the Ocean Sea, was in a very strange Ocean Sea.

He signed the necessary papers and received the necessary instructions for a week-long matriculation, and passed through a pleasantly green quadrangle, where some over-developed youths were playing touch football, and entered his dormitory, a huge, antiseptically-forbidding edifice, which smelled rather like a locker-room, where he was directed to Room 112. The dormitory contained a miniature post office, a sort of commissary where

45

candy bars, Cokes, peanuts and chocolate milk were dispensed by a succession of athletes who were earning their right to play games, and who were employed to salve the conscience of the people who were working off the mortgage on the Stadium.

The room contained a table, two beds, no bath, two straight chairs and a madman.

The madman was more or less seven feet high, a burly fellow of pleasant aspect. If you had to pick a room-mate, Craig thought immediately, this is the kind you'd look for. The man was blond, sunburned, with ingenuous blue eyes, and short-cropped hair. He was tremendously thewed. He smiled, showing an expanse of very white teeth. He shook hands cordially and announced himself as one Brown.

'Come in,' he said. 'Looks like the registrar has stuck us into this hole together. I'm George Brown. I flunked out of divinity school in another college, but I am one hell of a fine basketball player. I can say Hell because I am still a divinity student, not a basketball player, at heart, and divinity students can say Hell without being profane. Who're you, my child?'

'Child?' Craig said. 'What's this about *child*?'

'Well, you look kind of young,' Brown said. 'Excuse me. I'm kind of old. I'm twenty.'

'I'm fifteen,' Craig said. 'But maybe we don't call me "child". Where's I stow my gear?'

'Stow your gear?'

'Put my stuff.'

'Over there. In that closet. You haven't got very much, have you?'

'I got enough.'

Brown got up and snapped the bolt on the door. He watched Craig unpack his sparse belongings. Then he jumped up on one of the beds, and his head nearly touched the ceiling.

'Where do you come from?' he asked.

'The coast. Kensington, down on the east coast. Where do you come from?'

Brown's pleasant, healthy, athlete's face assumed a secretive smirk.

'Guess,' he said.

'I can't guess,' Craig replied. 'I just got here.'

'I'll tell you if you won't tell anybody,' Brown said. He looked over his shoulder. 'Swear you won't tell anybody.'

Craig stared at him with dawning nervousness. 'I swear,' he said, suddenly becoming conscious of the locked door. 'Where?'

'Heaven,' Brown said, rolling his eyes upward. 'From up there. I'm here on a Mission. You don't really know Who I am?'

'Brown, you said,' Craig answered, completely bewildered. 'That's who you said you were.' He looked again at the door.

'Brown isn't my real name, any more than you're whoever you

46

think you are. Who do you think *you* are?' The tone was belligerent and the face scowled.

'Craig Price. From the coast. Kensington, on the coast.'

Brown nodded his head with infinite adult wisdom. He stabbed a finger at Craig, and seemed to grow taller. His eyes gleamed with a hidden secret.

'You're no Craig. You're Isaac. And my name is really Abraham. Sometimes. I often take different shapes. Once I was Jesus Christ, but it *hurt* so. From time to time I am God Almighty, so I have the power to change Me into other people. Today I am Abraham, and I am going to sacrifice you, because as God Almighty I have told myself to be Abraham, and to sacrifice an Isaac. My Father's house has many mansions, and my Father's face has many forms. Today I am Abraham. The burning bush has told me so.'

He jumped off the bed and stalked the boy. His hands were hooked, held low, and white showed over his pupils. Saliva dripped from his mouth, and he worked his lips as if savouring a delicious morsel of food. He spoke:

'I was benched last season—me, Abraham, *benched*!' They'll know better than to bench me this year, after I've sacrificed my son!'

Brown began to approach the boy, who started to scream. The boy and the man circled the room, the man now reaching out his hands in the same leisurely fashion in which he would seek a savoury he is as yet unwilling to eat, saving the best for last. The boy continued to scream, while staying just away from the groping hands. As Craig darted away from the hands, he shoved the closed window with his shoulder, breaking the glass, and screamed louder.

'Help!' he yelled, his newly found man's voice breaking into falsetto. 'Help! He's trying to kill me! Help! Help!' He scuttled round the room, dodging, once kicking out at Brown's legs, another time feeling his shirt rip as the hands groped almost blindly at him, and the maniac's voice suddenly turned bland, soothing.

'Come here, now, come here, Isaac,' the voice said, 'it won't hurt at all. I've told myself that this is necessary, so they won't bench me any more. Just come here to your papa, and it'll all be over in a minute . . .'

There was a thunder of feet outside. Shoulders hit the door. Craig continued to circle, and continued to scream. More shoulders hit the door, which burst inward just as the maniac had the boy penned in a corner of the room. Half a dozen burly men leaped on Brown and knocked him to the floor, where the madman thrashed enormously until someone kicked him in the head. He lay, his lips froth-bubbling, his great chest panting sobbingly. Four men sat on him. One looked up.

'Who're you, kid?'

'Craig Price. I'm his room-mate. He's crazy. He tried to kill me. Said he was Abraham and somebody benched him and I was Isaac and everything would be all right as soon as he sacrified me . . .' Craig burst into tears. 'I just *got* here this afternoon,' he said, between sobs.

'Poor little bastard's still got on short pants,' one of the muscular men said. '*What* a way to start school. I always knew this guy was nuts,' nodding at Brown. Brown raised his head. 'Bust him,' the man said.

'What with?' one of the other men said.

'Christ, *Webster's Dictionary*, your foot, anything! We can't sit on him all day!'

'Hold him down a minute,' one of the men said. 'You got anything heavy, kid?'

'No,' Craig said. 'Not that I can think of.'

The man looked around the room. There was a flashlight on Brown's table.

'He won't need this, where he's going,' the man said. 'They ain't allowed in Dix Hill.'

He took the flashlight, wrapped it in a towel, and struck the maniac repeatedly at the base of the skull. The maniac slumped.

'Drag him out,' the man said. 'Somebody call the cops, and somebody else call the Dean's Office, and somebody else call the coach. You all right, kid?'

'I guess so,' Craig said. 'Is this guy really crazy?'

'He'll do,' the man said. 'He'll do. My name's Jimmy Wilbur. Most people call me Moose. I got a spare bunk in my room. You want to come spend the night with people who ain't God?'

'No, thanks,' Craig said. 'I think this semester I'll maybe room by myself, but thanks all the same.'

The man smiled. He was a tall, red-headed, compact man, with friendly grey eyes. His nose had been broken more than once, and his hips were so slim that his shoulders seemed deformed. The wide smile was kind.

'Good for you, kid. But if you have any more trouble, half the jockstrap scholarships of this school live down the hall from you. I run the store, and we got credit, when needed. Now let's get this son of a bitch out of here,' he jerked his head towards the unconscious man. Then he smiled again.

'How old are you, kid?'

'Fifteen,' Craig said, and suddenly squared his shoulders. 'Going on sixteen.'

'I think you'll make it,' the big, lean, compact man said. 'If you need any help, just holler.'

'What did you say your name was, again?' Craig almost blushed. 'This was sort of mixed up.'

'Wilbur. Jimmy Wilbur. Moose Wilbur.'

48

'Oh, my Lord,' Craig said. 'You're not the . . . the All-American?'

'So says Grantland Rice,' the big man said. 'Take it easy, boy. And if you need anything else, yell, because all us animals are right down the hall in this zoo. But what a hell of a way to start off a college career. Worse than mine.'

'Where did you start yours?' Craig murmured, feeling suddenly very faint.

'In a coal-mine outside Scranton, Pennsylvania,' Jimmy Wilbur said. 'And my last name ain't Wilbur. It's a name with a lot of "z's" in it. Good night, kid. Come on, you guys,' he said, 'let's get this nutty professional athlete out of here and let the kid get some sleep.'

They dragged the still-unconscious Brown out of the door. Craig closed and bolted the door, and then he lay down on the bed and really began to sob. Grandpa Sam Price seemed a dreadful distance away, as far as heaven, as long as eternity. He went to the closet, took the watch out of his pants' pocket and placed it under his pillow. The steady ticking sent him wet-faced off to sleep. The next day he got up and went to the gymnasium to register; at the same time his first room-mate was being taken in a strait-jacket to the insane asylum in Raleigh.

And that night, after the sweltering sign-posted registration day in the Tin Can, he had a fresh room-mate, newly in from Paris. The room-mate was wearing a furry fedora hat, and his name was Philip.

Philip had a rather small, heart-shaped face, with a tiny rosebud mouth and an air of great sophistication, His clothes differed from the popular John Held Jr. model, which embraced twenty-four-inch trouser cuffs, peaked lapels on a bottom-freezing jacket, a shirt dragged down past the Adam's apple and anchored by an enormous lump of necktie. At a time when young bloods wore painted slickers and drove raddled jalopies with slogans such as 'Hit Me Easy, I'm Getting Old' on the back, young Mr. Philip duFresne's fuzzy Italian fedora, black cordurory suit with narrow pants, and flowing artist's tie provided a distinct shock, coming just after the madman's introduction of Craig to College Life.

'*Moi, je m'appelle Philippe duFresne, et je viens de Paris. Zut, alors. Excusez-moi.*' He smiled winningly. 'I find it so difficult not to speak in French. I have spent the entire summer in Paris, France, *avec ma mère*. With my mother. My home is in Charleston, South Carolina. We live on The Battery.' He pronounced it 'Bottery' and seemed to expect applause.

'My name's Price—Craig Price. I come from not so far from you. Kensington, North Carolina. But we don't speak much French there.'

49

'My mother is a widow, and very rich,' Philip duFresne said. 'And the most beautiful woman in the world.

'That's nice. My mother ain't very pretty and we're as poor as church mice.'

'*Quel dommage*,' Philip said. 'What a shame. Then you have never been to Paris?'

'No. I've never been anywhere. Is it nice?'

Philip rolled his eyes ecstatically. '*Magnifique*. But wonderful. The women—ahh. *Magnifique*. I caught the clap in Paris,' this with great pride.

'You caught the clap?'

'*Alors, oui*. It was nothing. No worse than a bad cold. We say in Charleston, a man is not a man until he has caught the clap and screwed a nigger.'

Craig was aghast.

'H-how old are you?' he asked timidly.

'I am nearly eighteen,' said M. Philippe duFresne of Charleston. South Carolina, and Paris, France. 'Also I am a man. The lady who gave me the dose was not French, however. She was English, and her name was Iris March. I shall never forget her. She always wore a green hat. She has given me an idea for a novel. I am a writer, you know.'

'A writer?' Craig was overawed—overawed by the extreme age of his new room-mate. 'What have you written?'

'Oh, little things—*les petites choses*. But I am working on a novel now, a novel called *Barbellion*. I have the title from two words—barbarian and rebellion. Which bed is mine? I must stay in this beastly place until I am chosen for a fraternity. Stupid rules.'

'Over there—unless you'd prefer the one I slept in last night?'

'To a man, a bed is a bed. It is only who occupies the bed with you that is important. Excuse me. I shall go and tell the chauffeur to bring my bags.'

The grand stranger departed, and Craig shook his head. A maniac and a French-speaking novelist in rapid succession were a little too rich for a country boy. Presently, Philip returned, followed by a chauffeur carrying expensive leather luggage. The chauffeur made five trips.

'That is all until your trunk arrives, Mr. Philip,' he said. He touched his cap. 'Would you be wanting anything more?'

'No, Graves, that will be all for now. You'd better get back to the Inn and see if *Maman* needs you for anything.'

The chauffeur touched his cap again.

'Thank you, Mr. Philip,' he said, and went out.

'Decent chap, Graves,' Philip said, extending a package of cigarettes. 'Smoke?'

'Thank you,' Craig said, taking a fat, gold-tipped cigarette from a strange box. 'What are these?'

'Abdullahs,' said the exotic stranger. 'Egyptian. I never smoke anything else.'

'Do you always travel with your own chauffeur?'

To Craig, a chauffeur was somebody who drove an aged banker or maybe the head of the Atlantic Coast Line Railroad, around.

'It's a bloody bore, really,' said Philip, making a short dialectical trip across the channel to London. 'But the mater was obsessed with the idea of seeing me installed correctly in the university. Frankly, the old girl's between affairs right now, and is rather more bored than not.'

'Between *affairs*?'

'But of course. Since my old boy did a bunk—took off with some shocking tart—one can't blame poor old mum for finding a bedfellow from time to time. The last one was a bit sticky, though. An Italian. Greased his hair, and wore a dreadful perfume. What the mater saw in Raffaele *I* can't say. Told her as much, and she confiscated my allowance for a month, for being rude. Turned out I was right, too. Raffaele married some *frightful* peasant after he'd milked poor old mum of the best part of a year's income. I *told* her I didn't mind her spending *her* money on her boy friends but when she started holding up my allowance I was going to squawk to the trustees.'

'You actually get an allowance, Philip?'

'Call me Phil. A beggar's pittance, only until I'm twenty-one. A lousy hundred a month—plus expenses, of course. But then I write cheques. They aren't any good, half the time, but the lawyers always make them come right somehow. Do you drink?'

'A little bit. Not much. Do you?'

'Gallons. Never travel without a flask. Here. Have yourself a tiddly.' Philip produced a handsome pig-skin flask, silver-mounted, a long, thin flask of quart capacity, from his inner breast pocket. 'Had a special pocket made to hold it. It's French cognac. Best drunk neat.'

Craig tipped back his head and took a long pull at the flask. His eyes watered, but he fought down an impulse to cough. Philip gave him a look of near admiration.

'How old are *you*?'

'Nearly sixteen,' Craig said.

'You drink like you've been there before,' Philip said.

'Sho,' Craig drawled. 'I was weaned on Carolina corn. I had my first sugar-tit dipped in white lightnin'.'

'I think maybe you and I will get along pretty good,' Philip said, now crossing the Atlantic and speaking a Charleston version of English. 'Look. I've got a date'—he pronounced it 'day-et'— 'with the old lady. Would you like to come along and meet her at the Inn? She'll feed us.'

'I'd like to, but I haven't got anything to wear . . .'

'You must at least have some long pants?'

51

'I have. Look.' He went over to the clothes-closet and took down his other suit, the Sunday one. It was the snazzy plaid number with the twenty-four-inch pants-cuffs, and it had cost $18.75, tailor-made, at Solomon's.

'Jesus Christ,' Philip said. 'The old lady'd faint if you showed up in that Joe College thing. Look. We're about the same size. Wear one of mine.'

'I can't. She'd know immediately it was one of yours.'

'The hell she would. I bought a flock of stuff before we left London—not even paid for yet. She hasn't seen anything in the biggest bag. Let's look.'

Craig had never seen such clothes—tweeds, flannels, broad-cloths, sports jackets with complementing slacks. There seemed an endless family of hand-carved shoes—treed with oaken inserts, and Craig had never seen a shoe-tree before. There was a special vault for neckties, richly confected of names Craig had never heard—foulard, repp, piqué, satin and all the varieties of silk and wool and knit.

'Good Lord,' he said in awe. 'I never knew anybody had so many clothes.'

'Wait'll the trunk comes,' Philip said. 'This is just my travelling stuff. Which suit d'you fancy?'

'*Any* of them?'

'Take your pick.'

'Would it—would it be all right if I wore the grey flannel?'

'It's yours. But you better wear that maroon knit tie with it, against a white shirt. And *black* shoes.'

Craig's eyes dropped.

'I'm afraid I've only got brown,' he said. 'Maybe I just better not go . . . Or go as I am.'

'The hell with that. I wouldn't take you to meet a whore dressed the way you are. The old lady is awful particular. Here, try on some shoes. We're about the same size all over.'

Craig dipped into the shoe compartment, and chose a pair of black calf oxfords. He looked at the soles, and they were as pale as a Negro's palm.

'You never had these on,' he said, almost accusingly.

'Never had time,' his new room-mate said. 'Had the British boot-maker turn out a whole litter of them just before we sailed. I think those'll fit you.'

Craig took off his tennis shoes, and tentatively inserted a foot.

'Too tight,' he said. 'Sorry, but they're too tight.'

'Hell's delight,' Philip said. 'Of course they're too tight. Those socks you've got on weigh more than the shoes. Here. Try these socks.' He chose a pair of almost transparent black silk socks and slipped them at Craig. 'French silk,' Philip said. 'Feel better than a piece of ass.'

Craig slipped his feet into the socks, and the feet went into the shoes as if greased. He laced one, and then the other, and stood up.

'Feels like I'm wearing gloves on my feet,' he said.

'Jolly good,' Philip said. 'Long as I'm outfitting you, try one of those Italian silk shirts with that red tie. I imagine you have your own underwear?'

'Now wait a minute . . .'

'Oh, for Christ's sake don't be so touchy. I was just joking. All I want is for you to make a good impression on the old girl, so maybe she'll ask you home for the Christmas holidays. We have a lot of fun in Charleston around Christmas, and the poontang . . . Ahhhh.' Philip winked viciously. 'We got hotter pants in Charleston than in Paris. And less clap.'

Craig felt vaguely uneasy. But he dressed, slowly, in his borrowed plumage, and for the first time in his life experienced the sensuality that comes with the snug of good cloth around the shoulders, the braced hang of artistically tailored trousers, the cool feel of silk on his torso, and the stroking luxury of shoes that felt lighter than socks. He walked outside to the lavatory, damped his cowlick down, and smiled at his neat maroon knitted tie. He walked back to the bedroom.

'*Bis, bis*!' Philip applauded. 'Behold the *boulevardier*!'

Craig blushed.

'They do make a difference, don't they?'

'Nobody'll mistake you for sixteen, son,' Philip said. 'You look nearer twenty-one.'

'It's my whiskers,' Craig said. 'I was born with a beard.'

Philip stroked a nearly hairless face.

'My one big desire is to grow a moustache. Come on, I'll change now, and we'll go press a call on ma. Except we don't call her ma, or mama, or mother. We call her Julie.'

'Her name's Julie?' Craig said, stupidly.

'No, her name is *not* Julie,' Philip said cheerfully, stepping out of his trousers, and kicking them under the bed. 'Her name is actually Henrietta. But she doesn't look like a woman named Henrietta, so she settled for Julie. It's a lovely name, and I'm going to use it in my book, *Barbellion*. Julie March, after the girl friend who gave me the clap.'

'What about this book, exactly?'

'It's a story about the decline of the South, everybody decadent after the Yankees took over. Then . . . hell, I don't know what then, but I'll have a lot of sex in it, and some misce—some miscegen—a lot of screwing between white folks and black folks in it, and one lovely mulatto woman who steals the white hero from Julie March.'

'What's his name, the white guy, I mean?'

'Lesesne—possible Pierre. God knows we have enough Lesesne's in Charleston. At least I ought to be able to borrow the name.' Philip had just knotted a dull-grey silk tie against a white voile shirt. He inserted cuff-links—the first Craig had ever seen—in the double-barrelled cuffs, and shrugged himself into a dark blue double-breasted coat.

'How do I look?'

'Not so good as me,' Craig grinned. 'I think your tailor had me in mind when he made your clothes.'

'We're a fair entry, I'd say,' Philip reached for the flask again. 'Better have another slug before we brace the Duchess. A bit of tip to you, room-mate: call her Madame first, she likes it. And then, when she says: "Call me Julie", call her Madame Julie. That's about the time she'll tell you to call her Julie, seriously, without the Madame, and shortly thereafter she'll ask you to come and see us for Christmas.'

Craig said:

'I haven't got any money to go visiting to Charleston for Christmas. I haven't got any money at all.'

'*Merde alors,*' Philip said cheerfully. 'She'll send the car with the chauffeur to fetch her baby boy home safe and sound. Or better, I'm working on her to buy me a car. When we get there it's all on the house. I might tell you one thing else about Julie. She is only just twice as old as me. She had me early—and, I'm told, she got married for cause.'

It took Craig another twenty years to realize that what he had mouthed in answer was a cliché.

'You mean . . . ?'

'Your new room-mate is a near-miss, an almost-bastard,' Philip said gaily. 'And I don't think the man she married had anything to do with me. I look rather like a close friend of the family. My proper old man was a clot. I imagine Julie used him as a convenience.'

'Well, goddam,' Craig said. 'Nobody ever told me college would be like this. Last night my first room-mate went crazy on me, and tried to kill me. And today I got a new room-mate who is an almost bastard and who caught the clap in Paris, France.'

'And who is a liar, too,' Philip said cheerfully. 'I never caught any clap in Paris, France, or London, England, or anywhere else. As a matter of fact I'm a virgin. Are you?'

'Yes,' Craig said. 'I almost wasn't but I am. Technically I am.'

'Maybe we can improve the score,' Philip said, 'but in the meantime, let's go knock up Ma.'

Craig looked horrified.

'*What?*'

'Not what you think. It's an English expression. Let's go and rouse out the old lady. She'll be patting her foot.'

The boys walked down the corridor, and out into the street fronting on the Arboretum, heading for the Carolina Inn. They nodded courteously to everyone they met, and received very few nods in return.

'Friendly sort of place,' Philip said. 'About as friendly as Charleston, if your blood ain't blue. Another thing: I am not an almost bastard. My old man and Julie were engaged for eighteen months before they were married, and I wasn't born until fourteen months after the ceremony.'

'Then why do you lie?' Craig's tone held wonderment.

'Damned if I know, it just seems to be fun. Was it true your room-mate went crazy on you last night?'

'Crazy as a bedbug,' Craig replied. 'I don't lie except when I have to.'

'You're missing a lot of fun,' Philip said. 'Hello, there's the Deke House. I think I'll go Deke. What are you going to pledge?'

'Nothing,' Craig said. 'I haven't got the dough. Also I ain't social from Charleston.'

'Don't let it get you down, boy,' Philip said. 'Well, here we are. Let's go and beard the dragon.'

Madame Julie duFresne was indeed patting her foot.

'You're late,' she said. Then, turning her gaze to Craig. 'Who's this?'

'Friend of mine, Julie. My new room-mate. May I present Mr. Craig Price, of Kensington, North Carolina. His last room-mate went crazy on him after only an hour. This was last night.'

'He seems to be in a rut,' Madame Julie duFresne then turned a blinding smile on Craig. 'This one has been trying to drive me mad for years. What was your name again?'

'Craig, ma'am, Craig Price.'

'Nice name. It sounds strong. How old are you?'

'Fif—sixteen years old, ma'am.'

'Don't call me ma'am, for God's sake. My name's Julie.'

'I don't think I know you well enough to call you Julie, ma'am.' Madame Julie duFresne shot Craig a swift look.

'How old did you say you were?'

'Almost sixteen, ma'am.'

'How does it happen you're in college so early?'

'I skipped some grades, ma'am.'

'Look.' Philip's mother turned to her son. 'For the love of God, explain to your room-mate that this ma'am business drives me insane. Let's settle for something less formal.'

'How about Madame Julie?' Craig permitted himself a tiny smile. Madame duFresne looked at him sharply.

'As long as you're rooming with Philip, I think that "Aunt Julie" mightn't be too inept.'

'How about "Miss Julie"?' Craig smiled again. 'I'd feel easier, ma'am.'

'Miss Julie it is, and no more "ma'ams". You know, I think I like you, Craig Price.'

'Even in your son's suit and shoes and shirt and tie?'

Philip made a face. He put a finger to his lips.

'You didn't have to say that,' Julie duFresne said. 'I hadn't seen the clothes before. Why did you?'

'I don't know. I like your son. But he's a liar. He plays games with himself. He said you wouldn't like it if I came to meet you in my knickerbockers or my "college" suit, which are the only clothes I have.'

'Bloody little snob,' Julie duFresne said. 'So he got you to wear some of his, did he?'

'Yes, ma'am—yes, Miss Julie. We're about the same size. I don't know much about this.'

White showed over the top of Madame duFresne's enormous violet eyes. She jabbed at Craig with a long, crimson fingernail.

'See here, my boy,' she said harshly. 'You go out and tell my chauffeur to take you back to your dormitory, and to wait while you change your clothes into what you were wearing before Maurice Chevalier here came into your life. Then you come back and we will have dinner together, Price Craig.'

'Craig Price, ma'am.'

'And keep calling me "ma'am". I find I like it. In the meanwhile I will have a word with my child.'

'Yes, ma'am.'

As Craig went to look for Graves, the chauffeur, he reflected that the mother of his new room-mate, Philip duFresne, was the most beautiful woman he had ever seen in his life. It was not the severe black dress, the double-strand of pearls, or the first mink coat he had ever seen. It was not the Parisian shoes, or the elegant gloves. It was not even the enormous sapphire eyes in the white face from which the straight black hair was drawn to make a bun on the nape of her slender white neck, the wide humorous red mouth and the exquisite figure. It was not even the drawling, faintly accented voice which could sharpen from sugar into razor blades. It was the whole thing, put together perfectly into a package that was ready for a grown man to open. Craig wished fleetingly that he was a grown man.

'Wait here, please,' Craig said to Graves. 'Wait here until I change.'

As he stepped out of the beautifully cut trousers and pulled on his knickers, Craig Price said aloud:

'One day,' he said, kicking viciously at the wonderfully soft calfskin shoes. 'One day, I'll have me some clothes like this.'

He pulled on a sweater.

'And one day,' he said, 'I'll have me a woman like that. One day. And they'll all be mine. Not somebody else's.'

Wearing knickers, tennis shoes, and a sweater, Craig Price went back to the waiting limousine.

'The hotel, please, Graves,' he said, as he was helped into the back seat.

'And one day,' he said, 'I'll have a better car.'

7

THE trees crisped into violent scarlets and tawny golds, and the football season roared off with a bang. The team was good, that year, with a new coach—a tough, squat, serious, scholarly man who was paid to win and who won with hired material from the mining areas of Pennsylvania and West Virginia. There wasn't a Southern accent on the first two strings.

The athletes in the Aycock dormitory adopted a peculiarly paternal attitude to Craig, doubtless because of the violence of his entrance into college. Moose Wilbur, the All-American, seemed especially concerned with the boy's welfare.

'Look, kid,' the athlete said. 'Part of this deal I got with the school is looking after the store here in Aycock. I have to go to class in the morning and practice all afternoon, and I'm supposed to hustle a boarding house in the evenings. If you'd take that afternoon trick in the store for . . . You haven't got any labs, have you?'

'Not until next year,' Craig said. 'I'd be glad to handle the store, Jim.'

'Well, if you do, you can at least get your sandwiches and cigarettes and candy free, and maybe knock down a *little* on the cash. Not much, but enough for a movie. And listen, kid. It's hard for us to do it, and it's illegal as hell, but we—some of us—came by a lot of extra tickets. Good ones, down front around the fifty-yard line. There's a lot of business to be done just at game time, if you do it right, and careful. Say I got a couple of dozen choice ducats for you every home game, if you could get rid of 'em for a jacked-up price, us guys would be glad to split you fifty-fifty. Of course, if you got caught by the University cops, we don't know nothing. You just found the tickets.'

'It's kind of crooked, ain't it?' Craig grinned. 'Not that I mind.'

'It's no more crooked than the racket we work for,' Jimmy Wilbur said. 'I been going to school free ever since some scout saw me playing grammar school ball against Irontown and gave my old man a couple hundred to sign me up. You know I went to Peddie Military Academy first? I knew every play in this school's book before I signed up here my freshman year. We had extension coaches.'

'Why don't they just pay you a salary?'

Jimmy Wilbur spat, and ground the spittle into the concrete floor with the heel of his shoe.

'We're *amateurs*,' he said. 'We wind the eight-day clock, and jump over the suitcase on a bet, and hustle tickets, and hustle boarding houses, and work in the Student Union, and some old grad picks up the fraternity dues. We get our clothes free from the College Shop and somebody like old Ellis down there is representative for Doctor Pepper, and somebody else works in the Smoke Shop, and I tend bar at the commissary here, and it's all a bunch of crap. What makes it mostly crap is that all you can major in is physical education, because you got no time for real study. You got to show up three weeks early for the fall term, and after Christmas winter practice comes, and then you got spring practice unless you're playing baseball, and when the summer comes, they get you a job on a milk route or sawing logs or swinging a pick on a new highway project so you won't get soft. So you finally graduate and all you're fit for is a job as assistant coach in some jerk school somewhere, with the idea that maybe one day you might make as much as eight thousand dollars a year as head coach before the alumni get sore and fire you. Amateurs, for Christ's sake! Bums is a better word.'

He spat again, and left the spittle unrubbed.

'Come on down to my room, kid,' he said. 'I got a bottle of shine. Every time I think football I feel like getting drunk. You're a pretty good kid. Drink?'

'Not much. Some.'

'Don't let it throw you. A lot of guys get lost in the bottle. Come on, let's go strike a blow for Alma Mater.'

Seated on the bunks in Jimmy Wilbur's room, Craig said:

'How can you drink? You're supposed to be in training, aren't you? Isn't it bad for you?'

Jimmy Wilbur tipped the half-gallon fruit jar of white corn into a thick water-glass. He added a little Coca-Cola, and drained half the glass. Then he handed the jug to Craig, before he spoke.

'That's crap, too, like the rest of it. Why wouldn't I drink? I sweat enough to lose it. And I can still go on a Saturday. We got enough tame bohunks blocking for me to where I could do it on crutches. I made the official All-American last year. If I don't look good this year they'll just fire the coach. That, I'd like to see.'

Craig took a gulp out of his drink.

'Where does this come from?' he asked. 'It's not bad. I had worse down my way this summer.'

'Guy down the pike apiece on the Durham Road. Hey!' Jimmy Wilbur smacked his knee. 'I got an idea. I got an *idea*. The campus cop plays left tackle on the first string. There's a fellow over at Duke, comes from Jersey City, got a connection in the bootlegging business. He's a nice guy, an Irishman, and his brother is somebody in the New York-Jersey mob. How'd it be

58

if we sort of went in business together? He could get the alky from up North. We could put it together here, and start an unofficial agency. You could maybe work the fraternity houses on a steady basis—with me for a front, I mean. I'd take you around to a few of the lodges, and we'd buy the boys a drink, and I'd let the word drop that this could be steady service. They wouldn't have to go all the way out the road to pick up a jug. We'd cut the cop in, see, and split the take four ways—me, you, the cop and the guy in Durham. Well, maybe no. Maybe the Durham guy would have to go for half, and we'd split the other half three ways. After all, he's the supply. How's it sound?'

Craig paused before he answered. He thought about his one suit, and the day he borrowed clothes from Philip, his room-mate. He thought about the fact that, after buying books, and paying a month's board, he had less than ten dollars remaining to see him into Christmas. He thought about Sam Price, dying, and what the old man had said in the cowlot. He thought about Philip's lovely mother, and of Philip's beautiful clothes and shoes. He thought about his gold watch, and how much it was likely to fetch in a Durham hockshop.

'It sounds just fine,' he said. 'When do we start? But tell me something first, Jimmy, why are you guys being so nice to me? I ain't anybody.'

'I really don't know, kid,' the athlete said. 'I really couldn't say. Except that maybe you got a chance not to wind up smelling like jockstraps and shower rooms all your life. *I* don't know.'

He reached over and punched the boy roughly on the chest.

'Maybe it's just because you're a good kid with a chance not to be a bum. By the way, how're you getting along with that pansy room-mate you've got now?'

'All right, I guess. He's not a bad guy. He'll be moving out next quarter, anyhow. He missed the Dekes, but the Sigma Nus pledged him. He'll be their big glamour boy. Mama just bought him a green Pierce Arrow.'

'Oh, that's that big can I saw out front. And the dame in it. That couldn't have been his old lady?'

'Could, and was. Ain't she something to have a kid in College?'

'Man.' Jimmy Wilbur's whistle was reverent. 'Why don't I ever come up with a mother like that?'

'I'm going to visit them in Charleston for the Christmas holidays,' Craig said. 'Mrs. duFresne asked me. She thinks I'm a good influence on Phil. Philip, I mean.'

'Stand up, son.' Jimmy Wilbur looked at Craig keenly, and set his head to one side. 'Mmmmm,' he said. 'You'll owe me ten bucks if she don't. Here's the bet, paid now.'

He handed the boy a ten-dollar bill.

'What's this for?' Craig held the money awkwardly. He sat down.

'Call it a down-payment on a suit,' Jimmy Wilbur said. 'I might as well pay you now, because I lost the bet. In any case you'll level with me.' He cleared his throat. 'Tell me, kid. You pledging any fraternity? I'm a Phi Gam. I could fix it, okay enough. And no dough. Get you something to do.'

Craig squirmed.

'Maybe you'll think this is funny?'

'Try me and see if I think it's funny. Shoot.'

'Well, hell, Jimmy, I think this fraternity thing is a luxury you ought to pay for. It's not a thing you ought to earn, like waiting on tables or selling sandwiches and lemonade at night when the boys make the rounds with the baskets. I been rushed some— ATO's, Phi Kaps, Phi Gams, Phi Delts, Sigma Chis, Sigma Nus —everything but the Dekes, the SAE's and the Betas. But I don't play football and I'm not on the publications and my old man ain't governor and I ain't got a dime unless I make some. I just don't want to do anything on a free list. Maybe next year if I got some dough. . . . But if not, the hell with it. I don't want social charity. My old man couldn't make it in the Yacht Club back home, and it bothered him. It don't bother me a damn bit, except that it *does*, but I won't let it. You understand any of that?'

'More than you know, son. I'm on the free list in my lodge, and if they took Grantland Rice's All-America away from me I couldn't get in the door as a janitor. 'Have you met Brother Wilbur, the All-American?' Jimmy's voice minced. 'What they are saying is that this big Polack is in here for nothing, for free, and if he breaks his leg we'll start charging him dues. Christ Almighty.'

'About the bootlegging. I don't think I like that, either. I came here to learn something, not to get kicked out, and we'd be a cinch to get caught eventually. If nothing else, the pros on the Durham road would hear about it and gang us. If they're anything like the leggers in my end of the State, they got a working agreement with the cops.'

Craig spoke earnestly, learnedly.

'How come you know so much about bootleggers and crooked cops? A kid like you?'

'Easy enough. My grandpa was sick with cancer a long time, and he drank about a quart a day against the pain. When he got too feeble to go after his own booze, I went. I knew every bootlegger in Niggertown, and most of the white ones, too. Seems like every time I went after a jug, I'd run into a cop in somebody's kitchen. Got so I was hitching rides with them.'

Jimmy Wilbur laughed.

'It seems to me you know an awful lot for a short-pants kid,' he said. 'How about girls? You ever sample any of that coloured poon?'

Craig blushed.

'I pretty near did. We had a coloured gal named Iris—part Indian, part Negro, with a smidgen of white. What we call a Brass Ankle. She was about sixteen and pretty as a picture. This summer I got to thinking about Iris too much at night, and one day, when my mother went off shopping, I slipped down the stairs in my shorts, with something in mind. I guess the old lady read it in my eyes, because she cut my trail, circled back behind me, and caught me just as I was making a grab at Iris.'

'What did she do?'

'She beat hell out of me with a broom, big as I was. She said until the day she died, any time she caught any of her menfolks messing with the help, she aimed to grab a broom and wear 'em out. She would, too. She beat me something terrible when I was a little boy for running away from a fight with another boy. She hurt me so bad I went back and beat up the other boy.'

'Sounds like quite a woman, your ma. Say, we generally go over to Durham to one of the hotels on Saturday nights. There's some pretty good gals over there, and only cost two bucks, room and all. You want to go, some Saturday? You can't hang on to that cherry for ever.'

Craig blushed again.

'I'm in love,' he said. 'I would kind of like to be true.'

'Who in hell are you in love with? You only been here a month, and there ain't half enough girls to go around even for the society guys with cars.'

'Don't laugh,' Craig said. 'Jean Harlow.'

Jimmy Wilbur stared.

'That's kid stuff, that movie star business.'

'Not for me it isn't. I sleep with her every night. It's all I can do to handle her business.'

'Are you nuts?'

'No, I'm not nuts. I've got a funny kind of brain, though. I can generally dream about what I want to, if I concentrate hard enough before I go to sleep. Ever since I saw *Hell's Angels* I been concentrating on Jean Harlow. And by God, the other morning I caught her.'

'Tell me more, my young friend. This is a piece of scientific knowledge I'd like to share. How did you get so chummy with that blonde hunk of dame, at your age?'

'Well, a couple of weeks ago I dreamed I had her out in the woods near the lake. We were lying down on the pine needles, and I kissed her. Then she took her dress off. . . .'

'Does she wear a brassière, at all?'

'Nope. Not a stitch under that dress.'

'Not even pants?'

'Not even pants. Well, I crawled over close to her and was kissing her when the goddam alarm clock went off for my eight o'clock maths class, just as I was about to . . .'

61

'That's a pity. *What* a pity.'

'Wait a minute. I cut off the clock, and went back to sleep. And damn' if I didn't pick up the dream where I left off. I caught her, and caught her good. Of course I had to cut the class, but it was worth it.'

'How often does this happen?'

'Nearly every morning. I reckon I'll flunk maths, but somehow algebra don't seem so important.'

'You telling me the truth?' Suspiciously.

'Hand to God. I'm even getting her to where she comes to call a little earlier every day, and I been making the maths class for the last week. Not that it'll save me from a flunk. That X plus Y to the second power don't mean anything to me. After a session with Jean I can't seem to concentrate.'

'Boy, you are *the* goddamndest freshman *I* ever saw,' Jimmy said. 'Come on, let's have another drink, and then I got to practise. "Practise" *what*? Something I know more about than the coach?'

'You want me to take over the store today?'

'Sure, why not? And remember, don't steal much. Just movie money—although why you need it when you're going steady with Jean Harlow I couldn't know.'

Craig laughed, throwing his head back.

'Who can tell?' he said. 'Some day I may get tired of her and want a change.'

Jimmy Wilbur clapped himself dramatically on the skull, and burlesqued a stagger as he tottered off to practise, reeking of moonshine whisky. That next Saturday he ran a punt back from behind his own goal line for the touchdown that beat Duke, 7–0, and also kicked the extra point. But when he and a few select members of the varsity went to Durham that night to get their ashes hauled, his heart was not in it.

'What's the matter with you, honey?' the garishly cosmeticked blonde with the whore's bulging stomach asked him. 'Don't you like me any more?'

Jimmy Wilbur reached for his pants.

'It isn't you,' he said. 'It's me. I'm in love.'

'Who with? One of the coeds, and she won't put out?'

'No. Jean Harlow.'

The whore stared at him.

'I think you're getting punchy,' she said. 'All you athletes leave it on the football field.'

'You could be right,' Jimmy Wilbur said, making for the door. 'Baby, you certainly could be right.'

62

8

JULIE DUFRESNE'S house on Charleston's Battery, overlooking the river, was hidden from the world by a thick plaster wall. A niche in this wall proved to be an iron gate—locked—which was opened by a butler in a striped working apron—an elderly white-haired man with a bulbous nose as deeply pitted as a strawberry. He looked at Philip with a servant's lofty distaste as he produced an enormous iron key and the gate clanged on its pivot.

'Hello, LeBlanc,' Philip said. 'We're home. How is Madame?'

'Welcome home, Master Philip. Did you have a good trip?'

'That'll be enough of that "Master Philip" business, LeBlanc. I'm a big boy now. Yes, we had a nice trip. See that the car's washed. It's filthy.'

'*Oui, Monsieur* duFresne.' He accented the *Monsieur*. '*Madame votre mère* is having tea in the patio. She asks that you join her after you show your guest to his room and wash up, if you wish. How am I to call this gentleman?'

'*Mister* Price,' Philip said, as they moved through the formal palm-studded front garden, which was encumbered by so much marble statuary that Craig was reminded of a cemetery. Craig looked at the enormous tile-roofed white house, with its lacy iron-wrought balconies and galleries, presenting a formidable prow towards the river. He wondered why there was no front porch.

They moved directly into a dim, broad hall, with a staircase at the far end. A silver bowl of roses rested on a chest under a huge gilt-framed mirror to the left, and just past a door which probably led to the sitting-room, a vast carven chest held an enormous spray of some white flower with which Craig was unfamiliar.

Craig's eyes swept the length of the deep green thick-rugged hallway. At the far end a double entrance of carpeted steps led to a platform which sprouted what seemed to be a hundred yards of stairway. It had no balusters, just enormous hand-rails bolted against solid white panelling. Only on the next floor did the balusters begin—forming a square-ended horseshoe which extended two-thirds the depth of the house—slim white tooth-picks topped by the same graceful dark mahogany—to make a second hall. This hall gave the same impression of being out of doors, since enormous earthen pots circled by delicately wrought iron frames contained enormous fleshy green-fronded plants.

The walls on the second floor were white, as well, and seemed to possess an infinite selection of doors.

Over the stair-well hung a brass candelabra so huge that it covered nearly the width of the hall, and contained pointed light bulbs shaped like candle flames.

As they approached the staircase, Philip said:

'Where is Mister Price staying?'

'In the large guest room in Madame's wing. It is prepared.'

'Oh?' Philip's eyebrows lifted. He pursed his small mouth in a soundless whistle. 'Well, show Mr. Price to his room. I can still find mine by myself. LeBlanc will bring your stuff, Craig. Don't bother to unpack. He'll do it after we've gone to see Julie. Shake it up, son. I can do with a drink. That driving's thirsty work.'

They had come at a tremendous sustained speed in the new green Pierce Arrow, stopping only for gasoline and a sandwich. Roaring through the countryside in the lean, rakish car was another new experience for Craig, who up to now had only driven a Model-A Ford. It was a phaeton, and the wind rushed past its open tonneau, blowing Craig's eyelashes back.

'Can you drive?' Philip turned his head from the road, and narrowly missed a dog.

'Sure. Fords, anyhow.'

'This isn't a Ford, boy. This thing's got enough power under that hood to run a battleship. Want to try her out?'

'If you don't mind, I'd love to. I'll be careful.'

'Don't. It's the most dangerous way I know to drive a car. You just point her and let her go and she'll take care of herself.'

When they stopped for gas Philip slid out from under the wheel, yawned, stretched, and lit a cigarette.

'Take her,' he said. 'Take her as far as Georgetown, and then I'll run her on to home. You got any dough? I don't think I've got enough for the gas. She drinks it like it was whisky.'

'Yep.' Craig fished into his pocket and came up with a ten-dollar bill. 'Here.'

'Thanks. Julie'll give it back to us. I got in a crap game last night and it cleaned me out, almost.'

Philip paid the attendant, and absent-mindedly put the change in his pocket.

Craig eased the car into gear, and the silky power of the murmuring motors urged the monster into a floating sensation on the taut ribbon of road. The dense trees rushed by, and the sky was brilliant blue.

His assurance gained, and he gradually let her take the bit. As the Pierce Arrow roared through the moss-bearded-oak-rimmed road, Craig felt a tremendous exultation.

'I never been in an airplane,' he said, 'but I bet flying is something like this. *What* a wonderful car. How much do they cost?'

'I dunno,' Philip said, sleepily. 'Three or four thousand, I guess. If you don't mind I think I'll grab a nap. It was real drunk out last night.'

(*Three or four thousand*, Craig thought. *God Almighty. Just three or four thousand. And I got five dollars to my name. I wish he'd have given me the change back, but how the hell can I ask him when it's his car and his house we're going to—his food and his Christmas? What do I do about Christmas presents? I got to give his mother something, and I ought to give him something. But God, what a car!)*

As the car flashed along, Craig let the corners of his eyes dwell lovingly on the rushing scenery. This was his country, now, not the high hills stuck in the sandy plains of north and north-western Carolina, but the low, swampy coast he knew as well as he knew how to train a dog or catch a fish. Even in the wind the smell of salt and marsh-ooze was strong. The live-oaks and cypress and tall long-leaved pines held the road lovingly close. Only a few Negro shacks, shambling, with tar-paper roofs and sagging walls, stood by the roadside. To the left an occasional glimpse of water made him a little homesick, and he wished he were going back to New Truro, except that of course he had no place to go in New Truro, now that his grandpa's house had been sold. And oddly, for a boy so young, he felt no urge to see his parents, even at Christmas time. This feeling evidently was reciprocal. When he had written his mother that he was going to Charleston with his room-mate for Christmas, she had merely written back: 'That's nice. Have a good time. Here's five dollars. I wish it were more. Love.'

Craig let the car out another notch, and grinned at his sleeping friend.

'At least,' he said to the wind, 'I'm the best-dressed pauper in the freshman class at Chapel Hill, and at this moment I'm living high on the hog, even if it ain't my hog.' He grinned again, thinking that he sounded exactly like old Sam Price.

As they approached Georgetown, a small covey of quail ran high-headed across the road, and Craig braked sharply. Philip came awake with a start.

'Sorry, Phil,' Craig said. 'But some bob-white had the right-of-way.'

'Where are we?'

'Just about in Georgetown. Damn, this is pretty country, isn't it?'

'Too flat. Also they got a paper mill or something in Georgetown that stinks. When we get to the next filling station, let's stop and pee and have a Coke, and I'll take her on from here. How long was I asleep?'

'Bout an hour. I was glad. I was having a lot of fun with this car. I didn't want to talk.'

When they had finished the Coke, Philip pulled a wad of bills and some silver out of his pocket to pay the attendant. He looked at the bills.

'I'm sorry,' he said. 'I didn't give you back your change. Why didn't you ask me?'

'I figured you needed it worse than me.' Craig smiled. 'Anyhow, I had your car for security.'

'You're a strange one. You got any more dough?'

'Sure, I'm nigger-rich. Let's roll. I want to see Charleston.'

'You won't like it,' Philip said, frowning, as they pulled out of the station. 'The only reason Julie and I stay there is the trustees make us, most of the time. If it wasn't for that Julie'd be in Paris like a flash and you wouldn't even see the dust.'

'Maybe I'll like it, even if you don't. I know it's got a port and ships and coloured people and fried fish, and I was raised with ships and coloured people and fried fish, I can even speak a little Geechee. "Boy, where you get dem rope?" "Mah, I done t'ief um off de dock, yeddy?" '

'You'll meet damn' few Geechees in my house,' Philip said. 'We are what is known as blue-bloods, and blue-bloods are so proud they don't speak to each other even when they're married.'

'I hope I don't cause you any embarrassment,' Craig said seriously. 'About what forks and things. This is my first time away from home, except school.'

'You won't. Julie won't let you.'

'Excuse me, Phil. Tell me off if I'm rude. But I get a kind of feeling that you don't like your mother very much. I mean, you don't love her like people are supposed to love mothers, and she doesn't think of you as a son. More as a . . . a *person*, sort of.'

Philip took his eyes off the road and shot a swift glance at Craig.

'I don't mind talking about it. Julie's the kind of woman who can't let herself be a mother. She's too damn' beautiful to be a mother. I was raised—when she wasn't in Paris or I was home from boarding school—to feel that being a mother sort of got in front of her social life. Like I was a nuisance—a load she had to carry.' He raised his voice to a mimicking falsetto. ' "Poor dear Julie. Stuck first with a roaring drunk and now with that dreadful child. Do you suppose he'll take after his father?" Christ.' Philip's voice was bitter. 'Do you think I like it, to know about all the men I call "Uncle"? Uncle George, the summer gentleman. Uncle Peter, the Cap D'Antibes gentleman. Uncle This and Uncle That—one for Easter, one for Christmas, one for Thanksgiving. Ever since the old boy died I have had a succession of Uncles I never met before—nice slick gentlemen, mostly with moustaches, who pat you on the head and give you presents and say with their eyes that wouldn't it be nice if the little monster went to the movies. Or the zoo. Or to hell. Any place, so that whatever Uncle was around could get down to the business of going to bed with Mama.'

'But your *father*?'

'Oh, he was a great one. He went to a lot of doctors about this great love he had for the jug. The doctors told him he either had

66

to give up whisky or give up his wife. He chose the whisky. I don't remember him very well, except that my nurse used to tell me to be very, very quiet, because my father was sick. He was sick, all right. He was sick all over everything in the house. You ever know a real drunk?'

'Not really. Some of the boys in Truro used to get sweet on a Saturday, but . . .'

'I mean a real drunk, the kind that messes the bed and throws up at the dinner table and falls down all the time. Papa was a real talented one. He could throw up on places an average man couldn't reach with a stick. Also he had a habit of beating hell out of the old lady. He was a real fine one. And when the stupid bastard finally had sense enough to shoot himself, he couldn't even do that right. He messed up the job, more or less missed his head, and flopped around the floor an hour or so before he died. The flies . . . Lovely.' Philip shuddered, and the car swerved.

'I'm sorry,' Craig said. 'I didn't mean . . .'

'It's all right. Sometimes I like to talk about it. But when Julie looks at me she sees Jean-Pierre duFresne, flopping around and fouling up the rug with what few brains he had. And when I see *her*, all I can think of is Uncle George, the summer gentleman. *He* gave me a poodle puppy once. I named him George, and I'm afraid that when they took that puppy away from me they were dead right. Light me a cigarette, will you?'

'Sure. Sorry I brought it up.'

'It's okay. But I think the reason Julie took such a shine to you is that she wished you were me, and that there wasn't any me. I more or less resemble the other side of the family.'

'Let's skip it. I'm sorry I asked. How far are we out now?'

'About half an hour. I didn't mean to saddle you with my troubles.'

'Don't let it worry you,' Craig said. 'I got some troubles of my own.'

The bedroom was vast. It was obviously a woman's room. Craig whistled.

'Now, I wonder why the hell she put me in here?' he asked himself, half aloud. He looked about him keenly.

It *was* obviously a lady's room. An enormous canopied bed dominated the room, a careful exhibit of casual elegance. The walls were of a foreign-looking paper with very narrow satin stripes in yellow and white.

At the windows the under-curtains billowed in pale yellow silk which shed a golden quality over the room. The draperies and cornice were made of a floral print in the same scheme and were finished with a wide silk fringe. The draperies seemed to be made with white silk linings and inter-linings and were too thick, Craig thought. The rug was vast, a light golden carpet that felt fluffy underfoot.

Craig had a long look at the bed. The canopy seemed to be very old. This bothered him for some time until Philip told him later that it was hand-crocheted, and had been in the family for umpteen generations. The bedspread followed the draperies in design, but again seemed too thick to be practical. It had been turned diagonally back for the evening and disclosed a yellow silk blanket over embroidered, initialled linen sheets and pillow cases, and a tiny baby pillow which seemed to have no actual function.

Across from the bed there was a clothes press with two mirrored doors surrounded by intricately carved mahogany. A polished mahogany chest with a marble top stood across one wall over which was a portrait of an unsmiling female ancestor. Yellow tulips spilled out of a milk-glass bowl underneath the ancestor.

Two armless chairs squatted on each side of a round table which was draped in green velvet to the floor, and whose surface contained two books, a cigarette box, a lighter, a bottle of Scotch whisky—the first Scotch whisky Craig had ever seen—and a bowl of fresh fruit.

Next the bed stood a tiny stool which Craig thought must have been put there to help small people jump into the bed. A commode on the other side of the bed held a brass lamp topped with an opaque glass bowl and seemed established to provide light for the room when the two pairs of gilt sconces on opposing walls were off duty. The bedside table also contained a miniature painting of his hostess, done on ivory. Craig thought again how impossibly beautiful she was to be his room-mate's mother.

There was a fireplace of mottled black marble with a small round opening. The mantel was of white marble. Craig doubted that the fireplace was ever used since there were no fire tools and the opening of the fireplace was hidden by a gilt contraption that looked like an open lady's fan.

Craig leered at himself in the gilt convex mirror which threw him and the entire room into distortion. A round revolving rosewood bookstand sat in front of one of the windows. There was also a sort of extra bed which some years later Craig learned was called a *chaise longue*.

'Jesus,' Craig said aloud. 'There ain't no place here to sit down. I wonder if she thought her only child was bringing home a co-ed instead of me?'

The butler had arrived with Craig's one valise.

'The bath is there,' the butler said, 'and if I may say so, sir, she rarely puts anyone here. Shall I run your bath now?'

'If you please,' Craig said.

'May I press something for you, sir?' the butler asked, looking at the one shabby bag as if it were something he would really prefer not to touch.

'I don't think so,' Craig said. 'But would you open it up and hang my suits in the closet, please?'

He unconsciously emulated Philip.

'Very good, sir,' the butler said.

'Thank you,' Craig replied, and went into the enormous bathroom. It was done in green-and-black marble, with racks of initialled towels, and a tub the size of a cattle-dipping tank.

'Hot diggety dog,' he said softly. 'Now that is what I would call a tub. And how about me, with a butler and all? "Very good, sir." I bet Grandpa would blow a gasket if he knew. One day I'll have me a butler, too, but he'll be a damn sight cheerfuller than this one.'

He soaped himself and lay in the tub for only a minute or so, and then he went over to the black marble washstand, still dripping, and inspected his face closely. Blackheads, no. Pimples —a very few. But the beard was out again, stiff and black. Then he noticed to his horror that he was leaking water on to the marble floor. He seized a towel, marked by a great black 'dF', and hurriedly dried himself. Then he looked quickly behind him before he swabbed up the floor with the damp towel. He peeked around the door to see if the butler had left, and walked naked back into the bedroom. The butler had opened the little canvas bag in which Craig carried his shaving gear and toothbrush, and the scant toilet articles were laid out in a primly reproving line on the dresser. He picked up the razor, brush, and shaving cream and went back to the bathroom, where he noticed, for the first time, a glistening array of gold-stoppered flasks, labelled in scroll lettering with the names of various face creams and lotions and deodorants and perfumes.

'I think I like it here,' he muttered, as he lathered his face and proceeded to shave.

He hauled on his shorts and went to the closet. He looked intently at the clothing hanging inside. One was a grey flannel suit that smelled freshly new. One was a tuxedo that had never been worn. One was a sports coat of cocoa-brown flannel, with fawn flannel trousers. Two pairs of shoes, with trees—one pair brown buck, one black—sat snugly on the floor. A half-dozen neckties hung from a rack, and a half-dozen shirts were stacked on the shelf above the hangers.

He chose the brown sports jacket with the almost matching pants. When he was dressed, he looked at himself admiringly in the mirror. A man looked back at him. Not Craig Price, boy, but Craig Price, man.

'Maybe some day I'll be able to pay him back,' he said to himself, aloud. 'But it's sure nice to have athletes for friends.'

' You still going home with that fancy room-mate for Christmas?' the football player Jimmy Wilbur had asked. 'Or do you want to thumb a ride north and come home with me for a real Polack Christmas? My old lady is a hell of a cook.'

Wilbur had come into the dormitory store to check on the cigarette supply. Craig was sitting in a straight chair trying to make some sense out of a trigonometry formula, and was truly pleased with the interruption.

'Thanks, Moose,' he said. 'That fancy room-mate of mine *has* asked me down to Charleston to spend the holidays with his ma. Remember? I told you.'

'Yeah. I wondered if it was still on. I made you a bet.'

'I still got the ten. You want it back? And I still don't know what the bet was all about.'

'Skip it. You'll know when you're bigger.' He looked at Craig, who was wearing his knickers and a sweater.

Overnight—in less than three months—Craig had shot up suddenly. His former chubbiness was gone, and his face was almost gaunt. He was a solid six feet tall. He had quit combing his hair straight back, and now wore it parted on the side. What had been a cowlick was now a wave.

'Kid, you've changed a lot in a couple of months,' Wilbur said. 'I didn't realize it until I looked at you in those little-boy pants. You look like a grown man playing kid.'

'Thanks,' Craig said. 'I thought I'd wear the knickers down to Charleston and save my *good* suit to impress Phil's mama.'

'What good suit? Not that thing with the bell-bottomed trousers and the Joe College jacket? His old lady would like you better in short pants. God, kid, you can't go off to visit the quality folks dressed like you are. You need some clothes. You got any dough at all?'

'About five bucks,' Craig answered. 'Plus your ten.'

'Tell you what,' Wilbur said. 'You know Shevransky, works in the College Shop? He's from my home town. We'll go see him. Maybe we can fix a deal for some new duds.'

'I can't pay for any new clothes,' Craig said. 'I haven't got any money and I'm not likely to have any. I don't even know if I can get back in school next quarter, unless I can do something with the Loan Fund. I'm busted. My folks are broke.'

'The hell with it,' Wilbur said. 'Let's go talk to Shev.'

Shev was an enormous blond man of about twenty-two who was playing his final year as guard on the football team. He had made a Southern Conference selection for two years, and second-string All-American in his junior year. He had a wide, humorous Polish face and a broken nose. He was the campus representative for the College Shop, which sold good, stylish suits and haberdashery. He was paid a salary and a percentage on all the suits he sold when he was not practising or playing football. The salary

70

was provided by one of the alumni who still had some money left from the crash.

'Hi, kid,' he said to Craig. 'Hi, Moose,' to Jimmy Wilbur. 'Come to buy some of my fancy dress goods?'

'Maybe,' Jimmy Wilbur said. 'Look, the kid here is a friend of mine. He needs some clothes. He ain't got a plugged dime, but he's got to have some clothes.'

'We sell clothes for money here,' Shev said.

'You play football for *free*, too, don't you? You play it because you *love* the game. You play for Alma Mater. That's why you are such a good haberdashery clerk. Look. How many suits you got here?'

'I dunno. A hundred. Maybe two hundred. Who cares? Nobody's buying anything anyhow.'

'Nobody's going to miss one, two suits,' Wilbur said. 'And this kid's going to have some money pretty soon. Let's say we lend him some duds, and he pays you back a little bit at a time next semester.' Wilbur winked.

'I ain't going to have any mo——' Wilbur kicked Craig sharply on the shin. 'Shut up,' he said. 'Now pick out what you need, and I'll handle it all with Shev. Okay, Shev?'

'It's my job if I get caught,' Shev said.

'What the hell,' Wilbur said. 'You're through this year. That punt you blocked against Virginia—which I managed to fall on, making you a cinch for All-America, I might say—will get you a coaching job any place. You're only a punchy Polack, anyhow, and you couldn't pass a course in co-ed watching if you didn't have more muscles in your back than you got in your head.'

'Well, all right, Moose,' Shev said. 'Come on, kid, let's pick out some stuff and get it altered. You can write me a cheque in front of the tailor, to make it look good, and I'll tear it up when you get the clothes.'

'I haven't *got* a cheque,' Craig said. 'I haven't *got* a bank account. That's not honest . . .'

'Shut up, stupid,' Jimmy Wilbur said. 'They got blank cheques here. You know the name of a bank? Any bank? In your home town?'

'Sure. The National. But it went busted . . .'

'It'll do. A bum cheque on a busted bank ain't any worse off than a good cheque on a busted bank. Here. Sign there.'

They walked out after the tailor had finished. They went into Harry's restaurant next door. Harry was a Greek with a fine friendly reputation. He gave unlimited credit to athletes, and sometimes to their friends. He had the straight neck merging into the flat head of the Greek, a burlesque accent, and smeared his hair liberally with oil. Some of the campus wits occasionally remarked that Harry cooked with the same oil he used to tame his riotous hair.

71

He was behind the service counter when Craig and Jimmy Wilbur entered. The student waiters had not yet arrived to handle the supper shift.

'Hi, Moose. Hi, keed,' he said. 'Wat you wan'?'

'Two cups of Joe and a couple of slabs of pie. What you got besides oppla and peenoppla?'

'Stromberra and pits. Fresh.'

'Make mine peach. You, kid?'

'Strawberry, please.'

When the Greek leaned over to serve the coffee and pie, Jimmy Wilbur said quietly:

'You need a new waiter. The service is terrible here.'

The Greek started back and smote himself a mighty Hellenic blow on the forehead.

'Me? More waiters? These ottletes—peegs—already they eat me into poor-house. What I want with 'nother ottlete with oppetite like bozzard?'

'Relax. The kid's not an athlete. He's a friend of mine. Come on back to the kitchen for a minute. Drink your coffee, kid, while I have a talk with Harry.'

Craig was finishing his pie, wondering what it was all about, when the two men came back from the kitchen. Jimmy Wilbur had his arm around the Greek's neck. The Greek was shaking his head.

'Hokay, hokay,' he said. 'So I got a new waiter. Bot maybe we all go to jail, hey?'

'Not if we run it right,' Wilbur said. 'Come on, kid. You got a job starting Christmas. Only on week-ends—Friday through Sunday. Pays twenty-five dollars a month and your chow You'll probably die of ptomaine, but its better than starvation. Harry'll give you an advance on your pay now. How about ten bucks, Harry?'

The Greek grumbled, but fished into his pocket and came out with a soiled ten. He looked at it sadly.

'These wick,' he said. 'I lose twenty bocks instead of just ten.'

'You'll get it back, baby,' Wilbur said, and handed the money to Craig. 'You'll get it back, all right. See you.'

When they crossed the street and walked along the quiet campus pathway, Craig took the money out of his pocket and extended it to Wilbur.

'I don't understand any of this,' he said. 'The clothes, the job, the free food. It doesn't make any sense . . .'

'Sure it makes sense. Look, I put through that bootlegging deal I told you about. We handle the retail end through Harry. I don't trust many people, but you're smart enough to be my boy. It works like this: the word'll get around that you can buy a jug from Harry, but it can't be done on the premises. But a word to the right waiter—that's you—*and* the price in advance, will get

72

you a jar of corn anywhere you want it, delivery guaranteed in the dark of the moon. Your job is just to take the order and grab the dough and pass the word to my messenger service. It'll be having Cokes next door in the drugstore.'

'But where is the booze? Not in Harry's?'

Jimmy Wilbur smiled.

'No, not in Harry's, little boy. He's just the connection point for the week-end sports that run out of booze or can't get out to Botts'. You don't have to see it. You don't even need to know where it's stashed. You're just the middle man. It's better if you don't know. You can't get caught for just writing down a name, a fraternity house, and a figure saying "One" or "Two" or "Six". It's foolproof, and you get a cut on the gross sale. Not much, but some. It'll be good booze, because we're making the gin ourselves, and the alky's all right. It *ought* to be.' Wilbur smiled again.

'Where are you getting the alcohol?'

'Ask me no questions, pal, but I can tell you this. It's not from Durham or the bootleggers in between, and it's guaranteed not to make you go blind. We got no complications, kid. Come on. It's one way you can stay in school with a little style . . .'

'So,' Craig said, 'I will be sixteen years old in less than two weeks, and I am now a bootlegger. Or at least a bootlegger's assistant.'

'That's right,' Jimmy Wilbur said cheerfully. 'It ain't any worse to sell it than it is to buy it. If you got any moral objections, look at me—an *amateur* athlete. Who do you think built that new stadium, the angels?'

'Well, all right,' Craig said. 'But one question I have to ask. Who are your messengers—your delivery boys?'

'Athletes,' Jimmy Wilbur said, and smiled dreamily again. 'Mostly track stars. You see, in a way I am doing extra service for Alma Mater. Dashing all over this campus with a jug of hooch under their arms will keep them in steady training for the greater glory of the school.'

Philip poked his head in the door as Craig was buttoning his new jacket.

'Well, I'll be damned,' Philip said. 'Look at you. Where did you get the new duds?'

'I came into money,' Craig grinned. 'How do you like it?'

'Very elegant. Who's your tailor?'

'Credit,' Craig said. 'On the cuff. Don't you think we better go say hello to your mama?'

'Maybe we better have a drink first,' Philip's eyes roved to the bottle of Scotch. 'My God, boy, you struck a spark off Julie. We smuggled that stuff back from England, and it just isn't handed

73

out to everybody. And putting you over here, in her favourite room . . . hmmmm.'

He opened the bottle, and raised the neck to his mouth. 'Good stuff. Not cut.' He coughed and extended the bottle to Craig. 'Have some.'

'I don't think so.' Craig said. 'Later maybe. But I don't think Miss Julie would like it if we *both* came down smelling boozy. I'll wait.'

'Okay, then, let's go see Mamá.' Philip gave 'Mama' the English intonation.

A large arch revealed a fresh vista of flagged hallway as the carpeted elegance of the formal hall stopped just past the double entrance to the huge stairway. It was ceiled in a kind of festive canopy of red-and-white-striped silk which sagged slightly and gave Craig the impression that he was sheltered by a vast and ornate tent. Again the indoor planting made him feel that he was already in a garden, and seemed not to be in a house at all.

The flagged hall ended in another arch, thrusting you suddenly into an enormous patio, surrounded completely by the house. The second storey galleries were enclosed by white balustrade and the entire façade of the first floor was of glass. Here all was vast glass doors or huge sweeps of arched windows. It looked, felt and smelt like Craig's mental pictures of Africa or Polynesia. It was all a-jungle with tropical profusion. Enormous fronds of elephant-ear or towering palms, great trees of banana, creepers twining up the purely decorative French lamp-posts with the octagonal glass tops. A riot of small palms, pepper trees, pomegranates, was accented in a forest in which camellias peeped from plants unknown, and the entire vari-coloured family of roses seemed to climb the plinths with sluttish disregard of home or intent.

In the middle of the jungle was Julie duFresne. She was sitting at a glass-topped table with delicate wrought-iron legs, and next the heavily chased silver tea service was one slim crystal vase containing one long-stemmed and very elegant yellow rose.

The garden was so overblown with bloom that Craig felt he was walking into a hot-house. The patio was rendered fleshy by the enormous banana plants, sweet-sickly scented gardenias, the head-heavy roses and the purple bougainvillea which swarmed the walls.

In the tropical setting, she seemed more beautiful and much younger than before. She did not rise as the boys walked into the garden, but held out one hand and offered a cheek to Philip. Then she smiled at Craig, and held out the other hand.

'Come and kiss your old Auntie Julie hello,' she said. 'Let me look at you both.'

Her eyes swept Craig up and down, and then turned to her son.

'*He* doesn't seem to have improved much,' she said directly to

Craig. 'But *you* seem to have become a man, and a very good-looking one, too, I might say. I suppose living with Philip would age anybody, though.'

She waved at two chairs, one on either side of her.

'Sit down and have some tea. It's nice to have you home again, brat. And so nice you could come, Craig. Where are the knicker-bockers?' she shot the question suddenly.

'Upstairs,' Craig said. He smiled.

'That's a nice suit,' Julie duFresne said.

'Thank you, ma'am. It's the first time I've had it on.'

'It's not one of mine, Julie, if that's what you're thinking,' her son said hurriedly.

'I was thinking nothing of the sort,' she replied. 'Lemon in your tea?'

'Sugar, please,' Craig said.

She looked at her son.

'From the smell of you, I imagine you'd like a whisky?'

Philip blushed.

'No, thanks . . . ma'am,' he said.

Julie duFresne smiled at Craig.

'Maybe he hasn't learned much in class but I see somebody finally taught him a thing I've failed in. Manners.' She tapped a cigarette on the table. Craig was on his feet swiftly and struck a match. Julie duFresne smiled at him through the smoke, and raised an eyebrow. Craig sat down and picked up his teacup, and hoped to God he wouldn't break it.

'That's a very pretty room you've put me in,' he said tentatively, 'I never saw a room like that before.'

'It's too womanish,' Julie duFresne said. 'But it's my favourite, apart from my own. If you're wondering why I put you there, instead of in with Philip, I thought you might have seen enough of each other at school, in that dismal dormitory, and would want a little privacy.' She got up.

'I must go and change now,' she looked at her wrist-watch. 'Pants are fine for daytime, but . . .'

For the first time Craig, who had been busily watching her face, noticed that she was wearing slimly cut jodhpurs. It was the first time he had ever seen a woman in pants. She caught the look.

'No, I don't ride,' she said. 'But for knocking about the house, I like 'em.' She grinned, and held up her hands, which seemed immaculate to Craig. 'Believe it or not, I'm a gardener, and no matter what they say in England, you can't garden in gloves. Maybe you boys would like a nap? We'll have drinks about seven.'

She preceded the boys into the house, and it took a physical effort to prevent Craig from staring at her buttocks in the tight breeches. His head reminded him that this was his room-mate's *mother*, but the jodhpurs did fit her rather snugly.

Craig had never felt so much like a fool in his short life. He had been reading quite a lot of Somerset Maugham, and he was of the impression that all worthy people, everywhere, Dressed For Dinner. After Philip showed him briefly round the house, he went to his room and laid out his 'tux' on the bed. He had never actually worn a dinner-jacket, apart from the fitting, but it felt and smelt *festive*, like good dance music sounded, like pretty girls looked when they got all fancied up for the Saturday night dances at the beach, in the public pavilion.

He also remembered how handsome the tuxedoed *old* people—people of thirty or more—looked before the crash, when his parents had an occasional party and a small coloured orchestra was brought into the living-room in the big square brick house, with punch on the sideboard and folks making frequent visits outside to parked cars, to return smelling slightly more fruity than the punch.

He stroked the black broadcloth lovingly, and experimented with his jazzbo black tie. He laid a white stiff-fronted shirt atop the jacket, and found a wing collar and a small box which contained collar buttons and studs. He took out his new—unworn—black plain-toed shoes, and polished them briskly with his shabby knickerbockers. He took another bath, in which he wallowed a long time, and then savagely attacked his fingernails until he had buffed them raw. He scrubbed at his teeth, shaved again, although he shaved scarcely two hours ago and his skin was as smooth as a baby's bottom. He plastered down his unruly cowlick-turned-wave with stickum. And then, slowly, surely, lovingly, he inserted himself gently into his shirt and pants.

He had quite a bit of difficulty with the studs and with the cuff-links, and also with the collar buttons, but the black jazzbo hooked on very nicely. He slipped on his shining shoes and went to the long mirror to inspect himself. He snapped back his lips in a movie-actor's smile and reflected that he, Craig Price, was one hell of a handsome fellow, with the last of his deep summer suntan making the collar whiter, his teeth whiter.

'Pretty soon,' he muttered, 'I think I'll grow a moustache. I got enough whiskers for it, anyway. Something like Ronald Colman. But even without it I sure don't look sixteen.'

His eye dropped to the bottle of Scotch. Craig had experimented with whisky just a little—an allowed toddy or eggnog at Christmas time, and last summer, after he had graduated from high school and was playing big-for-his-age with a variety of maidens at parties and at the beach, he and some other rake-hells had slipped out to take an occasional nip, washed down with Coke, of the local corn. That stuff was clear white, burnt all the way down, and left a coating of fusel oil on the teeth. It came in half-gallon fruit-jars, not in slender graceful bottles that stood on tables in a delicate room in Charleston, S.C.

He decided that a man of parts such as himself—Beauregard Price, the well-known Charleston dandy—had best fortify himself with a drink before he joined the ladies. 'Joined the ladies,' he said aloud. He liked the sound. 'Joined the ladies', he said again, and took a tentative taste of the Scotch. He expected it to explode inside him, but it didn't. It went down as smooth as honey, as light as air, as strokingly hot as August in his stomach. He took another nip, and the glow mounted.

He lit a cigarette, which tasted better than any cigarette he had smoked since he first took up cornsilk and rabbit tobacco when he was eight. The Scotch did something to the tobacco's flavour. Then and there, Craig Price resolved that when he was rich, he would drink nothing but Scotch. He looked at his grandfather's old hunting-case watch. It showed a five-to-seven. Craig decided to have another drink and another cigarette while he waited. His cheeks felt a little warm, but his courage was mounting.

The suit had been expensive—$28.50—but it was worth it, if it made you feel like this. As for the Scotch . . . ah.

'Now that I'm gonna be a bootlegger,' he said aloud again, 'I might as well get used to what I'm selling.'

Just before Craig came to dress, Philip had said:

'Don't bother to wait for me. I'm going to grab a little nap. That drive made me tired. Go on down and talk to the old lady. She'll be in the drawing-room—that's the big door to the right as you came in the front—and don't be very late. She's a prompt one. Seven o'clock sharp will find her there—patting her foot.'

Craig took another look at himself in the mirror, combed his hair again, and drew a deep breath.

'Now or never,' he said, and plunged towards the staircase. Its curving mahogany rail was satin under his hand, and its carpeted stairs were so soft he could almost feel the softness through the thin soles of his new shoes. He went out into the long hall, past the flowers he did not know, and turned left into an enormous drawing-room. A fire hissed in a big fireplace of white marble, striking golden sparks off the massive dog-irons and the clustered tongs, poker and brass shovels on either side. Nobody was there, although a table next one wall was agleam with decanters and glassware.

Everywhere there seemed to be flowers—yellow roses in flat silver bowls, something he knew as delphinium from Grandma's garden, and enough gladioli to furnish a funeral.

It was the first time Craig had ever seen what he always thought of as a parlour with more than one sofa in it, and this one had three. Two identical small sofas faced each other on either side of the fireplace. They had curved backs and tiny legs and looked a little too frail to accommodate more than one person. They were upholstered in some kind of funny dull green velvet stuff. The third sofa was bigger than Craig's bed and it struck him as highly peculiar that it should be dead white. He had never seen any white sitting-down furniture before and thought how impractical it would be if you had a houseful of hounds. The white sofa faced the fireplace. There was a large cherrywood table in front of it, cluttered with a mess of silver pots: sugar-pots, cream-jugs, bonbon dishes and other implements of internal warfare he did not recognize.

The rug looked kind of faded but it was thick and silky feeling and large clusters of pinkish flowers grew off its white surface.

The walls were a nice pale green, he thought—like the woods looked in very early spring. Sort of like a green apple that would give you the bellyache.

The two deep bay windows that you could walk right into had yards and yards of green satin drapery edged with some sort of funny fringe. It seemed like a hell of a lot of material for a window. Next to the window-pane was something he had never seen before. There were two sets of curtains, like a sissy-looking nightgown, kind of white lace, evidently for the day time, because they could be covered up at night by pulling across enough green velvet drapes to make a sail for a sizeable boat. Each bay had a curved window and placed in front were matching tables made of some sort of gold stuff with inlaid flecks of other colours. Little velvet chairs with a deep fringe all the way to the floor were flung aimlessly around, but it was the three sofas and the enormous rosewood piano which commanded his attention.

A gold-framed mirror, as big and round as a cartwheel, with a snotty-looking eagle on top, occupied most of the wall space over the fireplace. Behind the piano there was another enormous mirror which couldn't seem to make its mind up what it was, since it was framed with wood and had a crazy-monkey picture painted in the top half of it.

The lamps were made out of a kind of pink glass, the exact colour of the camellias that floated around in bowls, like water-lilies in a pond. Most of the furniture was cluttered up with needle-point pillows, the same sort of woman-stuff that Miss Caroline used to work at for years at a time.

Electricity seemed to be lacking in this room, as enormous candle-holders of crystal and gilt stood everywhere, and while there was a large crystal chandelier hung from the centre of the room it appeared never to have been lit.

Craig had his back to the door, and was studying the vast circular mirror with the eagle on top, running his fingers over the most enormous piano he had ever seen, leaning over to sniff at a bouquet of gladioli in a large vase that rested on a strip of yellow satin flung over the gleaming surface of the piano, when the cool, slightly accented voice said:

'Hello, there. You're early, aren't you? Where's Philip?'

Craig whirled as if he had been caught stealing.

'He—he told me to come on down when I dressed . . . that . . . that you liked people to be prompt.'

'And so I do.' Her eyes roved briefly over his new finery, and if she was amused, she masked it admirably. One brow quirked briefly over the turquoise eyes.

(Some years later, Craig was recalling the evening for some British friends. 'I must,' he said, 'have been got up like a pox-doctor's clerk.')

She was wearing a long hostess gown—although Craig didn't know what to call it then—of a blue velvet, that hugged her closely up top and flowed swiftly from her hips to the floor, so that only the shining tips of her shoes peeped from beneath the hem of the gown. The bodice was cut to nothing in front, and she wore no necklace. The sleeves were long, and on one wrist she wore a massive bracelet in which blue and white and red stones appeared to leap out of the heavy twisted gold. She seemed all white from the bosom up until you got to the scarlet slash of lips, and moved to the eyes and the tightly drawn-back hair, into which, somehow, gardenias had been worked behind the tiny ears, which wore almost barbaric hoops of gold and seed-pearls.

'You look very handsome, Mr. Price,' she said. 'Although I'm not sure I didn't like you better as a scared little boy in your knickers.'

Craig's tongue swelled in his mouth, making speech difficult. 'I . . . you . . . this house . . .' He stopped. He couldn't very well tell her that she was the loveliest thing he'd ever seen.

'Perhaps you'd give me a cigarette,' she said, walking towards him. 'They're there, in that box. And would you like a drink? Sherry, perhaps?'

Craig fumbled for the box and managed to extend it without dropping it. He couldn't seem to find any fire, until she indicated a hammered silver lighter in the form of a swan. Craig managed to depress the little lever and produce flame without setting his hostess aflame.

'Sherry, please, ma'am,' he said. If she had said 'Arsenic' his answer would have been the same. She moved to the cocktail table, unstoppered one of the decanters, and poured a drink of pale amber fluid into a glass so fragile that Craig feared it would break in his fingers. She passed it to him with a smile, poured one for herself, walked over to the fireplace, and raised the glass to Craig.

'*Salut*,' she said. '*A votre santé*.'

'Yes, ma'am,' Craig replied, and downed the sherry in a gulp, setting the glass down swiftly before it bit him. When he looked, Julie duFresne was sipping her sherry, and looking at him with amusement.

'It's really for sipping,' she said. 'Try again.'

'I'm afraid to,' he said frankly. 'I'm bound to bust something.'

79

'No you won't. Pour yourself another glass, and let's sit down.'
She waved towards one of the two matching curved sofas in front
of the fire. She gestured towards the cigarette box, and Craig took
one, lighting it with trembling fingers. He sipped his sherry, and
could think of nothing whatever to say.

'You're a nice boy, Craig,' she said. 'I hope some of it rubs off
on Philip. He's rather spoiled. Will you continue to room
together? I haven't had a chance to ask him, and we don't
correspond very often—except when he needs money.'

'It must be nice, ma'am, to be able to write when you need
money.'

'Please don't think me rude. But have you any money at all?
What about your family?'

'I don't mind a bit. What little we had we lost. My father's been
kind of rattling around from pillar to post since the crash, when
all the banks closed. He had the same job for about twenty-five
years, but now he seems to get this job, that job, and don't any
of 'em pay very much. They manage to eat—and owe money,'
Craig smiled.

'What are you smiling at?' Julie duFresne leaned forward, and
the boy could not resist glancing at the deep shadow her cleft
breasts cast in the low-cut gown. 'What amuses you?'

'Me. I owe money too. But for different reasons. Except I'll pay.
My pa, he thinks that once he's borrowed, the money belongs to
him and he gets mad when somebody asks him to pay it back.
He figures they're trying to take something away from him.'

'What are you talking about?' Sharply, now.

'What *are* you all talking about?' Philip came into the room.
He was wearing an ordinary grey flannel suit. He struck a pose,
in mock horror.

'My God, Julie, who's your rich friend? Not'—more drama—
'not my room-mate? What did you do, Craig, stick up a filling
station when my back was turned? Get up and let me see that
suit. Where'd you get it?'

Craig coloured. It could have been the fire and the unaccustomed alcohol.

'Stole it,' he said briefly.

Julie duFresne looked coldly at her son.

'We always dress for dinner in this house,' she said. 'Go and
change immediately, Philip. Has three months of college made
you forget your upbringing? Hurry. Dinner will be on in fifteen
minutes. You're already late as it is.'

Philip started to speak, but his mother's eyes closed his mouth.

'*Oui, Maman*,' he said, and swiftly left the room.

Craig looked up. His face was still red.

'You didn't have to do that,' he said. 'I'm sorry. But it was new
coming here and I saw you and saw Phil's new car and heard so
much . . .'

'Hush.' Julie duFresne leaned forward, kissed her finger lightly and gently touched the end of Craig's nose. 'You're a sweet boy with all the right instincts, even if you aren't quite up to them yet.' Then a twinkle lit her eyes. 'But tell me, please, where *did* you get the suit?'

'I didn't borrow it,' Craig said. 'I didn't steal it. I got it on credit from the College Shop because I wanted to look good when I came here.'

'But how did you get it on credit if you didn't have any money?'

'I have a friend, a football player, a guy who's kind of looked after me since I first got to college. He is going to be a bootlegger in the winter quarter. He got me a job as a waiter, and I'm going to help him bootleg.' Craig was miserable, but he looked directly at her. 'I reckon I better leave now. You wouldn't want a waiter or a bootlegger in this house.'

Julie duFresne laughed, throwing her head back. She laughed as a man would laugh. Then she stopped laughing and took Craig's face in both hands, and kissed him lightly on the cheek.

'My dear, darling, honest boy, all flustered and ashamed. This house has known practically nothing but bootleggers since I lived in it, if none so young. And I am not unmindful of the compliment implied, that you should turn to a life of crime to do me honour. I have seldom been so flattered.'

Craig grinned uneasily.

'Maybe you don't mind then if I don't know much and do the wrong things?'

'My dear boy,' Julie duFresne said, and she was quite serious. 'In your life you may do a lot of bad things, but you'll never do a wrong thing. Now, I hear my progeny's footsteps. Will you escort me in to dinner?'

She took his arm, and as they entered the dining-room Craig Price felt that he stood just about eleven feet six inches tall.

He had expected the dining-room to be as large as the parlour, but was surprised to find it relatively small; not much bigger than his bedroom.

From the high blue white-lintelled ceiling another enormous chandelier hung directly over a smallish round mahogany table, and Craig reflected that there would be hell to pay if that thing ever came loose from its moorings. A whole covey of candles reached up from glass receptacles that looked like enormous transparent milk bottles turned upside down. A big silver something carved in grapes and other silver doo-dads stood in the centre.

The table was already laid for three and there was such an array of silver that he was certain he would never find out which fork to use on what, and he had no idea at all what the different-sized glasses and goblets would contain.

The walls were papered with a very light sky-blue with a design he liked, something like white peach trees with gay birds perched on the branches, but neither the birds nor the blossoms resembled anything he had ever seen in a fresh spring orchard around Kensington.

Enormous gold curtains with tucks in the top surrounded two narrow windows set into carved white frames with little yellow sit-down things under each window. They looked like a cross between a big saddle and a cobbler's bench.

Slim-legged chairs that again seemed too fragile to bear a man's weight were grouped around the table, with cushions to match the curtains, and the rug was the same material as the one in the parlour except that this time the big roses were yellow as well as pinkish.

Craig decided that he would never feel easy enough in this room to work up an appetite in it.

Philip handed his mother into her chair, and she motioned Craig into a seat on her right. The butler came in, removed the green, gold-flecked plates, and placed the heavy black silver-stranded napkins to one side. He served a greenish soup smoking from a silver tureen. Craig, panicky, looked quickly to see which spoon Julie used, and dipped the same kind into the soup. He was expecting some odd delicacy like shark-fin soup from the Orient—Somerset Maugham again—but was delighted with what he tasted.

'Why,' he said, 'it's turtle soup!'

'Is that surprising?' Julie duFresne asked, smiling.

'In a way,' Craig mumbled. 'Except I was surprised because it's what we had all the time in New Truro, when I was a boy—I mean when I was a kid. I sort of didn't expect to . . .' he stopped, embarrassed.

'Didn't expect to find it here? We're a seaport town too. We're all alike—Kensington, Charleston, Savannah, Jacksonville, New Orleans. Sea food until it runs out of your ears.'

Philip had recovered some of his poise, momentarily lost when his mother banished him to make up for Craig's *gaffe*. He was looking very handsome in a velvet smoking-jacket which obviously had cost considerably more than Craig's $28.50 splendour.

'Are you boys going to any of the Christmas balls?' Julie looked at her son.

'Not unless you make us. Please, Julie. They're still back in the Civil War, with dancing cards and a lot of dumb débutantes. Bunch of dam' standarounds. If you don't mind, we'd rather knock around on our own—and see a lot of you, of course,' Philip said hurriedly.

'I can't say I blame you too much. I think they're a bore. But how about our guest? Wouldn't Craig like to see some of

Charleston's blue bloods whirling around in their modern pantalettes?'

Craig made a clumsy attempt at gallantry.

'Wouldn't be anybody there as pretty as you, ma'am,' he said, and blushed. 'I mean . . . I wouldn't know what to do, and I'd feel miserable. I mean . . .'

Julie dipped her shining head in acknowledgment.

'Thank you for the second compliment,' she said. She rang the bell, and the butler arrived to clear away the plates, replacing them with a service casserole—something that smelled delicious, and proved to be white slivers of trout buried in a saffron sauce which contained tiny river shrimps.

He raised his eyes inquiringly.

'Trout marguéry,' Julie said.

'It's wonderful,' he said. 'I never tasted anything like it.'

'It's better in New Orleans,' Julie replied. 'Try some of that white wine. They go well together.'

Craig noticed that the butler had filled a small delicate long-stemmed glass with a faintly yellow wine, and a larger goblet with a ruby wine. He saw then that the white wine bottle peeped from an enormous ice-bucket on a side-table—a bucket flanked by a dust-crusted bottle of red wine, cradled at a 45-degree angle in a silver holder. Conversation faltered.

'Tell me,' Julie said a little later, as the butler replaced the fish with a peculiarly sauced broiled chicken flanked with broccoli, tiny mushrooms, and little inflated shells of Irish potatoes, with an oily green salad in a side dish. Craig observed that the butler removed the white wine glass when the chicken arrived, and that his hostess was sipping from the crimson goblet.

'Tell me,' she said. 'What do you plan on studying at school? What do you want to be?'

'A gigolo,' Philip said, pushing a piece of crisp French bread around in his chicken sauce. 'He's got all the makings.'

'Stop sopping your bread, Philip, and be serious.'

'They do it in France, and we're French, aren't we?' But he stopped, nevertheless.

'What *do* you want to be, Craig?' he asked. 'I'll be a writer if it kills me.'

'It probably will,' his mother drawled. 'Or me. But what, Craig?'

'I really don't know, Miss Julie. I'm awful young, and fresh out of the country. I'd like to try to be a writer, too, or maybe an artist, but it seems to me that's an awful tough way to make a living. It takes too long. I haven't got any talent for mathematics, or enough money to study to be a doctor or a lawyer or an engineer . . . and besides, it takes too *long*.'

'You must want to be *something*.'

Craig grinned shyly.

83

'Looks like right now I'm going to be a criminal.'

'What are you two talking about?' Philip said.

'It's a private joke,' his mother replied. 'Nothing that concerns you. Here's the dessert. We can talk about this some more over the coffee. The champagne now, LeBlanc.'

The third flat-topped shallow goblet suddenly contained a froth of bubbles.

'What happened to the Musigny, *maman*?' Philip managed a leer. 'You were awfully fond of . . . of Musigny in Paris.'

His mother fixed him with a cold stare. To Craig: 'Do you like cherries Jubilee?'

'I couldn't rightly say, ma'am. I never had any before. But it looks real wonderful.'

It looked wonderful, and tasted better. The black clustered cherries on the special ice-cream, with the butler setting a brandy sauce afire and pouring the flaming sauce across the top. Craig took a bite of the hot-cold dessert, and manfully reached for his champagne. The bubbles got up his nose, ticked unbearably. He sneezed—a sneeze, he felt, that was the loudest sneeze ever sneezed since people started sneezing. He went purple, and started to cough.

'Don't worry,' Philip said cheerfully, 'the first time I tried champagne I threw up, cherries Jubilee and all.'

'Philip, for heaven's sake! Are you all right, Craig?'

'I think so. Please excuse me, but it's the first champagne I ever tasted. Does it always do this to you?'

'Not when you're used to it. Personally, I prefer the still wines, like *Musigny*'—and again she fixed her son with a chill eye. 'When we've finished our dessert, let's go into the living-room for coffee.'

The butler or somebody had tossed a couple of fresh logs on the fire, and it leapt and crackled gaily, sending long black shadows roving up the candle-lit walls. It gleamed against the heavy silver coffee service, and struck diamond splinters from the crystal decanters which held liqueurs of a dozen colours.

'I think we won't have any liqueurs with the coffee,' Julie said. 'We had quite a lot of wine with the dinner.'

'It was the best dinner I ever had in my life,' Craig said. 'What do you call the chicken?'

'*Coq au vin*—chicken in wine with mushrooms and things. How do you have your coffee?'

Craig took a quick look at the tiny fragile shells and gambled. 'Black, please, ma'am,' he said. At home he had always had coffee in enormous thick cups, the coffee crinkled with cream, and at least three spoonfuls of sugar.

Julie reached for the cigarette box, and offered it to Craig, then to her son. Craig dived for the lighter and made a creditable effort to light his hostess's cigarette without sweeping the eggshell china on to the Aubusson rug. She leaned back on to the white divan, with a boy seated on a sofa on either side of her.

'Tell me some more about what you're going to do—what you want.'

'Everything,' Craig said suddenly, without thinking. '*Everything*. First I want to travel a lot—I don't know how. But I will. I want—I want to make lots of money. I don't know how I'll make it, but I will, somehow. All my people always been desperate—poor or middlin' poor. I don't like the idea for me.'

Julie duFresne looked at him gently, and without amusement. 'I somehow think you will,' she said softly. 'Would you like another cup of coffee?'

'Yes, please, ma'am,' he said, and leaned back to look into the fire. He had always been able to find faces in firelight, but there were no faces there tonight. Only shadows.

He finished his coffee, and strove valiantly to keep his eyes open. The wine, the food, the trip, the excitement, seized him, and his lids drooped lower and lower. He pulled himself together with an effort. He looked across Julie duFresne at Philip, who was frankly asleep.

'Some people are coming in later,' Julie said, 'but they're rather bores for you boys. I think you'd better go and get some rest, and we'll start it over tomorrow. That's a very long trip from the Hill to Charleston.' She reached over and nudged her son. 'Wake up, Philip,' she said. 'Time you young gentlemen sought some slumber.'

Philip shook himself awake. 'What time is it?' he asked, his voice blurred.

'Not late,' his mother said, 'but you've had a long tiring day and I think you both need some rest. Craig's very tired.'

'No, ma'am,' Craig said earnestly. 'I don't think I'm tired. To be honest, I think I'm drunk.'

'Not off the wine,' Julie said. 'Come on, off with you now, both of you.' She raised a cheek to be kissed by her son, and then turned her head to Craig, who awkwardly pecked the other side of her face. 'Sleep tight,' she said. 'Good night.'

When they reached the top of the stairs, Craig said to Philip: 'Do you always eat like this—live like this?'

'I suppose so.' Philip yawned hugely. 'Most of the time, anyhow, when we're both home. Good night, pal. I'm away to dreamland. I am really bushed. Tomorrow we'll go out and see if we can't rip the town apart.'

As he turned to go to his room, Craig said, with slightly alcoholic gravity:

'Philip, I really want to thank you for having me here to visit. I can't tell you . . .' Philip yawned again.

'Don't bother. Hell, it really wasn't so much my idea as *hers*. Go on to sleep now, and I'll see you in the morning. Ring that

85

bell by your night-table, and somebody'll bring you your breakfast. Ask for what you want. We never eat breakfast together in this joint. Nobody can stand the sight of each other in the morning. G'night.'

'G'night.' Craig went to his room and saw that there was a lit lamp by his night-table, and that one of his two pairs of pyjamas had been laid out across the bed. He was very tired, and drunk—drunk in the sense that liquor will take hold of a man who comes in from the cold after a day's hunting, and who feels the alcohol seize him when he stands before a fire. He felt more tired than if he had played four quarters of football.

He undressed quickly, found strength to hang up his new tuxedo, forgot to clean his teeth and pulled on his pyjamas. He dived into bed, and went straight off to sleep without remembering to turn off the lamp.

Once, early in the middle hours, he heard the sound of adult male laughter surging up from below, and knew jealousy which brought him sharply awake. For the first time in his life, Craig Price was deeply, seriously, in love, and with a woman more than twice his age. Sixteen was very young to be in love with any woman, especially a rich and beautiful woman, twice your age.

Fatigue conquered jealousy, and as Craig drifted off again, he muttered: 'I won't always be this young,' and snored.

Bright arrogant sun streamed through the windows when he woke, wondering briefly where he might be. He writhed under the soft sheets as a puppy might flex himself on awakening, stretched luxuriously, and looked at his bedroom again through sleep-blurred lids. Then he came fully awake, and had the momentarily horrifying thought that he might have disgraced himself. He got out of bed and went to the bathroom, suffering his first mild, but rather exhilarating hangover. His mouth felt fuzzy as he brushed his teeth. He stuck out his tongue, and didn't like the look of it, so he scrubbed at it with the toothbrush.

He remembered then that he was to ring for his breakfast, that nobody ever went down to have breakfast with anybody else. He had put his watch on the night-table: seven-thirty. Too early to disturb old whatever-his-name-was, or anybody else. He decided to go back to bed, and think a little bit. While he was thinking a little bit he fell asleep again, and was awakened at eight-thirty by Philip banging on his door.

'You had breakfast yet?' Philip was wearing a dressing-gown, pyjamas and slippers. He hadn't combed his hair. It bristled like a cock's comb. His face was rumpled.

'No, not yet. I woke up once but went back to sleep again.'

'So did I. Say, our Julie must have had quite a bunch in last night. They woke me up about one, and it sounded awful party-fied. Maybe we should have stayed up and watched the fun.'

'I heard them, too. But I don't think the grown-ups really

wanted us around. Anyhow, I was awful tired. And drunk.'

'Me too. I'm hung. I feel like hell. Tell you what, let's ring for old Applenose and we'll have breakfast here and then go look around my unfavourite city. Not that there's very much to see.'

'Do we dress, first? Before we eat, I mean?'

'Naw. Eat as we are. Julie won't be stirring until lunch-time. She leaves late, and gets up late. Bang on the bell.'

'Before I do, can you lend me a bathrobe? I haven't got—I mean I forgot to pack one.'

'*Mais oui, mon vieux.* 'arf a mo.' Philip was being tri-lingual again. He darted out of the door and came back with a blue silk dressing-gown which he threw at Craig. 'Now, jerk that cord. What do you want to eat?'

'Not much. Some eggs and bacon, maybe, and a cup of coffee.'

'You got a better stomach than me. I'm settling for a nip of that Scotch and a lot of coffee. Drowns the butterflies.'

'Drinking before breakfast? Ain't that supposed to be?...'

'I reckon.' Philip grinned and lit a cigarette. 'Everybody says I take after Pa. Here's your health.' He tilted the bottle and shuddered, but looked perceptibly brighter after he stopped coughing. 'One for you?'

'Great God, no. I had enough last night to last me a month. I'm just not used to this stuff. I think I'll take a bath instead.'

'Okay. I'll order for you. What do you want to see first— museums, old French architecture, all the historic old spots, Fort Sumter, what?'

'If you don't mind I'd kind of like to see the waterfront. I feel more at home on waterfronts. Let's go watch a ship come in, something like that. Down at the docks.'

'You know something, Craig? I'd really like to. I went to sea once. Here's LeBlanc. 'Morning. Mister Price wants...' The rest was drowned in the rush of Craig's bath-water.

When he'd finished bathing and shaving, Philip was back again, the better for a bath and a shave, and LeBlanc was bringing in a wheeled table with covered silver dishes which smelled delightful. When he lifted the cover from one dish, Craig saw some flaky crisp rolls.

'What are those?' he asked.

'*Croissants.* French breakfast rolls. Try some with that jam there. Coffee and *croissants* are about all the French—the French in France—eat. They call it *petit déjeuner*—little breakfast. Highly civilized.'

'Me, I'll still take ham and eggs. These look wonderful.'

They finished their breakfast and dressed. They strolled outside in the warm winter sun.

'Let's walk down to the docks,' Craig said. 'It's too nice a day not to walk. Also I think that green steamboat of yours kind of don't fit with stevedores.'

'I wouldn't say that. Us blue-bloods get along very well with the dockers. In a way we're a very democratic town, Charleston. We only fight among ourselves. The blue-bloods are always battling. Amalie is sore at Sophie, and Pierre has heard that Henri has told Armand . . . you know.'

'This doesn't seem like an American town at all. It doesn't even smell American.'

'It isn't. It's one part French, one part cracker, and one part African. We rule out the crackers and so it turns out like I imagine Algiers would be—not that I've ever seen Algiers—half French, half shine. But I can tell you a funny story about how the blue-bloods and the dock-wallopers get along.'

They were strolling slowly down a narrow, cobbled street. It was not too far from Yamacraw, the Negro settlement, and Craig noticed how black—coal-black, almost blue-black—the Negroes who thronged the streets were. He had heard Grandpa Sam mention 'blue-gum Niggers', but had never really seen any. These were not Negroes as he knew them, but straight West Coast Africans—Africans who talked the Gullah, as their relatives a bit further South talked the Geechee. The sounds were fascinating. The high-pitched babble of the unseen women, in little back courts, the deep bass voices of the men in the faded patched dungarees, the distant barking dog, the squalling cat, the lonely plinking of a cigar-box banjo, all melted into the smell of frying fish and damp mottled plaster walls that would never lose a nose-itching odour of urine and ancient garbage—the heavy smells of lush vegetation and rancid cooking-fat and horse-dung overlaid with dust—delved into his nostrils more deliciously than last night's champagne. He wished Philip would shut up, but Philip rattled merrily on.

'You know,' he was saying. 'We got a big event once a year. The stevedores and watermen are real proud of their rowing. Once a year there is a big regatta. The towns down this way—Savannah, Charleston and Norfolk—all enter the boat races, and for us it's as big as a World Series or the Kentucky Derby. They don't talk about anything else, and the main idea is that no matter what happens, Charleston has just got to beat Norfolk.

'So anyhow, a couple of years back, they were practising every day on the Cooper River, and about two weeks before the big event, the stroke oar caught a crab and busted his arm. You can imagine what that was like. Every man jack had bet a year's pay on the race, and here is the Charleston shell with no stroke oar, only two weeks before the big races.'

'Mmhm,' Craig said. 'So what did they do?'

'I told you we were a democratic city. The boys got together and had a conference. The captain of the crew said something like this:

' "Mon, we got trouble. We got to find a new stroke oar some-place. Any you guys know a mon can row stroke?"

'Somebody pipes up for a joke: "How about young Gaston LeJeune? Hees pretty good stroke. Win heemself big 'H' for sweater when he row for Harvard, heem. Maybe he row stroke for us, we ask heem right.'

' "Mon, hees blue-blood. He won' row with river-rats."

' "You can't tell. We don' lose nothing if we ask heem. We sen' three mon ask heem. Formal. Mebbe he play ball."

'Well,' Philip said, 'they went up to see Cousin Gaston—he is a cousin of mine, everybody in town is a cousin of mine—and the idea amused him. There's not much to do in Charleston and the idea that a *sang bleu* would be rowing with a bunch of water-rats for the honour of dear old Charleston would make a lot of party conversation for a long time. So Gaston said sure, and he went down and worked out with the boys every day. Everybody got to be fine friends. So the race is on.

'I must say, Cousin Gaston, apart from being a little fat and out of shape, was a pretty fancy stroke oar, and the Charleston shell jumped out ahead early and keep a good lead. But coming down the river about a thousand yards from the finish, the Nor-folk shell began to creep ahead. Its bow was just coming abreast when the Charleston coxswain started to yell.

' "Row!" he hollered. "*Row! Row! Row! Row*, you dirty sons-of-bitches—and *Monsieur* Le Jeune!"

'Yep,' Philip laughed. 'We get along fine, but on different levels . . .'

They walked through a dockside warehouse, stacked high with huge crates girdled tightly with broad bands of shiny iron ribbon. Gleaming black bucks, naked to the waist, with sweat-rags tied round their heads, chanted as they lifted and toted, heaved and pushed. Craig and Philip sauntered into the sunlight outside, to the edge of the mooring dock, and sat down on ancient, smoothly worn mooring bollards.

A ship—a tired, wave-abused ship—was tied up 'longside. She had come a weary way. She was of the ancient cargo vintage known as Hog Islander, relic of World War One, sow-like and ungainly, but an eminently practical beast of burden. Her rusted name-plate proclaimed her *Sundance*, and her stack wore the colours of the South Atlantic Steamship Line, home-based in Savannah. Abaft and above her foc's'le head and forward hatches was the wheel-house and officers' quarters. A 'midships hatch separated the wheel-house from the main deckhouse, which contained the engine-room, galley, and crew's mess. A ladder led downward to another stretch of hatches, to be surmounted again by the fantail, under which the crews slept—deck gang starboard, black gang port. They were separated by the steering-engine-room.

The *Sundance* had evidently not enjoyed a very clement voyage. She was a fairly light ship now, although the winches still rattled, as the after holds took on cargo. The red lead below her Plimsoll line was scabby and rusty-pink. Her grey paint job was scabrously eaten away, and sailors on rope-suspended stages were sloshing. paint on to her gaunt sides. They had not yet painted down so far as the port which discharged sewage bilge, and her outer skin, under this port-hole, was as streaked and foul as an island inhabited by herons. Her stack was smoke-blackened, and she looked weary and very, very sad.

'I think she's beautiful,' Craig said. 'I wonder where she's been? I wonder where she's going?'

'Not Tahiti, if that's what you've got in mind,' Philip laughed. 'Not this scow. This rust-bucket, and all her sorry sisters, make a regular run. They generally leave out of here, and they go to Liverpool, and then to Rotterdam, and on to Hamburg. Or they go to London, Antwerp and Hamburg. But they mostly pay off in Jacksonville, and start loading a little bit there. Then they take on a little more in Fernandina, and some more in Savannah, and they wind up here to top off the load and shove off again for Liverpool, Rotterdam and Hamburg. The bed-bugs don't go back into the bulkhead until you're about three or four days out, and it gets cold again. Also the food stinks. So does the cargo. This one's reversed her course. She's doing it all ass-backwards. She'll work south and sail from Jax.'

'How come you know so much about this?' Craig was frankly astonished. Philip laughed, deprecatingly.

'In my post-Boy Scout phase, I took sick with an urge for adventure on the high seas. This was just after I was kicked out of Woodberry Forest. Last year, Julie knew somebody important in Savannah, and they got me a job as workaway on one of these sad scows. No pay, sleep with the ship's carpenter—and what a nasty Swede he was—and work all day and half the night in port. Not for Philip, never no more.'

'What did you carry as cargo?'

'Beautiful stuff. Sheep-manure, sulphur, nails, and phosphate rock, with some logs for a deck-load. All I know about going to sea was how it feels to push a broom. Julie figured the sea-trip would make a man of me. It didn't. It damn' near made a woman of me, for every old wolf on the ship had a stab at me.'

'A stab at you? What do you mean?'

'I keep forgetting how young you are,' Philip's smile was patronizing. 'My poor innocent child, there are no women on ships. There are lots of old men—especially engineers—who spend their lives at sea. To them, a young boy is prettier than a woman. The same thing happens in prisons. I'm telling you, I pretty near had to stick a cork in my behind when I went to sleep. That's what I'm talking about, or do I have to draw you a picture?'

'But did you—I mean, how didn't—I mean . . .'

'*Once*. I didn't like it. It hurt. But he was a lot bigger than I was so I said, Oh, hell, go ahead.'

'Are you lying again?'

Philip grinned sheepishly.

'As a matter of fact, I am. A little bit. When it got too bad I went to see the captain and reminded him who I was, how I got on the ship, and who Julie knew. After that I didn't have any trouble.'

Craig frowned.

'Why do you go to all the bother to make up all these lies? Where does it get you? Why bother?'

'I really don't know. I like to think that it's the novellist in me coming out, but when I look at it honestly I guess I'm just a natural-born liar. I've always been a liar. I never told the truth in my life except from necessity. It's one of the reasons Julie doesn't particularly adore her one and only son. She thinks I'm weak. She may be right.'

'I don't understand it,' Craig shook his head in honest wonder. 'You've got everything. You've got a wonderful home and a wonderful mother and plenty of money and a car and you've been to Europe and . . .'

'Maybe that's the trouble. Maybe I don't want a wonderful home and a wonderful mother and plenty of money and a car. None of it's mine, including my wonderful mother. Maybe I want to be you—no wonderful nothing, but a wonderful something.'

'I don't know what the hell you're talking about,' Craig said. 'But I don't think I like it. Anyhow, I don't understand it.' He changed the subject abruptly. 'Tell me, Phil, what were the foreign ports like? London? Antwerp?' His change of subject sounded awkward.

'I don't know. I was so fed up with seafaring when we hit London, that I cabled Julie, who was in Paris, and joined her there. I completed my summer of culture in Fontainebleau, where Julie had a house.' The answer was terse.

'You just quit and ran off—and went away from the ship? Just like that?'

'You could hardly call it jumping ship. After all, I was just on the damn' thing as a favour to *Maman*, and they were probably glad to get rid of me. I wasn't much good at anything.' Philip looked intently at his feet.

Craig muttered to himself. 'I wouldn't have quit.' Then he looked up, straight at Philip.

'What?' Philip deserted the inspection of his feet.

'I said: "*I wouldn't have quit*." I wouldn't quit anything once I started it, not if it killed me.'

'I expect you wouldn't. You got a streak of bulldog in you that

I haven't got. Me, I do it the easy way.' Philip went back to inspecting his feet, as if he'd never seen them before.

Craig was silent. He was watching the men, slung over the side on the hanging scaffold, slabbering great streaks of paint on the ship's flanks. He noticed that the paint buckets were lowered over the taffrail by a line, and that the two men on each scaffold maintained a delicate balance to keep the plank at even keel—that they were constantly spattered by paint, and cursed monotonously as they worked. He also noticed a steady stream of men —obviously not employed on the vessel—who walked up the gangplank. Some came back immediately. Others stayed aboard.

'Who are those people—the ones going up the gangplank?' Craig pointed at the shabby human stream.

'I was a seaman long enough to answer that one,' Philip lifted his head. 'These are people out of work. On the beach, it's called. Most of those guys are ex-sailors—masters, mates, engineers, bosuns. They're broke and they're going aboard to bum a free meal. If the cook's in a good humour he'll give 'em a hand-out. If he isn't, back they go over the side again. I think there's something called a depression on.'

'There is,' Craig said. 'There certainly is.' Then: 'Tell me one thing, Phil. What was that business last night about the wine. Muse—Museen—Museeny, or something like that?'

Philip grinned, not nicely. He shrugged and spread his hands.

'I was having a little off-stage go at Mummy, as the British might say. Dear Old Mum had herself a big thing in Paris with one of my summer uncles. François, this one was. I can remember because he was just after Charles—he pronounced it "Sharl"—and just before Henri. He pronounced that "Onree". I think there was some talk of marriage but it was all very intense. Uncle François particularly fancied this Musigny brand of wine, and Julie particularly fancied Uncle François. She still drinks Musigny even though Uncle François eventually went back to Mrs. Uncle François, whom he had handy in the corner as an excuse all the time. I don't really think I care for my mother very much.' His voice was suddenly soft, and very cold.

'My mother's a whore.'

Craig jumped to his feet.

'Now, wait a minute,' he said. 'You can't talk about your mother like that! I'll . . .'

Philip smiled, and his face was infinitely, sadly old.

'Take it easy,' he said. 'She's *my* mother. If I want to call her a whore, I will. Because that's what she is—a whore. A beautiful, spoiled, gracious, charming, intelligent—whore!'

Craig hit him. Philip fell sideways off the bollard, and remained on the dock. A thin stripe of blood inched from the corner of his mouth and made its wavery journey down his chin.

'Get up, you bastard! Get up and fight!' Craig stood over Philip.

'No,' Philip said, 'not this boy. I like it down here on the deck. Kick me if you'd like. If it'll give you any pleasure. I don't fight over whores.'

Craig felt very weak, and suddenly sick to his stomach. Philip cradled his head in his right hand, lazily resting on his elbow, and made no effort to wipe the creeping blood off his chin.

'I'll tell you something else, Jack Dempsey,' he said. A drop of blood left his chin, and plopped on to the planks. 'She's had her eye on you from the first, young as you are. Not now—no, of course not, not *now*. But some day. You'll keep. You'll keep, all right. I've seen her plant it before, and you're on the chosen list. Even Julie hasn't got bad taste enough to crawl into your bed right now, but it's only a matter of time, my boy, merely a matter of time. Grow up and come back. Except you won't be here as *my* guest. You'll be *her* guest then, in *her* house, in *her* bed. You'll never be my guest again. You want to hit me some more?'

'No, Phil, I don't want to hit you. But I don't think I want anything to do with you any more, either. I'm sorry to say it but you are really *the* lousiest piece of . . . you just plain stink.'

'You might very well be right.'

Philip got up and reached for a handkerchief. He dabbed at his bloody chin. 'You got quite a punch. I always thought I stank. I even liked it when you socked me. I think I wanted you to hit me. Asking for it. Well . . .' He shrugged. 'What now?'

Craig looked at him, and felt something writhe in his stomach. It was a feeling not unlike the one he had when first he looked at the maggots working on the defunct Bell. A sort of . . . of . . . of violent distaste, mingled with nausea. Bile rose in his throat.

'My mother maybe got sick suddenly. She hasn't been well lately. If I can use your phone to call Kensington, I'm almost sure she'll be sick enough to want me to come home. I don't want to stay here any more.' He shook his head and flipped a wrist outward in total negation.

'If you feel that way, okay. We'll go back to the house and make the call. I'm sorry I loused up the holidays, but you did ask me about Julie, didn't you?' Philip shrugged again. He touched a handkerchief to his mouth. It had stopped bleeding.

'It'll teach me to keep my mouth shut. I'm sorry too, but I like your mother a lot. I like her . . . I like her a lot better than I like you.' Craig's voice had softened . . . sorrowfully, apologetically.

'That's obvious,' Philip said. 'Let's go home and make the call. If my *mother*'—he stressed the word *mother*—'isn't up yet, we can just fake it. It's only about three hours to Kensington. I could drive you . . .'

'No, thanks. I'll hitch-hike. It's easy.' For a second Craig tasted salty bitterness on his tongue. 'I wish I'd brought my Joe College

93

suit. It would make it even easier. Nobody would take me for a gentleman. As it is I guess I'll climb into my short pants, and maybe they'll take me for a boy. Overgrown, but a *boy*.' His voice hardened.

'But not your kind, Philip. Never your kind. Let's go. I'd like to say good-bye to your mother.'

'Miss Julie, I'm dreadful sorry,' Craig said. 'But I reckon I better go home. Ever since Ma had that measles thing, she's managed to catch every cold that came down the pike, and when I talked to Pop he said it looked like pneumonia . . . bad. I better go home and see what's going on. Christmas, and all . . . and Ma sick.'

'I understand completely, Craig. You wouldn't be happy here, worrying, and I suppose actually that Christmas is a time when any mother wants her child at home. Even one like mine. Are you sure I can't have the chauffeur drive you?' No mention at all of Philip by name.

'No, thank you, Miss Julie. I'll just grab a bus. There's one leaving at two-thirty, and I'll be home in time for supper. Easier that way. But sure has been fun, and I hate to spoil it.'

Julie duFresne took him by the arm, and walked him gently to the patio. Once again he was uneasily aware of the fleshiness of the banana fronds, the hot-house heat of the waxy flowers.

'Craig?'

'Yes, ma'am?'

'Come here.'

Julie took him by the shoulders and looked steadily into his eyes.

'I must do something about Philip.' Now the name. 'With the dentist, I mean. His gums are bleeding again.'

Craig looked at her and said nothing.

'Craig.'

'Yes, ma'am?'

'You will come to see me again some day?'

'If you want me to, ma'am. I'd love to come and see you again, ma'am.'

'Why did you hit him?' She fired the question.

'Hit who?' Craig's eyes widened. Julie duFresne shrugged.

'All right,' she said. 'I hope your mother's better when you get home. Craig . . .'

'Yes, ma'am?'

'He was right. I'm not a nice—'

'That bus is going to leave pretty soon, Miss Julie. I better go get my . . .'

'Of course. Kiss me good-bye, Craig.' She turned a cheek. He kissed her a short, savage peck.

'You know you're always welcome in this home.'

'Thank you, ma'am. I hope I can come back some day. But now I think I better leave.'

'One thing. Are you really going to be a bootlegger?'

'I guess so. It's one way of staying in school.'

'I wouldn't if I were you. You won't like it—later. Can I—this is hard to say—may I possibly help you, Craig?'

'Help Philip,' he said, roughly. 'He needs it more than me. Good-bye, ma'am. And thank you for everything.'

'Come back, Craig Price,' she said, and turned to walk into the house.

Philip dropped Craig at the edge of town over the Cooper River bridge, and in front of a shabby filling station.

'You ought to be able to hook something here,' he said. 'You still sure you don't want me to drive you home?'

'Thanks again, Phil. No. Like I told your mother—easier this way. I'll be home in three, four hours.'

'You still sore at me?'

'Not really. Yes, I s'pose I am. Not outside. Inside sore. Sorry. The kind of sore that don't . . . that don't scab over. But thanks anyhow. Good-bye.'

Philip looked at Craig, looked at him steadily as his mother had looked at Craig.

'Maybe I'll finish up at the Sorbonne,' he said. 'That Chapel Hill is awful goddamned dull. I really *do* prefer Paris, don't I?'

'I dunno,' Craig said, and turned away. 'I don't know what you want. So long. See you in Chapel Hill maybe, before you head for the Sorbonne.'

It was an enormous low-slung blue car, a Cord. The driver was bald and fat, not sloppy fat, but robust with the kind of fat that was neatly smoothed as by a trowel. The kind of fat that housed burst veins in the cheeks, to make a falsely healthy flush—the kind of fat that was fat all over, so that the collar was too tight, the coat wrinkled behind the neck, and sweaty under the armpits. The man swabbed his streaming red face with the back of his right sleeve. He got out of the low-slung Cord and said to Craig:

'Fill her up. Where do you go to pee?'

'I don't know, sir. I just got here. Back there, I reckon.'

'Oh.' The fat man took a raggedly chewed cigar from his wet lips, looked at it with distaste, and flung it away. 'I thought you were the attendant.' He looked Craig up and down. Craig was wearing his knickers again, and carrying his bag with the college sticker on it.

'College boy?'

'Yessir. Freshman. I'm hitch-hiking home.'

A gentle aroma of bruised corn came from the fat, flushed gentleman.

'Where you going, Buddy? Where's home?'

'Kensington. Home for Christmas.'

'That's where I'm going. I live there. Can you drive?'

'Yessir.'

'Tell you what. I'm so full my back teeth are floatin'. You tell the attendant to fill her up, and if you drive me home without both of us gettin' killed, there's ten dollars in it for you. Okay?'

'Okay. Thank you, sir.'

'Polite, ain't you? I like polite kids. Now . . .' The fat man with the flushed, vein-burst cheeks darted around the corner of the service station just as the attendant came out.

'Man says fill 'er up,' Craig said. 'Didn't say, but you better look at the oil. These things drink it.'

'You got one?' the attendant asked, unscrewing the cap to the gas tank.

'Not yet,' Craig said. The attendant grinned.

The fat sweaty gentleman came out buttoning his fly. He had a fresh cigar clenched in his teeth.

'Man, I feel ten years younger and ten pounds lighter. How much, son?' He turned to the attendant. 'She needed a quart of oil,' the attendant said. 'Your friend told me to check it.'

'That was smart of him. Already earning your pay, hey?' he smiled. 'Let's have a Coke before we start. You drink whisky?'

'Not when I'm driving somebody else's car,' Craig said. 'Not a car like this.'

'Good boy. Long as I'm the passenger, I think I'll have a snort. It's in the bag back there. Get it out for me.'

Craig opened the bag. It was filled with dirty linen, in which nestled a quart bottle of corn whisky.

'Good,' the fat man said, as Craig handed him the bottle. 'What a night. Mud in your eye.' He tossed his head back, and the bottle gurgled. He coughed and drained half a bottle of Coke as a chaser.

'I needed that one,' he said. 'I was afraid to before, because I got a bad habit of going to sleep when I drink too much. I can drink and I can drive, but mixin' 'em is too much for me. Thanks, Buddy,' as the attendant brought him his change. 'Let's roll. I think I'll crawl in the back and grab a wink. Man, that Charleston is a town . . . Maybe New Orleans is better, but last night . . .'

The fat man climbed into the car. He produced a hat from somewhere and pounded it into a pillow, wedged it into a corner and snuggled down. Craig eased in the clutch and the big car slid smoothly out of the filling station.

'You said you live in Kensington?' the fat man asked.

'Yessir. Between there and the Sound and sometimes in New Truro.'

'What's your name?'

'Price, Craig Price.'

'Any kin to Dick Price?'

'He's my father.'

The man laughed.

'What do you know? Him and me went to school together in New Truro. I was kind of sweet on your ma, too. My name's John Grimes. Shake.' He reached a hand over from the back seat.

'Sure. Nice to know you.'

The fat man took another long pull at the bottle, and nestled his head on to the hat. 'Home, James,' he said, and promptly went to sleep. He didn't wake up until they crossed the bridge over the Cape Fear River, on the outer lip of town. He took another ounce out of the bottle, and punched his hat into shape.

'That was quite a nap. We kill anybody on the way?'

'Nope,' Craig smiled. 'Not even a dog.'

'You must drive pretty good. You still live out Market Street?'

'No sir. Pa lost that one. We lived there for a while after, but Mother's got a job now down at the Sound. That hotel there. She runs the dining-room—kitchen, really. Dietician, they call her. I suppose it's another name for cook.'

The fat man looked keenly at the back of Craig's neck. Craig could see him through the rear-view mirror.

'You don't let yourself up much, do you?' The fat man was serious. 'That business about your mother being the cook, I mean.'

Craig stopped for a light before he answered.

'There ain't no point to saying she's a bank president. A cook is a cook. Where do you want to go, Mr. Grimes?'

'I got plenty time, and I've had nearly 'bout a night's sleep. Suppose you drive yourself home and I'll take over from there.' He worried at his pants pocket. 'And kid . . .'

'Yessir?'

'Don't take me wrong. I know your pa and I knew your ma. Here's your ten bucks, and Merry Christmas, and thanks for the chauffeur job.'

'You don't really have to do that. If anything, I owe you for the free ride. I couldn't . . .'

'The hell you couldn't. Take it and shut up. You earned it. And say. When you get out of school and maybe need a job, come see me. I got a lot of irons in the fire.'

'What do you do, sir? If I come to see you for a job?'

'Funny you made that crack about bank presidents. I'm a bank president. I just bought one. The one that didn't fail.'

'We had the wrong kind of bank. Thanks, Mr. Grimes. I'll take the money. And . . . thanks.'

'You're welcome, buddy. I got a kid about your age. A little girl. She's getting out of high school this spring, and she's going to Saint Mary's. She's goin' to be a real pretty little girl. Maybe sometime when you're in Raleigh you might look her up and take her to a movie or ask her to a dance or something.'

'What's her name?'

'Maybelle. After my two grandmothers. Matter of fact, why don't you come by the house for some eggnog Christmas afternoon . . . maybe . . . and maybe meet the family?' The man seemed oddly hesitant, as if asking a tremendous favour. 'We could talk . . .'

'I'd like to. Where's your house?'

'Well, it's . . . it's in Delgado. You see, I own some mills, too.'

'All those cotton mills?'

'Not all.' The fat man smiled now with pride. 'Only the one that ain't shut. Like the bank. The one that's open.'

He still held the money uneasily. He leaned over and shoved it in the general direction of Craig's right hand. 'Here. Take it. Buy yourself a present. And come see us, hear?'

'I sure will, Mister Grimes. Where 'bouts exactly?'

'Well . . . it ain't exactly in the mill district. It's in a place that ain't really got a name yet. It's not too far away from the new school. Big white house between the school and Winter Haven. Gonna have a nice name, that piece of ground. Forest Glen.'

'How do you know what it's gonna be named?'

The fat man achieved a blush.

'I . . . I own that land, too,' he said, and almost added 'beg your pardon'. 'I named it.'

'I was in the seventh grade at the school the first year it was built,' Craig said, suddenly finding a friend. 'I know your house, now. We used to go swimming in the creek behind it during lunch hour, and made the teacher awful mad. I did a lot of huntin' around there, too. There's a mess of quail back of the graveyard. They use there and flush into the swamp.'

'Looks like you been shootin' on my proppity', the fat man said. 'Maybe I better look me up some law.'

Craig laughed delightedly.

'You better be careful,' he said. 'The sheriff's a friend of mine. My huntin' partner. Who you gonna get to arrest the sheriff?'

The fat man slapped his thigh.

'I guess I'll have to take it as high as Raleigh,' he roared with laughter. 'I own most of that, too. Legislatures don't cost much, these days. I got me a tame one.'

They were breasting the big curve that crossed Ritchie's Creek and led through a cathedral of oak trees down to the Sound. They passed an enormous estate, barred from the common man by a huge iron gate.

'Fair Lea,' Craig said. 'It sure is pretty when the azaleas come out. But it's prettier in the fall, when the squirrels come out. I used to shoot a lot of squirrels out of this place.'

'It's a nice place, all right. You shot a lot of squirrels? I thought it was posted.'

'Well, it is. But there's a way to call 'em. You snick the safety of your shotgun on and off, and it sounds like a squirrel eating hickory nuts. Then you do a "*burrr*" sound with your tongue—like this.' Craig made the *burring* sound horizontally across his mouth, tongue against his front teeth. 'It'll fetch 'em every time.'

Mr. Grimes laughed again, very loudly.

'Damn me, if I was a squirrel, I'd come too. I knowed something was getting them squirrels, and it turned out to be you. You ain't shot any black swans lately?'

'No sir, they're too pretty, I . . .' Craig stopped. 'Don't tell me you own Fair Lea too?'

'I'm afraid so, son. They had a mortgage that didn't come out even. But up to now I ain't had enough courage to live in that big old house. I think it's haunted. I spent a couple nights in it, hunting, and it sure does squeak loud.'

'I'm sorry about the squirrels. I didn't . . .'

'Hell's horns and teeth, boy, they're a nuisance. But the next time you want to shoot some squirrels, don't waste a lot of effort tolling them across the road. Just walk in and make yourself to home.'

They rounded the second big curve, and the steaming marshy smell of the Sound filled Craig's nostrils. He took a big breath, and sucked in the fat sweat of mud and sun. The water stretched ink-blue before him, lightly flecked with breeze-tossed wavelets, and the few old grey, barnacly docks looked homely and battered —like well-beloved friends a trifle down on their luck.

'It's nice to be back home again,' Craig said. 'That first three months in college is a little lonesome . . . you know.'

'I *don't* know,' the fat man said. 'I never finished grammar school. I never been no place much but here and up in Shelby and once in a while to Washington to straighten out some business. Raleigh, of course.'

They arrived at the little hamlet, turned left, and went back up the Loop Road.

'That's home,' Craig said, pointing. 'There, across the street-car tracks. There ain't any driveway. I'll get out here, if you don't mind. And thanks, Mister Grimes. You sure you're serious about me coming around to press a call?'

The fat flushed man got out of the back seat and slid himself gruntingly under the wheel.

'Never more serious in my life. You're a good kid, Craig Price. A Merry Christmas and remember me to your pa and ma. See you after dinner Christmas afternoon.'

'Merry Christmas,' Craig said, and toted his baggage up the hill to the little red house which was his current home.

This was that year Craig's mother had forsaken fire insurance for a more reliable job as dietician in a small resort hotel half a dozen miles away from Kensington. The hotel was a square yellow stucco horror that overlooked the blue sweep of the sound which fudged in between a distant beach and the Atlantic Ocean.

Across the highway and on the other side of the street-car tracks sat the little red cracker-box which his mother and father had been able to rent so that Lilian Price could be near at all times to her kitchen in the hotel.

It had seemed rather an adequate house to Craig—comfortable enough and pleasantly placed next an orchard of fat yellow blush-cheeked plums gone wild, with a black forest of pine and live-oak thrusting its way almost to the back porch. Jays, brilliant blue, were raucous intruders. It was a nice little house really. Half of it was devoted to a living-room with a large fireplace and the rest comprised kitchen and two bedrooms.

It was furnished with others people's drab remnants and there never seemed to be any one chair on friendly terms with any single table. Meals came direct from the kitchen to the living-room and were eaten on two large card-tables which appeared to be in a state of perpetual indecision concerning their intent to collapse.

The little red house had seemed like a charming picnic site to Craig, who was rarely in it anyhow, except to sleep, since his boat claimed most of his attention. Now after a day and night in Philip duFresne's house in Charleston it seemed a squalid horror, a ratty compromise between the solid comfort of the old but now lost big house in Kensington and a share-cropper's shanty. His mother still had on her brown hotel kitchen uniform when Craig's new friend, Grimes, dropped him on the road.

'What are you doing back here?' Lilian Price said. 'I thought you were spending Christmas in Charleston with your room-mate.'

Craig went up the rickety porch-stairs and kissed his mother before he answered.

'I decided I didn't like it much down there in Charleston,' he said. 'It was a little too rich for my blood, and anyhow I have never spent a Christmas away from home'—he looked around him—'before. So I decided to come back.'

'You won't find a whole lot of Christmas here this year,' his mother said, looking at him sharply. 'You've changed, son. I think you've grown up. School all right?'

'All right. I made out. Where's Dad?'

'He ought to be in any minute.'

'Ma—a man gave me ten dollars for driving him from Charleston. Will you take it and buy you and Pa some sort of Christmas present?' He reached into his pocket and found the money. 'I'd like it if you would. He was a nice man, and he told me to buy myself a present with it.'

Lilian Price took the money. She held it in her hand, as one might observe a rat or a moist baby bird, or possibly a snake.

'He didn't try to do anything bad to you, giving you ten dollars just like that?'

100

'No, Ma. He was just a nice fellow. He said he knew you and Pa. He comes from New Truro. Named John Grimes. Little fat red-faced fellow.'

Lilian Price put the money in her apron pocket. She went over to a chair and collapsed into it. She stretched her varicosed legs straight out in front of her, and wiggled her feet.

'I could of married him,' she said. 'I could of had everything he's got now. Instead of *this*.' Her nostrils spread as she looked around the room.

'Who is he, Ma? He sounds awful rich.'

'Rich? He's got all the money in town. He's . . . He's . . . He's poor white trash from New Truro. His daddy was a cropper on your Uncle Jimmy's farm. I used to play with John Grimes when I was a little girl. What does he look like now?'

'Fat. Drinks a lot of liquor. But he told me he was a bank president and he owns Fair Lea and mills in Delgado. He said. And he asked me to come over to his house after dinner Christmas. To meet his daughter. She's going to school at Saint Mary's in Raleigh next year.'

'You go, boy. Maybe if he wants to he can help you in college. Somebody's going to have to, because we can't.'

'I don't want anybody to help me in college. I don't want to belong to nobody. Specially somebody I don't know. He was just a nice man.'

'I don't reckon he's a nice man. However he got to where he is I don't rightly know, but he couldn't be a nice man to do what he's done so fast, when everybody else is broke. It's wrong to be so rich when everybody else is poor. Wrong. Look at us. Lost everything. Sold the car—*no*. They took it back. Me working in a hotel. Your father selling insurance. *Selling* insurance? Nobody can buy any insurance. Nobody can pay the Piggly Wiggly bill. The only reason we're making it here is I can bring back enough stuff from the hotel to keep us from starving.'

She flourished the ten-dollar bill.

'That's the only cash money we got in the house right now and a shirt-tail boy had to bring it to me. My sister's working as a waitress, and glad to get it. Where's our house? This rat-trap? We used to have two cars. Your father played golf. And you—a shirt-tail boy—have to give me the only cash money in the house.'

Craig's mother burst into tears. Craig felt dreadfully embarrassed, and more than faintly hostile at the display. This did not seem a necessary time to weep.

'Don't cry, Mother,' he said. 'It ain't all that bad. Things'll get better . . .'

His mother glared at him. Her tears had stopped.

'Better? *Better?* How'll it get better? Me working in a kitchen like a nigger? Your father peddling insurance? Better?'

'One of these days I'll make it get better,' Craig said. 'Somehow. Somehow I'll make it get better.'

'Maybe you will,' his mother said. She sniffed into a handkerchief. 'But I doubt it. You sit here and wait for your father. I got to go to work—in a kitchen. Like a nigger wench. Like a nigger wench.'

She went out of the door, but turned before she left the porch. 'I used to play the piano,' she said bitterly. 'Before we sold it.'

'How'd he do it, Pa?' Craig asked, when his father came home. 'How'd he hit it? So fast and all?'

'I couldn't really tell you, Son,' Richard Price said. 'All I know about Johnny Grimes is that nobody ever beat him in a swappin' contest. Somehow he always wound up with the same knife and your best taw agate as well. He was a natural-born trader.'

'But how, Dad, *how*?'

'I told you, I don't know. We went to grade-school a little bit— that was before I came to Kensington, before your aunt Marge married the school-teacher—and he was a kind of dumb, fat kid. He didn't come from nowhere, his pa was a dirt-farmer, and he didn't make any grades. as I remember worth anything special. But he had this trader instinct. Seems to me, as I mind it, he started out medium-illegal. He was tapping pine trees and selling the turpentine before he was knee-high to a grasshopper. Then he did something with a ground-pea crop. Then he got mixed up in cotton trading. Everything he touched turned to money. Including his wife.'

'Oh?'

'Yeah. She was skinny as a rail and she was ugly. Kind of freckled, with white eyelashes. But she was the only daughter of old Holmes McCadden—you know, McCadden Mills. She was the apple of the old man's eye. I won't swear on the bible that John Grimes knocked her up on purpose'—Richard Price stopped speaking for a moment, suddenly aware that he was talking man-to-man—'anyhow she got into the family way, and somebody was guilty.' He looked over his shoulder. 'I wish to Christ it had been me. Old McCadden took down his shotgun and went looking for his son-in-law. He found John Grimes. There was a big to-do. Old Mac was so upset he died of a heart-attack just after the child —the girl—got born. And John Grimes wound up with a flock of mills. Turned out old Mac owned most of a bank, too.'

Richard Price cleared his throat, snorted, and lit a cigarette. He spat some phlegm into the fire.

'That is what is known as a success story. If you ever get a girl knocked up, try to find one with a rich father.'

'He seemed like a right nice man. I mean, he was nice to me.'

'You can be nice when you're rich. Why the hell wouldn't you be? It's easy. All you need is money to be nice.'

'I don't believe it,' Craig said. 'I know some people got money and they ain't very nice.'

'Try it out on me some day,' his father's answer was grim. 'I'll be the nicest son-of-a-bitch in town if I have a little money. Niceness will drip down my chin like honey. I'll sweat niceness. But you need money to sweat pretty. Then it ain't sweat and don't stink like sweat. It's perfume.'

He searched his pockets for another Lucky Strike. The packet was wrinkled, crumpled, and empty.

'In the meantime,' he said, 'I haven't got any cigarettes.'

'I got some,' Craig said. 'Have one of mine.'

'My thanks,' his father said, sarcastically, 'to my rich son.'

Christmas promised poor doings. Craig went out and cut a cedar tree, and his mother unearthed some battered old silver-speckled red-and-gold glass ornaments, so at least they had a tree. Lilian used the ten dollars well. She bought three cartons of cigarettes, a two-quart jug of local scuppernong wine, and a box of Christmas candy. Craig borrowed a shotgun from one of his shrimp-boat friends and came back with a brace of mallard ducks, which seemed obese.

'Where'd you get the ducks?' his father hefted them. 'They don't look like wild ducks.'

'They ain't, exactly,' Craig said. 'You could kind of call them wild ducks gone tame.'

'Fair Lea?'

'I ain't saying, Pa. But they sure are pretty, huh?'

'They'll eat good. Count our blessings as we may. I suppose you're big enough to have a snort?'

'I'm a college boy now.'

'Son.' Craig's father was serious. He fidgeted, clasped and unclasped his hands. Craig noticed that the first two fingers on his father's left hand were sallowed with nicotine.

'Yessir?'

'I don't see how you can go back to school. Seems like I just can't make a turn anywhere. Apart from what your ma makes right now, there just isn't any money—and God knows what your mother earns isn't enough. The banks . . .'

Craig smiled with a confidence he didn't really feel.

'I know a man that owns a bank. I'm going to his house for eggnog tomorrow, after we eat his—after we eat these ducks. Maybe *I* can make a turn. I'm going back to school, Pa, and I aim to stay in school until I get that sheepskin. Don't matter how. I'm going to finish college. You know something? College is like pants. If you got 'em you don't miss 'em, but if you ain't got 'em you feel awful naked. I need college.'

His father shook his head, sorrowfully, and stared at his feet.

'I went to the Morris Plan, to see if I couldn't raise the price

103

of your next quarter's tuition. I heard the man say: "Don't risk it —they're *bad pay*." I wasn't *always* bad pay. Until just recently. Seems like it's all changed now. I don't know where the hell we're headed.'

'I do,' Craig replied. 'Don't you worry, Pa. I'll make out okay. I got me some clothes, and a job, too. I'm going to be a waiter next term. It'll feed me and give me a little money beside. If I can arrange the tuition and dormitory rent, I'll make out fine.'

'I hope so. Some of us ought to. Well, Merry Christmas, son. At least we're eating.'

Craig looked again at his father, as at a stranger. Richard Price had gone very grey, and was completely bald on the top of his skull. His gaunt face was grey, too, the whiskers greenish-grey, and the lumps around the corners of his mouth stood whitely out. His prominent Adam's apple worked nervously, and his coat sleeves were frayed at the cuffs.

'Pa.' Craig spoke softly, hesitantly.

'Son?'

'We're about the same size, ain't we? Suit-size, I mean?'

Richard Price looked at his son.

'I reckon. You certainly got skinny in the last three months. I suppose so. Why?'

'I'd like to give you a Christmas present if you could see your way clear to take it. It's a new suit.'

Richard Price's nostrils flared, and his chin tilted.

'What you saying, boy? It's *my* business to buy *your* clothes! I can't help it if I can't . . .' He suddenly buried his face in his hands.

'Don't take on, Pa. I got this new suit—by sort of accident— and I got another one, too. I even got a tux. You'd like this suit, Pa. It's grey—just your colour. Like the ones you used to wear. Would you try it on, anyhow? I sure would like you to have it. Like it was a favour—like it was a Christmas present *to* me. Will you please try it on?'

Richard Price got up and walked to the window. He looked out for quite a minute. When he turned around, his eyes were level, if damp. The white lumps bulged more, at the corners of his mouth.

'Of course, son. Thank you for a very Merry Christmas. Where's the suit?'

'I'll get it. You put it on, and I'll put on my tux, and we'll surprise Ma. The two best-dressed gents on the Sound.'

The new, unworn, grey-flannel suit fitted Richard Price very well. As he looked at himself in the bedroom mirror, he said very quietly, 'Christ, I wish I was dead.' Then he walked almost jauntily into the sitting-room, to see Craig already dressed in his dinner-jacket.

'My Lord, we're a handsome pair,' Richard Price said. 'Your

mother won't know us. That's a good-looking tux, and this grey suit fits like it was made for me. How'd you come by this one?'

'*Some* people got credit.' Craig grinned to take away the sting. 'Naw, Pa, I got some prospects and some friends. I'll make enough being a waiter to pay off the College Shop.'

Richard Price turned bitter again. He smacked his right fist into his palm. 'Don't ever bank too much on credit,' he said. 'It's been my downfall.'

Lilian Price came through the door, still wearing her brown kitchen smock. It had grease stains in the front. She looked first at Craig, in his evening regalia, and then at her husband, sharply, newly resplendent in his son's suit. She smoothed the front of her blotched uniform with nervous red hands.

'I must be in the wrong house,' she said, with a forced smile. 'I guess I'm not grand enough for this kind of company. Maybe I better eat in the kitchen tonight.'

'We're just kiddin', Ma,' Craig said. 'Come on, sit down, and let me get you a glass of wine. We ain't got much but us, but it's Christmas and we still got us. That's better than what most people got.'

'I forgot to tell you.' Lilian Price looked at her son as if she were asking for a favour. 'I had a little time this summer, and I planted some Jerusalem artichokes. If you look in the kitchen cabinet you'll find a two-quart jar of pickles.'

Craig walked over to give her a great smacking kiss.

'If for nothing else, I'm glad I ain't in Charleston tonight. They eat real fancy there, but I sure didn't notice any artichoke pickles. That's *my* Christmas present, Ma—and I ain't going to give any of it to you and Pa. You wouldn't also happen to have some Brown Dogs, would you?'

Lilian Price got up and went over to a thick-varnished, scratched sideboard. She forced a warped drawer open, took out a box which once contained Whitman's Sampler, and removed the top. Craig saw a neat nesting of the little brown-sugar, peanut-studded circular candy which he had eaten from Foxtown from infancy.

'They aren't as good as the ones you used to get from Irey Ivin,' his mother said. 'But I thought you might like some. I did the best I could. I haven't had too much time lately.' She gestured futilely at the hotel.

Craig kissed his mother again.

'I bet they're better. Can I have one now before supper?' He made a fuss of taking a candy from the box.

'Don't eat too many. I have to go fix these ducks now. You and Dad just sit and drink a little wine and I'll see what I can do. Don't drink too much, hear? It's a family failing.'

Lilian Price went off to the kitchen. Her husband looked after her with almost a shamed distaste.

'I don't know what I'd of done lately without your mother,' Richard Price said. 'She's working herself to death, and her with the bad heart and all.'

'I don't either,' Craig said. He attempted to lighten t!.e atmosphere. 'Pass the wine. And maybe I'll give you one of my artichokes after all.'

Craig got on the beach car and went as far as Winter Haven. The motor-man stretched out an arm to hang the hoop neatly on the signal-stand's hook, and ground the brakes. Craig was the only passenger. He got out and began to walk. A big blue Cord roadster pulled to a stop beside him.

'I kind of thought you might be on this car,' the little fat man said. 'If you wasn't, I was coming to fetch you. You have a good Christmas?'

'Sure did,' Craig said. 'Hope y'all did too. Santa Claus treat you right nice?'

'Passin' tolable,' Mr. Grimes said. 'Passin' tolable. How'd he tend to you?'

'Passin' tolable,' Craig said. 'I got what we used to make a joke of in New Truro. Little cracker kid somebody asked what he got for Christmas, and he said: "A crokernut and a ournge." I got some Brown Dogs and a two-quart bottle of artichoke pickles. It was kind of slim pickin's this year.'

'I seen some,' John Grimes said. 'I seen some that didn't have no "crokernut" and didn't have no "ournge" and didn't have neither no Brown Dogs nor no artichoke pickles. My God, I love them things. Funny what you like when you get older. I can afford—I guess—all the fish-eggs come out of Russia, and a sirloin steak for breakfast, and all that fancy French cookin'. But what pleasures me most is a simple dish of ham-and-hominy or a plate of stew.'

They drew up in front of an enormous white-pillared house, with about an acre of manicured green grass in front. Tall pines shaded an avenue up to the porch. Just in front of the porch stood a huge living fir, gleamingly a-bristle with Christmas decoration.

'We'll turn on the lights when she gets dark,' John Grimes said. 'She was something to look at last night. Well, let's go in and see about that eggnog.'

He pulled the Cord up in front of the door. Craig noticed that the crushed-shell circular drive branched off in a Y-shape to an enormous garage, which contained three big cars and space for a fourth.

'You sure have got a lot of cars,' Craig said, as they got out of the Cord and walked up the broad steps. 'What else besides this one? She drives real sweet. I forgot to tell you.'

'Two Caddies and a Duesenberg. Mama has one Caddie and the other belongs to my kid. It's brand new. It's her Christmas

106

present. As a matter of fact, I was going to ask you for a favour. I haven't got the time to teach Maybelle to drive. If you'd give her some lessons over the holidays, if you're not too busy, I'd sure appreciate it. I don't trust Mama behind the wheel very much. She drives that big caboose like she's afraid it'll bite her.' John Grimes chuckled. 'And my garage repair bills say I'm right. Well, here we are.'

They entered an enormous room, done completely in red—red chairs, red-figured wallpaper, red sofas, red wall-to-wall carpeting, red drapes, accented startlingly by a dead-white grand piano, over which a red-and-black Spanish shawl was flung. Long-stemmed red roses flamed from silver and crystal vases. Another Christmas tree, lit, stood in one corner, and underneath its boughs, the carpet was heaped with presents, half unopened.

'I like red,' John Grimes said. 'I was in a fancy house one time when I was a kid and it was all over done up in red. It was the cheerfullest room I ever seen. Mama hates red. So to keep peace in the family we done about four or five rooms like this—a white-and-gold one for Mama, a yellow one for Maybelle, a green one for visitors and I forget the other colour. I ain't been in that one yet.' He grabbed a tasselled bell-pull, and a negro servant came silently into the room. Craig gaped. The servant's face was shining black, but he was wearing a white powdered wig, drawn back in a club and tied with a black ribbon. He wore knee-breeches and a kind of cutaway coat with brass buttons, revealing a frilled shirt. Lace dripped from his cuffs. Like everything else in the room, except the piano, the uniform was red—a velvet so dark it was almost plum-purple. He wore silk stockings, and black patent leather pumps with silver buckles.

'That's George,' Grimes said. 'George, go tell Mama and Maybelle we got company. Yes, that's George. I disremember his real name, but when I got him up in that rig he reminded me of George Washington, so George he is. How do you like him?'

'He . . . he . . . he sure is pretty,' Craig said. 'But ain't he kind of unusual? I mean, do most butlers dress like that?'

'Hell, no. Most butlers look like a flock of damned undertakers, creeping around like they was at a funeral. I like things cheerful. Every time I see George I feel better.'

· He walked over to a side-table, on which sat a vast silver bowl. He filled two chased-silver cups with eggnog, and handed one to Craig.

'I wouldn't go too heavy on this stuff,' he said, draining his own cup and swiftly refilling it. 'It's got enough rum in it to blow up the bank. That first one was for Mama's absent benefit. She don't like to see me swig. So I knock off the first one and sip the second. Here come the girls, now.'

Mother and daughter entered rather hesitantly, as if they were strangers in their own domain. Mother was a head taller than

John Grimes. She had a beaky nose, not much chin, and a long scrawny neck. Her blond hair was cut very short, and was tightly curled. She looked rather like a turkey hen, Craig thought. She was wearing a triple strand of pearls around her neck, and her chapped hands were ringed to the knuckles with stones as big as marbles. Her dress was flapperish.

Daughter was a complete carbon of Papa, except that she had more hair and less fat. She was pretty in a plump, rather vapid way, but her china blue eyes lacked Grimes' sharp animal intelligence. Her weight was mostly baby fat, but Craig had a sudden hunch that she never would do much about losing it.

'Meet the wife and daughter,' John Grimes said. 'This here is Craig Price that I told you about, the kid that drove me up from Charleston. Honey, Craig is going to teach you to drive your Christmas present. He's a real good driver.'

'Merry Christmas,' Craig said, not knowing whether to shake hands or not, and finally deciding against it. 'It's nice to know you.'

'Merry Christmas,' they replied in dubious voice that suggested it might as well be New Year's.

'You want some eggnog, Mama? How about you, Baby?'

'I don't think so,' Mama replied in a voice that suggested her husband had invited her to share a cup of deadly nightshade.

'I do,' Baby said.

'She's too young,' Mama said sharply.

'Aw, hell, Irma, this is Christmas, and she's nearly 'bout grown. Come on, Maybelle, one won't hurt you.' He poured a cupful and handed it to his daughter. 'Here, Craig, lemme full you up again. Let's set.'

They sat down in the enormous red chairs. Mama Grimes sat stiffly upright, her knees as prime as her expression. Baby emulated Mama in a stout and ridiculous caricature of extreme propriety. She crooked her little finger as she sipped her drink. Conversation lagged. Suddenly Baby said:

'Do you go to high school?'

'I did last year, but this year I'm in college. Carolina. I never saw you in high school, though.,'

'I didn't go. I went to private school. Miss Lacy's.'

'Oh.'

'Next year I'm going to Saint Mary's. In Raleigh.'

'That's nice. It's a real pretty school. But strict, though.'

Mama spoke.

'That's what makes it such a fine school for a young girl.'

Papa sneaked another cup of eggnog, and was observed by Mama. He hurriedly set it down on the table.

'I wish she was old enough to go to a good co-ed college, instead of some damned nunnery. She'll never learn anything about growing up if we keep shutting her up in these hen-parties.'

Mama glared at him, and said nothing. Papa shifted his feet. Craig fidgeted. Baby wriggled. Mama got up.

'If you'll excuse me, I got some things to do, and I think the menfolk have something to talk about. You'd better come with me too, Maybelle. It was ever so nice meeting you, Mr. Craig. I do hope you'll drop in often.'

Craig stood up. 'Thank you, ma'am.' He turned to the girl. 'When do you want your first lesson?'

'Tomorrow afternoon?'

He glanced at her father. 'Sure,' Grimes said. 'Sooner the better.'

'I'll come about three, then, if that's all right.'

'Fine. Pleased to have met you. Merry Christmas.'

She followed her mother out of the door. John Grimes heaved a gusty sigh of relief and went to a sideboard. He came out with a bottle of Canadian Club and two glasses. 'I've had enough of that bellywash. Let's have an honest shot before I ask you some questions. Mud in your eye.'

'Mud.' They drained their glasses, and Craig managed not to cough, although his eyes watered.

'I don't want you to think I'm nosy, Buddy, but I been asking around and I know your old man is having a rough time. We're laying off hands at the mill, but that's mostly hand-labour and I can always use a good office man. It won't pay much, but better'n he's doing now.'

'Anything would be better than he's doing now, I don't mind telling you.'

'But that still won't be enough to send you to school.'

'I'll make out somehow. The main thing is tuition, dormitory, books—things like that. I can always make out to eat. I got a job now, waiting in a restaurant. At least'—Craig laughed—'that's what they call it.'

'What do you mean, "that's what they call it"? It is or it ain't, seems to me.'

'Well, if you want the truth, Mr. Grimes, I'm going to bootleg for a living. With some other people—athletes.' Craig outlined his arrangement with Jimmy Wilbur.

'Hell's afire, boy, you don't want to get mixed up with no truck like that. Best you'll get is kicked out of school, and you might just wind up on the roads, swinging a pick for the State. And once a man's got a record on his back, every man's hand is agin him. He don't never stand a chance no more to make an honest living. You forget that bootlegging crap, and we'll try to figure out something else.'

'I *have* been trying to figure out something else. But nothing else seems to come out. I ain't an athlete. I haven't got any kind of scholarship. There aren't any real money jobs on the campus. Just free board for washing dishes, and the like of that.'

'What do you figure it would cost you by the month?'

'To go to school good? About a hundred a month. Just skin by, and do some work on the side? About fifty would do it. Take care of the fees and that sort of stuff.'

Grimes poured another noggin, and pointed the bottle-neck at Craig.

'No, thanks. I don't use it much.'

'Look, son. I taken a shine to you the other day—I dunno why, but I did. I like your daddy and your ma, and I'd like to help them get straightened out a little. But mainly I taken a shine to you. We never had but the one youngun, Maybelle, but I wanted a boy bad, and if we'd of had one, I would want him to be something like you. Now, I got more money than I know what to do with, but I don't believe in flinging it around foolish. More than that, I think a man ought to earn what he gets. It ain't worth nothing otherwise, I can throw *my* money like a drunk sailor now, but I earned it, and if I want to set it afire, it's my own business. I want to make you a proposition. I want to give you five hundred dollars a year until you graduate.'

Craig started. He hesitated before he spoke.

'I couldn't do that, sir. I couldn't let nobody give me anything, I'd rather bootleg and take a chance. I'm sorry, and I sure thank you, but I wasn't raised to take nothing from nobody. Thanks just the same.'

Grimes flipped an impatient hand at Craig. 'Wait a minute. Don't go off half-cocked. Don't be so techy—not that I don't admire it. It's one of the things I thought I saw in you. This is a business proposition. Look here, I'm a banker, ain't I? Don't bankers make loans? Ain't that how they make their money? I propose to make you a long-term loan. You sign a note and everything—the only thing is, I leave the date for repayment open. I could just as easy make it for a thousand a year, but I don't believe in giving people luxuries. Luxuries you got to earn. But it's damn' foolishness to throw away a chance to make something out of yourself for the lack of a few dollars for the grits-and-gravy.'

'But, Mr. Grimes, I wouldn't know when I could pay you back ... if I could *ever* pay you back. That's two thousand whole dollars you're talking about ...'

'Wait a minute, Buddy. I ain't so charitable as I sound. I like a return on my money same as the next man. What you're gonna do is work for me summertimes, and work hard. I'll pay you twenty-five dollars a week, and you get to keep five for spending money. I take the other twenty dollars, and it applies against the loan. You work for me three months and I get back three times eighty dollars—two hundred and forty dollars. That's half the loan, ain't it? So all I'm really risking on you is a thousand bucks, which you pay back after you graduate. But you damn' well *better* graduate, hear? You don't get the money in a lump either. I'll send you fifty dollars the first of every month. You can take a letter from me to the school people and make your own arrangements on the fees and stuff. Okay?'

Craig stood up and rocked uncertainly on his feet.

'I don't know how to thank you, Mr. Grimes. I just don't know what to say or how to thank you . . . about Pa and me and everything. I'll do the best I can, anyhow.'

'I know it, Buddy. Tell your Daddy to come see me Monday, and we'll work out something for him. Oh, and here. This is your Christmas present. Don't open it until you've gone. Take the Cord and drive yourself home. I won't be needing it, and you can drive it back tomorrow to give Maybelle her first lesson. So long, Buddy. See you tomorrow.'

Craig almost ran out of the door. He jumped into the car, and eased it gently on to the road. As soon as he turned a corner, he stopped, and ripped open the envelope. It contained a fifty-dollar bill and a note which said:

> Since you made it last fall all by yourself, Buddy, I feel like I owe you a bonus. Spend it on foolishness—the business agreement is after New Year's. Be careful with my little gal when you teach her to drive. Merry Christmas.
>
> J.G.

Craig was a big boy—big enough to drink whisky, big enough to drive a car, big enough to go to school, big enough to have a girl. He leaned his head over the wheel and cried like a small child. He was very, very careful with the Cord as he drove home to tell his parents the news. He didn't want anything to spoil the greatest Christmas he was ever likely to have.

Things seemed altogether different when Craig returned to school after New Year's. His father was back at steady work again. Not much of a job, perhaps, keeping books, but enough to eat on and pay the rent. Craig had Grimes' fifty dollars in his pocket, and there was another fifty dollars waiting in the Chapel Hill bank. Philip had not returned from the Christmas holidays, and since a lot of freshmen were dropping out because of the increasing stricture of hard times, Craig was not assigned a new room-mate. He was blissfully alone in the bleak dormitory room. He haunted the library, and read enormously. He was a fair amateur artist, and managed to get himself a job on the art staff of the college humour magazine. It paid him two dollars-and-a-half a month, but it published some of his cartoons, and more and more people started to speak to him on the campus. Through one new acquaintance he was able to get a kind of job hustling customers for a campus boarding house. It paid him nothing, but took care of at least two meals a day, and he was able to supply the third with a snack of sandwiches and Coke, at the dormitory store, where he still worked afternoons. He had very little more than occasional milk-shake money, once fees were paid, but he didn't care.

His first post-holiday conversation with Jimmy Wilbur the football player had been very pleasant—warm and easy.

'Hi, kid,' Wilbur said one evening in early January, when he dropped by Craig's room. 'See you got back all right from the Christmas wars. Where's your fancy roomie?'

'I guess he decided not to come back. I dunno. Haven't heard.'

'What happened down in Charleston with all the blue-bloods?' Wilbur flopped on a bed, and shook a cigarette at Craig. 'Did I win my bet?'

'If you'll tell me what it was I'll tell you whether you won it or not.'

'Well, it was kind of a three-way bet. One third was that you wouldn't like it, and would go back to your own home for Christmas. Next third was that you'd probably take a punch at that pansy room-mate, and have to leave. And the third was that if you didn't leave, and didn't sock your boy friend, then if you stayed on you'd wind up in the hay with Mama. Maybe there was a fourth end. I bet solid that our elegant young friend wouldn't be back in school if any of the first three things happened. That guy'll never finish anything he ever starts, any place, any time.'

Craig flushed. Then he laughed.

'You were almost right. I didn't stay but a night and a day. It was too rich for my blood. I did take a swing at Philip, and left.'

'What did you belt him for? He make a pass at you?'

'Nothing like that. But he called his mother a dirty name—a ... a whore, if you got to know, and I got mad and socked him. She's a real nice lady, and I did *not* wind up in the hay with Mama. God, Moose, I'm just a kid—and she's a rich grown woman. What would she want with a boy like me?'

'Plenty. I'll even bet you another ten that she grabs you before you're eighteen. That kind of rich, spoiled, travelling dame makes a pastime out of knocking off kids.'

'How would you know this?'

'I'd know it, all right. I got myself practically raped by the wife of a rich old grad when I was playing prep school ball, and wasn't much older than you. She was collecting young halfbacks that year. I was a punk, and didn't know what I had, but as I remember, she was real hot stuff.' Wilbur blew a smoke ring, and punched his finger through it 'Like that.'

'Well, nothing happened to me, so I lose the bet.' Craig reached into his pocket and drew out some bills. 'Here you are.'

Jimmy Wilbur laughed and shoved Craig's hand aside. 'Save it. At worst, you won three-quarters of it. I don't need it. But you going to work for me next week when we start this racket?'

Craig was a little shamfaced.

'I was going to bring that up. No, I'm afraid not. I'm going by Harry's today and give him back the money he advanced me, and pay something on the bill at the College Shop. I guess I won't be a bootlegger, after all. I'm sorry, Moose. But I ran into a kind of lucky deal. After I socked Phil and left, I was hitch-hiking, and this man . . .'

'I think he was dead right,' Wilbur said, when Craig had finished. 'He sounds like a hell of a fellow. He must have taken a real shine to you. You don't want to get mixed up in any crooked-ness if you don't have to. Me, I don't care. I'm sprung out of here in six months anyhow, and I'll give it a little play for road money. You're marked for luck, kid. Tell me, how was the daughter you taught to drive her Christmas Cadillac? Do yourself any good there?'

'I wasn't monkeying with my luck. Also she ain't much to look at, I'm afraid. Kind of fat and freckled, with light blue eyes. The old man's nuts about her, though. She's all he's got, because Mama is awful. I don't think the old man has much fun when he's home. Mama don't seem to like anything he likes. But I like him, apart from what he did for me. I'm going to drive him around and run some errands for him this summer. He owns about everything in town. Next year he says he's going to put me in the mills, and next year in the bank. Then he says he's going to put me to work steady, doing something.'

'Sounds like you got your future worked out just fine,' Jimmy Wilbur said. 'Take it easy. Oh, say. We're having a dance at my lodge Saturday night. Nothing much—little music and some eats. Bring-your-own-whisky kind of party. Like to come? It's formal, but I know you got a new tux. How's about it?'

'I'd love to. Except I haven't got a girl to bring. Don't know any.'

'Don't bother—there's usually a flock over from Duke or Greensboro, and somebody always gets canned, so there's plenty of spares. Make it about nine o'clock, hey?'

'I sure will. Thanks. Oh, Moose . . .'

'Yeah?'

'Mind if I buy a half-gallon jar?'

Wilbur smiled.

'You've come to the right place, sonny. That'll be two bucks. Cash on the barrel. And I'll give it my personal attention.'

There is something magic about the second quarter of college. The frightening strangeness has gone. The professors are no longer so awe-inspiring. The basic ropes are handy—the terrain is familiar, faces no longer seem hostile. A man—for a second-term freshman is a man, having survived the stress of the unknown enemy—walks a little taller, holds his head a little prouder. He is fighting now on his own terms, and there is a measureless exhilaration to coming back. Especially, Craig thought, when you know you aren't going to lose it. *This place is here for me to use,* he thought, as he dressed.

Craig Price had no way of knowing how a débutante must feel at her first big party, but he knew that he felt awful good, scared but scared deliciously, while still calmly certain of himself. He tied his bow-tie—clumsily, but he had abandoned the jazzbo and had bought himself a proper un-tied evening tie—and he hummed as he tied it.

'I got money in my pocket, and clothes on my back,' he sang, thinking all the time how wonderful it was that he had his future neatly settled, and smothering down a nasty thought that he was already in thrall to an obligation—that he was buying his life on the cuff. That nasty intrusion was trampled under the obvious fact that Moose Wilbur liked him enough to ask him to a party at Moose's own fraternity house, and that he was clad sufficiently well to shed credit on the great Wilbur, the All-American football player.

'By Golly, I feel wonderful,' he said—flushed from the shower down the hall, shaven and combed and shining in his dress-suit. He looked at his watch—eight-thirty. A half an hour to kill. It would be a long, a very long, half-hour. Read? No. Study? Not on Saturday night. Maybe somebody was home down the hall.

He walked down the dormitory hallway and rapped on Jimmy Wilbur's door. Wilbur was half-dressed, and he was talking to a big, raw-boned blond guy, as he fumbled with his cuff-links. There was a quart jug of white whisky sitting on the table.

'Gees, clock the kid. Pete—Pete Crane—this is a buddy of mine, Craig Price. He ain't very old, but he's awful smart. From what I know of this lad, he will be President of the United States when he hits the age limit. Pour yourself a drink, kid.'

Pete Crane got up and shook hands.

'This tramp athlete was just talking about you,' he said. 'Evidently you made some kind of impression on him.' His voice held a suspicion of the nasal West Country drawl.

'I'll say he made an impression on me,' Wilbur said. 'He can run around a room faster than anybody I ever met. He's the one whose room-mate went crazy the first night the kid was in school.'

Crane's left eyebrow quirked.

'Oh, that one? I heard about it. Must have been pretty awful, your first night here.'

'I got saved by the tramp athlete,' Craig laughed. 'I'm scared what's going to happen to me when he graduates. I never had a nurse before, but this is a very good nurse.'

'You don't know the half about this boy,' Wilbur said. 'Pour me a very little shot. I got to stay sober until midnight, anyhow.

114

We got some old grads coming in and the boys at the house need some new furniture, or something. No, Pete, you are looking at the only man in school who sleeps regularly with Jean Harlow. By the way, kid, how are you making out there?'

'She left me,' Craig said. 'She hasn't been back since I went to Charleston. Maybe she don't love me any more.'

'She's jealous of that Charleston rich-bitch,' Wilbur said. 'You can't cheat on your women, sonny, not even in a dream. Say, can anybody for crissake tie a tie?'

'I can,' Craig said. 'I been practising all day long. Here, hold still.' Jimmy Wilbur beamed at Pete Crane.

'You see what I mean? This is a very special kid.'

'I don't know what the hell you guys are talking about, but it wouldn't hold in court,' the big raw-boned guy said. 'But it sounds kind of interesting. Suppose you tell me for the record.'

'Crane's pre-law,' Wilbur said. 'Stop jerking at the ends. It looks all right. All pre-law guys talk about records and things not holding in court. Practising to be a shyster is a very difficult business—tougher than practising to be a coach. Ah . . . perfect. You'd make a wonderful valet, kid.'

'What about this Jean Harlow thing?'

Wilbur sketched Craig's vicarious amour with considerable profane embroidery. Crane laughed loudly.

'We got to do something about our boy,' Wilbur said. 'Apart from Miss Harlow, he ain't had no experience a-tall. What's loose at the co-ed shack? Anything noteworthy that the Dekes ain't snapped up?'

'Not a damned thing. But there ought to be a few town gals around tonight. There's one . . . *No*. I want her for me. I got seniority on that one. She's got the biggest pair of . . .' Crane sketched two halves of watermelons with his hands. 'Like they were cut in two and pasted on. Maybe we'll find somebody's sister for our young pal here.'

'Not *my* sister?' Wilbur threw up his hands in horror. 'Not *that*?'

'Oh, I forgot,' Pete Crane said. 'She's still in the hospital with the Old Joe. Or was it a baby? I guess we'll have to send for *my* sister. She was cured a week ago.'

'After the baby?'

'Of course after the baby. We had to get her married first.'

'Who was dumb enough to marry her?'

'Me, of course. After all, she *was* my sister, and it *was* my baby.'

'You're kiddin' yourself, son. It was *my* baby.'

'Suit yourself,' Pete Crane said. 'As a matter of fact, it was twins, and mine died.'

'Tragedy, tragedy. Maybe we better go now. I sent your jug over to the house, kid. With a ribbon on it.'

The conversation made no sense whatsoever to Craig, but it

115

fused him with a wild feeling of belonging—to be kidded, to talk foolishness, to not be patronized, to be poked fun at—all this was different from the thing in Charleston, his homecoming to Kensington, his stiff afternoon at the House of John Grimes. This was the Craig Price who had a tux, who could tie a black tie, who could listen to bad jokes about non-existent sisters, who could drink corn likker and be one of the boys, who was going to a party . . .

'Where do you come from?' he asked Pete Crane.

'Little town outside of Asheville. Waynesville. Nothing you ever heard of. It's famous for two or three things—my Uncle Ned, who is the best square dancer in Western North Carolina, the azaleas, and the drunkest Cherokee Indians known to God. As a matter of fact, I like your neck of the woods a lot better. You can get mighty tired of mountains.'

'Let's move,' Wilbur said. 'Will we take your limousine, Craig, or mine?'

'Oh, let's everybody take his own Cadillac,' Craig said.

'I prefer my horse,' Crane said. 'These new fangled gasoline buggies smell so bad.'

They walked out into the crisp, star-dappled night. The winter-weary bare trees stood lean like distant etchings against the winter sky, and the campus buildings bulked large, like huge friendly animals. Craig said, suddenly:

'You know what I feel like tonight? Don't laugh. It's the same way I used to feel when I'd sneak out of the house in New Truro to run off to a coloured camp-meetin'. Kind of a Sunday-go-to-meetin' feeling. Like something good was going to happen but you didn't know just what.'

'I know what you mean,' Pete Crane said. 'I mentioned my Uncle Ned. Us mountain folks don't know much about camp-meetin's, but a square-dance night is something to see. People come from all over the Smokies, and they tune up the fiddles and turn on the mountain dew. The fire's bright and nobody's mad at nobody. It's like going back to the way it was when the first settlers came in. They still speak a good part Elizabethan English, and all the square-dance songs are old English songs. When I was a little kid, sort of crouched off in the corner where nobody'd notice me, when they started a reel I kind of looked around to see if Sir Walter Raleigh had showed up yet. He never did, of course, but the feeling was like he just might if I watched real hard.'

'Us Polacks ain't so romantic,' Jimmy Wilbur laughed. 'We just tie *babushkas* over our heads and get drunk on potato whisky and fight. Or cry. Somebody gets hold of a guitar and begins to wail about the good old days on the *steppes*, and before long everybody's crying. What the hell they're crying about I don't know. I asked my old lady once, and she said: "We're crying because we're so happy." Well, here we are. Let us go and meet the noble brothers of the Phi Gamma Delta lodge. Somebody hit me if I get drunk. This is promotion-of-new-furniture night, and I wouldn't want the visiting grads to get the wrong idea of Brother James, otherwise known as Moose, Wilbur. That ain't what they pay me for.'

Craig felt only a moment's shyness as they walked into the great hall. A record player was going in the next room, and it was Ted Fiorito playing 'Willow Weep for Me.' There was a scent of crushed pine-needles, wood-smoke odour from the snapping blaze in the huge fireplace—a smell of whisky and cigarette smoke and of perfumed female flesh. It was a festive smell, mixed of music and women and whisky and clean people with no classes that needed to be cut tomorrow. Laughter mounted over the music, which had suddenly switched to 'A Faded Summer Love.' Twenty-five years after Craig Price left the University, a sudden sight, a sudden smell was able to reproduce almost to the minute some experience or person, with an accompanying song.

Her name was Mary Frances.

She was just sixteen. She was with her brother, Mark. She had come over for the week-end from the girls' school, Peace, in Raleigh. She was a large girl, tall, with a mature woman's body, and storm-tossed black hair. Her skin was that gardenia white only the Irish seem to achieve, with almost purple eyes, and a wide, rich, happy red mouth. She was dancing with her brother when the music stopped, and Moose Wilbur said: 'Hey, Mark. I want you to meet a friend of mine. He looks mighty lak' a pledge. Craig Price, Mark Malone. And . . .' He turned to the girl.

'Hi.' Malone stuck out his hand. 'My kid sister. Mary Frances Malone. She's over for the week-end. I smuggled her out of Peace, which ain't a mean feat. Said Ma was dying. This is Moose Wilbur, our most famous brother, and Craig Price. From where?'

'Kensington.'

'We aren't so far away. Goldsboro. Neighbours, practically. How 'bout a charge, Moose? I got a jug in my room. You kids want to dance while the grown-ups fade away?'

'Sure,' Craig said, uneasily. 'If Miss Malone . . .'

The girl looked at Craig and smiled.

'I'd like to,' she said. 'My brother's been trying to get rid of me all night. If you don't mind . . .'

Craig didn't know why he said it, but he blurted:

'I'm glad I'm not your brother,' as she slipped into his arms. He would never forget that a bandleader named Husk O'Hare was playing a tune called 'Tears', because Miss Mary Frances Malone said: 'So am I.'

The evening blurred, and Craig met most of the brethren who seemed nice, and most of the alumni who seemed nice—and drunk—and a plethora of pretty girls. Craig needed nothing more to drink, being already drunk with Mary Frances Malone in his arms.

Their conversation was compounded of all the clichés manufactured since young love became popular.

'You dance very well, Craig,' she said.

'I don't even know I'm dancing,' Craig answered. 'I'm flying.'

'How old are you?'

'Sixteen. How old are you?'

'Sixteen.'

'Can I please come see you on date night in Raleigh?'

'If you want to. Yes.'

'Where are you going to school after you finish at Peace?'

'I want to come here. But it'll take two more years before they let me. Also Bud—Mark, I mean, my brother—will be out then. I wouldn't want to cramp his style. Having a kid sister in school would.'

They danced inadvertently towards a side room, where a small fire flickered.

'Let's sit and smoke a cigarette. Do you smoke?' Craig steered her to a sofa.

'A little. But I don't inhale.'

He lit two cigarettes.

'Could I get you a drink?'

'Thanks. I don't . . . yet. Mark says it's not nice and the boys don't like it.'

'Then I won't. Look, Mary Frances. I'm not a fraternity man, but . . .'

'But that doesn't make any difference. But what?'

'Would you . . . would you come over for the Spring Frolics? As my girl, I mean? I know I haven't known you very long, but I sort of feel I have and . . .'

'And?'

'I mean you could stay at the Inn.' Craig made a swift resolution to steal a gun and stick up a bank and conquer the world, if necessary. 'And there'd be your brother. I mean for . . . to chaperone you, I mean.'

Mary Frances Malone smiled, and Craig felt suddenly blinded.

'I'd love to,' she said, and held up her flower face to be kissed.

It had come softly spring. It sneaked in as slick as a thief. One day the trees were bone-gaunt and obscenely naked. The remnants of old and coal-dusted snow filled small crevices in the wet red clay, trembling close against the clammy stones. The winds rapped impatiently, nervously at the door.

Now the blossoms burst. The peach trees rippled with bloom, and from the Arboretum, all the smells stole rides upon the gentle breeze, and crept inside the nostrils. The tiny shoots, fulfilled, blurted into tender leaves. Sap burst in jewels on the trees.

Suddenly birds, long winter gone, arrived in song, as in a tirade of trumpets. All was softly green, the young grass, even the feeling of the black night was green—not the sweaty lushness that would come with summer and its heavy smells, but the first intimation of new gentle time, as hesitantly soft as a baby's kiss.

Craig had flunked Maths Two that past winter quarter. He could not seem to focus his mind on calculus. It kept getting all confused with purple eyes and jet-black web-soft hair, and skin so soft and white that all the sines and cosines and symbols and stuff kept merging into a simple formula: 'If M to the second power equals Price, then I am in love.'

There was a deep-buried intangible quality in Mary Frances—a quality he sought the rest of his life. She was enduringly gentle and simply loving. She was not, even at a time when young women worked at it, cute. The Irish honesty of her uncomplicated self forestalled cuteness. She practised no wiles—she owned no professional woman's tricks. She refused to coquette when Craig took her to a Grail dance, or around to the Zeta Beta Tau house, where he had made a great many friends. The Zetes were Jews.

It had never occurred to Craig that Jews were different from anybody else. In his own home town they were portion to the aristocracy of the city. That they observed the Sabbath on Saturday did not seem unusual, nor was the presence in some houses of the *milchkedikh* and *fleischkedikh* eating-utensils, one for flesh, the other for dairy products. He loved the rich Jewish food, the noodles and the matzoth balls swimming in the chicken fat, the stuffed gefüllte fish and the rich desserts. The word 'Jew' meant no more to him than the word 'people', or that somebody was blonde or brunette. He had never heard the words 'Kike' or 'Sheenie' until he was exposed to the Northerners who came to Chapel Hill to take advantage of the cheap tuition.

Jimmy Wilbur took him over to the Zete house one night. The Zetes were throwing a party, and the left end of the football team had come down to the dormitory, sharing the corn-squeezings in Wilbur's room. This man, Jules Francovich, was possibly the only non-professional athlete on the football team. He played football for fun, and was the best left end in the Southern Conference. He was a lean, savagely handsome, olive-tinted boy from New York, who moved as sleekly purring as a cat, and whose black eyes and smooth hair gave him a Valentino stamp. He was enormously rich without making a display of it. He had a huge custom-built Auburn roadster that he very seldom bothered to drive. His father was a stockbroker in New York, and Jules' personal headlines in *The Times* when he blocked a punt or nailed a ball carrier behind the man's own goal line, had built him into a new-god in his father's collection of household deities.

Jules met Craig in Wilbur's room and asked him to the party. It was only a routinely quiet Saturday night, but Craig felt he had never met so many nice people at one time. There was one brother they called King Kong, a massive man who played first-string-guard—an impossibly ugly fellow with low-hanging arms and a gorilla's heft who was as gentle as a dove, and who was generally besieged by the village children when he walked the streets. There was a kid of Craig's age named Mike something, whose father was a theatrical producer. There was another named Lou, whose father was an artist. With the exception of King Kong, whose Louis Wolheim face made him almost beautiful, they composed a tribe of handsome, lithe, well-brought-up, genial people, and Craig immediately had a warm feeling of home-coming. They laughed easily, and possessed an indolent unstudied grace of family.

Their women—girl-friends and sisters—were invariably seemly, and were fragrant with a lush Oriental opulence. They were jolly girls, possibly a little pouter-pigeon plumper than the other girls about the campus, but quicker to smile, more eager to be 'nice'. There was no coquetry to combat. And the fathers and mothers —the big-busty mamas and the well-fed fathers, the little short fat ones and the tall spare ones, all seemed to share an enormous sense of fun with their sons and daughters when they came calling on a week-end. They swept Craig into a blanket embrace. It was not very long before he found himself dropping in on the Zete house at all sorts of odd hours, and he was ever welcome and he never thought of himself as '*goy*'.

The time for Spring Frolics had nearly come. Craig went to Mark Malone and asked formal permission to bid Mary Frances for the dances.

'They're having a week-end party at the Zeta Beta Tau house,' Craig said. 'The boys are all moving out. Would you mind if your sister—if Mary Frances—stayed there? They're . . . they're Jews . . .'

Malone grinned. He put a casual hand on Craig's shoulder.

'I'm Irish. My old man was a hod-carrier before he turned crooked and got rich. We come from uninterrupted peasant stock. And to put it politely, some of my best friends are Jews. You know who I'm having down for the hop? Francovich's sister, Sarah or I should say, Sally. If I'm real lucky I'll marry her. That's if she hasn't got any race prejudice about Micks. Let's see if Jules can't put our two girls in together, and why don't you come over here and stay for the week-end? You like this kid sister of mine, huh?'

Craig smiled, almost through sudden tears. He had been meeting too many nice people lately, and still wasn't quite used to it.

'If I'm lucky, I'll marry Mary Frances. That's if she hasn't got any prejudices against Protestants.'

'Welcome to the lodge,' Mark Malone said. 'But promise me

one thing. If you ever do get married, promise me you won't start all the kids' names with "M". My old man's got a phobia about "M's". Mike. Mark. Mary Frances. Mona, Monte, Madeleine. Christ. If I marry Sally I suppose I'll have to name the first boy Max, just to keep the tradition going.'

Mark Malone paused a thoughtful moment. He poked very gently at Craig's chest with his right forefinger.

'Price?'

'Huh? What?'

'I'm kind of fond of Mary F. You're both real young kids. If you do anything at all to this kid, anything at *all*, I'll kill you. Painfully as possible.'

'I wouldn't mind if you did. I'd rate it. Or I might even save you the trouble and do it myself.'

'You're a good lad,' Mark Malone said. 'The boys have been talking. You like to pin yourself up Phi Gam? They'd like to have you.'

'I can't, this year. No dough. But there's nothing I'd like better. Maybe next fall. I'll work this summer, and maybe have some money.'

'We'd make it easy for you. You could wait tables, maybe, or look after the accounting, or something like that . . .'

'Thanks a hell of a lot. But I'll come when I can pay my way like anybody else. But thank the guys, will you, and if the offer's open next year . . . well, thanks, Mark.'

In a life, of a life, there is possible perfection. Craig touched magic that week-end. Maybe there were other people around—at the Zete house, at the Phi Gams, in the Tin Can, necking in the Arboretum, strolling on the campus, dancing, singing, drinking milk punch at the K.A.'s, playing records at the Sigma Chi's, morning beer with the Phi Kaps—Hal Kemp playing the tea-dance and nobody dancing but just swaying and listening. And there was always Mary Frances—beautiful, quiet, unaffected Mary Frances—and so it had to be only natural.

They had gone for the afternoon to the big lake. The sun warmed them, sieving through the leaves, and the birds discreetly sang. They stretched, dripping from a swim, on the crisp young grass, and quite suddenly fell to kissing. The salty-sweet smell of wet, sun-warmed women suddenly got tangled with a clean cloud of black hair and wide red mouth acrid with want, with purple eyes rolled backward, with the feet of petal skin, with a small pocket of purest honey where the neck joined shoulder, where all the sweetness was, the intimate delightful crook of inner elbow, the plump bulge of inner thigh, all the wondrous nooks and crannies which spelt sugar and spice . . .

'I'm sorry,' Craig said. 'I didn't want . . I mean I didn't mean to. I mean I don't know what I mean. Except I'll love you all my life.

I . . . do you suppose we better get married and I'll get a job?
Suppose there's a . . .'

'Silly.' She pulled him down and kissed him, then turned swiftly
and kissed him once again, her hair falling in a soft shower over
his face. 'Silly. We can't get married for a long time. Let's just
play like we're married. And there won't be a . . . a baby. Not
for the first time. You know something? I always thought it
would hurt. It didn't. It felt . . . lovely.'

Craig was suddenly stricken by a fresh guilt.

'I promised your brother I wouldn't . . . I promised him. I
meant it, too.'

An ancient female wisdom, and even more ancient female
amusement, lit Mary Frances' eyes. She laughed, and it was a
joyous laugh.

'Don't you suppose Mark and Sally are in the same sort of
trouble with each other this very, very moment? Idiot boy. Come
kiss me sweet, silly, and shut up.'

When Craig went to bed that night, in the Phi Gam house,
after kissing his girl good night, with a new powerful knowledge,
his last thoughts before drifting into sleep were: *And to think I
used to be in love with Jean Harlow. I'm only sixteen years old and
I got at least fifty more to be in love with Mary Frances Malone.*

The jealous Gods ruin happiness held firmly in the hand, lodged
deeply in the heart, starkly graven in the brain. This was the
reason for it. It was possibly the fault of the drunks.

Craig went into the bathroom at the Inn. He had just seen
Mary Frances off, in her brother's car, looking over her shoulder
with a flung kiss, and he was heading back to his dormitory room
to be beautifully alone with his love, to savour and caress it far
from human view. He wanted nothing more than to think about
the fifty years he could devote all his time to being in love with
Mary Frances Malone.

He opened the door and heard a blurry voice from one of the
cubicles. Over the sound of rushing water, the whiskyed voice
said:

'I saw little Hot Pants over here. You ever try that? You know
who I mean. Mary Frances Moynihan . . . no, some other Irish
name or other . . . Mulligan. No, hell, you know. Goes to Peace
in Raleigh. Brother's a Phi Gam. They tell me she . . .'

'You mean the Malone girl. Her brother's a nice guy.'

'Yeah, but Ted Thompson said . . .' The voice dwindled to a
hum, and again there was the sound of a flushed toilet.

'But, my God, she's only a kid.'

'Doesn't make any difference. Ted said . . .'

Craig turned swiftly and walked away. His first impulse to
strangle both unseen voices sagged sickly in his stomach. He did
not want to see their faces. He had only fifty years to be in love
with Mary Frances Malone, and he could not, *would* not have

those years cankered by the sight of a remembered face in class, on the campus, in the drugstore.

It was all a lie, a filthy lie, the guys were drunk, stinking drunk, it was all a lie, a lousy lie, the guys were drunk, guys always talked, guys always bragged, guys always gossiped, it was all a lie the guys were drunk a lie drunk . . . But. She seemed to know an awful lot about what she was doing. And I didn't.

I was the virgin, Craig's head said. I was the one that didn't know what to do. The guys were drunk. Stinking drunk. Drunk guys talk a lot. All lies. Maybe they tried and couldn't. You know how drunks are. You know what liars are like. Liars like Philip. Drunks lie. Drunks brag. A lie. Remember Philip and the clap he never caught?

He prowled his room in a fit of sudden rage, too long withheld from not fighting the men in the toilet, too bitter inside him to compute—and smashed his fist into the plaster wall of his dormitory room. The wall was his enemy. He attacked the wall again until the knuckles of both hands were battered, bleeding.

Then he lay down on his bed, careless of the bloody hands, insensitive to outside pain, his belly twisting, and did not weep.

By God, they were right. Four days later he knew it. He *had* it. He had to have it. Everything his mother said had told him he had it. What the drunks said told him he had it. There was that itching, the burning, the discharge. And she had been such a wonderful girl, too. It couldn't be possible that Mary Frances had given him—you had to face the dirty word—the clap. The plain old clap. Not that sweetly held body, not that yearning face, not those lips which blotted out all thinking. Gonorrhoea? Great God. Mary Frances? Clap? *Christ.*

Craig got up and dressed. He raced to the Infirmary. It was midnight, the sky brooding black, plumped with lowering clouds, a moon peeping, a flicker of heat lightning to the west. Sweat stood in little hills on his forehead. He was acutely conscious of his groin, where an ache, an itch, a conscience, had suddenly come to live.

The night nurse was impatient. She was a horse-faced woman who looked more like a policeman than a woman.

'The doctor's asleep,' she said. 'Come see him in the morning or tomorrow afternoon, during his regular hours. There's nothing wrong with you. Not that I can see.' She sniffed. She reminded Craig of Miss Caroline.

'But there is, there *is*,' Craig said desperately. 'I got to see the doctor. I got to see him now. *Now.*' Some fierce urgency strode his voice.

'*Now.* I got to see him now!'

'You'll see him at your own risk, my boy,' the nurse said. 'He's had three deliveries today and an appendectomy. I wouldn't trust

123

his temper if you wake him. He lives next door,' she said suddenly, with a toss of the head. 'Over there.'

'Thank you,' Craig said, and dashed out of the door.

The doctor was not pleased. His hair was ruffled and his face was bloated, sleep-scarred, seamed, and puffed under the eyes. He was wearing a ratty red-flannel dressing-gown over his pyjamas, and his feet had been hurriedly shoved into sloppy run-over slippers. Alcohol clothed him. His name was McNab.

'Don't tell me you're pregnant,' he said. 'Although I'm prepared to believe anything. Come in, come in, for Christ sake, come in! Leprosy or what, at this hour?'

'Doctor, I . . . I . . .'

The doctor, McNab, grinned suddenly, a foxy grin, a conspirator's grin.

'Unbutton your pants. Strange as it seems, I was young once myself. Whore?'

'No, sir. A nice girl. That's why . . . that's why I can't . . . that's why . . .'

'They're all grey in the dark, me brave bucko. And the spirochete has no sense of social values. That applies to his cousin too. One lurks in the mucus, the other tackles the bloodstream. I should imagine you're fretted about the mucus. Old Charlie Clap. What symptoms?'

Craig stammered:

'Well, it hurts to . . . it hurts to . . .'

'Pee?'

'Yes, sir. And it itches and burns.'

'Lemme see. Hmmm. Nothing there. Bend over.'

The doctor took off his rubber gloves.

'If you want to, I can run a smear on you tomorrow. But it's a waste of time. All you got, boy, is a case of over-developed imagination. Where'd you pick up all this useless knowledge of symptoms?'

'My uncle's a doctor. My mother . . .'

'Oh, one of them, hey?' The doctor spat into the flickering fire. 'All about the birds and the bees and what'll happen if you're a bad boy? Christ, if I could close my fist on half-smart females, the sun would rise on a womanless world.' He paused.

'First time?'

'Yes, sir.'

'Well, then, goddamit, marry her, if you like her. But in the meantime, remember there's a drugstore or so in town, and try not to knock her up. You look a little young to be a father.'

'You're absolutely sure I'm all right? How about the other? The worst one?'

The doctor put a hand on Craig's shoulder. He was elaborately sarcastic.

'What's your name, *Doctor*? Don't tell me. Just go ahead and screw what you can catch. If you collect a bug, come see me, but don't let it spoil the fun. I had the clap three times when I was an intern, and every time it was a nurse. Quit worrying. It wrecks the sport. That'll be two dollars. After hours.'

Craig paid him.

The doctor looked at the bills as if they were a new culture under a slide. He shook his head, and handed them back to Craig.

'I suggest,' he said, 'that you run over to Durham and get yourself properly laid. Be my guest. Maybe your girl friend will like you better as a result. Good night, son.'

Craig sang loud as he walked back to the dormitory, his fears assuaged, his symptoms abated. He was singing an old shanty, 'Blow The Man Down'. All of a sudden he stopped in mid-verse. His mother's image floated past his eyes, and behind it was a succession of lectures, a succession of glossy prints in obstetrical textbooks, an unending flood of venereal close-ups in surgical volumes.

'God damn her,' he said softly to himself. It was the first time in his life he had ever used the words 'God damn' as an intended curse.

And then he thought about Mary Frances Malone, sang no more, and wished he actually had the clap. It would have made the break-off easier.

9

A HORN tooted dah-dah-de-dah outside the dormitory, and Craig looked out of the open window. The blue Cord was parked just at the corner, and Mr. John Grimes of Kensington, N.C., was leaning on the horn. Craig stuck his head out, and yelled: 'Don't wear it out! I'll be right down!' He rushed down the hall and took the steps three at a clip.

'I sure didn't expect to see you,' he said, as they shook hands. He noticed immediately that John Grimes looked older, very tired, and his once smoothly distributed fat now hung on him like pods, giving him almost an appearance of skinniness surrounded by loose bunches of flesh.

'Get in the car and let's go to the Inn,' Grimes said. 'I got a suite'—he pronounced it 'soot'—'there. Wanta talk to you. I was in Raleigh today buying up a couple of senators and I thought I might just as well run over. How you doin', Buddy? Everything goin' good?'

'Tolable. Flunked a maths course when I was in love. But I can make it up next fall by taking an extra course. Rest of the grades have been pretty fair. About a B average.'

'What's all this about love? No, don't tell me now. Wait'll we get up to the soot. I need a drink before I can listen to any love stuff.'

'You got some likker? If you haven't, I can . . .'

'I *always* got some likker.' Grimes turned his head from the road and looked keenly at Craig. 'Don't you go and tell me you're mixed up in that bootlegging business after all we had to say about it.' He barely avoided missing a co-ed, and turned his attention back to the road.

'No, I'm not mixed up in it,' Craig said. 'But my best friend is. It's good booze, too. I finally found out where they get the grain alcohol. Couple of the medical students supply most of it.'

Grimes shuddered, as they swept into the drive before the Inn. 'I'd hate to think what they drain it off of,' he shuddered. '*Brrr.*' To the bellman who opened the front door. 'Have somebody park the car, George, and send me some ice and ginger ale up to 303 and don't wait till next week. I'm thirsty.'

'Yassuh, boss. Yas, *suh*,' as Grimes slapped a bill in his hand. 'Right *a*-way. Yas, *suh*.'

'What's all this crap about love?' Grimes said, after he had poured corn whisky into the ginger ale. 'You got no business being in love so early.' He heaved a sigh. 'Man, that drink tastes good. You mind unlacing my shoes? My feet been swellin', and I'm too beat-out to lean over.'

Craig knelt and unlaced his shoes. Grimes wiggled his toes luxuriously. 'Tell me about it.'

'Ain't much to tell. She's real pretty, and a real nice gal. Her brother's a friend of mine. I had her up for the Spring Frolics. If I was older I'd think about getting married, but hell, Mr. Grimes, it's a long time before I can even think about thinking about getting married. That's what I told her when we kind of busted up.'

Craig was lying flatly and knew it, and Grimes seemed to sense it.

'I ain't going to meddle,' he said. 'But I got one thing to tell you. You kids get raised up with the idea that all the nice girls *don't* and all the bad girls *do*, and when what you think is a nice girl puts out, then you get all confused and think she's a bad girl. There ain't no such thing as a bad girl, not even a whore-girl. Remember it.'

'I'll remember it,' Craig said. And to himself, *I'll remember it, all right.* The complete capsuling of what Grimes had just said. The dirty, brain-tainting suspicion after the conversation in the bathroom, the juvenile inability to untangle the girl from the gossip, the soiling of what had been clean and beautiful, the evil impact so strong that all his mother's sadistic medical half-teaching had further fouled his feelings with an imagined venereal disease, the stupid youthful inability to return to the first purity of

126

feeling, to accept the girl for what she was, a delightful, beautiful, normally healthy girl who had felt springtime stirrings and thought she loved, physically, a young man, and who, in her simple honesty, and desire to please, gave that love unquestioningly.

'Yes, sir, I'll remember it,' Craig said to Grimes, and he thought of that night he prowled the woods, unable to sleep, after the empty excuses, stammered and half-spoken, of too much work, a lot of study to make up, mother's sick, got to go home for the week-end, all the senseless things people say when all they mean is that they can't accept a thing that used to be and isn't the same, so they want to leave it—want to go now.

Mary Frances hadn't helped his remembrances. Only *he* had changed.

'I understand perfectly, Craig,' she said, and placed a cool palm on his arm. 'You have a lot of work to do ahead and we're much too young to be in love. Maybe when we're older things will be different. I'm sorry about the other day . . .' And then with a flash, 'No, I'm not sorry a damned bit! Except it's changed you and now you almost hate me! If we were older and married you'd have thought it was fine, but now you're thinking I'm a campus widow! The hell with you, you, you . . . *dirty little boy!*'

Yes, he'd remember it, all right. He'd remember it all his life, and wonder where she went, and curse the space in time that found her too early. He'd remember all right. All his life, when his thoughts were sick and sore.

Grimes was talking across Craig's thoughts.

'. . . And this summer I want to do something I never done. Something nobody in my family never done. I want to go to Yurrop. I want to see that Paris, France, and that London, England, and maybe Rome, Italy, before I die. I ain't been very well in the last few months, and I done a lot of thinking. The missus, she won't go, she says she's afraid to cross the water and to be with all them furriners who don't speak English and that furrin food and all. And she won't let me take Maybelle. Says Maybelle too young to appreciate it and it would just upset her and spoil her for going to college back home and she'd pick up a lot of bad habits from them dirty Dagoes and Frogs and Limeys, and maybe get in trouble with some fellow. . . . I said the hell with it. I said, I'm going, come hell or high water, and if you won't go, I'll go by myself . . . or take Craig Price. You want to go to Yurrop, Buddy? Same deal we had, but we'd take a car on the boat and kind of rattle around . . .'

Craig gulped.

'You're serious? You're actually asking me to go with you to Europe? Oh, my God, Mr. Grimes . . . I'd swim to get there, I'd . . . I'd . . .'

Grimes reached out awkwardly and patted Craig on the shoulder.

'You won't have to swim, Buddy. And I'm serious. You and me are kind of cut out of the same cloth. Except I waited too long. You ought to do things like this when you're young, not when you're old and fat and tired and . . . Here, pour me another drink. Pour yourself one, too. We'll drink to Yurrop . . .'

Grimes swished his glass, and the ice tinkled.

'It sounds like sleigh-bells, don't it? Except I never seen a sleigh. Come to think of it, I really ain't ever seen nothing worth seeing. What I seen was cotton mills and turpentine camps and banks and crops and reports. I can't even talk English good. I got money and I don't know how to use it to get much good out of it. I got the biggest house in North Carolina and I feel like a stranger in it. I can buy the whole goddam legislature, but you think any one of them people I buy would ask me to their house? I'm a po' Bokra, I'm a cracker, and all them fine-haired starving blue-bloods look down on me and say I ain't got no right to have money. Why ain't I got a right to have money? I made it, one way or the other, tough or easy, honest or dishonest. I *made* it. I didn't have no long-nosed parents to cuss because they died off and didn't leave me nothing. I'm fifty-odd years old and never had no fun I didn't buy—a whore in a house, or somebody to be polite to me because if they ain't they know I can bust 'em. But nobody give me nothing.'

Grimes shrugged, and smiled half-apologetically. He sipped his drink.

' 'Scuse me, Buddy. I kind of got worked up. It ain't good for my heart, the doc says. But sometimes I get so goddam mad. Life's so short, and there had ought to have been something, something kind of fine, kind of sparkly, kind of exciting, something with frills on it . . . Maybe a beautiful woman to love you, maybe the moon coming up over one of them Indian temples, maybe a long view from a tall hill. Strange people, scattered all over the world, people that wouldn't know whether you was a cracker or the High Duke de Kallikak, long's you minded your manners and didn't spit on the rug.'

'You know what, Mr. Grimes?' Craig was reminiscently shaken by the outburst. 'The day my Grandpa told he was going to die pretty soon, he said just about the same thing. He said he'd sort of shuffled through life like a cropper that didn't care if the crop made or not. He said you ought to take a-holt of life and kick it around until it hollered "Uncle". He said he was going to die and he hadn't hardly had any fun at all, except a little bit when he went to sea. I never quit thinking about what he said. Sometimes it gravels me so bad I get up and prowl the floor like a lion in a zoo. I been reading an awful lot and sometimes I feel like I just can't stand it. I feel like I'll go crazy, and if I don't see all there is to see, and do all the things there are to do, and go every place there is to go, and have everything there is to have . . .' Craig blushed. 'I didn't mean to talk so much. Can I fix you another drink?'

'Yep. We both been running off at the mouth pretty good. But the thing about you is you know it in time to do something about it. Me, I always been so deep in the woods, like the fellow says, I ain't had time to pick out no particular tree. Me and you and your Grandpa all got the same idea, except your Grandpa was too lazy and I worked too hard. The idea is to work just hard enough to be able to be lazy. And to move around . . . see the Pyramids the same way you'd see the Washington Monument. Go to them islands where the girls got the big tits. See the elephant and hear the owl.'

'When are we going?' Craig was so excited he could hardly keep still. 'Where'll we go first?'

Grimes sipped his drink.

'I thought we'd leave around the middle of June. When's school out?'

'I think the fifth of June.'

'Well, that'd give you time to see your people a little. Then I thought we'd drive to New York slow and easy . . . Take a day in Washington. You never been to Washington. You could see the Smithsonian Institute and we could go to Baltimore and then drive up through Philadelphia and then take a boat out of New York, with the car aboard.'

Samarkand. The Taj Mahal by moonlight. Bali. Tahiti. The lost Atlantis, Popocatapetl. Mount Everest and the River Ganges. All translated into Washington, Philadelphia and New York, with the new world to come. Craig almost panted in his eagerness.

'Then where? *Where*?'

'London, first, I thought. Then we'd get on the boat train and take the car to France, and go to Paris and see the sights, and then drive slow through France until we got to Rome. See the vineyards and the castles. See the Colosseum and St. Peter's, maybe even the Pope. Then we might drive from Rome to Spain and maybe see some bullfights. That'd take us about three months, and we could be back in time for you to start school. Or almost. I can fix it with the registrar.'

'I don't know how I can make out to wait,' Craig said. 'I feel like the week before Christmas.'

'The time'll pass. It always does. You mind strapping me into my shoes, Buddy? I got to get along back to Raleigh. Got a few more people to see.' He heaved himself to his feet. 'We'll have us a mess of fun, Buddy. See some of them girlie shows in Paris, and the like of that. I reckon you're old enough now.' He winked salaciously.

'I'm old enough,' Craig said. 'I ain't too far off seventeen.' He winked back. His brain babbled.

'Try to keep your mind on your school work,' the weary old man said. 'But I must say I'm having a hell of a time keeping mine on my business—and the way things are about now, if you ain't thinking every minute you wind up selling apples. Things are real bad, real bad, all around. That's another reason I think I better take a vacation while I can.'

'Mister Grimes?'

He turned at the door.

'Yes, Buddy?'

'Why are you . . . *why* are you so nice to me? Me of all people? *Why?*'

'I don't know, son.' He smiled. 'I expect just because you're kind of like me, but with a forty-year head start. Come see me soon's you get home.'

Craig walked with him to the door, and saw him brace himself as he summoned his car. The bracing was a visible effort.

This was the year the jealous gods went crazy. Craig was less than scarcely surprised a few days later to pick up a copy of *The News and Observer* and see a headline: 'Carolina Industrialist Dead: Heart Attack Fells John Grimes.'

The body of the story said that Grimes had died in bed at his home in Kensington of a coronary occlusion—that his estate was in dreadful order, that his mills and his bank were temporarily closed. Craig therefore was not surprised when, on 2 May 1932, he went to the bank and was informed that no cheque had been deposited. John Grimes had made a personal thing of sending the money to the boy. That was all there was of John Grimes. There departed the friendship, the assured money, the future. There blew off the trip to Europe which was too good to be true, anyhow. Oddly, Craig was not so much disappointed about the trip to Europe for himself.

'If only,' he was saying to Moose Wilbur, 'if only the old man had just been able to do this one thing before he pegged out. He wanted to, so bad. He was a good man—a real sad man. But for some reason he liked me. We could of had a lot of fun, and I don't mean just because of him having money. I liked him . . . I liked him better than my father.'

'I been reading the papers,' Wilbur said. 'It looks to me like he was borrowing from Peter to pay Paul. From what I gather, if they come out of all the tangle with anything, his family'll be lucky. Seems like he mortgaged the mill to keep the bank going, and borrowed from the bank to keep the mill going, and hocked everything else to keep everything else going. It says in the *Observer* that even his house may be up for sale while the executors clean up the mess, and see who owes what.'

130

'I feel sick about this trip to Europe,' Craig said. 'The old man must have known that he didn't have too much time left, and he was pretty pathetic about wanting to get out and see some strange places before he died. Thinking back to that afternoon we had at the Inn, I was kind of certain, in a way, that he'd never make it, and that he thought so too. But he was kind of playing like he *might* have made it if he could hold out a little longer. The way he talked, it was almost like he was giving me the idea of it . . . as a sort of present, even if we didn't get to do it.'

Moose Wilbur cocked his head and was silent for a minute.

'You liked the old geezer a lot. Evidently he liked you. Then why the hell don't you go make his trip for him? Give him his present back. Go grab yourself a ship and get yourself laid in his honour in Paris, France, or some place. Go see a goddam museum. Go climb the Eiffel Tower. Give the poor old bastard his trip.'

The S.S. *Sundance*, moored at a Charleston pier, suddenly steamed into Craig's head. He remembered the gaunt hungry men, shamefully out of work, shambling aboard for a hand-out. He remembered that Philip had said the ships usually paid off in Jacksonville. He remembered the cargo, the ports of call . . .

Grandpa Sam also came suddenly back into his thoughts. The palms of Mombasa. Sydney Harbour. Takoradi. The only fun old Sam Price ever had . . .

He got up and paced the floor excitedly.

'Jimmy,' he said. 'You got a hell of an idea. I'm going to sea. Soon as school's out, I'll hitch-hike South and get me a ship, somehow.'

'Awful lot of people out of work,' Wilbur replied. 'Be mighty tough to land a berth. I was kind of kidding, anyhow, when I said run off and have the old man's vacation for him. You couldn't get a job sea-going, these days. Christ, kid, you told me yourself, you saw captains and mates begging for food in Charleston. How's a punk kid with no experience going to get a job when a skipper can't go A.B.?'

'I'll do it somehow. I'll bet you ten bucks I'm in Europe by the middle of July. And you can pay me now.'

Jimmy Wilbur grinned, and dug into his pocket. He peeled a ten off a thin roll of grimy bills and handed it to Craig.

'I believe you,' he said. 'And when you get back to Charleston, stop off and say hello to your old room-mate's mama. You're a big boy now, and about ready to pick. But damn' if I don't seem to be financing your life—love, and otherwise.'

Wilbur got up and paced, in time to Craig's marching.

'For two bits I'd go with you. But it looks like I'm stuck here. I got the news today. I'm the new backfield coach. Huh!' He snorted. 'Still with the jockstraps. Telling some other bum how to spin off tackle. Showing some other Polack how to throw a pass or kick it out of bounds on the five-yard line, and wondering how he didn't listen hard enough so it got blocked. Tailbacks, single-wings, double-wings, Rockne shifts. Balls. But it pays three grand a year, which feeds me. One day the head coach has a stinking year and all of a sudden good old Moose is head coach and making seven grand a year, until somebody fires him.' He shrugged. 'It's a living.'

Craig shrugged back. 'You make it tough. You make it sound pretty putrid. But congratulations anyhow. Any kind of job along about now ain't to be sneezed at. Wonder what they pay a deck-boy on a cargo ship?'

'About $7.50 a week,' Jimmy Wilbur smiled. 'Write me when you get steady work. Or seriously, kid, if you get into any bad trouble and need a buck, this new job of mine will always have an extra fin to feed you over a mean week-end. But what about school? You figure to come back in the fall?'

'I want to. God knows I want to. But I kind of got in the habit of thinking that Mr. Grimes had it all taken care of—the meat-and-potato part, I mean—and now I got to start thinking all over again. If I get a job on a boat, maybe I'll lay out a year and save some money and come back. Other people have done it.'

'You lay out a year and you find it awful hard to get to be a student again,' Wilbur said. 'It's like this damned football. It's awful hard to get going after a summer vacation. But I tell you something, and don't get all upset, one way or the other. I don't think you need college very much. It's the same way I don't need a coach. You got something—I don't know what, kid—but I don't think they can teach you enough stuff here to help you develop it. I spotted it the first night when I pulled that nut off your back. Your friend Missus duFresne spotted it. That gal, Mary Frances—and shut up, don't get your ears red—she spotted it. Certainly old Grimes spotted it. I don't think you're a student. I think you're a natural born bastard that'll either wind up president or in the clink, but I don't think college is going to help you or hurt you. Speech over.'

Craig applauded loudly, smacking his hands like pistol shots. Then he said soberly:

'But what do I do, Moose? Where do I go? I can't be a football coach or a writer or a lawyer. I don't know anything . . . I don't know how to do anything special. I go to sea, say, and wind up what? I don't want to work for people. I don't know what the hell I want. I don't even know what I *don't* want. But one thing I don't want. . . . I don't want to come back here and just skin through, washing dishes and hustling boarding-houses and begging off the Loan Fund and not getting anything out of an education but classwork and being ashamed because I haven't got enough dough to buy a quart, or having to bum cigarettes

. . . You know. I don't want to be a bum. I don't want to just skin by. Goddammit, I want . . .'

'What you want is to do like I said and get out of town,' Wilbur answered. 'I'm not kidding. Go off some place and look for something. Anything. Maybe after you've looked hard enough you can nail it down and find out what you want. The worst problem you got, sonny, is that you really never been a boy. You're a grown-up man, kind of, in a boy's breeches, like I said once before. You been cheated out of childhood, and you ain't got the patience to be an adolescent. Go be a man. Men don't go to college. Go be a man.'

'I'll see you in a hundred years or so,' Craig said. 'I ain't going to try to say thanks. I'll tell you what the girls are like in Paris, France, and you can tell me about the prospects in the freshman backfield. So long, Jim.'

They shook hands. They saw each other frequently before Craig left at the end of the spring term, but they had already said good-bye.

He didn't go to Raleigh to see Mary Frances. He didn't go home to Kensington. He stuck his thumb in the air and suddenly he was in Savannah, Georgia. He had about twenty dollars in his pocket—enough for a dingy room in a fifth-rate hotel across the square from the best one, and to keep him a couple of weeks until he got a ship.

'Dear Mother and Dad,' he wrote. 'I have decided to go to sea. I was able to get a ride down this far and so I decided it was better not to come along the Coast. I hope you all are making out all right. I'll let you know where I am. Love, Craig.'

Pompously to Mary Frances: 'I won't be seeing you for some time, as I have decided that travel is supposed to be broadening, and I feel I must go investigate Europe instead of keeping on going to school. I'll write you from Paris and London and wherever I wind up. It's not very often that a man can travel abroad at my age, and I couldn't refuse the offer. All expenses paid, and a salary besides. I might very likely live abroad.' He rejected the phrase, ' 'tis a far, far better thing I do,' and merely wrote: 'Take care of yourself. Love, Craig.'

He put the envelopes in the mail and then said, sipping a most unromantic milk-shake in a cool, fan-swishing dark moist-scented drug-store:

'Christ. The only thing I got to do now is to *get* to Europe, at least so's I can send a postcard home.'

And then he looked at Savannah.

Charleston had been different. He had not been alone in Charleston. His transport was assured, the warmth of a house and a hot meal in his belly were guaranteed. True, it was not of his

133

doing, but it was there, to be used. Then he also had the double assurance of his parents, just down the road, in Kensington. In Charleston he was a guest—a stranger, surely, but still a guest. It had been more or less the same in Chapel Hill. If he had a problem he could take it to the Dean's Office. Somebody would feed him—Jimmy Wilbur or somebody. And there was always home. But now, here, in the Georgia he had not seen before, his bridges burnt, the great wide world ahead—except how to get there?—he was truly alone for the first time in his life, and a great surge of wild exultation rose in him.

Now he was truly Lonesome Craig Price, the World Traveller, the Chief. The Captain-Admiral of the Ocean Sea was about to embark, and the only problem was: How?

The hell with *how*. Craig strode the streets, flicking an imaginary sword-cane at inoffensive objects. He felt he was already in Africa. The greenery was much lusher in Savannah, much lusher than in Kensington. The tall palms swayed low, the flowers literally sprang at you, the grass was almost poison-green. A slow breeze stirred the short palmettos lazily, and there was a smell of heat. The smell of heat is soft and lazy and full of languor, as stars crackle crisply on cold nights, and have the smell of diamonds, as the sun has a cheesy smell, and the moon is cold green ice-cream or warm yellow papaya, depending on its mood.

The River rode sluggishly yellow along the front street, Bull Street, and ships seemed to march along land. They did not move as ships are supposed to move—they seemed to be coaxed along by strings. They seemed also higher than the city, with the same eerie effect of the huge ships moving down the Louisiana bayous he had not yet seen.

The Negroes were even blacker than the Charleston gullahs. These were geechees—enormous plum-black bucks with blue gums deep-lipped over sugar-cubes of teeth—great black mammies with bright handkerchiefs tied round their heads. The picanins, often as not, ran naked from the navel down. There was a steady hum on the air—a hum of sun, of cicadas in trees, a murmur of distant voices, and always a hovering umbrella of green. Dust lay drifted on the streets, A bright winged tanager slices into the creaking fronds. There was the sense of earth turned, laid open and raw, but warm as a woman.

Craig went down to the water, the water he was assuming as career. This was purest Africa, now, more than Charleston. The goats were in the streets, the urine-dampened plaster smelling more strongly, the frying fish crackling louder in the spitting grease. A few small shops exhibited herbs—'Novelties,' the signs said. There was an unknown land of voodoo at his fingertips, and the eyes of the blacks who lounged along the narrow cobbled alleys were downcast and secretive. Always the palm fronds creaked in the wind. The shanties beckoned—come inside, they said, and we will tell you what the white man, the Bokra, don't know. Come inside and sit because it's a long time to hell and back and here we got fresh fried swimps, here we got dat fine crawfish soup, here we got de fried catfish and de jambalaya, jes' as good as N'Awlins, and here we got some voodoo drums and a little tetch High John de Conquerer powder, yeddy? You need charm, make yo' woman love you good, behave, not run off wid udder man? You come set here fo de fiah son, You jes' come here, makes to sit. Maybe makes to meet dis fine high yaller gal. A dollah ain't much fo' de rich boys. Times hahd, and fifty cents a power of money. She clean, too. Not like dem Bokra stop in de hotels.

Craig's heart bounded before the low-lidded eyes, leaped at the secret invitation to come to the Casbah. It was the prodding sense of forbidden knowledge to come—the implied danger behind the walls, the exhilaration of being outside his own terrain. *Implied* danger, and blood-steaming smells. Suggested adventure, and always the hot smells. Who can say what a guitar, pensively strummed in a Spanish back-alley, smells like? It smells like a dark-eyed buxom woman with a mole on her cheek and a red flower in her hair. Who can say what a bongo-drum evokes? A slave raid, an orgy in the wooded hills of Haiti, with a decapitated rooster spattering his blood, the rattle of bones, and a cat about to be skinned alive and eaten, quivering? Craig knew nothing first-hand of dark secrets, but he could smell with all his heart. The old spirituals, and fevered camp meetings he had attended as a kid, and again the savage music rolled and tossed in his head.

'White boy, what does you want down here?'

She was bright high brown, thickly lipsticked, oiled of hair, and wore a blue dress. 'You look fo' black gal?' She simpered. 'I only ain' ve'y black, but a gal right on. I got nice house. Only one dollah, yeddy?'

Craig shook his head. He was embarrassed to be broke in front of a Negro whore.

'I haven't got any money. Sorry. I just haven't got any money.'

She tossed her head and scorn clouded her eyes.

'In dat case, I'se wastin' my time. Not even fifty cent?' She flounced her bosom at him, tossing her head.

'Not even fifty cents.' He smiled. 'Maybe when I get rich I'll . . .'

'I hu'd dat one befo',' she said, and switched her hips in saucy rebuke. Craig watched her regretfully as she walked away. Some day, he said, I got to try some of that. When I got more money.

Craig sat quietly on the sun-warmed, tar-smelling dock and watched the ships. Two showed stern first, against the river, and one was hull down, coming his way. That ship would be along pretty soon, and maybe . . . maybe the Captain Admiral of the Ocean Sea would have something to go to sea on so his postcards

135

wouldn't make him look like a damned fool the way he was in Charleston.

The ship had docked. Craig watched, fascinated, at the necessary precision that warped her into her berth, the fluid communication between a swarming gang on the foc'sle head, the captain on the bridge, the other figures milling on the fantail. A burly man with an officer's cap shouted orders to his winchmen and the other seamen on the foc'sle head, seconding the shouted orders from a figure on the bridge. Another, short, squat officer responded to the weird linked-rhythm which centred on the flying bridge, where the captain stood sternly beside a helmsman. Light heaving-lines, of thin cord, with the old familiar turks'-head woven-weight bulking heavy on the end, snaked ashore, to be caught by waiting dockers. The thin line was fastened to the thick yoked hawsers, which then were looped securely to the incurved bollards. Then the winches rattled hoarsely and took a strain, and steadily drew the ship taut to the dock. A midships crew swung the gangplank from its deck-rail snuggery, out, down, and finally with a platform at right-angles to the shipside. All was made fast, and the groaning agony of the winches ceased. The ship was home.

The officers on foc'sle head, flying bridge, and poop, made negating signals with their arms, and the ship which had prowled the Atlantic's vast grey cemetery was as land-bound as an automobile, and much more neatly parked.

Men disappeared into the midships and afterdeck housing, and presently began to flow outward in a steady stream, some carrying sea-bags over their shoulders, bags like enormous canvas sausages, bulging and lumpy with possessions. Others, not carrying bags, appeared in shore-going clothes—shoddy store clothes— and left in a mighty hurry. A few remained aboard—the burly man with the blue officer's cap, who seemed to be everywhere at once, and some straggling seamen in sweaters and knitted watch-caps.

Suddenly there was a commotion. A thin scarecrow man, dressed in filthy blue dungarees and a sagging sweater, hatless, ran shamblingly forward from the midships housing down the ladder to the forward hatches, up the ladder to the foc'sle head, and stood, panting, staring round him, as a beast at bay. Behind him lumbered the burly man, leaping oddly nimbly for his size, swarming up the ladder to the foc'sle head, like a great cat. The thin man dodged round the winch which held its great iron necklace of anchor chain, and stood with his back to the aprons of the V of the bow, trapped, as the burly man went swiftly past the great bronze ship's bell and reached hungry meaty hands towards the thin shabby man, who attempted to shrink into the ship's iron skin.

The burly man grabbed him by the scruff and by belt, planted

136

his feet, surged, and heaved the thin man over the side. He fell and lay brokenly, then stirred, as the burly man looked down at him. Then he pulled himself painfully off the dockside iron sheathing, rising with separate creaking movements, like a folded rule emerging from its angled joints.

'You ever set foot aboard any ship of mine again!' the burly one stood with fists akimbo. 'You put so much as one flat foot on a ship of mine and I'll kill you, you son-of-a-bitch! I'll pull your head out of your neck like the string out of an orange, you goddam rumpot!'

The son-of-a-bitch-goddam-rumpot didn't answer. He dragged himself as swiftly as his bruised body allowed away from the ship, any place away from the menace of the man, any place away.

Craig got to his feet and walked forward to where the burly man still stood, watching the retreating figure of the shambling man, breathing satisfaction.

'Mister Mate,' Craig said, not knowing what else he was going to say. 'Mister Mate?'

The burly man looked at him over the ship's side. The mate had a meaty, blue-whiskered face, a broad sunburned nose, and little slits of piggy brown eyes. He had a hard flat mouth, and he was wearing a peaked uniform cap and a black turtle-necked sweater. It made a uniform.

'What do *you* want?' he bellowed. He never spoke, Craig learned later. He always bellowed.

'I bet you can't do that to me,' Craig said.

'Do what?'

'Throw me off the ship like you just did that guy.'

The mate stretched his neck veins ropy as he laughed.

'Come on up and see, punk. I'll eat you raw.'

Craig was serious.

'If you can't, eat me raw, I mean, can I have *his* job?'

The mate laughed again, hugely amused.

'If I can't, you can damn' well have *my* job. I ain't even got my morning sweat up throwing that rummy over the side. Come aboard.'

They fought solidly for half an hour. Craig was weedy, but he stood six foot high and what meat he had was solid. The mate was older, and heavier, but was deceptively fast afoot. He roared with laughter as he slung his punches, most of which missed. One didn't. It caught Craig on the bridge of his nose and he could hear the cartilage crunch. He fell backward on to the anchor winch, but as the mate came after him he kicked out and caught the mate in the testicles with the toe of his shoe. The mate clapped a hand on his groin and abruptly sat down.

Craig's nose was broken, gushing blood. The mate's face was twisted with pain from the kick in the groin. Craig went over and held out a hand. The mate seized it, and Craig yanked him to his feet.

'We going to do this some more?' Craig said. He sniffed, and swept blood from his face with the back of his sleeve. 'When you're ready, Mister Mate?'

The Mate laughed again, although the effort hurt him downstairs.

'No, by God we're not!' he bellowed. 'Of all the goddam crazy kids! You got yourself a job, sonny.' Then he suddenly swung his right hand. The fist caught Craig on the side of his jaw, and sent him swiftly to sleep. When he came alive again, the mate was standing over him, legs spraddled, looking down with vast amusement. The Mate reached out a hand and yanked him to his feet.

'You got yourself a job,' he said, 'if you still want it. The last punch was just to tell you I'm still the boss on this bucket. You think I'm the boss?'

'Yessir,' Craig said. 'You're the boss.'

'Can I throw you over the side?'

'You could of.'

'Okay,' the Mate said, and shoved out a friendly paw. 'Shake. It pays ten bucks a week and you're the Number Two Ordinary, and there ain't nothing lower than a Number Two Ordinary unless it's the cadet. What's your name?'

'Craig Price.'

'Say *sir* from now on. What was it again?'

'Craig Price, *sir*.'

'That's better. My name is Mister Cramer and I'm the chief mate and I'm the stud duck on this bucket. Don't you ever forget it. Now, you go get yourself cleaned up, get somebody to fix that nose, and come back here tomorrow. We're articling on a new crew. We sail day after tomorrow. Welcome aboard the S.S. *Wardance*. It's what's known as a hungry ship.'

He clapped Craig on the shoulder.

'You got guts, kid. Now get the hell over the side and see me in the wheel-house tomorrow at eleven.'

Mister Cramer turned and slid himself down the ladder to the foredeck, feet not touching the iron rungs, and never turned his head as he swaggered painfully, one hand still clapped to his groin, almost jauntily up the ladder to the midships-house, where he disappeared.

Craig swabbed at his nose, now puffed into a bread-roll, followed the mate, and went over the side down the accommodation ladder. He had a broken nose, eleven dollars and twenty-seven cents, but by God he had a job. He was going to see the wide, wide world, no matter what the other fellows said.

The Captain Admiral of the Ocean Sea finally had found his barque. The bounding main was stretched before him, and soon

138

his feet would tread a quarterdeck. On the S.S. *Wardance*, bound for Anywhere. That night the Captain Admiral of the Ocean Sea bought himself a steak. He felt he'd earned it, even if his broken nose hurt like hell when he chewed.

The waves smote the bow of the ship, savagely streaming sheets of water over the foc'sle head. The old Hog Islander was running bow-on into the gale. As she bucked, she groaned amidships, and when she buried her nose in a sea, her screws reared clear of the wrenching waves and thrashed painfully half-out of the water.

The night was blacker than the water, and colder than the Arctic ice that supplied the sea on this Northern passage to Liverpool. The night watchman was braced against the anchor chains as they stretched taut from the chain-locker to crimp round the winch. A night watchman was basically two people—the No. 2 ordinary seaman and the cadet. They each worked an eight-hour shift, from eight bells to eight bells or, rather, from 8 p.m. to 8 a.m.—two hours on lookout, two hours standby, two hours lookout, two hours standby. Seven bitter cold nights a week, each week.

The Captain Admiral of the Ocean Sea wore smelly long drawers, two pairs of pants, two wool shirts, two sweaters, a sheepskin coat, oilskins, a knitted cap pulled down over his ears under the sou'wester, two pairs of socks and hip-boots. The sheets of water smote him full in the face, streamed back over the iced foc'sle head and went plunging iron-heavy as an avalanche over the deck cargo of lashed logs, prisoned tautly to the hatch and bulkhead and tightened by turn-buckles.

A shadowy figure gingered its way over the logs, a feeble yellow tongue of flashlight licking out ahead of him. The tongue of the light stammered, and disappeared once altogether as the figure slipped or was knocked off an icy log. The shaky light reappeared, and then was snapped off as the figure climbed up the ladder to the foc'sle head. As his sou'-westered head appeared in dark profile, eight bells was struck on the bridge. The Captain Admiral of the Ocean Sea checked the starboard (green) and port (red) running lights, the mast-head light, answered the eight bells by hand-tapping the clapper of the brass foc'sle head bell, then cupped his palms to his mouth and screamed into the gale the required answer to the bridge: 'Lights 'r' bright, Sir.' The other figure walked over to the night watchman and shivered.

'You're relieved,' he said. 'How is it?'

'Another ten minutes and you'd have deep-sixed a corpse,' the relieved Captain Admiral of the Ocean Sea said. 'You'd think that Scotch bastard up there would at least set his lookouts on the flying bridge in the doghouses, wouldn't you, instead of down here on this frigging foc'sle head?'

'They don't call him Flying Bridge Muirhead for nothing,' the other nightwatchman said. 'He's still got the mate and the A.B. standing wheel-watch topside. He's bedded down in that nice warm chart-room with his bottle. Well, I'll see you in two hours, if I don't freeze.'

'Right, Cadet. Think about Savannah, it helps.'

'Not me, Ordinary. I'm going to think about Hell. It's warmer.'

The relieved Captain Admiral of the Ocean Sea, who was the No. 2 Ordinary Seaman, called Craig Price, took the flashlight and slipped and slithered, swearing steadily, over the sea-slimy logs leading to the midships ladder. He picked his way along the port passage-way, across the midships deck, undogged an iron door, slid into a brightly-lit passage-way, and dogged the door shut behind him. He stopped for a minute by the iron grating of the fiddley platform which stood atop the engine-room, peeling off his soaked outer clothing, kicking off the sea-boots, taking off his gloves and spreading his raw chapped hands over the blast of heat which blew up from the iron open-work of the fiddley, out of the engine-room below.

When he quit shivering he walked down the alleyway, seeing for the hundredth time the bullet-holes alongside the scabbed white doughnut life preserver, the axe-blade scars close where the red fire-axe and extinguisher hung in brackets against the paint-blistered bulkhead. The red stencilling on the life preserver said S.S. *Wardance*. She was a trouble ship, as well as a hungry ship, like the mate had said. She was bound out of Savannah from Liverpool, Antwerp, Hamburg and Bremen. Her cargo was timber, sulphur, phosphate rock, fertilizer, nails and scrap iron. Like Philip said. It stank.

The ordinary seaman, Craig Price, who was paid ten dollars a week, no overtime; who stood eight-hour watches at sea; who shortly would begin to rot his hands in a mixture of lye and water called *suji-muji* with which he cleaned the white-work; who helped shift the ship at night from dock to dock in his own time; who painted over the side in port; who swept the remains of sheep manure and phosphate rock and sulphur from the holds; who cleaned the stinking bilges in the deep-tanks; who helped batten down open hatches in company-time-saving defiance to maritime law when the ship was already at sea; who was part of the poop-deck gang when the ship tied up or cast off; who ate biscuits from which cockroaches were knocked; who worked under a Danish bosun named Svendsen who hated him and was doubly hated in return; who lived with seven other men in one room under the poop, next to the tortured grinding of the steering engine; who shared one reeking toilet with the same seven men and washed out of a bucket into which a steam-pipe had been twisted to heat the water—this ordinary seaman walked into the crew mess and bled off a cup of over-boiled coffee out of the huge zinc urn in the corner, sat down on a bench by the mess table, observed that

140

the 'night lunch' had already been eaten, and lit a cigarette. He cursed again—cursing ships and men and the sea and the spirit of high adventure which had got him into this mess.

Ordinary Seaman No.1 Joe Marjen walked shivering into the mess. Marjen was a Charleston boy. He had a pock-marked face, swarthy and pin-pointed by blackheads, and a broad turned-up nose.

'The skipper's on the mate's ass tonight for fair,' he said. 'I must have trimmed every ventilator on the whole frigging bucket three times. The Old Man says that the deck load is going to carry away, and I think he's right. *That'll* be fun, securing those logs when they bust loose and start to beat up the ship. Where's the night lunch?'

'The A.B.s ate it,' Craig said. Marjen swore steadily for two minutes without repeating himself. He quit when the Third Mate, a small short-coupled swart Canadian, came back and walked into the crew mess.

'Get going with that *suji*-bucket,' he said to Craig. 'You,' to Marjen, 'get up on the bridge and relieve the wheel. The A.B.'s sick, or something.'

Craig got the *suji*-bucket and the rags and went into the passageway to freeze his hands again and widen the cuts the lye had burnt into his fingers. He shut his mind to the hot-freezing cold and the chill-burning lye and began to think. Craig had found on the foc'sle head, where he wasn't allowed to smoke, that he could control his thinking, and by channelling it along pleasant lines, he could make the time pass more swiftly.

He thought of all the nice things he had ever done; the first shotgun, what Christmas cooking smelt like. He thought about the first double on quail and the first deer and how to make a good camp and how a bird-dog looked winding a covey in the broom-grass. He thought about the quiet of a Carolina swamp with the bass biting and an autumn afternoon on a lonely beach with the blue fish ravenous and the wind screeching outside a snug cabin whose walls trembled from a roaring fat-pine fire and red ham sizzling in the skillet. But he never thought about it all at once. He rationed it. It was too good to spend all at once. He would say: 'All right, Ordinary, what do we think about to-night?' and then he would think about every little tiny portion of it.

. . . A flight of mallards dipped their heads. They turned, circled to reconnoitre, and Craig called again. They swept behind him in a great curve, and came around, intent now on decoying. Keeping his head down, Craig shoved the gun up higher and slipped the safety-catch . . .

A shrill pick-up whistle from the bridge hauled him swiftly out of the duck blind and back to the *suji*-bucket on the hungry ship, *Wardance*, bound for North European ports out of Savannah. He dashed up to the bridge. The Mate was poised over the ladder, looking down at him.

'We've changed course,' he said. 'Trim the ventilators.'

'Aye, aye, sir,' he said, and went off to trim the ventilators which led to the cargo holds so that no dirty ocean damp would damage the lovely cargo of sheep manure, sulphur, phosphate rock, nails and scrap-iron for the Germans to make a new war with. The waves crashed over the decks as the ship changed course, and all the ventilators appeared to have been seized, rusted fast since they had been trimmed an hour ago.

When he went back to the foc'sle head, he was starving.

The bow was colder and wetter after the change of course and Craig had to wedge himself between the anchor chains to keep from being washed off the foc'sle head ten feet straight down into the well-deck. Still a couple of hours until dawn, the coldest, most miserable time of the fading night, when cold grey sky would merge with colder grey sea. There was nobody alive on the Atlantic but you, and the running lights and the unseen Mate and the man at the wheel, the God-head of Captain drunk, possibly in his bunk.

Standing braced, back against the chill-greasy winch, Craig switched on the separation-of-thinking process again, and went back to the ducks. He was now in a duck blind, just as cold, just as wet, just as miserable, but praising the lousy, snow-flurried weather that would force the clouds low and roil the water, so the ducks wouldn't snug up in the middle of the bay and refuse to fly. Waiting for the streaky dawn to give you shooting light, you were happy to be cold and wet and miserable, because the first flight of redheads or mallards or the occasional canvas-back would light a fiery furnace inside you and you would forget the weather as the gun heated under your hands.

But right then, right now, it was just a little too cold for Ordinary Seaman Craig Price to dwell lengthily on cold-weather duck shooting. In the first place, there were no ducks to look forward to—not even a sheldrake—only the necessary eight bells to tap out at eight a.m., and then relief from pneumonia on the foc'sle head. At least the breakfast would be hot, and you could spend the rest of the day in your sack, rolled up in the crumpled blue denim sheets that got changed once a week, listening to the roaring clank of the steering engine that lived between your foc'sle and the Black Gang's foc'sle. You skipped the midday meal, because it wasn't worth eating anyhow. And just looking at the bosun, Svendsen, his cigarette drooping from a quirked lipless mouth, with the smoke trailing upwards past one squinted eye, was enough to spoil your appetite even if the food had been much, which it wasn't.

. . . That day on the boat, after they'd finished collecting the ducks and the oysters and the fish and the shrimp and crayfish, the entire fruit of the morning harvest passed down into the launch's

galley, where Big Dan was chef. Craig had stoked himself pretty well with raw oysters and clams, but there was still plenty of space in the boilers for whatever Dan was making. What he was making was one big dish, and he made it in an iron cauldron big enough to boil a hog in. It was jambalaya—call it pilaff, payloo, pilau, paella, anything you want—but its main ingredient was rice and red peppers. Into this rice had been mixed shrimps, oysters, clams, crayfish, pork sausage, white slabs of fish, a chicken for the stock, and the whole business cooked together until it was one great big wonderful adventure. Dan had coloured the rice with saffron, and the juices from the seafood and the chicken had got married in a tremendous soupy ceremony so that the rice, while dry by grain, was damp by volume, and the hunks of fish and the shellfish lost none of their flavour, but were nuggeted through the rice. Dan served all this with great golden slabs of corn bread, a gallon of scuppernong wine, and finished up with coffee that was so strong you had to cut it to drink it.

Sitting, eating, with a basin of this stuff in your lap, soaking up the sun, listening to the birds in the marsh, watching the fish jumping in the sparkling, breeze-ruffled water, smelling the good salt smells of decaying oyster shell and marsh-grass mud . . .

It was now about ten minutes again, from finish-lookout and the same dreadful breakfast. Craig's foc'sle-head brain raced back again to the dinner Dan had smoking in the galley when everybody arrived triumphant with a *bateau* full of wild geese.

. . . There were oysters in the half-shell. There was a tawny-red soup called bisque, with the big crays, heads and all, in the wine-rich soup. Tiny teal broiled, embraced by bacon, like baby chickens, fell apart in the fingers. Each man had a big pintail, cooked to pieces, with carrots and onions and potatoes and apples and sage shoved into its inside . . .

Craig came off the foc'sle-head lookout at midnight, frozen stiff and wet through. When he thawed out a bit he was still hungry. The night-lunch wasn't much, coarse-grained cold bread, clammy salami, mummified bologna, and stone-hard rat cheese. There was little left but crumbs, because again the Able Seaman had eaten it all. Craig's belly was growling a long lament, and he kept thinking about that last meal. The thought process led inevitably to the officers' night-lunch. The officers on the *Wardance* did not eat the same food the men ate. The chief belly-robber was a long-red-nosed food-poisoner who believed that all the decent food belonged forrard, the swill aft. The officers' pantry included hard-boiled stuffed eggs, sardines, crisp crackers, good cheese, olives, onions, cold ham, goose-liver, lemon pie, Vienna sausages, and cake. And the coffee was only boiled once. Craig knew about this because occasionally the Mate would send him down when he was standby on the bridge to fetch him up a snack.

Once relieved he crept to the officers' pantry. He opened the ice-box and there it was, all the delicatessen his soul as well as stomach craved, and he ate ravenously. He was drinking a cup of boiled-once coffee—when he heard determined steps. The skipper had roused, either from ancient intuition or hunger, and was heading for the pantry. Craig beat him out of the door by a whisker, and for some stupid reason was still carrying the coffee-pot.

Still grasping that percolator, Craig took off. The Captain, wearing carpet slippers, looked once at his ravaged ice-box, the door gaped open, and the empty gimballed holder on which his coffee-pot had rested. He screamed like a banshee and raged on to the deck. Around, over, and practically under the ship Craig and the skipper went, aft to fore and fore to aft, the skipper cursing, stumbling, and blowing his whistle for aid.

Craig was young and sure-footed and he knew the ship, and what to him was a defined track was an obstacle course to the Captain, who kept generally to his cabin. The Captain fell over deck-cargo and barked his shins, slipped on the water-slick deck, collided with bulkheads, lost his footing on ladders, but continued to blow his whistle and scream for assistance. He aroused the off-watch mates, and the steward's department, and the deck gang, and the black gang, and he also roused Craig, who had flung the coffee-pot over the side, before he joined the herd of drowsy men. He made himself busy at all sorts of things, like trimming the vents and slapping *suji* on bulkheads, and when the skipper herded everybody into the crew mess to sort out the culprit, Craig was lost in the crowd.

There were over thirty men on that ship, and it's hard to pick a night-lunch thief out of thirty men. The skipper ranted, and roared, and swore that he would hang, keel-haul, and flog through the fleet the guilty party when he caught him, and in the meantime there would be no pay when they docked in Liverpool, and no shore leave at all. The Captain finally lost his voice, swore a husky oath of eternal vengeance, and departed, croaking.

The weather roughened. The winds clawed at the ship, and the great smoky-grey white-headed waves tossed the ship into troughs which caused the enormous massy bulk of the waves to loom fearsomely over the flying bridge. The ship rolled sickeningly. Foc'sle-head lookout was mostly impossible, now, and the lookouts stood their watches on the flying bridge, crouching miserably on the corners of the open topside bridge into little pillboxes called dog-houses. The wheel-watch stood below. Standby work was abandoned, and Craig went to work on his off-time as an apprentice helmsman. He steered a watch with the second mate, a former Charleston policeman named Rex Small. Small was a round, rather jolly man, sandy, rose-faced, but with the coldest eyes Craig had ever seen. When he smiled he smiled all over, but his eyes remained agate.

Small hated Mister Cramer, the Chief Mate, who relieved him after the mid-watch. He had heard, by now, how Craig had got his job. He deliberately set out to teach the boy, in a very quiet voice, to be a seaman. It was warm and dark and snug in the wheelhouse, smelling of hot paint, with the binnacle's tilting face glowing in the blackness, and the spokes of the wheel smooth and pliant to Craig's hands. There was no gyroscopic steering apparatus—the relentless urge of sea and stress of wind had to be computed in surplus left-or-right wheel-spin.

When Craig relieved the quartermaster, the Mate Small would say: 'She's eating a lot of that left stuff tonight. You better take two bends before you even think of moving her a degree. And for God's sake, keep her steady on. Ever since that night-lunch business'—Small permitted himself a smug smile—'ever since *somebody* stole the old man's coffee-pot and gave it the deep six, he's been as mean as a snake. He can feel a course change in his sleep. Keep her head on, and compensate, kid, for the love of God, compensate.'

The act of steering a ship was exciting, a hot battle snug inside against the unknown outer cold world of shrieking wind and buffeting wave. Craig developed a great pride in twisting two full turns into the slack wheel to keep a half degree each side of his course, feeling the security of knowing a little more than the sea knew, hearing from his back-antennae the moaning pains of the steering engine as it sorrowfully answered his deft hand on the smooth-grained handles of the spokes. The billygoat's head, the binnacle, told him that he was steering true, and Small's soft voice was commending.

'That's a nice clean wake you're making, kid,' he'd say. 'Nothing to start the old man out of his sleep. None of these rattlesnake wakes on this watch. Keep her straight like a ribbon, and some day you'll be a skipper.'

They talked endlessly in the night, softly so as not to arouse the ogre in his cabin behind the wheelhouse. Small told him gory tales of police work, raw stories of foreign places and people, and always wound up with one brutal statement.

'Stay with this business, kid, and you'll find out some day that a ship's your only home, you won't like it ashore, you'll never get any further than getting drunk in the first gin-joint closest the dock. Look at those tramps you're bunked with aft. Every A.B.'s got a master's ticket. Every Ordinary's at least a Second Mate. Except you. Get off the ocean, son. It ain't a place to make a living. It's a prison . . . a deep wet prison that needs left wheel one night, two turns to right wheel the next. It won't hold still.'

One night Craig said hesitantly:

'Mister Small, if you don't like it, how come you're here?'

145

'I had some wife trouble ashore,' he said shortly. 'For Christ sake, look what you're doing. You're steering 105.' And he spoke no more that night.

Eric was a white-haired old Scandihoovian, who never moved more than a block away from the dock. He would draw his pay when the ship struck port, and drink until he was returned, dried spittle crusting his lips, pathetically helpless and soiled, by some kindly whore or amiable policeman. Craig had seen it in Charleston—night after night while they loaded finally before they sailed with open hatches, Eric drunk and filthy, his eyes bleared and faded by drink and sun. But no matter how impossibly drunk the night before, he would turn to on time the next day.

Eric sober was a wonderfully gentle, well-read man, who took to his bunk with *The Decline and Fall* as an anodyne. Gibbon was his Bible.

'Look at Ericsen,' Rex Small said. 'Just look at him. *Look* at him. He's lucky to get a job as A.B. now. I wouldn't hire him as bosun. And he was the best master of steam—*and* sail—I ever met in my life. What he knows about ships, you wouldn't believe it. But he was skipper of one of the unlucky big ones—a passenger liner. He hit an iceberg, when he was drunk, and so now he sleeps aft with the bums. Every time he's sober he sees people screaming and jumping into lifeboats and lifeboats falling into the sea, and . . . he hasn't been off the dock in years. I bet you that in ten years of going to London he's never been farther away from the East India Docks than Charlie Brown's. Sea and whisky. Whisky and sea. The trouble with the sea is that nobody ever got around to convincing it that it was supposed to be mastered. You know a lot of things about it, but the sea don't know you know it. And don't give a damn. Give her a little more right rudder, and you won't have so much steerage way trouble. She's acting up tonight.'

The deck gang's foc'sle was a new experience in living for Craig. Eight men slept in double-decked bunks—the six A.B.s and the two ordinaries. It was aired by only the starboard portholes, since it joined on the room which housed the steering-engine, and it constantly smelled like a goats' nest. There was the one small toilet-washroom, in which the toilet possessed no wooden seat. The bathing facilities were a cross-hatched wooden platform, a faucet, a bucket, and the steam-pipe that heated the contents of the bucket. You stood on the platform, so that the water could drain into a scupper, and if there was anybody hanging around, maybe you could get him to throw a bucket of water over you. The filth from the toilet went into a bilge-port over the side, and striped the ship with excrement.

Eric, gentle, blear-eyed, ruined Eric, ground his teeth constantly, fighting in his dreams the dreadful night he ploughed the iceberg with his ship. Heavy, the leading A.B., snored, sending

146

gross bubbling noises from fat pursed lips. Flatulence punctuated the otherwise odorous night, and there was always somebody getting up, going on watch, and making a noise, or coming off watch, making a noise. There was one scarred degenerate, a man with a wolf's grisly roach, who crawled into Craig's bunk one night, and made violent love-offers. Craig toppled the man out of the bunk, and hammered him to the deck. The roused foc'sle hauled Craig off the man, as Craig was trying to pound his brains out on the bumpy concrete deck. They reported to Mister Cramer that the new College Ordinary had tried to kill Able Seaman George Evans. Cramer came down on the after quarters like an angel with a flaming blade. He looked at Evans, and he looked at Craig, who was still quivering with fury and outrage.

'He tried to gouge my eyes out,' Evans whimpered, pointing at Craig. 'He's crazy.'

Cramer walked over and struck Evans a tremendous blow in the face. Evans fell and sagged against the bulkhead, his head lolling, blood trickling from his mouth. Then Cramer walked over to Craig and lifted him off the deck by his jumper. He shook him violently.

'The next time, kill him before I get here, so I can log it as an accident,' he said. To the crew: 'You bastards leave this kid alone. He's a good kid. I hear one word of any more . . .' he glared. He strode across the deck to the A.B., Heavy. 'You see anything wrong back here?' His scowling face was an inch away from Heavy's face. 'Anything wrong going on back here?'

'No, sir,' Heavy said. 'That guy there had a nightmare and fell out of his bunk. He's always having nightmares.' Mister Cramer glared again, his blue jowls bulging.

'Okay. Turn to the watch. You, Eric.' His voice softened a moment, and it was almost possible to hear an implied 'Captain Ericsen'. 'Tell me what goes on back here. Everything.'

'Yes, sir,' Eric said. 'There won't be any more trouble, sir.' He smiled, his white-haired ravaged priest's face lit momentarily with an old brave light in the skimmed-milk eyes. Cramer clapped him sharply on the shoulder, his hand lingering briefly in what might have been a tiny display of affection.

When the Mate had gone, Heavy asked: 'You guys know each other before, or are you two going fruit? You keeping the kid on ice for each other?'

Eric reached carefully into his pocket and produced a long clasp-knife. He pressed a button and the blade flicked out, like a sudden bright leaf. He tested it on his thumb.

'What was that you said?' he asked. 'I'm a little hard of hearing. I thought you asked me did I know the Mate before. Was that what you asked me?'

'Yeah,' Heavy said, eyeing the knife. 'That's what I asked.'

'We used to go to sea together,' Eric said, and put the knife back in his pocket. 'When *seamen* went to *sea*.'

Eric became dead so suddenly. It all happened in the grey, miserable, early light of near-day, a fitting time for a portion of deck-cargo of enormous logs to strike their shackles and strive to destroy the ship within, when the sea strained its mighty sinews to kill it from without. Craig had the wheel on the dying hours of the morning. The logs . . . the logs lay like sleeping serpents, leashed over the hatch-tops on the forrard well-deck.

A mighty wave appeared from nowhere, catching the ship in the slumping hollow of its last departing enemy, and surged crashingly over the starboard quarter. The sleeping serpents came alive, and the boles of towering trees writhed and slammed against their prison, emerging through the boiling foam of the slashing water like evil crocodiles.

'For Christ's sake, give her some heavy wheel and head her into the sea!' The Second Mate turned, and rapped without respect on the Captain's door. 'Captain, the deck-load's carried away!'

The Captain's sleep-scarred face plunged through the door. His grey hair stood out at wispy angles.

'Take the wheel, Small,' he said. 'Boy, look alive and roust everybody out—cooks, black gang and all! Jump! Small, hold her into the sea as best you can while we secure. Goddam no-good stevedoring . . .' He disappeared.

Craig picked his way aft in the black wild night, slipping and sliding on the wet midships deck as he crossed from wheelhouse to main deck-house . . . stumbling, his face slashed by wind and wet, his nose red and streaming, his hands already freezing, as he'd taken no time to put on his oilskins when the skipper said 'jump'.

The men came sourly awake, cursing, groping for sea-boots and watch-caps, oilskins and sweaters. The engineers, accustomed to the fiddley's warmth, acutely hating anything to do with deck, cursed loudest. When Craig stopped off to raise the steward's department, Big Smitty, the chief cook, complained sadly. His eyes rolled white in his ebony face. 'Man,' he said, 'I'se paid to cook. Ah hasn't lost nothing on dat mean, cold foredeck.'

'You better get up, anyhow,' Craig said, running out of the door. 'Cap'n said everybody turn-to to secure ship.'

He raced back and ascended the ladder to the wheel-house.

'Take her,' the Captain said. 'Small, haul your ass down there with the men and get some chain on those goddam logs before they break us to pieces. Where the hell is the Mate? Oh, he's already down there. Ordinary, head her steady into the seas. I'm going topside so I can see what's going on. And if you take one wave on the beam, just one, I'll kill you.'

So Craig was left alone with the bucking ship in his hands, while angry mountains of black water plunged like white-maned enormous stallions, obscuring the foc'sle head, streaming in tons of solidly sheeted water all the way back to the wheelhouse bulkhead, sweeping rain-coated men off unsteady perches and hurling them to the deck, drenching them as they worked to tauten the slackened chains, slamming against the bulkhead while they laboured at the rebellious turn-buckles. It was grey light now, and it seemed to Craig that the scene below was like a madhouse in a hell composed entirely of angry-boiling water and malevolent living logs.

The First Mate, Cramer, was cursing as he screamed orders over the blasting banshee voice of the wind—over the great sodden blows of noise every time the ship took a sea over the bow. The Captain, on the naked bridge, was yelling orders into a trumpet. Small, the Second Mate, was supervising a gang headed by old Eric, and the Canuck Third Mate was working the opposite side of the ship with the bosun, Svendsen, and Heavy, the big A.B.

Craig was unable to pay close attention to the chaos below in the well-deck. He stood, legs spraddled, feet braced on the chequered-wood steering mat, his eyes pinned to the bow and the waves that completely smothered it. He had given up trying to keep a compass course, but was fiercely concentrating on holding the plunging vessel head on into the towering seas. The ship bucked like a bronco, groaned amidships, and lifted her high stern out of the sea as she bent in the middle when wave changed to trough and became wave again as it passed under the ship's keel. As it lifted her stern aloft, the nose dived into the next wave, and the *Wardance* bowed her back and then seemed to be trying to stand on her head.

Holding her head was a job for two men. She was taking two slack turns of wheel on one side, so that it was necessary to spin mightily to check her starboard sway. As she beat back, it was then necessary to let the spokes whir as she recovered lost slack, checking her just in time to keep her from carrying her full weight off course. Wandering off course. Wandering off course meant waves broad on, and men swept over the side.

Bit by bit, stick by stick, the drenched, frozen-handed seamen subdued the violent thrashing logs with chain reinforcements, jury-rigged restraints that would serve a makeshift purpose until the wind dropped a mite and permanent new harnesses could be poulticed to the creaking deckload. Already there were broken bones—hands, arms, and legs, but the last turnbuckles were finally being twisted.

Eric, the old sailor, was perched atop a log, just abaft No. 1 hatch, when an enormous wave crashed over the bow, avalanching in thousands of tons over the foredeck. It swept Ericsen off his perch near the bulkhead, where he had been giving a final tautening turn to the buckle which secured the load. It buried him beneath a seething lava flow of fury, and swept him aft. As the water streamed past, spending its abated anger on the quivering length of the ship, Ericsen lay in a crumpled heap, like a wet broken doll, at the water-bubbling foot of the wheel-house ladder.

Just as suddenly, the fierce wind began to drop in the clearing dawn, and while the heaped waves still fought the ship, it would not be long before their craggy mountain-tops smoothed into even weighty hills. Craig's shoulders bore a stabbing pain between the blades, and his arms felt as if they'd been hauled loose from the sockets.

The Chief Mate and the Captain came together into the wheel-house. They were both soaked, their eyes running, their faces cherry-red from wind-buffeting. The Captain looked briefly, impersonally, at Craig, and went into his cabin.

The Mate stood to one side of the binnacle, and peered through the glass at the rolling grey hillocks of water ahead.

'You did a pretty good job of keeping her nose stuck into weather,' he said. 'Everything below's pretty well secured for the moment. You got some relief coming in a minute, after they've had coffee. Poor old Eric.'

'I couldn't see,' Craig said. 'Is he . . .'

'Yes,' the Mate bit off the word. 'He's dead. He was all broke up. Not a whole bone left. Back on course now, kid. Let her go left fifteen degrees.'

Craig spun the wheel, and the ship responded.

'Was it . . . was it *my* fault?'

'No. Christ, no. Nobody's fault. Don't let that bother you. Eric was a sailorman, doing a sailorman's job. Nobody could have handled this tub of guts any better than you did, and Eric would be the first to say so. No, it wasn't your fault. In a way I'm glad. He was used up, poor old Eric. Just as well he went this way.'

Rex Small came into the cabin, followed by an A.B.

'You're relieved,' he said to Craig. 'Go get yourself some coffee and a sleep.' Craig reported the course and gave the wheel into the A.B.'s hands. As he went out of the door, and down the ladder, Small said to him: 'You did a good job, son. We'll use you steady wheel-watch from now on.'

Craig suddenly felt very proud, proud over the sadness. Half-way down the ladder he remembered he'd forgotten his oilskins, and as he came back, he heard Small say: 'He's laid out in the sick bay. Chips is sewing up some tarpaulin. When do we deep-six the poor old bum?'

The Mate turned fiercely on the Second Mate.

'He wasn't a bum. He was a great skipper.'

'You knew him, then?'

'I knew him, all right. I was fourth mate on his first big ship. Poor sad bastard.'

The Captain made his speech to the crew, commended the body to the deep, and they tilted the lead-weighted canvas package over the side, using a table top for the sliding operation. The canvas package made a tiny splash as the waves embraced it.

Craig was standing close to the Mate. He heard him murmur: 'So long, Captain Ericsen.'

The shortage of hands from the accidents changed the physical activity of the ship. The bosun was standing regular watches now, to replace the dead Ericsen, and Craig became a part-time A.B. He stood a regular wheel-watch instead of standby—two hours on the foc'sle head as lookout, fifteen minutes for coffee, an hour-and-a-half at the wheel, fifteen minutes for coffee, two hours on the foc'sle head, fifteen minutes for coffee, an hour and forty-five minutes on the bridge, and then blessed warm relief. He was regarded with a mild new respect in the foc'sle. Seldom had a raw ordinary seaman made it to a steady chore as quartermaster so swiftly.

There was little if any camaraderie on the ship. There was a solid running battle with the belly-robber, the long-nosed steward, whose depression-weary ship was victualled with weevilly flour, whose few fresh vegetables wilted, soured, and took on all the mouldy rank smells of the cold-room. The eternal bacon was fat-striped and lank. The cold storage eggs smelled like sulphur, and tasted worse. The cake that constituted the only dessert was coarser than the cheapest bread, and the coffee seemed steeped in iron filings. And always there was the smirking Svendsen with his lifted eyebrow and drooping cigarette and his constant boring monologue about seamen being soft and the food too good for them these days. He was a shameless lickspittle before the officers, and a martinet to the men.

In a very short time Craig had toughened into a man. He had swept holds in Jacksonville and Fernandina—phosphate rock that crawled into his pores, curled his hair kinky with white thick dust. The sulphur got into everything, until the ship was yellow-coated with it and it crept into his nostrils and gritted on his teeth. The bosun, Svendsen, had taken a particular aversion to 'de collitch sailor, taking de bread out of honest seamen's mout's'. Every unsavoury chore he could lay hand to he gave Craig. Once, when the midships latrine bilges had accidentally emptied on to a garbage lighter drawn alongside in Jax, it was Craig who was sent over the side to swab up the excrement. He was set to painting over the side, also in Jax, and the bosun slyly unhitched one end of the line which held the painting-stage horizontal, and Craig went plummeting into the river. This was a big joke: 'Haw Haw.' Only a Scandinavian can really laugh: 'Haw Haw.'

When necessary, Craig fought. Sometimes he won, sometimes he lost, but always he fought. He earned a reputation as a sore-head, and the men left him alone. He had two friends only on the ship—the second mate, Small, and the officer cadet, Jerry, who was ranked deeper down the social structure than Craig. They were companions in misery, since a cadet is always regarded as a company spy, little better than a scab.

In all respects it was a hungry ship, work-crazy, seething with dissatisfaction. But it was a time when a job was a job, a meal was a meal, and a hundred men begged for any job, no matter how mean. You took the Mate's abuse—Craig saw him haul a sick sailor out of a bunk one morning when the man refused to turn to and beat him to a pulp in the foc'sle—kick him to his feet, boot him out of the door on to the deck, and then log him a day's wages. Yet to Craig the Mate was capable of occasional small kindnesses, and taught him much of seafaring, even simple navigation.

Along in the black night, as the weather calmed, the cold receded, and the cockroaches and bed-bugs came back out of the warmth of the steam-pipes and lookout was stood on the foc'sle head once more, Craig would lean on the bow apron and watch the phosphorescent water splitting past the bow, and wonder, with vast homesickness and young desperation, where he was headed. To kill time he sang to himself. To kill time he attempted to make up songs. He continued to ration his thinking to the pleasant things he remembered. And somehow, the bleak, black time passed, the brass ship's bell gonged the hour, and the relief climbed up the ladder to set him momentarily free to sleep in his rumpled coarse blue sheets.

They had come by day past Wales, its emerald hills studded with castles and softly splotched by cultivation, past the Isle of Man, and were headed into the Mersey for Liver-bloody-pool, as the old hands called it. It was night now and Craig stood in the star-crusted darkness and the water made pleasant little chuckling sounds as it slipped smoothly past the bow. The lights of Liverpool were a twinkling promise, a far piece away. On the bridge, the mate of the watch tapped eight bells. Craig turned, repeated the bells on the bronze gong, and checked the running lights—red for port, green for starboard.

He looked at Liverpool's lights, faint in the foggy distance, and saw the Cinnamon Isles, Far Samarkand, Old Cathay—the Taj Mahal and the temples of Greece and the Pyramids, standing sternly safe above the shifting desert. Zanzibar lay straight ahead. He had safely passed the perils of Scylla and Charybdis—no siren song had lured him from his course. The Captain Admiral of the Ocean Sea had made his first landfall.

He turned to the bridge.

'Lights are bright, Sir,' he sang out, loud and clear. Then he turned again towards the oncoming lights of Liverpool. He rested his chin on his hands and looked into the soft distance.

'Very bright, Sir,' he said.

152

BOOK TWO

BOOK TWO

1

CRAIG PRICE rang for his secretary. The phone was onyx-on-ivory.

'Bring me another dozen copies of *Fortune*,' he said to a buxom zebra-dyed-blonde of indeterminate years. 'And another dozen *Times*, too. We got some company at the house for the week-end, and they might like . . .' He stopped, suddenly. 'People keep taking them away, and . . . call my wife, will you, Connie, and tell her I'll stay here in town tonight and drive down tomorrow. I got some people to see—you know, those Dallas people. I don't know why you can't talk money outside of El Morocco, but they seem to expect it. Better ring Twenty One and tell Grace we'll be a mob for dinner. Upstairs is better, I reckon. I won't have to kiss so many beautiful women I don't like.' He grinned. 'As a matter of fact, better reserve me the little room—not the Hunt, the little one behind it, the one with the piano. Texans can get noisy. I'd rather have the noise contained.'

'I thought they were wonderful pieces, Mr. Price,' the secretary said. 'I get a real charge—I am dreadfully thrilled, I mean—working for a man that everybody's suddenly discovered. I mean, *Time* cover, *Newsweek* cover, *Life* and now the *Fortune* bit—piece, I mean. It's almost like I was famous too, just being around you. Anything else?'

'Yeah.' Craig Price grinned again. 'Let's go some place and get laid.'

'Oh, *you*.' Connie the secretary bridled. 'You kill me, Mr. Price.'

'One day I may. Meantime, Toots, roll back that swinging door and pour me a bourbon and branch. Reading this crap makes me thirsty.'

Craig Price dismissed his secretary by dropping his eyes to a sheaf of papers—oil-drilling reports, stock-market reports, textile production reports, little pieces of paper with figures which meant something in later terms of bread and cheese, women and whisky, taxes and the avoidance thereof. At least one report on what could possibly be an oil-land play meant a fishing trip. Another meant that he had better fly over to check on his house in Villefranche, or it would begin to assume an aspect of non-deductibility as business expense.

He picked up a letter whose head bore the title:

'CRAIG PRICE,
Oil Producer,
Price Building,
New York 20.'

It was subheaded:

'B. C. STONE,
General Superintendent,
Production Department.'

He lit a cigarette, and read, moving his lips as if to memorize:

'Dear Skipper: How are you and the Yankees making it? Thought you might be interested in how things are running along down on the farm. Don't know if you can get the details from the drilling report or not.

'We finally qualified the Johnston and it is in the Unit with 195 feet credit. We didn't have to perforate any more than originally. . . . The Wahahrockah No. 3 had a channel job on the oil pay at 6,000. The gas sand above it broke in. Squeezed and got a good job, as it tested 16 bbls. per hour with AGR of 355-1 after the squeeze. . . . Down on the Five-Bar No. 3 we really cut some sands. Am completing it in the 6875' sand for a new field discovery with 140 bbls. allowable and dual in the 7,000' pay. Still have the sopic sand at 6450' which was assigned a new field discovery on March 4th by Camellia and the new gas sand at 5900'. So, am skidding 50' south of No. 3 and drilling No. 4 to take in these two pays with a dual. Nice thing is the No. 3 is higher than the No. 1 and No. 2 on the south end of the lease and when those wells are exhausted in the other producing sands we can open them up on the north end of the lease. That 7,000 sand perforated 6999-7000, only one foot open, flowed 165 bbls. on a $\frac{7}{64}$" choke. You just can't beat those Seco sands in my book. We are going to have to drill offsets to the Five-Bar to the east on the Scherffius, but won't get to that before you get back. . . . Guess you noticed the DST on the Texas Gulf State at 10,795 to 10,866'. I direct your attention to the BHP of 5590 No., both initial and final. This is a Penn. sand in the Bend. What happened was they didn't find it in the cuttings but the well kicked after a trip, which accounts for the long interval of the test. Looks to me like the same situation we have in the Gallstone down on the coast—high pressure, low income. It is a sand and should respond to some degree to frac. . . . The A.P. well up on the lake is a gas well, not too hot—couple of million, although it ran low as expected. . . . The Lone Star took a build-up test last week on the Neff-Godrey and the results were lush. Hopped right against the peg the minute it was shut in. Apparently no indication of draw down whatever. . . . Am preparing to frac a couple on the old MacIntyre lease south of the Julep "A". They are on the same contour on which we have obtained the best results on the Webb and Julep "B". Slid in a little electric vacuum pump on the Julep "B" and Webb and tied in the Sara Jones with a response of five bbls. per day on each of these three leases. Am carrying ten points. . . . The United finally started taking gas from the Marberry, but Coastal is not yet hooked up on the Adams—insists it is a matter of right-of-way trouble. . . . Oh yeah, they refused us a New Field Discovery on the Helen Borden, but nevertheless the Sinclair is laying over with an 8″ line (yes, I said an 8″) to handle that 330,000 feet per day. Don't understand why, but that's what they are doing. Expect to have it running by May 15th. . . . The pipe stocks are just a nub.

'We are having almost the same kind of spring we did last year. It has rained almost every day for the past week. Some flooding south of town and in the White Rock area. We are about 8 inches ahead of normal, the weather reports advise. Big front moved into Oklahoma last night, and it was down to 30 degrees in the northern part of the state—which takes out the fruit crop, as usual.

'Now for the gutter gossip . . . Charlie is tossing a big reception and dinner at the Petroleum Club on May 1st for the Officers and Board. I plan to attend to uphold the family honour.

'Cantreel announced yesterday to run for the Senate against Monroe, as expected. I suspect you already knew or anticipated this. The forces have joined for the fray—to the joy of the party faithfuls. May the money flow unrestrained!

'Stay out of the fleshpots, and keep that rotary turning to the right.

'Sincerely,
'Ben.'

Craig slapped the report down on his desk.

'Goddam Greeks,' he muttered. 'They do it with ships. I have to do it with depletion. What I need is a Panamanian flag and a tame prince.'

He picked up a column written by a female syndicated writer, which his secretary had clipped for his attention. The hen-columnist was being bitter about ladders in her nylons. Craig Price smiled as he read a diatribe about nylon stockings at present not being so serviceable as during the war. Then he glanced negligently at a blue-bound sheaf of statements labelled 'Price Mills, Inc.'

'Oh, how the money rolls in,' he murmured. 'Run, little stocking, wherever you are, and I will have a word with the engineers. Maybe they can build in a few extra potential ladders.'

His secretary had returned with the drink, which she had built at a bar concealed by a sliding walnut panel in the enormous office. He looked up, and accepted the drink, dark-red in a squat, heavy square-faced Steuben glass.

'Thanks.' He sipped the drink and waved the oil superintendent's report at her. 'Not bad. Not bad at all. You read these things? You read everything else I get, including the personals. You understand what the hell he's talking about?'

Miss Cornelia Woods squirmed.

'Ye . . . Well, no. Not really. It sounds like a lot of Latin to me. All I know it has something to do with getting oil out of the ground.'

Craig winked.

'I got, as they say, news for you, baby. Neither do I. It's all a lot of Texas talk and it makes me nervous. That's why Mr. Benjamin Stone earns his salary—*and* bonus. Mr. Stone *knows* about getting oil out of the ground.'

'Pardon me if I'm rude, but I never understand you, Mr. Price. I mean, why isn't Mr. Stone *you*? I mean, if he knows so much?'

'Mr. Stone isn't me because Mr. Stone doesn't know about drilling that twelve per cent interest speculation money downtown, from the money-changers in the temple. That's why Mr. Stone ain't me.' Craig slapped the report on top of a sheaf of papers, and picked up the lady writer's syndicated column. He pointed it at his secretary, almost accusingly.

'How many pairs of socks you ruin a week, doll?'

The secretary looked briefly at her fat legs, glossy in nylon, and then again at her boss.

'About one,' she said. 'It wasn't so bad before everybody started wearing girdles.' She stopped as if she had said a bad word. 'I mean there's a strain with the garters. I mean with the supporters anchored to the . . . I mean . . .'

'I know what you mean, sweetie,' Craig Price said. 'I sure do know what you mean. Ain't it a shame about girls and boys? Get lost now, I got some thinking to do. And tell the outside guys to send you a dozen pairs a week.'

'How long—how many weeks, Mr. Price?'

'Perpetually. For ever. We'll bury you free on the lone prairee. Give the *Times* and the *Fortunes* to Jazzbo, and tell him I'll want him at seven. Blow, Connie. I just got hit by an idea. Leave the bar open. Whisky helps me think.'

2

CRAIG PRICE sipped his drink and lit a cigarette. He slipped a copy of *Time* from under the mound of reports. The cover was surrealistic in the best Salvador Dali manner. The centrepiece

158

was a spider mounted on a web of oil rigs, factories, and long lithe legs of women, against a blue sky encrusted with dollar signs as stars. The face of the spider in the centre of the web was that of Craig Price, and the title was simply '*Legman Price*'.

The face was battered, and it was a face that Craig Price had seen for some thirty years in his shaving mirror, since he had started shaving at the age of twelve. Time and other people's fists had eroded it somewhat. Drink had cross-hatched veins on the cheeks, producing a false glow of health. On the right side of the twice-broken nose a small raised purple welt, called a 'devil's claw' by the belly specialists at the Albuquerque clinic, bespoke a discouraged liver.

The forehead was unduly steep, the brown hair curly, and you could not see the bald spot on the back of the head. The ears were large, not seriously outflanged, but big enough to warrant a carefully feathered Hollywood haircut as camouflage. The cheekbones were Indian-high and the right cheek carried a livid scar. His left eyebrow, permanently lifted in a sardonic quirk, showed a straight white pathway through the brow, ending where his hair began. Underneath the broken nose a white-threaded moustache accented an upper lip which was harshly straight, the lower lip redly full and softly sensuous. The chin was a rock, beginning to encumber itself with flesh. The curving nostrils flared deeply as he read.

The eyes appeared to operate separately from the face. The artist had caught them well. They leaped, they suicidally plunged, from the solid brown-stone of the face. The colour of the eyes was warm gold-flecked brown, and the whites owned that bluish pigmentation babies sometimes show. But the eyes were as curiously cold as frosted glass, as uncommunicative as the man hidden behind the eyes.

'Price never attends a directors' meeting,' somebody had said, for the benefit of *Time*. 'He just sends his eyes.'

The line made him smile. He got up, a square-shouldered, faintly bow-legged figure, a man whose walk combined built-in slouch with swagger, and sauntered over to the bar. He never hurried any more. He had hurried enough.

'Young man in a hurry,' *Time* had called him. But that was yesterday. Not now. He didn't have to hurry any more. He had, old Sam Price might have said, done arrived to where he was at.

Unlike most men of middle years, Craig Price had fined down. The ribbed blue suit (Brioni, Rome) rode him casually, exaggerating the breadth of shoulder and slimness of hips. The black silk tie (Sulka, Paris), snugged under a soft white collar (Brioni again), carried an opal pin (Sydney, Australia) hedged by diamonds. The cuff-links (Neiman-Marcus, Dallas) were gold Buddhas contemplating black sapphire navels. The black calf shoes were Peal (London) and they had twenty-four companions stoutly treed in each of three houses. The underwear was silk, and the shorts bore the same monogram the shirt carried—C.P. Initials figured largely in Craig Price's life, *Time* pointed out. His one child was also C.P.—Carol Price. The boy that they had buried was graven in marble as Craig Price II.

'He was called,' *Time* said, 'Cash Price when he started but he doesn't care much for Cash Price any more. He prefers Collateral Price these days.'

Craig Price smiled at himself in the mirrored wall of the built-in bar, as he tipped another slug of Jack Daniels Sour Mash into a fresh glass (he had a horror, *Time* said, of using the same glass twice) and said aloud:

'The hell I do.'

'He looks rather like a combination of Glenn McCarthy and Clark Gable,' *Time* said, 'with McCarthy's broken nose and Gable's ears. But he thinks of himself more as Rhett Butler as played by Clark Gable, and confines his resemblance to McCarthy only in oil manipulation and construction. McCarthy built the Shamrock Hotel in Houston: Price built the Price Building in Manhattan. Each man, after his own fashion, created his own pyramid in his own honour. Like most modern Pharaohs, they both owed money on their monuments.'

'It's *my* goddam pyramid,' Craig Price said. 'Except for the mortgage. At least it's got my name on it, and is that any worse than Rockefeller Plaza?' He went back to his desk and looked around happily at his office. 'And old Jack never had one like this one, the stingy old bastard.' Craig Price liked to talk aloud to himself. It helped him clear his thought processes, as a solid sneeze clarifies a chronic sinus.

'It was', *Time* said, 'a mighty office for a mighty man.' It was approximately forty by thirty feet, with a twenty-foot ceiling. One wall was golden-grey field-stone, housing a six-foot-high fireplace, with a swinging hob and a wrought-iron Spanish fire-basket with standing, ecclesiastically-headed dog-irons, in which a eucalyptus-log fire always snapped and crackled, breathing oily perfume over the room. 'Even in summer,' *Time* said, 'when New York swelters, C.P. keeps a roaring blaze, counterbalanced by stepped-up air-conditioning. Psychiatrists explain this as a form of contrapyrophobia dating back to early insecurity.'

'Contrapyrophobia my aching ass,' Craig Price said. 'I just like the look and smell and sound of a fire. Trouble with this town, they got to dig up a motive for everything. You lay a broad, you're in love with your mother.'

The office occupied the top of a forty-storey building in mid-Manhattan, just off Fifth. It was flanked by a series of functional outer offices, for hired help in the various Price enterprises—textiles, oil, advertising, administration. Thirty-nine more storeys contained the offices of people whose names Craig Price knew only from the rental lists. One half of Price Enterprises' floor was devoted to work by people whose names Craig Price did know. The other half was Craig's home-from-home. A suite of two bedrooms and one vast living-room opened to the left, as you stood at the office bar. This was secret country. Mrs. Craig Price had never seen the interior, as she had never visited the office.

'He has a passion for privacy,' *Time* said. 'He is a devoted husband and father on week-ends, but he is harshly obstinate about separating his family from his business life. Psychologists would also mine interesting ore from the exclusion of his wife from his city affairs. He is rarely seen with his wife in public, and she is forbidden entry to his office.'

'It's *my* office,' Craig Price said. He put his feet up on the desk, half-closed his eyes, and lit a cigarette with a gold Dunhill lighter which bore the initials '*C.P.*' in diamonds. '*I* made it. It belongs to me—not to nobody else.'

The desk measured roughly ten by five feet, and it was remarkably uncluttered. The huge brass rings on the drawers suggested a macabre joke. They had been bought from a coffin manufacturer.

Time said: 'The desk, which resembles a giant's coffin, lends really a rather cheerful note to a room which otherwise looks like an elephants' graveyard, or a cemetery for moribund animals of all species. Two African water buffalo glower at a visitor over the massive fireplace.'

'Inaccurate bastards,' Craig mumbled, re-reading *Time*, and re-grumbling. 'The *Newsweek* guy got it right. Anybody ought to know that a Cape buffalo ain't even remotely related to a bloody water buffalo.'

'The funereal air,' *Time* said, 'is further supported by the enormous vase of calla lilies on the desk's corner, and the lamp-base is a replica of a burial urn. Mr. Price laughs at intimations of morbidness, and says that like any sane man, he is practising for the future. "They won't have to cart me off," he explains. "They can just bury me in the desk and burn down the building. I already sent my own flowers. Call it a modern *suttee*, and regard my work as an Indian widow." '

'And it won't be the first house I ever set fire to, either,' Craig said.

'Mr. Price was regarded as more than mildly eccentric when he rebought his grandfather's old house in New Truro, North Carolina, completely redecorated it, and then summoned officials of the company which insured the house against fire, the village's fire department, and the local constabulary.

' "Is there any law that says a man may not destroy his own property, if he claims no financial gain, and is not a menace to

161

the community?'' he asked the assemblage. The firemen consulted hastily with the police, who talked again to the insurance broker. It did not seem to come under the head of arson, any more than a normal burning of trash, with proper supervision. Craig Price signed an absolution with the insurance people, and commanded the fire department to stand by.

' "Now, Gentlemen," he said, "we will proceed to burn some trash." He beckoned to the Negro boy who customarily drives his Rolls-Royce, and is a constant companion.

' "Jazzbo," he said, "did you fix the house? All the kerosene and cotton batting?''

' "Yassuh, Mistah Craig," Jazzbo Newton said, teeth gleaming in a shiny ebony face. "I sho' is done make us a monstuh bonfiah. Jes' lak de ol' days. Dis fat-pine house go up lak a bomb!''

'Price walked inside the house. He returned unhurried. In a moment, a fat greasy tongue of smoke licked out of the open windows. In a short moment more, huge flames seized the sky as the entire building caught, crackled, and roared into holocaust. In less than an hour, the roof had caved, and the house was a smouldering heap of fragrant ash. Price had watched it burn, with a curious air of satisfaction. When the roof fell, he turned to his Negro chauffeur.

' "Let's go invade the North again, Jazzbo," he said. "Gentlemen, I thank you for your kind co-operation." As he rolled off in the big English limousine, the police and fire department were still unclear as to whether Craig Price had committed a felony. But the town's hospital received a cheque for $10,000 the next morning.'

'Christ, they never get anything right,' Craig Price said. 'It took that house all of three hours to burn.

'Crap. All a lot of bloody crap,' Craig said as he read. 'None of these research bastards ever heard of a Viking's funeral. None of them ever even read *Beau Geste*. I sound like some kind of freak. It was *my* house. If I wanted to burn it down I wanted to burn it down.'

He touched a nipple on a fat bosom of buttons. Music came gently into the room. It was Lee Wiley singing the last bars of 'Moonstruck'.

Craig Price smiled. Lee Wiley always made him smile, as Satch made him happy, as the rollicking right hand of Bushkin stroked him, as Sinatra's rendering of the old Glen Gray specialities soothed him. This one had changed now to an old Ray Noble: 'The Very Thought of You.'

'Oh God,' he murmured. 'I wonder what ever *did* happen to Mary Frances? I wonder if she's fat, I wonder if she's happy, I wonder if she'd like it here? I ought to go back and dig up some of these people if I ever get the time.'

Time. Time said that three walls of Craig Price's office were

162

sheathed in Japanese grey-green grass-cloth, supported a Masai shield in red, white and black heraldic design, and were accented by an impala, a sable antelope, a greater kudu, a lesser kudu, a waterbuck, two Grant's gazelles and two mammoth elephant tusks leaning in a lazy ivory circle against the fireplace —an elephant's foot blooming with philodendron, a rhino horn shield for a paper-weight.

'A double-headed West Coast African god of fertility occupies the place of honour over C.P.'s desk,' *Time* said. Craig got up and walked over to the evilly smiling ebony figure—a figure which adorned his stationery and was wrought in iron on his gates. He patted the flat-headed, cheerful little ebony man who surmounted the long-faced, serious gentleman who depended from the cheerful little man's chin, by way of bracketed arms, akimbo.

'Keep working, Pop,' he said. 'We been lucky so far.'

He paced the huge room, nervously, and paused to flick an imaginary speck of dust from a long rank of books that lined, in five tiers, two of the walls. He pulled out a raw-leather volume on bullfighting and stroked it lovingly, holding it to his nose to smell the musty hide. He passed his hands as gently as a man might caress a woman over a mouldered, complete set of Somerset Maugham.

'Price reads enormously,' *Time* said. 'But he only reads old friends. He has no interest in new books. Anything later than *Turning Wheels* by Stuart Cloete is young Africa hat to C.P. He claims he doesn't wish to make any new acquaintances. As an impoverished youngster, he once went without lunch for a year to buy a matched set of Somerset Maugham. He believes that Mark Twain's *Life on the Mississippi* is the best book ever written by an American, since it duplicates the first part of *Huckleberry Finn*, a view shared by another of his literary heroes, Ernest Hemingway.

'In C.P.'s library, the *Wanderings of an Elephant Hunter* by a man named Karamoja Bell jostles the ponderings of Charles Fort and the collected essays of the early Westbrook Pegler and O. Henry, sharing space with Rudyard Kipling and Philip Wylie. He prefers Marjorie Kinnan Rawlings to Françoise Sagan, and believes William Faulkner to be unreadable. His tastes in music, also, reflect a desire to return to his youth. He likes no music written more recently than 1935.'

Mood Indigo breathed peace into the room. This one was a Sinatra.

'Why the hell should I *want* to hear anything more recent than 'thirty-five?' Craig Price asked himself. 'They going to improve on the Duke? You read this stuff and it makes you sound like a fag or something.' He paused in his pacing in front of the bar, and fixed himself another drink. 'There hasn't been any music, except Loesser, since I was a kid. When Porter and Gershwin and Yellen

163

and Ager and Arlen and those guys slowed down from the early pace, the stuff quit sounding like music and just made noise. Hammerstein sounds like somebody telling you to get up in the morning and Rodgers has been lost in the forest without Hart. Balls. Up to now the piece says I like fires, books and music. And I suppose, dames, but we haven't got to that yet. Yet.'

The door opened. His secretary, Connie, entered with a sheaf of opened mail.

'This just came,' she said. 'Some of it looks urgent, Mr. Price. Would you look at it, please?'

'I thought I told you to get lost. I'm thinking.' He frowned.

'But, Mr. Price, there's a thing here about that Canadian oil thing, and . . .' She paused in frustration, her hands almost supplicating.

'Look, doll-baby. Take it to bed with you. Lose it. Burn it. Shove it . . . Go *away*, sweetie. Mail is something I don't need today. The next thing I know you'll be following me into the bathroom with it. Now go home and dream a virginal dream, but leave me the bloody hell alone!'

'Yes, sir. Will I leave it in the basket?'

'Send it to my mother. She's in heaven, or someplace, but blow! I'm sorry, kid. I'll see you in the morning and we'll work like a couple of little Trojans, all right? I'll be a real good boy, and you can tell everybody how sweet I am, even if I'm ugly and talk dirty. Now for Christ's sake scram and leave me be.'

'Y . . . yes, sir, Mr. Price. Good night. Do you still want Jazzbo at seven?'

'I *told* you I wanted him at seven. For the love of God, have you got to have it in triplicate?'

'No, sir. Good night, sir.' Miss Woods, first-named Cornelia, called Connie, made a kind of curtsy as she backed out of the room, passing the correspondence helplessly from hand to hand. Her frustrated semi-virginal face wore a look of hopeless defeat. Her dumpy figure sagged.

'Girdles,' Craig muttered. 'If I ever saw a bloomer girl, this model of efficiency qualifies. Good God, bloomers, Pink bloomers, and the black ones the girls used to play basketball in. I'd forgotten all about bloomers.'

Craig shook his head, as a groggy fighter shakes his head to clear away the impact of a punch.

'I better watch myself,' he said. 'Next thing you know, I'll be going back to college to find the lost romance. Fitzgerald had a patent on the lost years. Lemme see. Five now, see the people at eight . . .'

He picked up the phone. This was a private dial telephone, separate from the network of organization 'yes-Mr. Price' efficiency. It buzzed a moment. Then a lazy low voice, with a cool arrogance which had started as a product of an unhappy marriage in Long Island, and had been refined by Miss Merriwether's expensive school for products of unhappy marriages in Long Island; which had been rendered loftily elegant by time in grade in Gstaad, Switzerland, and fashioned drawly by a London season and a flock of late nights in St. Germain-des-Prés; it was softly hoarse, purposefully ungrammatical.

'Mrs. Roosevelt?' Craig asked.

'Who else?' she said. 'You were expecting maybe Mrs. Eisenhower?'

'Not me,' Craig replied. 'You decent? I got a client.'

'Decent? *Me*? Never me. Naked as a jaybird. Thought you might call about Indonesia. Can I come over the way I am or are you commuting these days?' There was a low chuckle. 'You want to borrow some money for a cab, or what is all this undue attention about?'

'I flunked the Eagle Scout test, and my world is in shreds and tatters, not to mention ruins,' Craig said. 'Did you ever wear bloomers when you were a little girl? I *have* to know this.'

Indignation travelled the wire.

'*Bloomers*? Me, in bloomers? I never had on a pair of pants in my life. Think of all that time taking them off and putting them on, and all the fellows talking it up about how little Lola was the only girl in town with trousers. Do you think Lola would be a nice name for me? I'm tired of Sue.'

'I think Lola would be a lovely name for you, with or without pants.'

'What are you up to, Bud? You getting fresh or something?'

'Yes. Very.'

'All right. I give up. What time, and whose mother am I tonight? And if you say "Whistler's" I'll set a trap for you with ground glass. Remember Blue-Eyed Claude, the cabin-boy? We need a change of scene. And script.'

'I thought tonight you'd be a charming girl from Dal-ass Tex-ass. Kin you-all talk Tex-ass talk?'

'You watch your language, Hopalong, or I'll wash out your mouth with water. Certainly I can talk Tex-ass talk. *Tex. Ass.* There, see how easy it is? Man, I'm flat ready to ride. Ah got blue-bonnets in mah little ol' bloodshot eyes and the Cipango club is all rodded up, waiting for mah pretty cotton-pickin'-presence. What ever became of Neiman-Marcus?'

'Don't you go low-talkin' the New Alamo or I'll wash *your* mouth out with Scotch.'

'*Scotch*. That old mess? And furthermore, freyund, this telephone is gittin' to be too small for both of us. Isn't this a damn-fool way to talk when all you want to say is . . .'

'I love you?'

'Yes. Why do we do it?'

'I'm shy.' Craig smiled into the mouthpiece. 'Took cryin'-down with the shies. Maybe if you put your clothes on I might whip over before you get to be somebody's mother from Dal-ass, Tex-ass. What was the name again?'

'Lola. Don't bother to knock. Just lean them mighty shoulders on the door and batter it down, boy. What kind of diamonds do I wear later, clean or dirty?'

'Clean. The new ones. These are Texans, not Europeans. You ought to know better than to ask a question like that. And *not* the one in the navel. We are not entertaining Middle-Eastern oil people. You know something?'

'Mmm. *That* I do. And so do I, too, you. And when I think about how much, I always either have to make a lot of uneasy bad jokes or cry.'

'I don't cry much,' Craig Price said. 'Except out of gratitude for the good God's blessings. Consider I dropped a tear just now. And get those men out of your room, hear, or I'll have a fit.'

'Have it. Who needs you?'

'You. Now. In a hurry.'

'You may be right, Junior. Pardon me while I don't dress. More?'

'It's a long way, and my horse is foundered, but I'll make it, I'll make it. Mirages or not. But God, darling, please do try that new-fangled penicillin, because I get so tired of . . . I got all I can do to handle this cold.'

'Oh, shut up and hurry.' A kiss breezed sweetly over the line before the phone clicked.

3

CRAIG woke to the usual gag alarm at seven-thirty. It was a trick alarm. A friend had had it specially recorded. A soft sexy female voice began: 'Please get up, please wake up, Mr. Price, darling Mr. Price, please wake up, wake up, wake up, please wake up, dear Mr. Price . . .' The voice faded. Then, a man's gravelled whiskeyed voice said harshly: 'Get up, you bum, and make us a buck, put on ya pants and make us a buck! Make us a buck!'

He switched it off irritably, rolled over in bed, and buried his head under the pillow. He'd grab another hour, he thought blearily, before he had to face the grisly ordeal of dressing plus the inevitability of a weekend at home. Home. That would be Maybelle and Carol and whatever guests Maybelle would have accumulated to make the weekend a very jolly country fiesta. He groaned, and sought sleep, but his skin prickled and the sheets kept twisting in sweated shrouds, and finally he cursed and got up. He went to the bathroom, stuck out his tongue, grimaced, and turned on the shower. Before he entered the stall he rang a bell. He was soaping himself and feeling a mite less like death when there was a knock on the bathroom door. He'd go hide some place over the weekend and let the guests read *Time* and *Fortune*. If they already hadn't.

Without turning down the volume of the sheeting water, he yelled: 'Bring me a bloody mary! Bring me two bloody marys! And some coffee. Hurry!'

'Dat's all, Boss?'

'That's all. Shake it up. I'm dying.'

Mr. Jazzbo Newton, aged approximately twenty-five; colour, black; occupation, unclassified; shook his head and proceeded in a canter to the office bar, from which he produced the necessary ingredients for modern therapeutic handling of hangovers.

'Boss mus' is had hissef' a evenin',' Jazzbo said, and shook another gill of Worcester sauce into the Waring blender. 'He don' soun' real happy. I guess he got dem bad-time Sattidy morning blues.'

Jazzbo was about the size of a big jockey, or a small genie. His black face was round, his teeth a startling white. He had a tiny thread of black moustache, barely visible against the polished ebony of his face. He was wearing a chauffeur's cap bent into an Air Force's block, and while his suit was a decent grey whipcord, his tie a sedate black, on Jazzbo the garments assumed a completely zootish air. There was a hacking-jacket slant to the tails of his coat, and his ticket pocket also slanted. The sedate black tie was lumped in a Windsor knot. Jazzbo was sharp.

He picked up the glass mixer and one glass, noticed with profound self-approval that the mixture foamed stiffly, pinkly at the top, and proceeded to the bedroom.

'Where you want it, boss? In there or in here?'

'In there. I'll be finished shaving in a minute.'

'Yassuh. What us wearin'?'

'City clothes. Blue, grey, whatever. White shirt.'

'Check. I put de medicine on de bureau.'

Craig rinsed his face of the last of the lather, and dried himself. He reached into a squat, silver-and-crystal pillbox, and chose two red vitamin pills the size of peanuts, made a face and swallowed them. He gave his body a final buffing with an enormous white towel, monogrammed *cP*, and reached into a drawer for a pair of white silk shorts, also bearing the same initials—little 'c', big 'P'.

He combed his hair, and reached for a bottle of mouthwash. He swished the liquid around in his mouth, and spat. Blood tinged the greenish foam of the chlorophyll mixture. Craig lifted a corner of his mouth and observed that the gums were bleeding around his incisors. He turned on the ice-water tap, bent over the basin, and let the freezing water run through his mouth until the last traces of blood had disappeared.

'Better see a dentist,' he muttered, as he walked into the bedroom.

Jazzbo was sitting in one of the big wing chairs that flanked the enormous bed. He did not bother to get up, but waved a hand at the dresser.

'Yo' painkilluh, suh,' he said, and managed to bow without rising. 'I done had mine.'

Craig downed a glass of the vodka-tomato juice, shuddered, poured another glass, lit a cigarette, and sat down on the bed.

'Man, I don't feel good,' he said.

'Man, I doesn't feel good neither,' Jazzbo replied. He rolled his eyes upward. 'I think I is usin' too much gun,' and snickered.

Craig was shrugging into a shirt.

'What do you mean, too much gun?'

'Like you say 'bout what dem white hunters say when you in Africa dat time. I is usin' too much gun for dat Harlem game. When dey sees dat great big Rolls-Royce, dey jes' naturally flips. It takin' all de sport outa huntin'. I thinks maybe us better buy us one of dem little foreign cars, so's I knows whether de gals courtin' de car or me.' He chuckled. 'Man, it shootin' fish, jes' plain shootin' fish. How your huntin' comin' along, Boss?' Innocently. 'Seem lak you hunt from taxis mostly dese days.'

'Don't worry about my hunting. I do all right even without a Rolls. Incidentally, who belongs to that car, anyhow? I never seem to get to use it except when you don't need it.'

'Why, Boss.' Jazzbo's shrug was elaborate. 'You knows anything I got belong to you.'

Craig grinned, knotting his tie. There was never another like Jazzbo Newton, whom he had raised from a pup. Sometimes Craig wondered who was raising whom. Jazzbo managed to combine all services as chauffeur, valet, confidant, bartender, court-jester and friend with just the right degree of casual insolence—no, the word was not *insolence*, Jazz was never insolent—*equality*, I suppose, Craig thought. He kids the pants off me and I like it. I might be Craig Price, tycoon, to the world, but to Jazz I ain't nobody but Mistah Craig, home-folks. Well and good.

'You ain't goin' to eat no breakfast, Boss? Maybe a aig or somethin'?'

'No. I still got the butterflies. Where's the coffee?' He slipped into his coat.

'Out on de bar.'

'The coffee'll do me for right now. I got a little bit of last minute stuff to clear up before we go to the country. Come

168

back in about an hour. I'd like to get out pretty early, and there'll be traffic.'

'Yassuh.' Jazzbo opened the door. 'See you later.'

Craig sipped his coffee, lit another cigarette, and picked up a sheaf of papers. He felt a lot better. He liked working in the morning, early, before the office help arrived at nine. He did his best work in the morning, his best thinking at night. Quite often he would fall asleep in front of the fire, with the Hi-Fi playing softly, to awaken at three or four o'clock in the morning, like as not with a problem partially solved. He was a man who needed very little sleep, and he had never lost the habit of early rising, even after a tough night out on the town.

Such as last night. Poor Sue. Flanked on all sides by extravagantly admiring Texans, rendered excessively attentive by bourbon-and-branch, and excessively drunk later, from the champagne they had consumed at El Morocco. Sue had danced gallantly with all of them, and you would have thought she was having the time of her life. Only once did she complain mildly, after Craig had done his host's duty by the other girls, and they slipped into a slow foxtrot.

'My God, my feet,' she whispered into his ear. 'That little fat one wears his spurs, I swear, when he does a rumba. I'm one big saddle-sore from my sacroiliac to what's left of my toes.'

'You're doing fine,' Craig said. 'They think you're wonderful. And they're pretty nice people, at that. They just get a little exuberant when they fly in to catch the city sights. But they're all more or less partners of mine, and they give me the entire state when I'm in Houston or Dallas. I have to squire 'em around a little bit.'

'I know, sweetie. Don't worry about Susie. I have suffered more for worse causes. I have experienced the joys of an English hunt-ball, at a time when the samba had just percolated through the Yorkshire-pudding Iron Curtain. By comparison these hearty Texas types are Fred Astaires. Come on, we better go back to the table.'

That was one of the nicer things of all the nice things about this new girl, with whom he was certain he was in love. She *fitted*. Of course they'd been to bed, had lunched and dined together nearly every day for the last two weeks, but he would have been hesitant about asking most women he knew to suffer through a flock of Texans determined to crisp the town to a cinder before they climbed in their big aeroplanes and flew back to their oil and cattle....

This morning, Craig was having trouble with his work. He couldn't fasten his brain to figures and reports. It was a relief when nine o'clock rolled around and Jazzbo knocked and opened the door.

169

'Dey's a mess o' mail out there on Miss Connie's desk. You want me to open it up for you?'

'No. Leave it. It'll keep until Monday. Come on, let's go. Stop at Constance Spry's on the way out and we'll send a lady some posies.'

'Why don't I just call up and order 'em?'

'Nope. This is for a special lady. I want to pick them out myself. Let's roll. We might as well go home and get it over with.'

'Yassuh.' Jazzbo held the door open, and they got into Craig's private elevator. Outside the canopy stood an enormous black Rolls-Royce. Jazzbo reached the rear door, elbowing the doorman aside.

'No,' Craig said. 'I'll ride up front with you. It's a real nice day, ain't it?'

Jazzbo slanted his eyes sidewise.

'Fo' a man who was dyin' of a hangover a few minutes ago, you sho' has improved fast. You ain't in love or nothing like that, Boss? Not *again*?'

'Maybe. Here's the flowershop. Don't get out. I won't be a minute...'

4

THE big black Rolls turned off the main road just this side of Suffern and meandered half a dozen miles along a side road until it approached a great grey-stone wall with an ornate iron gate. One of the gate pillars bore the sign '*Price. Private.*'

Jazzbo Newton touched an electronic device on the dashboard of the Rolls and the gate swung easily inward. For an eighth of a mile the car crunched over a white gravel road through a dense forest of birch and oak and pine until it crossed a rustic bridge. On the left glimmered an enormous swimming pool, surrounded by flagged patio and a barbecue apparatus the size of a chalet.

The house stared arrogantly over a green sweep of approximately seven acres of close-clipped lawn dotted with carefully, artistically isolated groves of birch and oak and maple and dogwood. The long yellow gravel drive was flower-rimmed— pink geraniums now—Craig noted.

The house itself was Georgian, an immense pile of weathered red brick, which overlooked the grey-stone stables, the stables as big as an ordinary hotel. Bright-plumed pheasants walked condescendingly across the grass, giving the impression they owned it, and further, paid taxes on it.

Jazzbo braked the Rolls in front of the enormous brick house.

Craig viewed its white—but small pillared—doorway almost as a sightseer. The stone stables were way over there—stables without horses, and plenty of room for the groom, Craig thought bitterly. Sixty-eight acres and nothing to do with any of them.

'Does anybody ever swim in the pools?' He turned querulously to Jazzbo, as the car crunched to a halt on the swishing gravel. There were three pools, one outside a summer-house, on the main-house level, another half-way down a hill of sweeping green, the other big one at the very bottom of the long slope that vanished into heavy forest. The two upper pools were empty of water.

'Us ain' make much use of Number One and Two, Boss,' Jazzbo said. 'But Number Three been getting plenty trade from Miss Carol and she friends. It far enough away from de main house where de noise don't fret Miss Maybelle. What dese people you bought de house from *need* with three swimmin' pools, anyhow? Seem lak one enough satisfy anybody. And dem stable. Seem lak a stable ought to have maybe leas' one horse. Dem stable better'n mos' old-timey big plantation houses down South and nothing *happen* in dem stable. Dey don't even smell lak horses no more. I knows, because I lives in de groom's room, and it bigger'n de Waldorf. Dat is,' Jazzbo said, 'I lives dere when we is home.'

'I don't know,' Craig said wearily. 'Maybe this was another way to live, Jazz, like in the old days down South. But to me it just looks like so many English barns all scrambled together. Look, we'll be going back to town early tomorrow afternoon. Stand by, boy. It might be easier to make a late trip tomorrow night though, instead of bucking the afternoon traffic. Depends on the company. Tell the cook to feed you and stand by—in the groom's room, groom.' His smile was mirthless. 'While you're at it, groom, you might curry this noble steed here,' he patted the Rolls. 'It ain't up to its usual gleaming standard.'

Craig walked into the hallway, looked to the left at the old English, oaken-and-red-leather study, which was actually the drinking room, and turned right to an enormously high-beamed living-room bisected sharply in the middle by two back-to-back flowered chintz-covered divans and two mahogany tables. Huge fireplaces stood at each end of the room, whose leaded windows faced the long sweep down the sloping hill into the forest which rose steeply on the other side, past the big swimming-pool.

He swept his eyes round the room and considered that if you added up all the tables, chairs, sofas, banquettes and footstools you could very possibly hold a political convention in it without undue crowding, or the possibility of having it called a smoke-filled room.

The pictures which hung on the wall were expensive, if not attractive, because Maybelle had been in one of her doggedly

171

English phases in which anything short of Sir Joshua Reynolds or Gainsborough was regarded as radical.

There were bedrooms upstairs—how many Craig was never quite sure, since he had never counted them. And the dining-room, he thought, in all its elegance of dark wainscoting and grey-flowered paper, and crystal chandeliers, would be a simply marvellous place to commit suicide, but Maybelle had seen the house and loved it and wanted it and it seemed a cheap price to pay to keep Maybelle quiet.

Craig looked around him with the strange sense of unreality, as a tourist would feel in the Taj Mahal, perhaps. He yanked petulantly at a bell-pull. The butler emerged from a pantry, wiping his hands on his striped working apron.

'Oh, it's you, Mr. Price. I didn't hear the car. And how are we today?' He managed a smirk.

Craig looked at him with distaste. This was another of Maybelle's ideas—an English butler who looked as if he might have been written by P. G. Wodehouse and played by Arthur Treacher. Craig had wanted a Negro, or at least a Jap. This man, Denson, with his long pasty horse face, had a decided faculty for spoiling his appetite.

'I'm all right. Where the hell is everybody? I thought we had some people in for the week-end?'

'Madame and your guests went over to the club. Miss Carol is playing tennis, I believe. They are expecting you for lunch.'

'That's jolly decent of them,' Craig said, inadvertently mimicking the butler. 'Do you suppose you might find me a drink? Perhaps a gin-and-tonic?'

'Immediately, sir.' When the butler returned he was wearing a white jacket. 'There you are, sir. Would you be wanting to change?'

Craig took a pull at the glass.

'Take this back and put some gin in it. I'm already weaned. Yes, I suppose so.' Denson returned with the fortified drink.

'What shall I tell your—uh—man?' Denson always hesitated when the subject of Jazzbo came into play, as if he had suddenly sniffed an unpleasant odour.

'Nothing. I can still find my own pants. Don't let me keep you from your work. I'll just sit here and finish my drink before I dress.'

Denson disappeared, and Craig thought, suddenly, now why the hell do I have to justify what I do to that fugitive from a Noel Coward one-act play? Holding his drink, he walked up the broad softly-carpeted stairs to his room. It was a good room, he thought, very possibly because I held out for my own plebeian taste and avoided the chintz. It's the only room in the house that's fit to live in. He placed his drink on a small blond-wood bar, built into one corner, and walked over to the enormous cedar-lined clothes press which covered two sides of his dressing-room. He slid back a panel and chose a pair of grey flannel slacks, a brown Harris tweed jacket, a light yellow silk turtle-neck sweater and a pair of brown buck ankle boots. He stripped off the blue double-breasted town suit, kicked his black calf shoes half-way across the room, and flung the city clothes across the foot of the enormous four-postered bed. He walked into a vast yellow-tiled bathroom, washed his face and hands, and ran a comb through his hair, forgetting that he had yet to pull on the turtle-neck and would have to comb it all over again.

When he had dressed he inspected himself in a full-length mirror, and grimaced.

'Behold the country gentleman, all got up in his rusticating togs,' he said aloud. 'I must remember to buy myself a stout blackthorn stick for when I'm pottering around the petunias or primulas or whatever it is you do to justify the smell of manure and the gardening shears. I wonder who these people will be? And wherever does Maybelle find them?'

He looked at the soft green of the walls and the faintly breeze-stirring yellow curtains, brushed his eyes briefly over the half-dozen good water colours that relieved the green—one was a Dufy—and finished his drink before heading down the stairs. He opened the door and walked out on to the lawn just as a white Cadillac convertible, spilling young people, drew up. They all looked vaguely alike, except for the hair. The boys wore crew-cuts and jerseys and shorts, and the girls wore pony-tails and jerseys and shorts. They all look so goddam *healthy*, Craig thought, as he raised a casual hand.

'Hi, fellows,' he said. 'Come in and play with me. I'm lone-some.'

'Who's that?' a very pretty, bright-faced girl of about seven-teen said. 'Oh, I know. As I live and breathe, it's Daddy, fresh back from a whaling voyage. I thought he looked familiar. Hi, Pop. Buy us a drink? We're dying of thirst from all this strength-through-joy jive. You know most of the kids. Come on in, people.'

'You're all so big,' Craig said to nobody in particular. 'One minute you're babies and the next minute I'm building drinks for you. What'll it be, straight red-eye or will you settle for absinthe?'

'Coke, please, Mr. Price.' Little blonde dumpling. Cute.

'Do you have any ginger beer, sir?' Redheaded crew-cut.

'Seven-Up for me, please, Mr. Price.' Skinny brunette with ragged bangs.

'Gin-and-tonic.' No *please*. No *sir*.

Craig looked up. It was Carol.

'Gin-and-tonic?' His voice held mild surprise as he looked at his daughter.

173

'Sure. That's what *you're* having, isn't it?' The voice had flattened, hardened.

'Of course. But I was trying to save up on the gin. It's a habit I picked up from the butler. Here you are. Chin-chin.'

'Cheers.' Carol took a long pull at her drink and barely avoided choking. 'Dee-licious. Somebody put on the noise machine. You going to ask us to lunch, Mr. Price?'

'A pleasure, my pretty maid. That's if the grown folks will have us.'

Carol Price looked at her father with something nigh unto pity. For Christ-sake quit being coy, the look said, and act your age. And now that you've done your youthful parent act, why don't you just buzz off and leave us to our own devices?

Craig refilled his glass.

'If you people will excuse me . . .' his voice was absorbed by the blast that came from the Hi-Fi set. Nobody seemed to notice when he left.

Craig Price's daughter resembled him to a startling degree. The eyes were his—brown, goldflecked, level, and long lashed. She was a big girl, tall and already very well developed. Her nose was short and straight, the brown hair naturally curly. The long legs which sprouted from the white short-shorts were deeply tanned. A sprinkling of summer freckles starred her nose and cheeks. She was wearing a blue sweater and a vivid shade of lipstick. There was a decided belligerence to her chin, which again was a replica of her father's. The nostrils of the short nose had a tendency to flare.

She's going to be a damned good-looking woman, a dish, he thought, even if she does look like me. She's already losing the baby fat. Very good legs. And stacked, too. Now what kind of way is that to think about your own daughter? Except that I barely know the child, what with governesses and schools and me in town all the time. I don't think she likes me very much, either. How about that gin-and-tonic thing when all the other kids were having soft stuff? She knew damned well I wouldn't make a scene. Kids . . .

But I was drinking hard stuff and going to sea at that age, he thought. I had been with a woman. I was a man grown. Wonder if things have changed, or if this bunch has been indulged too much. They all go steady, and I reckon that old biology still works the way it used to. I wonder if Carol . . .

He bit off the thought with distaste. Mary Frances came briefly back to haunt him. She was only sixteen when . . .

What I don't understand about these kids is they're all so . . . so dull. The boys, I mean. The girls are little wives already. They drive the guys around like a herd of bloody sheep. They all go steady, and they plan for the future, and they sort of assume there'll be a future and a certain number of kids and the right mortage and a place in papa's business after they've finished school and done their military training. They start up with a life of infinite boredom and the only way it can get is worse . . . Oh, well. Never mind. Here comes Maybelle and her week-enders. I wish to God I was back in town, already. Wonder what Susan's doing right now . . .

'Hello, there,' he said, as a big Buick station wagon pulled up behind the kids' Cadillac. 'I was beginning to wonder if I was going to have to spend the weekend with the juvenile delinquents, except I'm a little old for the jitterbug or jive or whatever they call it . . .'

Maybelle crawled out from behind the wheel and reached her plump cheek towards him for a kiss. She was wearing a short pleated white flannel skirt, with white wool bobby sox and stout golfing shoes, and a pastel-pink angora sweater. Her blond hair was done up in some sort of bright bandanna arrangement. She looked flushed from wind and sun and quite pretty, Craig thought. Except for the eyes. The light-blue eyes always gave her away. They were a mite too prominent, a mite too moisty-misty. Sort of pickled eyes. Like onions in a Gibson.

'How was town?' And without waiting for an answer. 'This is my husband. Craig, this is Dr. and Mrs. Newsome, remember, I told you I met them in Mexico last year? Harry and Joan, my husband, Craig. And of course you remember Don and Betty Blackwell from Bermuda.'

Oh, God, Craig thought. Do I *not*. This is going to be a real beaut. They're the kind of people who talk *at* you.

'Hello,' he said, shaking hands with both men. 'Nice you could come. How was the golf?'

'We only played nine holes,' Harry Newsome said. 'I've got a kink in my swing. I can't understand it. I never used to have a kink in my swing. I seem to top everything when I'm not slicing. Or I'm undercutting when I'm not hooking. I guess it's got to be a kink in my swing.'

Man's sure got a kink in his swing, all right, Craig thought. Three strikes is out.

'You-all come in and I'll rustle us up a drink.' He shooed them into the door. 'I'll chase the kids out of the bar and into the rumpus department. How about some mint juleps, or some-thing long with gin? It's a hot day.'

'I'd love a julep,' Joan Newsome said. She was a big, busty, ash-blonde woman with a face which seemed a little too large for the chassis. She was wearing grey Bermuda shorts, and Craig mentally computed her stern at about six axe-handles across the beam.

'A gin-and-tonic for me, please,' Betty Blackwell said. 'Don-isn't-drinking-are-you-darling.' It was a command. 'You re-member the doctor said . . .'

'Oh, damn the doctor,' Don Blackwell said. 'Just because his wife drinks too much he puts everybody off the booze. He can't smoke so he puts everybody off cigars. I'll have a slug of bourbon, straight.' He leered at Craig, and made a defiant face at his wife. They both looked almost exactly alike. Fat, red-faced, her hair dyed in streaks, his white and absurdly crew-cut. Almost shaven.

'Julep,' Harry Newsome cackled. 'I don't have to chop anybody open until Monday. Let's live it up, for Monday they die.'

Funny, Craig thought. Nearly all the doctors I know look like undertakers—either tall, skinny ones, like this jerk here, or the short round jolly ones who rub their hands and call you 'old man', and laugh heartily after they've just threatened you with a carcinoma for your own good. The only one I ever liked was the one I couldn't see clearly that night, or maybe that one psychiatrist with the big laugh.

'You, sweetie?' to Maybelle.

'Just a little sherry, please, darling. You know I'm sort of taking it easy.'

Just a little sherry, darling, Craig's mind mimicked. *Just a little sherry*. My how we have come on, especially when we all know we will have a tiny little straight slug when we go to the can, and another while we dress, and then we will suddenly decide that we've had enough sherry and switch over to martinis and then, oh boy! Or rather, oh, brother.

5

CRAIG had dispersed the children, and the adults were sitting around on the red-leather chairs. The golfers had changed only from spikes to loafers.

'What's up for tonight?' Craig asked Maybelle, who was sipping decorously from her sherry glass. She had tarried overlong in the little girls' room—she always called it the little girls' room—and seemed visibly brighter as a result of washing her hands.

'Surprise,' she said. 'We're having a party in the stables. An old-fashioned party. Costumes. That's after the cook-out, of course. You're the chef for tonight. Jazzbo can help you. Then I've got an old-fashioned square-dance band coming. The idea is that we're all going to be hicks, like in North Carolina. You know those Jackson White people—the sort of half-Indian morons? They have the most entrancing repertoire of old folk music. They're divine.'

Well, damn me, Craig thought. Entrancing. Divine. My Maybelle has come a long way from Kensington. Old Man

176

Grimes must be twirling in his tomb. She's almost lost her Southern accent except when she's drunk, and then the repressed Scarlet O'Hara busts out all over. It's going to be a long, long evening. Entrancing repertoire or no entrancing repertoire.

'I hope you don't expect me to wear a chef's cap and an apron with a lot of witty mottoes on it, dear,' he said mildly to Maybelle. 'And do we really have to do costumes? To go to a square-dance, I mean? It isn't New Year's Eve or anything like that.'

'But I've got a lovely one all picked out for you,' Maybelle almost pouted. 'The girls and I have been working like mad. And half the county is coming. We haven't had a big party in just ages. But ages, lovie.'

'All right. How about it, folks? Should we have another drink now and go in to lunch? Or is it out to lunch? The kids want to stay, Maybelle. I don't suppose Carol was joking when she asked . . .'

'Inside-outside. Buffet, cold. Vichyssois (she pronounced it VitchySwah) and some ham and cold chicken and all like that. Salad and stuff. Fill your plate and pick your seat. I'm depending on you to stuff us tonight, Craig, and I want to leave plenty of room. Craig is the most wonderful cook,' she said to the guests. 'He adores to cook, don't you, darling?'

'Sure. I think it's divine. Let's see—three juleps if you count mine, one gin-and, a straight slug for Don, and some more sherry for Maybelle. That right?'

'That sherry's too sweet,' Maybelle said. 'Would you mind making me a martini on the rocks, dear?' She turned to the guests. 'I find that if I leave the ice *in* I don't get so tight so fast.'

'Off and running,' Craig muttered, as he turned back to the bar.

'What, dear?'

'Nothing. You want an onion or an olive?'

'Give me an onion.'

'Right.' He handed her the drink. 'I better go down to the play-room and tell the kids about lunch. Half an hour?'

'Yes. That'll give us time for a dividend. He's such a wonderful father,' Maybelle said in a loud whisper as Craig left. 'Carol adores him. The one regret of his life is that we couldn't have more children, but we lost the first one and after Carol, my health . . .'

'An amazing man, your husband,' Dr. Newsome said. 'Plain as an old shoe. Nobody would ever suspect the things he's done, and so young, too. I was reading that article in *Time*. It must be fascinating to be married to a man like that.'

'It is. Of course he's so busy I don't see a lot of him. He's got so much to do, so many places to go.'

'Does he play golf?' Harry Newsome asked. 'I'd like to shoot another round with a real good golfer tomorrow and see if we can't find out about this kink in my swing.'

'No, he doesn't play. Never seems to have the time.'

'What does a man like your husband do to relax?' Joan Newsome asked. 'He can't work *all* the time.'

'He hunts and fishes a little. Once he went to Africa and sometimes he goes to Canada or down South. We have a place in Carolina. Just a little shack where he goes to play poker with the boys. I think they probably drink more than they hunt but-you-know-men.' The three women momentarily excluded the two men from this intimate feminine secret, while Maybelle was thinking: *I know men, all right, and I know what the bastard does to relax, and I wonder who it is this time? As if it made any difference any more. This boy don't need no golf to relax. He's a natural-born relaxer from Relaxersville.*

'Have you heard the fast one about the horse with the green legs?' Don Blackwell said. 'Stop me if you have, but it seems there was this livery stable boy and he was in love with . . .'

'I think I'll have another little mart,' Maybelle said. 'Go on with the story, Don, while I . . . Can I help anybody else?'

'Let me.' Harry Newsome got up and collected the glasses.

Betty Blackwell had said nothing so far. She merely extended her pewter mug for another julep. Men liked Betty Blackwell. She kept her mouth shut except when she was drinking, and then opened it only to receive another swallow.

'We'll be having lunch soon,' Craig said to Carol, as he called her aside from the dancers in the rumpus room. 'About twenty minutes. It's a buffet. Tell your friends if they want to wash up or something . . .'

'Is it all right if we grab some food and just take it down by the pool?'

'Sure. I suppose so. Do you find us that repulsive?'

'Not you. I guess you'd be a very nice guy once a fellow got to know you. But those creeps mother hauls in . . . Do you know what you're in for tonight?'

'I've had the word. It seems we have a cook-out—my God, what an awful word—and I've got to play Boy Scout and burn off my eyebrows messing up a lot of good meat. Then it appears we are going to have a fine sort of Elsa Maxwell-type hillbilly party, where everybody comes as a moron in overalls, or something. To match the orchestra. Where in the hell does your mother come up with these ideas? I imagine we'll be fifty strong, at least.'

'She comes up with these ideas because she's bored out here on this dude ranch for about six days a week. So am I. You'd be too if you ever came home.'

'Listen, missie, watch your language. I didn't care too much for that crack you made earlier about me home from the whaling voyage. And I didn't care too much for that grandstand play you made about the gin-and-tonic when all of your friends were having Cokes and stuff. You're still a kid, and . . .'

'How would you know?' Carol's gaze was level, and her tone impersonal, as to a stranger. 'How would you know about me?'

'Look, it's lunch time,' Craig said, tamping down his anger at the tone. 'I've got to get back to the guests. Round up your friends and let's eat. Eat where you want to, but get cracking.'

'Yes, Master.' Carol dropped her eyes in mock humility. 'Don't beat me until after we've fed. Have fun with Mother's friends, like you always do. Give 'em the old Price charm.' She turned abruptly and started away. She stopped and spoke shortly over her shoulder. 'Why didn't you hand this one to Uncle Jimmy to handle for you, like always?'

Craig stood, dully pondering, as she swept away.

After lunch, the guests went to bed for a short siesta, and Carol and her gang dispersed on odd errands of their own. Carol muttered something about a movie and left in the station wagon, in a whish of scorched gravel. The kids had been very well-contained during lunch. They had filled their plates from the buffet, and had departed *en masse* for the willow-shaded upper poolside, where they sat cross-legged and ate dedicatedly. With the meal they drank mostly milk or Coke. Craig noticed that Carol and one of the boys had made a point of coming back for a bottle of beer. The kids had carried a little transistor radio to the poolside and seemed engrossed with whatever was coming in. Craig couldn't hear, but it was possibly the ball game.

After the guests had gone upstairs Craig said to Maybelle:

'You sleepy?'

'No. You?'

'Nunhuh. Let's go in the bar and have a brandy and talk a little bit.'

'Talk about what?' Hostilely. 'What would we have to talk about?'

'You loaded?' He almost said 'again'.

'No more than usual. If you drink, you get drunk. I had a couple of little marts is all. Let's go siddown and have a B. and B.'

'All right.' He touched her arm to steer her into the bar and she shrugged angrily away.

'I can make it on my own, loverman,' she said. She flung herself into a leather chair, stretched her legs, and held out her hand for the brandy and benedictine. 'What'd you have in mind to talk about?'

'Nothing very much in particular. I just wanted to talk to you away from those . . . those *people*.'

'What's wrong with those *people*, you call them? They're good as any of your people. They're all the people I know, people

179

like those people. Gimme a cigarette.' Craig flipped a pack at her lap. She caught it by squeezing her knees together.

'Thanks. You wouldn't have a match?' She ignored the lighter at her elbow. Craig started to say, for Godsake, why don't you use the lighter and there're cigarettes in that box, but got up instead, and held his lighter to her cigarette.

'Why can't we have one week-end out here alone, you and Carol and me?' his voice was almost pleading. 'Why do we always have to have some goddam barbecue or masquerade party and the place overrun with a lot of people I don't know and don't want to know? Why? Tell me why?'

Maybelle shook her head with mock puzzlement.

'Why? *You* tell *me* why. I get used to people. I get used to people instead of husbands. It seems natural to have the people around so everybody can see I actually got a husband, I suppose. When the husband shows up. I got to show off the great man to prove I got a husband. Otherwise Carol hasn't got a father. A girl gets used to surrounding herself with a crowd when she's got a long-distance husband. I guess it spills over into the week-end. Carol travels in a pack, too. Everybody travels in a pack or hadn't you noticed?'

She held out her glass. Craig got up and filled it quarter-way up with brandy and benedictine.

'I'd take it easy, sweetie. We got this party tonight. *Your* party.'

'Don't you worry your head about *my* party. I'll be all right. It'll be a good party. They're always good parties. You just take care of the hosting and don't be so goddamned condescending to everybody. Try to make out like you ain't bored to death. Give 'em the old Price charm.' She fumbled in the pack for another cigarette, and this time she used the lighter.

'That's the second time I've heard that one,' Craig said. 'Carol just dropped it on me, too. You-all rehearsing, or what?'

'Do you understand maybe you ain't very real to us peasants out here? You understand that mostly all we know about you is what we read in the papers? You understand that when you do come home it's kind of supposed to be like a royal visit? Everything's got to stop because the great man's home? You understand that maybe being with the great man could make me and Carol both nervous? And do you understand that I'm your wife and might like to get laid once in a while? Not every night, mind you, but like maybe twice a year or something like that. After all, we *did* start out that way. . . . I think I'll go take a nap. Like to come help me take it?' The last words were swift as a suddenly drawn pistol.

'Sure, sweetie. Sure.' What a he-whore I am, Craig thought. 'Let's go upstairs and catch a little shut-eye so we can hit the party with a fresh face. Come on.'

Maybelle sprang out of her chair, and her face was livid.

'Well, I don't want to go to bed with you, see! I don't ever want to go to bed with you again, you with your mind saying poor old Maybelle, I better give her a lay, it'll shut her up, and then I won't have to do it again any more for a while until she gets out of hand again! You bastard! You dirty bastard!'

She ran out of the room, sobbing, and a great crash of door echoed behind her.

Craig felt very tired.

'I bet it's going to be a lovely party,' he murmured. 'Just dandy. Costumes and all. I think I'll go have a word with Jazzbo, and maybe call Sue. I can use a little peace and calm.'

He walked over the rolling lawns to the stables, which were in a state of utter confusion. Jazzbo, the butler, the butler's wife, and some people Craig didn't recognize were all stripped to shirt sleeves. They were moving things, taking things out, bringing things in, erecting things, sweeping things, hanging things.

'Hi, Boss,' Jazzbo said. 'Looks like us gonna have us a ball. One of them old-time hoedowns. Mr. Denson there, he done put me in charge of the stage-direction. He say I the only one here apt to know what's goin' on. Also, I hears you is de cook. Kin you cook, Boss?' Jazzbo grinned malevolently.

'Shut up. We got a phone in here? An outside phone, I mean?'

'Sho. Up in mah quarters. Up in de groom's room. How you think I does all mah social business wid Harlem?'

'I think I'll go use it. No, don't bother to show me the way. I was inside of this palace once before when I bought the joint and the agent insisted. This ain't a bad lay-out, Jazz. Homey. Maybe I might move in with you some day.'

'You is welcome, Boss. Excuse me, I got to go see about de charcoal and de roastin' ears and chickens. Man, you gonna have your hands full tonight.'

'Yeah.' Craig walked up the stairs to the groom's quarters, and located a phone by an unmade bed he assumed was Jazzbo's. He turned down the blaring radio, checked a notebook and dialled a number. The voice on the other end was astringently cool.

'Yes.'

'Me.'

The voice warmed.

'Well, hello, Beauregard. This is Scarlett. Over to you, Mac.'

'Nothing in particular except I'm going out of my mind. I am in the camp of the Philistines and I needed something to save my sanity. I figured you were the best bet, so I sneaked out to the slave quarters and sent up a smoke signal. How do you feel?'

'I feel lovely. Thanks for the beautiful flowers. How did you know I'm mad for yellow roses? You don't sound so good. What are they doing to you out there on them manicured acres?'

181

'Worse than being staked out on an anthill. We got four creeps with kinks in their swings for house guests, and . . '.

'Kinks in their *what*?'

'Swings. Don't interrupt. Then we are having a cook-out party for fifty people, and I'm the chef. And then we are having a square-dance in the stables and everybody has to come as L'il Abner and Daisy Mae. Apart from that I was never lovelier.'

'Anything else?'

'Not much. My daughter has taken up insolence and gin simultaneously. She seems well acquainted with both. I know what Columbus said when he finally shoved off in the *Santa Maria*.'

'Be a nice man and tell me what Columbus said when he shoved off on the *Santa Maria*.'

'He said, quote, last night seems a mighty far piece away That's what he said, so he did.'

'One of them kissin'-and-tellin' fellers. Apart from Columbus, what did you have on your mind?'

'Nothing. Nothing at all. I just wanted to reassure myself that you were real. I wanted a breath of air. I wanted to hear you say anything. I wanted to hear you tell me that we are going to Cuba together. I wanted to hear you . . .'

Silence.

'I just wanted to hear you because I love you.'

'Oh, damn you. When can you get loose?'

'I guess it'll have to be tomorrow. I thought I might come in late tonight, but I have a feeling I will get very drunk in my capacity as chef-host. Can I come to your house sort of four-ish tomorrow? I will need a power of calm. Could you fix us a sandwich and we just sit around, maybe?'

'I'll have on my best toreador pants. The ones with the easy zippers. The tea-kettle will be singing on the hob. Come a-running. Sunday's always dull in New York, and a girl has to do the best she can. You know something?'

'What sort of something?'

'I'm putting you up for the Nobel Prize. That performance last night, after we decanted the Texans, was a spectacular thing. I think I'll do like the Coca-Cola people and have you bottled. How'd you feel this morning?'

'I quote my late grandfather,' Craig chuckled. 'I felt just exactly like a man that'd been slept with.'

'Well, now you know it. You better rush off and put on your chef's cap. Enough of this kind of talk will have me out on the streets accosting sailors.'

'What are you doing tonight while I suffer?'

'I'm suffering right with you, lieutenant. I am having dinner with my ex-in-laws. You ain't all alone in your misery. I figure if my man can take it, so can I.'

'Okay, we're both in this together. I'll see you tomorrow afternoon.'

'Right. Watch the grass-stains. I hear some of those country folk are murderous after the ninth martini.' She blew him a kiss. 'Bye.'

Craig surprised himself in a broad smile. He hadn't known her long but somehow Sue brightened his world. Even on this short acquaintance, a word with her could make his heart laugh. She affected him like the music that came constantly from his Hi-Fi set. All the old stuff that didn't bother you. Stuff as silly as . . .

Pearl Bailey was singing it now on Jazzbo's tuned-down radio. '*She's got, eyes of blue, I never cared for eyes of blue, but she's got, eyes of blue, and that's my weakness now* . . .' Silly damn song. No sillier than '*P.S. I Love You*', which is exactly how he felt about Mrs. Susan Strong; divorcée, five feet eight in her stockings, weight 140 when she was thin, long-thighed, neat-headed, brunette, corn-flower eyes, and easy. But *easy*. Sweet Sue.

'Brother,' he said, cradling the phone. '*Easy*. If all the women of the world learned that one word, there wouldn't be any divorces. There wouldn't be any lovelorn columns. There wouldn't be any suicides. *Easy*.'

He walked slowly back to the main house, feeling now that he might be able to face the evening.

6

It's got to end, Craig thought. *It's got to end sometime. Some hour soon they just got to go home. The war looked endless but it had to end. I imagine the prisoners of war just ignored the present and concentrated on V-J Day. Four o'clock Sunday—today—that's my V-J Day. That's my S-Day. My Sue Day. Meanwhile, there is always whisky.*

The stables were hung with Japanese lanterns, why, God knows. Approximately forty people survived from the original fifty. Half were dressed rustically in blue jeans and bandannas. Most were barefoot. Craig had discarded the kind of frayed straw hat that customarily belongs to cherished dray-horses, and had conveniently lost the clay pipe which accompanied his costume; old-fashioned overalls, chewed off at the knee, and held by a single gallus over the shoulders.

The Jackson White square-dance combination had departed, and had been replaced by a coloured rock-and-roll outfit from Harlem, which Jazzbo had hastily imported via the telephones and which had arrived all muggled-up in two Carey Cadillacs.

183

The smoke was thick, the noise deafening, but the party was a screeching success. One former pince-nez-ed editor of a come-to-Jesus magazine had already thrown up twice, once on his dancing partner. The doctor—what was his name, Newsome—was sleeping peacefully in one of the formerly aseptically clean stalls. Humour was rampant. Some people had misunderstood the rustic motif. One couple had come as a horse. Naturally the husband had arrived accoutred as the horse's rear. There was a Satan, a gaucho, and an Antony-and-Cleopatra team. There was a Caesar, a Hawaiian—not too bad, the Hawaiian, especially when you considered that she was espoused to the most fashionable Episcopalian clergyman in New York. His Highship better watch that 'un, Craig thought. She's taken three strolls around the property already, and her lipstick is beginning to blur. Funny how lipstick blurs more on the upper lip than on the lower.

Maybelle was having a ball. Right now she was got up in a Daisy Mae, one shoulder bare, and I hope to God she's got ample pants on under that fringe of skirt, Craig thought. She was doing a frenzied Charleston with—who?—oh, that fellow Blackwell, the one from Bermuda, the one who looks exactly like his wife. Whatever happened to her? Haven't seen her in a couple of hours.

Now Maybelle was doing the Black Bottom, rapidly changing hands to weaving crouched knees. She's all right as long as she keeps on to the Charleston and the Black Bottom, Craig reflected, standing in a shadow. It's when she hits the hula stage that the clothes begin to fly.

He looked around him at the harmonizers, the dancers, the amorous fumblers, and suddenly felt a need for air. He wasn't drunk, himself, although being subject to the pool-side barbecue through a peonage-process of serving fifty enormous steaks, a gross ton of sweet corn, fifty Rock Cornish hens and six or seven bales of mixed salad could be wearing on a man.

'Why is it?' he asked Jazzbo, his sweating assistant, 'why is it that the host has got to be the cook? Why is it that the host is never allowed to have any fun at a party?'

'Dat a easy one. You's de boss. Everybody know de boss got to suffer, jes' show he de boss. You doesn't work a crick in yo' back, you ain't democratic.'

'Well, then,' Craig said. 'I ain't democratic. I resign. You handle this modern miracle of stainless steel and electricity. Tote dat bale, boy, because de Massa Boss is going to refugee to the bathroom for a few minutes and wash that charcoal smell right out of his hair.'

Now he was standing on the dew-wet grass, as velvety as a putting green under his feet, sniffing at the stars and feeling the breeze touch his face with gently familiar fingers. The noise of the rock-and-roll band was sufficiently far behind him to blur, rather than to smite, inside his ears. He walked along the rim of the forest, idly musing, happy momentarily to be free of the contrived gaiety, trying to rid himself of the memory of one matron who had come in bra-and-diaper as a baby, another as a harem dancer, still another as Mammy Yokum, striped stockings, high button shoes, pipe and all.

'Having fun, Daddy dear?'

He turned swiftly and saw his daughter in the moonlight. She had evidently followed him.

'Why aren't you at the party?'

'Why aren't *you*?' Again the tone that had annoyed him earlier in the day.

'I'm too old for fun-and-games,' he said. 'I take my square-dances neat. Or did, anyhow. You forget I'm a country boy, not a city-slicker having fun on a Saturday night. Rich man's fun. To me it ain't funny.'

'Maybe I'm a country girl.' She matched his voice. 'To me it ain't funny, either. Especially dear mother doing the Charleston. She hasn't got the fanny for it.'

'Where are your friends?'

'Most of them got bored and took off for a beer joint in town. You don't understand, maybe. They get a steady diet of this. Every Saturday night is grown-ups' dress-up night. They get a little sick of seeing their noble parents necking in the garden. They get a little sick of being treated as "equals".' Her voice was bitter. 'They get more than a little sick of seeing the messes their parents are. For God's sake, why don't you people act your age?'

'Take it easy, chum. You don't have to be shrill. How come you're wearing a skirt and a sweater? How come you're not in a costume,' he gestured disparagingly at his overalls, 'like every-body else?'

'I'm ashamed. Look at you. *Look* at you. A clown. Why do you let her make a clown out of you? How can you stand her, her and her . . . How *can* you?' Her voice stamped its foot.

'Look.' Craig rested a light hand on Carol's shoulder. 'You wouldn't say you were going through a phase of something, or maybe somebody? We're a little silly, mind you, but not much sillier than you kids. Everybody's pretty silly, young or old. Take it easy.'

'You don't have the faintest goddam idea what I'm talking about, do you?'

'No. I don't. And I don't think you do either. And it's not necessary to swear.'

Carol shrugged pitifully, expressing depthless despair at the hopeless ignorance of parents.

'I don't think it ever occurred to you that kids want to be proud of parents—that they want to be kids *with* parents, not

185

equals? Not social equals with a bunch of grown-ups who are trying to be kids when they get loaded? Did it ever occur to any of you that maybe kids want to be kids for as long as they can? And that they want some dignity out of their parents? And that maybe a girl wants her daddy to come home once in a while and be nice to her mother? And that mothers shouldn't get drunk and do the Charleston? And that fathers shouldn't spend half their time in El Morocco with some—' She stopped. 'I'm sorry.'

Craig's voice was almost pleadingly patient.

'Sweetie. I work. I'm a busy man. I can't stand a whole lot of this. Your mother and I—we . . . we . . .' He shrugged, imitating his daughter. 'I don't know how to say it. Not to my child, I don't know how to say it.'

'Why don't you get a divorce?' She hurled the question at him. 'Why do you keep up this stupid game of being married? Why? Why?'

'This really isn't much of your business, Carol. You're seventeen years old. You've got about everything in the world a girl could ask . . .' Craig's voice trailed.

'Yes, I've got everything in the world a girl could ask for. I've got a drunken clown of a mother and a father who makes all the magazine covers when he isn't making all the models that go on the magazine covers. Yes, I've got . . .'

'I think that'll be quite enough for now,' Craig said sharply. 'Either go back to the party or go to bed. You're being very rude and besides you don't know what you're talking about.'

'You don't like it straight. None of you like it straight. None of you want to hear the truth. Well, I'm not going back to the party, and I'm not going to bed, either! Good night, Little Abner! Go help Daisy Mae do the Charleston!'

She turned and streaked across the lawn. In a few seconds Craig heard the grind of gears and the rush of rubber on the drive. The tyres shrieked as she took the turn below the swimming pool, and he saw her headlights probing the rise as the car headed towards the main road.

'The joys of parenthood,' Craig said, half-aloud: 'What do I do now, seize a cop and holler "Follow that car"? I doubt she'll break her neck. They never seem to. What really do you suppose she has on her mind? Boy trouble? The crew-cut redhead? Or the lean blond tennisy one? I don't know. Back to the scene of revel, I suppose, and count the corpses.'

He lit a cigarette and strolled slowly back to the stables, which appeared to be trembling with light and music.

This might be quite a nice place, he mused, if you could keep the people off it.

7

THE people had finally gone, thank God, and he had steered Maybelle painfully to her bedroom. He undressed her and more or less toppled her into bed, avoiding her mumbled declarations of love, her fumbling, embarrassing attempts at allure. He snapped off the light, and waited quietly by the door until he heard a steady, bubbling snore.

Then he crossed the sleeping wing and gently opened the door to Carol's room. He flicked the light switch. No Carol. He went downstairs and looked in the living-rooms, the bar, the play-room below. No Carol. As a final check, he walked across the rolling lawns to the stables. The downstairs lights were out, now, but a light still showed in the groom's room.

'Jazzbo!' Craig hissed. 'You still awake?'

'Yassuh. Be right down.'

Jazzbo came down, dressed in robe and pyjamas, turning on lights as he came. The last lights illuminated the smoke-smelling, alcohol-reeking, flower-wilting, dirty-glassed interior of the stable. The Japanese lanterns, smoked and scorched, swung drunkenly. The floors were mica-ed with shards of broken glassware.

'Man, we had us a ball,' Jazzbo said. 'I never see so many people get so drunk. Dat Mistah Doctuh Somebody, he was de las' word. I sho hate to get sick Monday so he got to cut me. . . . What's de mattuh, Boss? How come you look like dat?'

'I'm worried about Carol. She got mad at me about something and went off. She hasn't come back. I just came down here to finish checking. Get dressed and break out the car. We better go look for her.'

'Boss, you outa your min'? *Where* you gonna look for Miss Carol dis time o' night? Whichaway you gon' drive, look for Miss Carol dis time o' night? She all right, Boss. She probably still beatin' it up wid dem udder kids. You know how dem kids be, Boss. Don't worry. Dey all pretty good kids. Talk a lot and don't do nothin'. Here lemme fix you a drink. If dem people left anything to fix.'

Jazzbo bustled around the portable bar and found an un-cracked bottle.

'You doesn't mind, I think I have one wid you,' he said, and poured two stout slugs of Scotch into reasonably clean glasses. 'Here, Boss. Drink dis and you feel better. I guess you jes' discouraged from all da, cookin'. Down de hatch, Boss.'

'It ain't the cookin' that discourages me, Jazz.' Craig managed a grin. 'I guess I got a kink in my swing tonight.'

'You got a kink in yo' *what*?'

'Somebody else asked me the same question. Skip it. I suppose all we can do is wait. Come on up to the house and help me wait. This place stinks. We'll go sit in the bar and have a quiet ball of our own until it comes time to call the cops.'

In the early morning silence they heard the purr of the car, and went to the door. Lights traced an unsteady pattern on the road. The car ground to a halt in front of the door, its motor coughing out as it braked.

The red-headed crew-cut was driving. On the seat next him was Carol. She had been sick, and the front of her jersey was stiff with vomit. The kid behind the wheel was palely sober, and obviously frightened. He babbled.

'She wouldn't come home, Mr. Price! She wouldn't! I don't know what got into her! We were in this joint—this place we go—drinking some beer when she rolled up and she started drinking gin boilermakers. Everybody tried to stop her but she wouldn't stop! She raised hell, Mr. Price! They threw us out, and then she got sick, and the other girls all left, and . . .' The kid appeared on the edge of tears.

'It's all right, son. Thanks. She's all right apart from being . . .'

'Oh, sure, Mr. Price. She just passed out is all. She just got sick and passed out. She'll be fine tomorrow. She just got sick and passed out . . . She . . .' The boy stopped.

'She what?' Craig said sharply. '*What*?'

'Well, she . . . she was doing an imitation when we got thrown out. It was pretty funny, I guess, but the man that runs the joint didn't think so. She got on this little dance floor and started to do a strip-tease and said something about if it was good enough for her family it was good enough for the public and then she got sick and then we got thrown out and then she passed out and then . . .'

Craig patted the boy awkwardly on the shoulder.

'Easy does it, son. You want to stay here tonight?'

'No, my God, Mr. Price, my old man will kill me if I don't get home. This isn't even my car and . . .'

'No strain. It's mine, as a matter of fact. Jazz, take the young man home. But first, help me up the stairs with my daughter. She weighs a young ton. You wait here, son.'

Together Craig and Jazzbo wrestled the girl up the stairs and into her room, and dropped her on the bed.

'I'll take care of her,' Craig said. 'You take the kid home, and then get some sleep. I think we'll go in pretty early tomorrow.'

'Miss Carol a Mess, boss. What you gonna do about . . . ?'

'Don't worry. I'll fix her up fine. Now go on and drive the kid home, and tell him thanks again.'

'Okay, Boss. Good night. I ready when you is tomorrow—I means today.'

'Good night, Jazz. Thanks.'

188

Craig looked at his daughter, her clothes soiled, spittle caked on her lips, her hair a rat's-nest, her skirt rumpled. Her mouth was open, and she was very pale. He went to her bathroom and turned on the water, moistened a towel. He came back, took off her loafers, lifted her to a sitting position, and peeled off her sweater. Then he unzipped her skirt, lifted her leaden legs, and pulled off the skirt. He cradled her briefly until he could drop her head on the pillow. Then he carefully washed her face with the wet towel, straightened her limbs, and hauled the covers up over the bra-and-pantie-clad body. She snugged the covers under her chin, but she flung out one arm and moaned, then wriggled, just a little.

Craig stood over her, looking down at the relaxed childish face, the drunken sleep-parted lips, the moist hair.

He threw the skirt and soiled sweater into a closet, and walked over to touch the light switch. He closed the door softly. As he went to his room he murmured, softly:

'My God. This is where I came in.'

Craig leaned back and closed his eyes as the Rolls purred townward. He felt terribly tired. Morning had been pretty dreadful. Everybody had a hangover. Maybelle and Carol were both very pale, with circles under their eyes, and even the morning rounds of whisky sours had failed to quiet the tremor in Maybelle's fingers. Carol persistently avoided her father's eyes. Craig pointedly refrained from mentioning anything about the night before.

'That was quite a party, quite a party,' Dr. Newsome said, after his second whisky sour. 'I feel like the wrath of God. And I got a cutting session at nine o'clock in the morning. We better get in early, Joan, and catch a little sleep. I don't want to leave anything inside the customer.' He chuckled at his own wit. 'No, sir, it ain't fashionable any more to be absent-minded. They sue you.'

Nobody applauded. They reached for the Sunday papers or walked aimlessly out on the lawn. It was not a talking morning. Carol announced that she'd be missing lunch. She had a date with the kids to go to the club for tennis, and they'd grab a bite there. She didn't say good-bye when she left.

Craig managed to get through brunch, which was a dispirited affair of eggs Benedict, country ham, and broiled kidneys. After the coffee he mumbled something about a big day to-morrow, some briefs he had to study tonight. He shook hands, pecked briefly at Maybelle, and almost ran to the car when Jazzbo brought it around.

'Let's roll,' he said. 'I got to be in town by four.'

'Easy,' Jazzbo said. 'How Miss Carol? She in pretty bad shape dis mornin'.'

'She's all right,' Craig said. 'Hung over and ashamed, but okay. She took off early. Shut up and drive. I don't feel like talking.'

'Okay, Boss. But where we headed? De office?'

'Yes. I want to change. I left in such a hurry I forgot to take off my squire clothes. Then you're off.'

'Yassuh, Boss. Mind if I turn on de radio?'

'No. But roll up the glass. I don't want to hear anybody saying "How About That?" this afternoon.'

'Yassuh.' The dividing glass slid smoothly up, and Craig heaved a sigh. He put his feet up on a jump seat and thought that pretty soon he'd be seeing Sue, and then the day would brighten again.

8

HE remembered with vivid pleasure the first time he met Sue. It was a dreadful shrill party on Beekman Place, bunch of tatty people all posturing and noisily expounding their world-views. The tame author, full of himself, was trying to tell the tame director the difference between Prose and Theatre, and the tame pansy playwright was sulking in the corner because his boy-friend had been unduly nasty. The sounds were static. They probably hadn't changed except for topic, since the first knight tipped his visor and asked some dame: 'So what else is new?' The true connotation of 'dame' had foundered itself in the past.

One woman, in a horrid hat, was saying: 'But I don't *want* to go to Russia. I can't even get to the theatre. That cross-town traffic.'

Another, with three colours of hair: 'The solution to the Puerto Ricans is that they should stay in Puerto Rico. Who sent for them?'

'All I know is that I am keeping all sharp instruments away from my children. A do-it-yourself zip-gun isn't easy to live with, and that goes for rubber bands . . .'

'You know, I don't care what the papers said, she shot him in *his* room, not *hers*. And she always seemed like such a *nice* girl.'

'I didn't like her eyes. I can tell. I can always tell. Person's got bad eyes, they're rotten to the core.'

'Your eyes aren't so pretty.' The man smirked.

'I'm rotten to the core, like I said. That's why my eyes aren't so pretty. Mirror of the soul. I got a soul? I ain't even got a mirror.'

'But I don't give a good goddam about outer space. Who needs it?'

'Well, hell's horns, it's *up* there. Somebody ought to do something about it. *Something*. Anything. Parking lots, maybe?'

'The market dropped again. Thank heaven I put my money in Superstores. At least there'll always be frozen assets, if they start selling them again, when they run out of cold-storage eggs.'

'God is only *Dog* spelled backwards. Oh, don't hit me please, sir, I didn't mean it really.' Rolled eyes to heaven. 'Really, I didn't mean it.'

'A trip to the moon, on gossamer wings? Who needs it? I wouldn't go on a B.707, with Rickenbacker in the hot-seat and Lindbergh for co-pilot.'

'That girl's too young for him. But then, who *ain't*?'

'What right have the Jews got in Palestine? I mean *really*. Miami's more comfortable, and think of the Arabs. They must be frightfully annoyed with all those strangers barging in.'

'Why do all airplane accidents come in groups of three?'

'Something to do with spare parts. Pity they can't make them for people. Especially me. I could sure do with some—or at least one—spare part.'

'The trouble with the Russians is they got no sense of humour.'

'I saw better-looking hats on Clara Bow.'

'Whatever *did* happen to Helen Kane? Boop-boop-a-doop.'

'I quit reading the sports pages. They run the obituaries on the other side. Seems like everybody, but *everybody* I know, is dead.'

'But he was in his room, not her room, when she shot him.'

'It was a divine murder. Simply divine.'

'How would you describe the eyes, *bloodshot*?'

'Cancer. The last piece I read said you'd get cancer of the nerves if you didn't smoke. I wish they'd make up their minds. Damn this butane lighter. Anybody got a match?'

'I do *not* believe that television is permanent.'

'Look, maybe the French can cook, but what can they do with a colony?'

'Friendship's all right, but Jesus, when it starts costing you money . . .'

'But ain't there anybody, *anybody*, who could get to be President without a hobby? Golf's all right, but you can stretch it too far . . . Think of Hoover, fishing. Think of Harding, poker.'

'Personally, I always judge a man from his face, and I don't like his nose. On Bob Hope it's all right.'

'Don't tell me the Duke wasn't smart. He got out from under. Well, not exactly out from under *her*, because he's got . . .'

'Anyhow, come what may, sweetie, we still have Mr. John.'

Out of this din of something much less than nothing, a smiling serene face bloomed, crossing, transcending all the chatter.

It was the kind of cocktail party that will always be *that* kind of cocktail party. Why anybody ever goes to them is a mystery, but they have them, there they are, and there you go if you live in New York. Call them a needless necessity. Call them a poisoned thorn in the flesh of humanity. Call them a false festival of pale drinks, hot martinis, flabby strips of suppurating salmon. Call them shrivelled olives surrounded by cold bacon, call them bird-shot caviar on dead toast, call them little slivers of crinkled things to dip in cups of ancient onion-flavoured cream-cheese. Call them overfilled ashtrays, with the lipsticked ends of cigarettes crumpled in an unhappy marriage with the olive pits and drifting grey ash. Call them little slips of anchovy, lone and lost in a sea of stale hors d'oeuvres nobody wants, pitiful little anchovies, lorn from home. Call them cold hot-biscuits slimed with dis-interested butter. Call them sweetheart, call them darling, call them dear, but the right name is a crock of . . .

The people have all been locked out of their mental boarding-houses, or they wouldn't be there. Everybody looks like some-body you've met before, and the chances are you have.

There would be, of course, the stringed trio which strives valiantly to rise above the heavy hum of the noisy room. In-evitably, 'Tea for Two' gets played. And the whisky gets hotter, the martinis get melted-er, and this is no sort of a place to fall in love with, or in. But some people can manage to surmount any difficulty.

'Do you know anybody here?' Craig asked, crossing the room. *What* a pretty girl, he thought. Wonderful bones.

'More or less. Don't want to, very much, but the cat just died and there was Father's leprosy, of course. You know how New York is at this time of the year. Everybody busy, but then I always say Spain is a very poor country, like Arkan-saw. Or is it Arken-sass? Who are you?'

'Country boy out of his depth. By name of Craig Price. Lost in the cold canapé jungle. Who're you?'

'Y'all sound sort of Southren, honey. Ah'm a damyank by name of Sue Strong. We come North when there was a pantalette shortage in Jawja. Mama's name was Crimson. A distant cousin on the O'Hara side. What'll we do, go some place and get married or just neck?'

'Neck for a start. Do you always talk this way?' Craig steered her to a sofa in a small adjoining room. He beckoned a waiter who came with a tray of drinks.

'Only when I'm in love.'

'If you take your whisky with soda I'll leave you,' he said.

'Me sully mah whisky with soda? You outa your mind? You sure you're a Southren boy?'

'Thank you,' to the waiter. 'I beg your pardon, madam,' Craig said.

'Don't call me madam, Beauregard. I ain't even worked up

192

from the ranks yet, but I'm tryin'. What are you doing in this all-and-sundry?'

'Sundry, Mondry and always. Excuse *me*. That was pretty awful.'

The girl clinked her glass.

'Don't tell nobody, but I think you're one of us. Let me see your scars. I thought so. Secret agents everywhere.'

'You wouldn't be a little nuts, would you?'

She fluttered her eyelids in mock modesty.

'That's the nicest thing a man evah said to me. Mostly you got to die to be appreciated. You would be married of course.' It wasn't a question.

'Yes.'

'I just got un-.'

'I imagine the poor fellow couldn't stand the strain. The only reason I ain't un- is I don't go home much. You know, Boy Scout work, Daughters of the American Revolution, all that jive.'

'I had you put down from the start as a kind of steady kid. That serious talk gets me every time. I'm an intellectual. Only girl in New York knows how to tat.'

'I'm a tit man, myself. None of this tat stuff.'

'La, sir, how you talk. Maybe we can swap. Except it would have to be Tuesday.'

'I don't trade very much on Tuesdays but I am very firm about sundries. For instance, I would like very much to smuggle you out of this mess and go some place without all this *taka-taka*...'

'Accept. *Avec le sans regard*... What's "*taka-taka*"?'

'Swahili. I know a little. *Taka-taka* is junk. Rubbish.'

'You know some more? It sounds pretty.'

'*Mimi nataka lala kwa wewe*.'

'And that means?'

'I'll tell you after dinner. When I know you better.'

'Oh, a rude one, hey? I'll have you know, sir... I'll just creep off to the lady's loo and collect my coat. Do you do anything else worthy?'

'Only the Boy Scouts and the D.A.R., like I said. Well, hell, I was a Brownie once, but that was before the psychiatrists straightened me out. I think I was in school with your husband.'

'You were *not*. He went to Vassar. His parents had money. See you in a second... Craig?'

'Craig.'

'I don't think you have a chance,' she said, 'Darling' and swished off to find her coat.

9

LUIGI bowed them through the long bar. They stepped down into the dining-room, and then farther down into the garden, canopied like a gay carnival booth, in green-and-white striped canvas. A dense clipped hedge rose on all sides to the canopy's scalloped edges, and the tables were bright with red-and-white checked cloths. The floor was flagged. Small hurricane lamps contained candles.

Susan Strong sank into her chair and sighed exaggeratedly.

'My God, it's nice to meet another peasant. I had a horrible idea you'd drag me off to the Colony or Twenty-One. Do you really like scallions?'

'I love scallions. Let's eat us a bait of them. Twenty-One or Colony? And see all the people we just left? God Almighty, I have to spend enough time in those traps on business.'

The waiter brought a boat of ice-mounted radishes and green onions. Susan helped herself to a handful of the tender-green, slim, bulb-ended scallions.

'Yummy,' she said. 'Better eat a lot or we have to fall back on that tired old Cockney joke: "Breave on 'im, Alfie, and teach 'im a bloody lesson." '

'Watch me go. I never really got over the miracle of eating. And I damn well hate people who pick at food. Every time I see a steak I want to kiss a cow and say thank God for money.'

'I *did* know who you were, of course. I read the *Time* and *Newsweek* stuff. You don't sound very real to me.'

'I don't sound very real to *me*. It's a bad habit I have. I always feel like I was looking at somebody else, and wishing I was prettier. *I* know I'm kinda simple, but the outside people get me all mixed up with oil and textiles and insurance companies and stocks and bonds and electronics to a point where I feel I was poaching squirrels on somebody else's property. I was raised powerful simple, and never got over it.'

Craig reached for another onion.

'Funny. I was raised—reared, I should imagine—so terribly gently, Miss Merriwether, Scotland for summers, Barnard— and I never sort of recognized me in the process, which is why I talk a lot of damn foolishness, and most of it forcedly coarse. I suppose it's a kind of revulsion to Nannies and divorced idiot-parents and Long Island and woolly plaid steamer rugs. As a small child I always had a tremendous urge to say something vile at the table.'

'Did you have enough of that cocktail swill, or could you handle a martini or something?' The waiter hovered.

'I'd love one martini, very, very, very dry, and then let's leap into the Chianti. Not Valpolicella. I like my Dago red rough. And lots of that crusty bread. I'm feeling very starchy, and then red-meaty.'

Craig ordered spaghetti *al burro* and two rare steaks and salad, and a fiasco of Chianti.

'How much garlic?'

'All it'll bear, Buster. I told you I was a peasant. Gimme some more of them onions, and tell them to go heavy on the Roquefort on the salad.'

Craig shook his head, in wonder.

'I finally have found a girl to marry. Will you marry me—after I've murdered my wife, of course?'

'Naturally. What else? Breave on me, Alfiie, and teach me a lesson.'

There was a crash as a waiter on the far side of the room collapsed a tray, and the floor was paved with broken crockery. Craig smiled as the bus-boys rushed to the rescue.

'What's the grin about? My, this spaghetti is lovely. Tell me.'

'I was thinking about my home town, away down yonder, and a coloured waiter named Allen Jinny, my old man used to tell me about. They named him Allen because it sounded like a nice high-sounding name, and since he had no appreciable father, they called him Allen Jinny because his mother's name was Jinny.

'He worked for Cousin Kate in her boarding-house, and sometimes he worked on a schooner as cook for Cap'n Jack Morse. Allen Jinny had a besettin' sin, like most of us.' Craig's voice slurred into Southern talk. 'He was known to take a drink.

'Seem like all the local politicos were eatin' up Miss Kate's fine fifty-cent table-d'hôte one night in her boarding-house, and Allen managed to tip a tray of scalding soup on to the dignitaries.

'After the mess got cleaned up, and the hollering quit, Miss Kate took Allen back to a side-hall and read him a riot on what happened to the man who killed the goose that laid the golden eggs—meaning, I suppose, that if Allen didn't mind his ways and lay off the booze, he'd find himself out in the street, and far from home. Allen said: "Yas, ma'am, Miss Kate," and staggered off to the kitchen.

'The cook said:

' "Allen, boy, what Miss Kate done say you, she so hoppin' mad?"

' "I dunno," Allen said to the cook. "Miss Kate, she say some silly-son-of-a-bitch want to eat a goose, but I don't know who de hell gon' pick it." '

'You know, I find myself in the same thought process from time to time,' Susan Strong said, laughing through a radish. 'I don't know who de hell gon' pick de goose. Is there any more about Allen Jinny?'

'Too many. Just one more. One time he was down in Florida with Cap'n Jack, tied up at the dock in Jacksonville or some place. Old Jack said to Allen: "Goddamit, boy, I'm sick and tired of grits-and-eggs every night for supper. I want something new —something like a Welsh rabbit, anything.'

' "*Yassuh*, Boss," Allen said, and went ashore, where he got loaded enormously, mightily. He came back to the ship clutching two huge dead Belgian hares by the ears.

' "What the hell is this all about?" Cap'n Jack hollered."What you aim to do with those blasted rabbits?'

' "I gon Welsh de hell out of 'em, Boss," Allen said, and staggered off to the galley.'

Susan laughed. She had a very merry face. She was the kind of girl, Craig thought, who could laugh through a mouthful of steak and still look joyfully attractive.

'Let's have us a little *zabaglione*, if we can cram it down after this monstrous meat, and have a look at the town by night,' he said. 'Dance? Or go to the Blue and see what's new there? Copa? What? You call it.'

'I got cocktail-party feet, sweetie, and night-club nausea. Unless you're mad keen to stay up all night in Morocco, or something, I'd say let's go to my joint, take off the shoes, digest the dinner and hear some very low, non-abrasive music—as *Time* says about you, nothing later than 1935.' She smiled. 'It was a lovely dinner. Oddly, I've never been here before. Everybody's awfully nice. Who are they?'

'Just plain Wops. Friends of mine. I love Italians. These particular ones come from Naples. Luigi was born there. His old man fetched him over when he was about ten. They started a hole-in-the wall spaghetti joint around Mulberry Street. Prohibition fortunately arrived, and they already knew how to make home-stomped Dago red. They graduated from the rusty-red to the white—that old hand-hewn gin and the somewhat Scotch. Just like Twenty-One but more downtown. All good restaurants seem to start off as speak-easies, and work up to the class trade. Luigi did the same thing Jack Kriendler and Charlie Berns did with Twenty-One. When the depression came, and everybody was leaping out of windows, they took all the outstanding tabs, stamped them "Paid", and mailed them to the customers, with a note saying that their presence was still desirable, and that signing privileges still prevailed. A lot of people who might have been looking gloomily down at distant sidewalks decided against it. These same people made a comeback, and that's one reason why Twenty-One is rich today, and so is Luigi. Sheer gratitude, compounded annually. People do *not* forget, no matter what you say. I never forgot any small kindness or tiny slight I ever received. There are still some people on my *S*-list, and I'll have their guts for garters before

196

I'm through. There's quite a lot of fine folks on my God-bless-you list, too.'

'You sound a very fierce fellow,' Sue said. 'Let's go home and get into some sort of delicious trouble. Will you promise to beat me if I'm good?'

'Only if you're good.' Craig pulled back her chair. 'I like bad girls.'

'You'll love me. I'm filthy through and through.'

'I think I already do,' Craig said. 'I'm rotten to the core, also, and it takes two to know two, as the queer Siamese twins once said when they passed another set on the street.'

'No wonder Fred Allen failed in TV,' Sue said. 'Eighty-Third, corner of Fifth.'

10

IT was, Craig thought, his kind of apartment, as this woman seemed to be shaping into his kind of dame. It was nearly as big as his office, the living-room, and it had a fireplace vast enough to roast an ox in. The round coffee-table was large enough to put things down on, even without removing the serried ranks of bright-faced magazines and the odd book or so. The ash trays were moulded of massive glass and were as big as basins. An enormous white sofa dotted with fat crimson pillows curved around the table, with room enough for six people to sit comfortably. Opposite, a narrow, straight, green-black-mottled marble table sat squarely in front of a straight black leather sofa. Two wing-backed yellow leather chairs crouched on each side of the fireplace, in front of which was a hammered brass Arab *brazero* with its hollowed centre-piece spilling flowers instead of coals. To the right, in an alcove, was a bar—a functional bar. Craig walked over to inspect it.

'If I ever had any doubts about marrying you,' he said, 'this room dispels them. Especially the bar. Mind you, I approve of the books and the piano, since I think that a wall composed entirely of books is prettier than any picture, and a black Steinway with a jug of roses on it is a hard vista to improve on, but it is the bar that brings forth true character. You have true character.'

'My dear fellow, it took me twenty years of practice and a slight cirrhosis to evolve this bar. I hate cute bars. I hate bars with red-leather stools and funny ha-ha mottoes and pictures. I hate home-bars where people congregate. The purpose of a bar is to serve booze as neatly and efficiently and as swiftly as possible, so people can sit down and get drunk intelligently.'

'You got it made, Jack. This is the best one I ever saw. I especially like the ice-bucket bit.'

'I learned that from the airlines. The airlines think of everything, except how to unload luggage.'

It was a fine bar for anybody's apartment, as efficient as an old-fashioned saloon. It was only six feet long, and was built on to the wall of the alcove. Standing in front, it was possible to reach every glass, every pewter mug, every pottery Toby, on the four shelves, without moving your feet. A jolly family of necessities lived on the cork surface, to the left—a Waring Blender, Worcester sauce, salt, pepper, sugar, bitters, a plate with two fresh lemons, a vase of mint, a knife, spoons, corkscrews and bottle-openers. In the centre, an enormous silver ice-bucket, one of the pressurized kind, had been dropped below the bar surface, and its top was level with the bar.

To the right, standing proudly, were bottles of Scotch, bourbon, rye, brandy, rum, crème-de-menthe, bénédectine, sherry, gin, vodka, and cut-glass decanters of red and white wine. Beneath the bar-top were three compartments, with sliding panels. Craig slid back the first panel. Half-forgotten block ice from another age crouched on a platform, and was surrounded by beer, Coke, ginger-ale and tonic, each cradled on its separate rack. The centre compartment held the length of the ice-bucket and a cluster of spare syphon bottles. The left-hand compartment contained an army of bottles, the whisky, gin, brandy and rum standing primly in files on the spirit floor, flanked by various ages of sherries and anisettes and crèmes-de-menthe. Craig whistled.

'You mind if I come here to live?' he said. 'I particularly care for the faucet and the do-it-yourself sink behind the ice-bucket. I got a couple of places with bars in them, and each bottle seems to have a life of its own. The damn bar is always cluttered up with people telling you how to mix a martini. This is perfect.'

'I ain't un-proud of it,' Sue replied. 'I can literally serve twenty people in five minutes if they aren't asking for pigeon-milk frappé or something equally exotic. My grandfather was Irish, and he loved his poteen. He hated fuss. He said a man that wanted a drink wanted a drink and he wanted it fast with no goddamned nonsense, and there was no space in a service bar for anybody but the barkeep.

' "'Tis not a social cinter when it's in the home, lass," he used to say. " 'Tis not a place for pigs at the trough. 'Tis a shrine, a holy place, and needs but wan priest." '

Craig laughed.

'He'd have loved the red-bearded old goat who raised me. He had similar ideas. He figured that a half-gallon jug, if it held corn-whisky, needed no drinking glass unless you were putting on airs. He had a scar on his nose from the fruit-jar's rim.'

'I loved my grandpa,' Susan said. 'Brandy?'

'I think a Scotch and water. I loved mine, too. He was a kind of bum, I suppose, but he was about the only friend I had. I didn't cotton much to my mother and father.'

'Here. Glenlivet all right?'

'Lovely. Cheers.'

'Cheeri-awfully-bloody-ho. Mine wasn't a bum. He was a pirate. A black-bearded pirate who kicked over anything he couldn't jump over. Whether he bought it or stole it didn't make any difference. He started out as the classic hod-carrier and wound up like in the Horatio Alger stories. He owned the politicians and he owned the people who owned the politicians. He left a mess of money to my Dad, who wasn't—isn't—worth the powder to blow him from Newport to Palm Beach. I think the breed wears out with one man. Daddy plays golf and culti-vates exotic petunias, or something, and collects old spittoons, or something. What Mummy does I can't say, apart from having her face lifted and indulging in charity balls, but they ain't such of a much. They think I'm awful. When Daddy gets angry, he says I'm my grandfather all over again, which is the greatest unconscious compliment I've ever been paid. Thank Christ he didn't refer to me as a chip off his old block, or I'd have skulled his old block with an axe. Why don't we sit?'

'In a minute. I'm a snooper. I want to look at your books. I know your pictures are good—that Modigliani is lovely, and I like those Haitian primitives and the one of the three kids with a different expression. They must be looking at a dead dog, or something, because the little girl is all soft pity. The little boy in the middle will grow up to be a fag, and the other little boy will be either President, head of the Mafia, or hanged for murder. Whose is it?'

'Unsung Spaniard. Name of Solar. Friend sent it to me from Madrid.'

Craig prowled past the piano, and patted it on its mahogany-shining flank, as one would pat a plump pony.

'This looks like one of the good ripe old ones. You play?'

'Little bit. Nothing very fancy. I like the New Orleans stuff, and all the stuff Ella sings—the old Porter, Gershwin, Rodgers and Hart—you know. It said so in *Time*, that you know.'

'At least they were accurate there. I'm a music nut, but it has to hang to something in the past. Would that make me a senti-mentalist, apart from being a frustrated musician? Even today, I can't hear a certain song without feeling my belly twist. I can literally *smell* music. I can touch it—stroke its texture, I mean. I drive myself nuts. I'm tone-perfect in my head, and I can hold an entire musical comedy in my brain. I wake up with one song going, and I can reproduce it silently as Ella might, as Frank might, as Lena might, as even Satch might, but *I* can't sing aloud. *I* can't even play "Chopsticks". It's the big frustration of my life. I must sound awfully silly.'

'You don't sound silly at all. I'm a *writer* in my own head, and I can barely sign a cheque. I know how it should be, how it ought to be, and I would be a great writer except for one thing. When I try, nothing happens. I'm a magnificent writer who can't write. So I read. Like you listen. I read and I want to cry, because I could do it so much better if I only knew how.'

Craig offered her a cigarette, and grinned shame-facedly as he lit it.

'I'm a painter, too,' he said, 'so long as we're confessing. I could paint better than anybody—anybody from Michelangelo through Breughel and Van Gogh and Gauguin up to Norman Rockwell. Except I always lacked the one thing. I don't know how much turpentine you put into the paint.'

'So you play nylon stockings and sing oil-wells and paint stocks and bonds, is that it?'

'About it.' The smile was rueful. 'I could have been a better centre-fielder than DiMaggio, except I couldn't catch a ball very well. Story of my life. Let's have a look at these books. I want to see if anybody ever reads them. *Mmhm.* Mark Twain. All right. Conrad. The James boys. Unread—or at least unre-read. Good. All the Russians, also un-dog-eared. Hemingway. Steinbeck, thank God, rubbed slick. *Extraordinary Popular Delusions and the Madness of Crowds.*' He quirked his already permanently raised scarred eyebrow. 'Charles Fort and Rebecca West and Rilke. Maugham. All of Mr. Churchill. Ye compleat Evelyn Waugh. I like his brother better. C. S. Forester. What's this? *Finnley Wren* and *Professor Fodorski*? I *do* love you. I think Robert Lewis Taylor is the funniest man alive. Faulkner?'

'I can't read him, him and that Makalapawhichawaymultnomah County. Posturing bore. Writes in loops. You can take Mr. James Joyce and Miss Stein and . . .'

'Watch it. There ain't enough room there for both of them.'

Mrs. Susan Strong smiled evilly.

'I wish there were, and maybe we could cut you a new one, which would include all the delicate young men who write the precious plays, and all the world-weary boys from England and here, and possibly Françoise Sagan. I still got Kipling and O. Henry to keep me warm, and when all is lost we can always go back to Mencken and Joe Mitchell. You ever read Mencken's stuff about eating and drinking in Baltimore, and Mitchell when he gets on the subject of beefsteak parties, clams and terrapin? I drool. I positively drool like a boxer before feeding time.'

'I love food too, and reading about food. Maybe it was on account of the meals I missed.'

200

'When you were buying the matched set of Maugham₄ when you were young and tender and awful poor?'

'You *did* read that silly *Time* piece, then. And it's true. That old cliché about I'd rather read than eat was true in my case. I read anything—advertisements, the labels on vinegar bottles, "something something, malt, sugar, and salt", soap-chip descriptions and the fine print on toilet-paper wrappers.' He paused judicially.

'You perhaps care overmuch for horses?' Craig asked. Susan tilted her head.

'I *hate* horses.'

'So do I. They scare me spitless. They are always scraping me off on low branches or stumbling in holes or just plain biting me. One time—I swear this is true—a horse jumped through a library window with me aboard, at the house of a friend in the country.'

'I presume he was looking for something to read?' Sue snorted.

'I wouldn't put it past him. Probably the latest Paul Bowles. In this case I was the innocent prey. One thing more—you like bullfights? I mean, the business of the horses doesn't bother you?'

'Bother me? *Bother* me? I love to see a horse get it in the guts. When they started padding them I cried for days. I love bullfights, if only for the picador part.'

Craig reached out and swept her mock-dramatically into his arms.

'Is there anything so far we haven't got in common, so long as I am proposing marriage?'

'Up to now, nothing but bed.'

Craig tipped up her chin with one finger, looked steadily into her eyes, and kissed her very lightly on the lips.

'I have a hunch,' he said, 'that we will find we have *that* in common, too.'

11

'I REALLY don't know what it's all about,' she said. 'I suppose you'll think I'm a wanton woman, another one of the Park Avenue bums.'

'You're the loveliest Park Avenue bum I ever knew in my life,' he said. 'Mind if I sort of take a long look at you?'

'Charmed, I'm sure,' she said. 'After all we've been to each other, and that sort of rot . . .'

'You know I'm prepared to fall rather desperately in love with you,' Craig said. 'I hope you don't mind.'

'Not if you'll tell me now what all the Swahili talk was about.'

'*Mimi nataka lala*? Just meant I'd like to take a little nap with you, and I just did.'

'Rude man, to know your mind so early . . . How do I look?'

'You look like a very beautiful naked woman on a beautiful rumpled bed . . . And you have these great blue eyes and a skin that at least *I* love to touch. And you're big all over in the right proportion. Have you ever been to New Orleans?'

'Ask Jimmy. Ask Owen. Ask Tommy. Ask Dan. Ask Gasper. Ask Mary. Ask Seymour. Ask—no, you can't. Papa Celestin's dead. Yes, I've been to New Orleans.'

'Then would you be mad at me if I said I love you in a kind of back-Bourbon Street, un-Mardi Gras, way-down-yonder-sort-of-marvellous if-a-little-bit-early-to-talk-about-it-way?'

'I think I could accept that. *Mon cher.*'

'You know something else?'

'Maybe you wouldn't mind if I said you make me silly happy like a nigger camp-meeting. Notice I said *nigger*. None of my black friends ever minded. If you would sort of get up out of this well-trammelled bed while I go to the retiring room, and mix me a drink, I would like to tell you about what a camp-meeting is like. It would sort of be a present which I am jealous of owning, and don't like to pass around to anybody whom I don't love, don't trust.'

Unselfconsciously naked, Sue got up and kissed him coolly on the forehead.

'You jes' tell me about yo' camp meetin', honey. Ah's all ears.'

'You wouldn't know what it's like to be a little boy, thank God.'

'*Vive la différence*,' Sue said. 'Continue.'

'It was kind of like this. If you'll be a good girl and kiss me again.'

'I'm a good girl, and I just don't go around kissing anybody. Smack. So there. Tell me about your camp-meeting. We've been a touch short on camp-meetings in Long Island since the pantalette shortage drove us North.'

Craig accepted the drink and put on a pair of shorts. Sue had flung a sort of sarong around her salient points. Craig lit two cigarettes and said: 'It was like this, maybe better, maybe worse.'

From one end of two counties to the other, Craig prowled with his coloured friends. He was somehow accepted as an equal. He would be wandering idly around the little town and Big Luke, or somebody, would say: 'Don't you tell on me, Mista Craig, does you get cotched, but dey be a powerful big fish fry tonight fo' we starts a big soul-savin'. Ol' Satan, he take a mighty beatin' tonight out behind de Grove. I spects a mess of sinners gwine get saved from 'Ternal Damnation dis night, but de fish fry starts about eight, kin you sneak out, and de salvation come later, after de moonshine take hol' de preacher.'

And so Craig would make his manners, go ostensibly to bed, and then creep quietly down the backstairs when the old folks had settled for the night. He shivered with delicious anticipation as he walked out of the town and into the forbidding woods.

The onslaught on Old Satan would be held under an oak grove, or a palmetto patch, and there would always be makeshift rough plank tables to hold the food. If it was summer, watermelons, striped green-and-white, or dark, almost black-green, would be halved and quartered and stacked on the tables. If it was winter, the first course was always oysters, roasted under a tin slab, the fire fed by wet kelp. The lips of the big grey striated oysters parted slightly under the heat, and since everybody carried a Barlow knife, it was simple to cut the muscle. For Craig, the honoured guest, some little black boy was appointed to shuck the oysters, and to drop them into a tin dish awash with butter and hot pepper vinegar. Corn-cake or hush-puppies went with the oysters, to sop into the butter-sauce, emerging crumbling-soaked with the essence of oyster, butter, pepper and marsh-mud. It was difficult not to founder on the first course, but the knowledge that the fried fish and the late-fall collard greens cooked with sow-belly were coming up, to be followed by the chocolate cake, held a fellow back after the first two or three dozen. Craig usually cheated, when the oysters bore an inner burden of the tiny stowaway pink oyster-crabs, and he was never able to do respectable justice to the fish heads and the tails, as sea-trout, mackerel, perch and an occasional pompano came swift and golden from the three-legged iron spiders where the grease popped and spat defiantly at the black arms that turned the fish. ('Man, nobody got de right to say she a cook if she ain't got blisters. You's got to stand clos' to cook good.')

There would have been, in the black jungle-night outside the firelit circle, some steady traffic with harsh white corn liquor, homespun and cherished in fruit jars, and a few odd choruses of irreverent song, but the *al fresco* musicale was not allowed to take hold fully until the Sperrit called to Come to Jesus. And as the preacher said, Jesus was the first man to cast his bread upon the waters, and to make the fishes bloom like the green bay tree, and so the precepts of Our Lord were followed in the best Biblical sense until after dessert, which was mainly always chocolate layer cake. The good Sistern competed fiercely to see who could produce the highest, most-layered, blackest-icinged chocolate cake, else what de preacher gon say 'bout we when he hold another revival in Onslow County?

So they ate, and beautiful black faces gleamed with grease, and perfect teeth showed white in the firelight, and over there, a whippoorwill called, and here an owl answered. The young bucks had already sidled up to the young gals with the ornate pepper-corn hair-dos, each separately-crimped lock tied festively with candy-box ribbon instead of string, and were making pleasantries in the outer edges of the eating circles, with an eye to a convenient piece of romantic bush for later dalliance, after the preacher done shot salvation to everybody's soul. Mammy Laura used to say: 'Man, I can tell a chile age from de last successful camp-meetin'.'

Craig occupied the role of an ambassador plenipotentiary. Aunt Melissy: 'Chile, you ain't got near enough on yo' plate. Leaves I go fetch another piece fish, yeddy?'

Big Abner: 'Little Cap'n, I swears you eatin' like a hummin'-buhd. You jes' ain' tech no mo' than a gal chile.'

Aunt Galena: 'Mista Craig, yo' grandpa be shamed out of mind 'bout you, only two pieces cake. Ginst you don' lak choco-late, I go fin' some lard-cake I make myself.'

Preacher: 'Mista Craig, when you go be old 'nough sing bass in de choir? Yo' daddy, he sing a powerful bass. Sound almost lak he ain' white man. Us git hard up, smear he face with burnt cork, and put him to work wid Honeyboy Evans.' (Laughter.)

And so Craig stuffed himself, smearing greasy fingers against his pants'-leg, happy in the firelight, happy with the rich sound of Negro laughter, happy with the thought of what was to come when the congregation was replete, happy to be among friends in a backwoods celebration of true religion, which could have been described as a love of food, first; a love of God, next, and finally a love of fellow man, which would occur out of public view in the bushes.

And although he possibly was not aware of it, happy to be socially acceptable, although his face was white in a sea of black, which surged and heaved as the Sperrit took hold and the congregation came to the Lamb and the mourners threw them-selves upon the bench, and the preacher railed against Sin and its Master, Satan. As the smell of brimstone-to-come conquered the smell of frying fish and outvoted the fumes of home-cooked corn whisky, African voices swelled in songs which began on the Gold Coast; were richened by pain and sorrow on slave ships; by back-cramping toil in the canefields and cotton plantation; refined by sorrow over families split and sold in different direc-tions—and finally, mellowed by African humour and the realiza-tion that today is today so long as the moon shines and the fish fries and there is a buxom sweaty wench to toss sinfully after the soul is purged by the preacher, because de Good Lord, He ain't gon begrudge His po' chillun a little fun. Don't He say in de Good Book, multiply an' glorify My Name?

Conversation: 'What you do here, nigger? Seem lak I don' see you befo'. Where at y'all come fum?'

'I comes fum cross de river, udder side Brumsick.'

'What you comes here for?'

'I comes here to jazz, get drunk and sing bass.'

'Welcome, Brudder. Dey plenty gals and likker go round, and we needs a good second bass powerful bad.'

Sister Susannah, after Sister Snoree has tranced and frothed, outdoing Sister Snoree:

'Oh, my Saviour, I tries so hard to mortify de flesh, I tries so hard to behave, but when dem mens come nex' me, mah bones turn to jelly and seem lak I just cain' say no. Dere one man out heah right now de meanest man evah come down de pike. I wash clo', make money so he take it an' spend it on likker and udder women. I cut wood so I make fiah, cook food and he eat it. He make over me all de time, and my Lord, dis man touch lovin' in me I never know I had.'

'Praise de Lawd.'

'*Do*, Jesus.'

'*Do* tell,' from the congregation.

Single female voice: 'What dis man *name*?'

From a bush in the shadows:

'Nigger, keep dem big black cotton-pickin' han's to yo'sef. I ain't no easy meat for every nigger come askin'.'

'Aw, sweetness, little poontang never done nobody no harm.'

(Giggle.)

Sister Delorious:

'What happen de preacher?'

'He done through preachin'. He done take a walk wid dat light tan gal in de moonlight.'

'Huh. He say *don't* and he *do*.'

'Yo' nose jes' out of joint. You cut a eye at de Preacher yo'sef.'

'Dat a *lie*.'

'Don' you call *me* no liar, nigger.'

'Don' you call me no *nigger*, nigger, I scratch yo' eyes out.'

(Shrieks and confusion.)

The fires died, and the couples had paired, and only a few, taken unconscious by drink and religion, remained. Craig would walk slowly home in the moonlight, lonesome again now, and he could not tell you why, but he was happy in his loneliness. Away off, a dog howled, and was answered by another. The moon would be sinking, the stars fading, the skies beginning to lighten, and Craig would take off his shoes to creep up the stairs. He seldom slept until the bright sun came, as the savage spirituals rolled and sounded in his head.

Craig smiled, almost a sad reflection of half-forgotten pleasure.

'You must have been rather a lonely little boy,' she said. 'What else did you do? To pass the time, I mean?'

'I was *not* a lonely little boy.' Craig was almost fierce. 'Maybe

205

I was by myself because I didn't play a lot of games and have a lot of playmates, but I had a wonderful time. I read a lot and had guns and dogs and boats. Well, maybe I *was* lonely, in the formal sense, but I liked it. I liked it a lot. I'm a ham, honey, if you haven't caught it by now, and I liked dramatizing my loneliness. I *liked* to be solitary, and to feel sorry for myself, and then pretend that one day . . .'

'And one day?' The voice was an almost-amused caress. 'And then *one* day . . .'

'One day I'd have it all. One day, by God and by Jesus, I'd have it *all*. I was going to be Mysterious Craig Price with a look of eagles in his eyes, and a beautiful, mysterious foreign woman by his side, and when I walked into Anyplace, Anywhere, people would swivel their necks and say: "Here comes Mysterious Craig Price, with a beautiful foreign woman by his side." That's what they'd say.' He touched her nose with a fingertip. 'I suppose I sound a touch silly, and certainly too full of myself.'

'You don't sound silly a bit, my boy. I was more or less as gawky and teeth-bracey as a girl could be, and one day I was going to show 'em all. I was going to walk into the Waldorf with a King on one arm, and somebody like Rex Harrison or Gable on the other, and people would drop their drinks with a great clatter and say: "Here comes Sue Satellite, the famous star, and Winchell says that it is rumoured that a duel . . ." That's the kind of dreams I had, friend. Gloria Swanson wasn't in it, for me, and Garbo paled on the horizon.'

'You know a thing?'

'What sorta? Gimme a cigarette first. What sorta thing?'

'You ever go to lunch at the *Coq Noir* on Sixty-first?'

'Whenever I can find a boy-friend with enough money to take me. It costs you the earth just to sit down. Why?'

Craig was sheepish, honestly embarrassed.

'You won't tell if I tell you? Promise? This is one thing *Time* didn't mention.'

'Cross my heart and hope to die.'

'I own the goddam thing. You know that big pink banquette at the far end of the room, that's nearly always vacant?'

'Sure. I never saw anybody sit in it in the years I've been eating those platinum-cum-pearl lunches there. I wondered.'

'That's *my* table. I hate the joint, and the prices are ridiculous even for this silly town, and you couldn't catch me dead in it unless it was starvation time down South, but that table is always there. Always there for me. Mysterious Craig Price, the man nobody knows. So all right. I'm only a retarded fourteen-year-old, but let me tell you a thing, my dear good woman. I got turned down at the rope at the Stork Club once. The brief time I was in college I never made a fraternity because I couldn't afford one. Once I stole an alarm clock from a drug-store so I could get up in time to catch a class I was interested in. I know what it is to bum too many cigarettes. I been broke in a lot of places, and the smell of greasy dishwater on water-wrinkled hands is not, repeat not, pleasant. I know a growling gut from taw, and a one-armed joint makes one basically tired of beans and frankfurters. A firm by the name of Thompson, where you eat all you can hold—or could then—for two bits, had a lot of my trade. So I bought me a restaurant, the most expensive restaurant in town. And I stacked the prices to a point where I got these expense-account idiots bamboozled into thinking the food's extra special because it costs so much, like that French joint on Third Avenue, where they serve you hot martinis, spit in the soup, barbecue the cat, and get away with it because it's supposed to be so Frenchified-*chic*. When I go to Third Avenue, I eat at Costello's.'

'You are what is known as a disturbed personality,' Sue said. 'I think I shall put on some music, and pursue your tortured little teenage mind a trifle further. Or is it farther? For a would-be writer, I never got very far with basic English. What's with your choice? Sweet or hot?'

'I should think anything that connotes peace, tonight. You got anybody singing or playing "Autumn in New York" on a slow piano?'

'Bushkin?'

'Bought. Let it ramble from there. And I'm dry.'

'You need a lot of service, Mr. Price. Apart from my fair white frame.'

'Ah was raised up with mah own slaves, honeh,' Craig drawled. 'Mah front name ain't Beauregard for nothin'. Ah.' He purred as the music crept into the room. 'That's a nice song, that "Autumn in New York". Reminds me of mah sad past. Thank you for the drink. Come hold mah little old hand and ah'll worry the daylights out of you with some more history, sugar-baby. After we lost de wah . . .'

'You don't have to keep proving things,' she said, snuggled in a blue velvet robe that picked up the corn-flower in her eyes, comfy-cuddly as a big kitten against the white divan. She had lighted a fire, and the flames fingered tentatively up the walls. Craig was sitting cross-legged on the floor in his shorts, and the fire flung drapes of shadows over his shoulders. Sue said:

'You don't need to buy a restaurant just because you missed a meal or two. Why do you go to all this trouble?'

'Don't I, now?' Craig blew two streams of smoke through his nostrils. 'Maybe I *do*, plum. Maybe I needed a restaurant more than I ever needed anything. Maybe a restaurant was exactly what I needed. You ever knocked a cockroach out of a piece of hardtack? You ever built a whole week around one meal? You ever stole the skipper's night-lunch? Hunger in any form is one of the least attractive pastimes I can recommend. A beautiful woman walks past you on the street, and you don't think: My, what pretty legs. You wonder how she'd taste grilled with mushroom sauce, like a pheasant or something.'

'You sound like you lived in your stomach.'

'It was about the only home I had at the time. No less a prophet than Mr. Bernard Baruch has been printed as saying that a man's first thought on rising is: how will I feed my family today? And no less a man than Alexander the Great was quoted as saying that any army travels on its stomach. Man, my first impression of Liverpool, England, was a fish-and-chip shop, and when I left Hamburg I toted a roll of liverwurst as big as my thigh. Maybe the old folks don't get hungry, but as a kid I was always accompanied by a symphony which could have best been described as a growling gut. Bore you?'

'Not really. My family was always rich, saving maybe Grand-father's early hod-carrying days. I always thought of food as a necessary nuisance, although I must confess in school—boarding school—it left something to be desired. But we made that up with snacks we bought and smuggled to the rooms—candy and anchovies and bananas and all like that there.'

'What did you do when you finished school?'

'The usual. Not much. Knocked around Europe, after I finished Barnard. Went to parties. Nothing spectacular. There was a war coming on and I met young Mr. Steven Strong. Got married. Mistake, I guess. But he was mighty pretty. . .'

'You know, I really don't know anything at all about you, you lovely creature with whom I am about to fall in love. What do you *do*?'

'We talked about that over the antipasto. I'm nobody at all except a girl who didn't much care for the gent she married in a hurry when she was fresh out of Barnard. I've no talent at all. I don't write. I'm not in public relations. I can go to Twenty One by myself, and Toots Shor is nice to me. I read, I have an apartment, my ex- is a drunk, and the alimony's good enough to afford me a luxury or two. That's about all.'

'What really happened with the husband?'

'Good breeding. Excellent blood lines. Money. Not his. Lawrenceville. Princeton. Whisky. *Mucho* whisky. Life of the party. He was cute when he was a junior. He was cuter as a senior. Lovely clothes. He stopped being cute when he was a husband. As a husband he got progressively uncute. I don't know. We were both a mess—a kind of commuting mess. There ought to be a law against young people getting married without passing stringent examinations. There ought to be some sort of Prep. school, like Lawrenceville or Groton, for immature candidates for matrimony. Bed first, and then test your qualifications on somebody like Conant or Judge Landis. Don't you think we could give this away and go back to the camp-meeting? I feel like a session in the deep Carolina bushes, and I don't mean with the preacher. I won't mention "wife" until after.'

Wife. God Almighty. Craig turned over, placed his hands behind his head and thought: *Wife*. How long, as they say in New York, can a story get?

Well, first you go to sea.

How are you going to tell this new girl, this lovely girl, about going to sea, especially when you get married on the end of it? Tell her about the guy chasing the mate down the dock with the fire-axe? Tell her about the creature in Antwerp, who turned out to be a boy after you spent a week's wages buying it drinks that day? Tell her about the busted bottle, the bottle-scar on your cheek, or the people shooting at you from the top of a grain elevator? Maybe better tell her about the Russian broads and the bar-room brawls and then you can get around to *Wife*. Tell her about New Orleans?

'As a kid I used to hurt,' Craig said. 'I wanted to go *so* many places *so* bad, and when I got off that banana boat at the foot of Canal, with that big yellow rolling Mississippi at my back and the hot-garlic-bread French Quarter on my right, I knew I was home. By the time I hit Royal Street I was a Creole through and through, and by the time I lit on to Bourbon Street I was the King of the Zulus.'

12

THE loneliness that Craig Price had seeded as a boy fruited perfectly in New Orleans. He prowled the night-protected streets. He strayed like a rangy cat in the filthy, garbage-littered back alleys, wreathed in the grey-swirling fogs. The rough-cobbled streets were strangely soft and soothing under his feet, and the late-night odours—rotted bananas, refuse, old fish, charcoal smoke—filled his nostrils with the same exultation his soul felt when he heard the distant tinkle of a piano, the punctuating sobbing of a woman, the arrogant scream of a sex-tortured tomcat, the frightened yearning howl of a dog, the positive plunk of a guitar behind a wall. The thick fleshy wet fronds of banana trees jungled his feelings into a warm, salty exaltation. Bourbon Street with its blast and blare of horns, its reeling drunks, was pleasant enough, its roaring neon-lit bars pleasant enough, its beckoning street women exciting enough, but it was crouching close to a mournful dawn before Craig found what he sought in the snaking fog. This was the adventure-proneness which for ever haunted him—the hidden secret musky excitements behind the forbidding musty-mottled plaster walls—the intrigues he would never solve, the buried tragedies and wild unexplained excitements, the, the . . . Christ.

'I really don't know what the hell I was looking for,' he said to Susan, stroking her knee gently, absentmindedly, and speaking half to himself. 'I was a real peculiar kid, this Mysterious Craig Price I keep remembering. I had—can you understand?—a sort of built-in sense of tremendous potential power for excitement. In olden days I would have been a secret prince in mufti, looking for the fairy princess, but I didn't want her sparkling in tinsel. I wanted to find her in a wicked Emir's harem in Far Timbuktu. I wanted . . . I wanted to see a goat or a black cock slaughtered in a voodoo ceremony. I wanted to conduct a secret intrigue with a sloe-eyed girl on a balcony in Havana or Cuernavaca. I wanted . . . I wanted *all* the night, and be damned to the other people's day. I didn't want to see anything close-hand. I wanted the private intimation of the might-be of it, with nobody else looking over my shoulder. This make any sense?'

'Some. Some. You grant it might be a little hard to follow. But keep going. Press on, mate, and damned be he . . .'

'I don't know what I'm talking about half the time. It's like this: I was broke, real-gut-growling-broke, and I was pearl-diving—dish-washing in a grease-joint for my meals and a buck-a-day. The buck-a-day was moving-around money, and I didn't bother worrying about a room. I slept in the park or in the restaurant. When you're young you don't need much sleep. It was winter, and every night you could hear the fire-sirens scream, as somebody's pot-bellied stove got overcome with untested power and touched-off a fat-pine tenement. I used to follow the fires. Fire always fascinated me. His voice softened to a murmur.

'Tell me something, Mr. Price. Were you ever psycho-analysed? This fire fixation . . . I read about you burning down your grand-father's house.'

'Me? Psycho-analysed? *Me*? Not very bloody likely. I've seen some lovely products of that kind of voodoo. If you ain't nuts in the first place, you go nuts wondering why you ain't nuts in the second place, and in the third place I have known some psycho-analysts. One I knew had a wife who left him because she pre-ferred the dog in Washington to the man in New York.'

'I only asked because of that thing in *Time*. Burning down your grandfather's house. That didn't sound very mature to me, apart from being economically unsound.'

'That would be an even longer story. I'm talking too much tonight—you buy it at your own risk. If you want it, I'll tell you. Speak.'

'Gimme. It's only about five o'clock now. Tell me about burning down the house. This one really fascinates me.'

Craig crossed his arms and leaned his elbows on his knees. He shook his head, as if to destroy an unpleasant thought.

'You won't laugh at this one, please, or I dummy up on you.'

'I won't laugh. I don't laugh at what I'm interested in, only at what I'm trying to rid myself of. If that's a sentence.'

'Right. Story of my life. I had a certain kind of young childhood. Certain and secure and happy in that house. The beasts of the field were my friends, the birds warbled, the Negroes were happy and laughing in the cane-fields . . . all that Southern crap. Nightingales sang, and mocking-birds always warbled.

'The whole thing suddenly went to hell. Grandpa died and we lost the house. Southern people really never got themselves adjusted to the depression. All the props were knocked down, all the old securities wound up stone cold dead in the market. In short, we sold the piano.

'Sam Price's house went, as they say, under the hammer for something like six thousand dollars. This house was my castle, mind you. This house was my bastion as a fat little boy against the world. This is the house that the Captain-Admiral of the Ocean Sea came home to. This house . . . Somebody, I believe it was Jesus, said that his father's house . . . No matter. These were all my mansions. In one house.'

'If this bothers you, don't,' Susan said. 'I really didn't mean to unscab an old sore.'

'No, it doesn't bother me,' Craig said, his voice harsh. 'And it's not an old sore. I been wanting to tell somebody about it a hell of a long time, and you're the first one who seems a likely victim.' His voice softened, and he was no longer in the room. He was out in a sun-warmed row-boat, perhaps, or off with a dog in the fragrant piney woods.

'It was *such* a house. You could play underneath it when it rained. It was a house which was bulwarked staunchly by oaks, made beautifully fragrant by magnolia, rendered fertile by pecans and grapes, beloved by its flowers. It was The House on The Corner. It was *my* house. And it got sold up for six thousand lousy dollars. It got rented. It got rented to trash—poor white, and trash. It had their dung in the fireplaces, and dirty paw-prints on the walls. The wiring hung in loops. It smelt like a nest of goats. The roof sagged, and the porch was falling down. It was a poor house, a lonely house, a house that had been used and abused. It stank. The weed-choked grass was unmown, the cement sidewalk cracked, the fig-tree ruined, the garage a rotting wreck. Everything in and around this house had been soiled and fouled by the dirty hands of other people, unworthy people, and in the process the only youth I care to recall was filthed. Sullied, perhaps, is a better, milder word.'

211

'I didn't mean to call down all this lightning,' Susan said. 'Maybe I get you another drink, chum, and take you down off the rostrum?'

'You can get me another drink, friend, but I am still on the rostrum. Look, I had it reasonably rough in the early years. Rough enough, if I tell you some day—and as I think I love you, and will continue on this perilous pathway—you will know a whole lot about Craig Price that *Time* never touched. But it *was* rough and I was lucky and I made some money.

'I am not a nice man. The way I got started making money does not make me a nice man. If you ever want a close look at a gangster I suggest me—but not at this time. Leave it for other confessionals.

'I made some money—the kind of money I had thirsted for. Before I enjoyed the silky caresses of Mr. Sulka, before I touched even briefly on Tiffany, before Mr. Peal got my shoe business, I went back to New Truro, N.C., and I bought me a house. Before I ever checked into the Savoy the first time, before I built the Price Building, before I almost literally bought a pack of cigarettes, I bought me a house.

'I bought it for only four thousand dollars more than it was sold for twenty years ago. I spent three times the cost of the purchase to fix it up. I bought surgery for the trees, regenerated the lawn, crammed the flowers' hungry mouths full of fertilizer, nailed on some new shingles, re-laid the sidewalk, shored up the garage, re-papered all the rooms, sanded-down the wood-work. I bought a new stove and a new fridge, and put in a heating system. I bought a new grand piano and a whirling-douche sort of TV set. I added bathrooms and put in supplementary plumbing. It was the best goddamned house in New Truro when I got through with it. It was a house Sam Price would have been very proud of, and it showed its gratitude by withstanding some several hurricanes, including Hazel.

'*And then I burnt it down.*' His eyebrows clenched.

'And then you burnt it down.' Susan's voice was very gentle. 'Now I'll talk, and see if I'm right. You burn't it down because you wanted it all back. You didn't want other people's dirty-paw-prints on your youth. You made a memorial to your grandfather, the one you love, and you wanted it intact . . . you wanted your horse and your gun and your dog all shipped off to Valhalla . . . like, like . . . a Viking's funeral? Was that it?'

'That's precisely what I was doing. I was getting even for an unlost youth. I was sealing up my early happiness, so nobody else could ever touch it evermore. That, by Christ, nobody can take away. Do you possibly know what it could be like to see a precious thing fouled and mucked by strangers? Like pigs treading on an Aubusson carpet?'

'That I think I could say yes to. Tell me. All the things you've got now and all the things you've missed. All the things you've wanted and had to invent excuses for. You're certainly rich enough. What do you want now?'

'I'm rich now. Certainly. Sure I'm rich now. I was speaking retroactively.' Craig snapped. 'But I am not and never will be rich in my own mind. I still expect somebody to come and take it all away. I'm a poor boy right on. You rich people are raised in security. You accept everything. You accept the steak, the clothes, the house. And basically you accept your friends . . . they all resemble you and you form a club, a country club of the mind. You're immune from the coarser types, like me. But your hod-carrying grandfather would understand me. I still sit with my back to the wall in a corner on purpose.

'For a kid loose in the world, whether it's Washington or Hamburg, a guy like me don't—I said "don't", not "doesn't"—get a chance to meet the Miss Finch girls. A guy like me doesn't get to meet the sorority sisters of downtown Antwerp or Rotterdam on ten bucks a week for shovelling sheep-manure. A guy working from four p.m. to midnight on the W.P.A. in Washington is rarely invited by Mrs. Mesta or Mrs. Cafritz to the big-wheel parties. A guy hustling a new peanut stand in New York is really not welcome.

'There is a close conspiracy of the people who can afford the taxi, as against the subway bunch. And I may say, my girl, there is just as close a conspiracy in the outside bunch, against the inside bunch. I got the kind of face that won't get me past the doorman in Morocco, unless I pinned a neon-sign listing by Dun and B. on my Sulka tie, and even then they'll send for Perona to see if I'm un-leprous enough to make it to the Champagne Room. But I also got a peasant's puss that will make a tramp on a sidewalk ask me to dinner, pay the tab, and grant me her favours while slipping a buck in my pocket without embarrassment to insure my cookies and coffee on the *mañana*.'

Craig stopped, and smiled.

'I apologize for the vehemence. I must have been bitten by a yacht club or something when I was a child. But I'm basically sound in what I say. We of the have-not group have—or had—only the unacceptable to hang on to. I do considerable business, and I find that, invariably, the pushcart-pedlar comes good, the wildcat oil millionaire who started out roughnecking on a well, the Wall Street millionaire who hungered for the second meal when he was a runner, the baseball bum up from the bushes—we all constitute a very queer fraternity of the wary.

'Even whores fit into the picture in a most magnificent Steinbeck fashion. *You* people'—he almost spat the '*you*'—'will never get inside *us* people. We were the drifters and bootleggers and rough-neckers and roustabouts—we were the peasants that got it made, the reformed depression orphans, the dislocated nonwhiners who went out and kicked the situation in the balls. Your aristocracy of New York society goes to Morocco, Twenty One and the Stork. In that order. John Perona was a bootlegger, so was Billingsley at the Stork, so were the Twenty One boys. We're all a bunch of thugs, and the biggest bunch of thugs still got unfond memories of dirty fingernails and calloused palms. Because we're all honest crum-bums, way outside the drawled Long Island accent. We come more or less off the side streets, and have made the boulevards hold still for it.'

'You talk too much, son,' Sue said. 'What else bothers you? You're kind of ugly-pretty, you got all the money in the world, you're proficient in the feathers and everybody knows your name. What burrs your blanket? Wife, perhaps? I asked you about that before. You got everything and more than a man can possibly need. What are you so little-boying about?'

Craig spun round and looked keenly at Sue. She was leaning back against the circular divan, chin tilted, a lazy plume of smoke wreathing her face.

'I'm nervous. I confess it. I don't believe anything. I don't believe I've got money. I don't believe I'm any good in the hay. I don't believe I'm here with you. I don't believe the bank won't bounce the cheque. I don't believe the sheriff won't be rapping on the door. I don't believe I ever had Christmas dinner in a whore-house. I don't believe anything, except . . . well, maybe I believe in Jazzbo.'

'And Jazzbo is what?'

'I really don't know what Jazzbo is. Possibly my conscience. Certainly handy. Certainly the nice little bit that's left of me, as I remember me. He's a Negro from Carolina, and he's my good-luck charm. Ever since I found Jazzbo, everything has worked pretty good—beautifully, I should say. Hard to explain. I was raised in the sticks, and amongst people who wore conjure bags around their throats.

'I'm real superstitious about a little African god I picked up on the West Coast, and in the same way I'm superstitious about Jazzbo. I suppose everybody has to have a stooge, except that I'm more Jazzbo's stooge than he's mine. But he's a good simple man . . . I believe he loves me, and he doesn't care if school don't keep. Early or late, he's there for Mistah Craig. You know the William Tell bit? I got only one party trick. I'm good with a pistol, and I have a small target range at my house in Suffern. The party trick is that Jazzbo smokes a cigarette and I shoot it out of his mouth. It would never occur to Jazzbo that I might miss that cigarette and hit him. In any case, I've been lucky ever since Jazzbo cut my track.'

'Where did you accumulate this solid ebony paragon of good luck?' Sue wriggled on the couch. 'You mix me a drink. You're bent over.'

'All right.' Craig took her empty glass and walked to the bar. He took a fresh glass and filled it, lit two cigarettes and handed her one.

'Simple enough. When he was about ten he came to the house in Kensington and went round to the back door and asked the cook if he could have a word with Mistah Craig. We had lost a boy—the first and only one.' Craig shrugged with his face. 'Anyhow, he announced himself as the last of several score younguns by way of Big Abner, an old hunting buddy of mine, and expressed a wish to sign on for the duration. Big Abner and his mama were dead, he said, and he wasn't enjoying living ten-to-a-room with his big brother and family. He was a cute little kid, black as a tarbaby, with bright eyes and a wholly delightful sugar-loaf smile. His talents, he said without stammering, were varied.

' "I knows how to train houn' dogs and slop hogs," he said. "I is a good yard-boy. I runs a keerful errand, and I is honest as de day is long. I wants to improve my station. I can read and figger and I wants to amount to something. I wants to learn how to be a good house-boy and va-*lley* and shofer. Den maybe some day I be's yo' chief butler."

' "Where'd you get all these big words, boy?" I asked him. "Like valet and chauffeur and butler?"

'He grinned at me and almost winked.

' "I been studyin' up on how to git ahead in de worl'. Everybody talkin' 'bout how good Mistah Craig Price doin', him he so young, too, dat I figgah maybe I jes hitch myself to yo' wagon. Papa he say one time befo' he die, Papa say, Son, you de baby dis family, you mind what I say. You git ahold some quality white folks fo' yo' self, you go a far piece. Maybe even you go North, far as Richmond. So I has come to work for you." ' Craig smiled.

'He said this simply and with suave dignity. He knew he had me. His father had undoubtedly regaled the family with tales of how much squirrel-head stew and chitterlings I had consumed in the Big Abner household, when I was a kid and prowling the woods with a bird-dog. He knew about my secret rich life across the tracks with my coloured friends. He also knew I had lost a boy-child, and adjudged the time was ripe for the *coup d'état*.

'I took him in, naturally, more or less as an adopted son. I dressed him up and sent him to school, but school and he never got along very well. Our coloured schools at that time. . . . He could read, as he said, and write reasonably well, but progress stopped there. I tried tutors with the same result. I saw no reason to try to make an unhappy white professor out of a happy but simply specialized black intelligence. So I taught him to drive and build drinks and take care of my clothes and generally make himself handy. I must say he has been an all-purpose

215

black diamond, and I swear he would rather be my right-hand man than President of the World. He is a tyrant, of sorts, but in the old lost-world sense, when the black mammies ran the house for O' Marse and Ol' Miss, and set down a firm foot on the deportment of the white younguns.'

'You know something?' Susan stretched and yawned. 'I'm dead, paralysed dead, for sleep. Between sex, food and personal history, I am a real beat girl. I'm going to bed. Coming, Mother?'

Craig shook his head. 'I don't think so. I don't sleep well with people. I twist and sweat up the sheets and snort and grind my teeth and sleep with one hand trailing on the rug. Also I don't like to wake up with my beard sort of green and prickly, to contemplate the same grimy shirt and used-up suit I took off last night. I really don't mind getting up and going home in the dawn, if I can wake up with the reassurance of my own toothbrush. How'd it be if I kissed you sweet now and we met at the Laurent for drinks and a late lunch tomorrow—or today —about one-thirty? And what are you doing for dinner tonight, and lunch tomorrow and dinner, and lunch and dinner on Friday too?'

'You said you have a family. Don't you ever go home?'

'Not very much recently. I have that rare thing, a wife who really does understand me, I'm afraid. I get out for week-ends. Sometimes. All right for lunch?'

'I suppose so. I don't know what I'm letting myself in for. Oh well, in for a penny, in for a pound. I don't think I like it a bit, but I think I am about to be in love with you, Craig Price. Right now it's too late and I'm too tired to sort anything out, except you can't say it ain't been charming. The Laurent, you said? That's Fifty-Seventh?'

'No. Fifty-Sixth. Corner Park. Italians again. Friends of mine. And the brook trout is still kicking from Eisenhower's private stream in Denver. It's quiet, and has pretty pictures on the walls. It's a fine place to hold hands. One-thirty?'

Susan Strong bobbed her head up and down and yawned vastly. 'Mmmhmmm. G'morning, Mr. Price.' She stood on tip-toes and kissed his cheek. Craig turned to go, but spun around swiftly. His face had gone unbiddenly tender.

'You know a very silly thing? After a lot of sordid practice I think I'm really in love for the first time in my life.' And was gone, with a flourish that almost seemed as if he wore a cloak. That, or was being followed—followed unwillingly by something he feared.

Now, he said, *now*. *Now* I've bought it. All the time I've held myself away from it. All the time I couldn't let it interfere with what I had to do. All that I never had time for. All the sentimental bats and bugs I was frightened of, all the diversions and that kind of alarums that could get in front of my careful plans, all that sentimental crap that could cloud my judgment, all the loving grasping fingers that could jiggle my aim, all that personal involvement that could louse me up. All that love-jive, all them rosy future clouds, and now I just bought it, on the strength of one night's stand. How do we know it, and why do we do it? he asked himself, striding harsh-heeled, clacking along the greying dirty morning pavements. Why do we seek the trouble, the trouble we don't need, that we can't use, the complications that kill you?

'You tell me, Mysterious Craig Price,' he said sarcastically aloud. 'You tell me, Captain-Admiral of the Ocean Sea. Fifteen billion broads around and you got to go to one stinking cocktail party and louse up your comfortable life. Because you know you'll marry this dame who literally threw you into the hay with her blue eyes when you looked at each other across a stranded olive and a hot martini.'

Craig paused at a corner, and thumbed his lighter near a sign which said: 'Curb Your Dog.' The lighter spluttered impotently once but failed to produce a flame. He threw the cigarette into the gutter in a temperish fit and strode on. A slight fog was dwindling like steam from the streets to wreathe his head. A taxi lumbered, aimlessly stalking the dog-dunged, refuse-ridden streets. The driver paused hopefully when he spied Craig, and went despondently away when Craig shook his head and waved him on. A cop, alert to muggers, spun his stick and decided that the lonely, slightly weaving walker, intent on his thoughts, was not a likely member of the growing fraternity of night-blooming Puerto Ricans.

Craig rang the nightbell on his building. A bleared, white-whiskered night-watchman responded. He snapped himself to a mussy attention, and his swimming eyes lit dully with recognition.

'Oh, it's you Mr. Price. You're up early, aren't you?' This, with the brilliant wit for which all night-porters are noted, and which for ever condemns them to night-portering.

'Um.' Craig had long ago stopped responding to pleasantry from menials. 'You got a match? My lighter's busted.'

'Oh, yes, sir,' the nightman said eagerly, as if Craig had asked him for the key to the Treasury, and he just happened to have it with him. 'Here, let me,' as Craig slapped a fresh cigarette into his mouth.

'Quiet morning,' the nightman said, as the lift soared to the fortieth story, making Craig's ears, as always, pop. 'A little fog, gone now, but now it seems like we might have some rain.'

'Um,' Craig Price said, as he stepped out of the elevator. 'Good morning.'

'Oh, good morning, Mr. Price,' the nightman said. 'Thank you very much.'

Craig walked wearily through his office. He paused, briefly, to touch the smooth-gleaming elephant tusks, left the scattered lights on, and sought his bed.

He was pondering divorce possibilities, thinking about the division of properties, when he fell asleep.

13

WELL, girl, Susan said to herself as she woke, yawning, how about you for the feckless filly? Little Miss Round-Heels in person. Don't pay her no money. Buy her a meal and shove her into the sack. Or what's worse, you shove *him* into the sack. I suspect the guilt lieth within you, Susan, from the first minute you clapped eyes on that beat-up face. What *is* there about a broken nose? Up you get, my girl, and repair the ravages in time for lunch.

Funny, funny, Susan thought as she ran her tub. All the strange little peculiar hidden pockets behind the façade of public people. According to what I read, this Price man has been a ringtailed wildcat since he was twenty, and when you scratch him a little bit he's about fourteen years old today, broken nose, billion dollars and all.

She spilled some bath-salts into the tub, and lay at full length, wiggling her toes. I hopped into bed with him like a tart, she said to herself, like the cheapest floozie. Yet I don't think he held me cheaply. He didn't have to tell me all those things after he had, so to speak, already enjoyed the pleasure of my presence. Will anyone ever understand women? Not me. Half the gentlemen in the city panting after me and I practically knock the man down and drag him off by the hair.

But I must say the loose life becomes me, she said, as she sat in front of the mirror and began to fix her face. Up until six a.m., too much to drink, in and out of bed like a rabbit, and I look about twenty-five instead of my solid thirty-six. *Dear* Mr. Price.

One thing for very sure, she thought, as she slipped into her frock. For very damned sure. This is one to stop right now unless it looks like heading somewhere. The backstreet wife stuff is all right in the books, but it's highly impractical in New York, where everybody knows everybody. Being seen with this gentleman in public more than once is going to be an admission of something—of something I do not particularly like. And just be damned if I'm going to be one of these convenient women who waits with trembling breath for the master's infrequent knock. Well, let us see, Susan. How do we look in this blue?

We look just dandy, not to say radiant. And the hell of it is, she thought ruefully as she went out of the door, it's true.

Susan was five minutes early for the appointment, but Craig was already there, sitting at the bar and looking impatiently at the door. His face lit when she came down the stairs into the rich old room, and he almost bounded across the floor to meet her.

His eyes travelled swiftly over her face, dropped briefly, and unsuccessfully attempted to mask delight.

'You look sort of edible,' he said. 'Come and let's sit in the corner and hold hands, like I said. Larry'll feed us in all good time. I thought you'd never get here.'

He steered her across the room. Eyes followed them knowingly. Craig nodded to three or four people as he handed her into a divan behind a corner table. Susan had seen the look before. It was that old familiar what's-the-boy-up-to-now appraisal, the and-who-is-the-dish look.

'You ain't unknown here, my boy,' she said as they sat down 'Is this where you always bring your newest conquest?'

'Shush. This is a place where I only bring my better class of friends. You want a drink, or are you just plain hungry?'

'No drink. I'm starved. I missed breakfast, and I kept thinking about all that fancy food-talk we had last night. One thing you have to know about me, if you already haven't guessed: I'm a hearty feeder, day in and day out. God blessed me with good legs and a magnificent digestive apparatus.'

'Fine. We'll play seafood, maybe. You like little soft-shell crabs?'

'Love 'em.'

'We'll start with them, then.' He called the head waiter, ordered, and turned back to Sue.

'I'm sorry if I talked too much last night. I don't usually. But something about you brings out the long-play in me—the healthy urge to confide all. I suppose it's a matter of just finding the right person to listen.'

'I like to listen. I'm basically lazy. Also I learned a lesson very early. All men like to talk. Damned few like to listen. A girl can make herself a reputation as a brilliant conversationalist by just listening carefully enough to fire in a question once in a while.'

'I expect you're right. But apart from music, listening, and eating, not to mention the other thing, what do you *like*?'

Susan toyed with a soft-shell crab. She raised level eyes.

'I told you, I'm lazy. I like to sit in front of the fire and read. I like to lie in the sun and think of nothing at all. We've been through the music thing—the popular music thing. But I like concert music. I love the theatre. I like baseball. I love going to the zoo. I spend a lot of spare time in the Metropolitan Museum. I like to cook. I like beer. I like flowers and birds and

219

sunsets. I hate complications. I'm a square, I suppose. I can think of nothing nicer than being married to somebody you love and trying to keep everybody happy. I'm sore afraid, sir, that you've picked on a lump.'

Craig demolished a crab before he spoke. He pointed a fork at Susan's chin.

'I've been looking all over for a lovely lump like you. Don't you have any ambition at all? Don't you want to be a senator or a department store executive or a movie actress or a doer of good works with all their ensuing charity balls?'

She grinned at him.

'Foosh to the balls, you should pardon the expression,' she said. 'No. I want none of it. I should like to keep myself as clean and pretty as possible. I'm no femme fatale, and I know it. I'm a big dame with a reasonable figure, an ordinary face, so-so hair and medium blue eyes. I'd feel like a fool in a tiara. I've tried being a blonde once and didn't like it. Me and mascara don't get along very well. I, sir, am what you might call a modern milkmaid.'

Craig looked at the blue linen suit, with its white ruffly blouse and severe cuffs, the small gold arrow-brooch, the one good sapphire ring.

'I'd say anything else would be extraneous. If I ever need a full-time milkmaid, I'll keep you in mind. Shall we try some of the President's trout and maybe an avocado?'

'Wonderful.'

They ate in silence for a bit. Then Craig said:

'Would you mind terribly if we were a foursome for dinner tonight? There's a couple in town I almost have to see. I'm sorry, but dinner is a kind of business weapon with me from time to time.'

'Of course not. Who are they?'

'English. Or rather, he's English, she's Italian. He's part of my London operation. Very amusing chap, and she's a charmer. They've been awfully kind to me in London, and they're just passing through. It needn't be a late one. We can shake them after dinner if you like.'

'Of course. Usual little black, or something fancier?'

'Usual black. Take them to the Colony, I thought. I'll cocktail them first and then come and fetch you.'

'No need for that. Just ring and I'll take a taxi and meet you. I'm a big girl. I know about taxis. I'll be washed and waved about eight?'

'Eight-thirty. It would save me a step, sweetie. Nice of you.'

'Tell me something, Craig. This starts out to be protective coloration, or what? I mean, am I somebody's mother at night, but lunch is all right as a twosome, or what? I'd like to know. You being at least technically married, and not an unlikely item

220

for the gossip columns. Does it make any difference, because there's a press agent behind every philodendron in these places? I don't care, but what about you?'

'I don't care either. There's so much damned nonsense printed about everybody that I've found—I find—it a lot safer to brazen it out and hit the top spots rather than to try to duck around corners.'

Susan smiled.

'I noticed you changed your tenses on me. You've had a lot of experience at this sort of thing, I gather?'

Craig lit a cigarette before he answered. He smiled back.

'What would you have me say? I'm forty-ish. I have been untechnically separated from my wife for a long time. I am, I suppose, a public figure. I've found that a certain amount of safety is to be had in numbers.' He shrugged. 'One more item in Cholly Knickerbocker isn't going to break my back. Not if you don't care, Grandmaw.'

Susan shook her head.

'For me I don't care. I was thinking about wives and children, more. They read.'

'Possibly they've read so much, most of it untrue, that they don't care any more either. I know a lot of people, and am generally surrounded by same in public. Mostly the columns are pretty kind, and if they aren't . . .' He shrugged again. 'I don't make excuses.'

He glanced at his watch.

'I've got a board meeting at three. Want some dessert, or settle for coffee?'

'Settle for coffee. I've got to go to the hairdresser if I'm not to disgrace you in front of your friends. Been a nice lunch, Mr. P. I'll try to sparkle for your friends. Do I say "bloody"?' She was teasing.

They finished the coffee, and she slipped on her gloves.

'Where's your hairdresser?'

'Way uptown. Just pop me into a cab. Or do you want me to drop you, first?'

'Thanks. I'm just a hop and a skip. I think I'll walk.'

Craig handed her into a cab, waved, and started for his office. As he walked, head down, he was unable to recall one important thing that was said at lunch. He only remembered that Mrs. Susan Strong was prettier, if anything, in the daytime, and that his usual midday nerves seemed remarkably unruffled.

Susan sat under the drier, and let her thoughts roam. What a dull lunch, she thought. So different from last night. No laughter, to speak of. No real talk. Do you suppose that's reaction from last night, too many things coming all at once? It's possible even that my man Price is actually shy. Or maybe this is just natural,

221

and he's ringing in his English friends to keep the evening un-dull. But I think I am head-over-heels for this fellow. It's a poor business, at best. I've kept a very clean bill of moral health since Steve and I broke it off. I surely wouldn't care to be mixed up in something smelly. Last night was certainly a mistake, if a very pleasant one. But face it, Susan, you were about ready for such a mistake. Been too long a time, and old-maiding doesn't become you. I wonder what he sees in me, anyhow? God knows he must have been subjected to masses more attractive. I imagine they hurl themselves at him. Oh, well. We'll learn some more tonight, and maybe I can chart some sort of course.

She bit the inside of her lower lip.

'But damn it,' she said, half-aloud. 'I want him!'

The evening had gone very well, she thought, as she and Craig sat over nightcaps in her apartment. She had excused herself, after indicating the bar and switching on the record player, and had gone to ungirdle herself, wash her face, and slide into a house coat. Craig was sitting, gazing at nothing, when she came out of the bedroom and passed a hand gently over his head.

'Penny.'

'Nothing very much. Except that Nigel and Marisa both said they thought you were the most charming American woman they'd ever met, and I was inclined to agree. I noticed that you seem to know an alarming lot about England, and that the few people you mentioned all seemed, in Nigel's book, to be veddy veddy veddy top-drawer. Also you didn't say "bloody" even once. I thought that "little black" dress you wore was a kind of a stunner, myself. You looked, my sweet, so much more beautiful than anybody in the Colony that I'm quite sure all the ladies hated you violently, and of course all the gentlemen would cheerfully have poisoned me. I was very proud.'

'So I passed the first fingernail-test, did I? Didn't talk dirty or double-negative you into embarrassment or nothing like that there?'

'What do you mean, passed the first test?'

'I had a sort of feeling. I felt like maybe you were trying me on for size. Outside size, I mean. Fit for public consumption, and that sort of thing.'

'I don't know as I like that very much, Mrs. Strong. You wouldn't be going bitchy on me, would you?'

Susan sighed.

'I suppose I am. Being a woman is an involved business, at best. But I have this private thing of having to keep reassuring myself that I'm not just another well-manicured tramp. We fell into bed so easily . . . I mean . . . I mean I just wondered if it were only another laugh for you. You must be swamped in easy conquests. And I don't want to be one of these girls that everybody describes as 'Sue? Oh, she's a million laughs." I don't want to be a million laughs. I don't want to be even one easy laugh.'

'Here, here, take it slow, Mrs. Strong. Take down the fists. First, I do not consider last night as anything less than a magnificent accident. Second, I was *not* trying you on for size. And third, there is practically nobody that I'd care to display in front of Nigel and Marisa unless I was sure that I could be tremendously proud to present them. I was flaunting you in my buttonhole tonight, my good woman.'

Susan dipped her head in a mock-contrite bow.

'Sorry. I suppose I did sound bitchy. Won't be bitchy again. But maybe you can see my point. Just a tiny bit, anyhow. My late-blooming attack of conscience does not preclude the fact that we had frankly, last night, a charming unplanned roll in the hay. Worse people have rolled in worse hays. But there was quite a lot of love, or almost-love, talk going on last night, and dammit if I'm going to wrap up a heart and send it special delivery to be trampled. Not at my age. We can quit this one right now, my boy, and no harm done. But if we do decide to continue on, I want some sort of a future.'

'But . . .' Craig held up a palm.

'Wait until I've finished. I want some kind of a future. If I can't be a wife, I'll be a mistress. I don't care which. And that's a lie, there never was a woman, ever, who deep-down wanted to be a mistress, but I'll settle for the lesser if there's a mutual future and a chance of something else. Otherwise you can buy me an occasional drink in the Oak Room, and once in a while, if I'm exceedingly frustrated, I might just let you up my stairs in a weak moment. But when you're doing your late-night thinking, chum, try to think that the granddaughter of James Patrick Kegan Moriarty ain't a dame to be trifled with, and is too froward— and I don't mean forward—too goddam froward to truckle to a man in an ordinary casual weekend fashion.'

'Yes, Mummy dear.' Craig got up and started for the door. 'Already you're acting like a wife. See you around.'

'Craig.'

'Yes.' He turned around. 'What?'

'Come here and don't be a damned fool. Don't you know *anything* about women at all?'

'God pity me, I don't think so.'

'I don't know what gets into me, or any other woman. Maybe I was just trying *you* on for size. Believe me when I say I'm falling madly in love with you and was just sort of trying to knock it on the head before it started to hurt too much. Come and kiss me.'

Craig walked over, took Susan by the shoulders, and hauled her erect from her chair. His fingers bit into her upper arms.

223

'Look, my dear girl.' His voice was tensely savage. 'One of the things I care less about these days is games. I told you. I want to be in love. I want to be in love with you. I can be in love with you on a rainy Sunday when you've got the curse and there's nothing on TV and lousy double-features and the town closed tight. Even on this short notice I want to walk a long mile with you, Susan Strong.' He shook her. 'Don't you trifle with me, either, Babydoll. And don't try any tricks. I've had all the tricks, up to here I've had the tricks.'

'I said I was sorry. It won't happen again. Will you stay for one more drink?'

'Yes,' Craig said, and grinned. 'I'll stay. For one more drink.'

The next day at lunch he was light and gay again.

'Ever been to Cuba?' he asked.

'Oddly enough, no. Mexico, yes.'

'Well, I've got to go sometime in the next two or three weeks. Something to do with a manganese mine and a snide prospective purpose in a Cuban bank and the new political troubles. Be gone four or five days—maybe a week. If you were a good girl I might take you. It'd be fun. Like the idea?'

'It sounds lovely. Can you get away so long?'

'I can make the time. I need some relief from town, anyhow. I would like to shoot some craps at the casino and eat some Morro crabs and drink some daiquiris and loaf in the sun at Varadero. The actual business won't take much time. Come on, say yes.'

'Yes. I always heard this was how you started on a life of shame. They got a Mann Act applying to Cuba?'

'Not that I know of. It's the centre of the white slave trade. One of my other businesses. We need recruits. You look durable. Think how you can save all your money and then marry the sop on the corner.'

'Sounds charming. Will I need many clothes?'

'Very few. You can buy anything you want in Havana while I'm tying up a few tag-ends of business. We leave in about ten days. Week from this coming Monday. Sound like fun?'

'Sounds wonderful. I can't wait.'

(It does not sound wonderful, she thought. I don't like honeymoons on other people's time. Not that I'm not buying. I wasn't brought up to be a short-time girl. But after last night, I button the lip.)

'It sounds absolutely divine,' she said. 'More people tonight, or are we eating alone?'

'No people tonight. I think I feel like Third Avenue. A simple steak and a baked potato. All right?'

'Lovely. And afterwards, you know what I'd like?'

'What would you like? I'll get it for you.'

'I would like to go see a bad cowboy movie and then go home and crawl in the hay, early.'

'By yourself?' His tone held mock alarm.

'Strange as it may seem, yes. There are certain nights when grease on the face and general sloppiness are indicated. This is one of the nights. I've got a whole lot of thinking to do, and your presence disturbs me. Okay?'

'Sure. I could do with an early evening, myself. Ready?'

'Ready.'

Smart gal, Craig thought, when her taxi sped away. Already she knows how to ration a lover. It takes a smart one to know when Daddy needs a night off. And Daddy does need a night off, because Daddy has got some heavy thinking of his own to do.

14

Time said: 'In the Depression, latter-midst, Craig Price wearied of the sea. When he got his first job as a sailor, he gleefully relates, they called him "The Duke", because he had been to college. Several trips later he was called "The Iron Duke", and bore the scars to justify the title. Something drew him to Charleston, S.C., and when he paid off in that port he owned sixty dollars.'

Craig's lips had parted in a death's-head grin.

'Wearied of the sea. God. *Wearied of the sea*. Fancy, now. That's the understatement of all time. And it wasn't sixty dollars. It was sixty-three dollars, and fifty-nine cents, plus a few German marks. Something drew me to Charleston . . . I'll say, something drew me to Charleston.'

It was late spring of 1935, and he had paid off in Charleston. He was tired of roaming. He was tired of jobs, in between ships, in places like Washington and Baltimore and New Orleans, menial, stop-gap, deadly dull jobs, dirty jobs, which always seemed to pay just a little less than was necessary to maintain a full stomach and a clean pair of extra drawers. He was a little more than nineteen years old and felt, sometimes, an easy thirty.

Paying off in Charleston was an accident, of course, because a ship could pay off any place, but there he was in Charleston, where it all had started. He had a little money and more than one suit and as naturally as metal to magnet, his feet turned towards the Battery and a certain house. And he was nineteen years old—a man. He had decided that a man would do well to telephone first.

He had yanked at the bell-pull at the gate of the walled house, the walled house he remembered so well, proudly placed on the Battery. The same strawberry-faced butler opened the gate. He seemed much older now, and his pitted nose rested nearly on his chin. From him came a musty odour of age—the stale smell to be found in a room long unused.

'Craig Price,' Craig said. 'Madame duFresne is expecting me. You remember me, LeBlanc?'

'Please enter, sir. Of course. You came here a long time ago with Mr. Philip. Welcome home, sir. I must say, with your permission, sir, you've changed. I would not have recognized you if you had not called on the telephone. Madame is very eager to see you. She is in the patio.'

'She was in the patio before.' Craig looked around him. 'Nothing has changed much, LeBlanc?'

'Some things, sir. This way, please, if you don't remember.'

'I remember.'

Craig was wearing a new suit, a chalk-striped Oxford-grey he had bought in England. He was lean and hard as a rake-handle. He had, now, a moustache, a moustache burnt blond by the salty sun. Streaks of golden sunburn showed in his brown hair, waved unduly by the salt air. The nose, twice broken, rescued his face from handsomeness, as did the crescent broken-bottle scar on the brown of his cheek.

'Hello, Julie,' he said when he entered the flowering patio. 'I found you here before. You look lovely, as usual. Maybe even more so.' He could call her Julie naturally now, and tell her that she looked lovely. She *did* look lovely. She was wearing a halter and shorts, and was nearly as tanned as Craig and seemed very little older. The eyes were purple beacons against the rosy-brown skin, and if there was any grey in her hair, she she had carefully drowned it in dye. It was still as black and shiny as sealskin. She got up and placed both hands on his shoulders.

'Let me look at you,' she said, 'let me see you,' and pushed herself away, still holding him. 'Yes,' she said. '*Yes.*'

'Yes what?' Craig's voice was cool. He raised an eyebrow.

'The boy left. The man returned. I would have bet my bottom dollar. Pity I can't say the same about—' her voice suddenly brooded. 'Let's sit. Drink?'

'Please. Whisky, if there is some.' Craig sat in a chair on the other side of the same table he remembered.

'There is some.' She pressed a bell. 'LeBlanc is coming with it now.' She smiled. 'Do you still have the knickers?'

Craig smiled back.

'No, Miss Julie, ma'am. I'm a big boy now, I'm afraid. A sort of world-travelling big boy. Lot of strife and trouble since I left. But fun. How's Philip?'

'Philip? Here, LeBlanc. Soda or water, Craig?'

'Water, please.'

The butler mixed the drinks, in a vacuum of silence, left the tray, and departed.

'Cheers,' Julie duFresne said. 'Welcome home, Craig Price.'

'*Salut et bonne chance*, Julie duFresne,' Craig said. They drank.

'Philip?' Craig quirked his eyebrow.

'Why not *me*, first?'

'I can see *you*. All you've got is lovelier than I remembered. Possibly the sea is responsible. I mean, everything ashore seems lovelier than it used to. But Philip?'

Julie duFresne spoke soberly, bitterly.

'I'm afraid we've had a bit of bad luck with Philip. When you left, you were a boy, but you come back a man. Philip left as an exaggerated man, and has more or less degenerated into a nasty child. He's in Europe, still on allowance, with his hair curling on his neck. Possibly unwashed, writing bad poetry without capital letters, and picking up sailors in *pissoirs*. I'm afraid that there isn't much to say about Philip. Except, as far as I know, he hasn't taken to drugs yet. But then, the mail's been slow, lately.'

'I'm sorry, truly sorry. Now, what about you, Madame? I am really surprised to see no husband in the house.'

She shrugged and made a small *moue*.

'I've thought about it, and almost did it . . . several times. But then something always went wrong at the last moment—I couldn't face the idea of *him* or he got dissatisfied with the idea of a lifetime with *me*. I don't really mind being a lone, lorn widow-lady with an expatriate pansy for a son. Not, especially, if I can see you again, turned into the man I thought I saw inside the scared boy. You *are* a man, aren't you, Craig Price? At least you've interesting scars.'

'If that means I'm not a boy any more—' Craig grinned. 'Then today I am a man. A few years of my kind of hobo-ing is apt to scrub the boyhood off you with a stiff brush. It has to leave scars.'

Julie replenished his drink.

'I must hear *all* about it—all the places you've been, what you've done, what your plans are. Can you—would you please, stay a few days? I'm a lonely old lady, you know, and Charleston is so frightfully dull. It would be a favour for me.'

'I'd love to. I'll have to go and get my bag—my one bag—though. It's checked at the hotel.'

Julie duFresne flirted an impatient wrist.

'We'll send Graves. You remember Graves, the chauffeur?'

'Sure. That would be nice.' Craig's voice was suddenly wooden. 'Julie.'

'Yes?'

'You know why I came back?'

'I think so. Yes. I think so.'

227

'Philip isn't here any more. Is that why you didn't kiss me hello, like you used to?'

She got up swiftly and came into his arms.

A little later he said:

'Which room will I be staying in, now I'm here? The same one as before?'

'You know very well you won't be staying in the same one as before, Craig Price. Not if that's really *why* you came back,' and went fiercely again into his arms. The sun beat down in the patio, but upstairs it was darkly, gloriously cool.

'See here, my beloved boy,' Julie duFresne said. They were having post-lunch coffee in the patio.

'What? Cigarette?'

'Please. Thanks. But see here.'

'See here what, teacher?' He leaned back, stretched his legs, and fondled the sun with his body. 'See here what?'

Julie was serious.

'This will sound like a lecture. We've been sleeping together and it's been glorious. We both proved something I think is fine. You were always a man and now we both know it. But I'm too old for lotus-eating and you're too young. I have money; you don't. If you were ten years older I'd say let's get married and the utter hell with everything, age included, there's enough for us both. But I am just around the corner from a moustache and a menopause, my fine fellow, and you are just starting to tick over. Up to now you are just a sort of sea-going field-hand with possibilities of making foreman and maybe owning the plantation, if the women don't spoil you. I'm not going to be the woman to spoil you, although God knows I'd like to, twice a day, and three times on Sunday.'

'Let us go spoil me some, ma'am.' Craig almost wriggled. 'Ah feel lak' bein' spoilt some more.'

'*Tais-toi*. Shut up. I love you, Craig Price. I love you as the kind of son I'd like to have had, and I love you as an exciting lover, and I love you for something else . . . Something better than either. You're a hard man with a strong core of strength that I *won't*, I will *not*, see dissipated by ease. I am being selfish because I love you, and I am being selfish because I respect *me*. You can tell your grandchildren about the wonderful time you had sleeping with your room-mate's mother, and I won't care a hoot, I'll consider it a compliment. But I am not adopting any-body, at my age—especially somebody who will inevitably be saying to himself: "Poor old Julie, she's a touch long in the tooth, she won't really mind if I have to go to Jacksonville on business." I will *not* be held up in my old age as a figure of fun or an object of pity. I will *not* hear, second-hand, a lot of bad humour about cradle-robbing—"old enough to be his mother,

228

so sad a fine man like that is saddled with a woman twice his age no wonder he . . ." No *Merde*. Not for Julie. You can consider these last two weeks a honeymoon, for which I shall always be grateful, and for which I shall always love you, believe me. You've made me young again, and you've given me . . . well. You are leaving this afternoon, *mon cheri*. And I have decided after all to get married after a decent interval of mourning. There are several candidates for my hand, I'll have you know, and I think I shall choose Maurice Maréchal. He is ten years older than me, with a grown-up family that offers no problems. He has money and . . . and oh God, Craig, take me to bed one more time and then go away, go away, *go away*!'

15

CRAIG had been to sea. He had worked in Washington and New Orleans. He had been to sea again, and he had paid off in Charleston. He had been dismissed by Madame duFresne in Charleston, so once again, a creature of animal habit, his sparse money dwindling, he had traced the pattern of his earlier youth, step by step, and had followed his old trail to Kensington. There was nothing to call him to Kensington, really. Richard and Lilian Price were both dead. Richard's weak lungs had led to a fatal pneumonia. Lilian's adult measles had overstrained her heart. They had died within months of each other, and Craig had been in Germany at the time with no possible chance of getting home. In a way it was a relief. The lack of communication he had always felt about his immediate family was finally happily chopped short—severed at the umbilicus.

But still something drew him back to the old place. An oak tree, perhaps, the sun glinting on the breeze-dimpled waters, old Sam's house that was no longer Old Sam's house, the magnolia tree, the mocking-bird . . . who knows? He might just as easily have hitch-hiked directly north, or further south. Who knows? Not Craig Price. All he knew was that he was finished with the sea, he had been politely asked to leave the sheet-wrinkled love-tossed bed of his room-mate's mother, he had about ten bucks left in his pocket, and he turned sentimentally towards Kensington.

For luck he took a taxi to the same filling station at which he had started a life with John Grimes. This new saviour was a Yankee heading north from Florida. They had very little to say, except 'Thank you very much' when the Yankee dropped Craig at the corner of Third and Market and proceeded, unmerrily, on his way, after quarrelling with the Esso attendant over the high cost of gasoline in the South.

Craig was hesitant as he knocked at the door. In a way he was surprised that it was the same house in Forest Glen. The papers had said . . . but then he'd been away a long time, and out of touch. Possibly if his people hadn't died, they'd have kept him . . . Why would they, for God's sake? Who kept who in touch with anything?

He walked up the crushed-shell road. He looked at the garage he remembered so well, from when he was . . . from when he was a . . . a kid? There was no Cord, no Duesenberg, no twin Cadillacs. There was now a Ford. It needed washing. The lawn needed mowing, he saw. The house needed painting. The shrubbery needed tending.

Maybelle answered his knock. She was still plump, but very pretty in her bright dirndl dress. The eyes were still the same delft, but she was a woman now, not a fat little girl, not a carbon of her papa. Certainly not a reflection of her mama. Craig remembered she was nearly a year older than he.

'Won't you come in, Mr. Price?' She almost simpered. 'It is so nice of you to call. It's been such a long, long time. I didn't hardly know you with your moustache. It makes you look so old.'

'Thank you, Miss Grimes,' Craig said, as he walked into the room. 'But I did use to call you Maybelle when I was teaching you to drive, didn't I? Can we get it back on that level? Even if I do look so old?'

She was shy. She dipped her chin—which, Craig thought, would soon be plural.

'You never did come to see me in Raleigh,' she said accusingly, as she seated him in the same all-red but shabbier now, living-room. 'I just kept waiting and waiting and then somebody from The Hill told me you had run off and gone to sea. I was so mad I could of spit.'

'I hope your mama's well?'

The girl's face clouded petulantly.

'No, Mama isn't doing so good. She's in Nottingham Hill. That's in Greensboro. She got nervous something terrible after Daddy died. But they say she's doing fine for her. Can I get you a drink of something?'

'Tell the truth,' Craig said, 'I'm thirsty as hell. I'd love a Coke or a ginger-ale or anything like that. Can I help?'

'No. You just sit right there. I won't be a minute.' She disappeared, and there was a sound of the solid clanging of an ice-box door, the hiss of hot water on metal, and the icy clink of cubes. She came back swiftly, bearing a small ice-bucket which she plumped down on a corner table where a meagre collection of bottles, half empty, stood.

'How much, Mr. Price . . . I mean, Craig? Oh, excuse me. You said Coke or ginger-ale. You'd maybe like me to sweeten it up a little bit? I was thinkin' about havin' a little toddy, it's about time.'

Craig's eyes roved over the bottles and lit on a bottle of rum.

'Drop a little rum in the Coke, if it's not too much trouble. Maybe we can combine thirst with health.' He grinned sourly when he saw his feeble joke was wasted. Maybelle Grimes poured herself a stout two-fingers of bourbon, and knocked it back neat.

She handed him his mixed drink and then sat down. 'I feel like such a stranger with you,' she said. 'You been all-over, everywhere, all over to Europe and like that. Daddy set a lot of store by you, kind of like you were his boy. His own boy, I mean. He talked about you all the time. Just before he passed away, he was talking about taking you to Europe for a trip, and then putting you to work in the business. Yes, sir, Daddy set a heap of store by you.' She pressed her lips together, primly. 'Of course, there isn't much business left now, except the one mill and the house. I guess that's what drove the old lady nuts!'

The shafting statement drove through Craig's bored consciousness, which had prepared itself for Southern talk, and he looked at Maybelle Grimes with fresh interest.

'Drove her *nuts*?' he said.

'She's as crazy as a bedbug,' Maybelle said. 'Wild. The old man was lucky to die before she flipped. Like the song says, "Nobody knows the trouble I see, nobody knows but Jesus . . ."'

The sudden irreverent approach to parenthood shocked him. Craig studied his hostess. She was really quite a pretty girl, and she was sort of coming through the rye. Bosom, good. Legs, neat. The double chin, not quite yet. Not bad, not bad at all. And a little bit honest, too.

'I came round to call out of respect to your Pa,' he said. 'He had that idea of going to Europe, and taking me, and when he died, I went abroad as much for him as for me. I was fond of him, Maybelle. He was very nice to me when I needed somebody to be nice to me. I don't know if you understand?'

'I think I do. Would you like something tougher than that rum-and-Coke? I would. I would like to get a little bit drunk to celebrate that time you never did come to see me at St. Mary's in Raleigh. It's lonesome in this house with Ma in the nut-hatch and the shadows creeping all around. My pa's death was a real mess for everybody. He left everything all messed up. When the lawyers finally got it straightened out, there was this house and one lousy, but lousy, little mill. Papa's own bank went and everything else went except this house. And one lousy little mill.'

The phonograph was howling 'Tiger Rag'. The big red room was filled with cigarette smoke. Maybelle was sprawled

231

on a sofa, her non-drink-holding hand trailing to the floor.

'It's getting a little drunk, wouldn't you think?' Craig got up from his chair and walked over to the bar-sideboard. 'Why don't we have one more and then go somewhere and eat something?' I still got ten bucks, he thought. This is Kensington and you can do a big sea-food dinner on two bucks.

Maybelle stretched herself and yawned mightily.

'It's gettin' a little bit drunk and I love it. I don't want to go out any place. This is the first real good fun I've had since the old man died and we locked up Mama. Mama never wanted anybody to have any fun. Papa was away most of the time, or workin' hard, and whenever he tried to bring anybody home for a few drinks, Mama looked like the world was comin' to an end. He used to roll in fried and go right off to bed.

'It was the same way about the boys. Mama had some sort of idea that everybody was trying to rape me, or marry me for Papa's money, or something, and there wasn't any use trying to bring any kids home, because she clouded up and rained all over that, too. And I wasn't allowed to go out on dates alone with any boy, and now I guess the boys got out of the habit of asking me, because *nobody* ever comes here now. Maybe Mama bein' crazy scared 'em off.

'Nobody comes here, and I think I'm kind of cute.' She giggled. 'I'm kind of cute, I think, but nobody ever comes to see me. How can I be cute if nobody comes to see me? Gimme another drink, and in a minute I'll slap together some ham'neggs. Do *you* think I'm cute, Craig?'

'I think you're very cute,' Craig said. 'Cute as a speckled pup. Here.' He handed her the drink.

'Call that a drink? Ice tea's stronger.' She got up and walked, weaving slightly, over to the bar. She picked up the bourbon bottle and poured a stiff four-fingers into another glass, and killed half of it in a gulp. 'You think I'm drunk, don't you? Well, I'm not. I'm-cute-is-what-I-am-is-all.' She set her drink down carefully on the table.

'Sh—see. I got pretty legs, look.' She hiked her dress up to her hips. 'Got very pretty legs. I'm stacked. I'm built like a brick sh . . .'

'Careful,' Craig said. 'Watch it, baby.'

'Careful, my foot,' she said. 'Everybody sh—says be careful. Do'wanna be careful, wanna have fun. You mean to sh—say I'm not stacked as good as anybody? I'll show if I'm stacked or ain't stacked. You jus' wait.' In a swift second she tore off her blouse, scattering buttons like hailstones, and unhooked her skirt. It fell in a pool at her feet, and she spurned it to one side. She was clad now in blue-silk brief pants, a brassière, and stockings rolled above the knee. She kicked off her shoes and pirouetted slowly.

She looked at Craig belligerently.

'You mean tell me I'm not stacked? Mean say I'm not cute? If I'm so goddamn cute then why doesn't somebody do something about it? I sit out in this goddam house all day long and . . .' she started to sniffle. 'I bet you ain't so hot yourself. Show me something, tell me I'm wrong. Don't be sh—self-cons-sh-cious. Don't be modest. I'm not shy. Sh—see if I'm shy.' She unsnapped her brassière, and stripped off her knickers. She drew herself erect with drunken gravity, and gazed at him haughtily through lowered lids, with tilted chin.

'I'm not shy. You're shy. You probly got awful birthmark or something.' She lurched against him, and seized him around the waist, raising her face. 'Kish—kiss me,' she said, 'take—take me now.'

'I better go now,' Craig said. The sky was lightening. 'I better go before it gets to be real light. It won't look very nice if people see me coming out of here in the morning.'

Maybelle sighed and snuggled closer. She had both arms wrapped around him, the one behind encircling his neck, the other across his chest. Craig could barely manage to breathe. He lifted her left arm from across his bare chest and sat up in bed.

'Don' go'way. Please don' go'way.'

'No, honey, I better scram. I'll come back tomorr—I'll come back tonight. It'll be better that way. Honest.'

Maybelle wriggled, and put a hand on his naked thigh.

'Aw' ri'. But don't wait 'til night. Come for lunch. I'll make us nice lunch. Sort of picnic. Promise you come for lunch or I won't let you go.' Shamelessly she moved her hand higher. 'See? Got you. 'less I say so you can't never ever leave me.' She giggled.

'Okay,' Craig said. 'You win, honey. I'll be back about noon. I want to get my clothes and find a boarding house and maybe look around for a job. Going, now.' He kissed her briefly, gently removed her hand, and looked down at her flushed face, framed in damp-tousled curls. She closed her eyes, sighed, and drifted back to sleep with a slight smile on her parted lips. She looks like a fat little baby, Craig thought.

He pulled on his pants and went into the bathroom to comb his hair and wash his face. He dressed and crept quietly down the stairs, opened the front door softly, and stood for a moment under the pines, watching the last pale stars winking in the pinkening sky.

He decided he'd walk back to town. It was a nice cool morning for a walk back to town, and somehow his feet led him past the factory section on the outskirts of Kensington. It was longer that way, but the morning was cool and fresh, the breeze stirring softly in the pines, and he wanted another look at the mills.

Been years since I saw them, he thought. He walked in long strides, thinking.

There they were, the long buildings, bulking black like huge box cars on a siding, with the tall smokestacks etched black against the early lemon light. A few years ago, he thought, leaping blue lights would be glowing through those windows, the plants humming, clashing, roaring with life. No more. They would be barely making it on a two-shift, five-day week. He could barely make out the sign: 'Grimes Mills'.

'This is where I would have worked if the old man had lived,' he said aloud. 'One day these would have been mine. Mine. Old Man Grimes wouldn't have lived forever. Grimes Mills would have been Price Mills, one day.'

He walked on towards town. All of a sudden he stopped short. Old Sam Price's words came sharply back to him—the words his grandfather had spoken that day down by the cowlot, just before he died. What was it again, what was it the old man had said in his last pain?

'Don't go through life with this hookworm philosphy I always had—just settin' and lettin' it pass. Grab it and use it and kick the crap right out of it, and don't never, *ever* let it run you. You treat life like it was your enemy. Beat it on the head and knock it around until it hollers. Make it work *for* you. This world ain't no place for nice people. This is for dogs eatin' dogs, and the biggest son-of-a-bitch wins. . . .' Craig turned and looked back at the mill.

'And why not? Why not *now*? What's to prevent it? There's only Maybelle and the trustees. Only Maybelle, and Maybelle likes me enough to . . . Why the hell not?' He was startled to find his voice raised in a shout. A passing Negro and two yellow fice dogs looked at him in astonishment. 'I'll get a job, any sort of job, and stick around.' He took another, almost possessive, look at the mill, and strode briskly towards town.

That noon, when he arrived at the front porch of the Grimes house, he was dressed in his best grey-flannel suit. He had a flower in his buttonhole, and under his arm he carried a two-pound box of Whitman's Sampler chocolates. Craig Price had come a-courting.

16

IT was not a hardship at all, not at all, the courtship of Maybelle. It was not hard to take, Craig kept telling himself. She was quite pretty, amazingly affectionate, and almost insatiable in bed. Craig had found a job parking and servicing cars on the island filling station between Kensington and the Beach. It paid him ten dollars a week and it was comparatively easy to knock down another five dollars from the parking receipts. His room cost him two dollars a week, and he had at least one meal a day at the house with Maybelle. He was amply able to afford movies with Maybelle once or twice a week, and an occasional Saturday night dance. He joined the public library, and took home to his bleak rooming-house all the literature he could find on cotton and cotton-mills. Each night, when he left Maybelle's house, he would read until nearly dawn, trying to make some sense out of pickers and feeders and bobbins and frames and looms in relation to the long dirty-white tufts that were ripped from the bales and which emerged, finally, as garments. The lack of sleep did not bother him. He was young, and besides it was easy to curl up in somebody else's car and grab an hour's nap after the rush hours in the filling station were over.

One Sunday afternoon nearly four months after Craig had returned to Kensington, he and Maybelle were playing the gramophone after lunch. Maybelle was looking a little pasty, and slightly blue under the eyes.

'You don't look like you feel very good, baby,' Craig said. 'What's the matter? Girl trouble?'

'No,' Maybelle said. 'I wish it was. That's the whole trouble. It isn't . . . *that*, I mean. It hasn't been for three times now. Craig, I think I'm pregnant. I *know* I'm pregnant. Here. Feel.'

Craig touched his hand to her stomach. It felt firm, but not swollen.

'It could be any one of a hundred things,' he said. 'Why don't we call Dr. McGowan?'

'Oh, my God, no! If I am—and I know I am—everybody'd know. Craig, we have to get married! We have to get married right away. We can always say we got married and kept it a secret. Lots of people do. Mary-Ellen Grasham had a five-months baby, and nobody cared, because she told everybody Tommy and she'd been married secretly. At least they were married during the months when she really began to get big. Craig, we've got to get married. *Now*. Don't you *want* to marry me?'

Craig kissed her on top of the head.

'Of course I want to marry you, sugar. It isn't a matter of want or don't want. It's just that you know how things are. I'm not making enough money to support me, let alone three of us.'

'Oh, that!' Maybelle snapped her fingers. 'We've got the house. I've got a little income from the mill. And dammit, it's my mill. Well, anyhow, it's mine and Mama's. You could get a job in the mill if you wanted. I'm sure old man Soames could find you something to do. Especially if I said so and made the bankers make him give you something. We wouldn't need much to get along just fine, honey.'

Craig got up off the arm of her chair and paced.

'I don't know anything about cotton-mills,' he said. 'And I don't want it said around that I'm living off my wife. If we could wait a little bit maybe I could get a better job. Things are easing up a little and . . .'

Maybelle swung her arm violently, and knocked over a vase.

'Goddammit, Craig Price! This thing in my belly won't wait for times to get better! It's your baby I'm carrying, and I aim to see it has a father! Can't you see—can't you see I *want* to marry you, baby or no baby? I love you. And I don't want to be alone any more. Never again any more!'

She began to weep and covered her face with her hands. Craig patted her awkwardly on the shoulder.

'Don't cry, baby. Shush. Of course we'll get married. We'll take your car and run off to South Carolina—right now, if you'd like. Please quit crying.'

Maybelle's face emerged, tear-streaked but glowing, from her hands.

'Oh, Craig! You will? Oh, darling, I'm so happy . . .' and she burst into a fresh flood of tears. 'Here, blow,' Craig fished a handkerchief from his pocket and held it to her nose. 'You can't get married with your face all red and puffy. Again.' Maybelle snorted like a good child and looked at him happily.

'Think how happy this would make Papa,' she said. 'He always loved you, and he wanted you to work for him in the mills, and I think he hoped that one day you and I would get married. Oh, Craig, it's turning out just like in the movies.'

'I suppose so. But there's one thing, honey. I haven't got but about five dollars until next payday. Have you got any money? It costs money to get married.'

'Sure I have. Almost a hundred dollars here in the house. We can even have a tiny weensy honeymoon. Wait, I'll go pack, and then we can stop off for your clothes on the way through town . . .' She dashed happily up the stairs, taking them two at a time.

'Hey, careful!' Craig called after her. 'Mind the baby!'

He walked over to a mirror, looked at himself a long time, and sadly shook his head.

17

CRAIG did not literally have his hat in hand, since he owned no hat, when he approached the dehydrated old maid who had been secretary to the office manager so long she maintained an almost wifish, if virginally dedicated, interest in the factory. She was a caricature of the faithful secretary—the long nose red, the weak eyes watery, the hair skinned back to a drab pepper- -and-salt bun. Of course the glasses gold-rimmed, and the white shirt-waist chin-high. The shoes were common-sense, with built-in arch-preservers. Most certainly her underthings would be practical, possibly over-elasticized and safety-pinned against sudden onslaught. She diffused an odour of maiden-lady, who would most certainly have conserved her more intimate apparel with astringent sachet.

'Yes?' she said, in a tone implying that Craig had swept down from the hills on rape and robbery bent, and thank God she had the firm's funds tucked away somewhere in the corset that bulged and obtruded lumpy knobs and dislocated peaks. 'What was it you wanted?'

'I want to see Mr. Soames, please.' Craig was as humble as if he had been seeking audience with the Gautama Buddha, in some bygone age, and had suddenly been confronted by a temple priestess with a 'G.B.' on her jumper.

'About what?' The priestess stabbed him with a stare. (I know you, you beast, the stare said. You'll wait until I go to the ladies' and then you'll break down the door and . . . the word 'rape' was too delicious in her maidenly subconscious to be spoken, even to be thought of unuttered.)

'A job. My name is Craig Price. I'm married to . . . Mr. McMullen at the bank he said that he had called Mr. Soames and . . .'

'Oh.' Her lips disapproved. They drew themselves into a thin line. 'You're the man who . . .' She stopped, implying Attila the Hun had come to call without heliographing. 'Mr. Soames is very busy. I'll go ask him if he can see you now, but perhaps tomorrow would be . . . I'll go and see if Mr. Soames can see you.' Some uncrippled people are able to transfer a walk into a hobble. She succeeded.

Old bitch, Craig thought. Stale old-maid-bitch. One of us has got to go. She smells like a funeral, and looks like the guest-of-honour.

'Mr. Soames will see you.' She sniffed, with an implied but-I-don't-know-why, and would-you-please-wash-your-hands-first 'He's in *there*.'

It can't be true, the young Craig said to himself, it can't be true. Not that awful woman and Uriah Heep on the same day, as Mr. Soames came unctuously forward, rubbing his hands together with the dry crackle of parchment, and exuding an odour of ancient brown-lipped ledgers and dried-up faded ink. He was a little, skinny, bald man, grey-faced with wrinkles which ran in straight lines from nose to mouth, a man whose clothing could only be described as decent black. He smelt, and looked, as if he had spent a long time in an un-aired closet, and was pining for the mothballs.

'Oh,' he said. 'It's Mr. Price. Another Mr. Price once worked for me here. A Mr. . . . ah, a Mr. Richard Price. You would be a relation?'

He knows damned well I'm a relation, Craig thought, and he knows goddamned well who else I'm related to. What is all this horse manure, anyhow?

'Yes, Mr. Soames,' he said politely. 'I'm Richard Price's son. I've been away—in Europe—for quite some time. I was talking with the trustees at the bank, and they . . .' His voice trailed.

'Oh, yes, yes indeed,' Mr. Soames said. 'Please sit down, Mr. Price.' He giggled, as if sharing a new dirty joke. 'Please do sit down. And how is your father?'

You know goddamned well he's dead, you giggling old misery, Craig thought.

'Daddy passed away, last year,' he said, gravely matching unctuousness.

'Oh, my, how dreadful. I'm so sorry. He was such a nice man, so wonderful to work with. So quiet . . . But it comes to all of us, doesn't it?' His eyes almost lit in anticipation.

Old grave-robber. Let's get this the hell over, and all at once, Craig said to himself. Before I throw up. Where did my old friend Grimes find these creeps?

'The trustees said you might have a job for me,' Craig said. (That'll tell the cackling old bastard that I've come straight from the horse.)

'Well, Mr. Price, times are very hard, very hard, as you know, and I'm afraid there isn't much avail . . . Do you know anything about spinning machinery?'

'No,' Craig said, and started to say 'Sir' but didn't.

'Office work?'

'I can read and write. I can add and subtract.'

'Hee-hee.' Mr. Soames wriggled. 'Then, I suppose, due to the memory of *Mister* Grimes, who I believe was very fond of you, I suppose we had better start you off in the office. After all' —tee-hee—'you may be running this mill some day, due to your . . . er, ah . . . your close family ties.' He implied the tongue-in-cheek.

'What would the salary be, Mr. Soames? And when do I start?'

'I'm afraid the salary can't be but $25 a week, at the moment, but of course your wife's interest . . . You may start Monday if you like. Possibly, after you've learned the ropes, the trustees might see fit to . . .'

'I understand. Thank you very much, sir.' Craig stood up. 'I'll be in on Monday. What time, please?'

238

'The whistle blows at eight, hee-hee. Early to bed and early to rise. I always get here at *seven*.'

'I'll be here at seven, sir. Thank you very much.'

'I'm sure we'll get along together very well, Mr. Price.' The old man's voice now was almost a pleading whine. 'Your father was a fine man.'

'Thank you, sir. I'm sure we will. Good-bye.'

As Craig passed through the outer office he stopped by the secretary's desk.

'I'm going to work here next Monday,' he said. 'I suppose I ought to know your name? As we'll be working together, I mean.'

'*I* work for Mr. Soames. But my name is Mildred Mason. Most of the *old* employees'—she sniffed—'call me Miss Mildred.'

'All right, Miss Mason,' Craig said, 'as long as I'm a new employee I'll stick to the last name for a while.' He grinned wickedly and narrowed his eyes. 'Do I punch a time-clock?'

'Of course not.' Miss Mildred was indignant. '*We* don't punch time clocks. We're managerial *staff*.'

'Good-bye, Miss Mason. Thank you.'

She sniffed again. Attila the Hun had failed at . . . that awful word . . . but there was always Monday. And they say, she thought, that poor Mr. Grimes's daughter is at least four months gone. Beast. Pity there weren't more gentlemen like Mr. Soames. She bent to her typewriter.

Cloaked in dark suspicion and shadowed by outright resentment over his intrusion into the musty sanctum of Mr. Soames and Miss Mason, viewed hostilely by the millhands as a company-and-family spy, Graig dived insanely, unchannelled, into work. His office hours were confined mostly to papers—sorting papers, shuffling papers, making payroll sheets. He washed a dozen times a day to remove the filth of the ink of invoices and consignments. He practised touch-typing after hours, on a rickety old Underwood. He went to the bank for payroll money, and soon got to know the bankers. He signed up for a correspondence course in accounting.

At all times he was regarded coldly by Miss Mildred. At all times he was viewed with a sort of sneaky obsequiousness by Mr. Soames. Mr. Soames disapproved heartily—if Mr. Soames' juiceless body had been able to produce heartiness—of Craig's insistence on association with the millhands.

'It's not right, Craig,' he said. 'It's just plain not right for Miss Maybelle's husband to be hanging out with the hands. It don't look right for an office man to be out in the mill, talking to that bunch of lintheads all the time.'

Craig looked up from a stack of papers he was sorting, stabbing the carbons on a spike.

'It's the only way I know to learn anything about the mill

itself, Mr. Soames,' he said. 'I don't know anything about spinning machinery. I can't learn it in here.' He gestured at the dust-dingy office. 'All we got here is papers. If I'm going to—' he stopped, almost having said: 'If I'm going to run this place some day, I ought to know what's going on outside the office.'

'If you're going to *what*?' Mr. Soames looked at him sharply, his head cocked sideways. 'If you're going to what?'

'If I'm going to learn anything at all about the business,' Craig hastily amended. 'I mean, I think I ought to know all sides of it, don't you? Inside and outside, I mean?'

'Rome,' said Mr. Soames gravely, reprovingly, 'wasn't built in a day. Hee hee. You just do your work here in the office and the mill-hands will take care of themselves. It's not dignified to be on first-name terms with a gang of lintheads.'

'Yessir,' Craig went back to his work. I'll bet Old Man Grimes was on first-name terms with all of them, from the sweepers to the foremen, he said to himself. And I'll bet he stayed the hell out of this office.

Craig set out doggedly to memorize the processes of spinning, from the time the baled cotton arrived until it was rendered into cloth. He had small mechanical aptitude, but eventually—after nearly losing an arm a couple of times—he became at least familiar with the apparatus. At no time was he fascinated by the mechanical end of the business, but regarded it as a necessary evil to his future plans.

He despised the constant noise, the sameness of the daily internal belly-growling of the mill. But he forced himself to memorize the tortuous process which transmuted the bent backs of the field hands into fine yarns and clothes. From the first unbaling of the hard-packed cotton—from bale to feeder apron through conveyor pipes, from the picker to the thin fuzzy blankets that emerged to be cleaned, drafted and doubled into thicker laps; to the spinning rooms, where the spindles wound their fine-spun yarn around the bobbins—thousands of spindles, humming with the fast blur of wings, the bobbins expertly doffed of their fine white burden by nimble fingers, into the weaving rooms, where the clicking looms were fed smoothly by the travelling shuttles, finally to the fabric rooms—Craig haunted every process, speculating about short cuts, pondering on the possibility of more machines and less people. As he watched the miracle of cotton-boll to cloth, he kept thinking of spiders and silkworms, and their synthetic production of fine yarns from their own bodies. Just why, he couldn't say then, but somehow he thought there ought to be easier ways of making threads than the accepted battle against drought, wet, and the boll weevil. To Craig's untainted brain, there seemed to be too many processes —too much margin for error, too much opportunity for human frailty. In the meantime, he was getting to know the men, who at first thought it odd that the husband of the old boss' daughter could or would be in the slightest interested in routine jobs which meant so much an hour, so many hours a day, so many days a week, and which never changed from the unloading of the baled cotton on the sliding to the shipment of the fabrics.

In time he came to know them on a first-name basis and they no longer thought it unusual that young Mr. Craig seemed always sticking his nose into the works.

Craig's interest extended far beyond the mill. He was a country boy, yet, and sometimes, on a Sunday afternoon, he would climb into the Ford and drive across the river to where some of the cotton was grown. He would stop at well-remembered sites of his boyish hunting and strike up conversations with old friends among the Negroes. With the new background of mill work, his interest in the source of supply had doubled. With the sharecroppers, he talked endlessly—it seemed to Maybelle, waiting at home—about quail and deer and turkey and fat-backed sidemeat and how much the 'croppers were in debt to the various company stores.

Another county was heavily devoted to turpentine, the tower-ing pines oozing amber riches from the deep wounds in their rough-barked sides, the raw sap congealing into waxy balls like candle drippings, which were pleasant to chew. The turpentine still gangs were rough men, tobacco-chewing, hard-drinking, hairy overseers, shouting and cursing at powerful, plum-black, sweating Negro hands. They were dealing with a dying industry, and seemed to know it. But Craig found their company pleasant, and frequently slipped away for a few hours at night to sit by the fire, in front of the shacks, listening to the plunk of a banjo and drinking raw corn whisky with the cap'n and adju-tants. A bloody fist fight or a cutting marked nearly every shivaree, but somehow the roughness of it appealed strongly to Craig—if nothing more than as an antidote to the aseptic presence of Miss Mildred and the dry-rot of Mr. Soames, the relentless harsh clacking of the mills, and the flat expressionless faces of the millhands as they went robot-like about their never-changing chores.

Maybelle seldom went out now, and then only under protest, as the baby grew inside her. She was swollen and disagreeable, and she preferred to stay home and sulk. It had been an easy pregnancy, and she hadn't been sick at all. But ingrained shame at the sudden marriage, now that the cause of the marriage was painfully evident, bound her to the house. She refused even to shop, so Craig added the weekly grocery list to his other duties. He hired, for two dollars a week, a Negro woman to keep the house in some semblance of lick-and-a-promise cleanliness, and to cook a lunch for Maybelle and one major meal—mostly fried —for him when he came home in the evening. Maybelle was nearly always querulous, especially about his nocturnal prowlings in the countryside.

'I just don't see what you see in those roughnecks,' she said on an average of three times a week. 'Hanging around turpentine camps and talking to niggers and going out to the CCC camp in Onslow and messing around with the millhands. I declare, Craig, I don't understand you at all. What you goin' to gain from the likes of them?'

'I don't know,' Craig would grin embarrassedly. 'Maybe I'm a roughneck myself. Maybe nobody'll ever make a gentleman out of me. I guess they're my kind of people. Near as I can figure there are an awful lot of poor people around these days, a lot of hungry people, and I keep wondering how they got that way, and if they figger to stay that way. I couldn't tell you, Maybelle, because I really don't know.'

'We have a certain amount of responsibility,' Maybelle said primly. 'I mean, we got to hold our head up. It was Daddy's mill, and one day it'll be mine—ours, I mean,' she amended. 'It just don't look right, you bein' so friendly with the hands. I've been hearing a lot, lately, like that baseball business . . .'

'Sounds like you been talking to old man Soames,' Craig said. 'There's nothing wrong with the baseball thing. It hasn't hurt anybody.'

'Well, it don't look right, and I wish you'd stop it. You work too hard, anyhow, and treatin' the millhands like equals don't get you any respect. They just look down on you and laugh at you.'

Craig got up out of his chair and paced the room. Maybelle was sitting on the other side of the fireplace, knitting something which had momentarily come to rest on her distended belly. The needles stuck up like skinny rabbit ears from each side of the yarn. Craig spoke more to himself than to Maybelle.

'I reckon maybe you mightn't understand,' he said. 'But every time I go out to one of those CCC camps and see all those guys, most of 'em as old or older than me, working almost like chain-gang people in that Onslow County timber country I get a cold chill. Maybe it's a good idea to herd up people that can't get a job in camps with supervisors who ain't any better than shotgun guards, but when I think it could happen to me my skin crawls.

'I feel the same way about the millhands, and the sharecroppers, and the turpentine gangs, and all the people on relief. I feel even worse about all these shabby proud people busy living in the past, and starving to death because they're so proud. Proud of what? That they got all the fight bred out of them and don't know what to do now that Daddy's dead and the bank busted? There's a change coming, and it's coming pretty soon, and I

242

aim to figger me out some way to be ready for it when it comes. Maybe that's why I hang out with the roughnecks.'

'Oh, foot,' Maybelle said. 'The trouble with you is you think too much. Now that the Democrats are back everything will be the same again. It was the Republicans that wrecked the country. All you got to do is be patient and wait and everything will turn out fine.'

Craig glared.

'I don't want to be patient! I don't want to wait for everything to turn out right! That's the trouble with this goddam country down here! Everybody patient. Everybody waiting for everything to turn out right. A bunch of Micawbers!'

'You don't have to talk dirty, Craig. What's a Micawber, anyhow?'

'Skip it, honey. He was a man in a book who kept waiting for something to turn up . . .'

'Oh, a book.' Maybelle lost interest. 'You and your books. You've always got your nose in one when you're home. Seems like you don't hardly ever talk to me much any more. And the other thing'—she gestured helplessly at her distended stomach—'well, it won't be long now. Maybe we ought to be a little more careful next time.' She giggled, and Craig's nerves rasped. Maybelle's giggle was as irritating, at times, as old man Soames' nervous habit of clearing his throat, ridding his chest of ropy phlegm, and then swallowing laboriously with a nasal snort, or Miss Mildred's infuriating red-nosed sniff of constant disapproval. That pair of old vultures, Craig thought, if it's the last thing I do I'll get to a place when I can fire them both and hire a secretary with the biggest pair of tits in the county.

18

MAYBELLE'S irritated reference to baseball was funny. The baseball business had started off innocent in the extreme. Some of the younger millhands played baseball in the cool of the summer evening, after the five o'clock whistle, and occasionally Craig would drift over to the lumpy, hardbaked meadow to watch a pick-up game.

They made a shaggy-looking lot, playing in square-toed brogans from the Army-Navy store, their overalls rolled up to their knees to show fish-belly white skin, and when it was hot, stripping off their denim or chambray shirts to show baked red faces and necks contrasting sharply with the unhealthy pallor of their chests and upper arms. They were strong, physically, with square, thick-calloused hands and perpetually black-rimmed, broken or gnawed nails with thick white ridges in them.

But their faces were pimpled from a steady—or at times unsteady—diet of fried sidemeat and grits, navy beans, dried black-eye peas, potatoes and whatever else was going cheap. Although land was available the men's families never seemed interested in raising a few vegetables to supplement their diet, but bought nearly everything they ate from the company store.

Yet, like most Southern men of any station, they had been weaned on baseball, and they moved with surprising grace, that fitted oddly with their shabby, much-patched working clothes and clumsy thick-soled work boots. The spindle-men, who doffed their bobbins with one smooth motion, were very deft with their hands on balls hit to the ground, and while possibly slow afoot, made up for it in the ease with which they scooped a skidding ball off the bumpy infield.

From time to time, standing or sitting on the sidelines, a foul ball or a dribbled roller would come Craig's way. If it wasn't too much trouble, he would shag the ball and lob it back to the pitcher. He never intruded. He merely watched, sitting well back of third base. After a while the millworkers got used to seeing him there.

One day he showed up for the ball game and there seemed to be a shortage of players. Craig, as usual, was sitting on the sidelines by himself.

One of the players, a rough-thatched big redhead named Forney, a man of about nineteen or twenty, walked up to him and said:

'Mr. Price?'

'Yep.' Craig looked up. 'Hello, Forney.'

'We kind of shorthanded today. We got enough men to make two sides, but we short a umpire.' He pushed a sweaty lock of coarse hair out of his eyes. 'We was wonderin'—we was wonderin' if maybe you. You bein' front office and all . . . We was wonderin' if you'd umpire for us?'

'You want me to umpire? Sure. Be glad to. Where's the gear?'

'Well, we ain't got but one mast and one belly-protector. If you'd jest stand out behind the pitcher and call 'em from there. Less chance of you gettin' hurt thataway.'

'I can't call strikes from behind the pitcher,' Craig said. 'You can see high and low but you can't see wide or inside. I'll stand behind the catcher and try to duck the foul tips. Come on, let's go.'

'That's real nice of you, Mr. Price. Come on, you guys, Mr. Price is a-gonna call 'em for us.'

Craig crouched behind the catcher. He called a six-inning ball game. He missed more than a few decisions, but received nothing more damaging than a glare from the batter. It was a difficult job, since in addition to calling the balls and strikes, he was also supposed to judge decisions at first, second and third bases.

The men played two or three times a week, and Craig discovered that they made small bets on the games—a dime, a quarter, even as much as fifty cents. He was never invited to play, but as he continued to show up to watch the game, it was gradually assumed that he was the umpire. Somehow his position, small as it was, of being a front office man, gave dignity to his decisions.

One day, after Mr. Soames and Miss Mildred had gone home, Craig was still in the office, finishing up some routine paper-sorting. Big Red Forney knocked on the door and stuck his head inside when Craig called: 'Come in.'

'Ain't you comin' out to the game today, Mr. Price?'

'Thought I'd miss it, Red,' Craig said. 'I'm a little behind on some work. You can get somebody else.'

'Naw we can't. The guys don't want nobody else. We got a big bet on today. A dollar a man. That's big money. The guys want you to come call 'em.'

'Oh, all right.' Craig swept his papers together and shoved them in a wire basket. 'I can come in a little early tomorrow and finish up. Who's going to win?'

'Us. My arm feels real good today. We even got a new ball. That old taped-up ball nearly 'bout tore your arm off every time you th'owed it, and it didn't have no more life than a cannon-ball. Couple of the guys was knot-holing outside the reg'lar ball park the other day, when the Independents got their brains knocked out, and we come up with a couple of regulation balls that hadn't hardly been dented.'

The men played a six-inning game, only, and the score was tied at 10-all in the last half of the sixth. Red Forney's team, batting last, had a man on first base, with two out, with Forney at bat. He swung mightily at the first pitched ball, and hooked a double down the left field foul line. The runner on first tore around the bases and headed for home. The left fielder made a neat recovery of the bounding ball, and fired a peg at the catcher, who was straddling the plate. The base-runner, pounding in from third, hit the dirt in a slide, and the catcher tagged him in a cloud of dust. Craig jerked his thumb upward over his shoulder.

'Out!'

The batting team descended on him like a flock of angry vultures, all the players screaming at once and thrusting their faces at him. Big Red Forney raced in from second base to become the loudest screamer of them all.

'He was safe a country mile!'

'Goddam blind tom!'

'What else you expect from the front office!'

A few giggling millgirls, who had strolled by and paused to watch the game, took up the chorus.

'Kill the umpire!'

Craig faced the players calmly.

'Shut up and play ball,' he said mildly.

'Who's tellin' who to shut up?' This was a beefy, pimpled boy with almost albino hair and white pig-bristles for eyelashes. He shoved his meaty face into Craig's face and repeated: 'Who's tellin' who to shut up?'

'I'm telling you to shut up.' He turned to Forney. 'You asked me to umpire the game. Do you want me to umpire it or not? If you do, play ball. If you don't, find another umpire.'

'What's the matter? You yellow? You want to quit?' Voice from the rear.

'I said the man was out.' He ignored the voice. This is a damned silly thing, he thought. Just a pick-up baseball game and we got a row.

'Suppose I said he was safe?' This was big redheaded Forney. He moved a little closer to Craig. He repeated: 'Suppose I said he was safe?'

'You'd be wrong.' Craig was keeping his voice light.

'You callin' me a liar, then?' Forney was baiting now, and the delighted players thronged around, nudging each other.

'You gonna let him call you a liar, Red?' Again the unidentified voice.

'I didn't call you a liar. I said you were wrong. Or at least to my way of thinking you're wrong.' I been through this one before, Craig thought. I been through it in grammar school, high school, a little bit of college and a lot of merchant marine. Bullyrag the new boy especially if he's outside the mob.

'Oh, let him alone, Red. You asted him to umpire. If he wants to call you a liar he kin. He's front office, ain't he? He kin git away with it.' Again the voice.

Big Forney, hunching and loosening his ropy shoulders, tossed a lock of hair out of his eyes. He licked his lips in anticipation.

'For the last time, Price, you callin' me a liar?'

'If you want it that way, sure. I'm calling you a liar.'

'No sonofabitch calls me a liar . . .' Forney said. 'Specially a son of a bitch that gits a job in the front office by . . .' Which was as far as he got. Craig dropped his right shoulder and hit the redhead a vicious left in the pit of the stomach. As Forney gasped and bent double. Craig crossed a right to the side of his jaw and dropped him. He wiped a skinned knuckle on his trouser leg and looked at the men. Forney was sitting up, now, gasping for breath.

'Anybody else want some? How about you there on the ground? You want some more?' Forney was still gasping, but he got to his feet and aimed a wild swing at Craig. Craig ducked under it and buried a right hand to the knuckles into the same spot in the belly. This time Forney fell down and started to vomit.

'This can go on all day,' Craig said. 'But I thought you fellows came here to play ball. You want to play ball or do we just stand here and fight?'

'Aw, hell,' somebody said. 'Less play ball. Red was outa line. Come on, Red, quit throwin' up and less play ball. You willin', Mr. Price?'

'Sure.' He stuck out a hand and hauled Forney to his feet. 'No hard feelings, Forney?'

'No hard feelin's.' He mumbled, and shook his head. Then, 'Where'd you learn to hit like that?'

Craig grinned and touched his broken nose.

'I used to go to sea on a hungry ship,' he said. 'I learned it the hard way. C'mon, you guys, play ball.'

Forney's team lost, thirteen to ten, in the next innings, when somebody hit a homer with two on.

It was a small thing, a very little thing, a silly thing, as most fights are silly things, but eighteen men and a dozen women saw Craig knock Forney down, and the word spread around the mill that this feller Price, married to the boss's daughter or not, didn't stand for a lot of pushin' around. (Talking to a sailor in a beer-joint the other night down by the docks, and he said this Price killed a man in Antwerp, and gouged the eye out of another one. He ain't no man to monkey with, this fellow said. Leave's hit you with a bottle as with his fist.)

'Disgraceful, absolutely disgraceful,' Mr. Soames said, when he heard about it.

'You ought to be ashamed of yourself, brawlin' with the hired hands,' Maybelle said. 'Anyhow, I'm ashamed of you.'

'How'd you like to teach me that punch?' Big Forney said. 'Man, I thought a mule done kicked me in the stummick.'

'It's kind of simple,' Craig said. 'Idea is you hit fast and first. Especially first. Look, you get the leverage from dropping your shoulder. That way you get your body behind the punch, and a belly is hard to miss. Try it on me. Go ahead, swing.'

Forney aimed a clumsy left at Craig's middle. Craig moved just inside the swing, chopped viciously at Forney's left biceps with the hard edge of his left wrist, slipped Red's following right past his chin and stuck a hard straight right into Forney's face. He had pulled the force out of his defensive chopping left, and had swung his right hand punch past Forney's face. Even so, Forney massaged his left biceps vigorously, and grinned.

'You can nigh bust a man's arm that way, can't you?' he said. 'And he's wide open for that right hand. You coulda coal-cocked me.'

'That's the idea. He might hit you with one left but if you get him hard enough with that wrist he won't hit you with two lefts any more. Matter of fact, you'll have him fighting one-armed even if you don't flatten him with the right. It's a pretty good trick. There was a guy on the ship used to box professional and he taught me some stuff. It came in handy.'

'So the idea is to hit him with the left and cross with the right so fast that he don't have a chance to knock down the left, is that right?'

'That's right. You watch a man's eyes and you can generally tell when he's aiming to swing. You swing first and you got him.'

'You know a lot more of this stuff?'

'Some. Why?'

Forney scratched his head. They were walking back towards the mill together, now.

'Well, I was thinkin' maybe you could hold some lessons for some of the guys. We could dig up some gloves, maybe, and build us a ring. We ain't got much to do, kill time when we're off-shift. Be somethin' to do.'

'It's all right with me. Why don't you meet me down at the Greek's when you're off and we'll talk about it? I'll buy you a beer.'

'You'll have to, do we drink one. I'm busted.'

They met at a little Greek general store that sold 3.2 per cent beer, and took a couple of bottles outside and sat on the grass.

'I was thinking,' Craig said, 'that we could go a little bit further than boxing lessons. You guys got some pretty good ballplayers. If we fixed up a diamond and got some better equipment, and got more guys to turn out, we could make a couple of pretty good teams. If we got good enough we might be able to play some of the semi-pro teams. We could at least get some games with some of the other mills in the county. Like you said, it'd be something to do. Wouldn't take much money, either.'

'Much money. Hell's afire, we ain't got *any* money. That eight, ten dollars a week don't buy much fatback. Specially for a family.

'I know it. But we could start a nickel-and-dime fund. I'd put in, too. And maybe one day I could get the mill to help out a little bit, particularly if you guys got pretty good. Uniforms can wait.' Craig winked. 'I reckon we could steal enough cloth from time to time and it don't take much in the way of sewing talent to make a baseball suit. You can play in tennis shoes until you can afford spikes. Most of the equipment, gloves and stuff, you can get for next to nothing at the pawnshop.'

Red Forney scratched his head.

'Would you hold the money? I wouldn't trust most of these sonsabitches not to run off with a hot stove. Let 'em get five dollars ahead and they'd go off on a drunk and lay up in the woods for a week.'

'What makes you so sure I wouldn't go off on a drunk and lay up in the woods soon as we got five bucks head? You don't know anything about me.'

Red Forney spat.

'I don't hafta. You gonna run this mill some day. You hold the money, okay?'

'Sure. I'll sew it into the mattress. Talk to the guys and tell me what they say. By next summer we ought to have a pretty good ball team. And if you want to start the boxing now, you guys build a ring and I'll see if I can't talk Uncle Charlie out of a couple of pairs of gloves and a punching bag. I better be getting home. We got a baby on the way at our house.'

'Yeah. I heard. Listen, Craig. I didn't mean nothing the other day when I was ridin' you. I guess—I guess it's just the kind of thing we do. I dunno why. But in this town some people don't mind bein' lintheads, goin' around with their necks droopin' like a sick turkey. When you showed up to the ball games I guess we figgered you was somewhere between company spy and jest naturally nosy, always out in the back of the plant when you coulda stayed in front. But you got guts. Shake again, huh?'

'Sure. Be seein' you, Red. Let me know what the men say.'

As Craig walked home to supper he thought, wait until old man Soames hears about his new recreational programme. He'll blow a gasket. And why, he asked himself, do I get mixed up in things like this? He shook his head and walked home.

'You're late,' Maybelle said. 'Out with your linthead friends again?'

'Yes,' Craig said shortly. 'What've we got for supper?'

19

MAYBELLE was in her seventh month now, and flatly, stubbornly refused to leave the house, despite doctor's orders and Craig's cajoling. She regarded her bulging belly as a badge of shame, despite her earlier protestation to Craig that it happened all the time, and you could always say you were married secretly, earlier. She sat and she sewed and she ate, and Craig was certain that she reinforced her steady nibbling at candy and her passionate interest in desserts with a furtive interest in the kitchen bottle. Craig was drinking scarcely anything at all; he was too busy, too tired, and besides, even the cheapest blends in the newly opened ABC stores cost too much. But Maybelle had secret money of her own, and Craig was certain that she sent Floreen, the slovenly kitchen wench, out to buy a pint from time to time.

Food and inactivity had slabbered fat on a frame already prone to plumpness. The early hint of Maybelle's double chin was now a reality, and her body, in a wrap-around house dress, was nearly shapeless. Craig looked at her with concern, coloured slightly with distaste, one bright October Sunday just before lunch time.

Her hair was fuzzed untidily around the fatted face, which was slightly blotchy.

'Don't look at me like that,' Maybelle said. 'I know I look like a hoorah's nest. I can't help it. This baby weighs a ton. I'm too tired to fix myself up.'

'I wasn't looking at you like *that*,' Craig said. 'I was just thinking again that just sitting round is bad for you. You know what the doctor says. You're gaining too much weight and so is the baby. If he weighs a ton now he'll weigh two tons in another couple of months, and you'll have a hell of a time having him. Also you'll have a worse time getting your shape back. You ought not to eat so much, honey. And you ought to get out of the house a little.'

Maybelle made a face of disgust. She passed a hand over her stomach.

'Go out of the house looking like *this*? For everybody to laugh at, and whisper about? It's bad enough they all know why we got married. I don't have to show myself to them like a . . . like some freak.'

'You don't have to show yourself to anybody. Nobody has to see you. Tell you what. Let's you and me pile in the Ford and go for a ride in the country, cross the river. The trees are turning and it'll be real pretty. We don't have to do anything special or see anybody. But it would do you a world of good. How about it?'

'I don't want to. Stop nagging at me. I don't feel like it. Anyhow, bumping around in the car can't be good for the baby. No. I don't want to. Too much trouble, anyhow. You want to go, you go. I sit here by myself all week long, anyhow. A Sunday more or less won't make any difference.' Martyrdom bestrode her voice.

'Oh, hell, it won't be any fun by myself. I wouldn't leave you alone now without somebody in the house, anyhow. Look, tell you what. You go put on some warm clothes and while you do, I'll sneak back in the kitchen and fry a chicken and make some devilled eggs and stuff. We can take a couple of bottles of beer and have a picnic. I know a wonderful place not far from New Truro, little sort of hidden place by one of the creeks. We can build a fire and roast some hotdogs . . . Aw, come on, honey. Please.'

'Oh, for God's sake, all right. If you want to go play boy scout, I'll come with you if it'll shut you up.' She stopped. 'Oh, Craig, I don't really mean to be mean. I just feel so horrible, liked I was stuffed. And I look so awful . . .' She started to sniffle.

'You don't look awful at all. You can't expect to be very comfortable with a future All-American already practising place-kicks in your tummy. Come on now, honey, climb into some clothes. Don't worry about the hair. Sling a bandanna around it. Put on some slacks and a sweater and . . .'

Maybelle stopped her sniffles and laughed hollowly.

'Slacks. Slip into some slacks, he says. I couldn't squeeze into a pair of pants if they were made for Man Mountain Dean. You'll have to settle for a skirt and one of those goddam bibs they make pregnant women wear. All they do is make you look more pregnant.' She extended a hand. 'Help me up. You start the chicken and I'll come down and help you finish up. We got plenty of beer?'

'Sure. I brought home a half-dozen bottles last night. Be careful with those stairs.'

Craig went into the kitchen, and hummed cheerfully as he dismembered the carcass of a chicken, dipped the joints into salted flour and popped them into the spitting grease in the frying pan. He heated water and put a dozen eggs on to boil. He found a jar of sweet pickles in the pantry, and rummaged around for a market basket to stow the lunch in. He would stop at the first hotdog stand and buy some rolls and frankfurters, and the beer would be cold enough, especially if he put the bottles into the cold, swift-running little stream. Strange, he thought, even in summer that little crick never got warm. He remembered plunging his face into it as a kid, after a hot, sweaty walk in the woods, and it was almost like ice-water.

He whistled as he turned the chicken and lowered the flame. This would be fun, and it would certainly get Maybelle up on her feet and out of the house . . . Poor kid, he thought. Having a short-term one that everybody's bound to know about must be double-tough. Well, she'll forget it and so will everybody else, and by the time we have another one, and maybe another one, and everybody else has another four or five, there'll be so many young 'uns running around that nobody'll be able to tell one from the other.

He was draining the grease from the chicken, and had finished stuffing eggs with yolk, mustard, and mayonnaise, when Maybelle came into the kitchen. She had wrapped a bright paisley scarf around her head, and was wearing a light yellow woolly coat over a green wool dress. She had evidently taken considerable pains with her face.

'You look wonderful, baby,' Craig said. 'Here, we're just ready to go. Perch yourself on that stool and we'll split a bottle of beer while I get the salt and pepper and stuff. This is going to be a lot of fun. How do you feel?'

'A lot better. Maybe you're right, Craig. Maybe I should get up and around more. A baby isn't anything to be ashamed of so long as it's got a legal papa, even if you did catch him a little late.'

'Of course not. Half the married women in this town tried out their honeymoons before they saw the preacher. Come on, finish that beer, we're all set.'

They drove slowly through the city and out over the bridge

into what was almost unsettled country. They chose the river road, after stopping for raw hotdogs and buns, and threaded along the cypress-rimmed clay road.

'We'll come back on the hard surface,' Craig said. 'But I kind of like this old road if only because it leads past that old plantation. They named it Eden, and I guess they had some cause. Must have been wonderful living in those days, with nothing much to do but ride around on a horse looking at the cotton and tobacco, with three or four hundred slaves to do all the hard work. Nothin' much for Old Marse to do but hunt and fish and play poker and drink juleps and let somebody wait on him hand and foot. Of course, they lost it, like nearly everybody lost everything.'

'Well, all these cypresses make me feel real spooky,' Maybelle said, snuggling her chins into her coat collar. 'All that old grey moss hanging off the branches, and those big old oak trees and all. Don't much sun ever get through here. This place we're going for the picnic, I hope it's got more pine trees and gum trees and less cypress. I don't know why but swamps always make me feel sad and kind of scared, like there were ghosts hanging around.'

Craig patted her knee. 'Where we're going is as cheerful as Christmas,' he said. 'It always was my favourite camping spot when I was a little kid. You'll like it, but if you don't we'll have our picnic somewhere else.'

He drove carefully, and in silence, for some time. As the ground got higher, moving away from the river, the bearded cypresses and oaks diminished, giving way to the gloossy green of gallberry bushes, and huge stands of long-leafed pine. The gums, pin-oaks and hickories made a brilliant splurge of gold, yellow and darkest red against the black-green of the pines.

'Oh, this is pretty,' Maybelle said. 'It's lovely, really it is. Are we far from where we're going?'

'Not so very. Three or four more miles. Hungry?'

'Sort of. It's been a long time since I was on a picnic. We used to do it a lot in grammar school, but there was always some old teacher tagging along. I don't know what they thought we'd be doing at that age, they had to send a teacher.' She giggled. 'I suppose we'd of found something bad to do, though.'

Craig laughed, remembering Eunice and his experiments into the source of babies. I know where they come from now, all right, he thought. And it ain't from their mama's bellybutton, either, although Eunice wasn't too far wrong. Wonder what ever happened to her?

'Here we are,' he said, turning right off the road into two ruts that ran through the broomgrass and scrubby oaks. 'About two hundred yards more of the car, and then we have to walk a little bit. See the bridge up there ahead? The creek cuts back and sort of plays out in the shallows. It quits being a creek and be-comes a little brook. When I was a kid I used to kind of think that this was my secret country and I was king of it. It used to get a little scary in the late afternoon, when the doves started whoo-whooing in the swamps back yonder, but at this time of day it's wonderful. Here we are,' he said, stopping the car. 'End of the line.'

'I hope we don't have to walk far,' Maybelle said.

'Only about a hundred yards. Through that patch of young pine, there. Hang on to me. Those pine-needles can be pretty slippery.'

They walked through close-pressed young pines, following a tenuous pathway that Craig seemed to be able to see, but May-belle couldn't.

'Deer run,' Craig explained, when she asked him what he was following. 'I guess they don't use it much any more.'

As if to call him a liar, there was a whistling snort, and a white flag of tail disappeared into the thickness of the pine-stand. They could hear the rattle of horns and the crash of brush as the buck whistled again and went away.

'I guess I was wrong, as usual,' Craig chuckled. 'That ol' boy was laying up right alongside the trail. Another month, you'll be able to walk up alongside him and slug him with a baseball bat.'

'How's that? I don't understand. Oops! Hang on to me, I almost slipped. These needles *are* slippery, aren't they? How can you walk up to him and hit him with a baseball bat?'

'Well, I was exaggerating a little bit,' Craig replied. 'But this fellow just got his horns back—they shed them every year—and he's probably still got some velvet on them. Look.' He stopped by a hickory tree which was scarred at about a shoulder height. 'See those scars on the bark? That's where they rub off the velvet on the new horns. I guess it itches, or something, but when the velvet's off and the horns are all bone again, the buck is about ready to fight and breed.'

'I guess all boys fight when they're courtin',' Maybelle mur-mured. 'Much farther to go now? I'm tired.'

'Just a tiny bit more. Anyhow, come first frost, the buck's neck swells, and his horns are sharp, and he goes as goofy as any high school kid in love. He staggers around, not looking where he's going, with his mind on just one thing: Women. He'll travel twenty miles a night when he's rutting, breeding every doe he can catch, and between sittin' up all night and screwin' his brains out, he ain't got the sense God gave a crab-apple. That's why the late fall, October and November is the easiest time to hunt deer. A buck you couldn't get within a mile of will walk right up to you, plain punch-drunk, and if you get him in a corner, instead of running away he's just as apt to make a pass at you.'

'Men are all alike,' Maybelle said. 'Is this it, up ahead?'

'This,' Craig said, 'is it.'

They came into a tiny glade, green-grassy still, splintered with brown pine needles. Towering virgin pines, searching skyward for fifty or sixty yards of nearly branch-bare smooth-barked bole, formed a sun-pierced canopy over the dell, and little puddles of light picked out a golden pattern on the ground. The clearing sloped down to the little stream, which chuckled cheerfully as it bubbled over the clean white-sanded bed, peering from between green-lichened rocks, and slowing to a smooth, almost pool-still sheet of faintly brown, but very clear water. In the little pools, small fish swam, lingering quivering, hanging almost motionless in the deeper holes. The white sands along the pool bank, before the tiny green chickweed clustered flatly like clover at the water's edge, was scarred and re-scarred with a thousand tiny tracks.

'Look,' Craig said. 'The birds and the animals like it here, too. Those little bitsy tracks are quail. Those over there are coon, and that's a fox. There was a doe, and buck and two half-grown fawns here just before dawn this morning. I wouldn't be surprised if the buck wasn't the one we jumped back yonder. He fed all night, came for a drink, and then went to lay up before we stumbled over him.'

Maybelle looked at the tracks with vague interest.

'How can you tell it was a buck, a doe and two fawns? They all look alike to me.'

'Easy. The buck's toe tracks are more rounded, and more spread out than the doe's. See hers are sharp-pointed, and the width between the two toes is less than on the buck, because she weighs a lot less. And there had to be some fawns, because they're sticking close to the female, and they're about a third smaller than hers.'

'You know a lot about this sort of stuff, don't you?' Maybelle looked at him curiously. 'You like it a whole lot, don't you?'

'I guess so. I spent an awful lot of time running wild in the woods when I was a little feller. When we get things straightened out a little better at the mill—maybe next year—I thought I'd maybe buy a couple of bird dog puppies and train them around the house. There's still plenty of quail around there. Also a boy ought to grow up with dogs.'

'You're dead sure this is going to be a boy, Craig? Would you be sorry if it was a girl?'

'Hell, no. But I just kind of feel like it'll be a boy. Here, let me fix you up a seat, while I rustle up a fire. Just a minute.'

Craig disappeared into the surrounding woods, and came back with an armful of Spanish moss. He spread it thickly in front of a small boulder, near the water's edge, and then doubled a blanket over the moss. He took both Maybelle's hands and lowered her bulk gently to the ground.

'How's that? Comfortable?'

She looked up at him and smiled.

'Mmmmhmmm. Yes. You don't suppose it'll bother the baby or anything, me sittin' on the ground?'

'You're not sittin' on the ground, honey. You're sittin' on a mattress. Get to work on this beer while I stir up some firewood.' Craig opened a bottle, drank off the foaming top, and handed it to Maybelle. He scooped up the other bottles and took them to the top of the stream, where the water frothed and bubbled as it came through its narrow rock-studded channel to spread into the slow-moving pool. He stood the bottles on end, nesting them inside a small smooth cluster of stones, and wiped his wet hands on his pants legs. 'Cold as ice-water,' he said, and went out of the clearing into the woods again. He came back with more dry moss, and an armful of pine-cones. He dropped his burden and went back into the woods, emerging this time with a load of small sticks and tiny dry logs. He found three flat stones and arranged them in a rough triangle, bunched his moss into a wad, covered it with pine-cones, and made a small tepee of kindling over the top. He scratched a kitchen match on a stone and touched it to the moss, which flared and caught the cones. They glowed incandescently with rosy heat, and lifted tiny pursed lips of flame towards the sticks, which sputtered and broke into a steady blaze. Then Craig arranged a cartwheel of his little logs, ends pointing spokelike, slanting slightly downward toward what would have been the axis of the wheel. Plumy smoke lifted, grey and greasily aromatic.

'It smells wonderful,' Maybelle said.

'It's the pine-cones,' Craig answered, spreading a chequered tablecloth on a smooth piece of ground, and starting to unload the picnic basket. 'You ain't really tasted a hotdog until you eat one off a fire like this.' He put out paper plates, set out bottles of mustard and catsup and the salt-and-pepper shakers, and opened the bottle of pickles. He untwisted the waxed paper which contained the chicken and the eggs and arranged the food in the paper plates. Then he got up, walked again to the edge of the woods, and cut several lengths of long green, pencil-sized Indian-arrow shoots, and sharpened both ends, sticking one end into the ground just outside the little oven of rocks.

'She'll die down to coals in a minute,' he said. 'Then we'll roast the weenies. Meantime, I think I'll have a beer, too.'

Maybelle watched him as he went to the water's edge to retrieve a bottle of beer from the stream. My God, she thought, he's a good-lookin' boy. I guess I might be just the luckiest little old gal in Kensington to catch him, even if it had to be this— she looked briefly at her stomach—even if it had to be *this* way. And smart, too. I bet Papa is glad about us, wherever Papa's at. When we have this baby I'm going to be real careful about my eating and dressing up and all like that, and I'm going to have a real long talk with the bank and get them to pay him some more money. It won't be so long before I'm twenty-one and then I can do as I please, but I don't see any reason for making us wait. I really do believe he wants this baby, too.

Craig came back and sat down at her feet, his back to the fire. He had the beer-bottle wedged between his shoes, and he wrapped his arms around his legs and cradled his chin on his knees. He looked up at her and smiled.

'Craig?' Hesitantly.

'Uh-huh.'

'Craig, you really do—you really *want* this baby? You're not just . . . not just . . .' There was a note of pleading in her voice. 'You didn't just marry me because you had to, because of the baby and nothing else, I mean? I wasn't just a . . . a sort of accident that you got caught in and had to put up with?'

'Shush. Of course not, honey. Did you ever hear of a man that was a man that didn't want a baby? His baby? This is going to be a hell of a baby, and a lot of fun. There's a lot of things I know about I aim to teach this young 'un—stuff like about dogs and boats and guns and woods and—stuff like this, fires and picnics. Also we'll have to get him a brother one of these days. You want to name this one after your pa? John Grimes Price? It's a nice name.'

Maybelle shook her head.

'If it's a girl we could name it Joan Grimes Price. But as you seem dead certain it's going to be a boy, we'd best name it after its pappy. Craig Price, Junior. That's a nice name, too. Maybe if we have another boy then we could name him after Pa. Papa can wait. I'm hungry.' She reached for a pickle, and Craig laughed.

'I'd heard about pregnant women,' he said. 'You sure you don't want me to run back to town for some chop-suey? Here, chew on a chunk of this chicken and have an egg while I get the hot-dogs going.'

He took the frankfurters out of the picnic basket, and skewered a half-dozen on the sharp ends of the green wands, bending them forward over the coals at a forty-five degree angle. Then he took some cold buns, split them with his knife, and laid them face down on the hot stones to toast. In a short time the sausages began to sizzle, then to blacken slightly, and then to split their skins in jagged pink fissures. The grease dripped and sputtered in the fire. The smell, blended with the sharp odour of the pines about them, and the slowly glowing cones in the bed of coals, was tantalizing. Craig picked up a golden bun, used it as a glove to draw a frankfurter off its spit, placed it on a paper napkin and handed it to Maybelle.

'Careful,' he said. 'They're red-hot. Have some mustard?'

They sat by the fire, which Craig had refuelled with larger logs now, and ate the hotdogs, gnawed the chicken and devoured the eggs in happy silence. Somewhere off in the swamp a squirrel chittered angrily, and a bluejay cursed back at him. Deeper in the swamp a fox barked once, and somewhere a rabbit screamed as a predator seized him. The drilling of woodpeckers thumped drum-like on old dead trees, and in the silence the birds began to move. The yellowhammers, the golden flickers, swooped from tree to tree. Robins croaked in the distance as they explored burnt-off ground, and the little brilliant bluebirds darted and fluttered from tree to tree. Jorees walked through the dry bushes, their tiny footfalls sounding as loud as animals.

'I never realized, before,' Maybelle said presently, 'how noisy the woods can be if you'll just take the trouble to shut up and listen. The place is just plain full-up with life. Listen. Not a sound now, not a movement, now we're talking again.'

'I used to sit for hours, just listening,' Craig said. 'You stay quiet enough, and all the wild things get curious. I've gone to sleep and waked up looking right into the face of a wild turkey, and they're about the spookiest critter in the woods. You got enough to eat?'

Maybelle stretched and yawned.

'I'm as full as a tick. My God, that was good. I think you've got me sold on the outdoor life. Now, if we just had some coffee.'

'Easy. I stuck a thermos in before we left. Even cups, too. See.'

'You know something?' Maybelle laughed. 'I think you'd make a wonderful wife. Better than me. This has been a real nice day, Craig. I'm glad you made me come. I guess I was sitting around in that old house too much. But it's getting a little chilly. You reckon we better start pretty soon? I'm kinda tired, now, but pleasant tired.'

'Sure. Let me get rid of this junk, first.' He dumped the chicken bones, bread scraps, paper plates and other debris into the fire, which flared greasily. Craig scattered the cooking stones with a kick, and when the first had burnt down to ash, studded with a few coals, he scooped up handfuls of sand and buried the fire. Then he carefully tramped on the heap of sand until the ground was smooth again.

'First lesson for our young friend there in your tummy,' he said. 'Never leave a sloppy camp site. I had that engraved on my tail with a stick before I was five. Also it only takes one lousy little spark to catch in this broom grass and burn up a few million dollars worth of turpentine and timber.'

He hauled Maybelle to her feet, and then stooped for the blanket and the basket.

'There we are. Back to civilization, fat and sassy.'

Maybelle held his arm as they walked back through the wood, grown darker now as the sun was dropping, opening again into golden afternoon light as they approached the car. Craig handed her in, and then tucked the blanket over her knees.

'Look,' he said, as he trod the starter. 'It's plenty early yet. I'd kind of like to run down to New Truro and have a short look at the town—especially the old house. You mind?'

'Not me,' Maybelle said, snuggling into a corner. 'I'm as warm as toast and happy as a dead pig in the sunshine. You know, I've been down to Truro a few times—oyster roasts and maybe a square-dance over to the Beach, but I don't know anything about it. I thought it was a dump. Just a little fishing town, with nothing to do.'

'I suppose you're right. You're a city gal. But your old man came from these parts, and so did all my folks. You know what they say: You can get a boy out of the country, but you can't get the country out of the boy. I was raised in these parts, and I like 'em.'

'Papa used to talk about it a lot, too. But I never figured out what it was you-all did that made you like it so much.'

'I guess being young and half-wild was the main part of it. You give a boy a boat and a hound-dog and he don't want much else. Here we are, almost. Let's go have a look at Grandpa's house.'

He turned right, off the paved road which led to the cross-roads at the town's centre, with its one stop-light, which some one of the old shellbacks had remarked was as useful as tits on a boar, and drove a block on a crushed-shell street, completely shaded by ancient moss-dripping live-oaks. He drew the car gently to a halt across the street from the old house.

'There she is,' he said. 'But my God, she sure don't look like she used to.'

The house still dominated the corner, but its yellow paint, once so bright and cheerful, had scabbed and flaked, leaving stretches of unhealthy grey clapboard. The weathered roof, once coolly green, was now a mossed-grey, and whole files of shingles were missing. The grass of the side yard was over-grown with weeds, studded with naked dandelion stalks, and Miss Caroline's roses had long since lost their zest for climbing. Boards were missing from the front porch, and one, nailed to the cross beams on one end, was sticking up like a long warped ski at its loose end. The planking on the side porch was in even worse condition, and the steps had rotted and broken in the middle. The windows were boarded shut. Evidently the old house was between tenants.

'At least the magnolia tree looks the same,' Craig muttered. 'If we ever make any money, honey, I'd like to buy the old place back and fix it up. It would make a nice summer place for the kids, and I could use it winters for hunting and things like that.

I hate to see the old man's house gone to hell. I'll bet the inside is a wreck.'

Maybelle patted his knee.

'Sure, we can buy it back. You're doin' real good at the mill, everybody says, even old Soames says you work hard, and it won't be so long before I'm twenty-one and then we'll run the mill to suit us. And, Craig, I think you ought to ask for more money. After all, it is my mill. Kind of, anyhow.'

'I better wait a little longer before I go hitting up anybody for a raise,' Craig said. 'I ain't hardly got my chair warm yet. Well, let's go. Just looking at the old place makes me feel kind of bad. I remember it like it used to be, when everybody was alive and it was full of lights and nobody ever locked a door. We'll just drive down by the river-front and then head for home.'

Craig started the car and drove past the river-front, past the docks, past the ship-chandlery, the shrimp-house, the pilot house, and somehow it all seemed much smaller to him now, and very, very grey.

'I used to play a lot in that old shrimp-house,' he told Maybelle. 'We used to play all kinds of games. I remember once we were playing Tarzan, swinging back and forth from beam to beam. You'd swing by your hands, and then when you were going pretty good, you'd let loose one beam and swing over to catch the next one. I let loose one day, and my hands slipped on the next beam, and I fell about ten feet to the floor. Busted my left wrist. I remember how funny it looked, with a kind of sag between my hand and my arm. I was a big boy—about ten— but I started to cry. I wasn't crying because my arm hurt, because it didn't. I was crying because the quail season was going to open next week, and I wouldn't be able to hunt.' He laughed. 'Then, when the numbness wore off, I really started to cry. This time I was crying because it hurt like hell.'

'I somehow can't imagine you crying,' Maybelle said. 'You don't look like you would be apt to cry much.'

'Oh, I could cry all right. Mostly I used to cry when I was mad and had to fight. The harder I'd cry, the madder I got, and the madder I got, the harder I'd fight. Yep, I could cry real good.'

They drove in silence for a while. It was coming on dusk, and Craig switched on his headlights.

'I hate driving at this time of day,' he said. 'It's getting too dark to see, but it isn't dark enough to where your lights do you much good.'

'Well, just take it easy,' Maybelle said. 'You got three people— maybe four from the way I feel—in the front seat. Look, I can't keep my eyes open. All that food and beer and fire and fresh air. I think I'll take a little nap. You mind?'

'Not a bit. Go on to sleep and I'll wake you when we get home. It'll only be another forty-five minutes or so.'

Maybelle snuggled deeper into her coat, leaned her head back on the doorpost, and presently snored gently.

Craig looked at her out of the corner of his eye. He smiled. I believe she did enjoy it today, he thought. Maybe we can make out all right. She's a good kid. We started off kind of peculiar —maybe not like I would have wanted to—but we're in it now and the baby changes things quite a lot. I'm going to try to do the best I can by her. I'm all she's got, unless you count the old lady, and she don't really count. Not in that nut-house, she don't count. He put away the thought of the grim mechanics of their courtship and marriage.

Craig drove steadily, swiftly through the growing darkness. Once, on a curve, his tyres squealed, and he slowed down automatically, thinking that one way or another, they'd have to buy a couple of new tyres soon. Those front treads must be worn down to the fabric, he thought. I better see about that the first thing tomorrow.

He pulled to a halt at the intersection which marked the entry of the New Truro road into the main highway which led from Kensington to Charleston. He looked carefully, checking oncoming lights in both directions, and then pulled out on to the main road which narrowed into a causeway, built over and through a cypress swamp, leading to the long bridge which spanned the river which flowed from Kensington to New Truro.

It was a good road, newly paved with asphalt, shining black macadam whose slick surface could be very tricky when wet. Lucky, Craig thought, tonight it's not wet. He automatically checked his speedometer. This stretch was lousy with state troopers, especially on a Sunday. Fifty-five miles an hour. That was all right. He glanced again at Maybelle. She was still sleeping peacefully.

There was a long curve ahead which he knew by heart, and he automatically moved his car a little closer to the shoulder. A long tongue of lights licked towards him, as an oncoming car rounded the curve and poured straight down the stretch. Craig, dazzled by the light, trod on his dimmer button and his headlights dropped low to the road ahead. The oncoming car made no effort to dip its lights, and Craig did a sharp pat-pat—up lights, down lights—as a signal to the other car. The other driver paid no attention.

'All right, goddammit, you want some, have some!' Craig shouted, and jumped viciously on to his dipper-button. His lights lifted, reached straight over the blackout in front of him, and rebounded off the lightless rear-end of an ancient truck, barely crawling along at the beginning of the curve. Craig was on top of it in a fraction of a second. Half blinded by the blazing lights of the other car, now passing to Craig's left, he jerked viciously at the wheel to avoid running full into the unlit rear

260

of the creeping junk-heap which bulked elephant-like ahead. He heard his wheels scream, and felt the rear end sway as he swerved straight into the path of the oncoming car. Craig jerked mightily again at his wheel, this time to the right, and missed the approaching car by inches. Craig's car tilted up on two wheels, and as he twisted again to right it, he heard a loud report as his right front tyre blew. He sawed desperately at the wheel of the careening car with his left hand while his right arm went out to brace Maybelle's shoulder, and then the Ford slewed violently off the road and rolled over down the sloping embankment. It crashed to a stop, broken nearly in half against the upraised knees of a cypress tree.

Something must have jammed the horn mechanism, because it blew and blew and blew. . . .

'God Almighty,' the state trooper said to his mate, when they scrambled down the embankment to the wreckage of Maybelle's car. 'God Al*mighty*'

'Anybody alive in that I'll be real surprised,' the other trooper said. 'I called the ambulance, but I got a hunch it might just as well of been the meat wagon. Well, let's get at it. That's what they pay us for.'

The car was a smoking, twisted mass of tortured metal, its windscreen shattered, its steering post bent sideways, the back doors caved in, the right front door hanging loosely by a hinge, the hood flapped open, the fenders crumpled, the grille bashed in. There were deep dents in the roof. The horn, eerily, continued to blow, but it was becoming weaker and weaker.

'Cut off that damned horn,' the first trooper said. 'It's enough to give you the willies. How many people?'

'Two,' the second patrolman said, tiptoeing to reach inside the car, which lay on its side, wrapped U-like around the tree. 'Two in the other corner. One's half outside, jammed against the tree.' He flashed his light inside. 'I can't see much but blood, but it's a man and a woman . . . Jesus Christ!'

'What?'

The other trooper's voice was almost shocked in its surprise.

'They ain't dead!'

20

CRAIG regained consciousness in the accident ward. He looked wildly around. A face, a small white dot, far far away, came closer and closer, like the approaching headlights of a car. The dot got bigger and bigger and then it began to melt and reform into a face. The face was bending over him. He strugged to sit up, but hands pressed his shoulders back to the bed.

'Easy, there, boy. Easy. You've had enough trouble for one night.' He swivelled a shiny thing around in front of his eye, raised one of Craig's eyelids, and peered intently through a hole in the shiny round thing.

'I think he'll do, nurse. Concussion. Not too severe. And that cut. Why he didn't cut his head off when that windshield shattered I don't know. As it is, he's going to have a real good scar from the eyebrow up. There again, I don't see why he didn't lose an eye, at least. A half-inch lower . . . Hand me that syringe.'

'But wha . . . what? Where . . .' Craig's eyes dilated in panic. 'I remember! We went off the road. Tried not hit that car . . . My wife! Where's my wife . . . She . . . tried push her down so . . .' He lay back again. The room was spinning, and the man's face was going farther and farther away, fading, receding, until the little white dot disappeared.

The intern handed the syringe back to the nurse.

'That'll hold him for a bit,' he said. 'Keep an eye on him, nurse. These head cases. Keep him quiet. We don't want to move any blood clots or anything like that, not until we can have a better look at him tomorrow. What are they doing with the girl?'

'Took her straight up to surgery. She was bleeding terribly.'

'Goddam crazy kids,' the intern grumbled. 'Helling around in cars, probably half stewed. Was she cut up pretty bad?'

'No. She wasn't cut at all. They found her crumpled up half outside the car with the boy sprawled on top of her. But she was seven or eight months pregnant.'

'Oh, God,' the intern said. 'That'll be a pretty one. Well, call me if you have any trouble with this one. I got to go look at the Saturday night cuttin' cases. Keep some beds warm for the usual stream of battered Sunday drivers. The night is young, and you're so beautiful.'

'Oh, shut up,' the nurse said, and leaned over the bed to take Craig's pulse. She touched his bandaged head with light fingertips and went over to a lighted table in the corner of the ward where she bent over what appeared to be a crossword puzzle.

Craig came slowly awake in the early morning light. His head hurt horribly, great fiery streaks of pain stabbing into a steady, solid ache. He touched his head tentatively, and his fingers felt a thick turban of bandage. He moved his head slightly, and almost shrieked with fresh pain. One eye was bandaged shut, and his other eye was so puffed that he could barely see through the slit. He could smell, though, and the rank hospital odour scratched irritably at his nostrils.

'Nurse,' he called feebly. 'Nurse.'

The nurse came from her corner table, bent over the bed and took his wrist in her hand.

'Shhh,' she said. 'You'll be all right. Just a little bump on the head. You're a lucky young man, that's what you are.'

Craig moved his head uneasily.

'My head. It's killing me.'

'You mustn't move. It's bad for you. Here. Take this. It'll put you back to sleep, and you'll feel better.' She popped a pill into his mouth, and handed him a glass of water. He drank greedily until she took it out of his hand. 'That's enough. It'll make you sick to your stomach, and we don't want that, do we?'

'My wife. Is she . . .'

'Your wife's fine. Don't worry. Go to sleep now like a good boy.'

'But the . . . the . . . the baby. Is it . . . did it? Did she lose the . . .'

'Your wife's fine. The baby's fine. Everything is fine. Don't you worry. Just go to sleep now. Go to sleepgotosleepgotoslee . . .'

Craig sighed, and slept.

'Roll her out,' the resident physician said. 'Put her in a private room. She can pay.' He walked into the adjoining room and started to peel off his rubber gloves.

'Who is she, Dr. Springs?' The surgical nurse followed him.

'She's that little Grimes girl. Old John Grimes's kid. The one that married the Price boy. About seven, seven-and-a-half months gone, judging from what I could tell from what was left of the baby. I didn't think they'd been married that long.'

'They haven't. They ran off and got married three, four months ago. There was some announcement in the paper. He works at the mill, I think.'

'If it's the same Price, I knew his mother and father. Pity about that baby. It would have been a nice boy. Big little fellow. Head crushed . . .' the doctor grimaced. 'Untie me. I'm going down and have some coffee. It's early yet. My God, before I got into this hacksaw business I used to figure Sunday was a day off.'

Down in the diet kitchen Dr. Springs walked over to a table where the night intern was sitting, drinking coffee. He dropped into a chair and nodded to a student nurse, who brought him a cup of coffee.

'How's yours, Damon?' he asked the night intern.

'All right. Both eyes black, a ditch cut out of his forehead, pretty good concussion and a lot of gaudy bumps and bruises. I've seen worse come out of a football game. How's yours, my dear Dr. Springs?'

'She'll do. These young women are tough. I think she got socked by that tree-root when the door sprung when they hit.

Hard to say. Pity, though, because she was about a month off from popping a baby boy. Dead loss, of course. Anybody know what happened?'

'Yeah. Admissions said the State cops said as far as they could figure, from the skid marks, the kid tried to miss some old jalopy with no lights, turned into the path of a car going in the other direction, tried to get back on his own side of the road and did a somersault over the edge of the embankment. There wasn't a hell of a lot left of the car when the cops got to the bottom of the hill. Miracle they weren't both killed. Funny. The cops said the horn wouldn't quit blowing, sounded like it was trying to call somebody.'

The resident blew on his coffee. He tasted it and made a face.

'What is there about hospital coffee? What do they put in it, formaldehyde? It always tastes like it was drained off a subject. I suppose the cops collared the people in the jalopy?'

'Same story,' the intern replied. 'Charge, being improperly lit. Driver had an expired license. Coons, coming back from a Sunday fish fry. No insurance, naturally. What are you gonna do with people like that?'

'The other car stopped?'

'Not him. I doubt if he even knew the Price boy's car went over. He must have been going like a bat out of hell.'

A light flashed, and the squawk box cleared its throat.

'Dr. Damon, Emergency. Dr. Damon, Emergency.'

The intern got up wearily. He walked over to the sound box and flicked a key. 'Damon. Coming.' He turned to the resident. 'You might as well come too. It'll save wear and tear on the old girl's voice.' His voice sing-songed into poetical parody. ' "If Damon comes, can Springs be far behind?" Come on, grab your plumbing kit, Sawbones, and let's go patch up the new candidate.'

When Maybelle awoke she looked curiously around the white-walled room. It didn't look anything at all like her room. Her mouth tasted horrible. And she hurt. My God how she hurt. Especially her stomach. Her hands fluttered to her belly, and found no belly. What had happened to her belly, that she could fold her hands over like a fat old woman sitting in the sun? Her hands fell limply and now she touched her belly. Why, it was flat! Her belly was flat again!

I must have had my baby, she thought. I must have had the baby because this is a hospital room and my stomach is flat again. She opened her mouth and made a faint mewing sound, but no words came.

'She's conscious now, Doctor,' the nurse said. Two strangers walked over to Maybelle's bed. The male stranger was wearing a white coat. He looked down at Maybelle, then sat and took her wrist in his hand. He has a nice face, Maybelle thought. He must be the doctor. She smiled weakly at him and this time words came.

'My baby,' she said. 'I want to see my baby.'

'Not right now,' the nice-looking man said. 'You rest some more, first. You're very tired. How do you feel? Do you hurt?'

Maybelle touched her abdomen.

'Yes. I hurt down here. Did I have a very bad time with the baby? Was it a boy or a girl, doctor? My husband wanted a boy.'

'It was a boy.'

Maybelle smiled. She closed her eyes.

'I'm glad. Craig will be glad. I'm very sleepy. I think I'll sleep a little bit more and then you can bring me my . . .'

'She's still awfully groggy,' he said to the nurse. 'Let's keep her under sedation for another eight hours anyhow. The poor child actually thinks she's had a baby. Going to be a shock when she realizes . . .'

Maybelle's composure when she gained consciousness again was quite remarkable.

'Nurse?' Her voice was strong.

'Yes, dear. How do you feel?' The nurse walked over to the bed.

'I remember now. We were in the car and we had an accident. I lost my baby, didn't I? My baby is dead.'

The nurse put a hand on Maybelle's forehead. She nodded.

'I'm afraid so. Yes. You were very badly hurt.' She touched Maybelle's hip. 'The baby couldn't live. Poor dear.'

Maybelle turned her head away. Her voice was muffled in the pillow.

'It was . . . it would have been a boy?'

'Yes. It would have been a fine boy. I'm so sorry.'

'My husband . . . was he? Is he, too?'

'No. He cut his head badly. He had a concussion. But he'll be all right in a day or so except for the cut.'

'I wish it had been him instead of the baby,' Maybelle said bitterly.

'You mustn't talk like that. It wasn't his fault. And the people that found you—the police—say he tried to protect you with his body. It wasn't his fault. He did his best. Think how he must feel.'

'I don't care how he feels, I don't care, I don't care!' Maybelle burst into tears. 'Go away and leave me alone!'

'You mustn't upset yourself, dear. Try not to upset yourself. It's very bad for you. The doctor will be along to see you in a moment. That's a dear.'

'Well, she's tough as whitleather,' the doctor told the nurse. 'When she quits being sore she'll be as good as new. I don't think this thing scrambled her guts much. The baby took most

265

of the punishment. She'll probably have another six kids once she quits blaming her husband for what happened. They usually do. I've seen quite a few cases when a thing like this brings them together even when they're about to split off.'

Two days later Craig came into the room. His head was still swathed in bandage, his one visible eye still purple-black, but the swelling had gone down.

He walked over to the bed and took Maybelle's hand. She snatched it away.

'How are you feeling, honey?'

Maybelle didn't answer.

Craig tried again.

'I know how you must feel about the . . . about everything. There's no use me trying to tell you how sorry I am. It was all my fault for taking you out when you didn't want to go and . . .'

Maybelle looked him straight in the face, and her voice was as cold as her eyes.

'The next time you want to go on a picnic,' she said, 'find some other girl to take along.' And she turned her face to the wall.

21

IT was only natural that Maybelle's active hostility to Craig depleted with time, although both were careful not to mention the baby, picnics, or automobiles. The Ford had been smashed past repair, so they sold it for junk and went carless, since Craig's salary was not up to the purchase of another car, and for a long time Maybelle refused even to ride in an auto with friends. Craig pointedly refrained from suggesting that Maybelle buy a new car out of her own income. This income seemed to be a house secret, and only came into play when outstanding bills outweighed Craig's small salary.

A year had passed at the mills, and Craig had been given a ten-dollar raise, which brought his salary to thirty-five dollars a week. He had become quite an expert on grading the quality of incoming cotton, and Mr. Soames had gradually, without appearing to notice it, given over most of the final say on cotton-purchase to Craig.

Craig had suggested that the mill go so far as to advance certain seed supplies to some selected farmers in order to insure a better, more uniformly white grade of cotton, but Mr. Soames had snorted and said, with excessive unction, that cotton-croppers were a shiftless lot, at best, and that they'd probably sell the high-quality seed yield to somebody else, and go right on planting the darker grades.

On the trip to the bank, for the payroll, Craig had casually mentioned the selected seed idea to Mr. McMullen, the bank president, who had given him a lift back to the mill. Mr. McMullen said he was extremely gratified that Craig was taking so much interest in the mill, but perhaps it would be better if he left weighty decisions of this sort to Mr. Soames and the trustees, and confined himself to his job. Also, he thought that as the husband of poor John Grimes's daughter, Craig would improve himself by spending more time in the office and less out back with the men and the machines. And as for the sports programme... well. He shook his head ponderously.

'I've heard about your taking an interest in all this baseball and boxing business with the millhands.' He pronounced 'baseball' and 'boxing' as if he had been forced to say 'syphilis' and 'leprosy'. 'Mill-workers are shiftless enough without encouraging them to learn how to work at being lazy. Soames has mentioned to me that you want the mill to—to *subsidize*—a team, to buy equipment and uniforms and such. Ridiculous. All you'd get would be hands who are twice as tired and twice as lazy from *play*.' *Play* took on a connotation of fornication. 'You tend to your business, young man, and be thankful that you've got a good job when so many people are out of work.'

'Yes, sir,' was all Craig could think of to say, as he thanked the banker and got out of the car. A ten-dollar raise was a ten-dollar raise, even if he did suspect that it had been given him as a consideration against the medical bills for the accident. Ten dollars in 1935 was a fair weekly wage for a common mill-worker; as a raise it was considerable, since five dollars would buy a week's groceries and a carton of cigarettes to boot.

During Maybelle's convalescence, Craig came dutifully home every evening from the mill. He and Maybelle had very little to say to each other. They listened to Amos 'n Andy on the radio, and played some old, scratchy records on the gramophone. Maybelle read *Cosmopolitan* for romance and the *Saturday Evening Post* for heavy-duty intellectual content. Craig found time to study, and he read everything he could find on textiles, filled in his papers for the correspondence courses, and by 10 p.m. was yawningly ready for bed. They had almost nothing to talk about.

One night, bored with reading, his eyes itchy-aching, Craig put down his pamphlet and said:

'Maybelle, how often do you write your mother?' 'About once a month. Why?' She put a finger on the magazine page to keep her place.

'No reason. Just wondering. The poor old girl must be awfully lonesome. You haven't been to see her once since we've been married. Don't you ever go?'

'I went a couple of times. It didn't do any good. Those places give me the creeps. All those crazy people. I don't think it makes any difference whether you see them or not. The doctor up there said just as often as not it disturbed them more than it helped them, coming in contact with the outside world, that's what he said, contact with the outside world, and made them unhappy and dissatisfied. Anyhow Mama's crazy as a loon, and we didn't get along so well anyhow. And it's too much trouble and too expensive. It already costs a fortune to keep her in that place. If the bank didn't have to pay out so much I'd have more money. Even though they pay it out of her share.'

'Why didn't they put her in Dix Hill if she's as crazy as all that? I mean, don't they get about the same care in a public sanatorium as they do in a private one? And if she's insane it wouldn't make much difference where she is, so long as they feed her and don't let her hurt herself.'

Maybelle appeared shocked.

'Oh, we couldn't do a thing like that. A *charity* bug house? Anyhow, she's not that kind of crazy. Not violent or anything. Just kind of overall nuts.'

'What is "overall nuts"? What kind of crazy is she? What does she do, that makes her crazy?'

'Oh, a lot of things. She hears things and sees things. She always loses things. She keeps waiting for Papa to come home. Sometimes she thinks she's a little girl again, and wants to play dolls.'

'Seriously, play dolls?'

'Yep. She made herself a doll out of some old rags and slept with it just like it was a baby. Also she kept right on thinking I was a baby.'

It was, Craig noticed, the first time that Maybelle had used the word, baby, since the accident.

'Did you write her about . . . about the baby?'

'No,' Maybelle said sharply. 'I didn't. I couldn't see the use of it. I wrote her that we were married, is all. I didn't tell her *why* we got married. No point in upsettin' her, seems to me.'

'Did you ever think about getting her out of the place? Bringing her back here to live, I mean? If she's not really crazy, just a little queer? Half the people in Kensington have got some sort of peculiar relative. Seems a shame to keep the old girl penned up for her last days.'

Maybelle laughed hollowly.

'She was a pain in the neck sane. She'd be impossible crazy. Why are you so interested in Mama, all of a sudden?' She shot the question at him. 'You never asked me about this much before.'

Craig looked up at the tone.

'No reason, 'specially. And I guess I've been too busy, too many things have happened, to think much about it. How long has she been shut up, now?'

'Since a year after Papa died. Nearly two years, now. She came all unstuck when the old man passed away, and he lost his bank and the other mills and stuff. She always was kind of silly, and I reckon all the trouble at once scrambled up what brains she had. She just got queerer and queerer.'

'Then maybe she wasn't actually crazy so much as just in a state of shock or something like that. Who sent her off? Who committed her, I mean?'

'The estate. The trustees. The bank. I was just a kid, of course, not quite seventeen, and I didn't know which way was up. Before I knew it they had packed the old lady off. I decided not to go back to Saint Mary's the next fall. The trustees raised hell about me staying in the house by myself, but it was our house, Mama's and mine, and it wasn't mortgaged. The old man had put it in mine and Mama's name, so they couldn't touch it when they settled up the estate. Since then things just kind of ran along until you showed up.'

Maybelle was plainly bored with the conversation. She picked up her magazine. Craig interrupted her reading a little while later.

'Maybelle?'

She looked up irritably.

'What now? I'm trying to read this story.'

'You got any idea what it costs to keep your mother in the hospital?'

'What in the hell is all this? What do you care what it costs to keep Mama in the hospital? She's my mama, not yours.'

'I was just curious, that's all.'

'Well, I think it's fifty dollars a week, if you include medicine and stuff. You're certainly nosy tonight. Now hush and let me read.'

'Okay. Sorry.' Craig picked up his book on cost-accounting, but the fine print blurred in front of his eyes and he kept reading the same sentence, meaninglessly, over and over again. Fifty bucks a week, he thought. I make thirty-five, and knock my brains out for it. That's fifteen dollars more a week than I make. Fifty dollars times fifty-two weeks is $2600 a year, and she's been up there at Nottingham Hill for two years. Jesus, that's more than five thousand dollars. What I couldn't do right now with five thousand bucks as a down payment on anything, everybody as busted as they are. I could go into business for myself on five thousand dollars. I'll bet Old Man Grimes started with less. I got to do something about this. This is just plain money out of my pocket. For a moment, Craig had forgotten that the money was not even Maybelle's, but Maybelle's mama's money.

'I think I'll go to bed,' he said. 'I got a hard day tomorrow. That ten-buck raise seems to have been an excuse for old prune-face to hang about six extra jobs around my neck.' He got up, stretched, and yawned.

'You're lucky to have any job at all,' Maybelle said. Then, swiftly, 'Oh, I'm sorry, Craig. I didn't mean that. I know you work hard.'

'It's all right. Everybody keeps telling me I'm lucky to have any job at all. It gets a little tiresome.' He stooped and kissed her cheek. She put her book down.

'Craig.'

He had turned to go to bed.

'Yes?'

'I think I'm all right again now. Downstairs I mean. Could we go back to being kind of married again? Except we'll have to be very careful. I'd be afraid to catch another baby so soon after . . .'

Craig walked back and laid his hand gently on her shoulder.

'Sure we can. But not tonight. Not on top of Mama Grimes and my hard day tomorrow. Also I'll have to make a little sneaky trip to the drugstore tomorrow. Good night, baby.'

Maybelle sounded disappointed.

'Good night. I'll be along in a few minutes.'

As Craig undressed he pondered Maybelle with wonder. Maybe there's something wrong with me, he thought. She hasn't let me near her even though she's been all right for months. And all of a sudden, after her being kind of snappish about her mother and the questions I was asking, all of a sudden she wants to play house. I don't get it at all, he thought. Maybe it runs in the family.

He went to sleep adding how much an extra fifty a week would amount to in fifty years, and concluded that if Mama Grimes proved to be excessively long-lived, she would have cost him—them, well, Maybelle, anyhow—a power of money.

22

LIFE settled down in its accustomed pattern then, but with one exception. Maybelle insisted on extreme precaution against babies, was violently rabid on the subject, and Craig developed a complex against the performance of his husbandly duties. For some private reason, Maybelle was completely obstinate about what method of birth control they should use; she did not, she said, believe that foolishness about safe times, she knew girls who had got caught that way, and she believed definitely that women's contraceptives were insanitary. Gradually, more or less commanded to stand at stud, Craig came to regard his bounden duties with all the enthusiasm of an early Christian for an unfettered lion. He found himself thinking of extraneous business in the middle of the act, and only willpower forced him to drag his mind back from inventories and focus it on the project at hand. And Maybelle, her mind at rest, her fears of pregnancy exterminated by Craig's armour, proved well-night insatiable. Craig overheard a coarse analogy between two millhands on this vital matter, and the parallel kept coming back into his head at the oddest moments. One man had said: 'I wouldn't be caught dead usin' one of them things. It's like washin' your feet with your socks on.' Craig heartily, though silently, agreed, and felt his spurious ardour die.

As time passed, Craig often pleaded fatigue, pleaded the busy day tomorrow, pleaded headaches and bad colds and stomach disorders, but Maybelle was ever prodding at his side, even wakening him from sound slumber, as gently but as stubbornly as a puppy importuning single-mindedly for food. In the end it was generally easier to roll over, fumble for the packet of contraceptives in the night drawer, pull a shutter over his thoughts and give Maybelle her will. But the performance left him unsatisfied and frustrated, as if he had practised an uninspiring callisthenic, and sometimes the thought of a lifetime devoted to such a sterile relationship induced semi-panic. This in turn sometimes made him unable to comply with Maybelle's demands and earned him rousing recriminations.

His life, he thought, was getting to be more and more of a squirrel-tread. The mill, old man Soames, Miss Mildred with her sniffles, whistles to mark the shift changes, cotton to cull in the grading room, payrolls and timesheets, stale sandwich for lunch, invoices and outgoing consignment, papers, papers, papers, then the whistle, and home to Maybelle and a dreadful sameness of Amos n' Andy and work sheets from the correspondence courses, which Craig cursed himself for ever starting in the first place. Then the almost nightly ordeal with Maybelle's simple lust and the horrifying experience of washing his manhood out of the contraceptives because, as Maybelle pointed out, those things cost money. God Almighty, he thought, I'm not twenty-one years old yet and already I'm hooked, caught, finished. And you baited your own trap, Price, my boy. You better just grin and bear it a while longer, son, and see how things turn out. You can always go back to sea.

He attended the company ball games occasionally, and always umpired when asked. He had never had any more trouble with the men since his one brief brush with Red Forney, who had becomes his best friend among the millhands. The small start towards organizing a sports programme had worked very well. The men played in sweatshirts and bathing trunks now, and nearly all had tennis shoes. The petty-cash kitty which Craig still supervised was growing larger, swelling with nickels and dimes and occasional quarters, and was frugally dispensed by Craig when somebody broke a bat or the balls became lopsided from repeated pounding. Craig had also taught Forney what few tricks of boxing he knew, and Forney had appointed himself more or less head coach to anybody else who wanted to learn to fight scientifically. ('I don't teach them everything I know,' he grinned at Craig. 'I want to be able to whip any son of a bitch in the mill. You don't count. You're front office.')

Craig found himself developing a fondness for the big, rough redhead. Father Forney, he learned, had got himself squashed in a mechanical accident of some sort in another mill, up in Shelby, when Red was about eight years old, and the boy had been left as the man of the house, to look after his mother and a baby sister. His mother had worked in a mill, too, until arthritis—Red called it 'arthuritis'—crippled her so badly that she couldn't work any more. They had moved to Kensington to live off the grudging charity of an uncle, Red's mother's brother, and Craig gathered that the living had not been very bountiful or even painless.

'The ol' bastard had a way of getting drunk and coming home with boxing gloves on the brain,' Red explained. 'He beat on me until I was about twelve, but one night he took a swing at me and I hit him over the head with an axe handle. When he come to he kicked us all out in the street, me, Mama, and the baby. I sold some newspapers and stole some and when I was fourteen I went to work here. I was big for my age, and nobody worried much about them child-labour laws. Somehow we managed to make it, although my God, Craig, they was nights when you could hear my guts growl from here to Raleigh. Then the old lady died and left me with this kid sister. She's a hell of a good kid, smart as a whip, and if it harelips the Pope, I done swore me a swear that she ain't goin' to work in no goddam mill. Not if I got to kill somebody first.'

'What's her name, this kid sister?' Craig asked. 'How come I've never seen her around with you?'

'Libby. Elizabeth. I don't let her hang around the mills. She's fifteen now, and she's got a couple of risin' beauties that a girl twenty would be proud of. She already smells like trouble. Pretty as a picture. Got red hair, too, but it ain't carrot-red like this mane of mine. Soft and wavy, and more like a pretty roan horse. The boys in high school are sniffin' after her like dogs after a bitch, but they don't git very far. I take care of that. I let her have company in the house, but if she wants to go to a dance

272

with one of them sheikhs, old Pappy Red he goes along too. I'd like her to make somethin' out of herself, and I don't aim to have her knocked up by the first drugstore cowboy that tells her she's cunnin'. I reckon you know how them townfolks feel about mill girls, like as if they wasn't quite human. Just fall down for the first man come a-askin'. Anyhow,' Red laughed, 'she's too good a cook to lose. She can take a old shingle and make it taste like a sirloin steak. I et a sirloin steak once. When I git rich I aim to have one three times a day.'

'She sounds like quite a girl,' Craig said. 'She goes to school, of course?'

'Sure. She cooks my breakfast early and then makes me a lunch and then she goes to school. By the time I get back from work she's got that little house cleaned up as neat as a pin, and supper, such as I can manage, waitin' to go on the stove. Makes all her own clothes, too, and they ain't a better dressed kid in high school. She's gonna be a junior this fall,' Red said proudly. 'Don't get nothin' but A's on everything. By God, that's one Forney gonna amount to something, or I know the reason why.'

Craig was walking out of the mill-gate one Saturday after the twelve o'clock whistle, when Red Forney hailed him.

'Hey, Craig! Wait a minute for me. I want to talk to you.'

Craig stopped, and Forney came alongside. The breeze made a scrubbing brush of his coarse red hair.

'Where you goin'?' Forney asked, as they fell into step. It was a warm day in July—not smiting hot, but with the light wind stirring leaves which still bore a dusty remembrance of the tender green of spring. It was an exuberant day, with a profusion of birds, and the grass too was lush, stubbornly green against the inevitability of the searing August sun which would parch it into strawy strands. Even the sombre mill district looked faintly cheerful, despite the barrack-like, blind-eyed factories and the tall, jaundice-yellow chimneys smeared and streaked by the tars of smoke.

'Ain't this here a main bitch of a day?' Forney said. 'Makes a man want to jump up and crack his heels and do something real pure-T stupid, like runnin' off to be a cowboy or something.'

'I feel the same way. I thought I'd go home and work it off in in the yard,' Craig replied. 'Instead of running away to join a circus.'

'Man, you're shore housebroke for such a young feller.'

'I got a lot of early mileage on me. It's time I settled down.'

'How's the missus? She all right?'

'She's fine. She's pretty well over the accident now. I guess women are tougher than men. It's the men that wear the scars.' Craig touched the livid streak which split his eyebrow and ran upward to lose itself in his hair.

'Man, you sure got a face on you,' Forney said. 'You look like you been tromped on and forgot. Busted nose, windshield scars . . . How old are you anyhow?'

'I'll be twenty-one someday pretty soon.'

'You look thirty if you look a day. Craig, me and the guys were aimin' to say how sorry we were about the accident and all, but none of us are very good at that kind of stuff. I reckon you knew anyhow, without us havin' to tell you.'

'Sho. Skip it. All over now. One of those damned things you can't count on. I keep thinking that if we had come straight home from that goddam picnic instead of driving to New Truro, we never would have seen the car that wrecked us. If I'd of been drunk and drivin' fast, we wouldn't have hit that combination, either. Or if we'd gone to the beach, or . . .'

'If you'd been born the King of England or was a girl scout or a African cannibal or President Roosevelt,' Red said. 'There ain't no use iffin' yourself to death. You know what they say: "If the dog hadn't stopped to piss he would of caught the rabbit."'

'I came to the same conclusion,' Craig said. 'Things happen, they just plain happen. You can't back-track 'em and all the ifs and maybes ain't going to change anything. So I got a new scar, we lost a youngun, but we're still alive. Let her go, it's too nice a day.'

They walked in silence for a moment.

'Fine day to go fishin',' Red said suddenly. 'If you ain't got nothin' better to do than fart around in a garden, what say we go ketch a mess of perch or maybe a big-mouth or so? I know a coloured feller on Big Crick that'll lend us a boat and some poles and stuff. There's a million worms in that black muck along the crick bank. Come on home with me and have something to eat, and then we'll hitch a ride out to the crick.'

'Sounds like fun, and I ain't had much fun lately. Let's stop at the Greek's and I'll telephone Maybelle. I'll tell her I'm working or something. She don't approve of her husband hanging around with the help.'

Craig came out of the Greek's, and they caught a street car.

'I live on the other side of town,' Red explained. 'Mostly I walk or just thumb a ride. I pay a little more rent, maybe, but I didn't plan on Libby livin' in no mill-owner's shanty with all that millhand trash around her. We ain't got but the two rooms and a kitchen, but it's clean and it's close enough to school so Libby can walk.'

'You set a heap of store by that sister of yours,' Craig said.

'I can whip the son of a bitch says I don't,' Red answered. 'The way I figger it she's got a chance. All of us Forneys been poor white trash ever since the first one come over from Scotland.

We been millhands and sharecroppers and deckhands and roustabouts and railroad hands. Most of the women died early, frazzled out from work and younguns, and like I was saying a minute ago, Libby's goin' to be the first one to live decent and marry a gentleman—somebody that don't work with his hands. Maybe I'll have to stick up a bank, but that kid's goin' to college, if it's only one of them normal schools that learn you to be a school teacher.'

They rode in silence for a while, Craig thinking what a pretty town Kensington was once you got outside the depressing area of the mills and the niggertowns, where the starved cats prowled and filth littered the streets. The car clanged to a halt, and Forney said: 'This is where we git off.'

They walked half a block and came to a tiny clapboard house, one-storied, grey and dismal in its flaking paint, its asphalt-papered roof. It was set all by itself in the centre of an otherwise vacant lot, and was flanked by a sprinkling of china-berry and poplar trees.

'It ain't much to look at,' Forney said. 'But at least it's got a tree or three around it and it ain't in the milltown. Libby keeps it real nice inside. One of these days I aim to put in a bathroom when I get some money ahead.'

'How come the man built it so small?' Craig asked, as they walked on to the sagging little four-foot porch.

'It wasn't always so small. They cut this'n in two and drug half of it over here. Dunno where the other half is. Well, here we are. Libby!' he called. 'Compn'y.'

'Be right with you, Red,' a fresh contralto voice answered from the back of the house. 'I'm taking down some wash.'

'You like home brew?' Red asked. 'I usually keep a crock workin'. It's better than that three-point-two bellywash, and a sight cheaper.'

'Sure do,' Craig said, looking around as Forney went back to the kitchen. The door to one room was shut, and Craig judged that to be the sister's bedroom. The other room contained a kerosene stove, a long sofa he assumed was Forney's bed, a home-made white-pine table painted green, a battered, rump-sprung easy chair, and a couple of straight chairs. There were white-and-blue-checked curtains, made of something like gingham, and a pottery vase, filled with black-eyed-Susan daisies, stood on the table. A cabinet held some books—mostly school books, Craig observed—and was topped with another vase, which was rather a deep glass dish filled with purple-faced pansies floating in water.

Red came out of the kitchen with a couple of glass beer mugs filled with foaming amber brew.

'This is pretty strong stuff. I think Sis must have dropped a cake of lye soap in it, or something. But you can bet your ass she's stronger than any three-point-two. I stole the mugs. Try the brew.'

Craig drank, and his eyes popped.

'Whew!' he said. 'I tasted white mule that was weaker.'

Forney seemed pleased.

'Y' like my little ol' house? I told you Libby kept it nice and neat. We're a mite cramped for space but we make out. That's Libby's bedroom yonder—' he pointed at the closed door— 'and when she's got courtin' company I have to go shut myself up in her room until it comes time to kick the boy friends out, and then we swap around again.'

'I like it,' Craig said. 'And at least you got some privacy. You ain't living in somebody else's lap.' A door slammed in back. 'I guess that's your sister coming.'

A girl, smiling, walked into the room.

'Hello, Red,' she said. She looked at Craig.

'This is Mr. Price from the mill, you know, the feller I told you about. Craig, this here is my little sister Libby.'

'Hello, Libby,' Craig said. He held out his hand. 'Your brother was telling me all about you, but I don't think he did you justice. It's real nice to meet you.'

'It's nice to meet you, Mr. Price. Red talks about you a heap. He's told me about the ball team and all. He didn't tell me about that set-to you all had.' Her eyes lit mischievously. 'Somebody else told me about that, and I made old Red break down and confess that you kind of knocked the starch out of him.'

Red laughed.

'He did, too. My belly was sore for a week. Libby, me and Craig's goin' fishin'. Could you make us a sandwich or somethin'? Then if we ketch a real good mess of fish, maybe we could have us a fishfry later on this afternoon. How 'bout it?'

'Fine. I'll stir 'round in the kitchen and see what I can fix up for you men.' She went out of the room in a swirl of skirts.

'Ain't she somethin'?' Red asked proudly. 'And only fifteen.'

'Something ain't the word, boy,' Craig said. 'You better keep a tight eye on that one. She's a knockout.'

And knockout she is, Craig thought. A double knockout, with that hair and that shape. Whoooeee.

Elizabeth Forney was a tall girl, about five feet six or seven. She was wearing, that day, a simple chambray house-dress of vertical blue and white stripes. It was belted tightly, and her waist, Craig was prepared to swear, measured not much more than a big man's two-hand span around. The breasts above the narrow waist were, in a word, formidable. They were a grown woman's breasts, large, evidently firm and free of harness. They tipped upward and bounced slightly as Libby spun out of the room. The legs were long and beautifully shaped, and needed no high heels to effect a flowing curve of calf, for Libby was wearing white, low-cut tennis shoes.

Her skin was the whitest skin Craig had ever seen, that peculiarly milky colour most common to Scots and other Gaelic strains accustomed to generations of high, cold climate. It was a skin that would freckle at a mere suggestion of sun, as a talcumy dusting of freckles across her short straight nose testified.

Libby's hair, as her brother had said, was not strawberry or pink-red, the kind of hair that goes with white eyelashes, pale eyes and almost invisible brows. Libby's hair was a dark red, almost mahogany, nearly the colour of an Irish setter's coat. And the eyes were brown, almost black eyes, large and level under thick dark lashes and firmly curving dark brows. She had walked, Craig noticed, not with the lumbering flat-footed tread of the heavy-haunched mill girls, whose early faint cheap prettiness always faded into shapelessness after the fleeting magic kiss of young girlhood became the stolid embrace of womanhood. One baby—and they married young, sixteen, seventeen, sometimes even as young as fourteen or fifteen— just one baby and they blurred into a carbon of their sagging-breasted, broad-hipped mothers. This wouldn't happen to Libby, Craig couldn't help but think, if she had a dozen babies. She was lovely now; at forty she would be beautiful, and at sixty, handsome. He contrasted her briefly with a younger Maybelle, and hurriedly destroyed the thought.

She was coming back now, with two plates stacked with thick-breaded sandwiches. Craig noticed that she wore no make-up except a touch of lipstick, and the blush of natural rose high on her cheekbones, against the cream of her skin, seemed almost painted on.

'I got to apologize for the sandwiches, Red,' she said. 'I haven't been to the store yet. There's only some of that last corned beef, but I opened a can of salmon and mixed a little mayonnaise in it. It'll keep you-all from starving until I get to the store.'

'The reason she ain't been to the store yet is that I ain't give her any money yet,' Red grinned through a bite of sandwich. 'Here's ten bucks, honey. See kin you stretch it 'til it hollers.'

'Don't I always? Your sandwich all right, Mr. Price?' Her voice was faintly anxious but not in the least apologetic.

'Dee-licious,' Craig said. 'Or it would be if I could really taste it. But your brother's home brew burnt my tongue clear off. I'm just kiddin'. It's fine. And please don't call me Mr. Price. Your brother calls me Craig. I ain't got the kind of face that goes very well with Mister. Too many lumps and bumps on it.'

'All right . . . Craig,' she said. To her brother: 'Red, you-all don't mind if I go off now and get the shopping done? I got a

277

million things to do this afternoon, and if we can spare a quarter, I thought I might like to go to the movies before you-all get back from the fishing.'

'We can spare a quarter, sugar,' Red said. 'Who-all's playin' what?'

'My dream-man. Clark Gable. And Claudette Colbert. It's called "It Happened One Night." If anybody gets Mr. Clark Gable even in a picture I'm glad it's Claudette. Since I can't have him myself.'

'I used to feel more or less the same way about Jean Harlow,' Craig smiled. 'I know what you mean.'

'Run along, Sis,' Red said. 'Me and Clark Gable here'll clean up the dishes and stuff before we go.'

She said a breathless good-bye and seemed to float out of the front door. Her dark-red curls, cut shoulder length and pinioned by a ribbon, bounced on her neck as she left.

'She always runs, that kid,' Red said. 'But she don't seem to be running. You hear her ask me for the quarter to go to the movies? She always asks. She never takes nothin' for granted. I don't know how the hell she does it, but she'll feed us for two weeks on that ten bucks, dress herself, buy a couple of pretties and manage to look twice as good as the other gals with jest one hair-ribbon and a piece of dime-store jewellery.'

'She's quite a gal, quite a gal,' Craig said, as they walked to a hitch-hiking corner and stood off the sidewalk, looking properly hopeful as the cars sped by.

'I know it. And I aim to see she stays that way. Hey, there's a car stopping. Now wouldn't it be nice if he jest goin' right past Big Crick?'

Red's friend of the row-boat and fish-poles was an ancient wrinkled Negro who lived in a little shanty about a quarter-mile off the road which passed over the bridged Big Creek, and who looked like a very old monkey. Red fished in his pocket and tossed the old man a plug of apple tobacco.

'Henry don't chew it so good,' Red said, and winked at Craig. 'He's a little short on teeth these days. But you kin gum the hell out of it, can't you, Henry?'

'Dat I does, dat I does,' the old man said. 'Thankee kindly, Mistah Red. I kinda had a 'spicion you might come fishin' today, and seein' I didn't have nothin' better to do, I dug you-all a mess of bloodworms. Dey in de boat, in a tin can. I heard a power of fish jumpin' dis mornin'. Y'all ought to have good luck. Doesn't go to forgit old Henry when you comes back wid de boat. I sore hankerin' for fish I doesn't have to sell.'

'So long, Henry. We'll bring you back a bait of perch, any-how. Thanks for the boat and the poles.'

'Poor old bastard,' Red said as they walked down to the

creek's edge. 'I generally try to keep him in eatin' tobacco and a little cornmeal now and again. He's older 'n Noah, and he's got the rheumatiz, and he can't stir around as lively as he used to. Nobody to take care of him. Had some daughters but they all run away up North or some place, and his boys are mean triflin'. One cut another nigger so bad the nigger died and they electrocuted the boy. I think he's got another boy doin' a little free work for the State right now, swingin' a pick on the roads.

'I often wonder what happens to old people like that,' Craig said as the boat swung away from the bank into the current. 'Suppose nobody bothered to bring him a plug of tobacco or a sack of cornmeal? What then?'

'Oh, I'll come down here some day to go fishin' and find him dead. He ain't too far away from it now. Pore old feller. I suppose he could go to some kind of free home—I don't even know if they got poor-houses for niggers—but he's lived in the woods and on the water all his life. One sure way to kill him would be to pen him up. How about changin' the subject? Ain't nothing going to change Henry, one way or the other, good or bad, and we come here to fish.'

Red rowed the boat stoutly against the fast-running current. The deep stream was almost black in the gloom of the cypress shade, as black as the swamp on both sides of the broad creek. Presently he pulled around an L-curve, rowed another hundred yards, and then made his bow painter fast to an ancient finger-rooted tree-trunk up-ended summit-down in the middle of the creek. The boat yawed downstream with the current, and settled abeam of the half-sunken hulk of a long-abandoned boat. A patch of lily-pads covered the water in the still pool formed by the rotting vessel's beam.

'Ought to be alive with perch and blue-gills, anyhow,' Red said. 'Let's try the bottom with the cork-float, first, and a little later we can let the bait float down and maybe snag us a big-mouth.'

The men threaded the bloodworms on their hooks, and proceeded, almost monotonously, to pull in perch, fine fat fellows of a half-pound or more, each time the corks bobbed and disappeared. Presently they tired of bottom fishing, and let their unweighted baits float gently downstream in the current, close by the green-fronded upcurled lily-pads. They lit cigarettes and sat smoking silently for a while, absorbing the swamp noises, watching the small examples of insect life around them —the popping bugs, the swimming bugs, the zooming dragon-flies. Even the noise of an insect hitting the water was magnified by the stillness of the swamp into a sound that seemed as loud as a handclap. A mink, swimming downstream, made a small purring noise like a distant boat as he sliced through the water, leaving a bubbly, rippling wake behind him. A frog's plop was as loud as a beaver slapping his tail, and a released branch, as a squirrel sprang from one tree to another, twanged like a bow string before shivering into silence.

Red Forney cleared his throat, and it sounded loud as a clap of thunder. Craig jumped.

'Craig.'

'Yup?'

'I got a thing I want to talk about. I might as well put it to you flat.'

'Go ahead. Shoot.'

'You aim to run this mill some day. You're gonna be the boar-coon if it kills you. I got that sized up right?'

'I guess so. I'm going to bust a gut trying, anyhow.'

'How you aim to do it?'

'I dunno. I tell you frankly, I dunno. Being married to the dead boss' daughter ain't good enough.'

'How come? Don't she come into her stock or control or whatever it is when she's twenty-one? That's what they say in the shop anyhow. That when she rises twenty-one Craig Price will be the boss.'

Craig's cane fish-pole suddenly bent double, its tip thrashing as the fish fought. Craig yanked on the limber pole and a bass shot out of the water, leaving a swirl of froth and a small geyser of shining droplets behind him as Craig horsed him with one motion on to the boat's bottom. He flopped vigorously, scattering spray from his shining black sides.

'God that's a big one,' Red said, bending to unhook the fish, and then rapping him smartly on the head with an oar-lock. 'He'll go two pounds, easy. You really had him hooked good.'

Craig impaled a worm again before he spoke. He watched the wriggling worm float downstream.

'It ain't all that simple, Red,' he said. 'Not nearly that simple. We got problems in the family. Old Man Grimes left his stock, about seventy per cent, in trust for Maybelle's mother and Maybelle. Half belongs to Maybelle, the other half to her mother. The other thirty per cent is outstanding. I think the bank—the officers, I mean—got most of that other thirty per cent. There was some sort of deal of transfer when they were trying to straighten out the old man's estate. Also there's a mortage. Not a big one, but a mortgage right on, and the bank holds that. They're kind of happy to hold it, too, and they don't care if it never does get paid off. The interest comes in and they got all the security in the world. You understand this?'

'I think so. I ain't got much book-learnin', but I can figger. Yeah. I understand it good enough to hold water.'

'Well, the thing is, seeing I'm married to Maybelle, is that her third of the stock would give me some say-so if she was talking for her mother, too. But the old lady is shut up in an insane

280

asylum and the bank has got the handling of her share until she dies—seeing as how she's insane—and then it all comes back to Maybelle. Hell's afire, her mother could live another twenty years, and all that time the bank would be running the business. So what it amounts to is that until the old lady kicks off, we just sit on Maybelle's one-third. Drives me nuts. I ain't been mixed up in this business long, but I see ways to double it if it wasn't for old Soames and the people at the bank. They ain't had a new idea since 1900.' Craig shrugged. 'Don't think I haven't been giving this a lot of thought. But I'm stuck. I'll get a raise here, and a raise there and some day, when I'm bent over with age, too old to enjoy it, old lady Grimes will die and I'll be president.'

Now it was Red's rod that bent, but as he jerked the pole, the fish gave an angry shake of his head and threw the hook. He raised a two-foot shower of water as he crashed.

'That was a whale,' Craig said. 'Damn near twice as big as mine. You couldn't have had him hooked real firm, though.'

'The hell with the fish. We got enough fish. I been studyin' you for a long time, Craig, even before you beat hell out of me that day. I think you gonna be the head man around here, and I don't think it's going to take you too long. I'll be honest with you. I want to hang on to your coat-tails. I want to go where you go—foller you up. That's why I hailed you today, to talk about such as this.'

'But, Red, I'm not much bigger than a clerk. I wouldn't have got the job at all if I wasn't married to Maybelle. No use kiddin' about that.'

'I ain't kiddin' about anything. I got a hunch in my belly says you ain't goin' to need all the time in the world. Craig, I know I ain't very long on learnin', book learnin', anyhow, but there ain't nothing about the back end of a cotton mill I don't know. I started out sweepin', and now I'm the best damn' spinner in this mill. Old Marvin McCracken ain't goin' to live forever as spinnin' foreman. I want that job, and I want it pretty soon. I told you, that kid sister of mine is goin' to college. On Marvin's pay I kin make out to send her, and then some.'

Red stopped, and coloured. He took a packet of Bull Durham out of his jumper pocket and rolled a cigarette, twisted the end, and lit it before he spoke again.

'I take a chance that this all sounds biggety, and you'll put me down for a blowhard. But I *know* I can do a lot of things better than a lot of people, even if I don't know jest how I know it. Craig, I am to straw boss this whole mill some day. Right now I know we ain't got anything but foremans runnin' the different departments, but one of the main things this here shebang needs is somebody to boss the foremans and keep all the detail out of the front office. That man's gonna be me, some day, you watch and you'll see.' He stopped talking, embarrassment showing pink in his face.

Craig looked at him earnestly for a moment.

'Red, as far as I'm concerned, if I was the boss-man today you'd be running that spinning room tomorrow. But I'm not and I don't know when or if I ever will be. You got my word on one thing: If I ever am the boss, you're the foreman of the spinning room, and from there on it's up to you. But right now I got a better idea with more future for at least one side of your family. What's your kid sister studying in high school?'

'Libby? I guess the usual writin'-'rithmetic-history stuff. She ain't only a sophomore, risin' third-year.'

'Well, you listen to me. You tell that sister of yours to sign up for all the business training stuff she can take for her last two years. A good stenographer can always get a fair job, and a good private secretary makes a lot of money, especially up North. A good private secretary—and 'specially one as pretty as Libby—also meets a lot of people. Your sis stands a hell of a lot better chance to make something out of herself that way than if you send her off to some half-assed teachers' college or a nursing school.'

'But, Craig, all these years I had my heart set on seein' she got educated proper all the way. Now you're sayin' she's better off bein' a secretary or a stenographer or somethin'.'

'A good office girl makes a lot more dough than a school teacher,' Craig pointed out. 'The North is full of women executives that came right out from behind a typewriter or out of a stock room. I was thinkin' specially about textiles. Department stores and women's wear shops don't hardly hire anything else but women boss-help any more. And there ain't any better place to learn textiles than at the bottom—and that's a textile mill. And you believe me, from what I read cotton's going to take a back seat pretty soon. It's already starting to. They're going to make a lot of stuff from now on where the boll-weevils can't get at it—in a laboratory. Rayon's just the start.'

'You sound like you know what you're talkin' about. Where do you know all this from?'

'Reading. And maybe just smelling. But just look at those Enka Mills outside Asheville. Made a fortune already, those Dutchmen, out of synthetics. But that doesn't concern your sister right now. From what you say and what I can see, she's a hell of a smart girl. And I will promise you one thing: When and if I do get my free hand in that mill the first thing I do is fire Miss Mildred Mason, even before I sit down to tell old Soames he ain't needed any more. And if your kid sister studies her typing and shorthand and business correspondence and all the rest of that junk, she's got a job with me the day I walk in the door as boss. We might as well keep it in the family,' Craig grinned.

'As long as you seem bound and determined to run the back end of the mill, we might as well let Libby run the front end. And then I can go fishing every day, and raise bird dogs.'

Both men had simultaneous bites. This time Craig's bass threw the hook, but Red landed his, flopping fiercely. It would weigh at least four pounds.

'I reckon that's a good sign,' he said, rapping the fish with the oar-lock. 'That's a damn' fine fish to ketch on a pole with a worm for bait.' Then he started to laugh.

'What's so funny?' Craig said.

'I got to laugh at the pair of us,' Red replied, still laughing. 'Here we are, two shirt-tail boys, practical, sittin' here fishin' out of a nigger boat with two cane poles, a handful of worms and damn' near a bentpin. And we talkin' like you already president and me general manager and Libby runnin' a whole office full of stenographers and clerks and stuff. I bet if you turned us upside down and shook us you couldn't pick up five bucks between us. We like little boys talkin' about runnin' away and findin' a gold mine in Alaska or some place.' He sobered. 'Talk's cheap, they say, but somehow I don't think what we're talkin' is cheap. You got to start to think somewhere. And I reckon the luckiest day of my life was when I give you that bad red-ass time and you hauled off and slugged me in the guts.'

'You're right about one thing, sure,' Craig said slowly. 'Talk may be cheap, but it don't hurt to start thinkin', and thinkin' big, somewhere early, or you find out you're too old to start. Come on, big shot. We got enough fish. Let's go home to your house and cook some. I'm hungry.'

Craig noticed with appreciative amusement that when they stopped off to thank the old Negro for the use of his boat and fishpoles, Red gave him the biggest bass and at least half-a-bushel of perch. He also noticed that he, Craig, switched his grammar and dropped his g's to meet the occasion. What exactly would you call that, he wondered.

They were lucky again in thumbing a ride, and they had the fish nearly cleaned when Libby came in. Her cheeks and eyes were glowing, and she had changed to a yellow dress and shoes with high heels.

'That musta been some picture,' Red said. 'You look like you're about to catch a-light. Claudette get a-holt of Clark all right?'

'She sure did, but she took an awful long time about it,' Libby said. 'When he blew the horn and the Walls of Jericho finally fell down I was as limp as a rag.'

'I dunno what she's talkin' about, do you, Craig? Reckon you could fly back from Hollywood for a minute and fry us a mess of fish, Sis? They so fresh they still kickin'.'

283

'You boys must of had real good luck,' Libby said, tying on a white apron. 'Go have some more of that home brew and I'll call you when the fish are ready. How about some cornbread to go with the fish, okay?'

They drank the home brew and later ate the fish, dunking the cornbread into the potlicker that came with a side dish of collard greens, and chasing the last greasy morsels of the fish around with fragments of the crumbly golden bread. Craig ate to a bursting point, and they listened to Libby's excited chatter of what Mr. Gable did to Miss Colbert, and what Miss Colbert did to Mr. Gable, and when Craig got up to leave he seemed to have had more fun than any day since the picnic. And he hurriedly put the picnic out of his mind before he got home and was informed by Maybelle that he was late again. He had difficulty eating two suppers, but bravely managed to choke down a dinner which consisted of fried fish, collard greens, and cornbread.

23

THE summer slipped swiftly into fall, the bright leaves turned and fluttered into black mouldy compost, and nearly a year from the day of the accident, old man Soames fell sick with a variety of agues common to the old, terminating in pneumonia. Craig, less than a year away from majority, found himself literally saddled with the executive operation of a mill. True, the bank had to be consulted for signatures on major transactions, but in effect Craig Price was Grimes Mills. Old John Grimes had run, always, a one-man stud-horse operation, and Soames had been little more than an expanded chief clerk and head book-keeper. There was no board of directors for the mill, apart from the trilogy of bankers who now supervised the general operation until such time as control might revert to Maybelle and her mother, at Maybelle's coming of age and her mother's return to sanity. Calculations had slipped, more than slightly, since Mrs. Grimes had been tucked away in Nottingham Hill, one of the more genteel sanatoria in Greensboro, a city whose maniacs were often described as nervous patients, just as Asheville's tuberculars were often called paying guests until their rotting lungs terminated the holiday with a formal cough. Confusion had been such that when Grimes had died, and Mrs. Grimes had suffered her collapse, the bank had informally assumed the stewardship of both blocs of stock.

In January, when Mr. Soames had still not returned to work, the bankers had checked the books and noticed that both sales and production were measurably up for the last six months, with an unwonted sharp climb in the last quarter. They debated heavily as to whether this could be the fault of improving times or possibly due, in part, to Craig's youth and energy. They further argued as to whether Soames should be replaced by a new and older man than Craig, but decided that older men might come dear, and that for a raw-eared boy, this young Craig Price, moustache and all, was doing a very creditable working job and might be left alone for a spell. Subject, of course, to consultation and veto. The gentlemen spoke in chambers, without banking formality.

'If that's so, then,' Mr. Norton, the first vice-president said, 'we got to pay him a little more money. And give him some sort of title. Frankly, the title is more important than the money. It would give us some sort of excuse to ease out old Soames on a little pension. What'll it be?'

'General manager?' Mr. McMullen, the president said, and then hastily amended his own suggestion. 'Of course not. Not even Soames ever held that position. He was only called office manager.' When speaking with clients Mr. McMullen generally salted his conversation with repeated throat-clearing and the use of the word 'hum' as a glottal stop. With his familiars his fusty public elocution had a tendency to swerve to succinctness.

'How about assistant office manager?' This was Mr. Carroll, the second vice-president.

'That's no good, either, not if we're going to kick old Soames out. Who'd he be assistant to, Miss Mildred?' McMullen snickered at his own joke. 'She could have used a young buck thirty years ago.'

Norton spoke again, ignoring the humour.

'He's been overseeing the grading and doing most of the buying for the last year. Why don't we call him purchasing agent? It sounds good, and he can't buy anything very much anyhow unless we okay it. He couldn't make very many expensive mistakes. What's he making, now? Fifty a week?'

'No. Thirty-five. You know that as well as me.'

'Hell, man, he can't be purchasing agent even in name only for thirty-five dollars a week. What is old Soames getting for doing no work?'

'Used to be one hundred and thirty-five dollars a week,' McMullen said. 'On the cutback, ninety dollars. He ain't worth fifty, even when he's working, if you ask me.'

'I say retire him. Give him twenty-five dollars a week and turn him out to pasture. It's more than he's worth, but he's been working in the mill for thirty-five years,' Mr. Carroll said.

'If this mill had gone under like the others, he wouldn't have had anything,' McMullen replied. 'He don't rate any hundred dollars a month. If he hasn't saved any money in thirty-five years he don't deserve to live in luxury. I say fifty dollars a month is more than plenty. It's as much as some of the hands get.' He snickered. 'And old Soames was always one for holding down costs, when it came to the hands.'

'What do we pay the boy, then?'

'Give him another raise,' McMullen said. 'Give him fifty dollars a week. For a shirt-tail boy it's a fortune. I remember when I was his age I . . .'

'That's settled then,' Norton said hurriedly. He had been laved before by his superior's reminiscences, which invariably began with a twenty-mile hike through the snow to the little red schoolhouse. 'Suppose we continue Soames' salary for six months and then give him fifty dollars a month for life?'

'Full salary for six months is too much,' McMullen said. 'Three's a-plenty.'

'All right. Three months for Soames, and a fifteen dollar raise for young Price. Agreed?'

The other men nodded. Norton winked at Carroll, after McMullen had left. 'You don't suppose all this has got anything to do with the daughter coming of age at the end of this year, do you?'

'Won't make any difference if she does,' Carroll said. 'She only comes into thirty-five per cent. We vote the old girl as long as she's shut up. I still say we ought to have had her committed to the State asylum. Cheaper, and permanent. A mess of money mounting up to invest with. Don't forget, that fancy bug-house she's in is costing us—her—fifty dollars a week.'

'Well,' Norton said, rather coarsely for a banker. 'It ain't any skin off my ass. The estate pays the bills, and she can't spend much where she's at right now. When she kicks off it'll all go to the daughter anyhow.'

'They live for ever, these nuts,' Carroll said. 'I'll see you tomorrow when we talk to the boy.'

Miss Mildred brought the tidings.

'The bank just called,' she said. 'Mr. McMullen.' Her sniff suggested that Craig finally was to be brought to book for embezzlement, at least. 'They want you to get down town right away. They said it was important. Before Mr. Soames got sick . . . .' Now the sniff implied that Mr. Soames' illness had been personally induced by some foreign germ imported by Craig, and that in the hale presence of Mr. Soames, the bank would never have gone so far as to soil its hands on Craig, even via the telephone.

'Cheer up,' Craig said. 'Maybe I'm fired. Did anybody say what they wanted with me?'

'No. Just that you should come right away. You'd better not keep them waiting.' Miss Mildred went back to her desk, the knobs in her undergarments more than ever pronounced by the indignation of her carriage.

286

Craig checked himself over in the mirror in the men's room. He looked good enough to see the bankers. He had bought a blue suit and he was wearing a white shirt and a blue tie. He dampened his hair and brushed it and went outside to flag a trolley for downtown. Wonder what these buzzards want, he thought, as the trolley jarred his spine on its seats, seats as woodenly wrinkled as a roll-top desk, with the heated car smelling of tobacco juice and musty people. I don't think I've made any bad mistakes lately. He got off at Queen Street corner and walked a block to the bank. He entered gilt-barred doors and nodded at the first teller.

'Had a message at the mill, said Mr. McMullen wanted to see me,' he said. 'You know anything about it?'

'They've been having a meeting of some sort in Mr. McMullen's office,' the cashier said. 'Told me to tell you to come right up.'

'Important?' Craig asked.

'I wouldn't know,' the teller said. 'I just work here. But you better get rid of that cigarette. Mr. McMullen's asthma . . . you know.'

Craig knew by now. He tossed his cigarette into a sand-filled pot and walked up the one flight to the president's office. It was not much of an office, even for a bank president, Craig thought, nodding at the runnelled-necked, gold-rimmed-eye-glassed, chinless maiden lady who sat at a typewriter. Where do they *get* them? Craig wondered. They all look alike. Maybe their wives won't let them have pretty ones.

'Mr. McMullen sent for me,' he said. 'I don't know what for.'

'They said to come right in,' the secretary said. She jerked her head towards the door behind her. 'Knock and go in.'

Craig knocked and went in.

'Well, that was quick,' Mr. McMullen said. 'Come in, son, and sit down. Of course you know Mr. Carroll and Mr. Norton.' Craig nodded and said of course he knew Mr. Carroll and Mr. Norton. They were grouped in phalanx, in order of seniority, Mr. Norton, first vice-president, on Mr. McMullen's right, Mr. Carroll, second vice-president, on Mr. Norton's left. The shields of their bankerhood almost interlocked in mutual protection.

A straight chair, empty, was placed directly before—but at a safe distance against cold germs—Mr. McMullen's desk.

'Sit down, son,' Mr. McMullen said again. 'We're not going to eat you.' He chuckled. Seeing the chuckle, Mr. Norton chuckled, and was seconded by Mr. Carroll.

'We have a surprise for you,' Mr. McMullen said. Mr. McMullen had a heavy shock of theatrical white hair, and a fine tracery of broken veins over his cheeks. The flush gave him a look of hearty well-being. His nose also was guttered with burst veins. He was wearing a grey worsted suit, a blue-and-white polka dotted tie, and his glasses dangled from a cord around his neck. He picked them up and perched them on his nose, then cleared his throat, and glanced, right and left, at his cohorts. He looked like a caricature of a moving-picture banker.

Mr. Norton was indistinguishable from the protective coloration of his senior, except that he wore brindle-brown worsted, and was cadaverously thin. Mr. Carroll was shiny bald, with a strand or so of hair combed across his bone-white skull. He wore a pepper-and-salt suit. The desk they surrounded, one behind, two on the flank, was of square flat-topped yellow oak, protected by a skin of bluish glass. It contained only a mock-onyx pen-set and an oblong glass tray which held paper-clips. The carpet was coarse green worsted, harsh underfoot, and there were some black-framed pictures on one wall, pictures of Mr. McMullen in dress clothes surrounded by admiring people, also in dress clothes, sitting in attentive array on each side of Mr. McMullen, who was standing in an attitude of speech before white-clothed tables.

'How would you like to run Grimes Mills?' McMullen said. 'Well, not exactly run the mill, but ah—er for the hum moment, hum since poor Mr. Soames is ah—er indisposed, yes, indisposed, hum, well to ah—er run the mill?' He looked at Mr. Norton and Mr. Carroll, who nodded gravely.

'To take over temporarily for Mr. Soames, is that right, Mr. McMullen?' Mr. Norton asked.

'Only to take over for Mr. Soames, temporarily,' Mr. Carroll said firmly, as if daring any man to dispute his decision.

'I don't know quite what you mean,' Craig replied.

'Well, hum, it is ah—er possible that Mr. Soames will be absent for some time with his er—ah unfortunate ah, hum, er—ah illness. We were wondering here if you might look after the office until Mr. Soames returns, or until such time, hum, that we er—ah, ah—er, might see fit to replace him with another man if his illness er—ah, hum . . .' Mr. McMullen allowed his voice to die.

'Until such time as,' Mr. Norton said.

'Exactly,' said Mr. Carroll. 'That's right.'

All three men looked inquiringly at Craig.

'Yes,' Craig said.

'Yes, what?' Mr. McMullen almost pointed a stabbing finger at him. Craig was about to say 'Yes, sir', remembering his ancient tutelage in manners, and then recalled that they probably were asking him if he could handle the daily business detail of the mill until old Soames came back or they replaced old Soames with somebody else.

'Yes, sir, I think I can handle the office all right. I've been doing most of the work since Mr. Soames got sick. I think I

288

know most of the detail by now, and something about the actual millwork out back. I mean . . .' Craig resisted a coy impulse to cast down his eyes.

'I believe you can, my boy, I believe you can,' Mr. McMullen said, losing his er-hahs and hums briefly in a fit of inner heartiness that caused his nose to glow. 'My partners and I, as trustees of the mill, consider it a sacred duty to discharge er—hah hum,' he coughed. 'My asthma is very bad today. Perhaps George will explain.' He coughed again and hawked something substantial into a handkerchief. 'George?'

'I think I should say that we—Mr. McMullen —I mean—' a slight bow—'have decided that you should be given a chance. Of course we recognize that your extreme youth should be held against you, but there are certain other considerations . . .' Mr. Norton looked warily at Mr. McMullen. 'There are certain other considerations, yes, certain other considerations.' Mr. Norton stopped, satisfied.

Mr. McMullen had recovered from his momentary asthmatic seizure, and the glow that suffused him previously had subsided somewhat.

'It is not so much that you are just *any* employee, hum,' he said. 'But there is a special, an er—hah *special* consideration to be considered, hum, since you are a member of the er—hah family, hum? I mean to say, hum, a *member* of the *family*. And thus, er—hah, entitled to more, hum, consideration than . . .' He hawked again into his handkerchief.

'Yes, sir.' It was all Craig could think of to say. He hoped he looked inquiringly intelligent.

'Perhaps, then,' Mr. McMullen said, 'we had better discuss the er—hah gruesome details, as it were, hum—the details?' He looked at his henchmen for approval. 'Shall we get on with the details, hum?'

'Yes,' said Mr. Norton, looking at Mr. Carroll.

'Yes,' said Mr. Carroll, looking hopefully at Mr. McMullen.

Craig sat in his chair and said nothing at all, afraid to speak for fear of punctuating his phrases with er-hah or hum.

Craig's interview with the banking gentlemen was brief, and somewhat less than violently satisfactory. They continued to congratulate him freely on his elevation to a position of such great trust, and volubly commended themselves for their generosity in doubling his salary in less than two years time. Men had worked hard all their lives to earn less than fifty dollars a week, they assured him solemnly, occasionally punching his chest with grave stiff fingers, and some had never achieved a position of such great trust and responsibility in such a short time. A whole great textile mill practically under his hand, so to speak . . .

'Can I hire and fire and promote?' Craig asked.

Well, not exactly. Not right now. Not just yet. Things were running along very well, and it was up to the foremen to suggest hiring and firing and promotion, and for the moment approval of those recommendations had best remain with the bank. After all, a man of Craig's extreme youth had enjoyed very little managerial experience, and his current position was more or less of a temporary nature pending a scrutiny of results. Perhaps some day, when he was older and more experienced, then of course . . .

'How about machinery replacement? Some of the stuff is just making it on spit-and-string. The looms alone . . .'

For the moment, such things as any large capital outlay for machinery was out of the question. One day, perhaps, when we see that the upturn is permanent, instead of possibly a flash-in-the-pan. But at this time perhaps we had just ride along as best we can, and let the maintenance men earn their pay.

'How about . . .' Craig looked around him at the banking faces, pale, flushed, roach-haired, thin, bald, well-fleshed, conservative—bankers' faces—and quit.

'Thank you very much, gentlemen, for the raise. I'll try to earn it. And the title, for my signature, is *purchasing agent*? That means I buy cotton only, and such things as office supplies and light bulbs?'

'That is correct,' Mr. McMullen said. 'And raw cotton only to the extent of minimum inventory. Apart, some consultation with us will be necessary. Congratulations, young man. You have a fine opportunity for er—hah, hum, success. Hum.' The interview was over.

Craig shook hands and left. Oh, boy, he thought as he left the marbled men's-room bleakness of the bank. I have now got two jobs—all of mine and all of Soames'. I can do everything with this new title but hire, fire, promote and purchase anything larger than a rat trap for plant improvement, and the minimum inventory of raw cotton. But I'm rich. Stinking rich. I now make fifty whole dollars a week. I *am*, by God, rich, he thought, suddenly sobering. Fifty dollars is a mess of money these days. And I got a big house and a wife with money of her own. I think I will just take another look at the books one day pretty soon and try to figure out just how much money of her own my wife has got. She's always been awful close-mouthed about it. Apart from that hundred I borrowed for the wedding and the honeymoon, there hasn't been much Maybelle money scattered around. And I'm still paying off the bank for the loan they made me on the hospital bills.

He passed an automobile showroom and stopped, almost like a child with its nose pressed against a toy-shop window. A lean, sleek Cadillac stood alone in the centre of the floor in haughty grandeur. It was gleaming black, with white side-walled tyres—only a two-door coupé, with two small seats in back, but wearing the sincerely rakish air of expensive elegance. He looked at the price-tag. Eighteen hundred and seventy-five dollars plus tax, plus carrying charges from the Acceptance Corporation, of course. Nobody ever paid cash for a car. So much down and the rest when they caught you, or else a ram-shackly rusty heap for a trade-in, and so much when they caught you. If you were real smart and traded every year you never got out of debt, but then you always had a new car and only a slightly longer debt. No Caddie for me, right now, Craig sighed. The bank would say I was living too high on the hog for a kid. No Cadillac for Maybelle, either, although she could sure afford one for less than what it costs to keep her mother in that country-club nut-house. But I suppose the bankers would poor-mouth all over that, too, and I never would get my new looms. Maybe I won't get my new looms anyhow.

He walked on, and stopped before another automobile show window. This was a Dodge. Two door, five passengers, black—just as black as a Cadillac, but no white-wall tyres—with a bucking ram for a radiator decoration. That's more my style, at eighty-seventy-five, plus tax, plus carrying charge. Nice solid car, too, for a young executive. And I am a young executive. The man said so, and said I ought to be grateful to be so rich so young. Wonder what they'll take as a down payment? Walk in and see. Won't hurt. Always get the down payment from the bank.

I look pretty good, Craig said, watching himself in the re-flecting glass of the show-window. Scars, yes, and the busted nose, but the white shirt and the Arrow collar and the blue tie and the neat blue suit and the shined shoes, because today was banking day and today I am a man about to buy a new car, the first car he ever bought. I think I'm getting a little heavier, too. It's that solid citizen look. Maybe the moustache helps.

'I like the looks of that one,' Craig said to the man with the little pin-stripe blond moustache and the big bat ears. (At least my moustache is thicker than his moustache, Craig thought. I look like a lot of things but I don't look like a fairy.) 'How much is a down payment, the least you'll take, I mean?'

'You don't have any car to trade?'

'No. I had an accident. The car was a wreck. A dead loss.'

'Oh, then I suppose you'd have trouble with the insurance,' the man with the pin-stripe moustache said. He had pimples on his forehead, too.

'No, I wouldn't have trouble with the insurance. The wreck wasn't my fault. How much?' Craig lit a cigarette and looked for some place to toss the match. He dropped it on the floor.

'Two hundred dollars down. The rest in eighteen months.' The man looked nervously at the dropped match.

'As much as two hundred down? That's nearly a fourth.'

'I'm sorry. I don't make the rules. If you haven't got a car to trade, then it's two hundred down.'

'You wouldn't take a note for the whole amount?'

'We're not allowed. I don't . . .' The man looked over his shoulder at the closed door to an office.

Craig held up a hand.

'Don't tell me. You don't make the rules here. That car ready to drive?'

'Yes, but it's the only one of its type we've got in stock until we send for another one for the showroom . . .' the bat-eared young man was flustered. He looked once more at the office door.

'Drive it out to the kerb. Gas it up and get the papers ready. I'll be back in half an hour with the money. Don't bother about the time payments. Okay?'

'Yes. Yes, sir.' The clerk seemed already to be counting his commission. 'I'll have it ready, sir. It's unusual but . . . I'll have it ready, sir.' He headed swiftly to the office. Craig was certain there must be a dragon in it.

He walked rapidly back to the bank. He spotted Mr. Norton at his desk, behind the mahogany railing at the end of the room, near a window, past the grilles of the cashiers' cages. He bobbed his head, and Mr. Norton beckoned him to come in. He stood in front of Mr. Norton's desk. Mr. Norton let him stand, and then said:

'Pull up a chair, Craig. Forget something?'

Craig seated himself, and looked more closely at Mr. Norton. Earlier, Mr. McMullen had claimed his fascination.

'No, sir,' he said. 'Not really. I guess I'm here as a customer.'

Norton smiled bleakly. He was a thin, ginger-coloured man, with dry dandruffy brown hair which matched his brindle skin and suit. He had big yellow horse-teeth which he bared in a smile that was not reflected in his eyes.

'Something important?' The teeth again, as if to say, whatever would you have of any importance to bother *me* with now?

'I would like to borrow nine hundred dollars, sir, to be added to my other note. There's only about a hundred dollars left to pay from the hospital bills. It would come to about an even thousand, altogether.'

Norton leaned back and placed his fingertips together. He rolled his eyes heavenward.

'Why, nine hundred dollars, that's a lot of money, Craig, a whole lot of money. Let's see, that's about a third as much as you'll be earning this year. That's a *lot* of money for a poor banker to let out without security. What do you want so much money for? You planning to buy another mill?' Norton allowed himself a chuckle. 'I know you just got a raise, but it's not even marked on the payroll yet.'

Craig spoke seriously.

'Mr. Norton, if I signed over my raise to the bank, so that I never saw it at all, I mean—if I signed over my raise, could I have the nine hundred dollars now. Just take it out of my pay cheque until the whole thousand dollars was paid? It would only take a little more than a year, at sixty dollars a month. This means a lot to me, Mr. Norton.' Craig had almost said 'please', but choked back the word in time.

'Maybe if you'd tell me what you needed so much money for in such a hurry I might see my way clear to arrange it,' Norton suggested purringly. 'But a garnishee is not legal except by court order, and suppose you got fired—not that you will, of course, but suppose you did—why then I would be left with your paper and no endorsement and then where would I be? In trouble, that's where I'd be. I'm afraid it's impossible, Craig, that much money without security. You'd think, from the way you came in here in such a hurry, that you wanted to take delivery on a Cadillac or a yacht or something like that. Of course, if you got your wife to endorse the note, why then—'

'It was a yacht, Mr. Norton,' Craig said. 'I'm sorry I bothered you. I guess I can get along without a yacht this year after all. Maybe you're right. I could get fired, and then where would you be? Excuse me, Mr. Norton. I guess I'll get back to the mill.'

He left Norton looking after him with a puzzled expression. Snotty kid. Nine hundred dollars this snot-nosed kid wanted, Norton thought, nine hundred dollars. I wonder if he's got some girl in trouble or what? I hear he and the Grimes girl haven't been getting along so good since they had that accident. Mr. Norton took a penknife from his pocket and began to pare at bitten nails.

Craig was blushing hot under his collar, his neck red, when he left the bank. Crossing to the other side of the street, away from the auto showroom, he walked quickly past, shielded by parked cars, and saw that the salesman had driven the coupé out of the building. It was standing by the kerb, and the salesman was giving it a few final dabs with a chamois skin to remove the last flecks of showroom dust.

There was the Morris Plan on the corner.

No good there, either. Not without security. Craig took Grandpa Sam's gold watch out of his pocket. Only eleven o'clock. Plenty of time to borrow money at the Morris Plan, if only you had some credit that didn't need a wife's signature. He looked at the gold watch again. What did you do when you were flat broke? Why, you hocked a watch. Where did you hock a watch? You hocked a watch at a pawn-shop. And suddenly, swiftly, Craig's legs carried him down Front Street to the sign of three golden balls, depending over a flaked gilt sign proclaiming the establishment as *Uncle Charlie's—Loans*. Something Grandpa Sam had said once before came vividly through: 'Mostly, you'll find that the poor look after the poor,' old Sam had said. 'And along them lines I'll take a crooked pawnbroker over an honest banker any day in the week.'

And somewhere, some time, Craig had read an English novel in which the phrase: 'And so he fell into the hands of the Jews', had stuck.

'I'll fall into the hands of the Jews,' he said, aloud, and walked into the pawnshop. It was not the first time he had been there. The last time had been for the purpose of persuading Uncle Charlie to sell him some used boxing gloves and a punching bag very cheaply, for the greater amplification of the mill-hands' athletic aspirations. Craig and Uncle Charlie got along very well, because Craig was old Sam Price's grandson, and the two old men had been friends.

The shop was empty, apart from Uncle Charlie and the dusty, massed array of old mandolins, guitars, fiddles, trumpets, saxophones, hunting knives, pistols, suitcases, athletic equipment, shotguns, assorted jewellery, second-hand clothes, and a vast array of watches.

'You are coming to buy, to sell, or just to visit?' Uncle Charlie asked. '*Wie gehts*, Craig, and how is my prince of commerce today? Already I hear the news. You are to be the new general manager, is it, of my poor friend Grimes's mills. Perhaps a glass of wine to celebrate?' The old man smiled and extended his hand.

'How does it get to you so fast, Uncle Charlie? I just now heard it myself. I get a raise, even if the title isn't general manager. Purchasing agent, except I can't buy anything, is my title.'

'A title is nothing. A work is everything. Sit down and talk to an old man who is tired of giving people money for merchandise they will never redeem.' The old man looks like a cricket, Craig thought. Little and scrooched up like he was about to jump, a hundred years old at least. He looks more like a Chinaman than a Jew, with his little stringy beard and the skullcap on the back of his head. I'll bet he was a heller when he was younger, because he's got a wicked twinkle right on, Craig thought, as suddenly he felt at home, felt friendly, felt like he used to feel with the fellows in the Zeta Beta Tau house so long ago— it seemed—in Chapel Hill.

'How does it get to me so fast, the news that you are coming up in the mills, that today they tell you that you are now making —what is it—fifty dollars a week already instead of thirty-five? It is a trade secret among people who sometimes bank the bankers.' Uncle Charlie twinkled again. 'Do you not know that all banking starts on kerbstone trading, and that the only difference between Uncle Charlie Lipschutz and the House of Rothschild is a matter of degree? And preference? I prefer the climate here to the pogroms of Poland or the fogs of London. Less snow, and no ghettoes.'

Craig gulped. Suddenly he had made up his mind.

'Uncle Charlie, tell me one thing. In this business of yours, do you ever play a hunch? Give somebody too much for something that's a bad risk for you, just because you feel something, lucky, maybe, or turn down something that you know is worth more than what you would have to give for it? Just on a hunch? Just because of the way you feel that day or the way the person looks or the way the weather is? Do you? *Do* you?'

The old man looked at Craig, and stroked his beard. He smiled.

'Just what is on your mind Craig? Tell Uncle Charlie. And for the love of the good God, sit down in that chair there. You make me nervous. What is so serious with such a young man who is doing well if all the reports along the bourse are correct? A man who has married well and who is working well and making respect for himself? A man whose grandfather could be proud of him? What is all the sudden concern of my rich young friend? Tell.'

'It's not a very big thing. Maybe you know better than me. Today I need some money, and I don't need it for anything important except to me. Okay, you can laugh, but today I want to buy a car. I don't want to buy it tomorrow. I don't want to buy it next week. I don't want to ask my wife for the money. Uncle Charlie, I need two hundred dollars real bad and for no damn' good reason at all except that I feel like what you say in the bar mitzvah, today I am a man. I could get it from the banks if I crawl and say yessir and let them get their hands on my personal life and I don't want to. So I suppose I came here to hit you up for a loan with no security except maybe Grandpa's watch, but you got more watches than you'll ever sell and you wouldn't want Sam's watch anyhow so I guess I'll be going and I'm sorry.'

'Such a long speech from such an excited young man. If you must babble, you should take up politics or at least religion. You would make a wonderful preacher, so persuasive. So you come to pawn a watch and remain to pray, or at least to have a soul purge? So today you got to have a car. Not tomorrow. Not next week. Not next year. Today you must have a car. Why?'

'I don't know. All of a sudden I was walking down the street and I saw a car and it was important that I had a car today. Because I broke up my wife's car? Because I killed my baby when I broke up my wife's car? Because today I got a raise and nothing else except a phony title from those people in the bank? I don't know, Uncle Charlie. Maybe I'm crazy.'

'Not so crazy. Young, perhaps, foolish, perhaps, but not so crazy. It is something to be young and crazy with want. Better maybe than being old and not wanting any more. The young prune has much juice to squirt. The old prune . . .' he shrugged. 'I am an old prune and I have no more juice. Maybe a little in the head. Nothing any place else. Perhaps some people would call the juice in my head water on the brain.

'You want two hundred dollars to buy a car? How will you pay the rest, because it must be a new car, a shining new car, or you would not want it today. You would be content to have it next week. How will you pay the rest?'

'The two hundred's only the down payment. I can pay the rest on tick in eighteen months. They'll give me that much time to pay the rest, if I have the two hundred.'

'And this chariot, this fiery chariot of Elijah's, it costs in golden talents how much? In the gelt of our time?'

'Less than nine hundred dollars.'

'You should have been a Jew. Not much more than eight. Not much less than nine? Ay, what supreme, what superb confidence. Less than nine. My boy, you will go far, very, very far.' Uncle Charlie spread his fingers. 'Of such thinking is born high finance. So I will tell you what I will do. I am an old man and foolish. I squander my money. I will help you buy your car. I will give you the cash, and you will give me a paper. I will give you nine hundred dollars and you will pay me a thousand. Why should the finance company have the interest? You will have twenty-four months to pay. If I do not live for two more years, you do not have to pay.'

'Do you want me to sign over the car as security? Suppose I don't pay? Suppose I lose my job and can't pay?'

The old man smiled.

'What would I do with a car as security? I can't drive a car. You cannot put a used car in a pawnshop window, like a fiddle or a concertina. I am not in the used-car business. You will pay, and you will not lose your job. And now you are asking yourself, why is this old fool doing this?'

The old man held up a hand.

'No, don't deny it. I will tell you a secret about an old Jew who came from Warsaw a long time ago, who pushed a pushcart like all Jews from Warsaw seem to do, and who made some little money as a pawnbroker. I will do it only because once when I was young I wanted something very much and could not have it, and when I finally could afford it I didn't want it, it was ashes in my mouth. I have nothing to use money for now. My wife is dead and my children educated and ashamed of their papa who runs a pawnshop. I cannot eat much or drink *schnapps* and I am many years away from my last woman. I indulge myself in old man's foolishness, that is all.'

He went into the little back room behind the shop, and Craig heard the clicking of safe-dials. In a moment the old man came out, with a sheaf of hundred dollar bills and a piece of paper.

'Here is the money. The paper is only an I.O.U. for a thousand dollars. Sign it here. You can pay me back ten dollars a week. Drive your car in good health, and do not say thanks. I am not accustomed to being thanked, only cursed as a pawnbroker by the people who come to me from hunger. Good-bye, Craig. Bring the money in person so we can talk a little. It is often lonesome in this warehouse of misfortune.'

Craig stuffed the money in his pocket and went out into the street, his eyes stinging. He was reminded, once again, of the rough kindness of his old friend, Jimmy Wilbur, of the clumsy intuitive friendship and embarrassed generosity of old John Grimes. Nobody would ever believe this, he thought, hurrying to the auto salesroom, nobody would ever believe that I walked into a pawnshop with nothing to pawn and walked out with nine hundred dollars in my pants pocket. Nine whole hundred dollars, more money than Craig had ever touched at one time except when he went to get the payroll money from the bank.

'Here's the money,' he said to the salesman, and planked down the nine one-hundred dollar bills. 'Give me a receipt and the registration papers and I'll take delivery now.'

'Don't you want a demonstration before you pay?' the salesman asked. 'It's customary.'

'No,' Craig answered. 'Just give me the papers and the keys. I'm in a hurry.' He tapped his foot irritably until the salesman fumbled through the papers and finally handed him a keyring. Craig stuffed the papers in his inside pocket and walked out to the car. If the salesman hadn't been looking, he would have patted it like a pony. Instead, he walked around the car, viewing it with what he hoped was a judicious eye, got slowly and deliberately into the car, and leaned luxuriously back on the grey plush seat. He sat for a moment in the lemon winter sunshine, sniffing eagerly the wonderful new-car smell, of hot burnt oil and paint and clean metal and wax-rubbed polish and just plain *newness*, before he slowly pressed the clutch and drew the car away from the kerb. He wanted a long ride, even though it would have to be slow, but right now he would have to settle for getting back to the mill. It was going to be a long time until five o'clock this afternoon.

24

IT was five-thirty before Craig finished the day's work, locked his desk, and went out into the growing darkness. The car stood at the kerb, and half a dozen millhands stood around the shining vehicle. Craig knew all of the men, but Red Forney was not among them. Craig nodded, and they looked at him in surprise when he unlocked the car and got in.

'Whose car is that, Craig?' one of the men asked.

'Mine,' Craig said. 'Just bought it today.'

'She's a beaut,' the man said. 'Musta cost a lot of money.'

'It did,' Craig said, and suddenly threw back his head and laughed. 'It did. But today I came into a lot of money,' and pulled swiftly out from the kerb.

Automatically he pointed the nose towards home, and as suddenly pulled over to the side of the road and made a U-turn. Almost without knowing what he was about, he headed in the direction of Red Forney's little house. He wanted to share this car, this triumph, this first luxurious thing that he had ever owned, with somebody—somebody who would be truly joyous at his fresh good fortune. He wanted to stand on his head or walk dangerously along the top of a fence. He could not, or possibly would not, have been able to explain to himself or to anybody else why he didn't drive the car swiftly home to May-belle, except there was a vague foreboding that a lack of enthusiasm on her part would rub some of the glitter off his spirits. He didn't want to muddy his brand-new acquisition for a little while with a long explanation of how he got the money, or to explain that the bank wouldn't lend it to him. It was the same shapeless impulse which had moved him not to try out the car before he bought it. He had felt strongly that if something were basically wrong with his new baby, he didn't want to learn about it until much, much later. He sniffed again, luxuriously, at the hot new-car smell, as he parked in front of Forney's house.

He leaped up on to the rickety little porch, and rapped on the door, jiggling slightly with impatience. The door opened and Libby stood framed against the light.

'Hello there, baby sister,' he said. 'Where's Red? I got something to show you-all.'

'Come in, Craig,' Libby said. 'I don't know where Red is right now. Off with some of the other fellows, likely. You want to wait? And what have you got to show us? You look all excited.'

'Put on your coat and come see,' he said. 'It's chilly outside. Hurry. This can't wait.' Libby looked mystified, but she darted into her room and came out shrugging herself into a coat.

'What is it? You got me all excited, too.'

'That!' Craig said, sweeping a dramatic arm. 'That!'

'But it's a brand-new car,' Libby said. 'A wonderful brand-new car. It can't be yours, Craig. Oh, it's lovely,' passing a hand over one of the fenders. 'I wish it was lighter so I could see it better.'

'Hop in,' Craig said, opening a door, and Libby slid under the wheel and over to the far corner. 'I'll take you for a spin.' He pressed the starter button, and the motor leaped smoothly alive. 'Listen to her purr,' he said, delightedly. 'And look. A radio and a heater and everything.' He snapped on the radio. 'I haven't tried that, or the heater, either.' He turned on the heater, which murmured softly and sent a wave of cold air around their legs. 'Motor needs time to warm up before you feel the heat,' Craig said, and snapped off the heater. He twiddled the knobs of the radio and 'The Very Thought of You' came into the car. 'That's a Ray Noble,' Craig said. 'Hasn't it got a pretty tone?'

'It's all wonderful,' Libby said. 'But whose *is* it?'

'Mine, by golly,' Craig said. 'Mine. All mine. I bought it today and you're the first person except me to ride in it. I feel like busting a bottle of champagne over the radiator, like they do when they launch ships.'

'But how did you get a new car like this?' Libby said, awed. It's not your . . .' she stopped.

'No, dammit, it is *not* my wife's, like you started out to ask,' Craig said. 'She hasn't even seen it yet. It's mine. I got a little raise today, and a kind of title, and . . . wait. I want to tell it all to Red, too, and I don't want to tell it twice. Let's ride out to the lake and back and by that time he'll probably be home. I want to try this baby out. It's a pity we can't open her up until she's got more miles on her.'

Libby sat quietly in the corner as he drove, his eyes intent on the road, both listening to the music that filled the inside of the car. Her hands stroked the soft cushions, and she looked eagerly at the gaudy green-and-red lights on the speedometer, the red bulb which flashed when the headlights came on full force. She tentatively opened the glove compartment, and fingered the nickelled window and door handles timidly.

'You know,' she said softly. 'I never rode in a new car before. I didn't know they'd smell like this. Sort of like the Five-and-Ten at Christmas, but different. All I ever rode in was one of those cut-down old Fords some of the fellows at school have. Nothing like this. It seems so heavy, but it goes along so smooth.'

'Are you sixteen yet?' Craig almost touched her on the knee, then hurriedly withdrew his hand.

'No. Not quite. Almost. Why?'

'Well, when you are, I'll teach you to drive. You and Red'll be having a car like this some day, yourselves, and maybe you'll even have one of your own. You'll need to know how to drive, and I'll teach you.'

'Oh, Craig, that would be wonderful,' she said. 'I love driving along, 'specially with this music playing. I wish we could just drive and drive and drive all night, going somewhere, anywhere. I never really been anywhere yet. Not that I remember.'

She leaned her head back on the seat, her chin raised, her

curly hair spilling over the seat, and Craig felt a sudden great surge of . . . what? Warmth, protectiveness, affection? Not so much to kiss her, although her lips were half-parted, in young abandonment to sensuous enjoyment of the new car, and the line of her profile into her neck was lovely. He shook his head slightly, as if to clear it.

'We better turn this thing around and head for your house instead of driving and driving all night, going anywhere,' Craig said. 'Your brother'll be home and wondering what became of you and hungry to boot, and then I'll have to fight him all over again, and now I think he knows more than me and can probably whip me.' He laughed, and to himself it sounded forced and strange.

'Red's awfully fond of you, Craig,' Libby said. 'We talk about you all the time. Red was just saying the other night he sure wished you'd drop by the house more often. We know it ain't . . . isn't . . . much, not like that big place of yours . . .'

'Maybelle's,' Craig said harshly.

'. . . but you're always welcome to what we've got, such as it is.'

'Thanks, Libby.' This time he did pat her knee fleetingly. 'You're a swell kid, and you've got a good brother. How's school?' His voice was abrupt.

'About the same as usual. I got elected to the Student Council.' Shyly. 'And I'm going to be head cheer-leader next year. And I've been taking the business course, like you told Red I ought to. I'm pretty fast on the typewriter already, but I'm having a terrible time with shorthand. I guess I'll learn, though. Everybody seems to.'

They drew up in front of the house. Craig cut his headlights just as Red stormed out of the door. He had evidently been waiting at the window. He dashed across the sidewalk to the car just as Craig walked around to open the door for Libby.

'God damn it, Libby! I've told you a thousand times I wouldn't put up with you runnin' around in cars after dark with boys, and by the time I get through with this . . .'

'Oh, shut up, Redhead,' Craig said, walking around in front of the car. 'It's me. Craig. Nobody's going to run off with your precious sister. Simmer down.'

'Oh, Craig,' Red's voice relaxed, and he unclenched his fists. 'I came home and couldn't find Libby and the lights were on and then I saw this damn' big car drive up and I thought it was one of those sheikhs from school with his daddy's new car—you know what I mean. Come in out of the cold. Where'd you steal this boat, anyhow?'

'Didn't steal it. Bought it. Today. I'm a big shot. You like it?'

'I like it, but I don't believe it. Set down and tell me all about it. Sis, pour us a couple drams of that home brew. I guess we got to celebrate somethin' or other.'

300

'Can I have one too, Red? To celebrate, I mean?'

'No you can not have one Red to celebrate I mean,' her brother mimicked her. 'And if I catch you at it until you're grown I'll warm your tail. Just like I used to. You ain't too big for a spankin'.' He winked at Craig.

'What happened, you got a new car and all?' Red asked, as Libby came back with the home brew and sat down by her brother on the divan. 'Somebody die and leave you a fortune?'

'Nothing like that. But the boys at the bank called me in today and said that they were going to retire old Soames and I could take his place for a while before they decided whether or not they would have to hire somebody else to take his place. They gimme a raise, too. A big one. I'm makin' fifty a week now.' He dropped his final g's as he so often dropped them in Red's company.

Red whistled.

'Fifty a week. My God, that's all the money in the world. No wonder you bought a car. I'd 'a bought a steamboat or somethin'. So you gonna be runnin' the place now?'

Craig smiled wryly.

'Not likely. If you mean doin' the work, yes. I'll be doin' mine *and* Soames' work, for half the money he was getting. I got a half-assed title—excuse me, Libby, I'm sorry—but it don't mean a thing. So if you're getting all hotted up about that foreman's job, you better relax. I can't fire anybody, I can't hire anybody, I can't really buy anything. Far as I can see nothing's changed except I make more money. I ain't spittin' on the money. It bought me that new baby outside.' He jerked his head at the door.

Red handed his beer mug to his sister, and nodded his head at Craig's drink. Libby took both mugs and went to the kitchen for a refill.

'Well, at least you're movin',' Red said. 'While I'm still doffin' bobbins. And you're rid of old Soames. The next thing I reckon is old Mildred. We got to start figgerin' on how to make room for Libby in another year or so.'

'There'll be room for Libby in another year or so, don't worry your head about that. And the next new car that drives up to this door—unless you beat me to the punch—is going to be a Cadillac.' He pounded his fist in the flat of one hand.

Craig drove slowly, feeling something more than slightly guilty. He had spent an hour drinking home brew and laughing and talking with Red Forney and his sister, consciously putting off going home. He had, he knew, come within a whisper of kissing Libby in the car, although he was not really aware of it at the time. The clean fresh smell of the girl mingled with the wonderful equally clean smell of the new car, in warm close

301

quarters with the peculiar bug-in-a-rug intimacy of driving at night, the triumph of the new possession, his first real big possession, a decent wage and what was really, he thought, a very good job in a very short time. . . . All of it mixed up at once could have got him in all sorts of trouble. And any kind of trouble was a thing he was fighting shy of until he got that goddamned mill ironed out to where it would sit up and beg.

'You better stay a far piece away from that girl, Price,' he said aloud. 'She's too young and she's Red's sister and you're married and you don't need any more trouble, not right now. You better stay away from that house, too, and concentrate on how you can get a free hand with that mill and get that bank out of there. And right now you better concentrate on explaining the new car and the new raise and how come you're late to supper to Mrs. Craig Price, who will be waiting at the window just about like Red was when he thought Libby was out gallivanting with one of the city slickers. I'm glad I was me and not a city slicker when old Red came boilin' down off that porch. At least he trusts me with the kid.'

He turned into the drive of Old Man Grimes's house, and pulled up to the front steps with a flourish. He honked the horn rapidly. Porch lights came on, and Maybelle appeared at the door. She looked puzzled.

'Who is it? Oh, it's you, Craig,' as her husband stepped out of the car. 'Whose new car is that?'

'Mine,' Craig said, and it seemed to him that never had one word, one little word, meant so much.

25

MAYBELLE did not, it appeared, want to try out the car. Not at night. 'We'll wait until Saturday afternoon,' she said. 'When it's good and light.' And then, 'I don't really see how we can afford a new car. Supper's late. Come in the house.' She dismissed the car.

'Wait'll I put the baby in the garage,' Craig said. 'Isn't she pretty?'

'Umm,' Maybelle said. 'I guess so. Hurry up. You can tell me all about it while we eat.'

Over supper—sauerkraut and boiled frankfurters—Craig outlined, rapidly, the happenings of the day, skipping his visit to Red Forney's house and his short ride with Libby Forney.

'It's wonderful about your new raise and the new job and all,' Maybelle said. 'You sure have come a long way in a powerful short time. But I don't see what you're so mad at Mr. McMullen and Mr. Norton for. It seems to me they've been awful nice and 'awful generous, doubling your salary from your startin' pay in less than two years. And lettin' you replace old Mr. Soames just like that.' She snapped her fingers.

'But, Maybelle,' Craig said slowly. 'Can't you understand? They haven't *given* me anything. I'm still an office boy, the way they think. I do two men's work for half the money and they still feel like I'm an office boy, married to the boss's daughter. And when old Norton wouldn't lend me the money for the car—without *your* signature—' Craig bit the words—'without *your* signature, I just felt like I was butting my head against a wall.'

'But the banks always act that way,' Maybelle said. 'They got to have security. They know how much money I make out of the mill. They could always take it away from me if they had my name on your note and you didn't pay or anything like that.'

Maybelle shook her head righteously, as if possessed of superior wisdom. It was a mannerism that always unreasonably infuriated Craig.

'And I still don't understand you going to a pawnshop. A common pawnshop, like a . . . a drunk or a tramp or a thief. That dreadful old Uncle Charlie Whatsisname. That's awful, Craig. Just awful. What'd people say if they found out?'

' . . . what people would say if they found out. I don't give a good goddam what the people would say if they found out. Uncle Charlie lent me the money when the bank wouldn't. On my name. On my signature. Not yours or the bank's or anybody else's. Mine. Not yours or ours or his or theirs. Mine.'

'But, Craig, you know everything I've got is ours.'

'Is it? Is the house ours? Is the money you get from the mills ours? I know you pay some bills. Sure. We had to, to live. But I don't know how much money you've got or how much you get. I can guess, but you never told me. Maybe you don't like to talk about money, but I do. I like to know about money. Me and Uncle Charlie have some of the same ideas about it. It's worth what you can buy with it, and what you can do with it, and that's all it's worth.'

Maybelle's voice was meek, placating.

'But, Craig, honey, you never really asked me. You made all sorts of fuss about us livin' as best we could on what you made at the mill. We could of had all sorts of extras if you had just said something. I'd of bought us a new car any time you said, if you had just said you wanted one.'

'Maybe you don't understand how I maybe wouldn't want to suggest to my wife that she buys me a new car after I've busted up one that wasn't mine, killed a baby and put us both in the hospital? What in hell do you take me for? I live in your old man's house, I work in your old man's mill, I . . .' Craig put both hands to his head and pressed his temples. 'Let's go in the living-room,' he said, 'I'll bring the coffee.'

'I don't understand you, Craig,' Maybelle said over the coffee. 'One minute you want to be you and the next minute you want to be us, and then you don't want to be us. You get all upset, and I don't know what you want. If I'd of known you wanted a car so bad you wouldn't of had to go to a pawnshop —like a . . . like a nigger. And if Mr. Norton wanted me to sign a note for you I'd have signed it gladly. All you had to do was tell me. All this fuss about a car and notes and things.'

Maybelle wagged her head again, slowly. This time she conveyed elaborate puzzlement.

'I didn't know you felt that way about money. All I get is about three thousand a year from the mills—maybe a little more lately, since you went to work'—this with a small attempt at mollification—'and you can have every nickel I got if you want it. But I don't know what you'd do with it and I wanted to save something for a rainy day and . . .'

'Save something for a rainy day. Save something for a rainy day.' Craig repeated the words in cadence. 'It don't rain tomorrow. It rains today. It rains yesterday. Ah, the hell with it. So I went to a hockshop and bought myself a car because I got a raise, and I didn't need my wife's money. I didn't need my wife's name.'

'All I know is you got me awful confused,' Maybelle said. 'Now if you really want to straighten everything out, I'll give you nine hundred dollars and you can go straight downtown to Uncle Charlie's tomorrow and pay him right straight back and if you want to you can pay me back or just call it a present and forget it. Or if you feel so high and mighty about what's yours and what's mine then I'll sign your note and you can pay interest to the bank. You're making my head ache.'

'I'm making my head ache, too,' Craig said. 'I'll try one more time, and I'll talk slow and keep my voice down. Look, everything about everything is tied up in the same package. Before you say it, I know I'm lucky to have a job, I know I'm doing real good to be so young, I know I ought to be grateful for everything, and I'm not. I'm not a goddam bit grateful for anything. I just know what kind of a job I'm doing and I want a chance to keep on doing it and I want it my way. It's the only way I know. I had enough favours from enough people—you, the bank, your father, Uncle Charlie. I don't want favours any more. I don't want to be real smart for my age. I want to deliver the goods and be recognized as a man grown or I want to quit. But be good and goddamned if I want to be an office boy.

'Maybelle, can't you see? The way everything is now, I'm still an office boy, married to the boss's daughter, and lucky to be eating and living in a fine big house I didn't buy, working in a fine big mill I didn't build, eating fine food I couldn't buy if I hadn't knocked up the boss's daughter, and we get right back to the same thing in the same circle. I ain't going to spend the rest of my life being grateful for the fact that I knocked up the boss's daughter and so got a job in the boss's mill so the boss's daughter could have a papa for the baby that the papa killed in a car wreck. That's rough, maybe, but it's how I feel.'

Craig stood up, and began to pace.

'Oh, for God's sake, sit still,' Maybelle said. 'Every time you get something on your mind you start to prowl like a tom cat.'

Craig stopped pacing, and faced her.

'Maybelle, can't you understand about this car? This car and why I wanted it explains everything. I'm big enough and yes, smart enough, to run a mill. If I'm running a mill, God damn it, I want to *run* a mill. I don't want to have to raise my hand like a snot-nosed kid asking the teacher if he can go to the toilet every time I want to replace a piece of machinery or fire some bum and hire somebody who ain't a bum. I can't go to the bathroom without permission from Mr. McMullen, Mr. Norton, and Mr. Carroll. We just can't fiddle along doing the same things the same old way they were doing them when old Soames was a boy, with your father making all the decisions.'

'Well, I don't see what you're so upset about. What do you want to decide?' Maybelle's voice was plaintive.

'How the hell do I know what I want to decide?' Craig's voice lifted to a shout. 'I just want to know that if there is something I *do* want to decide, then I can decide it and not have to go sit down with those old maid bankers and let whatever it is die of dry-rot. We need new machinery, we need to expand the help, we need new buildings, we need—oh, Christ.' Craig pounded his fist hopelessly in his hand. He shook his head. 'Maybe I ought to just throw it all in and go back to sea. I suppose I could take the car back and get most of the money back. Old Uncle Charlie wouldn't be out too much money.'

'You wouldn't go to sea and leave me? You wouldn't leave the mill? Who'd run it now? I'd lose everything and Mama would...'

'The banks could run it. Like they're running it now,' Craig's voice was clipped and cold. 'Into the ground.'

'But what do they do *wrong*?' Maybelle's voice was plaintive. 'What is it that they do *wrong*?'

Craig exhaled an exaggeratedly patient breath.

'It's not what they do wrong. It's just that they don't do anything. They just drift. Old King Cotton. What was good yesterday, when Daddy was a boy, is plenty good enough today, and no young whippersnapper with a lot of crazy ideas is going to change the way we did it since Eli Whitney invented the cotton gin.'

'Well, what do you *want*?' Maybelle's voice shrilled.

'I'll tell you what I want. I want legal, actual control of the

305

mill. I don't want a goddam banker telling me anything. I want to run it, and if I run it off a cliff I still want to run it. And there ain't but one way I can run it and that's if you help me. You want me to stay here? You want me to work in your father's business. Or do you want me to quit—quit you and quit the mill and just go back where I came from? It's going to be one or the other. It's up to you to say.'

Craig got up and walked over to the window, his fingers laced behind his back. Maybelle looked at the impassive shoulders.

'You know I'd die if you left me,' she said. 'I'd just lay right down and die. You tell me what you want me to do and I'll do it, I swear I will. Just tell me is all and I will. I love you, Craig, and you're all I've got.' Maybelle began to weep. Craig walked over and put his hand firmly on her shoulder, exerting a gentle pressure with his fingers. 'For God's sake, Maybelle, please don't cry now. We might as well talk this thing out and crying won't help us. Please don't cry.'

'All right, I won't cry.' Maybelle lifted her chin. 'See? I've stopped.' Craig bent and kissed her. 'That's a good girl,' he said. 'Now listen carefully to what I've got to say.'

'We got anything to drink in the house?' Craig asked. 'I feel like a snort while I work this thing out.'

'There's about half a bottle of Golden Wedding, I think. Wait, I'll go see.' She got up and walked towards the kitchen.

'Bring some ice, too,' Craig said. I feel like drinking tonight, he thought. I'd like to get a real buzz on. Because I got a feeling that tonight's one of those now-or-never things. It all depends on Mama Grimes.

'Brown it up good,' he said to Maybelle, as she poured the drinks. He accepted the one she handed him, and looked at it against the light. 'I suppose we might as well drink to the raise and the new car,' he said. 'And maybe to tomorrow.'

He took a long pull at his drink, and waited for Maybelle to settle herself.

'It's January now,' he said. 'You'll be twenty-one in a month. I'll be twenty-one in December. When you're twenty-one you inherit your share of the mill stock. Thirty-five per cent.'

'That's right,' Maybelle said. 'But I don't see how that changes anything. I'll keep right on getting the same income I'm getting now, whether I have the stock or don't have the stock. And I'll still just have a one-third say-so in how the mill's run.'

'If you had your mother's stock you'd have some more say-so. You'd have better than a controlling interest. Instead of running the whole shebang, the bank would be in the spot you're in now, and still gonna be in when you come of age—minority stockholder. But if you could vote your mother's stock, instead of letting the bank handle it, then you'd be a majority stockholder.'

306

Craig spelled out the words slowly. 'Then you could do anything you wanted to—sell out your interest, hire, fire, do anything you wanted to do.'

'I wouldn't know how to do anything,' Maybelle said. 'I wouldn't want to do anything. Business just confuses me.'

'*I* would,' Craig said grimly. 'I sure as hell would. Business doesn't confuse me, not if you keep it simple.'

'I don't see what we're wasting time talking about,' Maybelle said. 'It still don't make any difference as long as Mama's alive and crazy. The bank's gonna run the mill, right on.'

'Look,' Craig said. 'When you come of age maybe we could sue for control of your mother's stock, but the question of her insanity and your—our youth—would come into it, and by the time we dragged it through the courts and paid off the lawyers there probably wouldn't be any mill left. So I reckon a lawsuit is out.

'Then what are we arguin' about?' Maybelle said.

'This. Your mother was not certified insane—you know, with a flock of doctors and things like that. She was put in that sanatorium just like you'd put any sick person in a hospital. Nottingham Hill is as much a hospital as it is an insane asylum. To all intents and purposes your mother had a nervous breakdown after your father died and all his businesses went to hell. She's not actually crazy. She was just plain sick. And you were too young and confused to do anything about it one way or the other—you said it yourself, you didn't know which way was up—and I suppose you could almost say she was railroaded into that place in Greensboro. She's probably no crazier than I am.'

'Well, if she's not crazy, then why hasn't she hollered to get out?'

'I been asking around some. It's a lot easier to get in one of these places than it is to get out, if you're old and confused and some responsible people put you in. The people in the hospital don't want you *out*. Especially if the money comes right on the dot every week, or month, or however it's paid. Your mother probably thinks she can't ever get out. There's enough bars around to make it look like a jail, even if they call it a hospital. And enough pills—enough sedatives to do what they call "relax" the patient. Remember, we're not dealing with a state asylum. This is just a private hospital, run for profit, and it's probably got as many drunks in it as it has nuts.'

'So?' Maybelle got up. 'You want a freshener?'

'Yes, thanks,' Craig held out his glass absently.

When Maybelle came back with the drinks he took a long breath.

'This may cost some money,' he said, almost to himself.

'What may cost some money?'

'What I'm about to suggest. Maybelle, we want your mother back. We've got to have her back.'

'What, Mama crazy? In the house? I told you I wouldn't have her.'

'We've been through that. She won't be any trouble. We can hire her a practical nurse for ten bucks a week. Hell, we could hire her a registered nurse for thirty-five dollars for twenty-four-hour duty. But we don't need one, because your mother's not crazy.'

'Who says my mother's not crazy?'

'I do. I say it. She's as sane as you or me. She just had a hard time, with her troubles and all, I expect a late menopause might have played some part in it—she just had some trouble and needed treatment and rest she couldn't get at home, with your father dead and you just a girl and all.'

'You making this up or what?' Maybelle frowned at him. 'You sound as crazy as Mama.'

'No, I'm not making it up. I'm speaking the truth. As soon as you come twenty-one, we're going to get in the Dodge and ride up to Greenboro, and we're coming back home with your mother if I have to drag her. Mrs. Irma Grimes has spent too much time in the hospital when she's got a grown daughter and half-interest in a house and plenty of private income and a son-in-law with a good job. A son-in-law who is pinin' for his dear old mother-in-law.' Craig's grin was wolfish. 'I really never did know how much I missed the old lady around the house until I set down to study on the matter.' He burlesqued a country drawl.

Maybelle began to laugh.

'I swear, Craig, you're the limit! For a moment I declare I thought you were serious. I can just see you and Mama here in this house together. I'd go crazy as a loon just watchin' you. You'll have to put *me* in an asylum if that happens.'

'I'm not kiddin', honey. Mama's the only answer. We need Mama real bad. Look, Maybelle. Wouldn't you like to get out of this two-bit town some day? Wouldn't you like to be rich, big rich, live in New York, go to Paris, have big cars, mink coats, yachts, go all around the world? We can do it. We can do it with one mill. We can do it with one mill if I run that mill, because I'll run that mill into a lot more mills. If I don't run that mill we can just sit here and get old, seeing the same dull damn' people, kissing the bank's behind every time you need a new hat, practically. But with Mama . . .'

Craig kissed his fingertips and blew the kiss towards the window.

'Mama ain't goin' to live for ever,' Maybelle said. 'We could wait, maybe.'

'Your mother could live another twenty years, easy, maybe more. We need her alive and we need her now—at least as soon as you're of age, so you can claim her legally as next of kin. You don't have to prove anything, except that you're of age,

308

that you can afford to look after her, that there's a home to go to. There's nothing to it, except maybe a couple of little pieces of paper.'

'And sayin' we get Mama, and bring her home all sweet and happy, what then? What do we do with Mama when we got her? Keep her for a pet or teach her tricks or what?'

Craig shook a finger at his wife.

'Maybelle, Maybelle, you mustn't say things like that any more. This is your dear old mother you're talking about, the mother that we're going to bring back so she can spend the rest of her days with the only family she's got—you and me. "It's not as if Mama was crazy," is what you're supposed to say, "it's just that she was upset and had to go away where she could be taken care of until I got older and could take care of her myself. Now I'm married to Craig, and he's doing so well and all, now we can bring Mama home." That's what you're supposed to say.' He grinned again, less wolfishly.

'Just exactly what have you got up your sleeve, Craig Price? I kind of know, but I don't know exactly. Be serious.'

'All right. I am serious. When your mother comes out of Nottingham Hill, of her own volition, into your adult care, into your own home, your mother is once again a sane woman—in full possession of her faculties, is what they say. Better than that, she never was insane, she was just sick. Listen to me carefully.

Craig held up his hand, the fingers spread.

'Now she's well.' Craig ticked off one finger. 'That's one.

'Now you're twenty-one. That's two.

'According to the terms of the will, the bank no longer controls your shares nor your mother's shares. They were just held in trust for you until you came twenty-one. The only complication was that your mother had a breakdown, and the bank naturally looked after her business. That's three.

'Now all that's over, because you're twenty-one and she's cured of her breakdown. You have your shares, your mother has her shares. Between you, you own seventy per cent of Grimes Mills. That's number four.'

Craig looked at his thumb, standing stiffly erect over the clenched four fingers of his right hand.

'And that's five,' he said, holding his thumb in front of Maybelle's face. 'The Big Five.'

'Suppose you tell me what five is? I know anyhow, but tell me.'

'Five is me. Five is Grimes Mills. Five is Price Mills. Five is a million dollars, ten million dollars, a hundred million dollars, maybe a billion dollars.' He waggled his thumb. 'But that's for the future. Right now five is just you and me and your mama. Five can go up.' He swooped the thumb towards the ceiling. 'Five can go down.' He turned his hand so that the thumb was pointing at the floor. 'Or five can go away.' He made a motion like a hitch-hiker, passing his arm swiftly before his chest, with the thumb pointing to the door. 'It's up to you to say.'

'What do you want me to say, then?'

'I want you to give me a power of attorney to vote your stock, and, as your husband, to run your mill as I see fit. And I want the same thing from your mother. That, or for her to turn over her interest to you. I don't want to sell the shares. I don't want the income from the shares. I just want to replace the bank in the running of the mill, that's all. You can pay me a better salary to run the mill, if you like, or vote me a share of the profits, if you like. But as far as your actual ownership of your stock is concerned, it's still yours, and can't be sold or mortgaged without your express permission. The same would apply to Mama Grimes.'

'And suppose I say no? Suppose I say I won't have the old lady in the house. Suppose I say I won't give you control of my stock, and won't make you president—I suppose that's what you want to be, president—suppose I won't?'

Craig got to his feet. He made the hitch-hiking motion once more, his thumb pointed towards the door.

'That's all,' he said. 'You heard what I said before. Out. Away. I don't care where or what. Just out. Tomorrow, as soon as I can pack.'

'You'd walk out? Just like that? You'd go off and leave me, just like that?'

'Yes. I'd go off and leave you, just like that. Yes I would. And yes, I by God will.'

'Then you never loved me at all. All you wanted was the mill and you just used me as an excuse to get your hands on it. You never really loved me.' Maybelle's voice was flat, not accusing. Craig put a hand on her shoulder.

'That's not true, not true at all. I did love you and I do love you but I can't be and won't be anybody's puppy dog. Christ, Maybelle, I don't want to steal the mill from you and your mother. I just want to run it right, and make more money, and build something, for you and your mother and our children if we ever have any more. But I can't do it with that goddam bank on my back. It's a comic-opera bank in a small town, and I got ideas that don't fit the bank, don't fit a small town. And I can't do anything with those ideas unless I have a free hand. God Almighty, don't you *want* to do something big with your life?'

'I do, if you're in it. I don't, if you're not. I haven't got anybody but you, Craig, and you know it. That's why you talk so mean.' Her voice crumbled, presaging tears. 'All right. I'll do what you say. Even with Mama coming back. Much as I hate it, I'll do it. But suppose you can't get Mama to come around to your way of thinking?'

Craig laughed. He closed his thumb into a complete fist.

'See? Number five has gone away, all settled.' He opened his hand, tilted her chin, and kissed her lightly on the lips. He laughed again.

'Don't you worry about Mama. Mama will be eating out of my hand. Oh, baby, it's going to be wonderful! We'll be rich and go everywhere and do everything! You just wait and see! We really ought to get drunk tonight, to celebrate!'

'We can't. There's nothing left in that bottle,' Maybelle said. 'We killed it on the last drink.'

'There's still Captain Bill's, out the old Jonesboro Road,' Craig said. 'Let's tie one on. We're gonna be rich, we're gonna be rich, we're gonna be rich stinking, filthy, dirty, rotten rich! Come on, get your coat. You haven't even tried out your new car yet, and you better hurry, because it won't be too long before we trade it in for the biggest, longest Cadillac in North Carolina!'

Craig had a splitting head the next morning, when he went to work, and Maybelle only moaned and rolled over when he got out of bed. His mouth tasted like an old rubber boot, and when he drove up and parked his new car in front of Grimes Mills, he thought for a moment that Captain Bill's bootleg booze had affected his eyesight. For a fraction of a second, he could have sworn that 'Grimes' had been erased, and replaced by 'Price'. He blinked his eyes again, and 'Grimes Mills' had returned.

'But not,' he said aloud, as he got out of the car, 'not for too goddamned long!'

When he passed Miss Mildred's desk, he was whistling. She looked up in annoyance.

'All that noise over a raise?' She delivered her habitual sniff.

'So you know already?' he said.

'The notice came in from the bank this morning,' she said. 'I suppose now you may be replacing Mr. Soames?'

Craig's voice was very gentle.

'Yes, Miss Mildred,' he said. 'Some day, maybe not tomorrow, but some day, I may be replacing Mr. Soames.'

26

MAYBELLE'S long awaited majority finally arrived. Craig suggested a party. Maybelle refused, flatly.

'I don't know anybody I like. I just don't know *any*body,' she said. 'Of course I reckon Mr. McMullen and his wife and the other bankers would come, but we never really knew many people in this town, even when Papa had money. I haven't got any real friends.'

'I remember,' Craig said. 'He talked to me about it once. What did he say? Something about he could buy and sell half the town but nobody would come to his house because he was new-rich or something like that. Everybody looking down their noses at him. The old man never got much use out of his money, I reckon. We'll get some out of ours. We'll have it and we'll rub their noses in it and then we'll just take off and leave them to stew in their own lousy juice in this lousy town. It won't take much longer and we'll have them crawling up the driveway. I'm younger than your daddy was, when he made money.'

'I declare, Craig,' Maybelle said, 'you talk just like we were already rich as Croesus. You goin' to spend it all before we got it?' She giggled, and for once Craig didn't mind the giggle.

'I already spent some of it before I got it,' Craig said. 'Happy twenty-first birthday, honey.' He handed her a small, white-satin jeweller's box. Maybelle's fingers fumbled as she tried to untie the ribbon.

'What is it, what is it?'

'Here, give it to me.' Craig took the box. 'Now, close your eyes. Hold out your hand.'

He took a small diamond ring out of the box and slipped it on the third finger of her left hand. She stood like a child, her eyes squeezed shut. Craig kissed her. 'Now open your eyes,' he said. 'See. Now you're formally engaged.'

Maybelle held her hand high to let the light catch the stone, and tears came.

'Oh, Craig,' she said. 'Oh, Craig.'

She came into his arms and wept softly on his shoulder. He patted her rather roughly.

'There's no call to cry,' he said. 'It's not a very big diamond. But it's the best I can do right now. One day I'll buy you a dia-mond as big as a bar of soap.'

'It's just lovely,' Maybelle said. 'Just lovely. But how . . . ?'

'Ask me no questions and I'll tell you no lies. Maybe I stole it,' Craig said. 'Maybe I found it in the street. But I *didn't* get it from Uncle Charlie, so don't start worrying about that. Nobody ever had that ring on a finger before.'

'But it must have cost a fortune,' Maybelle said.

'No it didn't, either. Just wear it and hush about where and how I got it. Telling you would spoil it. Just figure that Santa Claus brought it, a little late.'

Craig was not going to tell her that he had parked the new car in front of the town's best jewellery store, at a slack time of day, and had casually inquired about engagement rings. The sleek and shining car had been credit reference enough, when Craig casually established his identity with his auto-title. The ring had cost three hundred dollars. It was worth more, but as the jeweller said, nesting it into its lush little ivory-satin box, damned few people were buying diamonds this year. He accepted a twenty-five-dollar deposit, and promised to send the bill to Craig at Grimes Mills. Craig might take a year to pay, he said cheerfully, if he didn't mind a slight credit charge. Craig said he wouldn't mind at all, he was a little pressed for cash, having just paid for the new car. The jeweller said he knew how it was, the bills he got every month, his wife must think he was made of money. He tactfully failed to ask if it weren't just a little bit late to be buying an engagement ring.

'I've got something else, too,' Craig said to Maybelle. 'Two bottles of real champagne. I slipped them into the icebox. They'll be cold in a minute. We'll drink a bottle here, and then go to the King Crab for dinner.' The King Crab was the most expensive restaurant—or roadhouse—in the area. It featured fancy seafood, thick grilled steaks, and an open fire in winter.

'I know it costs a lot but I don't care,' Maybelle said. 'I think you're just wonderful.' She kissed him again. 'I'm goin' to get all dolled up so you'll be proud of me.'

'I'd get dolled up myself except I don't have a tux any more,' Craig laughed. 'I got a little broke one time and sold it for a couple of bucks. Remind me, when we get a little bit richer, to buy myself a new tuxedo. I guess you'll just have to settle for my banker's suit tonight.'

'Oh, it's wonderful to be twenty-one,' Maybelle almost carolled, as she went to dress. She leaned over the banisters and threw him a kiss. 'And tomorrow I'll give you a present. We'll go down to the bank and straighten everything out with my stock.'

'No,' Craig said. 'No. It's bad luck to talk money on a party night. This is a party night.'

Maybelle kept saying what a lovely time they were having, a lot better than a stuffy old party, just the two of them out together. They had drunk the first bottle of champagne at home, and Maybelle had giggled when the bubbles got up her nose, but after a while the bubbles didn't get up her nose any more. They had an enormous sirloin steak and finished the second bottle of champagne and danced some to the music from the juke box and finally they went home and Craig found just enough whisky in the kitchen bottle to make a nightcap. When they went to bed, Maybelle curled into his body like a burrowing puppy, and went soundly off to sleep right in the middle of a stout statement that she didn't care whether he used one of those awful old rubber things or . . . She snored gently. Himself slightly fuddled by the unaccustomed wine, Craig gently disengaged the arm on which her head rested, turned over and went to sleep.

Craig came home early from work the next day. Maybelle met him at the door and kissed him soundly.

'Didn't we have a lot of fun, just, last night?' She almost squealed. 'I never had so much fun in my life. I guess I was a little tight from all that champagne when I got home. I just remember getting up the stairs. I was feelin' awful sexy, too, but I guess I just went to sleep, didn't I?'

'That you did, that you did,' Craig said, slipping out of his overcoat. 'You had something in mind, but you caulked off in the middle of whatever it was. Just as well, I guess. I was kind of tired from celebrating, too.'

'I went down town today,' Maybelle said. 'I had some business to tend to, and some shoppin' to do.'

'What sort of business, and what sort of shopping? God, I'm tired. I really had a rough one today, and last night's champagne didn't help me concentrate any.'

Maybelle giggled.

'Don't be mad at me, will you please not be mad at me, Craig? I spent a lot of money, too. You're not the only one in this family who can spend money. But I'm rich, now I'm twenty-one, even if it's only credit. You just sit down now and put your feet up and let me bring you a drink. I got some sour mash bourbon and some vermouth and I've got some old-fashion's sittin' in the icebox. Just like Papa used to make when Mama wasn't lookin'. You just sit there and read the paper a minute.'

Maybelle scurried out of the room. In a moment she was back with a tray, which contained two glasses of dark red old-fashioneds and a cut-glass dish of cashew and brazil nuts.

'Drink your drink now, and then you close your eyes,' she said. 'I got to go upstairs, but I'll be back in a minute. When you hear me comin', close your eyes.'

Craig lit a cigarette, and sipped his drink. I wonder what all this is about, he thought. But I must say she mixes a swell old-fashioned, and I sure need it.

'Here I come, ready or not,' Maybelle said from the stairs. 'Close your eyes.' She plastered a kiss on his cheek, and put a long, oblong cardboard carton on his lap. 'Now open,' she said. 'Hurry, open it up and tell me if you like it,' She hopped up and down with excitement.

Craig opened his eyes and saw the box, with 'I. Kramer, Tailor' on it in fancy curlicued letters. I. Kramer was the best ready-to-wear tailor in town. He carried Kuppenheimer and Hart Schaffner and Marx suits and Knox hats and Arrow shirts. Craig broke the string and saw a dinner-jacket, a lovely double-breasted dinner-jacket with sleek satin lapels. Maybelle had her hands behind her, and she swiftly dropped another tissue-wrapped package on top of the dinner-jacket.

'These are some shirts and bow-ties,' she said. 'Oh, Craig, try it on, try it on right now!'

'Maybe after supper,' Craig said, not knowing what to say. 'When I said that about not having a tux any more last night, I didn't mean . . . It was just a thing I said. I didn't mean to . . . to hint or anything like that. It's beautiful, Maybelle. I don't know how to thank you, but you shouldn't have. You just shouldn't have.'

'I suppose it won't fit very well,' Maybelle said. 'But Mr. Kramer said you could come down any time and have it altered. But I wanted to bring it home to you tonight as a surprise, just like you brought me the ring last night as a surprise. Please try it on, Craig. Don't go upstairs. Try it on right here. I sent Foreen home tonight. I'm cookin' dinner myself.'

'All right,' Craig said, and shucked his clothes. 'You're a real sweet kid, Maybelle, you know that? A real sweet kid.' He drew on the trousers, with their long, unhemmed bottoms flapping like penguin flippers over his stocking feet until he stooped to tuck up the trousers. He started to put on the coat, but Maybelle stopped him.

'No, no, the tie first!' she said. 'The tie first! There's two kinds, one of those snap-ons and then a tie-it-yourself kind. I didn't know whether you knew how to tie one yourself,' she said. 'We've never been anywhere in a dress suit.'

'I used to know how,' Craig said, stripping off his four-in-hand. 'It was one of the few useful things I learned in college. Let's see. It's better if I close my eyes and do it by feel. There. How's that?'

'Perfect. But put on the coat, put on the coat! Oh, Craig, it's beautiful. It fits just perfect. Go look at yourself in the mirror. Isn't it just beautiful?'

'I look like a matinée idol,' Craig said. 'Look at me. If you took away the busted nose and the knife scar and the autom —the other scar—I'd look just like Clark Gable. It fits perfectly, honey. I'll just stop off tomorrow and have old Izzy hem up the trousers, and then, by God, we'll invent some place to go to wear it. Come here and snuggle up. Doesn't it feel nice and smooth and sort of cosy?'

'It smells good, too,' Maybelle said. 'I reckon nothin' smells better than new clothes.'

'New clothes and a new car, they both smell good,' Craig said, climbing out of the dress pants and reaching for his ordinary trousers. 'I better get out of the fancy new duds. I wouldn't want to spill anything on them. Thanks a whole lot, Maybelle. It was kind of wonderful of you to think of it.'

Maybelle bridled.

'It wasn't anything, just not nothin' at all,' she said. 'I got more fun out of it than you, I bet you. Here, give me. I'll hang 'em up in the closet right now, and then I'll get you another drink. I've got some things I want to talk to you about. Buyin' that Tux wasn't all I did today.'

She came back, and dropped crouching to the floor, and put her chin on Craig's knees, looking up at his face.

'I stopped off at the bank today,' she said. 'I went in to see Mr. McMullen. He seemed kind of surprised to see me.' She giggled at the memory. 'It was kind of like I'd caught him doin' somethin' bad, like a naughty little old boy.'

'What did you want to see him about?' Oh, God, Craig thought, I wonder what she said. Take it easy, boy, he said. Real easy. 'What did you say to Mr. McMullen?'

Maybelle's tone was airy.

'Oh, I just told him how nice I thought it was that you had the promotion and all, and how happy I was—as a stockholder—to know that the mill was doin' so well, and that you had turned out so fine, and how sorry I was about old Mr. Soames bein' retired and all like that. Just a little social call.'

'You're a little late, aren't you? About thanking him for my raise and promotion, I mean? That was quite a while back.'

'I explained I hadn't been downtown much. And then I asked him if he knew what day yesterday was. He looked a little startled all over again.'

'What did he say?' Here it comes, Craig thought. 'What did he say?'

'He said: "Tuesday". Then I said of course I knew it was Tuesday, but it was another kind of day, too, and maybe it slipped his mind. He kind of coughed and snorted, you know how he does, like he was going to lose his breath and explode, and then he said:

' "Oh, yes, Mrs. Price. I do remember, er—ha hum now hah," ' Maybelle's mimicry of Mr. McMullen's professional asthma was not bad. ' "It's hah—er your birthday, hum. Your twenty-first, er—hah hum, birthday hah." '

'We can do away with the imitation, honey,' Craig said. 'I heard it often enough. What else did he have to say.'

'Well, he said that he had been planning to call me on the phone to ask me to come down and talk to him and the directors about me coming into the mill stock and all, but Mr. Carroll had a cold and the papers weren't quite ready and he thought it would be better if all the executors were together at once to talk about what the future held, something like that. Of course, he said, in spite of my legal age, my youth and inexperience er—hah hum . . .'

'I heard that before, too. What else?' Craig was feeling better. Maybelle hadn't stubbed her toe so far. 'What else?'

'Well, I said I was busy, and I didn't know whether I'd have much time right now, I had a trip I was maybe goin' to make, but whenever the bank was ready to talk they could just call you. I said I was leavin' everything in the business part up to my husband. Did I do right? Did I, Craig?'

Craig leaned over and patted her knee.

'You did fine, just fine and dandy,' he said. 'Was that all?'

'About all. He said he'd call me in a day or so, and I said not to bother about me, just to call you. Then he said I'd have to sign some things, and I said to tell you because I didn't understand any of it very much and when they got ready to sign things then you would tell me what to sign and all.'

'That's just great, baby. Now what we are going to do is just let 'em keep right on handling your stock, keep right on running the mill, until it gets time to give it to 'em all at once, in one bundle. I mean after we've got Mama straightened out. You've got to remember, I'm not quite twenty-one yet. Until I am, there's no use upsetting the Three Blind Mice.'

'The who?'

'I just thought of them. You remember, hickory, dickory, dock, the mouse ran up the clock? That's how I think of them. Norton is hickory, Carroll is dickory, and old man McMullen is dock. Old Dock McMullen.'

'Oh, Craig, you're such a fool. But it's funny.' She paused. Then: 'Craig, would you like to have another baby? An on-purpose baby?' Maybelle's brain had skipped nimbly away from the bankers.

'I reckon. Sure. Wouldn't you?'

'Now? I mean start one now? Like tonight?'

Craig rubbed his chin, then his nose.

'I wouldn't think so, honey, not right this very minute. I think we got too many things to straighten out first. An awful lot of business. And this thing with your mother. And the bank. We're awful young, and we've got an awful lot of things to do. Maybe next year, when all's settled down and we can kind of concentrate on a baby. We don't want to start too many things at once, and the next few months are going to be powerful important to all of us. I'd say wait a little longer. In a way I'm a fatalist. Maybe we mightn't have been meant to have this other—the poor little fellow we lost.'

'I guess you're right,' Maybelle sighed. 'I guess we ought to wait for a while. But let's not wait too long, Craig. Let's please don't wait too long.'

'We won't. Come on, and let me see some of this supper you're so proud of. And thank you, baby, thank you all over again for the lovely surprise present.' He put his arm around her as they walked back to the breakfast-room near the kitchen where they took most of their meals.

Craig called Mr. McMullen early the next day and said that if Mr. McMullen could spare him ten minutes, he would sure like

317

to have a word with him. Mr. McMullen said to come in at eleven. Mr. Carroll had a cold but Mr. Norton would be there, if it was anything important. It was something important, Craig said, and he would like it if Mr. Norton were there, and it was a pity about Mr. Carroll. Sometimes those colds just hung on and on. on.

Craig wasted no time at all. Once seated, he said:

'I believe my wife was in to see you yesterday, Mr. McMullen?'

'Yes, Craig. It was nice of her to drop by. She had some very nice things to say about you. That's unusual, these days, for a wife to have anything nice to say about a husband. Right, Norton?' Mr. McMullen had chosen momentarily to abandon his er—hahs and hums.

'I'll come to the point, as I know you gentlemen are busy,' Craig said. 'My wife is young, and perhaps—perhaps a little bit over-likely to favour me. As you must know, I am a little younger—not much younger, but some—than my wife. But where I have knocked around quite a bit—as you must know—and have worked quite a bit—as you also know—Maybelle has been pretty well protected and sheltered. Even after that unfortunate accident, when we lost the baby, she is still more or less a little girl.'

'What are you trying to say, Price?' Norton asked. Both bankers leaned forward. The avuncular 'Craig' had already been abandoned in favour of the surname, a compliment, Craig thought. 'What are you trying to say?'

'Only this, gentlemen, Mr. McMullen, Mr. Norton. I am not of age yet. I have a lot to learn. My wife is of age but she knows nothing at all about business—the broader things of business, such as you gentlemen in the bank are well acquainted with. But she is my wife, and she trusts me, and perhaps her estimate of my ability is maybe a little bit over-developed. You can understand that, I suppose, both of you being married men?' Craig almost twinkled while he said to himself, you phony bastard, oh you phony bastard.

'Of course we understand,' Mr. McMullen said. 'Although he'll find, won't he, Norton, that as time wears on his faults will outweigh his virtues. Isn't that true, Norton?'

'Yes, yes,' Mr. Norton said. 'But you still haven't come to your point, Price. What exactly did you have in mind?'

'Yes, yes, come to the point,' Mr. McMullen said.

'Just this. I have advised my wife,' Craig said, 'to leave the full administration of her property in the hands of the bank for an indefinite period of time. I have neither the legal right nor the time to look after her equity. I'm too busy at the mill. I believe you understand that, Mr. McMullen? Mr. Norton? And frankly I'm too young yet to concern myself with things that my elders understand better than me.

'So, with your permission, I do not—on behalf of my wife—want a transfer of stock from your custody into her hands at the moment.' Craig permitted himself a small laugh. 'You know women,' he said, 'They don't know the value of a dollar. She'd probably sell her stock to a Yankee or somebody and go rattlin' off to Europe to play with the Frogs and the Limeys and eat caviar.'

Mr. McMullen winked at Mr. Norton. Mr. Norton winked back at Mr. McMullen. They both winked at Craig. All boys together, Craig thought. The Three Blind Mice.

Mr. McMullen stood up. His er—hahs and hums were still lost in the distant forest.

He looked first at Norton for confirmation.

'I must say, Norton,' he said, 'that our early judgment has been solidly confirmed. We knew we had a good boy, but we didn't know we had a good man. I can safely say that I knew it all along, but it is better to be borne out by Old Father Time. I feel, sir, that Miss Maybelle's interests will always be safe in your hands, because you exercise a remarkable judgment for a man so young. I tell you, Norton, blood will tell, every time. I want to shake your hand, Craig. I can confess it now, but for an awful moment, when your wife came by yesterday, I thought maybe you two—excuse the word—you two harebrained kids might have some outlandish idea of taking over the mill. That right, Norton?'

'That's right, Mr. McMullen,' Norton said.

'In that case, gentlemen,' Craig said, 'I'd better be getting back to work. Us millhands, you know . . . And I can swear on a stack of Bibles, neither I nor my wife have any *harebrained* ideas about taking over the mill.'

He went out of the door. After it closed behind him, McMullen said to Norton, 'You suppose he got mad when I said "harebrained"? I meant it as a compliment.'

27

'Do you reckon she'll be glad to see us?' Maybelle said, as the car rolled towards Greensboro. 'It's been a pretty long time since I went to see her. Maybe she's mad at me.'

The car rolled smoothly over the well-banked road. It was late March, and the dogwood was in bud, the forsythia showing sprigs of yellow, and azaleas glossy green by the roadside. The sun shone warm, for March, but outside it was still chilly, and Craig had the heater on, with the radio playing softly.

'Sure she'll be glad to see us. I wrote this doctor—whatsis-name, Zimmermann, Immermann—that we were coming. I wanted to make sure that your mother was expecting us, and I also wanted a long talk with him about her condition.' He slapped his breast pocket. 'We may not need this, but you never can tell about foreigners. And brain doctors aren't always like other doctors. I've heard you have to be a little bit crazy yourself to live around nuts. Or at least, that it helps.'

'That's a lot of money, that two thousand dollars you've got in your pocket,' Maybelle said. 'The man at the bank like to of had a fit when I drew it out. It leaves my bank account kind of skinny. I suppose the first thing the teller did was to run upstairs and tell old man McMullen and the other Two Blind Mice.' Maybelle had fallen into Craig's habit of designating the bankers as Hickory, Dickory, and Dock. 'Dock'll blow a gasket.'

'They'll probably think we need it for house repairs, or something like that. Anyhow, it's your money, and none of their business. We can probably put it right back in day after tomorrow. But I thought we might need some money if that square-head doctor kicks up a fuss about signing the discharge papers. If what I've heard about these nut-doctors is true, they're about half racketeer, anyhow.'

Maybelle lit a cigarette and handed it to Craig.

'Thanks,' he said, and put one hand on her knee. 'Don't worry about your mother. She'll be all right, and we'll be all right. I wish we'd had time to stop off in Chapel Hill, but we'll do that some other time. Right now I can't wait to get to Greensboro.' He accelerated slightly. 'Don't worry,' he said. 'Everything is going to be fine, just fine.'

Nottingham Hill looked, as is generally customary with expensive sanatoria, more like an overgrown golf-course or an English deer-park than a place of locks and bars and padded cells. It was operated more as a select country club or resort than as a prison-place of confinement. This hospital was a conversion from a former vast private estate, sold up in 1929 when its multi-millionaire owner's financial dream-world collapsed and he decided that a bullet was cleaner than prison. Some harshly spoken friends had said that if he hadn't shot himself while mad, he could have ended up as a paying guest in his own home.

Its nine-hole golf course was now a truck garden, in which some of the patients worked for therapeutic reasons, but apart from the golf-course very little had changed. The former caretakers' elaborate cottage was now the chief doctor's residence and office. The stables housed the other doctors and the nurses. The ivy-clad grey-stone mansion served as the main hospital, and various other buildings, mostly old, some new, contained dormitories, isolation and violent wards. Great maple trees, just budding now, would shade the rolling grassy lawns and yellow-gravelled walks. There were ranks and ranks of azalea bushes, groves of dogwoods, and enormous oaks and pines. In another month it would be as lovely as in its more cheerful yesteryear. Apart from a certain professional concern with locked doors, matches, and sharp instruments, it ran as smoothly as when the former owner had a few score people up for the week-end, and the whole estate blazed with lights and rang with drunken laughter.

'It's a real pretty place,' Craig said, parking the car. 'If I had to be crazy I'd as live come here as any place. I suppose the food's pretty good, too. Who are all these people walking around?'

'Nuts,' Maybelle said. 'All nuts. They don't shut 'em up much in the daytime. When I was here last Mama had the run of the place. But come sun-down it's kitty-bar-the-door for all of 'em, half-nuts, medium-nuts, or all-nuts.'

Craig looked at the people with morbid curiosity. It was the first time he had been inside the grounds of an insane asylum, and it had given him a queasy feeling to halt the car before the locked twelve-foot iron gates, while a sort of sentry took his name, made a phone call from a box, wrote down his licence number and then waved him on. The same feeling you would get, Craig imagined, about going to jail. Except that he would be free to leave when he wished.

The strollers all looked like more or less ordinary people. Mostly they were middle-aged, some even bent and old, but there were a few young women and a couple of men no older than Craig. They were dressed cleanly enough, but they shared one thing in common. None of the women's hair seemed well-tended, whether grey with age or still dark or fair with youth. The hair seemed lifeless, and stuck out at bushy angles, as if it had been rudely shingled more for convenience and cleanliness than for appearance. And the clothes, although some were formerly expensive and all were of good quality, seemed oddly twisted and ill-fitting, like hand-me-downs. The women's stockings were wrinkled, seams twisted askew, and their feet possessed a hesitant shuffle which indicated that they might be more accustomed to carpet slippers than to shoes. The men's clothes hung more neatly on their bodies, but their walk was an odd, too-tentative, semi-shamble, as if they were permanently undecided about going forward or backwards.

The men, Craig noticed, strolled mostly alone, poking at things with sticks, but the women walked in twos and threes and fours. The men walked silent, with heads bent, while the women chattered. Here and there, rustic benches were leaned against the boles of the great trees, and on these benches sat people holding books and papers. But the papers and books sprawled limply across their knees, and they stared at them with dull eyes. Craig shivered.

'I'll be glad to get out of here,' he said. 'Let's go see the doctor. It's time. I guess that's the administration building over there, isn't it?'

'That's where I went before,' Maybelle said. 'They'll let Mama come and sit in one of the sitting-rooms with us. Really this place isn't too bad, 'specially once you're used to it.'

'We'll talk to the doctor, first, I reckon,' Craig said. 'Then I'll say hello to your mother and then I'll go back and see the doctor alone. Come on and let's get it over with.'

They walked up on the porch of the glossy-ivied building, and rang the bell. The stout, brass-studded oaken door was opened by an attractive young dark-haired woman in a tailored grey shark-skin suit over a yellow cashmere sweater.

'Come in,' she said. 'I remember you, Miss Grimes. I'm Miss Swanson, Dr. Immermann's secretary. But of course you wouldn't be Miss Grimes now. You'd be Mrs. Price, now.'

She looked at Craig.

'This is my husband, Mr. Price,' Maybelle said. 'How is my mother, Miss Swanson?'

'She's fine, just fine. You'll be seeing her in a moment. But Dr. Immermann wants to talk to you a moment first, the same as last time. If you'll step this way,' she beckoned to a corridor, 'the doctor is waiting.'

Dr. Immermann turned out to be a handsome, well-fleshed middle-aged man in a shaggy brown Harris-tweed suit. He had a high Nordic colour, wore rimless glasses, and his short-clipped hair was thick and sandy-grey. A row of pipes was racked on his large desk, which otherwise contained only a pen-set and one clipped sheaf of papers. He got up from a green leather swivel chair, and extended his hand. His voice contained only the mildest trace of accent, mostly to do with v's and w's.

'I am glad to see you again, Mrs. Price,' he said. 'It has been a long time since we met. Very warm for March, is it not? And you are Mr. Price. I am so glad to meet you, and I must congratulate you both on marrying such fine young people. Please do sit down.' He waved to two red leather straight chairs.

'Does a pipe annoy you, Mrs. Price?' Maybelle nodded no. 'Thank you. I am afraid I am a hopeless slave to the weed.' He selected one of the pipes from the rack, tamped the tobacco with his finger, and lit it. 'I am a creature of habit,' he said. 'Every morning I fill all the pipes under the delusion that I save time by not having to do it again all day. Silly, the habits one acquires.'

He puffed his pipe alight, and waited.

'We want to know about Mama—about my mother,' Maybelle said. 'How is she? I mean, is she . . . better? Better than she was?'

322

'Do you mean is your mother insane?' the doctor puffed at his pipe and looked at the ceiling. 'Who of us is not, at some time or other? No, I would not say that your mother is insane. I would say that she came here very much in need of psychiatric attention, and certainly of supervision, but I would not say that she is or was actually insane. Certain oddities, peculiarities, yes. But then most of us become a trifle odd with advancing age.'

Craig spoke for the first time.

'Then she could leave if she wanted to?'

'I see no reason why not. She signed herself in of her own volition.' The doctor flipped through the sheaf of case-history. 'She came here with two gentlemen—let me see, a Mr. McMullen and a Mr. Norton, bankers, I believe, trustees of Mrs. Grimes's husband's estate until Mrs. Price—then Miss Grimes—should come of age. Mrs. Grimes was plainly in a disturbed condition, with certain—ah—peculiarities, which the gentlemen described as wanting hospitalization and care. I suppose for formality's sake these gentlemen should accept responsibility for her discharge.'

'Suppose my wife accepts responsibility for her discharge?'

The doctor looked over his glasses.

'She is of age? She is able to care for her mother?'

'Yes.' Maybelle and Craig spoke together. The doctor shrugged.

'Then I cannot see any objection, unless your mother should prefer to stay here. In this case, as she is an adult, as she pays her bills promptly, she is welcome to stay. We have certain patients who do not want to leave. This is not a prison. It is a hospital, a sanatorium.' He had deliberately switched from *sanitarium* to *sanatorium*. 'We cure—or at least care for—sick people here. But enough of this. I think now we should go and see your mother. She is waiting in the living-room. I will leave you alone with her, and then you can come and see me in my office here a little later.'

Feeling slightly set back, disarmed, Craig dipped his head and said:

'Thank you, doctor. I would like to talk a little more before we go.'

'Very well. Miss Swanson will take you to your mother, Mrs. Price.'

Miss Swanson escorted Craig and Maybelle into the living-room, a warm, thickly-carpeted room with flowers—daffodils—in vases on gleaming side tables, and a small fire flickering in a grate.

'Just wait here,' Miss Swanson said, indicating wing chairs flanking a divan in front of the fireplace. 'I'll send for Mrs. Grimes.' She went out of the door. Maybelle looked inquiringly at Craig.

'He seems like a pretty nice fellow,' Craig said. 'I don't think

323

maybe we're going to need this money. I guess I was mistaken in this fellow. I kind of thought we'd have to buy her out, pay him off to say she wasn't crazy, or something like that.'

'Hush,' Maybelle said. 'Here she comes. Hello, Mama.' She got up to kiss her mother, who recoiled slightly.

Mrs. Grimes still looked like a rather flustered peahen, Craig thought. Her nose was still beaky, the chin retreating, but now her neck was wattled and crêpy. The ash-blonde hair, once so tightly curled, now stood stiffly away from her head in a sort of Dutch-boy bob, giving a peculiar, almost obscenely flapperish look to the lined, dry-skinned face. The slightly popped blue eyes wandered restlessly, and she twined the fingers of her veined, knobby-knuckled hands, clasped tightly together in front of her. She was wearing a blue knitted wool dress that was neat enough, but bagged in unlikely places. The nurses, obviously, had dressed her specially for the occasion, or perhaps she had just come upon a hidden lipstick or rouge pot, because she had painted her lips thickly and great splotches of feverish red highlit her cheeks. She couldn't have been much more than fifty, but she looked sixty, at least.

'Hello, Mama, how are you feeling?' Maybelle said again. 'Let's all sit down,' she laughed nervously, 'so we can talk. You remember Craig, don't you, Mama? You remember he came to see us one Christmas before Papa . . . before Papa passed away.'

Irma Grimes looked at Craig suspiciously. The look hadn't changed any, either, Craig thought. That's how she looked at me the first time she ever saw me.

'That's the one you married, is it?' she said. 'I wouldn't have known him with the moustache. He looks a lot older and a lot different from what I remember him lookin' like. Of course I didn't see him very long because he and your papa wanted to get to drinkin'.' She made a face of disapproval, and looked Craig up and down, disconcertingly.

'What happened to your face?' she said directly. 'It didn't use to look like that.'

'We were in an accident, remember, Mama, I wrote you? It wasn't our fault, but Craig got cut up pretty bad. It's lucky we didn't get killed.'

Irma Grimes sniffed. 'I always told your papa he was a fool to give you that car for Christmas. You never know what kind of people you'll get mixed up with gallivanting around in cars, a girl your age, no more than a baby.'

Craig attempted a little feeble levity, not much, he thought, but a little.

'Maybelle isn't a little girl any more, Mrs. Grimes. She's a big girl. Twenty-one years old and married.'

324

'Hmf,' said Irma Grimes. 'Married to a shirt-tail boy with a broken nose and a face full of scars.'

That'll hold me, Craig thought. She ain't so crazy at all. A shirt-tail boy with a busted nose and a face full of scars. That's me all over.

'Do you like it here, Mama?' Maybelle asked. 'Are they good to you?'

'Why wouldn't they be good to me? I pay my way. I like it here all right except the food ain't so good sometime. I didn't like it at first but I got used to it. It's kind of pretty later on in the spring, and there's lots of real nice people to talk to. Some of them are a little funny at first but you can get used to anything. When they get too funny they take them away for awhile and when they come back they don't act so funny any more. The only thing wrong with it is you can't get out without somebody to look after you when you go downtown.'

Maybelle looked at Craig desperately.

'How would you like to go back home and live with Maybelle and me? We're . . . we're sort of a family now. We'd sure like to have you,' Craig said lamely. 'That's if you'd like to come back home to your house.'

Mrs. Grimes looked at him with infinite, lofty wisdom.

'Oh, they wouldn't let me,' she said. 'They wouldn't never let me in a million years. It would be too dangerous for them. This is the only way they're safe, with me kept here.'

'Who, Mama? Who do you mean?'

Mrs. Grimes looked cautiously around the room, and lowered her voice.

'Those men who kidnapped me and put me here. They're afraid I'll tell your papa what I know about them. They wouldn't dare to let me out. Your papa would put them right smack dab in jail where they belong if I told him what I know.' Her eyes narrowed and she nodded her head wisely—quite a lot like Maybelle when she is being infuriating, Craig thought. That's where she got it. Mama.

'What did the men look like, Mrs. Grimes?' Craig asked.

'I don't know. I can't remember. It was dark and I couldn't see their faces. But I'd recognize them again by their voices, I bet you.'

'Well, they won't bother you any more,' Craig said heartily. 'I won't let them. Maybelle and I won't let them.'

'You got a face that would scare 'em off, all right,' Mama Grimes said with a flash of candour. 'It would scare *me* on a dark night, I can tell you.'

'Hush, Mama, you mustn't be rude to Craig,' Maybelle said.

'Men,' Mama Grimes said. 'Men. Drinkin' and carryin' on and never comin' home. Kidnappin' people and shuttin' 'em up. It was an evil day when John Grimes come a-courtin', an evil day, and like my mama said, no good would ever come of it.'

Maybelle looked at Craig and nodded slightly. Craig got up.

'I think I'd better go see about the car,' he said. 'It'll be a long trip home.'

'That's right,' Maybelle said. 'You go see about the car and I'll talk to Mama.'

'You took your own sweet time this time to come talk to Mama,' Mrs. Grimes was saying, truculently, as Craig went out the door. 'You must have been pretty busy with that boy with the broken nose and the moustache. I don't know what your papa ever saw in him, anyway, bringin' him around that day like he was kinfolks on Christmas.'

'This busted nose of mine is going to take a power of living down,' Craig said to himself, as he walked back along the corridor and knocked at the door of the doctor's office.

'How did you find her?' Dr. Immermann asked, as Craig sat down.

'I don't see much difference, except maybe she's older. I never met her but once, so I couldn't be expected to know. It's hard for me to tell whether she's grown older or what.' Craig laughed. 'She doesn't care much for my face, right now.'

'That's nothing, nothing at all. She's child-like in some ways, and she day-dreams a lot. Did she tell you about being kidnapped?'

'Yes, that came up right quick. Two wicked men who are keeping her here for some reason that I couldn't quite make out.'

The doctor smiled and lit his pipe.

'Nothing very serious about that. She came here after dark, under mild sedation, terribly disturbed. Possibly the past months had assumed a dream quality. It is hard to say. I sometimes feel a bit unreal myself these days. Then there is very possibly some childhood dream, some real or fancified fright—of being frightened by a cruel prank, or by some old wives' tale, who can say?—and they all get mixed up into fantasy which is sometimes more real than actuality. It is a very small aberration, like a child being afraid of the dark, and of the faceless people who live in the dark. I should imagine, once away from here, happy at home again, the memory will lessen and eventually disappear. Nothing, nothing to worry about.'

Craig spoke very slowly, frowning.

'What I do not quite understand, Doctor, is this: 'Is she legally sane? Is she cured? Or almost cured? Or what?'

The doctor stretched his long legs and spoke more or less to himself. He passed his hand over his brow and backward over his short-cropped hair before he spoke.

'She has not been declared by law insane. She has not been committed, against her will, to a public or private institution,

326

as insane. Odd, yes, but where does oddness stop and where insanity begin? She is not a clear-cut manic depressive. She is not paranoiac. She is not catatonic. She is not dementia praecox. She is only mildly schizoid, like many ageing people. What is she? I don't know what she is. She is a product of possibly a too rigid upbringing, having a tremendous resentment to normal sex because of early childhood training, with any number of images, mother or father is not important, clawing at her psyche. I imagine she was not a very attractive child. Certainly she would have some guilt complex about what might have been an early brief enjoyment of sex, especially pre-marital sex, against a subconscious will, which developed into a revulsion against marital sex. I don't know. All I know is that her world fell apart and she became, for a time, a child. Physically she is healthy. Certainly she is not dangerous, and certainly she knows right from wrong. No, insane she is not, if you demand a definition.'

'That doesn't answer me,' Craig said, stubbornly. 'I don't know all the words you are using. Father-images and unconscious resentments, and things like that. What I want to know, is she legally sane once she is outside of here? Would a bargain she made, a paper she signed, for instance, be legal? Or would the fact that she's been shut up here for a couple of years prevent her from acting as a . . . as a competent adult witness, say?'

'Many people have pleaded insanity, at least momentary insanity, as an excuse,' the doctor said. 'Very few have ever pleaded sanity as a defence. Insanity is used as an apologetic reason for one thing or another. But I wander: I will answer your question.

'Your mother-in-law has been a sick woman. She has been treated, and to all practical intent, cured. The word normal is not definable. Perhaps she has never been what we call normal. But she is as normal as she was before it was found necessary to send her here for rest and care and treatment. Would you condemn a man who had sustained an operation for appendicitis for a scar? We all wear scars of one sort or another,' he bowed almost apologetically. 'You wear scars on your face. Would it not be likely that some people wear scars inside, on their psyches? Perhaps you would say souls. Would you go through life condemned because you have a broken nose and a scar that splits your forehead?'

Craig smiled.

'You still haven't answered my question, yes or no.'

The doctor sighed.

'I imagine you find me pedantic. I shall try again. Your mother-in-law is neither sane nor insane. To all intent, when she walks out this door, she is a competent adult until something else happens which might stamp her as dangerous to herself or to others. It would then be necessary to mark her "insane" by having competent physicians certify that in their opinion she was not of sound mind and should be committed for her own good. In Vienna,' the doctor said, 'I once knew a physician who signed such a document, and because of red tape and delay he was waiting in the madhouse as a patient when the person he had certified arrived.' The doctor laughed shortly.

'Can she sign documents?' Craig was persistent.

'I imagined that your interest might lie in that direction. Yes, of course she can sign documents. She signed her own admission. She will sign her own discharge.' The doctor narrowed his eyes. 'The legality of those future documents might be open to question if it could be proven that she was insane at the time of signature. That is very difficult to prove, and generally takes such a long time that the answer is usually provided by death. Does that answer your question?'

Craig had sufficient taste to blush.

'Yes, sir,' he said. 'But it's a pretty important matter. Concerns her welfare as much as some others.'

'That is generally so,' the doctor said, 'when families arrive post-haste to retrieve buried relatives. There is nearly always a probate court or something similar lurking behind sudden solicitude, because no one really wants a queer and often bothersome relative around the house if other people can be paid to accept the dreary details of her responsibility. I am right in gathering that extreme concern for your mother-in-law's happiness did not entirely dictate your arrival at these gates?'

'I'm afraid you've got me, sir,' Craig said. 'I'm afraid you're right.'

'I shouldn't let it bother me too much, if I were you,' the doctor said. 'But I would be interested to know one thing: What were you prepared to offer me as a bribe for a certificate of complete and permanent sanity? If there were such a thing, which there isn't.'

'I wouldn't . . .' Craig went scarlet and half-clapped a hand to his breast pocket. The doctor threw his head back and roared with laughter. Tears came to his eyes, and he drew a handkerchief from his breast pocket and wiped them.

'What was it? Five hundred dollars? A thousand? I should like to think it was a thousand? How much?'

'Two thousand,' Craig said. He drooped his head for a second, and then looked squarely at the doctor.

'Two thousand,' he said. 'Here.' He tapped his pocket.

'You must want something very badly,' the doctor said softly. 'Would you say that you were entirely . . . sane? To want something so badly as to pay two thousand dollars for nothing of any value whatsoever? Is that a mark of sanity, as the word is so often, so loosely defined?'

'I feel ashamed of myself, Doctor,' Craig said. 'I don't often admit that. Not really ashamed of myself, but ashamed of my ignorance and ashamed of . . . well, just ashamed of my ignorance.'

Dr. Immermann got up from his chair. Craig rose, and the doctor put a hand on his shoulder.

'I will sign papers that your mother-in-law is discharged at the request of her next-of-kin. If you will have your wife step in to sign the papers, your mother-in-law may sign her own discharge after the nurses have packed for her.' The doctor laughed again.

Then he said seriously:

'As I have told you there is no law in the land which can accurately define the sanity or lack of it in some of the actions of your mother-in-law, no law which can keep her here if you are willing to accept her. The human mind cannot be measured in that exactitude. But the body in connection with that mind is measurable to a degree. Excitement, fear, unhappiness, even change, can work sudden bodily changes, exactly as it happens in children. Extreme nervous stress might cause—what is the lay term for an epileptoid spasm—a fit, you would say, of short duration and of no particular hurt to her well-being. It is common in children, and might be due to anything from an imbalance of bodily fluids to a deficiency of sugar content in the blood stream—to physical or nervous exhaustion or a sudden shock or fright. You will also find that in people of your mother-in-law's history there is a tendency to incontinence—inability to restrain bodily functions—even as small children sometimes wet their clothes when laughing hysterically or playing too hard. She may be a bit difficult around the house. If I were you, which I am not, I would be tempted to leave her here, and not intrude her into the daily living of young people.' He shrugged, and got up. He smiled and extended his hand. 'But I am not you.

'Try to look after her, and tend her well,' he said with marked irony. 'I am sure that she is worth the effort. And if your charitable effort should come to a lawsuit, and you need a psychiatrist to confound the simple legal peasants, I am at your service, at a very nominal fee. Not,' he said, 'two thousand dollars. But I'm sure I should be worth that much if the look on your face at this moment is any index to my ability to confuse.' Craig did not think it very funny that the doctor found it necessary to guffaw again.

It was raining gently when they left, and they felt close and comfortable inside the Dodge. Getting Mama to leave had been easy enough. One of the nurses had packed her things swiftly. When Craig finished stowing the three bags that comprised her luggage—most of her clothes were still in the house in Kensington—Mama was curled up in the back seat, asleep. ('The nurse gave her a pill just before we left,' Maybelle said. 'I've got the

329

bottle. The nurse says give her another if she wakes up on the way home. I believe she's glad to be going home. Did you notice? She couldn't wait to sign the papers.')

Craig drove silently, swiftly, in the rain, for most of the six-hour journey back to Kensington. Neither he nor Maybelle felt very much like talking, not merely to avoid disturbing the sleeping passenger, and after a while the steady thrumming of the tyres on the wet road sent Maybelle off to sleep. Craig drove in the night, his mind racing in rhythm with the motor. The idea, he thought, is to get her to trust me. That and only that, because if she trusts me it will be easy to persuade her that the bank is the villain—that the bank shut her up, the bank is the two mysterious strangers who kidnapped her, and the bank will put her back in the asylum unless I protect her. There's no hurry, no hurry at all. I've got nine months before I can do anything, anyhow. No good trying anything until I'm legally of age. I guess the only thing is to take care of the old girl and some day when she's in a good temper, sweet-talk her into transferring her stock to Maybelle. Better Maybelle than me. They surely can't blame a mother for turning over her holdings to her daughter, but if she signs over the stock to me everybody will swear that she's still falling-down nuts and I bamboozled her into it. Then, once the stock's made over to Maybelle, it'll be a simple matter to get Maybelle to make me a power of attorney. Nothing simpler or more logical than for a wife to turn to her own husband to run her business, is it? The bank might raise a stink about the old girl being crazy and easy to persuade, but legally they haven't got a foot to kick with. If Mama was to die, Maybelle'd get the money anyhow. So what's so bad about Mama making the transfer before she dies? Nothing, Craig thought, it's done all the time. The only thing is, we're stuck with her. We can never send her back again once we've declared her sane, and made it stick. Oh well. Another year, just another short year, and I'll have this whole thing by the balls. But, boy, it's going to be a long, long short year. He drove on through the night, savouring the soft rain, the gentle whish of wiper on windshield, the whispering tyres, and his brain a-buzz with plans.

28

THEY got home around midnight. Irma Grimes allowed herself to be led, like a sleepy child, to her room. Maybelle undressed her, took her to the bathroom, and then fed her another pill. She tucked her mother in, and Craig said:

'I think maybe you'd better sleep with her tonight. She's

going to be terribly confused when she wakes up in the morning. She's been accustomed to waking up in the same place for the last coup!e of years.'

'Sleep with her?' Maybelle was aghast. '*Sleep* with her? It made my skin crawl just to touch her when I undressed her. I'd as leave sleep with a rattlesnake. Old women, they smell, they—' Maybelle was exhausted. Nervous tears trembled on her lashes.

'I don't mean in the bed with her, honey. I meant we'd put in a cot. If she wakes in the night, or when she wakes in the morning . . . . she'll need a familiar face and she hasn't got used to mine yet. She'll think the boogie-men have got her for sure. It's only for tonight, maybe tomorrow, until she gets settled down.'

'If you think I'm going to—oh, all right,' Maybelle said abruptly 'Tonight and maybe tomorrow night. Not more. Then we get a nurse. I'm not going to spend my time cleaning up after her. Just look at her. Would you like to spend the night in the same room with her?'

'After all, she's your m . . .' and Craig stopped at the dangerous light in Maybelle's eyes. He held up his palms protectively. 'I know. It's my fault. It was my idea. Leave the door open so we can hear her, and come on downstairs. We'll have a nightcap. You've had a long hard day.'

Seated in the living-room, finishing his drink, Craig stretched and yawned.

'God, I'm tired. That's over five hundred miles, that drive, plus all the rest of it. We didn't have a chance to talk much in the car. Was she very hard to persuade to come home? She seemed agreeable enough when we left.'

'Craig, I don't care what you say, or what that doctor says about Mama, she's still as crazy as a coot. As far as I can see, she hasn't changed a bit. She was like a bad little child when you left to talk to the doctor again. She wanted to come and then she didn't want to come, and then she cried and said nobody loved her and that the men would get her if she ran away. *Ran away*, was what she said. I tried to tell her that she wasn't running away, she was just going home, and finally I guess I got her mad and told her that if she didn't come I'd *send* the bad men to get her. She shut up then and came as sweet as cream. Craig, I don't like this. I don't like it a bit. And just having her around is going to be hell, do you realize that? You'll be off at work every day, but I'll be here in the house with her. All day long I'll be here in the house with her.'

Craig got up and rested a hand on her shoulder.

'Cheer up, honey. It can't be all that bad.' He started to say she wouldn't be half as much trouble as a baby, and thought better of it. 'I'll go fix the cot, and then I'm going to hit the hay. I'm a day behind, and more, at the mill.'

'Well,' Maybelle said. 'I slept most of the way home and I'm just not sleepy a bit. I'm going to sit here and read a little more and maybe have another drink before I go to bed. Put my green silk pyjamas on the cot and I won't have to bother you when I undress for bed.'

Craig bent and kissed her good night.

'You're a real honey,' he said. 'You know that, don't you?'

'No, I don't know it, but it makes me feel good to hear it,' Maybelle replied. 'Go on and get some sleep, and if you hear me scream, come rescue me. I never slept with a maniac before.'

'Shush,' Craig said, touching a fingertip to her lips. 'Don't talk that way about your mother.' He went up the stairs, and in a moment Maybelle heard him curse as he pinched a finger opening up a cot.

The old lady was rather pathetic when she came awake in less than half-remembered surroundings. Maybelle was sleeping soundly when Irma Grimes awoke, looked wonderingly around the room, fingered the counterpane, looked at the drapes, noticed the figure on the cot in the corner, and then searched frantically around for a bathroom. There wasn't any bathroom that she could remember in the fog of transition and sedatives, and in her panic she wet the bed. Then she broke into tears, flung back the covers, and charged, all green-shadowed bony angles in her sopping nightdress, over to the cot where Maybelle slept with her face turned towards the wall.

'Nurse, nurse!' Irma Grimes sobbed. 'I couldn't find the bathroom, I couldn't, Nurse, and I've peed in the bed! Get up, please, Nurse, I'm hungry and I can't find my clothes! Somebody's moved my room and they didn't have to because I'm not funny any more. I haven't been funny in a long time. I didn't need to go away!'

Maybelle awoke, and saw her mother standing over the cot, her grey hair standing stiff as quills, her slight body pathetic in the soiled nightgown, her face tear-sodden and white showing over the pupils of her eyes.

'You're not my new nurse!' her mother screamed. 'They've taken me away! Those men have taken me away!' She stretched her arms out straight before her, fingers spread against an unseen presence. Her mouth gaped open, and her eyes dilated. 'Don't touch me!' she screamed. 'Don't touch me!' Then saliva slid ropy from the corner of her mouth, her eyes dilated, and she sagged to the floor in a faint.

Maybelle shook herself fully awake. She had been momentarily terrified by the picture of her mother standing over her like something in a horror movie, and it took her a second to recollect where she was, and why her mother should be standing over her bed. Then she bent over the frail, crumpled figure on the floor.

She was surprisingly heavy, Maybelle thought, for so skinny an old woman, as she half-dragged her across the floor and lifted her on the bed again and pulled the rumpled wet gown down around her ankles. She called twice to Craig, but got no answer, for Craig had risen earlier than usual and had already left for work. For lack of anything better to do, she chafed at her mother's wrists, and in a moment the eyes opened.

'You're not my nurse,' Irma Grimes said, in a calm voice. 'You're a new nurse. And you haven't got on a uniform,' she added primly, disapprovingly. 'Where is your uniform? You ought to know better than to run around in a pair of pyjamas, showing everything off.'

'I'm not a nurse, Mama,' Maybelle said. 'I'm Maybelle. Your daughter. Maybelle. Don't you remember? We brought you home yesterday. You're home, Mama. You're home, home, and you're all right.'

'Oh, Maybelle.' The eyes flickered in comprehension. 'It's you. Then they brought you here too. You were acting funny and they brought you to this place too. Don't worry,' she said. 'We'll be all right pretty soon and then we can go back to the other place. We won't act funny very long.'

'Mama, Mama, Mama! You're not in some other place. You're home! Home! Craig and I went to get you and brought you home yesterday. We came in the car. This is your bedroom. You're home!'

Irma Grimes's voice was cross.

'If I'm home, then where's your papa? Your papa would be here if this was home. I don't care whether I'm home or not. In the other place my real nurse always brought me breakfast on a tray. You're just trying to fool me.'

Oh, God, Maybelle thought. I can't leave her and that lazy slut of a nigger hasn't come yet and Craig's gone to the office. At least I can call and get him back. He can be here in a few minutes. But then I'll have to go downstairs and use the phone and God knows what she'll be doing while I'm . . .

'Mama!' she said sharply. 'Mama! You've been bad, wetting the bed like a baby! Get up this minute and come with me to the bathroom so I can change you and you can take a bath. Then I'll get your breakfast, and you can help me in the kitchen.'

Irma Grimes giggled.

'You'll have to help *me*, Nurse,' she said, and giggled again. 'I just did number two.'

Maybelle groaned, and stripped the filthed sheets from the bed with one hand while she hauled her mother to her feet with the other.

'If it's going to be like this every day,' she gritted, as she herded her thoroughly soiled mother to the bathroom, 'if it's going to be like this every day I just don't see how I can stand it.'

333

'Craig,' Maybelle said that night, as she ran out into the yard to meet him. 'Craig, I'm not going to be able to stand it. I can't tell you what it's been like all day. We've got to get some sort of nurse right now—tomorrow. I tried to call you a couple of times, but Miss Mildred said you were out back in the plant or had gone some place. You haven't got any idea of what Mama's like. She's a child, Craig, a baby. She eats and she smears food all over her face, and she has tantrums and cries, and throws up, and she wets herself and does the other thing and she had a kind of fit . . . Craig, I can't stand it, I can't stand it! Let's take her back, let's do anything, but get her out of the house.'

'Where is she now?' Craig put an arm around Maybelle and walked her to the door. 'In bed?'

'No, not in bed. She's dressed and waiting to see you. She's sitting in the living-room and right now she's as sane as anybody. Ever since this afternoon, when she finally got over whatever kind of spell it was she had, you'd think that she was a duchess.

'She's been all over the house, criticizing this, telling Floreen how to do that, meddling in the kitchen—Craig, right in the middle of the afternoon she said she had to make some cookies for you or you'd be mad at her—God Almighty, she's all over everywhere and Floreen says she's goin' to quit and . . .'

'Take it easy, baby, take it easy. The first day in a thing like this is always the hardest . . . the doctor said . . .'

Maybelle looked at him in rising anger.

'How the hell would you know about the first day being the hardest in things like this? You never been through a thing like this! I don't care what the doctor said! We get a nurse tomorrow or you can stay home and take care of her yourself!'

'Calm down, honey, calm down. Let's go and have a drink and things'll look a little brighter. Come on, now.'

'Drink! We can't even have a drink in the house right now. Our own house! You remember how Mama was about the old man and his toddy? Well, while she was rooting around in the kitchen she found a bottle of whisky and poured it in the sink! She said nobody was goin' to drink in her house, not if she could help it. And then she went into a half-hour lecture on the trouble with Papa was whisky and if he hadn't of drunk whisky we never would have had the trouble we had. We're goin' to have to hide the whisky and drink in the back yard.' Maybelle trembled with frustrated anger.

Standing in the hall, Craig patted Maybelle on the behind. 'Take it easy, baby. I stopped off at the ABC store. There's a couple of bottles in the car. We'll put her to bed and then get plastered, if you want to.'

'I want to,' Maybelle said. 'My God, you'll never know how I want to. Come in now and talk to the duchess, while I go see if

I can calm down Floreen enough to get some supper on the table. Here's Craig, Mama,' she called, as she went on to the kitchen. 'Here's your new son-in-law come to get acquainted with you.'

Mrs. Irma Grimes had been repaired, considerably, by the combined efforts of her daughter and the Negro cook, Floreen. Maybelle had washed her hair and had tamed it with bobby-pins, but it still stuck out in a stiff, crinkled aureole of steel wool. Maybelle had put her into an old black silk dress that hid, somewhat, the scrawniness of her figure. Maybelle also had dug up a costume-jewellery pearl necklace, and with her face lightly made up, Irma Grimes looked completely calm and composed as she sat in the red living-room, in John Grimes's old red easy chair. She was sitting perched forward, her knees primly together, when Craig entered the room.

'Welcome home, Mrs. Grimes,' he said. He had debated the idea of calling her 'Mama,' and had rejected it as a little bit previous. 'You're looking wonderful. Did you sleep well last night?'

She surveyed him coldly.

'Well enough, for a strange bed. I had got sort of accustomed to another kind of bed in that place—that place I stayed in while I was away—one of those that lift up when you turn a crank. No complaints, I guess, except the house seems a little run down. I suppose it's the help you have to put up with these days, triflin' niggers. That's how it is, the minute you turn your back, everything gets run down. Nobody takes care of anything that ain't theirs. I suppose it's a cross we have to bear when we get old, but you would think that a body could go away a little while without finding everything changed when she gets back.' She looked at Craig as if to include him in the major change.

'You can sit down,' she said. 'Over there,' indicating the chair Maybelle always sat in. She sat calmly appraising him.

'You look like a nice young man,' she said. 'And I don't suppose you can help your face. It might have been—it was, one time—a pretty nice kind of face, as I mind it, before it got all messed up. It must of been a real bad accident. You wasn't drunk or nothin' like that?'

'No, ma'am,' Craig said. 'Nothing like that.'

'Well, I suppose it can't be helped now,' Mrs. Grimes said, resignedly. 'That's how life is, I guess.'

'I guess so,' Craig said.

Irma Grimes looked at him keenly.

'Maybelle tells me you're a real hard worker and a pretty good provider, is that right?'

'I hope so, ma'am,' Craig said. 'We make out. I try hard.'

'That's good,' Mama Grimes said. 'Mr. Grimes was always a real good provider. Anything my heart desired. He couldn't do

335

enough. If he hadn't of drank . . .' she sighed. 'We take the evil with the good, I reckon. It's a woman's lot. Things was different when Mr. Grimes was alive.'

We're showing progress, thank God, Craig thought. At least she has properly disposed of her husband, and isn't waiting for him to come through the door with whisky on his breath. She's got him real good and dead.

'Seems like when Mr. Grimes passed on everything got all mixed up. Those people—that bank, and all those people like that—kept sayin' we had to sell this and couldn't have that and this had to go and my rings and all.' She touched the glass pearls at her throat, and sighed. 'These was all I was able to save from the wreck.'

'It's a pity, it's a shame,' Craig said earnestly. 'But you know how banks are. When you don't need money they force it down your throat, and when you do, they won't give it to you. All they want is to take it away from you.'

'You never said a truer word, young feller,' Mama Grimes said. 'Never a truer word. Why, it was a positive scandal, the way those people acted, me sick and all, signing this, signing that, selling this, taking that, you would have thought they *owned* it.'

'That's right, what you say,' Craig said. He looked again at the cheap pearl necklace. 'You're sure right.'

Craig thought of a lot of things to say. It was too early to play any cards right now, but obviously Mama Grimes wasn't going to be too tough a customer to turn against the evil symbol of BANK. Lay back and wait, boy, until she's gentled down and knows you better. Just take it easy and wait.

'I hope you don't mind, Mrs. Grimes,' he said, after a long pause. 'I hope you don't mind about me and Maybelle getting married and me living in the house and all. I sure would be unhappy if you minded. But you were sick and Maybelle was all by herself and I sort of figured that maybe a man around the house . . .'

'You'll always have house-room with me, young man—what is it, Craig?—so long as you mind your ways,' she said grandly. 'I'm right pleased Maybelle had sense enough to take up with a serious feller, instead of one of those drinkin' no-good drugstore cowboys that stay out all night. Me bein' off sick, like you say, and Mr. Grimes passed to his reward, why I think it was right neighbourly of you to step in and look after Maybelle, seein' to her well-bein', and all. A young girl's got no right livin' all by herself in a big house with nobody to look to her good.' She smiled at him, perched in the chair as pertly as a bird.

'Of course,' she continued, soberly. 'I ain't sayin' I wouldn't have liked more say in choosin' a son-in-law. But with the way young folks run around these days I reckon I'm downright lucky to have any sort of son-in-law at all. I vow,' she said, 'what *can* that child be doin' about supper? We had meals so regular when I was away visitin' in Greensboro. You can say all you want to against hotel livin', but at least the meals are *regular*.'

That's pretty good, Craig thought. Now it's a hotel. Now it's visiting. I'll see if we can't concentrate on the hotel business. It's better than having her say, 'When I was off locked up in a madhouse.'

'Excuse me, Mrs. Grimes,' he said. 'I'll just go look into the kitchen and see if I can lend Maybelle a hand. That nigger of ours ain't the best in the world, but with niggers all workin' in the factories these days, I guess we're lucky to get any sort of help.' Craig noticed his dropped g's again, and grinned inside himself. 'Old rabbit ears,' he said, and went off to the kitchen.

'That's a nice young man, even if he is ugly,' Irma Grimes said aloud to nobody in particular, as Craig excused himself. 'Polite as pie and goin' off to help Maybelle in the kitchen. There's not many young fellers would help their wife in the kitchen. John Grimes never so much as put his face past the kitchen door. Maybe Maybelle did right well to marry this young fellow, especially if he's a good provider. And I'll find that out,' she said ominously. 'I'll find that out, all right.'

In the kitchen, Craig whispered to Maybelle.

'For the love of God, hurry up. She's hungry again.'

Maybelle was peering into the oven. She turned a hot, flushed face to him. 'I'm doin' the best I can,' she said. 'It'll be ready in a minute. Go back and keep her amused until I get it on the table.'

'Supper'll be ready in just a minute, Mrs. Grimes,' Craig said returning. 'Meantime, I brought you a box of candy. I was meaning to give it to you after supper, but maybe one or two pieces of candy right now won't spoil your appetite.' He nodded towards the kitchen. 'Just so long as we don't tell Maybelle,' he said in a conspiratorial voice. 'You know how *they* are about eating before meals.' *They* implied enemy.

Mama Grimes clawed greedily into the candy-box which Craig had produced from his overcoat-pocket in the hall. She smiled at him and spoke with her mouth full, her lipstick blurred with chocolate.

'You're a nice boy,' she said. 'A thoughtful boy. Why don't you call me "Mama", too, like Maybelle does?'

'Thank you, Mama,' Craig said. 'That I will. I haven't had a Mama to call my own in a long time. Well, I can hear Maybelle in the dining-room. Maybe I'd better put that candy-box away until after dinner, all right?'

'Put it in my bedroom, under the bed,' Mama said, reaching for one more chocolate. 'Where I can get at it if I get hungry in the night. You're a good boy . . . son,' she said, and got up to go in to supper.

Mama ate regally, one finger crooked, but demolished the supper with an appetite undiminished by her stolen moment of secret chocolate consumption.

'Mr. Grimes always used to say I didn't hardly eat enough to keep a bird alive,' she said, through a mouthful of country ham and hominy grits, some of which trickled down her chin. 'I always was a picky eater, even when I was a girl. Not,' she said, looking coldly at her daughter, 'like some people I know.'

Supper ended with apple pie, and Mama had two pieces.

'The crust is soggy,' she said. 'I guess I better get that nigger in hand tomorrow and teach her a few things about cookin'. You'd think,' she said, again looking almost balefully at Maybelle, 'that this girl hadn't had hardly any raisin' at all. Imagine. This poor young feller comes home all tired out from workin' all day and gets fed stuff you wouldn't ask a hog to eat.'

Craig kicked Maybelle under the table. The kick said *don't* and Maybelle's angry flush subsided.

Mrs. Grimes announced, after dinner, that she was used to early bed and early risin', and she hoped that Craig and Maybelle wouldn't be the kind of people that sat up all night, not with a day's work to be done. Maybelle took her mother upstairs, while Craig looked at the paper. After a few minutes Maybelle came downstairs, looking fretted and more than a little puzzled.

'She says she won't sleep a wink unless you come up and kiss her good night,' she said. 'What have you been doin' to the old lady?'

'Nothin',' Craig said, smiling. 'Nothin' at all.' He went up the stairs.

29

IN practically no time at all, it seemed to Maybelle, Craig had become her mother's son and Maybelle was something caught between an easy object of abuse and an unpaid chambermaid who specialized in the dirty work. The first talk of hiring a professional nurse had come to nothing. It had been decided—at least Craig had decided—that a registered nurse was out of the question, even though they could easily afford it by using the money that had previously been spent every month on Mama Grimes's medical care at the sanatorium. Craig had put his foot, very firmly, down.

'It doesn't make any sense to the whole plan,' he told Maybelle one night, after he had dutifully kissed the old woman good night, now a ritual in the household. 'If we hire a real trained nurse, and ask the bank to give us the money we—they—were spending on Mama's asylum bills, you know what the bank's going to think.'

'What is the bank going to think? Sometimes I get so goddam tired of what the bank thinks and doesn't think, I could . . . What'll the bank think?' It had been a bad day for Maybelle. Floreen the cook had quit again for good, sayin' she couldn't stand it no more, that old sick woman in the kitchen all the time and messin' the bed and all like that. She might be black but she always worked for quality folks and havin' that old woman always stickin' her nose into everything she done in the kitchen . . . Floreen accepted her wages and went away with the righteous carriage of a wronged woman who was not coming back for evermore. That she would be back tomorrow had nothing to do with Floreen's flouncy intent as she stormed out of the door with her lip run out, but it meant Maybelle had to cook two meals, do most of the housework, with her mother nagging persistently at her heels.

'The bank,' Craig said, 'is going to think that we just changed asylums, if it's necessary to have a trained nurse on twenty-four-hour duty. They're going to think it especially if we ask them for some of your mother's money to pay a nurse, and we can't afford it out of what I make. Anyhow I don't want a trained nurse in the house. The first thing old McMullen will say is: "If that old woman's as well as they say, then what do they need with a trained nurse in the house? If you ask me, she's still batty, and that boy's up to something." That's what McMullen will say, and the other Two Blind Mice will say yes. I don't want to touch a dime of her money. Let it mount up in the bank. We'll just have to spend some of yours. After all, getting Mama loose from Nottingham Hill didn't cost us a cent. We put that two thousand back, and you can use some of it if the bills run too high. It won't be much longer, now.'

Maybelle's voice shrilled.

'You're off in the mill all day, you don't know what it's like! She follows me foot to foot. I can't hardly go to the bathroom without her tippin' behind me. And she talks, my God, she talks all day long. She criticizes everything, she pokes her nose into everything, and when she goes into the kitchen to cook there's flour on the ceiling and butter on the floor and she dirties up all the pots and pans . . . and . . . if I was a nigger I'd quit too.' Maybelle was near to tears again, a state, it seemed to Craig, in which she was prone to over-indulge these days. 'And, Craig, she's so filthy! She'll get excited over nothin' at all and pee in her clothes, and she hardly ever takes the trouble to get up at night to go to the bathroom. I change those sheets every day, and I can't blame Floreen for not wantin' to wash them, so I have to wash them every day myself, and it's just awful . . .'

'I know, I know it's awful, baby,' Craig said soothingly. 'But we have to put up with it for a while. Let's do this: Let's get another servant, a white one, a kind of practical nurse that'll help with the housework and keep an eye on the old lady. She can live in, and it won't cost a whole lot. Say maybe fifteen dollars a week. There are plenty of mill families that have got an aunt or a sister out of work that'd be glad to make the extra money. This way all the bank can say is that it's wonderful that Craig Price is so considerate of his mother-in-law *and* his wife, without having that thing about registered nurse hanging over our heads.'

'Anything, my God, anything at all,' Maybelle said, 'if it'll just keep Mama out of my hair even a little bit. Way I feel right now I'd hire a gorilla if only it would eat the old bitch.' Maybelle's lips were tight. 'And don't tell me not to call my mother an old bitch. Old bitch she was and old bitch she is, and a filthy one, besides. Even if she wasn't filthy, just having her in the house all day is enough to drive you nuts. I used to think I was bored stiff when I was alone here. Now, my God, what I wouldn't give to be alone here. You could hear me all the way to the mill, whistlin' while I work.'

So a succession of practical nurses—chapped country wenches from farms, unwanted poor relations from the mill town, white and black and copper in colour, relentlessly came and as relentlessly went. Floreen quit at least twice a week, but at least she was constant in her returns.

Mama Grimes was something more than impossible with the practical nurses. She quarrelled at them steadily. She seemed now to delight in fouling her bed and clothes, and ceremonially met their muttered grumblings with a farrago of abuse. She refused to allow them to dress or undress her. She refused to let them sleep in the same room with her, because she wasn't used to sleepin' with niggers and white trash and country wenches. In the end it was Maybelle who settled the whole matter of help.

'I don't know why in hell I didn't think of it before,' she said to Craig. 'I guess I stay so turkey-feathered mad at Mama all day long I never really get time to think. Look, these dam' wenches we get to help out don't really do anything but eat their heads off and complain. In the end I have to do it all myself. I got a solution.'

Craig was prepared to smile indulgently at any solution Maybelle might have to offer.

'What, baby?' He had come down from kissing Mama good night and he and Maybelle were having a drink before their own evening meal. They had developed an elaborate pretence of eating with Mama, while not eating at all, but watching in horrid fascination as gobbets of food clung to her lips and collected on the front of her dresses, then putting her to bed and retrieving a bottle of whisky out of a hiding place and having a couple of nips before they ate a warmed-over supper in the comparative peace and quiet of a house freed at least momentarily from an abrasive extra presence.

'What, baby?' Craig said.

'It's so simple. We use a diaper service, just like we had a baby. We only have to buy some more sheets. We'll let her mess herself to her heart's content, just like she was a baby, and we'll do some pretending, too. We'll just send all the mess to the diaper service and let them take care of it. This way,' Maybelle said, 'I really don't mind it so much, thinkin' of her like she was a baby.'

'I think you are a wonderful girl,' Craig said. 'I think you are the smartest girl I ever met.' He got up from his chair and made a ceremony of kissing her. 'We've got the meal thing more or less settled, like she was a baby, and now we have the bed clothes and dirty drawers thing settled, like she was a baby, and now let's do something else, like she was a baby. Or at least, I'll I'll do it. Let's give her a prize for being good, sort of. I'll take her to the movies every Saturday afternoon, and you can take her a couple of times a week. How does she feel about dogs?'

'She hates them,' Maybelle said. 'Wouldn't ever let Papa have one around the house.'

Craig's face fell in mock despair.

'I had thought for a minute,' he said, 'that I might buy her a puppy. To keep her busy, I mean. You wouldn't mind cleaning up after a puppy too, would you?'

'We could try her on a cat,' Maybelle said. 'She might love cats. At least we could get a sand-box for the cat.' They both laughed uproariously, until Craig's face suddenly sobered.

'It's not too bad an idea. Not too bad at all.'

'What? The sand-box? We could try that on Mama too.'

'A cat. A kitten. Didn't you tell me she was back to playing dolls when the crack-up came? And that she thought you were a baby, too?'

'Yes,' Maybelle's voice was dubious. 'Yes, that's right. She did have this baby thing.'

'Well,' Craig said, 'I wouldn't go so far as to build her a real baby, you got enough to do'—his laugh was light and more than faintly false—'but let's try her on a kitten. It might keep her amused, and off your neck during the day.'

'I'd give her a crocodile if it would keep her off my neck,' Maybelle said grimly. 'It's worth a try, anyhow. But you'll have to bring the cat to her. She thinks the sun rises and falls in you.'

Strangely enough, considering the hostile beginning, Irma Grimes did think the sun rose and fell in Craig. She was as impatient as a child for his arrival in the evening, from the office. She fretted and worried that he might have had another accident, if he was as much as a few minutes late. She played an interminable game of dressing up for him in the afternoon, and her conduct with Craig was almost coquettish. She had a way of dismissing Maybelle from the room when Craig arrived, and she talked excitedly of all her doings of the day—a cake she'd baked especially for him, cookies she had made, fudge and penuche and brownies she had painfully confected, despite, she implied, a solid front of hostile interference in the kitchen. When he brought her the kitten, a tiny, cuddly, topaz cat with its eyes barely open, she held it to her cheek and insisted that it sleep in bed with her. Cunningly, she narrowed her eyes, and announced that what she was going to name the kitten was a secret. Then, childishly unable to contain herself, she blurted that if it was a little boy cat she was going to call it 'Craig'.

'And if it's a girl cat?' Craig teased, refraining from suggesting that she look and find out. 'What'll you call it then? Maybelle?'

'No, not Maybelle,' Mama Grimes said. 'I'll call it Craigie. That would make a nice girl's name . . . Craigie. I hope it's a little-boy cat, though. But I think I'll call it Craigie anyhow, boy or girl.'

Craigie proved worth its weight in peace. Mama Grimes held the kitten as possessively as a little girl might clutch a doll, and only the resilience of Craigie's young bones kept it from being crushed. But the kitten seemed fond, too, of Mama Grimes, and appeared perfectly happy to allow Mama Grimes to fall asleep before it made its nightly determined climb to the mantel-piece. If Mama Grimes woke in the night, she called Craigie, and Craigie would spring down on to the bed again. Now that Craigie had come, Mama Grimes stayed more and more in her bedroom, and Maybelle seemed visibly younger as a result.

Craig seldom came home without some sort of gift for Mama Grimes. A stroke of sheer accidental genius, he freely admitted, was the canary bird, a surly creature who refused to sing, but who proved fascinating to the cat. The cat would not leave the bird's presence, hoping in its feline optimism that some day the door of the cage would come ajar. And Mama Grimes would not leave the cat. A more effective barricade against her down-stairs presence could not possibly have been more strongly erected. She could barely bring herself to leave the cat and the bird alone, even for her daily safari to the kitchen to make cookies for Craig. Then she brought cat and bird-cage with her.

In a curious way, Craig found himself fascinated by his mother-in-law. She made nothing whatsoever of her visits with Maybelle to the movies, but she looked forward to her Saturday afternoons with Craig with fierce intensity. She would plan a whole week on what to wear, and pointedly refrain from seeing any especially choice picture with Maybelle. She held tightly to Craig's hand during the tense portions of the films, and laughed with childish delight at the pratfalls, and was especially fond of Westerns. Indians and a running fight with a stage-coach made her bounce up and down with excitement.

Afterward, Craig always took her to the Greek ice-cream parlour down the street from the theatre, where she gorged herself on banana splits or chocolate sundaes. But she always ate with great decorum, with only a suspicion of whipped cream or chocolate syrup clinging to her chin. After the treat at the ice-cream parlour, they would gravely stroll, with Mama Grimes stopping excitedly before shop windows, or accompanying Craig on any small commissions he might be performing for himself or Maybelle. When she met people she knew, they would pause briefly to exchange greetings, and it was nearly always: 'How do, Mrs. Grimes? How are you feeling?' And Mama Grimes would reply: 'I'm feelin' just fine. Do you know my son-in-law, Mr. Craig Price, who's doin' so well at my husband's mill?'

People said that this young fellow, Price, couldn't be nicer to the old lady even if she was his own mother, and she didn't seem crazy at all, no matter what people said about why they sent her away. Why, she talked to me just as human as I'm talkin' to you. And this boy, Price, he never seemed to be drunk in the roadhouses or steppin' out on his wife like so many men that married money did. He tends to his business and pays his bills, and ain't too proud to take his old mother-in-law out to the movies and shoppin' and all. Why, that Harry of mine, he won't even speak to my mother, and we been livin' in the same house with her for twenty-three years.

30

THE *ménage à trois* had settled into a bearable routine. Maybelle and Craig almost never went out at night, because they were afraid to leave Mama Grimes at home. The sameness of their patterned existence caused the months to flee. It was late September, now, six months since they had taken the old lady from the mental hospital. Apart from her incontinence, and an occasional flight of fancy, she appeared largely normal. A husky sleeping pill generally got her through the night, and although she had frequent nightmares which caused her to mumble and occasionally to scream, she seldom woke.

Her fondness for Craig increased and he thought with assurance that it would be just a few more months, now, before he got Irma Grimes to sign over her stock to her daughter. Then he, Craig Price, would be over twenty-one and free to walk down to the bank one day with a couple of very important pieces of paper, correctly signed and notarized, in his hand. He would stop at the Cadillac showroom on his way back from the bank, and he would drive that Cadillac, a few days later, over to Red Forney's house so that he could tell Libby she had a job when she graduated from high school in the spring. Craig mused often as to just how much he would pay Miss Mildred when he retired her, and he thought with pleasure how happy Red would be when Craig told him about his new job as foreman of the spinning room. . . .

It was a warm Sunday afternoon when Mr. McMullen drove up to the house in his Packard. The banker rang the bell and was met by Craig, who was wearing a flannel shirt and an old pair of dungaree pants.

'I hope I'm not intruding or anything,' Mr. McMullen said. 'I er—ah was just driving by, hum, and I thought I'd stop off and pay my respects to Mrs. Grimes, that's if she is hum, well enough.'

'Come right in, Mr. McMullen,' Craig said. He gestured apologetically at his clothes. 'You'll have to excuse the way I look, it being Sunday and all, but Mama Grimes and I have been trying to do something with the rose garden for next year and I'm afraid I'm not very clean. You come right in and sit down. Would you like a cup of coffee?'

Mr. McMullen allowed that he would love a cup of coffee.

'Well, Maybelle's gone off some place or other, but I'll get my mother-in-law to fix us some coffee and stuff. Excuse me just a minute while I go find her. There's the Sunday paper and the *Saturday Evening Post* if you haven't seen it. I think there's a new *Life* magazine, too. Excuse me a moment.' He went off, calling: 'Mama Grimes! Mama Grimes!'

Mr. McMullen looked around him at John Grimes's happy red room. He remembered it well from the old days, when John had that nigger all dressed up like George Washington, and there was always plenty to drink after Mrs. Grimes left the room. The room looked a little too red without that nigger. But Mr. McMullen noticed that it was extremely well kept, with flowers in vases, the furniture dusted, the floor around the carpet edges shining with wax, the brass dog-irons in the fireplace burnished, and the ashtrays clean. Mr. McMullen shook his head approvingly. The young Prices kept themselves so much to themselves that he hadn't known quite what to expect. That was quite a strange boy—man, that young Price—Mr. McMullen thought. Does his work, stays out of trouble, and he or somebody else keeps a nice house. And I know for certain he hasn't touched a cent of the old woman's money since they got her out of that nuthouse we put her in. For a long time I thought he was maybe trying to pull a fast one but I guess he's just a good boy. I wonder what she's like since we put her away?

Craig had dashed upstairs and held a hurried conference with his mother-in-law.

'Mama,' he said. 'You remember Mr. McMullen, the bank president? He stopped off to say hello. He's downstairs and Maybelle's gone off some place with the car. Would you serve him some coffee for me—some coffee and maybe some of those brownies—and just sort of talk to him for a minute? It's real important to me, Mama.'

'You know I don't like him, Craig, I never did, all stuffed up with his own importance. Makin' me sign this and sign that and all, just like he owned it. I never did like him even when Mr. Grimes had him come a-callin' to the house.'

'Please, Mama,' Craig said. 'This is important to me. We do some business together and the only way I'll ever get rid of him is to be nice to him. And we want to get rid of the bank, don't we? We don't want the bank making us sign things and sending us off to other places, do we? Please, Mama, be nice to Mr. McMullen for just a minute.'

'All right,' Irma Grimes smiled at Craig. 'If you say so, son. But I don't look so good in this dress. Better change.'

'That's all right. I told him we'd been working in the garden, just trying to explain away how bad I look. You look fine.'

'No, I don't. You help me out of this dress and get me that grey crêpe-de-Chine that you like, out of the closet. I guess it's all right for you to see me in my shimmy.' Mrs. Grimes almost blushed. 'You're in the family now. That's right. Now button me up the back. You go down to the kitchen and start to heat the coffee and I'll come down the back stairs and bring it out.'

'You'll be real careful, Mama? About not spilling the coffee, I mean?'

'Don't tell your grandmammy how to lap ashes,' Mama Grimes said with a stern note of reproof in her voice. 'You go start the coffee while I do somethin' with my hair.'

Craig raced downstairs and put the percolator on to boil, got out some brownies of Mama Grimes's confection and arranged them on a silver tray. Oh God, he thought, don't let her fall flat and throw the whole mess in old McMullen's face. Then he went back to see the banker, who was leafing though a *Life*. Mr. McMullen looked up.

'Sorry to keep you waiting, Mr. McMullen, but you know how ladies are. Especially old ladies.' He grinned. 'Mama Grimes said she wouldn't dream of coming down to see you in her gardening clothes. She has to primp a little first.' Craig sat down in Maybelle's chair.

Mr. McMullen leaned close, and dropped his voice.

'Before she comes, tell me, Craig. Is she . . . is she er—hah you-know, hum?'

'Do you mean crazy?' Craig shook his head gravely. 'I'll let you be the judge. According to what the doctor told me, when we went to get her, she's as fine as can be. Remember, Mr. McMullen, when the crash came and everything turned upside down—well, remember that a whole lot of people got very upset. You remember Jesse Hutton, don't you, at the Cotton and Corn across the street? There never was a finer man than Jesse Hutton, my father used to say.'

Mr. McMullen frowned at the memory of Jesse Hutton.

'You couldn't say he was typical of the banking business,' he said. 'Maybe his books were a little messed up and when the bank failed he blamed himself. He didn't have to go so far as to cut his throat. I didn't cut *my* throat. John Grimes didn't cut *his* throat.'

'Some people are just stronger than other people,' Craig replied. 'You're one of the strong ones. But I guess, or so the doctor said, that Mr. Grimes's death and the crash and the depression all coming at once made Mrs. Grimes a little nervous at the time. You were right to put her in the hospital. But Maybelle thought that she didn't need to stay there any more, if she was well, and there was a . . .' Craig coughed delicately.

'Man around the house?' Mr. McMullen finished the sentence. 'I think you may be right. Every house needs a man around it. Women . . .' he let his voice trail.

'Here comes Mrs. Grimes,' Craig said. Mr. McMullen got up. He harked at the sound of approaching footsteps as if he were waiting a wild beast. What he saw was a grey-haired lady in a grey crêpe-de-Chine dress, her hair neatly combed, carrying a tray containing a small coffee pot, two cups and saucers, and a dish of cookies.

'Let me take the tray, Mama.' Craig said, and swiftly relieved her of the burden. He set the tray down on a coffee table, and looked at the old lady with pride.

'You remember Mr. McMullen from the bank, don't you, Mama? He just stopped by to say hello.'

Irma Grimes extended her hand as if she almost expected Mr. McMullen to kiss it. He took it and then dropped it.

'Please sit down, gentlemen,' she said, with dignity. 'I will pour the coffee, Craig, and then I'll leave you-all to talk. My husband always said that a good wife knew when to leave when two gentlemen were talkin'. How are you keepin', Mr. McMullen?' she said, bending over the coffee tray. 'Sugar? Cream?'

'Two lumps,' Mr. McMullen said. 'No cream, please. I'm

doing as well as could be expected, what with age and business. I must say, Mrs. Grimes, you are looking wonderful.' Mr. McMullen's mouth looked as if it was about to say something like: 'And I wouldn't have believed it on a stack of Bibles if I hadn't seen it.' Instead he said: 'It's real nice to see you looking so well.'

'Thank you, Mr. McMullen. Please do have one of these brownies. Craig just loves them, don't you, Craig?' She beamed.

'Nobody makes them any better,' Craig said. 'I just can't keep her out of the kitchen. I'm getting fat off her cooking.'

Mr. McMullen twinkled ponderously.

'And just what do you think of this new son-in-law of yours?' he said with heavy jocosity. 'Stealing away your girl kind of behind your back?'

'I couldn't have done better if I'd picked him myself,' Irma Grimes said staunchly. 'Craig and me, we make out real good. You-all please excuse me now. Maybelle left me a million things to do. I declare, that child . . . If it wasn't for Craig . . . It's real nice to see you again, Mr. McMullen,' she said, and gave him her hand again. 'Please give my regards to your wife and please come to call again soon, hear?' She swept slowly, with great dignity, from the room.

'Well I will just be a dirty son-of-a-bitch,' Mr. McMullen forget his banker's dignity for a moment. 'She's saner than both of us. I don't know what I expected but damned if she don't look better than she has in twenty years.' He waggled his head. 'And the night I took her up to Greensboro, she . . . I don't understand it. I don't. I don't understand it.'

Thank God you don't understand it, Craig thought. By God, wasn't the old lady a wonder? No grand duchess ever made a better entrance or departure. Good old Mama.

Craig got up and reached for the banker's cup.

'Another cup of coffee?'

'No, thanks. I got to go myself. I just stopped by for a minute. Tell your wife I'm sorry I missed her. And, Craig?'

'Yes, sir?'

'I want you to know I think you're doing a very fine thing. A very fine thing, my boy. Not every man would take their mother-in-law out of a mental hospital and bring her home to live—not if she could afford to pay her way in one of those places that make a business out of looking after old ladies. An older person in the house isn't easy.'

'I know, sir,' Craig said, modestly. 'But she's old and all she's got is Maybelle and now me, and we didn't want her to end her days in a—a place. You understand that, don't you? Especially since she's not sick any more.'

'I understand, my boy, I do indeed,' Mr. McMullen said solemnly. 'And I honour you for it. I've known all along that you had good stuff in you. I just didn't know how much until recently. I'll say good-bye now. Give my best to your pretty wife.'

Craig showed him to the door. 'Yes, sir,' he said. 'Thank you for dropping in. We live sort of simple around here, but you're always welcome. Please come back again soon. Good-bye, Mr. McMullen.'

He waved as the banker's car went out the drive. Then he went back to the bottle's secret hiding-place and took a long swig, straight out of the neck.

'Jesus,' he said aloud. 'That was a close one. Just suppose she'd picked this time to have a fit?'

A certain extra force, practised sometime by children and people of occasional mental imbalance, got Irma Grimes through the ordeal with the banker. She would have recognized that voice anywhere. She forced herself to remember him as Mr. McMullen, banker, not the man with the unseen face, the remembered voice. She forced herself to remember that Craig had asked her to behave herself in front of the banker. She had clenched her mental teeth, closed her mental fists, straightened her mental spine into one burning thought: don't spill the coffee on the banker because it will hurt Craig, the Craig who brought her presents, who took her to the movies, who always kissed her good night, and stood between her and the threatening faceless men who lived in the dark. As long as Craig was there nobody would hurt her, and nobody would take her away to places that had bars, where they locked you in at night, where you couldn't cook in the kitchen because of the rule against matches, even if they would let you in the kitchen which they wouldn't. Don't spill the coffee, don't embarrass Craig, she had thought, and then she had covered her swift panic with an actress's steely determination. She made it to her room before she collapsed. Craig wouldn't want me to fall down in front of his friend, she had thought, because it might hurt his business. Then she fell backward upon the bed, as the voice reached its dark hooked hands towards her throat.

'Where's Mama?' Maybelle asked, when she came in a few minutes after Mr. McMullen had left. Craig laughed.

'Don't you worry your head about Mama. She was the greatest testimony to sanity I ever saw in my life. Old Dock was flabbergasted. Hickory and Dickory will be too, when he tells them tomorrow. Mama came downstairs looking like the Queen of Rumania. She served coffee and cakes to McMullen like some duchess or other, and I swear she made an exit out of the living-room like she was going off to be president of the D.A.R. If we ever need a witness to Mama's sanity, when we get around to this business of signing the papers, McMullen is our best bet. Mama did just fine, just dandy. We sure don't have to worry about Mama.'

'Don't we?' Maybelle's voice edged. 'Well, I do. I still say she's not fit to be loose, Craig. I wish we'd never taken her out of the asylum.'

'For Christ's sake, quit calling it an asylum, Maybelle! Hospital, hospital, *hospital*! She was in a hospital!'

'All right, hospital. When are you going to work on her to sign her stock over to me? You know she doesn't care an awful lot about me. She'd rather do it for you—to you, I mean.'

'I've told you a thousand times I don't want her to make over her stock to me. It's not natural, it'll attract attention, it's not right! If she makes it over to you and then you let me run it, that's a different matter. She can even think she's signing it over to me, if she wants to, but legally it has to be made out in your name.'

'Oh, all right, all right,' Maybelle said, wearily. 'Anything you want. Just get me a drink and then I'll go up and put your rich girl friend to bed.'

The kitten cried, and cried again.

'That goddamned cat,' Maybelle said. 'You and your presents. I know, I know, I was in favour of it. *And* the canary bird. At least the damn' bird is quiet. It hasn't sung a note since it came.'

'Well, Mama Grimes likes them both, and it makes it easier on you, having her in the house.'

The kitten yowled.

Maybelle got up.

'I guess I might as well see what's what. I tell you one thing, Craig. Some day I'll have me a house without cats *or* parents. Some day.'

She walked out of the room and up the stairs. The kitten's cry and Maybelle's scream mingled.

Craig bounded up the stairs. Maybelle was standing in front of the bed, pointing at the rigid figure of her mother. The topaz cat was crouched on Irma Grimes's breast, head down, rump up, tail swishing. It cried monotonously, digging its fore-claws into the stuff on Irma Grimes's frock.

'Look—look at her face!' Maybelle said, pointing with her left hand, the back of her right hand protecting her opened mouth. 'Look at her face!'

'Get on the phone!' Craig said. 'Go downstairs and get on the phone for the doctor! Hurry!'

He reached over and made a motion to remove the cat. It spat and struck at him with its paw. Craig seized it by the loose skin of its back and flung it crashingly into a corner. It mewed feebly and then was still.

Irma Grimes's face was cyanosed, purple-swollen to a third-again its normal size. Her eyes were open, staring. Her teeth were clenched, her nostrils flared. She lay as stiffly, as rigidly, as if she had been stretched. Saliva stood in foamy flecks on her lips, and some of the moisture had dripped down her chin. Craig looked desperately around him. Something he had read or heard, something about artificial respiration, he discarded, and then remembered something else about people swallowing their own tongues. He tried to move Irma Grimes's clenched jaws and could not.

'Maybelle!' He shouted at the top of his lungs. 'Maybelle, bring me a table knife!'

'She had a convulsion of some sort,' the doctor said. 'I couldn't say what caused it. She swallowed her tongue and choked to death. Did she have any sort of shock or anything like that?'

Maybelle looked at Craig.

He shook his head.

'Not that I know of. It was a very quiet afternoon. Nothing happened except that Mr. McMullen, you know, the banker-McMullen, a friend of the family, dropped in. My wife was out, and Mrs. Grimes made us a cup of coffee. Then she went upstairs. She seemed fine. I tried, I tried, Doctor, to prise her mouth open with a knife, but I guess she was already dead. How long does it take to choke to death?'

'Not long,' the doctor said. 'Not very long.' He looked at Craig. 'Don't I know you?' He answered himself. 'Sure I do. Price. You were the boy with the busted head, from an automobile accident. And you would be Mrs. Price, who lost the . . . I was intern on the emergency that night. Name's Damon. I've been taking Dr. McGowan's calls this week-end. Nice neat scar you've got there, Price. Where's the phone? I have to call the coroner.'

'Down there, at the foot of the stairs, Dr. Damon,' Craig said. He looked at the body on the bed, then he looked at Maybelle. They could hear Dr. Damon dialling, the buzz of his voice as he gave names and address.

Maybelle's voice was low, steady. Her eyes held more cold knowledge than pain.

'Well,' she said. 'You've finally got your goddamned mill.'

350

BOOK THREE

BOOK THREE

1

'EXCITED?' Craig said, as they settled back in their seats.

'Terribly. I go all fluttery just getting on a plane. Especially a big four-motored one with a foreign language at the other end of the line.'

'You look excited. You look about fourteen years old, all dressed up in grown folks' clothes. You look beautiful. That summer tan against that white sharkskin suit. I didn't get any tan this summer. I'm as pale as your suit. We'll remedy that in Cuba. That August Cuban sun, boy. Except you never feel sticky hot in Cuba like you feel in New York. You can sweat rivers and still feel cool.'

Susan Strong did look beautiful. The smooth honey of her tan lightened the cornflower eyes and accented the vivid red slash of lips, and her cheeks had flushed. Her brown hair was touched with golden points from the sun, and she wore her hair short and curly. A blue silk blouse almost exactly duplicated the blue of her eyes. And she had the long full body to make a severe suit seem a little extra-sexy.

'Hold my hand,' she said, as the pilot revved the motors prior to take-off.

'Scared?' Craig smiled at her, hiding her hand in both of his.

'Of course not. I just like to hold your hand. This is an excuse. Tell me, do I have to speak Spanish in Cuba?'

'Of course not. Not around Havana. All the middle-class people speak English, and the rich folks speak French. Havana's got awfully Frenchified in the last few years. I'll speak some Spanish, though, because I like the sound of it.'

'I'm glad you can speak it. Mine was the product of a few forgotten courses in school and a couple of trips to Mexico. I don't speak anything very well. That's why I am sort of fascinated with the way you switch your conversation from semi-illiterate to an almost-written prose.'

'You can get by with me in Spanish on one short declarative sentence. "*Te quiero*." I love you. And maybe "*sí*". Never say *No*. Always say *Yes*, except if I should ever ask you to go away, or if you want me to go away. Then say "*No*!"'

'*Sí, señor*,' Sue said, releasing his hand. 'The sign says we can smoke now. What's the first thing we'll do in Havana?'

Craig grinned lewdly. Susan blushed, and struck lightly at his hand.

'I was serious. What'll we do? I want to know more about you. This will be the first time, do you realize it, that I've seen you

353

truly outside your New York self? Outside of restaurants where everybody knows you? Away from business friends? The only place I really know anything about you at all is my apartment. So what'll we do?'

'We'll have fun. We'll relax. We'll let one thing flow into another. We will make few plans and see few of any people of any importance. That suit you?'

'Right down to the bone. But business?'

'Three phone calls, one lunch date—without you—and three cocktails while you get your hair done some afternoon. Actually I could have fixed it all by phone, or have made the people come to New York. All I really wanted was an excuse to get you out of town. Satisfied?'

'Yes, sir,' Sue dipped her head. 'If you say so, sir. Just so long as it's fun.'

Havana did promise fun. The plane tilted, circling Rancho Boyeros Airport, the earth curving up almost bloody ochre, marked green-jungly by palm, the airport blinding white in the sun. Craig held Sue's hand again as the '*abroche su cinturón*' sign flashed on, and they levelled off to land. She pressed his fingers.

'I still get a big rear out of this *pueblo*,' he said. 'The first real vacation I ever had was here. I don't count all the early sea-going. But this was a vacation where you had enough money to stay in a decent hotel, and gamble at the Summer Casino. It was quite a few years before the war and Maybelle and I were having one of our rare streaks of getting on pretty good and business was just starting to bounce. We stayed in a little hotel close to the Presidential Palace. It was cheap and the bar was in the habit of buying a drink. You could see the curving sweep of the Malecón through the palms, and Sloppy Joe's was just up the street, and so was the Paddock, and you could hear the street-cars clanging by, and the blare of the street orchestras, and then there was the Floridita and the Zaragozana. There was the Havana Country Club and the Yacht Club, where some friends got us temporary membership. There was *Las Fritas* and later Matanzas and Varadero. I was just young enough still to be excited at the idea of travelling first-class. Also it was the first time Maybelle had ever been out of the country, and she was excited more than I was . . . I . . .' Craig paused, almost in an embarrassment of memory. He had spoken without thinking of Maybelle. Then he thought, the hell with it. No use trying to fight shy of mentioning Maybelle. Susan knows I'm married—has known from the first.

'Well, here we are. We'll buy us a watery tourist-bureau daiquiri while they go through the customs nonsense. Then we'll dash off to the Nacional. This is going to be real good, honey. I feel about twenty years younger already.'

Craig leaned back in the Packard limousine. This was his second trip to Havana in three months. God, but how the town

354

had changed in twenty years. Not only counting dictators. Neon lights everywhere, now, and enormous great Cadillacs everywhere, even a velvet rope at the Floridita, from which Constante was for ever gone. The beggars no longer clutched at you from the sidewalks, and there was air-conditioning everywhere. Even Marina's gracious old cat-house had closed its old-city head-quarters, and where had Chori and Alberto and Clara gone to, from that joint in *Las Fritas* where Chori played the *timbales* and Clara and Alberto danced a rumba—the real, old, voodoo rumba, in which shoeing the mare was simple jungle sex, with Clara arching her back and opening her legs as she lay on the floor . . . where had they *gone*?

'Clara's dressing-room was also the men's room,' Craig said to Sue, as they drove into town through the fleshy green red-earthed countryside. 'I was drinking a lot of rum and bodily urgency finally made us quite good friends. She was medium brown, and very pretty, and Alberto was a thin black blade of fine gentleman. Clara was doing the rumba quite a piece before Arthur Murray got hold of it. The *Fritas*—the "fried", meaning hot-dogs-and-hamburger carny section—was considerably rougher in those days. You could get your head bashed very easily. But, like always, I seemed to fit into the seamier side of the *barrio*. You suppose there's something really coarse about me that makes the bums love me?'

'I love you, and I'm no bum,' Sue said. 'Then again maybe I am. And like you said, it takes two to know two . . .'

'I hadn't been to Africa or the East when I first came here,' Craig said, as they drove past the Cristal, jewelled among its lush trees, and later past Marina's new, but non-*simpatica* fancy house, past the enormous concentric circle of fountain which had been built with public funds and which was called, with Cuban tart humour, the *bidet* of the sister of a past president who had not become poor during his administration. The president had remained honest, in token, but sister had handled the slush-fund. Sternly, in a family way.

'I hadn't been to Africa or Hong Kong, then, but this town hit me like New Orleans. I knew I was home. Somehow the ripe smells are always the same in any tropical or semi-tropical town which remembers Africa's hot history still—or any of the Oriental sly pervasive influence. Ever been to Singapore?'

'I'm afraid not. Is there any place you haven't been?'

'Russia and Inner Mongolia. Unwant. No like. No reason, no desire. But when we do the town tonight, before we go down to Varadero tomorrow, you'll see what I mean by this special smell. It's very special and awful universal. Singapore smells like Savannah's coloured quarter. Babati or Dodoma in Tanganyika smell exactly like New Orleans's French quarter. The *village nègre* in Sidi bel Abbès smells like the poorer parts of Cuernavaca, and backstreet Havana is blood kin to the Asian slums of old Nairobi or the Kasbah in Algiers or the Medina in Tangier. It never fails to excite me.'

'You suppose it's the smell of age, of decaying older civilizations? Or what? Or just what you read into a lot of ancient stinks?'

'Maybe. Actual age, perhaps, but more of living people from an older time—the pre-pre-pre-television-aircraft era. People living as they lived when things were much simpler, but more violent, and you built a stout wall to protect your possessions, and masked your women with *yashmaks*, and built a castle on a hill so you could roll down rocks on your known enemies or unbidden strangers. An age when a man kept his intimate, personal life safe and solidly secret against suddenly brusque intrusion.'

'You have a tremendous thing about privacy, don't you?' She turned and looked at him seriously. 'Everything considered, including gags and double-negatives and a generally rude jeer at the world, always surrounded by a flock of people, you are the most passionately selfishly private person I think I ever knew. Everything's rough outside, and you're all walled up in your own Kasbah. If I knew you better, I'd say you've invented the false crude exterior so that the part of you I like best can't possibly be bruised by handling. A stout rough cage for a very delicate bird, so to speak.'

'Shush. I'm a lover and a fighter and a wild-horse rider, and a right fair windmill hand.' His voice had slipped into a drawl. 'That's Taixus talk, ma'am.' The voice changed again. 'I think you may be right. You remember Lonesome Craig Price, the boy-type mystery man? I haven't changed much. Lonesome Craig still rides tall in the saddle on the lone cliché.'

They drove along the lovely palm-fringed concrete curve of the Malecón, looking seaward to the grim old Morro, where the opponents of the *status quo* used to be eased gently down the chutes for the special delectation of the waiting sharks. Now they simply shot them. Across the bay was Guanabacoa ...

'Smell ...' Craig mused. 'All the flowers, all the bougainvillea, all the frangipani, all the night-blooming whatever can't kill the smell I mean. It is that same fine smell of scabbing ancient plaster sodden by urine over the ages, a sour smell, the smell of heat and dampness, of charcoal fires and donkey droppings, of dust and open gutters and curry powder and rotting vegetation, of moulding refuse and plants so brutally lush they ought to be called animals. I wonder why that smell hit me so hard the first time in Charleston, next in Savannah, next in New Orleans, then around the world of Africa and its neighbour, Southern Europe. Sicily and Sevilla are sisters under the skin. God, I should have been an early Phoenician ...'

'Well, here we are,' as the car drew up to the Nacional. 'A noble establishment, with a noble bar, by the noble pool. A little Israel. All the Miami Americans refugee here. All the Cubans refugee to Miami. They even go there to shop. What a wondrous thing is reciprocal trade abetted by cheap air-fare. This has a smell, too. A stink of riches. I used to look at it and wonder if I could ever afford it. Turns out I can. They bow at me now.'

Sue turned to look at him, just before they started to alight.

'You ever, ever going to get over that little boy hunger complex?'

Craig grinned. He extended an arm to hand her down.

'Sure. Just as soon as we've had a swim and a drink and changed, we're going to yell for the car and go downtown to the Floridita. There, my good woman, I can assure you we will conquer the hunger complex. I intend to gain ten pounds this week, on a steady diet of nothing but Morro crab, avocados, and pompano, ably bulwarked by *paella*, *zarzuela* and *arroz Cubana*.'

'Greedy gut,' Sue said as they walked into the vast cool lobby. 'Do we register?'

Craig cocked an eyebrow. He looked shocked. 'Register? *Register?* Of course not. Do you think we're peasants? I keep a suite here, year round.'

'Oh,' Sue said. It was a very eloquent 'Oh.'

'It's altogether too plush for me, *guapa*,' Craig said later. 'The whole town. The whole island. All the *Vedado*. That damned great building with the fancy-schmancy bar on top. The TV studios. All the French restaurants. The velvet rope. The no beggars. The air-conditioning . . .' He swept a hand at the entirely elegant room in the Floridita, the tensely hovering waiters and captains. 'We might as well be in the Colony or Twenty-One.'

'*I* like it,' Sue said. 'And I am mad for this *cangrejo moro*, it says here on the menu. Also I like the drinks and the service and especially I love that gorgeous suite at the hotel. I think I shall accumulate a little extra all-over colour on the front porch. You said you kept it, the suite I mean, all the year round. Why?'

'I like to feel secure,' Craig replied. 'Also it's deductible. Also you'll accumulate your extra colour at Varadero. Maybe the Kawama hasn't changed too much.'

'Kawama? You mentioned it before. Tell.'

'Little club. Main building like its name—turtle. Wonderful little *casetas* scattered all around. Room service from the main club, but where everything else is concerned, you're on a honeymoon. And that's what I intend this trip to be. Present sentimental intentions apart, I want to get out of this transplanted Miami and go some place where the shuffling land-crabs and the rustling palm-trees understand me. My God, this restaurant in the old days . . .'

2

HEMINGWAY, then, would have been sitting, reading his *Diario* in the corner nearest the bar, behind a potted palm, on the banquette against the wall, his spectacles perched on the end of his nose, his hair just beginning to grizzle. Nobody asked him for any autographs. They knew who he was but the tourist flood had not then begun, and a man could read his paper and drink a daiquiri in public privacy. It was understood, via Constante, the inventor of the perfected frozen daiquiri, that nobody bothered the *gran maestro*, who was just one other member of the club. The tourist went to Sloppy Joe's or the Paddock. The old pros and wishful young ones came to the Floridita.

Constante, grey-haired, thin, elegantly grave but with a face-lighting smile of honest happiness, would look up from polishing a glass. He owned the restaurant, he owned the hotel which housed it, but wore a white barman's jacket. He had started from nowhere in a mine in Oriente and he had begun the bar which became a restaurant which became a hotel which became a gold mine, and he still thought, with harsh Basque practicality, that a bartender's place was behind a bar. Always the same salutation, with a grave dip of the grey head.

'*Buenos días, Señor Price. Como siempre, bienvenido. Usual?*'

'*Sí, por favor, mi maestro.*' Shy smile of acknowledgment. He was a slight man, but his hands were muscled as a strong man's arms are thewed. He would gravely—always gravely—cut a grape-fruit in two, take it in his hand and give a mighty squeeze, forcing every drop of juice from the fruit. Constante never allowed an assistant to make the *ideal*. He invented it; the patent was his. So was the *fuerza*—the force.

The strained grape-fruit juice went into a shaker, together with gin and an extra something of his own devising, and was poured foaming, with a sure flourish of the wrist, foaming into champagne glasses. On the bottom two flat almonds rested. Constante would bow, and then pour himself a half-glass.

'*Salud señor. Pesetas y amor mucho tiempo para gastarlos. Y buen apetito, también.*'

'*Igualmente señor. Muchos años. Y las tapas son magníficas, como siempre.*'

By then a trap of *tapas*—hors d'oeuvres—would have arrived, and it was entirely possible to make a full meal on those *tapas*—*salchichones, camerones, butifarra, anchoa*, three kinds of *queso, jamon duro, aceitunas, huevos duros.* . . .

'*La vuelta por favor, señor.*' The round trip.

'*Pues sí señor.*' Another expulsion of the juicy vitals of the grape-fruit.

'God,' Craig said. 'You never got drunk. You couldn't get drunk. You sat and listened to a three-piece trio, two guitars, and maracas, that strolled in from the street—we were open to the street then—you sat and drank *ideales* and ate the *tapas*—the anchovies and hard ham and shrimps and olives and cheese and hard-boiled eggs—and listened to the music and the gossip and the latest joke against the current government. The *lotería* boys would drift in with the newest hot numbers in the *bolita* and you would buy something just on a hunch.

'I forget what number the spider represents—thirty-eight or thirty-nine, I think. You know all the numbers have images—the dead is one number, even a ladies' unmentionable indisposition is another, so if you collect a funeral or the curse you play the unhappy hunch. This was the illegal lottery, like the numbers racket, played daily.

'Well, I found a spider in my shoe that morning so I played the *araña*, on a hunch. The old spider hit, at thirty to one, or something, and my last ten bucks suddenly had fresh dignity. It was a very nice day. I took the lot out to the Summer Casino and toyed with the freckled cubes a bit and went up against the blackjack, and I was on fire. I paid for the whole trip that day. Paying for the whole trip was important. It was kind of *my* money, and had nothing to do with Maybelle or that bloody mill.'

Somehow he had straggled into the murky grotto on the way to Marianao, the one next to the shooting-gallery, and there was a little band going. The leader's name was Caralinda—'Prettyface' —and he played a fine guitar. Chori, the drummer, touched his drums with a willow withe he cut on his way to work. Chori looked like an unwashed bear, wore the same shirt for a week, was constantly high on marijuana, and drank anything alcoholic anybody would buy him. Caralinda was uglier than Chori. Clara and Alberto danced the rude chicken-goat voodoo rumba when the mood struck them, and there was a charming, drunken Negro, a female pickpocket black as the sins she had forgotten, with her hair in pepper-corns, whom everyone called 'Sheerly Templay' or *Shirley Temple*. This particular Shirley Temple spent half her life in jail, and the other half in Chori's. They were altogether quite wonderful friends, and the blackest Congo jungle opened and smothered you in warm wet liana-creepered sensual mystery when Chori, under the influence of the newest *tu-bae*, deserted his *timbales* and began to pound the walls as a drum when '*Elube Chango*' started, and all the old bad snake gods stirred and began to crawl.

'*Qué quieres tomar, tú?*' Craig would ask Chori, when the formal time came to buy the band a drink.

'*Usual. Un tu-bae.*'

'*Un tu-bae? Cual es un tu-bae?*'

'*Es del beisbol. Sabes, hombre, los baises, los tres baises, cuando*

el golpeador—el batter—ha golpeado un golpe para dos baises.
Un two-bais heet. Pues, posen, un tu-bae es una copita de ron malo
sin Coca-Cola. Hombre, tú eres analfabético!'

'What's he talking about?' Maybelle had said suspiciously.
'And why do you talk to these dirty niggers in this filthy place
anyhow? And dancing with that black woman!'

'I like 'em,' Craig said gently. 'Chori was just saying that he
wanted a two-base hit. It's slang for baseball. It means he wanted
a straight shot—from the translation, a straight slap of bad rum
without Coca-Cola.'

'It was a lot of fun,' Craig told Sue, as they drank their coffee.
'For me, but not for Maybelle. She took it as a personal affront
that a lot of people in Cuba spoke Spanish. I was able to butch
along in my high-school Spanish, but she seemed to think that
they had no business to be black or brown, and that the Chinese-
Cubanos should have stayed in China, and that finally, more
people ought to speak English. Most of the locals were just a
touch too *colorado maduro* for Maybelle. She came from that
deep old Sooth.

'What Maybelle liked was the Havana-Biltmore Yacht Club,
where all the nice folks went for a swim and drinks and lunch
and a *bocadillo*—a sandwich—which was named for its inventor,
Elena Russ, and which was composed of turkey, ham and jam.
She liked the Country Club even better, because that's where the
nicest, stuffiest folks went. No matter. How did you like the
cream-cheese with the fresh coconut conserve?'

'Yummy,' Sue said. 'God, you talk a lot. When you're not
eating or the other thing.'

'You ain't heard nothing yet,' Craig said cheerfully. 'Wait'll we
get to Varadero. Then we'll really make some hole.'

'Are you being rude?'

'Dirty-minded girl. I was talking oil talk. Making hole is
digging deep, to make progress.'

They went to Templete, which used to be a reasonably dingy
waterfront café with the sidewalk beggars ever at you, and the
nine-o'clock gun firing practically beside your table, and now it
was all men's-room bright and painfully clean. Beggars were
disallowed and the food had suffered from tourist-blight.

'I'm not taking a chance on my other hang-outs,' Craig said.
'I couldn't stand it if La Perla and Los Tres Hermanos have
cleaned themselves up. I used to drink beer with the waterfront
bums in those joints, and for twenty-five cents you could get a
miraculous plate of black beans and rice, with one Hatuey beer
included. Let's don't press our luck. Let's whip down to Varadero
tomorrow, and see if there's one illusion left in this nasty, naughty
over-chrome-finished world.'

They caught the Varadero plane from the military airfield, and, thank God, the Kawama was still there, although there was an enormous hotel in Varadero proper, and a lot of new sort of Americano motel-type buildings scattered all along the strand. But the beach-sand was still brilliant white and sugar-soft, and the wind joked with the rattling dry fronds of the palms, and the palm-trunks' beards still shivered in the ocean breeze, and the waters were still smoothly opalescent, with the bright fishes darting.

'I love this place, darling,' Sue said, when they went to the little *caseta* with the tiny screened lanai. 'Could we stay a week, maybe?'

'Sure,' Craig replied. 'Why not? Technically I'm down here on business, anyhow, that bank thing.'

'What does your wi—' Sue stopped.

'I'm away a lot.' Craig bit the words short. 'I can always extend a leave. And anyhow I get the progress reports on what's cooking. And my *wife*, as you almost started to say, knows about the demands of my work.' His face was suddenly cold. His former, easy reference to Maybelle chilled under the word 'wife'.

'Isn't that a lovely sky?' he said. 'Let's do a little Gene Austin. Nothing but blue skies from now on.' His voice rasped.

'Look, sweetie,' Sue said. 'We are practically strangers. Don't get mad at me for asking things. Would it bore you terribly if we devoted a little time to me finding out more about you? That's twice I've said it. Seriously, darling, I feel I know you so well in a way, and don't know anything about you at all in another.'

'First,' Craig said, and kissed her lightly, 'let's go swimming and then we can turn on the inquisition. Okay?'

'Yas*suh*, boss,' Susan said. '*Po' favo*'.'

3

'SHE probably read that take-me-now line in a book somewhere,' Craig told Susan. 'Actually she was a virgin. Poor, sad, not very bright little kid, all alone in a big house and only a lousy little mill to turn to.'

'It *was* a lousy little mill,' Craig said, 'and the lousy little mill had a lousy little mortgage on it, still. But its beat-up looms worked, when they weren't being repaired. And of course, when Maybelle got pregnant, something had to be done, and marriage seemed the likeliest answer.

'Looking at myself honestly,' Craig said to Sue, as they sat in the sun-soaked patio at Kawama, 'I am afraid I made a definite planned play for Maybelle. It wasn't hard, God knows, because I was young and randy as a goat, and she was quite pretty in addition to being over-sexed. But I think I would have been able to find more attractive quarry if it hadn't been that thing about the house and the mill in the background. I will not say my sentimental thoughts were unmixed with practicality—spindles and cotton and what might be done with a going concern with a big house laid on and an income assured.'

'Did you ever love her—*like* her even—at all?'

'No, not to love. Yes, to like, and yes to feel sorry for. She was there, and she was lonely, and her mother was clapped off in a madhouse, and she was a nice girl, if a trifle hot in the pants, and I had liked her father very much. We fell into bed as naturally as two lonely strangers strike up a conversation in a bar. And I had that old feeling about hell, if it isn't me, it'll be somebody else, and I was not a particularly nice young man at that time. I was not looking for Juliet, nor a world well lost for etcetera. I was on the make for anything, but I did *not* impregnate the lady on purpose..I ask you to believe that. But I must also confess I was not astonished when Maybelle gave me the last word, and asked me what I proposed to do about it.

'I believed her when she said she was pregnant, and that I was responsible. She was an ingenuously honest girl, and sincerely, I believe, in love with me. At least in a fleshly fashion. Her life, between the old man's sudden shuffle-off, and the old lady's craziness, had become a tangled skein, something like my own, and we were both orphaned strays. Loneliness is a dreadful thing, and so is working in a filling station, which is what I was doing at the time.

'I told her simply that I could barely afford to keep me and that a wife and child, at my tender age, was impossible economically.

' "There's the mill," she said. "You can always work there. They pay me a pretty good income now. Maybe with you working there we'd make more money. Anyhow we've got the house. We won't starve." '

'And so,' Craig said to Sue. 'I began my life of shame.

'Perhaps you never saw a mill town. Every time I am forced to take a train into New York from a week-end in Bucks County or any place else outside that thriving commercial leprosarium of ours, I look at those impossible dreary buildings, smoke-bleared by the passing freight-trains—those awful tawdry block-houses of dirty glass windows and ugly brick, which have a rusty sign saying the Some-Something Bolt and Valve Works, stretched like discarded shoe-boxes from Hoboken to Hell and back—and I wonder about who sits in the paper-dingy offices, figuring out consignments of things, and whether the poor bastards who lean over the machines have anything at all to say when they dash to the corner saloon for a beer when the whistle blows.'

Craig made his voice mince bitingly.

'You'd think they might say: "We turned out another five thousand gross of prefab toilets today. The foreman got his thumb stuck in the afterskinnis of the fregastis. We made more paper cartons out of acetate than we ever made out of paper. We are thinking of going into extra fittings for old-fashioned railroad brake-shoes. This year we tackle innersprings. We're rolling with the times—we won't call them brake-shoes any more. We'll call them slippers. We must be making money, because we are taking advertisements in all the better Republican-minded journals, and the boss is writing the copy himself."

'I don't think they say that at all. I think they say: "Y'think the Yanks win it again?" I think they say: "An' I told my old lady to shut up, or I'd belt her in the puss." I think they say: "Dunno what's wrong wit' de young kids. Dey got everything. I raise dat kid of mine like he gonna grow up to be Mickey Mantle, and arready he's two-time arready in de ju-ver-nile court." I think they think, but don't know how to say: "O my God, why have all the houses that live alongside railroads got to be painted cow-flop brown, and why do all restaurants have to be run by Greeks, and why don't the old lady cook something once in a while except goulash or sowbelly?" This, of course, would depend on the location.

'A milltown,' Craig said, 'is a milltown, is a milltown, and you need a Miltown, pillwise, even to think about what is a milltown. The filthy skeletons of machinery, the grimy prison aspect of the buildings, the blowing of the whistle, the locking of the gates, the inexorable punching of the clock, the sameness of the sameness, day after dismal day, the ... the terrifying idea, if the human factory-beasts have ideas, that for thirty unshaven years they have done the same thing, with minor variations, to the same material, the same grease-sweating machinery. Punch, cut, sew, weave, weld, tread the treadle, swing the crane, check the dial, watch the pump, feed the furnace, investigate the rattle, hear the doomsday thump, nerves tuned to the clatter ... Whether it's cotton or cars, people who work in factories ought to have a special place in the hereafter, for God knows, purgatory owes them a due bill against a fine hotel suite in Hell.

'When I wake up grinding my teeth at night I dream that I am a working-stiff in a factory—a brick-maker, or a flour-miller, a fashioner of pistons or nuts and bolts or valves or window sashes or portions vital to the growling guts of the automotive industry. Today I don't really blame the organizers, except when they try to organize me. Today I think Reuther has a point. Anybody who works an assembly-line—anybody who has to spend five or six days a week in any place which reduces man's rudimentary thought to taking something off a crawling gridded-metal snake and putting it on to another, anybody who spins his life away, anyone who always sows but never sees what he reaps, anyone who stands upon a permanent escalator—an escalator on which fear is the co-pilot . . . Jesus God. Somebody ought to pay them something extra in whisky or marijuana just to compensate for a life of demoniacally exquisite boredom, surrounded by flatulent noise and industrial stink. Out comes the Cadillac and all the man who puts the last bang on the fintail can think, when he sees the car he will never drive, on his private Sunday surrounded by weak beer, runny-nosed children and inferior baseball: "I hit dat car a real good bang in de ass." The joys of automatic transmission will never be his. His epitaph is: "I hit dat car a real good bang in de ass."

'A milltown,' Craig said, 'whether it's making paper out of pulp, or a fresh pulp out of old paper, stinks. When you take a noble fir to convert it into newsprint for the society columnists to befoul, the process stinks only slightly less than the finished product from the columnist. Coal is extensively used in heavy industry and smogs the air, and dingies the English sparrows. I have not, thank God, ever been down in a coal mine, but I have difficulty leashing my sanity when I invite the claustrophobia of an elevator or the controlled madness of a department store. I shudder to think of my reactions if I were forced to delve into the secret earth to rid it of its carbonized accumulation of detritus. I wouldn't mind, so much, taking the exhumation process a step further and converting the concupiscent anthracite into diamonds, especially if I could get some non-political Zulus to do the dirty work. Except for the fact that I basically dislike diamonds.

'Oil, I might say, is the only good thing that comes out of the earth, apart from fruit and flowers. You can send a rotary bit grease hunting, and only the steel, tortured into shape in Pittsburgh at the expense of God knows how many million tons of *coitus-interruptus* coal which was timidly practising to be a diamond, only the steel sees the inner secrets of the Jurassic substructure. Only the steel peers and probes, like an eyeglassed gynaecologist, into the womb of the world.

'And in all this stink and sweat and noise is one thing: Money.

'When you hit pay-sand—where the oil is—what you see in the microscope looks like rock-candy,' Craig said. 'Oil is a big rock-candy mountain. Built on fish and bugs and trees and sand. They rotted, honey, and the stinking sweat of their rottenness got to be part of the medium in which they smothered. And of the life within which we live and the death we die. Sweet to the sweet. Stink to the stinkers,' Craig sighed, mocking himself.

'God, how I wander on. We were talking about milltowns, and we wind up with Jurassic substructures and oil-bearing sands. But that oil is what makes the spindles bob, and what makes the bobbers spin, and what puts the pretty clothes on the pretty ladies, and what clothes their lovely legs with two-thread glamour, and hoists their tits in salute to the ladies' magazines, and makes possible the Paris fags that make the ladies' magazines possible, and what runs the pretty big-assed cars that use the lovely two-toned paints and . . . Back we go to cold and discomfort and the kind of glass windows on factories that seem to have had streaming noses blown on them.

'And I have not, as yet, let you into the house of the happy vegetable who works in factories, for this-much an hour. We must inspect a home, some time, after office hours of course, of Mr. Stefan Plinski, the economic baron's by-product. Perhaps we will skip this one. Stale grease and oil-paper offend me.

'Shall we go swimming, and pretend we're looking at tidelands, my darling? Or sunken treasure, or what?'

'Let's just go swimming and then come back and drip on the tiles, and pick the other half of the rum-blossom,' Sue said, pulling on a cap. 'I think you've depressed me enough for right now.'

4

'I MENTIONED before,' Craig sipped his third daiquiri, his body glistening with salt and sun, 'if you wanted to meet an original thief, I'm your boy. We went to Cheraw, S.C., and we got peace-adjudicated. We spent our honeymoon in a motel, much before the swimming-pool era. And then we went back to Kensington and broke the happy tidings to the trustees, who seemed something less than overjoyed to make my acquaintance. Apart from what I'd read, I didn't know a bobbin from a robin, when I turned up and asked the manager to find me a job as anything befitting the incipient boss's husband. He put me to work sorting papers, figuring that I would possibly fall into a loom and cost the company money if he put me out in the clicking-and-clacking part of the store. That was all right with me. Machines make me nervous.'

'They make me nervous, too. So does hunger. I'd like some lunch now,' Sue said. 'Let's not go in the dining-room. Let's have it out here in the sun. Could I have that lovely avocado stuffed with the crab again, pretty-please? And the same *arroz-con-pollo?*'

'We're in a rut,' Craig smiled. 'And for dessert we'll have cream cheese and coconut, and tonight we'll have the clams with the green sauce, and you'll have indigestion and throw up.'

'That's how I keep my figure. It's a kind of birth control. Pleasure without penalty . . .'

Craig beckoned the waiter. 'Two more daiquiris,' he said, 'and *almuerzo* same as usual.'

'I am not going to bore you,' he told Susan, as they tackled the crab-stuffed avocado, 'with a detailed account of my sordid rise

365

from ex-boss's daughter's husband to chairman of the board. But in my case it *was* penalty without much pleasure. Old John Grimes was smart. I think he had some ticking presentiment that he'd conk off in a hurry, and that neither his wife nor daughter would be capable of keeping the shop open and the weavers weaving. So the old boy set up a rough agreement with the bank to hang on to anything that might be left from a crash he was sure was coming, shaped to keep his only chick from bestowing the frayed patrimony on some strolling adventurer, until, at least, she came of age.'

'Like you?' The smile lacked merriment.

'Like me. Suspicion is not the word for what the trustees viewed me with. Hostility, certainly. But they couldn't refuse me a job . . . especially when Maybelle's condition was becoming apparently less and less delicate, more and more visually gross. They set me to work in that office job . . . One hundred whole dollars a month salary. Christ, I still shudder. Piles of paper, invoices, out-voices, consignments, salaries, piece-work time, wages-and-hours . . .' Craig burlesqued a shiver.

'I paid, my dear. I *paid*. Dives in Hell never paid a dearer price. Lazarus had more latitude with his leprosy. I *learned* that damned mill, from bottom to top. I *memorized* it. I listened to all the bitching from the labourers. I studied raw cotton supply against consumer demand for shoddy drawers. I went visiting back to the sharecrop cotton plantations, and talked to the Negroes about how much they owed the company store for sidemeat. And I watched the union organizers growing stronger and stronger and stronger. We had finally Castonia, N.C., as an object lesson.'

'Maybelle came twenty-one, and now she voted some stock for herself. In a couple of years I had become purchasing agent, and more or less was running the business. The bankers adored me, by now. They said what good luck it was that Miss Maybelle had married such a smart, hard-working young man, such a nice serious fellow, and what a pity it was their first child got killed in an accident. I had breasted the mediocre man's high tide of success. I was earning a whole fifty bucks a week. And then Maybelle's mama conveniently died.

'I must say this was considerably frustrating, since by dying the old girl wrecked a devious plot to con her into signing over her stock either to me or Maybelle, whichever seemed easier. But there I was, twenty-one years old, president of a whole great big textile plant. To say that my pantaloons failed to contain me would be one of the vaster understatements of all time. I now owned—or at least controlled—the keystone of what I planned on making into a very large arch indeed. Expansion was what I needed, and expand is what I did.' Craig grinned, almost sheepishly. 'Something had to give, because my britches wouldn't hold me any longer. It turned out that the ever-loving banks did most of the giving, with a little dishonest—if only slightly—aid and assistance from the boy tycoon.

'I had done a certain thing about a strike... We never had one. It never came off, and the Russians retired happy.' Craig grinned, sharkishly. 'I made a deal first, of course, with the head agitator, a gentleman named Kolinski. He was the friend of a friend. The friend was an athlete named Jimmy Wilbur, and he recommended me highly to Mr. Kolinski.

'Rayon was here, and nylon, and the other synthetics were already over the practical hill, and the silkworm crop was a source of trouble to the war-planning Japs, and I had always been a ladies' man. I kept thinking about secondary sexual characteristics and female vanity. In short, ladies' legs crying for beauty. The cellulose world was breathing hot upon us.

'The answer seemed to be a new mill which would devote itself to the new stuff. As president of this splendid plant, as both president and purchasing chief, I hit upon a rather unoriginal idea.

'I did it all very simply. I bought me a very large mill that was under the hungry hammer, and talked Maybelle into selling Pa Grimes's house for the necessary loot for the down payment.'

Craig's voice was dreamy.

'My, but we started little and meek, and everybody said I was nuts to go heavy into stockings in my small holdings. Stockings, I said, went on women's legs, and for every woman there were two legs, and the female population was rising. We would get to the other daily double, brassières, later, and eventually we would hit the buttock market, because each girl has two of each, crying for restraint, but right now let's get the stockings on the road, and while we wait for the right brand of nylon, leave us screw silk and concentrate on rayon, the poor man's thumbed nose at the silkworm. Let Cannon handle the towels, I said, but there is nothing wrong with a rayon shirt, a rayon dress, a rayon anything.

'This needed money. I found that, in moments of pregnancy, women used a popular cliché that they were eating for two. As president and general manager and purchasing agent, I found I could eat for two, as well. So I bought for two. I bought everything for two, and debited it to Grimes Mills, and siphoned off the extras to Price Mills. It was really disgustingly simple I had wonderful advice.'

'Why do you tell me all this really? I know the answer, and I find I don't like it.' Sue's face was displeased.

'I thought you wanted to know something of the manner of man with whom you're in Cuba, and with whom, I believe, in love.' Craig's voice was light. 'See me starkly for the black villain I am, and then cast me from your doorstep. To continue: while Grimes Mills sagged, Price Mills flourished. It was easily understandable. The former was dehydrated from malnutrition, and the latter was being force-fed with all kinds of goodies. Sort of like a mother pigeon loses weight while the squab balloons.

'There came a day when I dropped in on the banking gentlemen in New York and suggested that it would take a mess of money to revitalize Grimes Mills' creaky machinery and outmoded facilities if it worked as a separate entity whereas I was in a position, with my flourishing new Price Mills, to absorb . . . Except for the matter of money, but pawnbrokers are pawnbrokers and we made the deal. It was only paper again . . .'

'I don't understand anything at all about how you do these things.'

'Neither do I, really,' Craig said. 'Never have and never will. What I was proposing to do was to buy Grimes Mills by borrowing in advance against the money Maybelle would make by selling her old man's emporium. It was slightly involved because it was necessary for me to hock Maybelle's money, which she didn't have yet, in order to pledge these moneys as security. You understand that? And I had to have come confidence money. Fifty grand.'

'No,' Susan said.

'Well, I'll try to put it another way.'

Craig paused and lit a cigarette.

'It was rather a dandy deal. I bought Grimes Mills with money I borrowed against the purchase price of the mill, so that I could pay the money to the estate so that the money I borrowed to create a fund against which I could borrow the money could be made possible. I'm sure Maybelle was baffled, and of course Mama was dead now, and couldn't have cared less. It was sound business all around, and almost semi-demi-honest. Now I owned the two mills. I took a tremendous hunk of tax credit when I bought Grimes, because I was able to deduct its losses against the profits of my own company. Then, when we merged, I was able to do a bit of dickering on capital gains, on Maybelle's end —and of course she gave the money back to me, although it was still escrowed against my loan, which was becoming less daily— and then I was able to siphon some of my profits from Price Mills back into the anaemic ex-Grimes, so I could show a jolly decent loss on gross earnings at Price for a bit. One day or other, I was suddenly in business with two fine textile mills, free of supervision, and any moment, any wonderful moment, along would come the brewing war. And by that time I would have a million mills. And some friends in Washington.' Craig hooded his eyes, and smiled. 'And, oh so many, so very many, delightful friends in Washington. It is so easy to make friends in Washington. You simply give people money.'

'Tell me one thing,' Sue said. 'That day, that first big day, when you knew you had it all wrapped up—before you worked out all the later details with your bankers and people—what did you *do*? Actually *do*?'

'You want it in the correct order?' Craig's voice was lazily indulgent.

'Please. I'm curious.'

'Naturally, first I went to the local bank, after a decent period of mourning. Just as ambassadors do, I presented my credentials —namely, Mrs. Craig Price. And when it had been ascertained to everybody's unwilling satisfaction that I was the new president of Grimes Mills, due to the demise of a mother-in-law and a small power-of-attorney giving me the working control of seventy per cent of Grimes Mills stock because of my wife's implicit trust in my executive ability, I went down to the Cadillac people and picked up a car I had thoughtfully ordered several days before. They were glad, nay, delighted, to accept the Dodge as a down payment. Then I drew a thousand dollars in cash from the bank —on my signature, which they seemed frantic to honour— especially as I had parked the new car in front of the bank, in between the No Parking signs. Then I pressed a call on Uncle Charlie Lipschutz to take care of the balance on my IOU for the Dodge. He wouldn't let me pay. Then I picked up Maybelle in front of the dress shop where she was ordering some new clothes and we drove home. Then I drove to the mill and fired Miss Mildred—retired is a better word—as I had a new secretary in mind. Then I put a small mahogany, gold-lettered board on my —Mr. Soames', the former manager's—desk. It said "President". Then I took it off and threw it away. And then I went back to the spinning room and fired the foreman, because we wouldn't need him any more. And then I went to pay a call on the new foreman of the spinning room, a man named Forney, and on his sister, a girl named Elizabeth . . . I had a couple of promises to keep.'

5

NEVER had there been a day like this, Craig thought, wakening early to a bright sunshine dustily glinting through the blinds. Never would he forget this day, this shining day of all the days, the biggest day he would ever see in all his life. He had slept little, but he woke refreshed, eager to dress, eager to eat, eager to get down town. First he brushed his teeth, tasting the mint of the paste pleasantly. He showered, lingering long in the hot water, and then shaved carefully. He knew what he would wear: the blue suit, the dark blue tie, the white shirt. He whistled as he combed his shower-damp hair, and dug deeply with the file into his nails. Dressed, he inspected himself, and wondered if he had

369

forgotten anything. Yes. One thing. One very important thing.

He walked back to the bed and gently shook the sleeping figure.

'Maybelle,' he said. '*Maybelle*. It's time to get up. We got a lot of things to do today.'

This was the great day, the day he would take Maybelle to the bank, the day he would walk into the bank as young Craig Price, boy substitute for an old man, as Craig Price, husband of old John Grimes's daughter. And he would walk out as Craig Price, man, nobody's husband. As Craig Price, president of Grimes Mills. And the bankers would stare respectfully at his back as he left, shaking their heads in wonderment. Craig went out into the frost-fresh morning, and walked up and down on the silvered-brown grasses, each blade bravely bearing its hoary burden of frost now becoming dew under the rosy warmth of the morning sun. They looked like snot-nosed little boys, he thought. What they used to call *me*—until today.

The breeze was freighted with pine-smell, and somewhere in the distance someone was burning brush. A robin croaked, and it occurred to Craig that he had read all his life of robins' singing, but when they came to Carolina in the fall, all they did was croak. Maybe they left their singing voice up North with the Yankees.

He fingered the paper in his pocket, and took it out to read it again. It was all there, signed, witnessed, sealed by the notary. Such a simple little bit of paper, he thought. What a tiny little piece of paper, to mean so much. He could not remember what paper cost, per sheet, but the notary's fee had been two dollars. Two lousy little dollars, that was a million dollars, ten million dollars, a hundred million dollars, a billion . . . A bluejay shrieked angrily somewhere off in the pines.

'That's right, God damn it,' Craig said to the invisible blue jay. 'I said a billion and I meant a billion.' The blue jay was silent.

He could see Mr. McMullen's fat flushed face paling with surprise, Mr. Norton's horse-teeth showing and sombre eyes unbelieving when he and Maybelle walked into the president's office of the bank and tendered this tiny piece of paper, this puissant piece of paper, not even many words on it. All so simple. It merely said that Maybelle Grimes Price hereby granted an unlimited power of attorney to her husband, Craig Price, for all activities pertaining to the operation, control, or expansion of Grimes Mills, which she, as majority stockholder . . .

'Have you met our young Mr. Price?' he murmured to himself. 'He's president of Price Mills, you know. I tell you, they don't make many boys like that any more. Why, he took over his wife's father's mill when he was only twenty-one, the mill was going to hell in a hand basket, and in two years he . . .'

'Breakfast's ready,' Maybelle called from the house. 'What are you doing out in the yard?'

370

'Just gettin' myself a breath of air,' he said, coming towards the house. 'It's a real nice day. You look awful pretty, honey.'

She did. She was wearing a black broadcloth coat-suit which firmed her figure, and the ruffled breakfast apron she wore gave her a sort of French-maid-y look. She has real pretty legs, Craig thought.

'What have we got for breakfast?' he asked, kissing her on a plump pink cheek as he came in the front door. 'I'm starved.'

'What you like. Battercakes and honey and those little sausages. You look good, too, Craig. Excited?'

'A little bit. Not much. It's a big day. Maybe the biggest day of my life. New life opening up, kind of. And I owe it all to you. I won't forget it.'

'Oh, fiddle.' Maybelle was embarrassed. 'Come and eat your breakfast and then let's get on down town and tell the Three Blind Mice the news.'

Craig had two cigarettes and two cups of strong black coffee after the pale golden freckled pancakes and the tiny little wrinkled sausages. He excused himself to go to the bathroom, and while he was seated on the toilet he ran over his farewell speech in his mind for the hundredth time. He had painfully composed it over the period of weeks of necessary mourning for Maybelle's mother.

'I would like, gentlemen,' Craig murmured, 'to work closely with the bank in all things affecting . . .'

It was a good sound exit speech, he thought, washing his hands. Dignified. Not brash. The whole thing would be dignified. He touched his inside pocket again. It would have to be dignified. He had the dignity right there in his pocket. He walked out of the bathroom into the hall.

'Come on, honey,' he said. 'Let's go down and give the boys the news.'

If he had expected excitement, expostulation, or even implied resentment from the bankers, he was disappointed. Old Man McMullen had made the necessary polite er-hums and ah-hers, and when Craig had thrust the power of attorney into his hand, he had adjusted his glasses, read the letter thoroughly, and then passed it on to Mr. Norton without comment. Mr. Norton read it and passed it on to Mr. Carroll. Mr. Carroll finished reading and handed the letter back to Craig.

'Well?' Craig said.

Mr. McMullen inclined his head.

'It seems to be in order. Norton, arrange for all the necessary papers to be put in order, the necessary transfers to Mrs. Price, a copy of Mr. Price's power of attorney to be filed, and an immediate audit of the mill to be made. I congratulate you, Mrs. Price, Mr. Price. It goes without saying that any assistance which the bank can render is yours for the asking . . .' He stood up. It was as simple as that.

Craig made his little speech, and it sounded a trifle hollow in his ears.

'I would like, gentlemen,' said Craig, as he and Maybelle rose to go, 'to work closely with the bank in all things affecting the major operations of the mill. You have been very kind to me in the past; I hope you will bear with me in the future. I will do my level best not to abuse the great trust that is now invested in me. John Grimes was a friend of mine—in a way almost a father. I have the interests of his only daughter firmly in heart and mind. I hope I will be allowed to call on you frequently for advice and assistance. Thank you very much for everything. Come on, Maybelle, I know you've got things to do in town. Good morning, gentlemen.'

He opened the door to McMullen's office, and he and Maybelle walked slowly, with dignity, down the corridor. Maybelle had some shopping to do, and he had several chores of his own. Quite a few, as a matter of fact.

'Well,' Mr. McMullen said. 'Well. I guess there isn't anything you can do about it or about him. I heard about it before, but I never saw it done in practice. This young fellow literally screwed himself into a fortune.'

'Surprise me if he don't screw himself out of a fortune some day.' Mr. Carroll said. 'You can reach too high, too fast.'

Both Mr. Norton and Mr. McMullen shook their heads.

'No,' they both said, and looked at each other.

'No,' Mr. McMullen said. 'This is no wild-eyed young marsh-pony we're dealing with. This is a smart boy. If it hadn't happened one way it would have happened the other. He had the old lady twisted around his finger. I saw it that afternoon, the day she died out at the house. It was just a little matter of time before he got her to sign over the stuff to him. I doubt very much if we'd have had a leg to stand on trying to break it. But lucky for him he didn't have to put it to the test. He just fell into a pile of crap and came up smelling like a rose. He's the kind that always will. I think we just go along with him. Within reason anyhow.'

The phone rang, buzzed through from the secretary's desk. Mr. McMullen answered, irritably.

'Tell him yes,' Mr. McMullen said, and hung up with a bang.

'What was that?' Mr. Norton asked.

'The cashier was calling, wanting to know if it was all right to let Mr. Craig Price have a thousand dollars in cash.'

All three men nodded together.

'Yes,' they breathed. 'It's all right to let Mr. Craig Price have anything he wants—within reason.'

6

'HELLO, Uncle Charlie?' Craig said. The Cadillac stood, almost panting, in front of the pawnshop. The shop was empty. Craig called again and the old man emerged from the back room. He wiped his glasses and adjusted them more firmly on his nose. He looked, Craig thought, another hundred years old. That makes him two hundred, at least.

'Oh, it's you, Craig.' The old man looked past him at the enormous sleek black Cadillac with its dazzling white-side-walled tyres. 'For a second I thought that the Governor was in town and needed sudden money, he should come in such a car, paid for by the state. Where is the motor-cycle escort?'

Craig laughed almost apologetically.

'Don't kid me, Uncle Charlie. You know it's mine. I came to pay back the loan. All of it.'

The old man permitted himself a tiny smile.

'For a moment I was frightened. I thought that perhaps you had come for more money to buy a car like that. I don't keep so much in the safe. Burglars, you know. It is a lovely automobile. Do you like it better than the other one?' He flashed the question.

'No.' Craig paused, hesitant. 'No, I don't. But it still means something. Something big.'

'I know. How did they take it, the bankers, when you made your triumphant trip to tell them that today you are president of Grimes Mills, Incorporated, and tomorrow president of Price Mills, Incorporated?'

'I . . . I hadn't got around to that yet. I mean, I hadn't . . .'

The old man smoothed his wispy goat's beard and smiled gently. 'That will be next year, will it not, when you come to see me in a steam yacht or your own airplane? Or possibly the year after. I hope I should live so long to see it. So.'

Uncle Charlie spoke sharply.

'So. Now you who was a smart little boy now is a smart big man. What do you intend to do now you have got the thing you want? And so suddenly. It is a pity,' he said, 'that poor Mrs. Grimes had to die so conveniently. Had you planned to get her to sign her stock over to you or just to your wife? Excuse me. I must not be rude, but I was interested to see exactly how you would work it. Now that you are a merchant prince, what do you intend to do?'

'Expand,' Craig said, and exhaled a breath. 'Expand, Uncle Charlie.'

The old man nodded at the slinking great black beast at the kerb.

'*That* is expansion? That thing with the automatic everything

373

on it? What do you expand to next? You will buy a railroad to get you from the office to the house?'

Craig repeated:

'Please don't kid me, Uncle Charlie. I came here mainly just to tell you thanks for that day you gave me a year ago. It was a very important day, Uncle Charlie. Maybe the most important day in my life—even more than today.'

'Craig,' Uncle Charlie said softly. 'Importance is every day. To not do something bad and to know it is important. To do something bad and not know it, that is not important. To do something bad and know it while you do it is very important and can be very bad. You have a big chance, Craig, a bigger chance than most of the young men. Try to think a little each day. Not too much, but a little—think a little before you do it. If you think a little you will not hound yourself so much for the mistakes you make. Try to make only intelligent mistakes. Dumbness—a *dummkopf*—no excuse is available for a *dummkopf*.'

Craig reached into his pocket.

'I want to pay what I owe, Uncle Charlie, with thanks. If you could tell me?'

'Wait a minute.' The old man shuffled back to the room behind, and again Craig heard the dials twirl, the tumblers click. Uncle Charlie came back, like an old mandarin with a priceless scroll, holding Craig's IOU gingerly between thumb and forefinger.

'You smoke, I know,' he said. 'You have a match? Good. Light it.' The match flared and Uncle Charlie held the IOU to the flame. He dropped it when the fire-browned edges of the flaring paper threatened to singe his fingers. He browned the charring paper out under his foot.

'So,' he said. 'So. You owe me nothing. Call it a house present, Craig, and see that you return it to some one, some time, who wants and needs and can use. But for this you have to do me a favour.'

Craig was momentarily flustered.

'I can't take it, I can't . . .'

'Of course you can. You can always accept an old man's whim. But you can do something for me that I have always wanted to do, to be.'

'I'll do anything I can, Uncle Charlie,' Craig said, 'but I still say I can't . . .'

'Be quiet. Come outside.' The old man walked slowly around from behind the counter. He produced a ring of keys, and locked the door. They stood together on the sidewalk.

'Now,' the old man said. 'Help me into the back seat of your magnificent new car. Close the door carefully. So. Very good. Now drive me around the block—better than that, drive me to Market Street and back again. Drive me past the bank, and drive me up Front, so I can see how the wealthy *goys* used to live. I

374

have always wanted to be rich,' he said. 'And young, while I was rich. It is a pity, sitting in the back seat of this new car, with such a handsome, successful chauffeur, that I do not smoke cigars.

'But at least, Craig,' he said, and chuckled. 'Would it hurt your dignity very much if I whistled at a girl or two, especially a *shiksa*, and they thought it was you?'

Old Uncle Charlie, Craig thought, after he had dropped the old man back at the pawnshop. Old Uncle Charlie. He makes me a little nervous. He makes me feel uncomfortable, and a little guilty. He makes he wonder about me. That crack about what am I going to do and I said expand and he looked at the car and asked me if that was what I meant by expansion. Suddenly he made me feel guilty for having the car at all, for having done what I've done.

He spoke softly aloud to himself, as he drove back to pick up Maybelle.

'I don't know, I don't know, I don't know. I say that to myself at night or once in a while if I'm alone and I don't know. I don't know, I don't know. I don't know about me, I don't know about Maybelle, I don't know about tomorrow. All I know is somehow I got do it the best way I know how because nobody'll do it for me, ever. And if it means trampling down some people and running over some backs, well, then I got to do it, that's all. I want—I want—Jesus Christ, how I *do* want—and how do I *know* what I want? I just want so hard it eats into my guts.

'I'm in a spot right now that could be everything and could wind up nothing. Age against me, the way I came into the play against me. I don't want Maybelle, I want something better, but without Maybelle, without Maybelle's money, without old John Grimes, before Maybelle, without Uncle Charlie, how do I get what I want when I don't know even what I want?

'Is this what I want?' Craig squirmed his behind on to the grey velvet seat cushion of the Cadillac, looked at the jewelled dashboard. Is this what I want? A house? A car? A woman? A work? Is that what I want?

'God almighty Jesus Christ I wish I knew what I want and how will I make it, how will I ever make it with Maybelle when what I want is something that comes out of the sea in a cloud of mist? What do I *want*?' What cripples me that I want it so?

'And what sort of price do I want to pay, me so young, me so unsure on the edge of fortune, me so . . . me *so* . . .'

Maybelle was waiting for him in front of the best department store in town.

'What kept you? The new car?' Maybelle's eyes swept the long black magnificence as if it offended her. Craig opened the far door and she climbed in spilling bundles.

375

'You don't seem surprised we got a new car.'

'I'm not surprised. Not at all. I knew it was the first thing you'd do. And I knew you'd have had it planned all along. But what really kept you?'

'I had to go see Uncle Charlie. I wanted to pay off the note on the Dodge. He wanted to take a ride in the car . . .' Craig drew away from the kerb. 'Isn't it—isn't it lovely, Maybelle? Just look.'

Maybelle sniffed. Her nostrils spread.

'It's lovely, all right. Lovely. So I wait on the corner so you can take that dirty old Jew for a joyride? After this morning in the bank? A Jew pawnbroker comes ahead of me?'

Craig sighed inwardly. If this girl ever needs a job poisoning wells I can write her a recommendation, he thought. The day started out so bright and beautiful and now . . . It isn't a very pretty car at all.

'Oh, Lord, Maybelle,' he said, turning on to the main street that led towards home. 'Uncle Charlie's not a dirty old Jew. He's a wonderful, kind, sweet old man. He wouldn't even let me pay him the rest of the money I owed him. All he wanted, he said, was to take a ride around town for a few minutes, just a very few minutes, to see how it felt to be . . . to be rich and young, he said. Don't make me feel like I committed a crime or something. Not because Uncle Charlie wanted to ride in a new car.'

'So tomorrow,' Maybelle said spitefully, 'tomorrow it'll be all over town that you're takin' charity from a Jew . . . let alone—' she stopped. She put her hand to her mouth.

Craig pulled the new Cadillac over to the kerb. His voice was deadly.

'I hope that you weren't going to say what I think you were going to say. It's not too late yet. I can still go back to sea.'

'I didn't mean anything, Craig. Really. Really, I didn't. You know how I am. Waitin' on the corner and you come drivin' up in a great big new car that I didn't have any sayso about, and all of a sudden I find out you've been joyridin' with a Jew pawnbroker and I guess I just got mad after the business at the bank and . . .'

If she says 'and all' I swear I'll kill her with my bare hands. Craig's brain clenched, like a fist.

'All,' she finished, and Craig started to laugh. He threw his head back and roared, like the doctor had laughed at the mental hospital in Greensboro. Maybelle's voice lost its note of faint apology and harshened again.

'What's so goddam funny?'

'Me. You.' Craig was still laughing. 'Just you and me. We sit here in a brand new Cadillac with the world in our laps and you accuse me of unfaithfulness for taking a nice old man out for a spin around the block before I pick you up. And what are you mad at the car for, anyhow? It's a good car. The best. I thought you'd be pleased.'

'I don't know,' Maybelle said, when he started the motor again. 'I guess I never will understand you, Craig. I guess I never will. You do things—you do things too *fast*. It's . . . it's almost vulgar, the way you do things too fast. You seem to be tryin' to keep provin' somethin' all the time. It ain't—it isn't *nice*. It's like a nigger on Saturday night, drunk and buyin' up the town knowin' he'll be busted tomorrow. It would have been nicer if you'd let me help you pick out the car.'

'Sister,' Craig said. 'Nobody ever summed me up any better. Congratulations. Now I know exactly what I am and why I act the way I do. I'm a drunken nigger on Saturday night and I'm buying up the town, and I don't give a country fart if I *am* broke tomorrow. Do you hear? I don't give a good goddam!'

He pulled into the drive with a brutalizing wrench of steering wheel and a squeal of brakes. He was still furious. They sat in the car silently for a moment in front of the house.

'*You* don't understand *me*?' he suddenly shouted, making an exclamation of the question. 'I'll never understand you! One minute you're as sweet as pie and smart as a whip and the next minute you can pour cold water on anything so that all the pleasure goes out of it! You don't understand what a—what a *gesture* can make! This was a day that had to have a Cadillac in it, if just to prove to the world that I'm of age, that nobody is going to shove me around, that I can afford a Cadillac! I can stand off a bank, I can run a mill, I can goddamned well buy a Cadillac! This ain't a car you're sittin' in, it's me! Me, Craig Price, your husband! Me!'

'All right,' Maybelle said, calmly. 'I give up. I'm sittin' on you. But you better remember one thing, big boy, when you start to holler. Up to now *you* been sittin' on *me*. Don't yell, it isn't necessary. I know you're smart and I know you work hard but when you came here a couple of years back you didn't have a pot to piss in. I may be dumb but I am not a fool, Craig Price. You can make ten billion dollars and I'm still goin' to remember how you got started. Papa first and me next and then Mama and now the bank. So we got a Cadillac. All right. But how we got it is a thing you better remember. *I* will.'

'So will I,' Craig said. 'To my dying day, I'll remember. Let's get out of this—this pest-house—' he looked with distaste at the car. 'It looked so pretty a few minutes ago.'

'Mama would have liked it,' Maybelle said, getting out of the car. 'If she'd lived to see it, which she didn't, thank God. I reckon I couldn't have stood two crazy people around the house.'

They went inside and Craig sat down in the living-room.

'You want a drink?' Maybelle asked. She was still standing.

'No. No, thanks. I've got to go back to the mill.'

'Well, I do. And I haven't got to go back to the mill. At least I can drink to one thing. The old lady's gone and you've got what you want and maybe now there'll finally be some peace around here. You sure you don't want one?'

'Sure.' Craig watched Maybelle pour herself a half-glass of bourbon. She held the glass high, for a moment. Then she turned to Craig.

'To. the new president of Grimes Mills,' she said, sarcastically, 'and to his new Cadillac. And to dear old Mama, who made it possible. Dear old Mama. I wonder if they've got a diaper service in heaven?' She downed half the drink at a gulp. She sat down and looked at him stubbornly, mulishly. 'I wonder if Mama appreciates all you did for her at the bank this mornin'?

'I want to get some things straightened out around here,' she said. 'Gimme a cigarette,' Craig handed her one, and struck a match. She inhaled deeply, and looked at her glass.

'You know I'm sorry about your mother. You know I feel like it was my fault. Almost as if I killed her by getting you to take her out of the sanatorium and bring her here. I've told you I'm sorry. What I had in mind was for everybody's good. I didn't want your mother to die so I could get my way. I just wanted . . .'

Craig's voice now was placating.

'Oh, for Christ's sake,' Maybelle said. 'Don't come pall-bearin' to me. I know better. Get that deacon look off your face.' She drained her drink, and looked at him absently. Her voice was almost impersonal.

'She wasn't doin' anybody any good alive,' she said. 'She was just a nuisance to me and you and everybody else. I suppose maybe it wouldn't have happened if we'd left her in the hospital, but we didn't and that's that. There ain't any use cryin' over spilt milk.'

'I'd think you'd feel a little bit more about your own mother, Maybelle. After all she *was* your mother.'

Maybelle looked at him pityingly.

'You know goddamned well and good I never cared anything about my mother,' she said. 'As a matter of fact, I never cared any more about her than you did. Even before she died when you were bein' so sugar-sweet and bringin' her candy and takin' her to the movies and stuff, all you were doin' was tryin' to wind her around your finger. Well, now she's dead and now you've got your wish and I don't have to clean up after her. I don't have to wait on her hand and foot any more. I don't have to watch her eat and have her nosin' into everything and followin' me around all day talkin' her head off.'

Maybelle pointed her finger at him. Her voice now assumed command.

'You can make sorry faces in front of everybody else and go around lookin' like you're mournin' for Mama, but don't try it on me, Craig Price. Not on little Maybelle. All you ever wanted out of Mama you got. I reckon all you really ever wanted out of me you got. Now I don't give the first good goddam about the stock or what you do with it. You run your mill to suit yourself. Pay yourself whatever salary you think you're worth. We'll split the income. I'll keep my share and you can have Mama's share. You can call it blood-money if you want. But don't ever try to sweet-talk me about Mama. When she choked to death she did us both a favour, and saved us both a lot of time and trouble. Forget her. She's dead, and you got yourself a mill to play with. And also, you got me to consider.'

Craig started to say something, but Maybelle held up her hand.

'Wait a minute. I'm not through talkin' yet. Things are goin' to change around here. We got considerable money now and we're goin' to start livin' like we got money. I want some decent help in the house, and I want to do the house over. I want to buy a lot of clothes. I want to make some friends and take some trips and go out nights. We've been sittin' home for one reason or another ever since we got married and I'm sick and tired of it. I'm twenty-two years old and I never been anywhere, never saw anything. I want to join the Country Club and the Yacht Club and have some parties and have some fun. Do you understand that? You've got the mill, but I—we—are goin' to have some fun.'

Craig looked at her for a moment.

'Making friends and joining the clubs won't be so easy as all that. Your papa wasn't able to do it, and you didn't do so well at it coming up as a girl. And God knows my folks didn't amount to a bale of hay in this town. It won't be so awful easy just to strike and suddenly declare ourselves the belles of the ball.'

Maybelle laughed loudly, harshly.

'Don't give me that crap. We can do anything we want to. You're about to be the youngest big shot in the town. You got the bank behind you because the bank has to be. We're both young and today we drive a Cadillac—which reminds me. I want a car of my own, right away, I think a red one—we've got more than enough money to compete with this po' *Bokra* society that's come up since the depression. There ain't any quality people in this town with enough money any more to call the turn on who's social and who ain't. It's been coming into the hands of the crackers since the banks broke and the wrong-side-of-town people started buyin' up the quality folks' mistakes. 'Bout the only quality people in this town with money are those that got crackers for partners. You get to work on them with some of the goose-grease you used on me and Papa and Mama and the boys at the bank, and see if you can't persuade us right into society.'

'Persuasion isn't enough.' Craig's tone was dubious, still placating. 'You can't just start out from scratch and . . .'

Maybelle laughed again.

'The hell you can't start out from scratch. You never stopped at anything you wanted yet. I'm surprised you'd be so backward about this. Look, you're going to do a lot of business with a lot of people from now on. A lot of people will need your business. A lot of people got do business with you to keep their own business alive. You think they won't come to our parties? We'll throw the best parties this town ever saw. They'll come, all right. You'll see.'

'Okay, we'll see. We'll see. But I've got to go now,' Craig said, looking at his watch. 'I've got to get back to the mill.'

'For what?' Maybelle asked, still nastily. 'Why? You're the president. Why can't the president take an afternoon off on his first day as president?'

Craig looked at his wife without love.

'As president of Grimes Mills,' he said, 'bad taste or not, drunk nigger on a Saturday night or not, I have certain duties. I have to fire two people. I have to hire two people.'

He got up.

'I'll be home early,' he said. Evidently the bourbon and the anger had seized firm hold of Maybelle.

'Be sure and hire one with big tits,' she snapped, and poured herself another drink.

Craig decided not to answer. Not right now, anyhow.

7

CRAIG walked into the office. He looked around him. It looked the same. There, Miss Mildred. There, his desk. There, Mr. Soames' old desk. He shivered. A depressing place, this office, brooding with a stink of death. Well, by God he'd change that, starting tomorrow. Tear the whole damned place down and start all over. Even if he had to paint the whole thing red.

He nodded to Miss Mildred and walked over to Mr. Soames' desk. He took a piece of gilt-lettered mahogany out of his pocket and put it on Mr. Soames' desk. It said: *President.* He didn't like the look of it on Mr. Soames' desk. By God, he'd buy himself a desk as big as a drydock. And keep the new secretary outside.

Miss Mildred pursued him with her eyes. Craig looked at her with fresh interest, now he was going—within the next few minutes—going to fire her. What sort of person was he going to fire? It occurred to him that he'd never really seen the old girl before. All he really remembered of Miss Mildred was a disdainful sniff, and the musty old maid smell that went with the office.

What lay beneath the tightly bound bosom, what secrets

380

cowered in the stiffly corseted body? What hid, cringing behind the face that met the world as a beak-nosed, chinless frontispiece? Did Miss Mildred have real breasts underneath the baggy-seated oatmeal tweed suit she was wearing today? What flights of forbidden devilish thoughts sneaked into that red-nosed head of nights, when she tossed and twisted on her virgin cot? Did she dream deliciously of carnal embrace with a man? What did she think when she observed herself unbeautifully naked when she bathed, the lank body withered and unused, but equipped with fallow traces of all the standard knobs and orifices? Did she weep, smothering her face into the pillow, for a man she never knew, the man who might have caused to bloom her cheeks, who might have crammed her barren womb with children, the man who might have led people to call her 'Millie' or 'Mil' instead of Miss Mildred? Did she ever letch after old Mr. Soames? Had she ever been pretty enough to attract the casual vagrant lust of old John Grimes? What did she do on her days off? Movies? The beach? Did she hate dogs and keep a cat? Had there ever been a parrot? Had there ever been a lover, somewhere, blotted in a war or cancelled in an accident or merely run off to sea, some gay laughing lad who might have violated her undesired chastity and freed her painfully, happily from her old-maid sterility? Did she burp? Did she break wind? Did she secretly envy Myrna Loy? What was her last name? It was Mason, Craig thought. Mildred Mason. A name to fit her face, a name to go with endless cleaning of typewriter keys, a name to match an unearned menopause, a name to rhyme with rubber plant, with canary bird, and with limitless careless children of brothers and sisters, who called her Aunt Mildred and wondered how soon she'd leave when she paid a call on a holiday to bring them gifts.

'Miss Mason,' Craig said. 'I'd like to talk to you.'

Mildred Mason looked him firmly in the face. The levelness of her gaze was disconcerting.

'When do you want me to leave?' she asked, softly. It was odd how much dignity settled firmly on to the rabbity face with the skinned-back hairdo and the negligible chin. Craig felt suddenly disarmed. Miss Mildred saved him the necessity of a question.

'When you walked in the door here the first day I knew it was a matter of time. It didn't make any difference who went first, me or Mr. Soames,' she said. 'One of us would go and then the other would go. Old machinery . . .' she shrugged. 'I can leave today or tomorrow or whenever you wish . . .' she hesitated. 'When you wish, Mr. Price.' She did not sniff. Her nose seemed less red, her chin stronger.

'How long have you worked here, Miss Mildred?' Craig lit a cigarette nervously. He had never fired anybody before.

'Thirty-two years,' she said. 'I was working for Mr. McCadden before Mr. Grimes married Miss Irma and came to work in the mill. Like,' she paused, 'like you came into the mill.'

I can't do it, Craig thought. She's as out of place as the furniture and she's as dull as dishwater and she's set in her old-timey ways but she's been here thirty-two years and I can't do it. *I can't do it?* The hell I can't do it. I'll do it now.

'Miss Mildred,' he said as gently as he knew how. 'I guess you know that I run the mill now.'

'I saw the sign on your desk,' Miss Mildred replied. 'I knew when Mrs. Grimes died that it would be just a few days before there would be a sign on your desk. Yes, Mr. Price, I know you run the mill now.' She wouldn't help him further.

'I think you've worked hard enough and long enough,' Craig said, haltingly. 'I'm going to change things some around here—people and furniture and everything. I think maybe you've earned a rest . . . some free time to enjoy yourself . . . I think Mr. Grimes would have said the same thing . . .'

'When do you want me to leave?' She repeated the question.

'I don't see any sense in stretching things out,' Craig said. 'As soon as possible. And Miss Mildred?'

'Yes, Mr. Price.'

'I want you to understand that this is not a dismissal, not any reflection on your work. You will be retired on half-pay.' Craig had intended to say three months' notice, but lacked the courage.

'That's very nice of you, Mr. Price. Very kind indeed. I certainly couldn't ask for more. When will you have the new girl? Would you want me to show her around?'

'She'll be in to work in a couple of weeks or so. After I've had some work done in the office. But if you could clear your files I'd like to have the carpenters in next Monday. Then if you'd be so kind you might come back for a few days and help the new girl get settled. That would be very kind of you, Miss Mildred.'

'Would that be all for now, then Mr. Price?'

'Yes, Miss Mildred. Except if you would change the payroll sheets, please, to your half pay—' he spoke swiftly on impulse—'Starting six months from now. We—*I* would like you to take a vacation, and if you want the money in a lump sum . . .'

'I thank you again, Mr. Price. But I have some money laid by. I won't need the money in a lump sum.'

She turned to leave.

'Miss Mildred?' She halted and turned to face him again.

'You know I hate to do this? You understand I don't like doing this?'

'I understand, Mr. Price. Of course I understand. Don't you fret yourself. It comes to everybody.'

Craig desperately did not want her to leave, not for just a moment more. He was lonely, miserable in his first executive decision.

'What—what will you do, Miss Mildred? After you've quit, I mean? What'll you do?' It suddenly seemed important for him to know.

'Mr. Price,' she said. 'I have worked in this office for thirty-two years. I really just can't say what I'll do. I'll find something to keep me busy, I expect. Was that all?'

'Yes, Miss Mildred. That's all.' Craig looked at the sign which said *President* and suddenly threw it into the waste paper basket. It would look better, in gold letters, on a frosted glass door when the office was remodelled. He grimaced.

'I might as well get the bastard new-boss business over,' he murmured. 'Christ, I feel like a criminal. Two years I've looked at the dried-up old bag, just waiting for this day, and now I feel like a bastard. All she ever did was sniff and look at me like I was an office boy, and now she really makes me feel like an office boy. Jumped-up and out of my station. A crook. Well, there's no sense in putting off the rest of it.

'I'll be back in the shop for a little while, Miss Mildred,' he said loudly as he left the office. 'If anybody wants me for anything serious I'll be in the spinning-room.'

'Yes, Mr. Price,' Miss Mildred said. 'You'll be in the spinning-room.'

When you're hungry, Craig thought, walking towards the spinning-room, you gulp it down and never notice the taste. You reach for whatever's handy and just choke it down. You don't bother to taste it on your tongue. I suppose when you fire somebody you're supposed to just fire somebody, not roll it around in your mouth. I've known ever since I walked in that door that I would fire Miss Mildred, that I would fire old man Soames, if he didn't die or quit, and after that fishing trip with Red Forney that I would fire the foreman in the spinning-room. I don't think I really like being an executive, Craig thought, but you got to do what you got to do and executives hire people and fire people. For Christ's sake, Price, he said to himself, that was what you were quarrelling with the bank about when they made you purchasing agent. You got to fire to hire. You can't hire unless you fire. But how in the name of God will I tell old Marvin Mc-Cracken that he isn't wanted any more? Miss Mildred made it easy for me. Maybe old Marvin won't. Old Marvin. I don't really know old Marvin.

'Marvin,' he said, sticking his head through the door, where the thousand spindles whirred. 'Marvin!' The old man cupped an ear to hear, and then stumped towards the door. Craig nodded at Red Forney, operating his spindles, doffing the bobbins with the same ease that he unhooked a bass or threw a baseball. Red winked at Craig, and then turned his eyes back to his work.

Old Marvin McCracken came to the door, staring suspiciously behind him, as if he were afraid to leave the work for a moment.

'Come on out with me into the yard where we can talk,' Craig said. 'You can't hear yourself think in here.'

'Something wrong, Mr. Price?' Marvin McCracken was nervous. 'I hope it ain't got nothin' to do with my department. Production's up and . . .'

'Here, have a cigarette,' Craig said. 'No, Marvin, nothing's wrong with your department. Nothing at all.'

'I thank you kindly, Mr. Price. I don't use 'em. Coffin nails, that's all they are, coffin nails. I'm sure glad there ain't nothin' wrong with my department. I give it my best druthers.'

'I know you do,' Craig said. 'I sure as hell know you do, Marvin.' He inhaled his smoke and looked at the old man. Here is a new one, he thought. Old Marvin McCracken, about to be fired. Old Marvin McCracken, his working life about to end. I never even saw him before. He looked at the old man. His hair was white, his eyes were watered blue, brown liver-spots freckled his face and hands, his teeth were obviously false, and vertical lines of wrinkles ran from under his nose into his thin upper lip. More wrinkles, vertical and horizontal, bisected each other on his forehead. He had a large brown mole with a stiff stand of hair in it on his left cheek. Marvin McCracken, boss spinner. Foreman of the spinning-room? For how long?

'I hearn the news, Mr. Price,' Marvin McCracken said. 'I hearn tell you are the new pres-y-dent of Grimes. That sure is fine, you so young and all. I mind well the day Mr. Grimes, God rest his soul, I mind well the day he come to work here, him no older than you. Mr. McCadden he owned the mills in them days. I wasn't no more than a sprout when I first come to work here for Mr. McCadden. My, but he was a fine man, was Mr. McCadden. He was Missis Grimes's papa and he died just like his daughter done and left Mr. Grimes in charge. It sure do seem history takes a hanker to repeat itself,' Marvin McCracken said. 'What did you have on to your mind to say, Mr. Price, when you called me, like?'

Craig spoke gently, tentatively.

'How long have you been working here, Marvin?'

'Nigh on to forty year. Stiddy. You look at the time book, Mr. Price, you see I never taken off sick. No sir, not Marvin Mc-Cracken. Don't drink, never smoked a cigarette in my life, chew a little maybe, but take off sick? Not Marvin McCracken. No sir, not Marvin McCracken, Mr. Price.'

Oh, Jesus, Craig thought. This is worse than I expected. I stand before a man without sin, mortal or otherwise.

'How old are you, Marvin?' he asked.

'I couldn't rightly say. Sixty some, mayhap. I was country born. We didn't kind of keep no registers in the country. I'd say sixty some.'

'How's your health?'

'Well, my back devils me some, and when it's wet I git a little stiff in the joints. But it never gits in front of the work. You jist look at the book, Mr. Price, you see. I never taken off sick, not like some-'uns I could mention.' The old man looked back balefully in the direction of the spinning-room.

'You married?' God, the things you really didn't know about people until you had to fire them. 'Children, I reckon.'

'Widdered for the third time, God rest her poor soul,' the old man said. 'A doin' woman if ever I seen one. Work from dawn to dark and never a whine. Took down with the gallopin' consumption and died just like that there.' He snapped his fingers. 'A minute she was, next she warn't.' The old man's voice was fretful now. 'I reckon I'm too old-cagey to take on a new wife now, Mr. Price. I reckon the women don't want no old man except maybe for their money. I make out with my dotter, Sarah. She taken a husband and catched a child off'n him, but he run off somewhere and Sarah she moved in with me and my departed. I don't know where that man run off to or why he run off, but Sarah be a power of comfort around the house and the youngun ain't really too worrisome. A well-behaved youngun but a little slow. Got a big head. Sort of a swole kind of head.'

'Could you make out all right with Sarah—your daughter—to look after you if all of a sudden you took sick and couldn't work any more?' Craig was still fingering his way along the wall of indecision. 'What I mean, Marvin, have you got any money saved up against your old age?'

The old man's expression was shocked, hurt.

'Naturally, I got money saved up. I been workin' all my life and all the time I saved a leetle. I put it in the postal savin's. I got anyhow about a—I got enough.' He looked almost truculently at Craig. 'I don't have to ask nothin' from nobody.'

'I know you don't have to ask nothin' from nobody,' Craig said gently. 'You bein' such an old hand around here.' Marvin McCracken smiled with an old man's conceit.

'Anything I kin do to help, you jist call on Marvin McCracken.'

Craig paused, then leaped.

'What do you think of Red Forney?'

The old man grunted.

'A fair hand. Does his day's work. Don't take off sick much. Keeps out of trouble. I reckon you'd say he was a fair hand.'

'Well,' Craig said. 'I been thinking that maybe it was about time we thought about retiring you, and maybe Red . . .'

'Me retire? Me retire?' the old man bristled. 'Why hell, Mr. Price, I wouldn't know what to do if I retired. What'd I retire on? That Red Forney take my job? I don't forgot more than he'll know in forty year. You just a-funnin', Mr. Price. The work's goin' good and the production is more'n you got marked on the chart. Retire? I ain't hardly more'n started yet.' The old man laughed falsely, and the laughter dwindled as he looked at Craig's face.

'I guess you ain't funnin', at that,' he said, with dignity. 'All right, Mr. Price, if you want it that way. All right. I ain't never asked nobody for nothin' and I'm too old to start now. When do you want me to knock off?'

Craig put a hand on the old man's shoulder, and Marvin McCracken moved out from under the hand. He looked angrily at Craig.

'You'll be on half pay, Marvin,' Craig said. 'I know we don't have to do it but I would like to put you on half pay. You'll be comfortable, living with your daughter.'

Marvin McCracken looked at him icily.

'I don't need no charity,' he said, coldly. 'I worked here forty year and I earned every penny I ever made. I don't need no charity. I'll make out. You can take your half pay and shove it up your ass.' He spat. 'Mr. Price,' he said, and walked away.

He'd change his mind of course when the money started to come, Craig thought. If his experience with Miss Mildred and Marvin McCracken was any sample of an executive's life, he reckoned maybe it would be easier to be a hired hand. But at least, he thought, walking back to the office, the pleasanter part is yet to come.

8

SOMETHING sent him to Mr. Wilhelm's flower shop on Front Street. It wasn't much out of the way anyhow. Most people didn't buy cut flowers in town except for funerals and wedding and such, but Craig had a hungry hankering for flowers. Perhaps there was the funereal urge to celebrate the passing of Miss Mildred, of Marvin McCracken? I come to bury Caesar, not to ask him to dance?

What flowers, he wondered, would go with dark-red hair and almost-black eyes? Strange what you don't know, he thought, pulling up in front of Mr. Wilhelm's. I went to high school with Jessie Wilhelm and Peter Wilhelm and Max Wilhelm, and I know the old man has a nursery farm, a big one, down towards New Bern, but I don't know a thing about flowers, about what flowers you can take to a girl with hair like an Irish setter's, a girl who is going to be your new secretary about the same time her brother starts to run the spinning-room.

I know, Craig thought. I'll stop off at the ABC and buy a jug, and that'll settle Red. Then the flowers can be for the house and I don't even know what colour they have to be to go with hair

386

or eyes. Some red roses will do, hot-house roses with the long stems, a dozen's enough I guess. First flowers to a girl, really, except the dance corsage for Mary Frances. Now this is a real strange one. I am going to give two new people a new lease on life, I guess, and I'm taking *them* presents. You reckon anybody'll ever bring me a present? I doubt it, he thought, harshly. I haven't got the face for it. Uncle Charlie gave me a present, a big one. Maybelle gave me a present, a big one. I guess I got the kind of face that will only ever get the big presents, the ones you don't really like. Well, Maybelle did give me the dinner jacket. What are you feeling sorry for, Price, you stupid bastard?

The dozen long-stemmed American beauties were on the Cadillac's seat by his side, nestled against the bottle of scotch, when he leaned heavily on the horn outside Red Forney's house. Lights were on, the people had to be home. The horn blared, and the front door opened, and Red Forney's bristly head came out on to the porch. Craig honked the horn again in a shave-and-a-hair-cut-two-bits rhythm. Forney's head turned against the light and he called something to his sister. They came out together to stand beside and marvel at the car.

'I told you,' Craig said. 'The next time I parked a car here it would be a Cadillac. Look at us. Look at us, Foreman. Look at us, Secretary. Just look at us. Everybody's rich. Here, Libby! The flowers are yours. Here, Red! The whisky's ours. Here!' He took Red Forney by one hand and Libby by the other and did an impromptu dance on the sidewalk.

'You ever kiss a president of a textile mill? Now's your chance,' he said to Libby. 'Right there! Shake hands with the president, Red, the new president! Shake hands with your new boss, Libby! And mind you call me Mr. Price in the office! Hop in the car! You drive Red, and then let's go drink some of that bottle and smell Libby's flowers! This day's been a long time a-comin'! And right now I feel like for the first time that it was here!'

'I think we better have a drink and put the flowers in some water and kind of calm the new president down, Sis,' Red Forney said. 'We'll just pat the car a couple of times and maybe drive in it a little later. It's too pretty to wear it out right now. By God and by Jesus, Sister, we'll have us one too, one of these days. I swear I never knowed they could put nothin' together this pretty.'

'Come on in, Craig,' Libby said. 'Come on in and sit. Red, you fix us a drink while I fix the flowers. And can I have a drink too, to celebrate? You wouldn't give me one the last time.'

Red looked at Craig.

'I guess it ain't every day I get to be foreman and Libby goes to work for the new president with the Cadillac parked outside the door,' he said. 'Fix yourself a toddy, Lib. I guess we got to celebrate. I don't know what to say, Craig, now it's here. I just dunno what to say.' He looked at his hands unbelievingly. 'Me,

Red Forney, with that spinnin' room to run. Me, Red Forney, with his kid sister runnin' the front office. Me . . . me . . . with the weavin'-room ahead, and ahead of that . . . me. I don't believe it.'

'That Cadillac says yes,' Craig said. 'It's sitting out there in front of your house. It says I'm president and Libby is going to be my new secretary and you're foreman of the spinning-room and one day you'll be general manager of the mill and . . . that Cadillac says yes.'

'Rich man,' Craig said to Red Forney. 'The inside toilet business starts right now.' He walked over and once again kissed Libby on the cheek. 'I hope you don't mind my kissin' my new secretary in a kind of cousin fashion, or else you can't be the new foreman of the spinning-room, which means you won't ever have an inside toilet and Libby won't have a car of her own and go to Bermuda on her vacation. Oh, goddam, people, let me babble for a minute. I'm happy fit to bust. Look out the window.'

'We already seen it once,' Red Forney said. 'If you wasn't a boy I'd kiss you myself.'

Craig stood between the pair, his arms around brother and sister.

'By God and by Jesus, like Red says, at least this part of my family likes what happened today. I plan to spend about five hours telling you about what Uncle Charlie said about the Cadillac, and how the bankers took it, and I think we'll all get drunk. Can my new secretary get drunk, Red?'

'If she's old enough to work she's old enough to get drunk,' Red Forney said. 'Libby, fix us another one.'

'How was it, Craig?' Red Forney said swiftly, as his sister went to make the drinks. 'Bad? Old Marvin, I mean.'

'Rugged. Rough. I tried to put him on half pay and he told me to stick it up my ass.'

'That kinda figures. I hope I won't have to tell you the same thing some day. That's a joke,' Red said. 'Did you have much trouble with Miss Mildred?'

Libby came back from the kitchen with the drinks.

'I'd like to know about that, too,' she said. 'Was she terribly upset? Take on something terrible?'

'As a matter of fact, no. She wasn't. She didn't. Not to notice, anyhow. Maybe inside she was. She said she knew it was coming from the first day I walked in the door. She made me feel like a real sad bastard, she took it so good. I tried to soften it up some just because my conscience hurt me. I have her six months on full pay and then she retires for life on half pay.'

'I feel bad about her too,' Libby said. 'I feel kind of guilty. Maybe she doesn't have anything to do now for ever more. To keep her alive, I mean. Maybe she never had anything to keep her alive but the office. Poor sad old woman. Like getting divorced and having no place to go.'

Craig looked at Libby in surprise.

'For Christ's sake, stop it,' Craig said. 'This is a celebration, not a wake. I'm the boss. Let *me* do the feeling bad on my own time. We got what Mr. Roosevelt calls a New Deal. Here's to the new foreman and the new boss of the president's office. Down the hatch.'

'You didn't have to retire anybody,' Red said later, after Craig had sketched the outline of the day. 'You could of just canned everybody. How come?'

'I don't know. Softheaded, I guess. It's funny, but I can't stand the idea of firing anybody. I killed a man in a fight once in Europe and it didn't bother me too much. But old Marvin McCracken and Miss Mildred are going to fret me the rest of my life. And I haven't even done them a bad turn. New secretary, my glass is empty. Among your other duties . . .'

'Yes, Boss.' Craig looked at her with new eyes. His eyes seemed to have taken on a fresh appreciation of everything this day. The girl was gone. The woman was here. That remark about Miss Mildred. The fine long body was no fuller than before, but some of the childish chubbiness had been replaced by cleaner, sleeker lines. Her face had always been beautifully boned, but now . . . It was frightening how her face was now. It was not only lovely with its winged broad brows but the brown eyes suddenly contained a woman's secret wisdom.

He tried to make a joke of it.

'You reckon I'm safe in the same office with this gorgeous sister of yours, Red?' Craig made a nakedly obvious effort to conceal what he felt was nakedly obvious in his face.

'You better be. I'm running the backside of the shop. You read about them industrial accidents every day in the paper. My old man got mashed up permanent. It's even happened to mill presidents.' Red Forney laughed but there was little mirth in his eyes. 'I reckon you're safe with my little sister,' he said.

'Little sister might have something to say about that,' Libby said lightly, and both men glared at her.

'Sorry, gentlemen,' she said. 'Here are your drinks.'

9

THE office was unlike anything ever seen in Kensington, North Carolina. It had a rough-stone-fronted woodburning fireplace, and there was a white circular divan in front of it. It had a small, blond wood bar in one corner, a bar which housed a small

389

refrigerator. A flat glass dish containing michaelmas daisies stood on the bar top. There was another vase of yellow roses on the corner of the boss's enormous desk. Two lushly upholstered green easy chairs were placed at each side of the boss's desk. A low round coffee-table stood in the centre of the room in front of the divan, and bright green-and-red chintz drapes rustled against one enormous window which gave a close-up view of a very large weeping willow tree. One wall, next the fireplace, was lined with books, mostly in bright jackets, and if you stepped down two steps, you entered a smaller office, where a smaller desk, blond wooden filing cabinets built into the wall, and one easy chair with smaller coffee-table, chaperoned a typewriter and two telephones. There were flowers on the smaller coffees table, as well, and the telephones were painted white. Both room-were carpeted wall-to-wall. The carpet in the big office was apple green, and the carpet in the smaller office was honey-blond. Private bathrooms depended from both offices. The boss's bath-room contained a shower.

The offices had cost one hell of a lot of money. They had taken two months to do, and were spoken of as a scandal in the mill. Looks like a goddam bedroom, some said, not an office. Looks like a whore-house, others said. Who ever seen an office with a chandelier?

Craig had picked up Libby in the new Cadillac to take her to her first day of work. As they entered the door which said: *President*, in tiny golden letters against the dark walnut, Craig suddenly, impulsively, caught Libby up in his arms and carried her across the threshold. He plumped her to her feet with a thud, and kissed her on the forehead. He swept one arm to cover both rooms in one grandiose gesture.

'Welcome,' he said. 'Your new home. I hope you like it.'

Libby granted the room only a scanty glance, and looked deeply into Craig's eyes.

'It's lovely,' she said. 'I can't believe this is all coming true.'

'I wish you were a bride instead of a secretary,' Craig spoke almost to himself, knowing when he said it that it was only a matter of where and when.

'I like your new office,' Maybelle said. 'I'm surprised you don't leave the house and go live in it. Especially with all the modern conveniences and your fancy new red-headed secretary. You didn't waste much time, did you, boy? She qualifies on the tits real good. That's a real dish you got there. This makes it a real pleasure to be delayed at the office. Can she type? Or is that necessary?'

Craig chose to ignore the heavy sarcasm.

'Don't you get any wrong ideas about me and Libby,' Craig said. 'Her brother's my new spinning foreman, and he'll kill the

man that lays a hand on her. It's just that she's smart as well as
pretty, and I can't see any reason for having ugly old people to
work with you or ugly old places to work in. There seems to be
some sort of general idea that all offices should be ugly, all
secretaries should be chinless old maids, and that there should
always be somebody like old Soames around to give the place
an air of dignified dreariness, like an undertaking parlour. I
happen to think different.'

'I know,' Maybelle said. 'And you're the new president, so
you're allowed to think different. But did you *have* to have two
new bathrooms?'

'I didn't *have* to have the two new bathrooms. I *wanted* two
new bathrooms. I don't like the idea of going to the bathroom
that my secretary's just left.'

'She couldn't use the one the other help uses, I suppose? She'd
be too grand for that?' Maybelle's voice was elaborately sarcastic.

'Look,' Craig said. 'Please don't make me mad. Leave Libby
alone. This kid never had an inside bathroom before. We can
take the cost out of my salary, or charge her a nickel every time
she pees, if it bothers you.'

'How was she fixed for flowers before?' Maybelle's voice
flickered viperously at him. 'You're going to wind up with a real
tidy bill for flowers here if this gets to be a daily habit. Do you
have flowers and a special toilet to make shirts that shrink?'

'As a matter of fact,' Craig said. 'I do. Perhaps some other
people don't. *I* do. And they *don't* shrink.'

'You've come a long way from the hungry sailor, haven't you?'
Maybelle purred now. 'Boy-oh-boy. Did you have a special toilet
when you were going to sea on the *Wardance*? Did the bosun
put flowers on the mess table?'

'No.' Craig's voice flattened. 'That's why I have to have a
special toilet now. And flowers. And a Cadillac. And good clothes.
And a nice place to work. Just because I had to bathe and go to
the toilet in the same place with eight other people and the bosun
didn't put flowers on the table. I knocked cockroaches out of the
biscuits. I had to eat and sleep with people I didn't like, and
most of them were ugly. That's why I've got a pretty secretary
and a nice office and two toilets and flowers and a fireplace.
Would you like to shut up about this now and consider it the
price of being married to a man by the same name?'

'I'll shut up,' Maybelle said, 'as long as your fancy ideas don't
eat too deep into the profits, or you may kind of find yourself
without that power of attorney. And I wouldn't work too late at
the office too often if I were you. You know how the help talks.
You wouldn't like it back at sea, going to the john with eight
other people, and no flowers on the table.'

So she gives the sea business right back to me and the trouble
is, Craig thought bitterly, she's right. Like all women, she can

smell what isn't actually there before it happens, because she knows some day it'll be there. I'd a hell of a sight rather be working late at the office with Libby than be staying home with Maybelle—and Maybelle already knows it before I've even had a chance to prove it.

Working with Libby was a delightful habit. Just looking at Libby was a delightful habit, and habit was all you could call it. Craig found it awfully easy to leave his breakfast table five minutes earlier in order to pick her up at the little house. He found it just as easy to time his work-finish so that he could drop her off before he went home for supper. This became increasingly easy since he had incorporated the small ice-box in his bar and obviated the necessity of going home for lunch at all. Libby kept the ice-box stocked with cheeses and fruit and the makings for sandwiches. It was easy to send out for coffee until Craig decided to put a hotplate in the corner and instal an electric percolator, so that now lunch could consist of hamburgers and hot soup and decent coffee instead of the soppy stained cardboard cartons from the Greek. Lunch grew into a small ceremony, a happy time of the day when all the hands were off on the lunch hour, the phone was still, and there was no noise in the plant. The implicit peace of that hour was almost profound. Craig would say:

'Hey girl! Drop that typewriter and come make your boss a martini. We've worked hard enough for right now.'

Libby would hood her eyes demurely, and bat her lashes in the best approved Southern fashion.

'You know I don't approve of drinking during working hours,' she would say. 'It's bad for the morale of the help.'

'Oh, hell,' Craig would say. 'Unbend. Relax. A little martini never done nobody no harm. What are we having for lunch?'

'Baloney sandwiches or some of that canned crab you bought the other day. Or cheeseburgers.'

'Settle for the crabs. Won't be the first time, either. By God, girl you make a fine martini. Lookin' at you, sweetie.'

'Lookin' at you. Boss.' With her small smile.

A tiny bow, each to the other, and then Libby would bustle about the ice-box, put something on the hotplate, make the coffee, and Craig would think: *This is better than being married. This is almost like being in love, without all the trouble. It's like a picnic every day,* and then he winced when he thought of the word 'picnic'.

He looked at the girl.

She was wearing a black linen suit and a simple white shirt-waist. There was nothing obvious to detract from the mahogany roan of her hair, which she had taken to wearing off her neck, high-piled on her head. She used no cosmetics except lipstick. She kept her fingernails short and uncoloured. She was, Craig thought, the most ornamental piece of furniture in the office, or possibly in the world.

'Anybody ever tell you how very, very pretty you are?' he asked.

'Sure.' She flashed a smile. 'You. You always do. Every morning when you pick me up, and every day about this time, and every night when we have the one toddy before you take me home.'

Craig slapped himself lightly on the head. 'I must be losing my memory,' he said. 'I thought this was the first time I ever said it.'

'You said it the first time you ever saw me when I was a little girl,' Libby said.

'So I did, so I did, and I was right. Except you come along fine like a good garden. You get prettier all the time and I don't know how I can stand it if it keeps up. Not working with it all day long.'

'You fired Miss Mildred,' Libby said. 'Maybe I'll be next when I'm old and ugly. Have some of this cold crab and let's quit talking about me. It makes me nervous.'

Once in a while, Craig would say:

'I don't feel like working any more today. Do you?'

'You're the boss, Boss. But there's an awful lot of correspondence we haven't . . .'

'The hell with the correspondence. Let's go some place and play. Let's go fishin'. Let's go down to the Fort and watch the waves roll in. Let's go to the movies and see two Westerns. But don't let's work. It's too pretty an afternoon.'

'Who'll take the calls?'

'Stop being practical. What have we got a switchboard for? I went over to Brunswick to look at some cotton samples or something. I went to London to look at the King. But let's go some place away from all these goddamned invoices and the last letters from the union gents. Let's go swing in the trees and pretend I'm Tarzan, and you're Jane.'

'Let's pretend you're pretty silly for a president of a textile plant. I've got work to do. And so have you.'

'You're fired then. Fired unless you come with me, and right now.'

'I can't afford to be fired. You know that. Wait'll I tidy up and I'll be right with you. Tarzan, Sir.'

10

CRAIG had thought, when he carried his new secretary over the threshold of his new office, that it was only a matter of where and when. He had thought the same thing, really, that first day he

393

ever saw her when he went to the Forney house for beer and sandwiches before they went fishing. He knew it, knew it surely, the night of his first new car, when he took her riding before he even showed the car to Maybelle. He believed that Libby knew it, and that her brother Red knew it inevitably, but damned if he was going to do anything to soil this beautiful kid who wasn't a kid any more, but a glowing woman as ripe as a blush-peach for the plucking.

Libby was now a creature of temptation to touch. Every time she brought him a batch of correspondence or fixed him a drink or merely crossed his field of vision, there was a temptation to fondle her flank or lightly touch her shoulder, as innocently as one drops his hands to the head of a beloved dog or unthinkingly strokes the cat or even rubs the shabby spine of a favourite book or gently enjoys the mirrored-sheen of a good piano. Or, on the other hand, as un-innocently as one unhooks a brassière.

Libby was a flower, just unfolding its dewy petals in a joyous morning sun, and Craig wanted to smell it and see it and touch it, but something in him recoiled from the actual cutting of its stem. That the stem-cutting was inevitable he knew. This he found vastly puzzling to himself, because it had nothing to do with his marriage, nothing to do with infidelity, nothing to do with Libby's brother's fiercely protective attitude. It was almost as if he were trying to shield himself, to shore up and preserve one last shred of his boyish—would *niceness* be the word, he asked himself? For he remembered Mary Frances, and always with pain and abashed chagrin, and perhaps Libby to him was another Mary Frances, and he was chary of risking his own feelings, shy of ever again committing himself to positive tenderness.

Craig's almost virginal physical avoidance of Libby persisted for a year. He often worked her late, and he always drove her home, and the home-coming became almost a ceremony, too, because her brother Red had formed the habit of waiting for their arrival, and there was always a quick drink before Craig said: 'Christ, I wish I could stay, but I got a wife waiting supper at home, and you know how wives are . . .' or something equally trite. 'See you in the morning, Casey'—or Mike or Buster or Looie—any name he could devise to keep himself physically aloof from the girl in his own mind, and which was actually less descriptive of his feelings than 'darling' or 'sweetheart'. Away he would go into the night, fully frustrated, with the stench of frustration clinging to him as strongly as the scent of a heated bitch. Maybelle could smell, all right, and the scent of her husband in frustrated rutting season was as palpable as an observed infidelity.

394

11

THAT the young Craig Prices had had no friends of their own age, no intimate friends, was in a sense not their fault. Maybelle's unwed pregnancy, then the fatal accident, finally the presence of Irma Grimes in the house, had precluded much of an effort towards a wide circle of acquaintance. Now, of a sudden, they found themselves swept up into the limited society of a small coastal city whose former aristocracy of cotton, of shipping and real estate, had recently been devoured by the depression. There was no longer an aristocracy in the old sense, except as shabbily shown by the rotting old houses along Front Street, unpainted, termite-ridden, literally crumbling on their wet foundations into the yellow mouth of the river. The few acres that John Grimes had been able to preserve, sweeping outward from the town, overnight became valuable building sites. An entirely new community of post-crash people began to spring up. People made tidy fortunes from dairy plants and ice-cream factories and shirt factories. There had been shipyards during World War One—the dull mutter of an approaching World War Two inflated real estate in the vicinity of those mouldering old ways.

The young Prices suddenly found themselves in demand among Kensington's upper classes; classes in which poor whites come freshly affluent were no longer barred because a grandmother had painted her gums with snuff; because a grandfather had said 'hit' for 'it' or 'putt' for 'put'. Craig had John Grimes's white-pillared house repainted, and presently the Caddie was joined by a red Chrysler for Maybelle. The Chamber of Commerce beckoned, and Craig answered. And he had become a man among men, there was no doubt of that.

Two years after Irma Grimes died—1938—Craig Price was a man of commanding presence. He was twenty-three years old and looked thirty-five. His face had hardened and set into an adult mould and his eyes, which had never been very young, tended to wrinkle at the corners from concentration, giving him a mild and attractive squint which could lighten into laughter. His body had heavied in the shoulders, firmed into compactness. But mostly the eyes commanded. They never seemed to leave you when Craig was talking, especially when he was talking persuasively.

Maybelle had become what the daily paper might have described as a handsome young matron. She had lost first, her babyish chubbiness, then her pregnant fat, and now was a smoothly upholstered young woman. Both Craig and Maybelle were very well-dressed.

Once the young Prices started to entertain, they served the best food and were lavish with the best liquor, and, of course, were the first young people to install a swimming pool. This was conceded to be the mark of ultra-elegance, since Kensington was a seaboard city and the citizens had hitherto been content with piling into a car to go to the beach. Craig and Maybelle had another advantage, their extreme youth. The people in their economic stratum were of necessity considerably older, and those 'nice Price kids, he's as smart as a whip' became almost a vogue among the beginning-to-grizzle Country Club set. A few tentative pressures here and there, after Craig began to take an active interest in civic work—and especially after he was no longer accused of merely being John Grimes's lucky son-in-law, especially as he achieved an increasingly powerful position at the bank —soon firmly installed them in the meagre social constellation of the city.

12

THERE was nothing really too wrong about Maybelle except the drink and the fact that her husband didn't love her, didn't like to sleep with her except at pistol-point, and she damned well knew it. No, there had never been any real serious trouble with Maybelle except the drinking, and her resentment of his work, and his growing social stature in the city. And of course his secretary. That red-headed little bitch. But then most wives are jealous of their husbands' work and also of their secretaries, if the secretaries are pretty, and it is likely that the jealousy is more markedly posed against the work than against the woman, who is only parcel to the work. Women generally despise undue success in a husband, because it makes the husband more attractive to other women, more a public property, and also less dependent on wives, to a point where wives become unnecessary, the work a mistress, a narcotic, and the secretary who shares the work a devil's advocate. Maybelle had a valid point in her mounting animosity towards Craig. She felt he had used her body coldly as a stepping stone, and now that the stepping stone had become cemented into solid foundation, the body no longer was necessary either to his pleasure or professional use. Also Maybelle didn't like the constant reference, always acidly, by her girl friends to Craig's long hours in the office. Things like:

'I'm certain your husband will go a long way. He surely spends twice as much time at the office as my husband. That pretty red-haired girl wouldn't have anything to do with it, would she?' Giggle. Or:

'That little new girl your husband has at the office. She's pretty enough, but wouldn't he find that distracting in the office?'

Or: 'Did Craig really have to hire the whole family to run his—

pardon—your mill? Wouldn't the brother have been enough if he *did* have to adopt a lint-head into the family?'

Or 'I never seem to see that secretary of your husband's at your parties. I suppose you reckon he sees enough of her in the day-time, and would be bored by having to see her at night. But my old man always has *his* secretary to *our* parties. We couldn't run one without Ethel. She's plain, I got to say, but she's a real honey.'

Maybelle knew very well that when Craig stayed on at the office until nine or ten at night, when he phoned to say that he'd just grab a snack and she should go on ahead with dinner, that he was scourging himself towards an eventual aim that was marked clearly on his mental calendar: *'The expansion of Grimes Mills into Price Mills. The day he would have something of his own.*

She knew her man well enough now, she thought, to know that he wouldn't be stupid enough to sleep with the help, and that above all things he wanted something of his own—something that hadn't been indirectly given him by her or her father or her mother or any other damned body. And she knew also, that while he generally satisfied her sexually, it was a sterile satis-faction, almost a masturbation on her part, and that Craig himself no longer achieved much in honest physical excitement from the simple act of sexual congress, although Maybelle had attempted several variations on the simpler theme. She had dis-cussed, with the alarming candour of used wives, the entire processes with some of her new women friends, and they had reached a conclusion that all men were bastards, and all husbands bores after a certain lapse of time. So they drank.

Maybelle had always liked her toddy, but the liking increased after her child was killed in the accident. It was always, in con-versation, her child never Craig's child, with an intimation that Craig might actually have done it on purpose. The same implication attended her mother's death. 'If Craig hadn't insisted on bringing her home from the hospital, Mama would be alive today . . .'

Quite often Maybelle would be snoring asleep when he got home from the office, and there was no way of telling whether she was dru k or sober, because drunk or sober, Maybelle always snored. And Craig had formed the steady routine of the martini before the lunch that Libby made him, the extra drink or so if the work ran late, and always the one drink with Red and Libby when he took her home. When he fell into bed, he usually went swiftly off into a fatigue-drugged slumber, only to be awakened when Maybelle's half-conscious demands roused him to acquies-cence, and mostly he went through the chore only about half awake himself. Maybelle never woke when he got up in the morn-ing. It was easier that way and it was getting to a point where he sometimes did not really see his wife all week until a Saturday night party at the Club or somebody's house on Sunday.

Looking backward, Craig remembered isolated instances of coming home to find her in a state of high gaiety with 'the girls', two or three other wives of the new business friends, all much older than Craig and Maybelle, wives who had very little to do with their spare time, since coloured servants could still be had for six dollars a week, and Papa was off to that old office all day. Although the house was huge, most of the drinking seemed to occur in the kitchen—the women sitting around the kitchen table, their hair screwed in curlers under bandannas, grease smearing their unlipsticked faces and their bodies covered by wrappers or slacks and blouses. They experimented with each other's hair, and manicured their nails, jabbered about God knows what, and were generally head-waggingly drunk by lunch.

Lunch would consist of a tomato-and-bacon sandwich, or a piece of cold fried chicken. After lunch they would drive their Buicks and Chryslers uncertainly to their houses, sneak another stealthy shot from the kitchen bottle, and sweatily sleep most of the afternoon away. Then they would arise fur-tongued and swollen-faced about five, bathe, make up their faces carefully, draw on stockings and squirm into a girdle and a slip and a bra, and prepare the cocktail fixings for the master's return from commerce. With the precaution, of course, of a preliminary tot or so against the master's homecoming.

Personally different, they were a strangely similar group in looks, mood and habit. In their fashion all had been pretty, but the early prettiness had been blurred, some of it by age, more by daily infusion of alcohol. They had all married young, generally before they finished their complete educations, some because of pregnancy complications, some because lil' old Joe, or Pete, or Dick was simply the *cutest* boy, I swear, honey, and had the cutest car, and was a Deke or a Beta at Chapel Hill or Raleigh or else his parents had a ton of money and we don't *have* to start off poor-mouth with me doin' all the housework.

The chip-diamonded fraternity pin on the left breast, for all to see, and the promise of a honeymoon in Florida or maybe even in New York, plus a little spring moonlight, a good dance-band and the smell of jasmine and tuberose on the gentle night air, some drinks down in the bar of the fraternity house. . . . Or a crisp scarlet-and-gold autumn football week-end with the fire blazing and the drinks taking firm hold after a nippy afternoon of cuddling under a blanket in the stadium, and Hal Kemp providing magic with 'Heart of Stone' or the Dorsey Brothers being sentimental gentlemen from Dixie . . .

All these, and an appalling early ignorance of the latest contraceptives, had helped to form the club of young matrons. A girl was not really criticized because she failed to graduate from St. Mary's or Peace, and missed the mass début in Raleigh, in order to elope, always to South Carolina, which was pretty informal about short-order marriages. Of course it was better to make the début, and to get married in church with a long trailing dress and a veil and all, and so in some instances the drugstores did a thriving trade in ergonol, and the girls who had never stirred a foot at any sport livelier than dancing suddenly took up horseback riding and attempted daring jumps from lofty ladders. Then it was all right again—(I've come around, honey, silly ol' me, I guess I was just late)—and so the début could be held, the marriage arranged, and Miss Deborah Ann Mitchell became Mrs. Robert Rodd Emerson III, and was thereinafter referred to as the 'attractive' or 'beautiful' or 'talented' young matron in the local society columns which devoted barren shores of flotsam space to Country Club bridge benefits and charity auction sales. Not forgetting the Little Theatre.

The husbands worked nine-to-five in banks or real estate or mills or fertilizer factories or insurance firms. They all made what was known as 'enough' money, and generally lived out close to the Country Club, where all their other friends were building now and which was very closely screened against Jews and other undesirables, such as Negroes, Republicans, Holy Rollers, and in some instances, Catholics. ('Of course, I haven't got anything against Jews, some of our best friends are Jews, and I suppose Catholics are all right, but really you don't want to live with them. You treat them even a little bit decent and pretty soon they want to joint the Country Club and are always droppin' in on you just when you don't want them.')

They made, now the Depression was easing, 'enough' money. They had a salty-grey-shingled beach cottage for the summer, and they all belonged to the Country Club and the Yacht Club and a cotillion society at which white gloves and tails for the gentlemen were mandatory at the New Year's Ball. They played golf twice a week—Wednesday and Saturday—and got violently, generally nauseatingly, drunk every Saturday night either at the Club or at somebody's house. They were rigidly moral in town, nearly, due mainly to lack of easy facility, and with a few exceptions, wonted infidelity was confined to a hurried smudgy kiss in a garden or a fumble in a car parked outside the Club. One lady got herself discovered in a rumpled compromising position behind the bunker at the eighteenth hole by another couple also seeking *al fresco* sanctuary at the Club, and the town buzzed deliciously for months. Occasionally, an expense account trip to Raleigh or Charlotte or even Washington produced an evening of revel which included whores and a brief attack of conscience to fatten the hangover.

Almost to a woman, bar the few nymphomaniacs, the childbearing wives had never experienced an orgasm. After the first sweaty excesses of legalized fornication had dulled to formal routines—Sunday afternoon after a big dinner of chicken-and-dumplings and strawberry shortcake, or an infrequent recurrence of ancient lust at 2 a.m. after the Saturday dancing—intercourse meant only children and throwing-up in the morning and three's enough for any family, don't you think, honey?

The men, immersed in golf, sailing, fishing, quail-and-duck hunting in the fall, looked at their women dully, tragically apathetically. Somewhere, away back, there had been that girl, the girl with hot parted lips, a girl whose mouth was parched by desire, that girl who suddenly was unashamed of a bared bosom on the moonlit beach, the girl who danced and laughed and swirled and paid extravagant compliments (I swear, honey, in that white coat you 'bout the handsomest ol' thing I ever did see), a flashing dagger of a girl, the one all the stag-line cut in on at the Spring Frolics, so you couldn't hardly dance with your own girl, and who had more late dates than *any*body. This was the girl whose left teat trembled delicately to the touch when you hung the fraternity pin on her, making her irrevocably yours in the eyes of God and man; this was the girl who said tremulously, later, when you were getting rid of compromising sand or jamming the dislocated seat back into the car, 'I declare, I don't know what came over me, I swear I don't. I guess you must think I'm just awful, but I never went *all* the *way* with anybody else before.' Tears, and the embarrassed pat, and then the Galahad approach. (Don't you fret, we'll just get married, honey, sweetie-baby and everything will be all right.)

The husbands looked at the wives, and now saw *wives*. The wives looked at the husbands with uninterested dull hatred. Betty hadn't lost the weight she gained after the last pregnancy. Ate her head off, no matter what the doctor said, while she was carrying little Charles. Mary-Beth is drinking too much. Honest to God, it's getting to be worth your life to take her to a party. The other night at . . . I don't know what's come over Nancy. Once in a while when I try to do the husbandly duty she just rolls over and says she's got a headache. God, I don't know about Jill. She's after me all the time. For Christ's sake, doesn't she know I work for a living? If she had her way we'd be in bed all day long, and I wonder now just what she'd been up to before we got engaged? So innocent and all, that night after the winter Festival. A nice girl, a *wife*, ain't *supposed* to be teasing all the time, like she was a . . . a *girl-friend*. Why, she grabbed me by the . . .

The tragedy progressed when Dick started calling Marjorie 'Mama', and Marjorie started calling Dick 'Daddy'. It was the children's fault, of course, until it got to be an adult habit, and they finally used it against each other in direct address. 'Darling' and 'Dearest' vanished into the forgotten fogs of youth, and became replaced by 'dearie' and 'sweetie', two words from which all the original velvet nap had been worn slick, becoming as impersonal as 'you there'. Finally, it was factual that no bed had been encumbered happily in a long time when Mama referred to Papa, in his absence, as 'Jones' or 'Smith', and Papa referred to Mama, in the presence of his clients or cronies, as 'the wife' or 'the madam'. Where had the 'Harry, darling', or the 'Mary, dearest' fled away, to be replaced by 'lovie' and 'sweetie' and 'dearie'?

The children claimed the mother's first attention, as the office held its mistress's clutch on the father. The painful parody of the evening greeting eventually ceased. No longer did Annie say: 'Anything new at the office today, Ben?' and no longer did Ben reply: 'Nothing much, 'bout the same. Maybe have some trouble with that new contract.' What contract in question was never amplified, either by question or answer. No longer did husband ask: 'What's going on around the house?' because the answer was always the same. The pipes had burst. The baby had a suspicious-looking rash. Dr. Smith came by and said . . . (I'm gaining too much weight. I heard about the most divine diet, nothing but carrots and . . .)

They just nodded, now, and the man says: 'Jesus, I'm really beat. Easy on the vermouth.' And the woman replies, making the martinis: '*You're* beat? Try running this house just once, just *one* day.' And the conversation lapses into newspapers until dinner, after which Father snores in his chair, and Mother looks at him with blooded stilettos in her eyes.

The dripping red steak of Saturday romance had long since become Monday's meat-loaf. There sits Romeo, there sits Don Juan, there sits the young Clark Gable, with his chins slumped on his chest, his five o'clock shadow deepened into darkest midnight blue, his burgeoning belly unleashed by a loosened belt and the first two buttons of his trousers undone. His coat is off and the shirt-tail billows, and he has kicked off his shoes. A copy of the *Saturday Evening Post* or *Esquire* is equally somnolent, face-down, on the floor beside him. And Mary or Marge or Janie or Beth thinks:

Christ.

No more than that. Just: *Christ.*

This was the world of Craig and Maybelle, a world of infinite boredom with themselves and with new friends, and, generally, with work. Craig was not bored with his work, and as much as possible he avoided his friends, all of whom were older than he, and his wife's friends, so assiduously that Maybelle's commonest complaint was the whining 'but we never do *anything* and you never take me *anywhere*'.

13

THE new little house sat there, primly, like a nice girl in a party dress, with her ankles crossed and her hands folded in her lap. A nice little girl like Libby looked the day I first saw her, Craig thought, as he drew his Cadillac into the kerb behind a gleaming new black Ford sedan. Hot diggity damn, he said to himself, everybody's rich. Even me. Hooray for us.

The little new house was gleaming white, of painted brick, and if you left it alone in the weather long enough the bricks would show rosy pink through the scabbing paint. In time it would have some eager ivy or rambler roses groping along its sides. Right now it looked more like a man with a fresh haircut, or a girl with her hair still tight-curled from the beauty shop, before the curls have had time to be combed and fluffed out into a halo.

It was one of a hundred thousand similar houses, costing about $6500 with a twenty-year first mortgage, with an added burden of second mortgage, if you couldn't get up the down payment. It was a house which would be outgrown if there were children. It was a house with a patch of just-starting undecided lawn, with some just-beginning lonely bushes, probably hydrangea and azalea. There was an ill-at-ease pinetree or two, and a couple of discouraged maples, and a clump of weeping willow from which the leafy tears had not quite commenced to flow. The little new house had been cookie-cut, rubber-stamped from a classic master plan which lacked imagination but offered plastic toilet seats. If you turned it one way, and reversed it to face the microscopic backyard, or glued it on to another house, you could multiply it by half a million and throw it down in any place in the land, and it would tell you one story: This is the first clean, the first new house that people who have never lived in clean, new houses before, have ever owned. On a twenty-year payment plan, of course.

Craig beat on the polished imitation-brass knocker.

'By God,' he said, 'it's a castle. Let the poor folks into the castle, or do I have to come in the back door?'

'Nobody carried *me* over any thresholds,' Craig said to Libby Forney and her brother Red. Craig was cradling a bulky bundle. 'I feel real hurt, I feel so hurt I ain't gonna give you your new house-warming present.' He pointed a finger at Libby. 'At least you got carried over the threshold of *my* new house. Office, that is. Maybe I should have said *our* house.'

'You weigh too much,' Red laughed. 'I don't aim to get me no ruptures bein' polite to the boss. It ain't in the contract.'

'What contract?'

'The one you're gonna have to sign some day with these

union fellers. They's more and more of 'em around, talking to the help. Foreign-lookin' fellers. Some others, people from upstate.'

'That'll be a frosty Friday,' Craig said. 'Leave the business. Damn the unions. Here, Libby. You're politer than your brother. If you can manage to untie some of these strings you'll find a present for your new house. And I must say it is a lovely new house.'

Libby's fingers flew eagerly at the wrappings. The discarded paper disclosed a chased sterling silver tea-and-coffee set, complete with tray, pitchers for cream and hot water, and a squat round sugar-bowl. The coffee-pot bore the initials 'RF' and the teapot 'LF'. The others utensils were monogrammed simply with a large curly-tailed 'F'.

'Oh, Craig!' Libby dashed at him and threw her arms around him. She kissed him soundly on both cheeks. Tears started in her eyes. 'I can't tell you how . . .'

'Don't,' Craig said shortly. 'Just show me around the new house. I didn't want to come prowlin' around until you people had it fixed up to suit you. It sure does look pretty outside.'

'I ain't much good at sayin' thanks,' Red Forney said. 'It don't go with my hair or general disposition. But in your case I aim to make an exception. I reckon that day you knocked me windin' when I was givin' you a hard time at that baseball game was the luckiest day Libby and me'll ever see. When I say thanks, Craig, it ain't just for a silver coffee-pot or that new Ford out front or this new house or a way me and Libby can hold up our heads now. It's more'n that. Now I've said it. Thanks. Have a snort.'

'Why, Red,' Craig said, 'I do believe you're a sentimentalist instead of a redheaded ex-po' *Bokra* who also happens to be the best stud-hoss foreman in the textile business. Come on, you fellows, show me the house. The drink can wait.'

'It isn't a very big house, Craig,' Libby said. 'But look. It's got a living-room and a dining-room *and* a breakfast nook and this big kitchen. And we've each got a big bedroom and a private *bath* each. See, what a lovely bath.'

'I reckon Craig don't appreciate what a power of importance we lay on private baths,' Red said. 'But unless you've lived most of your life washing out of a tin tub and going outside to—'

'Shush, Red,' his sister said.

'I reckon Craig does appreciate private baths,' Craig said. 'Don't forget that Craig was raised in the country and went to sea for a living before he broke into the silver-coffee-pot-and-new-Ford-car set. Why'd you buy a Ford, Red?'

'Well, hell, you had a Cadillac and I didn't want to start no competition with the boss. People would talk it around that I was gettin' uppity. Also, by the time we got the down payment paid on this house, and the down payment paid on the furniture, and the down payment paid on everything else, we just didn't plain have no more money left for such as Cadillacs. I reckon that Morris Plan bank can live on us for ever. It don't need no other customers. Maybe next year we'll work up to Chevvies, but there ain't no real hurry. Libby's got her own private chauffeur, and he's got a Cadillac. Sis don't really need no better transportation than a Cadillac and a chauffeur, do you, honey?'

Libby smiled at Craig.

'I'm satisfied,' she said. 'I'm real satisfied. As long as my chauffeur's satisfied. Do you really like the house, chauffeur, sir?'

'I wish I lived in it,' Craig said. 'I guess you people share my tastes. I love that green in the living-room and the yellow in the breakfast-room and the grey-and-yellow paper in the dining-room. I guess I'm what you might call a kind of crazy springtime kid. Also these chairs and that sofa seem to be the kind you're supposed to sit down on instead of look at.' He kissed his fingers, then blew the kiss at the house.

'What I like about it most, forgettin' the mortgages,' Red said, 'is that nobody but us never lived in it before. Every time I go to the can I can't help feelin' that nobody ever sat on it before but me.'

'That's crude, Red, and it's the second time you brought it up,' Libby said.

'I don't care if it's crude or not crude,' Red replied. 'To me, poor white trash, livin' in my own house with my own bathroom is better'n bein' President Roosevelt. You got to be poor a long time to really appreciate bein' able to slam a door so nobody can come into your private doin's.'

They went back into the living-room and sat down. Red went to the kitchen and returned with three drinks.

'Look,' he said. 'Real, honest-to-God ice-cubes from a real, honest to God refrigerator. It suddenly strikes me that we're rich. We ain't poor no more.'

'Poor no more,' Craig said slowly. '*Poor no more*. It seems to me that you just said a mouthful, Red, my friend. I reckon that's the story, more or less, of everybody's life. Any day a man wakes up he wonders, even before he goes to the bathroom, inside or outside, how he's gonna feed his family that day, and how he's gonna keep himself from being poor any more. Especially if he's been real tough poor, and now he knows what it's like to have two pairs of shoes instead of one and an extra bottle of beer in the ice-box. I don't think you people will ever be poor any more. Christ, I sound like a preacher. Here's all the luck in the world to you both.' He raised his glass, and drained it. 'I got to be moving along now. It's a lovely house, and I hope to spend a lot of time in it.'

As he moved towards the door, Libby kissed him on the cheek

again. 'I haven't really said thanks, Craig. I'm saying thanks now, for both me and Red.'

Craig turned.

'I'll pick you up in the morning as usual, Mike,' he said. 'It's a pity this brother of yours ain't front office and has to go to work so early in the shop, else I could be his chauffeur, too. 'Bye.'

A strange emotion crawled behind Craig Price's eyes as he drove away and caused them to cloud, ever so slightly.

God damn, he said to himself. Look at those kids, with their new house, shining new house, new car, shining new car, new ice-box, shining new ice-box, and now a shining new life, even if it does include a lot of shining new time payments. And to think that I had a little bit to do with it. To think that Libby's new tea service and Red's Ford all came out of old man Grimes picking me up on the road, and me getting Maybelle knocked up, and me having a fight with Red, and us going fishing, and me firing old Mildred and old Marvin, and now Libby and Red are quality people.

Red said once that when he got rich he was going to have sirloin steak three times a day, and now he can have it, on just a little more money, that little more money that makes the difference. Now he's got his inside toilet and Libby's got her own bathroom and all on just a little more money—a little more money that came about by me murdering Maybelle's mama, more or less, and bamboozling the banks, and being a he-whore with Maybelle. What was that thing I read in college—'*Deus ex machina*'? That's what I am, he thought, a goddam *Deus ex machina*. And possibly one of the unhappiest goddam *Deus ex machinas* ever seen. I wonder what will happen to them now, in their neat little white brick house with the breakfast nook and the *two* bathrooms. Red'll never get any further than straw boss of the mechanical end of the mill, because he hasn't got the education to be the general manager, and I think he knows it, and doesn't mind it. But Libby? There's no end to where she can go. I hope she marries a nice guy in the blue-blood class, because she's worth being a member of anybody's country club. Or I hope she goes North and does something about meeting a nice man who'll give her a good home and a good life. By God, if it weren't for Maybelle . . .

He put that thought swiftly out of his head. He was going home to Maybelle now and he wasn't taking any thoughts of Libby with him. He shook his head sharply, and turned into the drive. It would be nice if Maybelle were reasonably sober.

'I think he's the sweetest man I've ever known, Red,' Libby said, as she poured coffee from the new silver pot with the 'RF' on it. 'The kindest and most thoughtful.'

'I don't know about sweet and kind and thoughtful,' Red said, 'but I guarantee one thing: he's the toughest son of a bitch I ever met. I don't mean nothin' about how hard he can hit with his fist, although I know something about that too. What I mean is just plain all-over tough, inside and out.'

'He's the best friend you've—we've—got,' Libby said. 'You oughtn't to say things like that.'

'He may be our best friend now, and don't get me wrong, because I like the guy . . . maybe as much as you do?' Red cocked an eye at his sister. 'How much *do* you like the guy? It's something I been wantin' to ask you. But before you say a word, let me tell you somethin'. Craig Price knocked up Maybelle Grimes because he wanted in at the mill, and plantin' the dead boss's daughter with a baby was one way in. And Craig Price dragged the old woman out of the booby hatch with just one idea—gettin' control of her stock. And Craig Price fired old Mildred Mason and old Marvin McCracken just as cold as a dog's nose so he could give you and me jobs. Just because we're his friends—now. He didn't care a fart in a whirlwind about either one or how long either one had been working there, any more than he didn't give a good goddam for his mother-in-law or, for that matter, for his wife. Now I ask you again. You're a big girl now and I can't hand you that "little Sis" stuff. How much do you like the guy? And I don't mean as a boss. Forget I'm your brother and tell me like I was a friend.'

Libby looked at her brother with almost-pitying woman's eyes. 'You don't know that I'm in love with him? Red, you're smart, and you're so dumb. I've been in love with him ever since the day you brought him in the door of the old house. When I was wearing hair ribbons and tennis shoes. When I made you some tuna-fish sandwiches and then fried you some fish. When he came by to take me for a ride in that new Dodge. The first thing he ever owned, he wanted to share with me. You don't *know* I'm in love with him? I'd marry him if I could, and the minute he asks me I'll go to bed with him, but the trouble is, God dammit'—it was the first profanity Red had ever heard her use—'the goddam trouble is that he never does anything about me. It's like he was scared of me. Every time I want to touch him or more, want him to touch me, he shies off. I'm happy enough just being around him all day, fixing him a drink or a sandwich and working with him, but if you want an honest answer, brother, what I really want him to do is tear off all my clothes and throw me down on a beach or in the back seat of a car or at the corner of Market Street and Front, I don't care!' Libby burst into tears. 'I don't care!'

Red was plainly shocked at the outburst. He had known his kid sister had been a woman for a long time, apart from the necessary impedimenta and moods which distinguished women

406

from girls. But back somewhere in a brother's brain is the grained idea that it is always somebody else's sister, not your own, who moans and writhes and twists in your arms, whose mouth is wet on yours, whose nipples stand erect under your stroking hand, whose hips swirl and rise to meet you. Red had been with a few whores and some of the mill girls, but it really never had occured to him that they had brothers. Sisters were . . . well, *sisters*. They didn't talk as Libby was talking, like a whore, like an easy piece of milltown poon. Red shook his head. He reckoned he was out of his depth, and he wished he hadn't brought the subject up.

'I don't like to hear you talk like this, Sis,' he said, awkwardly. 'It ain't becomin' to a nice girl. It ain't . . .' He patted her on the shoulder. She stopped crying and glared at him.

'There ain't no such things as a nice girl!' she cried. 'There are just girls! Just girls, made for men to love and to hold close and take to bed! Just girls! Girls that go to the toilet and have the curse once a month and fall in love with men that they want to. . . . You know what I mean. You use the word all the time. You want me to say it? I'll say it. F . . .'

'Don't say it. I don't want to hear you say it.' Red held up his hands defensively. 'I never reckoned to hear my baby sister talk like this. I looked after you so careful and all. I tried to take care of you. I wanted the best for you and now you talk like a . . . like a . . . wantin' to take up with a married man. I reckon you better quit your job. You can still go to college.' Red Forney looked trapped and baffled.

'I will *not* quit my job. I will *not* go to college. I'm going to stay right here.'

'If that Price lays a hand on you I'll . . .'

'You'll do nothing at all. I'm not a child any more. And if you dare say a word to Craig about this I'll . . . I'll try to kill you, Red! I'll sneak up on you at night and brain you with a poker! I'll run off with the first sailor I see! I'll . . .' White showed over the top of Libby's pupils. Red shoved her gently on the shoulder.

'Calm down and listen to me. You ain't gonna do any of the things you say. Look, I respect Price, and if like you say, he ain't made any grabs at you, I respect him twice as much more. You're a woman, and a damned pretty one. If you was *his* sister, and we was workin' together all day long, I ain't so sure I wouldn't . . .' he smiled. 'I ain't so sure I wouldn't kind of help you along.

'But there ain't no future to you goin' crazy over Craig Price. He's married, and I expect he aims to stay so. Maybe he don't give the first cuss about his wife, but she's part of the mill, and he's sure as hell married to that mill. There's gonna be more mills, and more everything else, and one day he's gonna be too big for this town. And all you'll be is left with a bastard brat and a busted heart. If they was any future I'd say go ahead and grab him, but that man ain't good for no woman and for damned few men and you mind my words. He's a wrecker. He called me a stud hoss today. Man, I ain't even a Shetland-pony mare alongside this feller. I was wrong about tellin' you to quit. You'd see him anyhow, maybe more and for worse than just seein' him every day in the office. But listen to your big brother. You find yourself a nice boy friend, and make some plans about hangin' on to your cherry until you get married. There ain't much market for damaged goods anywhere, and once it gets around that you're Craig Price's fancy woman you ain't got a prayer in hell of ever catchin' a good husband and raisin' a nice family.'

'I'd rather have a bastard brat by Craig Price than a whole litter of legal children by anybody else I know!' Libby flashed. 'I tell you now, I don't care about anybody else, and any time he wants me he can have me, and if I have to be his fancy woman, as you call it, I'd rather be his fancy woman on the side and work with him all day in the office than be married to the Governor!'

'That's little-girl talk,' Red said. 'You been seein' too many movies. What I do suggest is that you consider it ain't real nice to go poachin' on another woman's man, and what you have to do on the side, in the dark, eventually gets to be like a toad or a snake or anything else slimy that lives in the dark. All the fine-haired love in the world don't last unless it gets a little sunshine and a whole hell of a lot of public approval. Maybe I ain't got much education, but at least I know that.'

Libby sighed.

'I know you're right, Red. My head tells me you're dead right. But I'll tell you something about women. Unless a woman's scheming to get something she wants for the rest of her body, her head doesn't figure much in her make-up. My head tells me I can't have him but all the rest of me just yells that I got to have him!'

'Well, then, there's nothin' more I can do about it,' Red said. 'I'm sorry. I can't follow you around any more and keep you from neckin' with the drugstore cowboys like I used to. And there ain't any use of my sayin' anything to Price, who would just tell me to go to hell, hit me in the chin and probably fire me into the bargain. And it looks like there ain't anything I can tell you.'

Red looked around him at the sparkling new house, the fresh paint, the new furniture. Suddenly he swept his arm and knocked the coffee service to the floor. Coffee dribbled from the spout and stained the new rug, and the scattered sugar made a tiny snowdrift.

'All this we got we didn't have before!' he said. 'If I'd of knowed about how we was goin' to pay for it I'd of killed him before I walked him in that front door in the old house. I'd of worked as a mill hand and used a backhouse the rest of my days before I'd have brought him in that door!'

Libby darted into the new kitchen and came out with a wet dish-towel. She started to mop the coffee stains from the rug. On her knees, she picked up the pot and scattered cups and the half-emptied sugar-bowl and put them back on the coffee-table.

'I'm sorry, Sis,' Red said, and got down on his knees. 'Give me the rag. It needs a little more moppin'. I'm sorry. I just got mad the way I do. I keep sayin' I'm sorry.'

His sister looked at him coldly. She shook her head in sober, mock puzzlement.

'I wouldn't have thought it,' she said. 'I really wouldn't have thought that we could have dumped so much dirt over so much niceness.'

She got up and went into her room, and came out with her handbag. She walked to the door. Her shoulders were haughty.

'Where you goin'?' her brother asked.

'Out,' she said. 'And don't bother to wait up. I've got my own key and I'm a big girl now. Like you said.'

Red Forney looked dumbly after his sister, his baby sister, at her women's buttocks as she walked coldly out of the door. Why, he thought, she *is* a woman. I kind of never thought she would be, that maybe she always would be a little girl. Then he went to the kitchen and wet the towel again and came back with a box of salt. As he went down on his knees to scrub again at the coffee stain, he sprinkled some salt on the carpet. He had heard or read somewhere that salt would take out coffee stains. He wondered as he scrubbed if you could take out other stains as easily with a little scrubbing. When he got up to take the dishrag back to the kitchen he had decided that maybe there was a stain on this day that would need more than perpetual scrubbing. But then Red Forney was a man of spare book-learning, and he might have been wrong.

Libby walked angrily, her heels clicking harshly. She was angry at Red, even more angry at herself for the sudden revelation of her honesty to herself and to her brother, and sweetly, rather happily angry at Craig for having roused the honest female beast in her. Virginity had not troubled Elizabeth Forney. She was a pretty girl, and she had had her share of dates. But brother Red had been stricter even than a father about the better-class boys assuming that a mill-girl was easy pickings, and she had assisted Red with a reverse snobbishness. *She* looked down on the people who were supposed to look down on *her*. It put an impossible barrier between her and the kids from the Country-Club set. She was frankly bored by the boys of her own station, who were for the most part clottish young pigs with white eyelashes and bad complexions, sons of mill people, boys with no humour and little imagination. Libby had become the ultimate snob. She refused to expose the poverty of herself and Red to equality, scorn or condescension. She refused to be the easy necker, the easy petter, the ultimately easy lay, just because somebody's grandson with numerals after his name owned a snazzy car, went to Carolina, and was out scouting for easy stuff. She refused double-dates when someone of her classmates suggested that she knew two of the *cutest* boys, and she also refused the fumbling advances of the poorer element from Castle Street and Delgado who clumsily assumed that everybody was in the same boat, the same slum, and why not go behind the nearest sand-dune at Carolina beach and—she thought of the word which she yet had not said aloud. She had almost said it today when she was scrapping with Red. But it was a horrible word, horribly descriptive, but in a way not so nasty as some of the excuses people made to avoid saying it.

Now she, Elizabeth Forney, was caught. She had refused the attentions of the upper classes, and had scorned the possible attraction of the lower classes, and there wasn't really a middle class, in Kensington, North Carolina, not if brother Red was watching. Because brother Red was as proud as she, and if he and she weren't good enough for one, they were too damned good for another, and the middle-classers would have sneered at their early poverty, too. Libby felt suddenly cheated.

I've never even soul-kissed with a boy, she thought. I've never had a man's hand on my breast or up my leg. I've never even had a crush on a fellow, not even an athlete. I am well known as the dullest drag in the date department.

And look at me. I'm a good-looking girl. I've got a good figure and a nice face and pretty red hair. I've got a good job and a nice brother, even if his English isn't too good, and a new house and a new car and the nicest boss in the world. I'm in love with my boss, who has got a wife and who had a baby and who doesn't even look at me. He's kissed me on the cheek like you'd pat a dog a few times. I know he doesn't love his wife but he doesn't love me, either. I'm the girl who answers his phone and makes his drink and fixes him a sandwich. I am still Red Forney's Little Sister, and by God I don't want to be Little Libby any more. I am Elizabeth Forney, woman grown, and as long as we are talking frankly, Libby, she thought, I don't want to be un-soul-kissed or un-touched any more. I want not to be a virgin any more, and the man I want to un-virgin me is named Craig Price. My boss. And since he is such a stinking gentleman, it's up to me to do something about it. I've got Red tamed about the whole idea. I want this man, and I want him soon, and how I get him doesn't really make any difference. Why, Elizabeth Forney, she said, what terrible thoughts you have.

Then she quit walking and went into Belk's and bought a pair of shoes with very short uncomfortable vamps and very high heels.

14

IT would be difficult for either Craig or Libby to say how or why they had suddenly commenced kissing. It had been like something Druid-sent from the forests, some tiny secret sign, some small smell, some slight unplanned musky indication of need to each other. Perhaps it had been the fresh flowers in the bowl, perhaps the intrusive breeze that stirred the curtains and let the sun-bright day bow unbidden into grey-faced business. Or even perhaps the way Libby's skirt rustled when she brought in a tray of stolid correspondence, or the crispness of her shirt-waist, the liquid swing of her hips, or the shape of her small, neat ears. Perhaps a birdsong, faintly heard, perhaps the memory of a good breakfast, perhaps the cheerful clanging of the mill machinery as it spelled harsh profit.

Libby placed the tray of correspondence on Craig's desk, and he could see the curve of her breasts as they fell forward from her body when she leaned over the desk. Suddenly he was out of his seat, kissing her, holding her close, with both their bodies blended, straining towards each other. Then Libby pushed him suddenly away.

'No! No, Craig! Not here. Even in the yard. Even in the street. Anywhere else but here or in our house.'

Craig looked honestly surprised. He looked at the closed door, a door that could be locked against intrusion.

'Why not here? Why, of all places on earth, not here? We live here. It's our home.' Craig shook his head. Women, my God, women.

'That's it, Craig. That's just it. We have to live here. And work here. And it's not—not *ours*. Craig. I love you, Craig. But this is a good part Maybelle's and her family's. But it's not ours to make love in. And my brother works in the back of the mill. It's like having him in the same room with us. No, Craig.'

Craig looked baffled, and more than a little hurt. She had kissed him as fiercely as he had wanted her ever since the first day he had seen her.

'Where, then? Where do you go to love somebody you love?'

'Not our house, either. That's Red's—*Red's*. Actually Red's. Not yours and mine. You can have me when you want me, but it has to be some place that's ours. I don't care if it's a sand-dune or the back of your car or even a hotel room. But not here, and not there.'

Craig frowned. Flooding memories of Mary Frances suddenly drowned him. He remembered the day that . . . that spring time when. That time by the lake at school. He closed the trapdoor on his memory. No. He didn't want that again. He didn't ever want to take a woman he loved in a circumstance of former loving—

not a woman as close to what he considered the love he had thrown away as a stupid callow boy. And now the hot spontaneity had cooled from his first embrace with Libby, although the warmth of her body and the scent of her body were still printed on his person. What had begun in happy heat had now of necessity become a plan, and Craig did not like the idea of its having become a plan. He shook his head again, and grinned. The Great Avoider, he thought.

'I need a drink, girl,' he said. 'A stiff one. Suppose you do me a little bourbon-and-branch, while I collect my scattered brains. You had much practice kissin' fellows? That one was about two hundred proof.'

Libby smiled as she walked over to the liquor cabinet.

'I never had no practice a-tall kissin' fellows like that before. But I think it could shore git to be a habit.'

'All right,' Craig said. 'We don't need the hillbilly dialogue just because I'm nervous. Don't feel you have to put me at ease just because we suddenly attacked each other. And we did, didn't we? Attack each other? Ferociously, I mean?'

'I wouldn't say *you* attacked *me*.' Libby matched his grin with more calculated lasciviousness than one would expect from a girl in her latest teens. 'Let's just say that I been practisin' up so I could attack you. So when I attack I make it stick. You got a lot of lipstick on your mouth, boss.'

'You practise real good,' Craig said. 'Thanks for the drink. I know I got lots of lipstick on my mouth. It tastes just dandy. You havin' a drink?'

'I don't think I need one,' Libby said. 'I'm too young to kiss the boss *and* have a drink on one and the same day.'

'Seriously,' Craig said. 'Seriously, Sugar.' They drove along the beach road to the old Fort. Libby was sitting very close to him, and he could feel the pressure of her breast on his arm, the warmth of her long thigh pressed close to his. 'Seriously, it's a hell of a problem, and the way you put it, I didn't want to talk about it in the office. I want you more than I ever wanted anything, my girl, but it's got to be a half-way house and that I hate. I'm still married with all the complications you know about. In a town like this we can't go scampering in and out of hotels, such as they are. And there's something dirty about these motels that I don't want to rub off on us. You know—too many people there before. I don't seduce lightly, do I?'

Libby shivered slightly, and Craig could feel her tremble.

'Let's stop here so I can kiss you again,' she said. 'So I can get you back again. Right here. There's nobody around for miles.'

The little fishing-shack had a 'For Rent' sign on it. It sat on a high sweeping dune overlooking the beach on which the heavily white-plumed rollers pounded. It had a little rickety, precarious flight of planked stairs leading from the small porch to the beach below. Sea-oats surrounded the cottage's salt-grizzled shingles, and silver gulls screamed and braced their wings as they rode the stiff breeze.

'What a sad, lonely little house, all by itself away from everybody,' Libby said. 'I know what this house feels like.'

'All alone on this beach where nobody ever comes except to fish and then only in the fall,' Craig murmured, half to himself. 'I always loved to fish. You know, darling child, I think I will take up fishing as a hobby. I've been working too hard lately.'

He threw the car into gear, and Libby looked at him in surprise. He hadn't kissed her again.

'Where are we going now?' she asked. 'You're driving so fast, Craig.'

'To the hardware store,' he said. 'I have to buy some fishing-tackle and some camping equipment because I have just rented myself a fishing-shack. I hadn't realized how much I missed fishing until that day I went with your brother, and that's not real fishing, that bent-pin-and-worm stuff. I'm a surf caster at heart.'

Craig left the office after lunch for three days. He had not kissed Libby again, but had stayed so stiffly aloof that she looked hurt.

'What will I say if anyone calls?' she asked, rather plaintively on the third day.

'Just say I'm back in the plant and to leave a message. Or else I've gone across the river and will be back by six. I will be back by six.' He blew her an airy kiss. 'Look after the store, Pete.'

Saturday morning Craig got up late and dressed in rough clothing. He produced a rod-and-reel, a tackle-box, and a bait-bucket from the hall closet.

'What's all this?' Maybelle asked. 'You being a Boy Scout again?'

'Yes,' Craig said. 'I'm going fishing.'

'Who with?'

'A couple of fellows from the office. I'll be back by dark.'

'You want me to fix you a lunch?'

'Don't bother. We'll grab a sandwich somewhere. 'Bye.'

'Don't be late. You know we got people comin'.'

Craig took down the 'For Rent' sign and threw it into the sea-oats. He produced a key and opened the door.

'Come here,' he said gruffly, and this time, when he picked Libby up in his arms to carry her across the threshold, he did not set her down with a thump or kiss her on the forehead.

'I love our house,' Libby said. 'It's not a sad little house any more. It's a very happy little house. And I am a very happy big girl.'

'I reckon I might say I ain't real miserable,' Craig said. 'Here, woman, put on my coat and fix us a pot of coffee on our happy little stove. It won't be the last you'll fix so you might as well get in practice.'

'Yes, Master,' she said, and Craig looked at her naked, as she slipped into his coat, looking a little silly in a man's coat. He wondered, almost sadly, if anything so beautiful would ever happen to him again. Pessimistically, he rather thought not.

'I think we should pass a law,' he said, as she moved over to the tiny stove. 'I think it should be against the law for you to wear clothes. Ever again, even in the office. Except that coat of mine of course. Enough of it slips apart so I can get an occasional glimpse of what's inside.'

'Well, it isn't nice for girls to go to work naked,' she said, and turned swiftly to fling herself on him. 'Oh, Craig, tell me, tell me true, was I—was I *nice*? I don't know anything about these things. I didn't ... I didn't disappoint you? I wasn't too—too *eager*? Too dumb? Too—shameless?'

'I have been drinking entirely too much coffee lately anyhow,' Craig said, with his face buried in her tumbled hair. 'Let the coffee go and come back here where you belong. I'll answer all your questions ten years from now.'

It was not a bad little house at that, Craig thought, watching Libby dress, and wondering afresh at the beauty of the girl— wondering specially anew at the frankness, the eagerness, the honest innocent passion of this former child, this new young woman who had come to vibrant life under his hands. That she was virgin he indisputably knew. Physically she had certainly been virgin, but in her heart, and surely in her head, she had not been virgin. A troubling thought occurred: she had come eagerly to him as surely and as intuitively expert as Julie duFresne had come smoothly practised by experience.

'Were you planning to ask me if I still loved you, now I've had my wicked will?' he asked, chuckling.

'Not at all,' she said, doing something with her hair, standing frowning into a wrinkled mirror. 'I was expecting you to ask me do I love you, now I've had *my* wicked will. I believe I do.' She turned from the mirror and her eyes hurt him. 'Oh, how very, very much I do, and I always will. Oh, Craig, I've thought and thought about how it would be and never knew it would be anything like this until I feel almost ashamed of myself. I feel wicked because I'm happy. Aren't girls supposed to cry and carry on and things like that? Should I cry and carry on to prove I'm a nice girl?'

'No, but seeing as you're still in your slip, you can take it off again and come back here. I never want to leave here, this funny little house of ours, with its little tin stove and all the awful things I put in it this week including this bed. You're going to have to do a lot of redecorating, my lovely woman.'

'It was sweet of you to send flowers,' Libby said. 'Are you sure we ought to—again?'

'I'm sure we ought to—*again*,' Craig said.

'You're late,' Maybelle said. 'Did you catch a lot of fish?'

'No,' Craig said. 'A few little ones. I gave them to the fellows.'

'I don't know why you still insist on minglin' with these mill-hands,' Maybelle said. 'Now you're president and all. Was it that red-headed Forney fellow you're so fond of you made him foreman?'

'No,' Craig said. 'It was a couple of other fellows. Look, I'm tired. That surf was awful rough. I'd like to turn in early.'

'Well, you can't. You know very well we've got the Millers and the Wrights comin' any minute for some drinks, and we're all supposed to go to the King Crab for dinner later. You better hurry and get dressed. Maybe you better have one drink first. You're lookin' awful peculiar.'

'That's not a bad idea,' Craig said. 'Fix you one?'

'I already got one,' Maybelle answered. 'You go on up and shower some of the fish-scales off you, and I'll fix you a stiff one and put it on your dresser.'

'Thanks, sweetie,' Craig said, and went up the stairs.

15

THE shower beat down on him, washing away all exterior traces of Libby's body, washing away everything except what was inside him. I wonder if Maybelle knows, he thought. I don't think so. But how she could miss it I can't say. I feel as guilty as if I had come in naked, full of lipstick, all chewed up, with a signpost on my chest saying Craig Price spent all afternoon banging his secretary with whom, ladies and gentlemen of the jury, he is desperately in love. I got Libby all over me and all inside me, but right now Maybelle is fixing me a drink. And then the Millers and the Wrights will come in and we will talk textiles and gold and unions and banks and local gossip, and by God I'd like to give 'em some local gossip. His mind mimicked: 'Have you heard the latest, folks? Craig Price, the youthful president of Grimes Mills, the one who is married to Maybelle Grimes, spent all afternoon in a fishing-shack down by the old Fort. Mr. Price one of the city's brightest young men, spent the afternoon deflowering Miss Elizabeth Forney, Mr. Price's pretty red-haired secretary, who couldn't be more than eighteen years old, if that. Mr. Price, a lusty young man, possessed Miss Elizabeth Forney three times this afternoon, and was figuring on a fourth despoliation when he looked at his dead grandfather's watch and said Christ, I'll be late for getting home and Maybelle has got some awful duds in for drinks and dinner later at that well-known tavern and clip joint, the King Crab.

'Miss Forney, whose brother is foreman of the spinning-room of the mill which Mr. Price acquired by impregnating his present wife, and later by contributing to the indirect murder of her mother, was proven beyond all doubt to be a virgin, but oddly the defloration of Miss Forney, who is called Libby by her friends, was unaccompanied by the usual nuisances generally attendant on virginity. In fact, Miss Forney showed a rather unusual and unmaidenly interest in the yielding up of her greatest treasure. Mr. Price, when interviewed, told the press that he was first astounded, then pleased at her proficiency, and hoped that several subsequent fishing-trips would yield the same catch.'

You cold-eyed son of a bitch, Price, you impossible bastard, Price, Craig said to himself. Now you will check yourself in the mirror for any possible tooth-marks or fingernail scratches, take a drink which your wife has so thoughtfully left on the bureau for you, and proceed to clothe yourself in purple and fine linen. Then you will go downstairs with all the stigmata of your love miraculously erased, trying to not remember Libby's soft, happily-wounded-oh-Craig eyes when you dropped her at the house, or how you felt when Red mixed you a drink and said: 'Where the hell you-all been? You workin' the kid on Saturday afternoons now, slave-driver?'

'As a matter of fact, no. I been over in Brunswick, fishin' with some folks I know, and I almost ran over Libby on Front Street. So I reckoned as how I'm her chauffeur I'd bring her home.'

'What movie was it this time, Sis?' Red asked.

'I hate to confess this, Red, but there's a re-run of *Hell's Angels* and *It Happened One Night* at the Bijou, so I went back to see them both all over again. I wanted to see if Jean Harlow'—she winked wickedly at Craig—'had anything that I didn't.'

You wonderful adorable kid, Craig thought bitterly, that I am already turning into a competent liar, a slick liar like me. You checked the papers just in case. Somehow I wish you hadn't.

'Did she?' he asked. 'Really have anything you haven't got?'

'Only some lower-cut dresses,' Libby said. 'Let me fix you a drink, boss, before you go home.'

People are always fixing me drinks, Craig thought. I must look like a man who always needs a drink. Right now I really do need one, standing in front of Red Forney after I've just spent the entire afternoon ruining his kid sister, the kid sister he has tried so hard to protect. But in defence of himself, he thought, I had the kid sister's complete co-operation, above and beyond. It still don't make me feel any better.

''Scuse me if I drink and run,' he said, knocking back the drink. 'I think we got some people coming in at the house.' And you would give anything you've got to spend the night with Libby, he thought. You would love to take her to that double feature she lied about—but had sense enough to check on—and hold her hand and eat popcorn and then take *her* to the King Crab and dance and then go to bed and wake up Sunday morning with all warm delicious fragrant presence in the Libby-smelling bed, Libby snuggled close and curled and fitting into you, so that then you could get up and *really* go fishin'. You bastard, he said to himself.

'Thanks, Red. Thanks, Butch. See you in the jute-mill Monday.' He waved and walked out of the door.

'There goes a real nice guy,' Red Forney said, as the door closed. 'A real nice guy.'

'There never was a nicer guy,' his sister answered. 'You hungry? I'll fix supper.'

'A little. Is there anything wrong with you, Sis? You look a little peculiar. Kind of . . . peaked. I don't know.'

'Nothing at all, Brother. We had a pretty tough week at the office, and I had to catch up this morning. I guess looking at two long movies tired my eyes some more. And then there's . . . you know. Girl trouble. I'll just go wash up and see what we'll have to eat.'

'Oh.' Red was embarrassed. 'I'm sorry. I didn't know. Don't go to too much botheration. If you'd like, we can go out to eat. It's Saturday and all.'

'No, I don't think I want to. I'm real tired tonight. You fix yourself another toddy and I'll just throw something together and we can listen to the radio, unless you want to go out yourself?'

Red grinned, a little sheepishly.

'Well, I didn't know what you wanted to do, but there's a gal I just met and I thought I might take her to the movies. You know I never seen neither of them pictures you mentioned. The Bijou, you say?'

'Bijou,' Libby said, and then said to herself, thank God I checked the picture ads in the newspaper.

'You'll love them both. Who's the girl, Red? Anybody I know?'

'No, I don't think so. She's the new seventh grade teacher at Forest Glen. I was comin' home one evenin' and she was havin' some trouble with the sprocket chain on her bicycle. I stopped the Ford and fixed it for her. She seemed like a real nice girl and I been out with her a couple of times. She's tryin' to improve my

417

English.' Red blushed. 'I reckon it's a hopeless proposition.'

'This sounds serious,' Libby said. 'What's her name and where does she come from?'

'She's a country girl. Named Nancy Ann Morrison. Black curly hair and black eyes. Real pretty. Comes from some little hick town outside of Dunn. Kenly. You'd never know it, though. She had two years in college, in Greensboro, and she goes to Chapel Hill for summer-school now. Kind of,' he said wistfully, 'like I wanted you to do.'

'Don't you worry about me,' Libby said. 'I'm fine. You just go call your girl and I'll hurry supper so you can be sure to get to the show on time. Next time, Red, why don't you bring her home for dinner? We've got a home to be proud of now, you and me.'

'That'd be real nice, Sis,' Red said. 'I'm certain you'll like her. I'll run around to the corner and call her. We got to get a telephone put into this place when we can afford it.'

Libby went into the kitchen and looked through the ice-box. There were some pork chops which would do all right, and some lettuce and tomatoes, and she could fry some potatoes in a minute, and there was half an apple pie from yesterday. That'd be all right. She was glad Red was going out because all she wanted was to sit home and think about today. So old Red's got himself a girl, hmmm? Maybe that's why he said I looked different. Maybe having a girl or a fellow gives you new eyes. She looked at herself in the kitchen mirror. I think I *do* look different. God knows I feel different. I don't even feel like me. I feel like some strange girl I might have seen in the movies. I feel like a shell that somebody's pulled all the insides out of, and put a stranger inside my skin. 'So this, Elizabeth, is what it's all about,' she said aloud, and began to slice potatoes.

Red finished his apple pie and coffee and said: 'That was real good, Sis. You sure you don't mind bein' by yourself?'

'No, honey, run along like a good boy. I'm going to do something about my hair and fingernails and then go to bed. Run off and get your girl.'

'I thought if you were still awake I might like to bring her by for a beer or something after the show. So you could meet her, like, and tell me what you thought. I wouldn't want to . . . not if you weren't awake. I mean . . .'

'Oh, for God's sake, Red, this is your house. I'll leave some snacks in the ice-box, and if I'm up, I'll have a beer with you. If I'm not up bring your girl in and give her a drink. This isn't a kindergarten. It's your house.'

'It isn't my house,' Red said, leaving. 'It's *our* house. And I don't want to bring any girl here unless you're up.'

'Well, don't bring her tonight, then,' Libby said. 'Buy her an

418

ice-cream soda and then go park in Sunset Grove and neck her some and take her home. I'm going to bed.'

'Why, Libby,' Red said. Then he went out to take his school-teacher to the movies. Girls were certainly peculiar, he thought, as he opened the door of the Ford.

Our house, she thought as she got undressed to bathe, and inspected curiously this new body which was no longer hers alone to command. *Our* house? Oh, no, brother Red. Not *our* house. *Our* house belongs to Craig and me, a little grey-shingled house that stands on the edge of the beach down near the Fort. Our house has a kerosene stove for heat and a bed that really isn't big enough for two people. It has a little stove to cook on, and some oil lamps, and one table and two chairs and no running water except from the pump in the back. Our house has an Indian blanket for a rug, and another on the bed. Our house has an outside toilet—just like we always used to have, she thought—and a tin coffee-pot and a shelf where you put the pepper and salt and coffee and maybe a bottle of whisky and a can of sardines. *Our* house has some flowers on the little oilskin-covered table. Dear Craig. He must have worked like a Trojan, cleaning that place up and buying sheets and blankets and the other stuff. And the flowers. He must have driven all the way down there this morning just so there would be some roses on the table.

Libby got into the tub, and let the hot water stroke her. Why is it I feel so *good*, she thought. Why don't I feel *bad*? I haven't had a wedding or even a real love affair. I have just been in bed all afternoon with a married man who right now is at home with his wife. He won't—he *couldn't* go to bed with her, not this after-noon! Her new thoughts shrieked in her head. She stifled the shrieks and then thought dully: But as long as he lives with her he'll have to go to bed with her. And he'll be going to bed with me—in the afternoon in that *ugly* little house. With the kerosene stove and the oil lamps and the Indian blanket for a rug. That *ugly* little house. Libby suddenly began to cry, and suddenly, down below where love had entered and changed her from a girl to a woman, she began to hurt. The physical hurt was there, as if she'd been riding a horse, but it hurt worse in her breast, worse in her head. Libby saw herself naked with hostile eyes as she dried herself, and when she got into a nightgown she went to the kitchen and poured herself a stiff slug of bourbon. It was the first drink she had ever taken alone. Then she went to bed and buried her head under the pillow, but she could not get Maybelle out of the room. Maybelle was sitting right there on the side of the bed with her. It wasn't Craig who was spending her wedding night with her, alone in a bed while her brother was at the movies. It was Maybelle, Craig Price's wife. Or perhaps, if Libby had been older, she might have called it conscience.

CRAIG looked very sharp in his blue suit, with grey-figured tie. He looked well-showered and unmarked by any other women.

'Hello there, John. Hello, Helen. Hi, Hank. Hello, Marge. I'm sorry I'm a little late showing. Maybelle taking care of you all right? Everybody got himself a drink?' He swept his eyes around the room.

'Everybody but you,' Helen said. 'My, you look handsome, Mr. Price.' Helen looked exactly like Marge, except that one was blonde and the other brunette. John and Hank looked exactly alike, Craig thought, except that one was bald and the other had hair. One was fat and one was thin but they looked just exactly alike. Everybody in this damned town looks exactly alike, except some of them are old, some of them are young, some of them are men, some of them are women, but they all look exactly alike.

Helen was the blonde one. She must have been quite a dish, Craig thought, making himself a drink, and noticing with approval that somebody had thought to put olives and almonds and potato chips and peanuts on the coffee-table. Helen had brown eyes to go with the natural blond hair, and three or four babies had comfortably plumped out her figure, but she still wouldn't be too bad on a dark night on a desert island. Marge was one of the lean horse-faced ones with a huge fleshy red mouth that looked as if it would be able to suck all the reluctant nectar out of whatever unhealthy blossom she buzzed over. I'll bet she's a caution in the cot, Craig thought, lifting his drink in a toast.

'Both you gals never looked prettier. Mud,' he said, and speaking of being drained dry, he thought, if I can make it through this evening without falling on my face, I will be very surprised indeed. Hello to all my dearest friends.

'Where've you been fishing?' Hank asked. Hank belonged to Marge, and looked it. He looked depleted. He was the bald pasty one with the tobacco-coloured pouches under his eyes. Seen sideways he had a nasty little fish mouth, fit companion, Craig thought, for his wife's rapacious lips.

'Any luck?'

'Down by the Fort. No luck to speak of. I took a couple of my people from the mill down there.'

'Now damn my eyes,' John said. John was the chubby one with the too-much hair. He belonged to Helen. 'I knew it had to be your car. I was down there looking at some land somebody wants to sell me, just this side of the Fort, and I saw a black Cadillac that couldn't have been anybody else's. Were you parked just by that little shingled fishing-shack?'

'That I was,' Craig said, thinking thank Christ I didn't say I was in New Truro. 'That was me. There's a damned fine slough cuts in there, and it's generally good for some bass or at least a sea trout or two. Nothing much today, though.'

'That's a pretty high hill, there by that house,' John said. 'Break a leg mighty easy getting down that hill.'

Craig handed cigarettes around.

'Not really. That little shack, I don't know who owns it, has a pretty good stairway—well, ladder—built all the way down to the beach. It's not very tough to handle if you're sober. Which I was.'

'The trouble with fishing,' John said, 'is that there is always some damned fool who wants to fish.'

I'll kill him, I'll claw out his eyes, I'll cut his throat, Craig thought. I have heard that one exactly seventeen thousand, four hundred and fifty-one times. But this time he's right. Today I wasn't some damned fool who wanted to fish. Wouldn't you know somebody would spot that car, though? And wouldn't it be this clown?

'That's a nice little house,' he said smoothly to Maybelle. 'I'm thinking about renting it. It doesn't cost anything. I've been working too hard lately,' this broadly to the others. 'And Maybelle's not too much of an outdoor dirl. I thought I'd get in a little fishing once or twice a week. Like you sail, John. Like you play golf, Hank. There's something about being there with the sea and the seagulls and the kind of peace and quiet that does the same thing for me that a good stiff wind or a solid tee shot does for you fellows. And it's so close . . .'

'When will you rent it?' Maybelle asked. 'And for how much?'

'This week, I think, honey. Remember when I bought those rods? I ran into some fellow in the hardware store who said he had this shack and I could have it for five bucks a month if I wanted it and would look after it. All it needed was a stove and some salt and pepper and like that.'

'Take me down to see it sometime,' Maybelle said. 'Before you rent it. Maybe I can learn to like to fish.'

There I go, Craig thought, trapped before I start—almost. But not quite. I think I'm off the hook on that one. Maybelle is no fisherman. I guess I settled those sons of bitches by almost telling the truth. Oh God, I wonder what Libby's doing right this very moment, this very, very moment?

'I don't care if he is a Democrat, he's still a Yankee, and there never was a Yankee gives a damn about what happens down here except to slap some more taxes on our industry,' John was saying. 'I personally think he's a Jew, anyhow, with a name like that.'

'You voted for him, didn't you?' Hank said. 'I know I did.'

'Yes, but I didn't know then he was going to close up the banks and start all the alphabet-soup agencies when I voted for him. I just voted for him because I was tired of Republicans and Hoover.

'I swear, I can't get a nigger wench to work for me that isn't

421

more shiftless than the last one,' Helen was saying, the words cutting across the men's conversation. 'Niggers just aren't the same as they were, any more. Uppity? My God, you wouldn't believe it how uppity they are.'

'It's all this schoolin' does it,' Marge said. 'You send a nigger to school and you lost a good worker that knows their place and the first thing you know they'll be wanting to vote and ride on the trains and in the front of the streetcars. I swear, I'm half-afraid to go out at night. Did you hear . . .' and the voices hummed in low feminine conspiracy.

I got to buy another car, I guess, Craig was thinking, as the voices droned on in endless trite monotony. A little second-hand Ford or something. That damned Cadillac is too much of a landmark. There just aren't enough of them around. Maybe pick up some jalopy for a couple hundred bucks that won't attract so much attention. One way or the other I'm apt to get hung on that, too. You can't keep anything quiet in this town.

'. . . Don't you think so, Craig?' John's voice sliced into his thoughts.

'Huh? I'm sorry. I was thinking about something else. Just woolgathering. I've had a lot of stuff on my mind this week, and all this fresh air today has made me a little groggy. What was it you asked me?'

'Unions. I don't aim to let a bunch of Yankee Jews come in here and tell me how to run my business. But that fellow Rosenfeld in the White House, looks like he's behind them heart and soul.'

'I don't want anybody telling me how to run my business, either.' Craig's voice was mild and light, in a feeble attempt at humour. 'But there must be a Yankee, somewhere, who isn't a Jew, and as for Mr. Roosevelt, I would think that his old Dutch ancestors would rise again if they knew how many times people mention Jew, Yankee and Roosevelt in the same breath. Here. Your glass is empty. Let me fix.'

'I don't care what anybody says, they ain't the same as us.' This was Maybelle. 'I don't think they're quite people. Niggers smell different, for one thing, and you can't trust one as far as you can throw him. That last one we had in the kitchen, I swear . . .'

'Every time I get to shootin' in the eighties something happens and I'm right back in the nineties again.'

'We luffed on the port tack before we could . . .'

'The most darlin' dress today at Miss Antoinette's . . .'

'I think it'll take war to get us out of the Depression . . .'

'Cotton's down again . . .'

Oh, my God, Craig thought. This, I'll have to hear this all night. It'll be a little better when they get a good can on, because

422

then they'll start to tell jokes and talk about other people's scandals, and at least you don't have to listen to John's jokes because he always slaps you on the knee just when he comes to the punch line. And dinner'll take up a certain amount of time. But don't ever let anybody tell you that you don't pay for your sins. Right now I'm paying for mine.

Craig turned with a trayful of drinks just as the group broke into raucous *whah-whah-whahs* of laughter.

'You'll have to tell that over again, John,' Helen said. 'Craig missed it.'

'No, you tell it, Helen.'

'No. You tell it. You tell it better than me.'

'Well, all right. It seems that there were two Jews ...'

An hour later, Craig said:

'Maybe we'd better be getting on to eat, folks, I guess we better take all three cars and then we won't have that dropping-off business after. Come on, Marge, you ride with me. Maybelle can go with John, and Helen can go with Hank. Come on Marge, I always wanted to get you alone in a car on a Saturday night.'

'Now you just quit bossing us around, Craig Price. All us girls have to go powder our noses, and you show the boys where to go.'

'The boys know where to go,' Craig said. 'The yard is good enough for the boys.'

Marge gave him a playful push. 'Aren't you just dreadful,' she said, and the implied translation was: You might have thought you were joking about getting me alone in that Cadillac of yours, big boy, but five minutes in that back seat and I'd have your tongue hanging out, friend.

As the girls went off, en troupe, to swap gynaecological lore in the process of mass urination and lipstick repair, Maybelle was thinking: I never did trust that bitch. I don't like her mouth. Give her an hour and I'll bet she'd ... Like a mink, I bet.

Helen was thinking: Wonder why that handsome son of a bitch didn't ask *me* to ride with him instead of that big-mouthed slut Marge. I'm a lot better looking than she is. And I wouldn't be surprised if she did something to him even while they were driving.

In concert, both Marge and Helen said: 'Oh, Maybelle, these new curtains are so cute. They just *make* the powder-room.'

And Maybelle said: 'Anybody in a hurry for the throne, speak up.'

'Well, I am,' Marge said. 'My back teeth are floating. If none of you ladies mind, I'll play through.'

Downstairs, the gentlemen, having watered the lawn, were grouped around the drink table. Craig made an attempt at conversation after mixing them all a final short shot for the road.

'Can either one of you old married men—you've both been at it a lot longer than me—can either of you tell me why all women

423

wait until the last minute to go to the bathroom, and why they always go together? It don't seem quite nice to me. What in the name of God do they talk about? Why do they always go together?'

'I don't know,' Hank said, wearily. 'I gave up tryin' to understand anything about 'em years ago. But can you tell me why it's against the law for a husband to ride in the same car with his own wife? It ain't but a ten minute drive from here to the King Crab.'

'I reckon that's easy,' John said. 'If you're as tired of yours, always clack-clacking away, as I'm tired of mine, anybody else's wife is a relief, even for ten minutes. And you know as well as me we'll all go to somebody's house for a nightcap, and then Craig will have to ride with Helen, and I'll ride with Maybelle, and John'll ride with my ball-and-chain. Dam' sight simpler if we all went in one car.'

'I can already see the fuss when we get to the Crab,' Craig said. 'They will try to figure out who rode with who, so the one that rode here from my house can't sit next to that person, but at the same time, also can't sit next to his wife. And this adds a new problem, because if we go anywhere else, then we have to wind up driving with our own wives just to keep the cards straight. Otherwise . . . No, let's see. If we have a round table I can sit between Helen and Marge and John can sit between Marge and Maybelle and Hank can sit between Maybelle and Helen. Now if we don't have a round table, I guess one of the boys will have to sit at each end of the table with somebody else's wife on each side of them . . . the hell with it. Let the dames worry about it.'

'What are you-all talkin' about?' Maybelle said, as the girls came chattering down the stairs. 'We're all ready to go.'

'The anatomy of strange tribal customs in the deep South,' Craig said. 'Come on, Marge. If we're ten minutes late, nobody'll mind much, will they? Oh God, almost a tragedy. I nearly forgot the jug. Wait a minute.'

He tucked a bottle of bourbon under one arm.

'Come on, Marge,' and handed her into the Cadillac.

As they swung down the gravelled lane to the main road, Marge snuggled into the opposite corner, hoisted her knees up on the seat, and looked at him under lowered lids.

'You want a cigarette?' she asked.

'Thanks. Wait a minute.'

'Don't bother. I've got some here in my bag. I'll light you one. Where's the lighter?'

'There.' He touched a knob, and she moved her legs so that his hand swept across her knee. She left the knee where it was. She lit his cigarette first, and handed it to him. Its end was oozy thick with lipstick.

She leaned out of the corner, and blew a stream of smoke in his general direction.

'You're a very strange boy, Craig Price,' she said. 'A very strange boy. I'd like to know what goes on behind those brown eyes of yours.'

'Nothing very much, I'm afraid, Marge.' He was driving with his brown eyes pinned inflexibly to the road. 'Nothing, I'm afraid, much more than what goes on behind anybody's eyes. Work and a little play and a lot of worry.'

'I don't mean that.' Marge put her hand on his knee, now. 'I mean what do you think of most of us—all the ones who are a few years older than you are. All the people you know now. All the people you go out with. Sometimes, the few times I've seen you, you look at us like we were a lot of nasty bugs or something. You don't seem like any of the men—the older men, and God knows not like the boys—at all. Sort of like a foreigner.'

Craig smiled, and took the deep inside of a curve. The tyres whished on the asphalt.

'I am a foreigner. Hadn't you heard? I come all the way here from New Truro. Thirty miles away. I'm a country boy.'

'If you're a country boy, I'm Gloria Swanson,' Marge muttered. 'But I want you to know that all of us aren't as dull as you make me feel like you think we are, Craig. For instance I'm not as dull as I sound when we girls get cackling around cocktails. You'd find I'm not dull at all, Craig. If you'd care to investigate. Some afternoon, Craig, when work's slow at the office, if you'd like to call me . . . or if you'll just pull over into the first side road for a minute right now I'll give you a sample of just how dull I'm *not*.'

Great God, Craig thought, feeling like a man who had just been offered a bag of peanuts after a six-course meal.

'I'm certain you're not dull at all, Marge.' His voice was falsely light again. 'But I am, you know, awfully dull. But who else is *not* dull is Maybelle, especially when I'm as much as a minute late. Sometime soon, maybe, Marge, but right now I think we better step on the gas and be waiting at the gate when the others get there.'

Marge laughed, or rather, barked.

'Henpecked, huh? I didn't really expect it of you. All right, young man. The offer's still open. Hank plays an awful lot of golf, or at least that's what he says. And things get pretty poky around the house for me, since I seem to be one of the few *young matrons*—' she minced the words—'one of the few young matrons who isn't bowed down under a litter of brats.'

She took her hand off his knee.

'Christ, I hate this town. At least Charlotte's big enough to lose yourself in. How I ever got . . . Never mind. Personally I don't think you're shy at all, or dull at all, or dumb at all. I think you're very cagey. I think you've got a girl. You look like a man that's got a girl. You look like a man that's just had a girl. Are you sure you went fishing? Not that I'll tell.'

God Almighty, it can't be that plain, Craig thought. Or can it? He kept his eyes steadily on the curving ribbon of road.

'Me? Got a girl? No, ma'am. I got a mill that keeps me busy. I got no time for girls. Apart from that, I got a wife. She keeps me busy, too.'

'I got a husband, too, if you could call Hank a husband.' Her voice was bitter. 'He doesn't keep me busy. And lots of men with wives have girls. Well, here we are. You won't have to wipe off any lipstick this night, more's the pity. Some other night you might have to. It's nice we'll be waiting for the others when they drive up. No nasty suspicions, or anything like that.' As she opened the door to get out, she said: 'I hear you've got the prettiest, smartest secretary in town,' and Craig thought that if a shark could smile, you could call the shark Marge. If you wanted to call a nice, honest, decent shark, Marge.

The waitress knew everybody and was real pleased to see them, and real pleased to sit them at a real nice quiet table away from the juke-box, and was real pleased to bring some setups and cracked ice, and real pleased to ask Craig please not to put the bottle on the table, implying that it would give the place a real bad name. Whisky was real legal in North Carolina if you bought it by the bottle at the ABC store before sundown, but in a really chic place, like the King Crab, you weren't supposed to leave it sitting up there on the table for everybody to look at, because people would think you *drank*. That wouldn't be very nice to have people think you drank, because it might affect business in one way or the other. Of course, it was all right to leave a bottle of Chianti or something like that on the table, because a bottle of wine, which could be legally sold away from the ABC store—and at night—did not carry with it the moral stigma of a dirty big old bottle of booze sitting right smack up there on the table. Only the very nicest people drank wine, except the impoverished drunks who drank fifty-cent Muscatel.

There would be the nearly unvarying menu of shrimp cocktail with the limp lettuce or crab cocktail with the limp lettuce or devilled crabs and there would be any kind of fish such as flounder, or trout or mackerel or bluefish. And there would be those great big, black-topped thick steaks, a rarity, because in the King Crab they actually broiled the steaks so that they came out almost edible instead of as corpse-greyish slabs of fried boot with the corners upcurled. Oddly enough, too, nearly everything in the King Crab lacked the hair-oil grease content of most local restaurants. The King Crab rated very low on ptomaine poisoning, and employed waitresses who did not obviously appear to be waiting out professional personal engagements between Sugar Hill in Kinston and a third-class railroad hotel in Rocky Mount. Everybody who was anybody in Kensington came to the King Crab, largely, as Craig once remarked, because there wasn't any other place to go except the hotdog joints and the few Greek short-order houses, with the hair-oil cooking fat.

It was several years before Craig Price discovered that nothing much had changed from Kensington to New York, but Saturday night was head-counting time in the King Crab, unless there was a dance at the Club or a big private party going, and anybody who wasn't to be seen at the King Crab wasn't *any*body. People traded freely between tables, exchanged snorts of bourbon or blend from the sub-rosa bottles, and swapped babble in which *I declare* and *you-all* were as basic ingredients as the fat that fried the softshell crabs.

Craig attuned a listening ear to the hubbub, but switched off his brain. The eyes remained alert to the next flock of visiting fire-folk, but his secret brain was back with Libby Forney, and his secret heart was keeping company with his brain. I wonder what she's doing right now, poor kid, he thought. I wonder if she really got hurt today. We were pretty violent a couple of times there. I don't know much more about these things than she does. But she didn't seem to hurt. I mean, she seemed to want it, and more and more as we went along. I mean if she hadn't wanted it she wouldn't have done it, would she? Or if she hadn't wanted to carry on with it, she wouldn't have, would she? I got to solve this car situation somehow. Or find a new place to go. And how about that bitch-wolf Marge? That you could call an open invitation to . . . dance. Never have I seen one in heat like that one. Stay away from that, Price, my boy, even on the dullest, meanest day of your life.

'Dance Marge?' he said. 'That's a nice tune. Who put all the money in the machine?'

'Some sucker from the corner table,' John said. 'Dance, Maybelle?'

'Dance, Helen?' Hank said.

And they all got up to dance. The tune was 'Stars Fell On Alabama'. Glen Gray was playing it.

Marge's hips moved fluidly against Craig in the half-lit patch of dance floor.

'It's nice the floor is so small,' she whispered, one hand on the back of his neck. 'You can dance this way without all the people talking too much. You like to dance this way, Craig?'

'I like to dance this way,' he said, and her body pressed perceptibly closer. 'But then,' he said, rather hollowly, 'I like to dance with anybody I don't have to carry, and I sure don't have to carry you, sugar.'

'Don't you be so sure,' Marge said, and the fingers of her left

427

hand ever-so-softly crept along the back of his neck. 'You dance very well, Craig. And it's nice music.'

'Thanks,' Craig said. 'So do you. I think Glen Gray plays real good.'

They danced silently for a moment, and Craig was thinking: It takes a bitch in heat like this one to make you appreciate what I left this afternoon. I'm glad I inherited old Marge tonight. It makes me feel a little bit better about me and Libby. Every time this one grinds herself into my groin I can think about this afternoon and this afternoon gets sweeter in the head. Jesus, this one really ought to charge ten bucks for a dance. I had worse lays in Antwerp than she's giving me now for free except I don't want none. I don't want *none*. I wonder what Libby, is doing, exactly, this very moment, right now? Whatever it is, I wish to God I was doing it with her instead of grinding around the floor with this bitch.

'There comes the girl with the steaks,' he said. 'I guess we better go sit down.'

They ploughed through the meal, and then they ploughed through a discussion about whose house they would go to for the nightcap, and Craig won, figuring if they came back to his house, at least he wouldn't have to drive home drunk, and tonight he would be drunk as a skunk. This time he inherited Helen for his driving companion. Helen was full of whisky, wine, crabmeat and steak. And the remembrances of things past which had led to offspring. Helen sat quietly in her corner of the front seat and suddenly started to hiccup.

'Stop the car, Craig!' she said, suddenly. 'I'm going to be sick!'

'Hold it if you can!' Craig said. He braked sharply, and pulled swiftly over to the shoulder, jumped out of the car, and hauled her head towards him, trying to stand away from her retching while he supported her back with one hand, and held her head with the other. Her body racked. She heaved. Sweat came on to the forehead Craig was holding with one hand, and she heaved again.

'All right now?' he said. 'Here. Here's a handkerchief. You sure you're all right?'

'I think so,' Helen swabbed her mouth. 'Did I get any on us?'

'No,' Craig said. 'You didn't get any on us.'

'I don't know what happened,' Helen said, pale and quivering, as they got back in the car. 'I never get sick. I just never get sick.'

'It's the oldest joke in the world,' Craig said, 'but it was probably something you ate. I don't feel so good myself. Seafood. Good one night, bad another. You just can't trust it. We'll be back to the house in a minute, and Maybelle will make us some coffee and I'll give you a drink and you'll be fine. Just fine.'

Just fine, he thought. What is Libby doing right now while I'm holding a drunk's head and defending my honour from a man-eater? Is there anybody there to hold Libby's head while I take this drunken bum back to the house to feed her coffee so she can get well enough to have another set of drinks that'll make her sick again? If Libby's feeling lousy can she tell Red, can she tell her brother why she's feeling lousy? I wonder if I can get by there tomorrow? That's no good. I got no excuse to get out of the house or even to just drop in their house on a Sunday. You never have an excuse to get out of the house on a Sunday.

'That's a real hard bunch to lose,' Craig said, looking round him at the heaped ash-spilling trays, smelling the fug of the lingering cigarette smoke, seeing the lipsticked edges of smudged glasses, regarding without pleasure a brown cigarette scar in the rug. 'And that last bunch that followed us on from the Crab was extra special durable. For a while it looked like they planned to stay on for breakfast.'

'I wish you wouldn't be so snotty,' Maybelle said. 'These are the nicest people in town. You always look at them kind of like they were interesting bugs or something, but not as if they were really there. You act so—sort of *superior*.'

'That's the second time tonight I've heard that one. I must definitely look at these people like they were bugs, or something. The second time must make it stick. Bugs.'

'When was the first time?'

'Going over in the car with Marge before dinner. She said it.' Maybelle snorted.

'Marge, hey? That bitch. I was almost surprised when you beat us to the restaurant. I figured she'd drag you into the bushes by main force.'

'Oh, I ain't as cute as all that.'

'You don't have to be cute for Marge to drag you into the bushes. If you've got pants, all you just have to be is *there*.'

'I thought she was your dearest friend,' Craig said, picking up glasses. 'Come on, help me take this stuff to the kitchen. I want to go to bed. And I don't want to get up in the morning and see all this mess. That Helen's a beat, isn't she? I suppose you know she got sick and threw up coming back here.'

'She got sick and threw up again after we got here,' Maybelle said calmly, opening some windows. 'We barely got her to the john in time.'

'She's lovely, Helen. I suppose she's your second best friend?'

'You tryin' to pick a fight?' Maybelle was belligerent. 'What the hell's been wrong with you all night? You know all these people and what they're like. They ain't a bunch of rank strangers. We've been out with them a lot before.'

'Maybe that's the trouble.' Craig picked up two ash-trays and dumped the ash-smothered crumpled cigarette ends into a waste-

429

basket. 'Very possibly that is the trouble. We've been out with them before. I don't know how you feel, but this town is gettin' smaller all the time. I feel like a man wearing a shrunk shirt or a pair of pants that are too tight.'

Maybelle's voice was sarcastic, now.

'If you mean you're gettin' too big for your breeches, you could be right.'

'Let's don't fight. Go on upstairs and get undressed. I'll douse the lights and sort of check around to see that we don't have any left-over guests abandoned for dead in the rhododendrons. I'll be up in a minute.'

Craig walked out into the yard. A half moon rode high in the sky. The night was sweet and soft, with just a hint of chill. He took a deep breath, and sniffed the night smells. Even the faint odour of skunk, wafted from a far hill, was not unpleasant, and night creatures made their usual satisfactory *clunks* and *pops* and *whistles*. A mocking-bird suddenly burst into a mad scherzo of trill, the silvered notes flung from its throbbing throat. The sky was exceptionally clear, and the stars swung low. A faint breeze caressed the pines into grateful murmurs.

'It's all so nice without the people,' he murmured aloud.

'Oh my God,' he said then, thinking of Libby and vaguely of life. 'Oh, my God.'

He sighed, and went upstairs to bed. Maybelle was already snoring. Hours later, in the middle of a troubled sleep he woke, to feel her hand on him. He rolled over on his stomach, and turned his back to her, but the hand was persistent. He rolled over on his back again.

'Well,' he said, 'if you really want to. Wait a minute while I go to the bathroom.'

17

'LET's go for a drive,' Maybelle said, after a late Sunday breakfast. Craig looked up from a welter of Sunday papers. He subscribed to them all, now, the Raleigh *News and Observer*, the Charlotte *Observer*. Papers that provided some news of the outside world and did not indulge in headlines like the one in the local paper's sports page about the House of David team beating the Independents. 'WOODS WOULD WIELD WICKED WINNING WILLOW', the headline said, intimating that somebody named Woods, with a beard, helped the cause of the House of David by getting a base hit at a crucial moment in the history of the sacred sport, even if it was Class D sacredness. He had observed that Maggie was still belting Jiggs over the head with a rolling-pin, and that Mutt still had a definite advantage in height over Jeff, and that Sydney Smith's Gump family still worshipped tragedy and money as exemplified by Uncle Bim. A Negro prize-fighter named Joe Louis seemed to be doing very well.

'Where do you want to go?' he said, pushing aside the stack of papers. 'I could handle another cup of coffee before you make up your mind.'

'All right. I'll make some fresh.' Maybelle, wearing a white quilted house-coat and blue backless high-heeled mules, clacked off to the kitchen. Craig looked after her with sick eyes. I performed well last night, he thought. I stood very well at stud. If I were a stallion I'd be worth my weight in oats. I reckon, boy, you can do anything you have to do, because you sure have got a strong stomach and the morals of a monkey. He picked up the papers again. Lou Gehrig still had an unbroken string of performance at first base for the Yankees. Me and Lou Gehrig, Craig thought.

Maybelle came back with the coffee. She was having one of her cheerful, helpful days. She was cheerful and helpful always after a successful session in bed.

'Here's your coffee, honey,' she said, and patted Craig's head. 'I'll just go get into some clothes. Let's ride down by the Fort. I want to see your little house that you're going to rent.'

'It's not worth the bother,' Craig said shortly, thinking swiftly, God, it's still got the flowers in it. 'I haven't got the key yet anyhow. Let's go somewhere else. Soon as I get time I'll fix it up and then take you down. If you feel like a picnic.' He came in high and hard like Walter Johnson, the old pitcher, with the word *picnic*. The word did it.

Maybelle's face went cold.

'No thanks. I've been to a picnic. Let's just skip the whole idea and stay home with the papers.'

'I'd rather, really. I'm real hung from last night, and I'm plain worn out from all this reorganization at the mill.' Craig talked fast. 'You know, I've got a dead set against going for Sunday drives, anyhow. I've got kind of a dead set against Sundays, as a matter of fact. I remember Sunday as being the worst day of the week when I was a little kid, whether it was here or in New Truro.'

Maybelle decided to play. She sat down, poured herself a cup of coffee, and reached for a cigarette.

'Why? Sunday school?'

'Not so much Sunday school. I didn't have much trouble with my people about Sunday school. They weren't very strong about the church-going. Also when we lived in one neighbourhood I was a Presbyterian. In another I was Episcopalian. And when we moved out of town it was too much trouble, and there wasn't anything but Methodists and Baptists and maybe Holy Rollers in New Truro and Mother didn't care much for what she felt was the lower orders of religion. No, it wasn't Sunday school. It

431

was the fact that a kid didn't have anything to *do* on Sunday.'

'I think maybe I could use a drink,' Maybelle said. 'How about I make us a couple of old fashioneds?'

'Sure. That'd be fine. I got the creepy-crawlies in my stomach. We didn't drink on Sundays in those days. We practised nothing but boredom. You ate the biggest dinner anything could dream up, and it was always the same. Stewed chicken and dumplings and mashed potatoes. There seemed to be some sort of law that Sunday was for taking some stringy old hen and parboiling her until she was fit to stew, and always there had to be dumplings.'

'I like chicken and dumplings,' Maybelle said. 'Here's your toddy. As a matter of fact, we're having it today.'

'Oh, God,' Craig said. 'I don't really mind chicken and dumplings. It's just that they mean Sunday, like turkey means Christmas and Thanksgiving. I'd rather have turkey on Sunday and chicken on Thanksgiving, and maybe a steak on Christmas, if you get what I mean. It's the thing I hate the most about this neck of the woods. Everybody's always doing the same thing. Always with the same people. At the same time and in the same place.'

'Well, honey,' Maybelle said reasonably. 'There's only so many places and people and things to do. Like the Ureys have asked us to their house tonight for cocktails. If it wasn't the Ureys it'd be the Miltons or the McGuires or the Paynes.'

Craig groaned.

'I know, and that's why I hate Sundays—hated them even when I was a kid. You weren't allowed to play baseball on Sunday. You couldn't fish on Sunday. You couldn't hunt on Sunday. I remember when you weren't even allowed to go swimming on Sunday. What you did was eat that big chicken dinner and then everybody piled into the car and went for a Sunday afternoon drive. Jesus Christ, I can still smell Grandma's bombazine and see her jet beads. It was about three hours of the most punishment I ever hope to take. And it happened every Sunday. I love to drive a car, and I am happy when I'm going somewhere. But to just go for a drive. Ugh.' He shuddered. 'It was like if it wasn't the Ureys it'd be the Miltons or the McGuires or the Paynes.'

A bell rang.

'Hello,' he said. 'There's somebody at the back door. I'm dressed. I'll go see who it is. Who in hell could be ringing the back-door bell at this time of day on Sunday?'

'Whoever it is, tell them we don't want any, especially if it's some of those Jehovah's Witnesses,' Maybelle said.

Craig walked through the kitchen and opened the door. On the stoop was a small, very black boy. He was dressed very cleanly and neatly in denim trousers and a shirt which had obviously been sewn down from a man's. He wore a kind of sandal made from cutting up discarded automobile tyres. He held a man's floppy cap in his hand, and he stood proudly erect. He smiled, showing a vast snowy expanse of teeth, and his eyes followed the upcurl of his lips. He was as black as The Imp, and he wasn't much bigger than a minute.

'I begs yo' pardon, suh,' he said, and made a kind of bow. 'You is Mistah Craig Price.' There was no hint of a question here. He stood then more or less at military attention.

'That's right,' Craig said. 'And who might you be?'

'I is called Herbert Hoover Lincoln Newton. Most folks calls me Hoov. You doesn't know me, but I knows you. In a way I knows you. I is Big Abner's last youngun. I 'us just about bo'ned when you was a boy, used to shoot quail-buhds mah pappy's place. I knows you remembers all the other younguns, Booker and Jefferson and Woodrow and Hardin' and all them gal chillun. We mus' is had about twelve, fo'teen head, and I de las'.'

'Well damn my soul,' Craig said. 'If you ain't a member of the family. You come in the kitchen, Herbert Hoover Lincoln Newton, so we can sit down and talk like family folks. Maybe we can find a glass of milk or a Coca-Cola or something for one of Big Abner's younguns. Which'll it be?'

'Coca-Cola, pleas suh, Mistah Craig,' Herbert Hoover Lincoln Newton said, 'I thanks you very kindly.'

Craig picked him up and swooped him on to a kitchen stool. He reached into the ice-box, got out a Coke, opened it, and then took H. H. L. Newton's man's cap out of his hand and placed it on the sink.

'Here you are, Hoov,' he said. 'Tell me. How's your pappy makin' out? And your ma?'

'Pappy he done pass on las' year 'bout cotton-pickin' time,' Hoov Newton said. 'Mammy, she don' pass on 'bout fresh-corn time.'

'I'm sorry to hear that,' Craig said. 'I'm real sorry to hear that. Many's the glass of scuppernong wine I had with your daddy in *your* kitchen when I came in all tired from huntin' birds. Where you livin'?'

'I's livin' in a house wif' my brother Hardin' and he wife and some of they younguns and some of Pappy's gal chillun ain't ripe 'nough marry yet. It powerful crowded in dat house. Dat is why I has come to press a call on you and make a propotishun.'

'A what?' Craig looked puzzled.

Herbert Hoover Lincoln Newton seemed slightly annoyed.

'A propo-tishun, suh. I aims to work for you, if'n you have me, and I come to work out de terms lak dey does in de company sto' ginst how much fatback, how much lard, how much cornmeal dey gives you fo' so much cotton nex' yeah. A prop-o-tishun.'

Craig bent his head in apology.

'All right, I'm sorry. Just what exactly is this propotishun?'

'My daddy, Big Abner, he say jus' fo' he die, he say, Hoov, you de baby dis family, you mind what I say. You git ahold some

433

quality white folks fo' yo' self, you go a far piece. Maybe even you go North, as far as Richmond. So I come to work for you.'

'That's very nice, Hoov. But what can you do?'

'I know how to train houn' dogs and slop hawgs. I is a good yard boy. I runs a keerful errand, and I is honest as de day is long. I wants to improve my station. I can read and figger and I wants to amount to something. I wants to learn how to be a good house-boy and va-lley and shofer. Den maybe someday I be's yo' chief butler.'

'That sounds fine. Where'd you learn all those big words, son? Like valet and butler and chauffeur?'

Herbert Hoover Lincoln Newton grinned at Craig.

'I ask aroun' some. I ask people what I kin do to git ahead in de worl'. People say all de time, ovah Brumsick, dat young Mistah Craig Price, dat man used think de world of Big Abner, used shoot Big Abner's buhds and drink scuppernong wine in kitchen jus' like he ain' white folks—dey say all time how good Mistah Craig Price doin', him so young an' all. So I ask people what I kin do go work for Mistah Craig Price, and dey say learn how be good house-boy, first, den learn be shofer, never tell story, never steal, work hard, and den some day maybe you be chief butler and go North. So I jus' figgah maybe I hitch mahself to yo' wagon, seein' you lets me, ob co'se.'

'How old are you, son?'

'I doesn't rightly know. I reckons bout ten, twelve. I had three year schoolin', though, and I reads and writes good.'

'Well, I'll tell *you*. You sit right here and finish that Coke and I'll go get my missis so you can meet her and see if you want to work for both of us. If you like her, and if she likes you, then I don't see why we don't get in the car and go see your brother and find out how much I'll have to pay you to run my life.'

Herbert Hoover Lincoln's eyes became enormous.

'Oh, you doesn't have to pay me nothin', Mistah Craig. I works gladly for nothin'.'

'That's no way to do business, son. You wait here a minute.'

Craig walked back to the living-room.

'Who's that kept you so long in the kitchen?' Maybelle looked up from the papers.

'A little coloured boy. One of Big Abner's brood—you know, that old coloured farmer friend of mine. I used to shoot quail on his place when I was a kid. This is his last young'un. Abner's dead.'

'What's he want? What's he doing coming to the house on Sunday anyhow?' Maybelle sounded querulous.

'He's a real cute kid and seemed like he's smart as a whip. He wants to work for us. Yard boy, house-boy, anything. He tells me he wants to hitch up to my wagon because I'm Craig Price, suh, doin' so good and so young and all, and one day, he informs me, if he plays his cards right he can get to be my shofer and my va'lley and my butler and maybe make it North as far as Richmond, even. He says he'll work for nothin'.'

'What in the hell can we do with a nigger baby around here? My God, Craig, the ideas you get in your head . . .'

Craig held up his hand.

'Whoa. Stop. I knew this family, all of it, nearabouts. They're good people. You're always yelling about the trouble you have with the help. Here we got a chance at training a real good man. He can earn his board and keep just working in the yard and doing odd chores around the house. We'll send him to school, but he can work afternoons. And one day we've got us a real jewel like you read about, instead of some slut who's always leaving in the middle of the week just when you need her most. Come on, honey, be a sport. I'd like to have this one for a present. Come on.'

'What's its name?' Maybelle asked.

'Herbert Hoover Lincoln Newton.' Craig grinned. 'We got a Republican in the house. I hope your old man don't mind having a black Republican for a kind of grandson.'

'Well,' Maybelle said. 'We had George Washington for a butler once. Let's go see the newest dependent.'

Herbert Hoover Lincoln Newton slid hurriedly off the stool when Maybelle came into the kitchen. He bowed his head.

'This is my wife, Miss Maybelle,' Craig said, watching keenly.

Herbert Hoover Lincoln Newton kept his hands stiffly at his side.

'Hidy-do, Miss Maybelle,' he said. 'I is pleased to make yo' 'quaintance.' He looked up at Craig in supplication. What do I do now, Boss? the look inquired.

'Hello. My husband says you want to come work for us. You willing to work real hard?'

'I works real hard, ma'am. I tries hard to learn anything *you* wants to teach *me*.'

Good boy, Craig thought. That's giving it back to her. Good boy.

'Well, I don't know. I swear, Craig.' She was speaking now as if Herbert Hoover Lincoln Newton was not present. 'I don't know what use he'd be. He ain't no bigger'n a jazz-bow, and he's about the same colour.'

'Jazzbo,' Craig said. 'Your name ain't Herbert Hoover Lincoln Newton any more. Your name is Jazzbo. Your new missus just hired you and christened you all in the same breath. Didn't you, Maybelle?' he shot her one of those-I-can-always-go-back-to-sea looks.

'I suppose so,' Maybelle said. 'I guess so. And Jazzbo is a kind of cute name. And if we dressed him up real cute he'd be real nice to help serve at parties and things like that. I guess so.'

'He's a little too young to serve at parties and things like that,' Craig said. 'We'll talk about that later. Come on, Jazz. It looks like you're hired. We better go talk to your brother now and work

435

out the details. I'll be back in an hour, Maybelle. In plenty of time for lunch.' He grinned. 'There ain't much you can do to hurt a stewed chicken. Or the dumplings. I'll hurry.'

'Dis a power of car,' Jazzbo said, when they drove off in the Cadillac. 'Boss, I ain't never see no car like dis. Close up, I means. You reckons some day I learns to drive a car like dis?'

'We'll start now, for a few minutes. Come over here and sit in my lap. I'll do the gears, but you can steer her. How's that?'

'Man, I is nigger-rich,' Jazzbo said. 'She steer sweet as cream. I only ever ride a bicycle. Dis ain't no bicycle. How ol' I gets to be 'fore I can drive all by myself?'

'Hop down now, because we're coming into traffic. I'd say that as soon as your legs get long enough to touch the pedals, we can adjust your age to fit the licence. Since you don't know how old you are, anyhow. Where's your brother's house?'

'Brooklyn. Back Red Cross Street. Ovah de bridge and dere us is.'

Craig drove for a moment, silently, weaving in and out of the Sunday traffic.

'You know, Jazz,' he said. 'You make me feel lucky.' He reached over and rubbed his hand over the little boy's kinky hair. 'I think you're my good luck charm. I think somebody sent you to me on purpose.'

'I glad you thinks so. Kin I ask one question, Mistah Craig?'

'Shoot. Fire away.'

'Who does I work for in yo' house? Does I work for you, does I work for Miss Maybelle, or does I just work for everybody?'

'That's a good question, Jazz. You work for me. You do what Miss Maybelle says, of course, and you mind your manners, but anything bothers you, you just come see me. Miss Maybelle ain't gonna ask you to do anything I wouldn't approve of. No. You work for me. But we got a lot of things to think about, like getting you to school on time. I reckon a bicycle is the answer. We'll go pick one out tomorrow when the stores are open.'

'A new bicycle? Mah ve'y own bicycle? Wid a bell and a basket and all?' Jazzbo's eyes were billiard-balls of excitement.

'Well, you got to go to school,' Craig said. 'And since you're gonna be my shofer some day, I damn well ain't gonna be yours. You got to work up from that bicycle before you take on a Cadillac, my boy.'

'You calls me yo' "boy". Does you mean I is really yo' boy, Mistah Craig?'

'Sure.' He ruffled the little boy's hair again. 'I haven't got a real boy of my own. I guess you'll have to do. Sure you're my boy.'

Jazzbo made a manful effort not to cry. He wiped his nose with the back of his hand, and blinked his eyes rapidly. Then he wiped his eyes with his sleeve and looked Craig straight in the profile.

'I's black,' he said. 'You's white. How can I be yo' boy?'

'Don't let it bother you. Anybody ask you whose boy you are, you just say, I'm Mistah Craig Price's boy. Mistah Craig Price didn't have no boy of his own, so he took me to raise. That'll tell 'em who you are. Craig Price's boy.'

Jazzbo started to snuffle again.

'Stop it,' Craig said. 'There ain't nothin' to cry about, son.'

'I sorry I's cryin',' Jazzbo said. 'But I just thinkin' how happy Papa be in Heaven if he know dis. You reckon he know about dis, Mistah Craig?'

'Sho' ', Craig said. 'Your papa knew pretty near everything. He's duty bound to know about this. Your papa was so smart he even knew how to keep young turkeys from drowning themselves when it rained. He don't figure to get no dumber in heaven.'

'Dis ain't de way to mah house,' Jazzbo said, a moment later. 'You's goin' de wrong way roun'.'

Unthinkingly, Craig had taken the road which led to Libby's house. He laughed shortly.

'I had my mind on something else,' he said. 'For a minute, Jazz, I thought I'd stop off and see some friends and show 'em my new boy.' Once again he passed his hand over Jazzbo's tight-curled skull.

'But I guess not,' he said. 'I guess I better not monkey with my luck.'

He drove on past Red Cross, over the bridge, to Brooklyn and Jazzbo Newton's brother, Harding, who would, of course, be delighted at the prospect of one less mouth to feed.

18

THERE was tremendous mutual shyness when Craig stopped off at Libby's house on Monday morning, to take her to the office.

'Hello,' Craig said.

'Hello,' Libby said.

Silence.

'You have a good weekend?' Craig asked.

'All right.'

'You sure ain't very talky this mornin'. Cat got your tongue?'

'No.'

He took his eyes off the road, and flicked them lightly over the girl. She was sitting primly, her knees together, staring fixedly at the road.

He reached over and touched her knee with his right hand.

'Was it that bad?'

'Yes.' Libby whirled suddenly. 'Yes! Yes, yes, *yes*! It was that bad! It was worse than bad! I spent the whole week-end with your wife! I couldn't get her out of the room! Every time I closed my eyes, there she was in the room with me! It was horrible, Craig, horrible . . .'

He squeezed her knee. A car cut out of the traffic line and crossed ahead of him. Craig cursed.

'Goddamned hillbillies, they oughtn't to be allowed a driver's licence . . .' He paused. 'Sorry, sugar. I had a kind of edgy week-end myself. With only one good thing in it. The rest was dreadful.'

'I'm sorry, Craig,' her voice was now contrite. 'I don't mean to be a bother. Really. I know all about us and what we're up against. But Saturday night I was so—*so* vacant. I felt like that sad little house, left all alone. *Vacant*. A house nobody wanted. And I kept wondering what you were doing, and Red went to the movies . . .' She laughed, a little hysterically. 'He went to see a double-feature. "Hell's Angels" and "It Happened One Night". With his new girl. With his new girl, Craig, and I was all alone and you were out with all your friends and your . . . your wife. I had to lie about seeing the double feature. But Saturday night I wanted to go see it with you.'

Craig's laugh was a bark.

'I guess we've got the same kind of head. I wanted to go and hold hands and get all smeared up with the butter from the popcorn. All night long when I was having to be polite to those idiots, through the cocktails and the dinner and after, I wanted to be eating popcorn, or doing anything else at all, with you. But there's nothing you can do. So then you mix another drink and what the hell.'

'Craig?'

'Yes?'

'You didn't . . . you *didn't* . . .'

'Hush. You damned well know I didn't if you're meaning what I think you mean. How could I?' Oh you lying bastard, he thought, this is one that even the God of Wrath will forgive you for.

'How could I? After you?' His voice was very sincere.

'I know it's not my place to . . . to . . .' She tilted her chin suddenly. 'I'm old enough to have realized that you have to . .. to . . . sleep with your wife!' She snapped the words. 'But please, Craig, please, please, never just before or just after you and I . . . Please, Craig.'

'You know I wouldn't,' he said.

'I feel better,' Libby said. 'I'm sorry I made a fuss. But this doesn't happen to a girl but once, and I guess it's kind of important. I mean it only happens to a girl once and it's kind of important and . . .' She smiled, a little girl's smile. 'I guess I mean it only happens to a girl once and it's kind of important. But I said that, didn't I?'

'Do you know something?' Craig asked.

'What?'

'I ought to fire you. Fire you right now, out of hand. Do you know we have circled our mill on the Loop Road three times? We're both late, and what will happen to the textile business if we don't quit this merry-go-round and go to work?'

'I guess we'll all starve,' Libby said. 'I'm sorry if I've been sort of like—sort of like a new bride. But it was such a short honeymoon, Craig, to be left at the end of it.'

Craig turned into the parking space which said 'President'.

'Sweetie-pie, there is not just one goddamned thing that we can do right now, and maybe not for ever. You've got to understand this. Maybelle is there, and she is there just like this mill is here. It's a thing we have to recognize and realize. She's there and the mill's here, and unless we just run off all of a sudden and go to live in the South Sea Islands, we are going to have to face the fact that Maybelle and the mill are here. I'm sorry, but that's how it is.'

'I know. Please don't be mad at me. I'll get over being a girl right now and be a very smart secretary. Please don't be angry.'

'I'm not angry. I'm sad. Here is you and here is me and there is Maybelle and we are entering the mill that feeds us. Good morning, Joe,' to one of the pensioners who raked the yard. 'Nice day, isn't it?'

'Shore God is,' Joe said. 'Mawnin', Mr. Price. Mawnin', Miss Forney. Shore God is a hell of a pretty day.'

'Now that,' Craig said, as they entered the office, 'is what I would call a very picturesque yard-raker. "Good mawnin', Miss Forney." This shore God is a hell of a pretty day seem any brighter to you?'

'Lots,' Libby said. 'Heaps. But we better get to work. There's a pile of correspondence a mile high.'

'I don't want to work right yet. I want to talk some. The work can wait. Damn the work. Reach into that ice-box and give us a Coke. I guess I forgot to tell you I'm kind of the father of a nigger baby.'

The Coke fell out of Libby's hands and rolled over and over on the rug.

'I'm sorry,' Craig said swiftly, and retrieved the bottle.

'I'm not *really* the father of a nigger baby. I just kind of adopted one yesterday. I took him to raise.'

'Look,' Libby said. 'Don't scare me like that. What sort of nigger baby?'

'Well, I told you a nice thing happened yesterday. A little kid used to belong to a huntin' friend of mine came a-calling, and he announced himself as a member of the household. So now I

439

have a rather black son. His name is Herbert Hoover Lincoln Newton, and his nickname is Jazzbo, and he could be ten, he might be twelve years old, but he runs a keerful errand and is honest as the day is long, and some day when he grows up to be my butler and va-lley and shofer, he aims to go as far North as even maybe Richmond. This he informed me in the kitchen, and I didn't really have much choice, did I?'

'The door's closed,' Libby said. 'May I kiss you, please, boss, before we start the day's work? Somehow I feel like I had a honeymoon now.'

'I strongly disapprove of kissing during working hours,' Craig said, 'but so long as the door's closed . . .'

Oh good Lord above, Craig thought. I am really in it for fair. Now I've got an office wife. I love her, I suppose, but what in the name of Christ am I going to *do* with her? Every day she's here, and let nobody fool you, young man, it'll get to be a couch business, whether brother Red works in the shop or not. It'll get to be a couch business. You want to win a bet, Price, you dirty bastard?

'Libby,' he said.

'Yes, boss,' she replied brightly.

'Lock the door.'

'Yes, boss.'

He took her brutally into his arms.

'The correspondence can wait,' he said, and thought, it's an awful long drive down to the Fort anyhow.

19

CRAIG thought everything over very carefully in the shower before he came down to breakfast. I better bounce this one in easy, he thought. What I don't mainly want is a married holiday. I don't want it with Maybelle, and I don't want it with Libby. And I don't want a fist fight with anybody. Especially Maybelle right now. New York, I want it for me to look at all alone. He grinned nastily at himself as he shaved. Lonesome Craig Price, he thought. Investigating a new Ocean Sea. Or at least a new jungle. This time it's New York. All by his little lonesome self.

I guess maybe I just better throw it in, and Uncle Charlie can always help me here. I know how Maybelle feels about Uncle Charlie.

He felt good. He felt that he looked good. He felt excited as he walked down the stairs and smelt the pleasant odour of cheerful morning cookery. Young Jazzbo was just going off to school. He looked very clean and neat in knickerbockers and jumper, as

440

he pushed his bicycle along the drive, his school books tucked into the basket of the bike.

'Good morning, Jazz,' he said.

'Mo'nin', boss,' Jazzbo replied. 'You please excuse me, suh, but I is got to git movin'. Dat history class. Good-bye, boss, I sees you dis afternoon.' Jazz took the curve to the main road on a bobsledder's bank.

That seems to be working out all right, Craig thought. I'll know more when he's older. But I sure don't know how deep that history is digging into my little black sort-of son. Well, here we go to face Maybelle. The hero leaves the ranch. I feel like I was going off to a war, kind of.

She was already at the table reading the paper when he came into the breakfast-room. She was wearing now a pink quilted dressing-gown, and her face was smoothly greased. A turban hid the pins in her hair.

'Maybelle.'

'Yes.'

Craig dropped the bomb over breakfast, which consisted of waffles and little sausages.

'I've got to go to New York for a couple of days.'

'Oh, wonderful! When do we leave?'

'I don't think *we* leave. I thought I'd go by myself this first time. It's all business. We can go together later on, maybe around World Series time. Stay a couple of weeks and see all the shows.'

'What kind of business in New York that's so important I can't go?' Maybelle pouted. 'I've never been to New York.'

'I know. Neither have I. I never been further North than Washington, unless you want to count Europe. But I'm thinking hard about spreading out some. We may make the stuff here, but New York's where you sell it. There's a lot about finance I don't know much about, and I've got an appointment with a man, a factor, named Nate Mannheim. I've had a letter of introduction.'

'What's a factor?' Maybelle didn't sound very interested.

'A factor's a man who deals in accounts receivable. He's a kind of a pawnbroker, I guess you'd call him. He lends money on risk—not so much on the credit of the man he's lending the money to, but on the strength of the man's accounts and assets and the credit standing of the man's customers. It's as if he lends money on what he can take and sell if you don't pay. And I need some money. Bigger money than I can promote here. Funny, this Mannheim is a nephew of old Uncle Charlie. It was Uncle Charlie suggested maybe I ought to go have a talk with this Mr. Mannheim.'

'You still see that Jew pawnbroker? I never will understand you.'

'Sure,' Craig said. 'I drop in once in a while and have a chat with the old fellow. We got to talking business and expansion and Uncle Charlie said that if I wanted big capital I'd have to go North for it. I guess he's right. Winken and Blinken and Nod'—Craig had changed over from Hickory, Dickory and Dock when he referred to the bankers—'they wet their pants if you talk a loan any bigger than five thousand dollars, and I need about fifty thousand dollars cash *and* some heavy credit. There's another mill I can buy if I can just—' Craig clenched his teeth—'if I can just talk somebody into bankrolling me for just a little bit. Uncle Charlie, he said one pawnbroker is like another. So I'm going to New York, to Wall Street, and have me a little talk with Mr. Nathan Mannheim.'

'You and your beloved Jews,' Maybelle said. 'If you're goin' to spend all your time with them I don't want to go to New York anyhow.'

'I believe New York has got more than one Jew in the city,' Craig said. 'If we ever go there to live you might have to get used to them.'

'When are you leavin'?'

'Tomorrow night's train. Be gone three, four days, all together. If I can just get this thing settled I reckon we'll move up there to live some day. It's where the big money is.'

'I like it here,' Maybelle said. 'I wouldn't know anybody in New York. I despise Yankees, anyhow.'

'Where'd you ever know any?'

'I met a few on the beach. Stuck-up. Always lookin' down their noses at you and makin' fun of your accent. They all talk through their noses, too.'

'You're not mad at me for going off, then?'

'I'm not mad at you. But I don't see what you want with another mill. We got a mill. We got a swimmin' pool and two cars. You're a real big toad in this little puddle.'

'I want a little bigger swimming pool,' Craig said. 'That's why I'm going to New York. I want to be a lot bigger toad in a much bigger puddle.'

20

'I NEED a lot of dough, Uncle Charlie,' Craig had said. 'A whole slew of it. That Jordan mill can be bought. They're in trouble. But it'll have to be some fast cash and a large under-write. I haven't even bothered talking to the bank here. They don't deal in that kind of money.'

'You come perhaps to ask that I lend you the money?' Uncle Charlie twinkled. 'A car for you I can buy. A cotton mill, no. This kind of money does not come from unredeemed ukuleles and watches that turn green before they stop keeping time.'

'No, I didn't come to hit you up for a loan. I just thought you might maybe have an idea about how a dumb country boy could rassle up enough dough to buy a mill. Up North, maybe. I don't know how it's done. I know it is done, but I don't know how.'

'Well,' Uncle Charlie put his fingers together as he thought. 'If you are rich, the banks are falling over themselves to lend you money. If you are poor, the banks are saying phooey, get out of here, *schlemiel*, *goniff*. If you are very poor and have something to offer as security, there is always a pawnshop with an Uncle Charlie. But there is a middle way. There is a thing called a factor. It happens my sister Sarah had a son named Nate Mannheim. A Yankee, yet. But he is very big in the Yankee pawnshop business, which is factoring. Also he charges sometimes as much interest as twenty per cent because his business is risks, like mine, except much bigger. You are a risk, my friend Craig. *Oi weh*, what a risk.' The old man twinkled again.

'What exactly is a factor, Uncle Charlie?'

'A pawnbroker, yet. I said it already. Except he has money and he will lend it to people that the banks will not lend to, at an interest the banks will not dare to ask. In return for this he wants a lien on your rents, on what people owe you, on your market. He wants to know about the credit of the people you do businesss with. That is a factor. I think he is a good man, this Nathan Mannheim. I think perhaps you should go to New York and talk with him. Even if he will not give you money he will give you good advice. Wait. I will write a letter to my nephew. You will write him and then he will answer and you will go see him. Wait. I write it now.' Uncle Charlie busied himself with an ancient quill pen. He finished writing, and handed the letter to Craig.

'So. Now I ask a question?'

'What?'

'You need another mill? You must have another mill to be happy? You cannot live without another mill?'

'I want another mill,' Craig said. 'Thanks, like always, Uncle Charlie. Yes. I need another mill. For myself.'

Uncle Charlie shook his head.

'Another mill. Like two cancers. Wear it in good health,' he said.

'There's a letter here from New York,' Libby said. 'From a Mr. Mannheim. It says . . .'

'Gimme,' Craig said. 'I'll read it myself.'

'Dear Mr. Price,' the letter said, 'I have received your letter and also the enclosed letter from my uncle Charles Lipschutz, who seems to feel very highly about you. I would be pleased to see you at any time within the next month with the exception of week-ends. Please telephone me when you arrive in New York. Yours very sincerely, Nathan Mannheim.'

'Feel that writing paper, sugar,' Craig said. 'It must be an inch thick. We'll have to get us some of that some day. How'd you like to go to New York?'

'Oh, Craig, could we?' Libby's eyes were almost as round as Jazzbo's, when he heard about the bicycle. 'Could we really, Craig?'

'I think we could. I think we will. But we'll have to be careful.' He disliked the pall that shadowed Libby's enthusiasm.

'You know, sweetie,' he said. 'You *know*. Red and Maybelle. Maybelle and Red. Is there any place you could logically go for a week? You haven't had a vacation in a year. Maybe some day I could take you along as my secretary, but I've already told Maybelle she couldn't go, that I'd be too busy . . .'

'No. There's no place I can think of that I could go. I don't know anybody out of town. I haven't got any relatives. I could tell Red right out, I suppose. No. I wouldn't want to tell him right out. Maybe he knows but I wouldn't want to tell him. It's like he never brings girls to the house unless I'm there. And . . .'

'And?'

'The first thing your wife would do would be to call the mill the day after you left. And if I weren't here to answer . . . No. New York will have to wait, Craig. But I would so love to be alone with you in a town where we didn't know anybody, to be with you all the night, to wake up with you in the morning, to see any other place but this, with you to show it to me. Oh, Craig. Why do you have to go to New York and make me know that I could almost but not quite be there with you?'

'Libby, for the love of God, don't cry,' Craig said. 'Please don't. We'll go to New York. We'll go some day, and we'll shop on Fifth Avenue and see the World Series . . .' I already said that before, to Maybelle, he thought. 'We'll go and go right when I move there to live, and I'll need you to look after me and you'll have your own apartment and . . .'

'And your wife will go too.' Her tone was flat. 'She'll go, too. She'll always go. Wherever you go she'll go.'

'I suppose so. I guess you're right.'

'I told you, I don't mean to be a nuisance. But it's getting inside me, Craig. It's not . . . it's not *nice*. Like about the other house and the other car. And the office, too. I feel so—so *outside* you.'

'The other house and the other car were necessary,' Craig said. 'You know that as well as I do. And the office. Well, it's our office. We can do what we want with our office. If we don't do it too often.'

It had damned well been necessary, he thought swiftly. That day Maybelle came a-roving and nearly caught us. Thank God I was actually fishing and Libby was off far enough down the beach to hide when she saw that red Chrysler drive up. And thank God there weren't any girl things hanging in the cottage.

'I think your fishin' shack is real cute,' Maybelle had said, sniffing around with a beagle's suspicion. 'Remember, you were going to bring me down here? But it sure could use a woman's touch. You want me to fix it up real fancy for you, honey? That Navajo rug really ought to go.'

'No,' Craig said. 'No thanks. I like it rough the way it is. It suits me just fine.' (*Where are you, Libby? Where are you right now? And I hope to God you've got sense enough to duck behind a sand-dune.*)

'Well,' Maybelle said brightly, dismissing the coffee-pot and the kerosene stove, 'I mustn't keep you from your fish. I didn't have much to do and was just drivin' around and thought I'd look in. It's a real nice place, Craig. I'm glad you rented it. And you look a lot better since you started fishin' the late afternoon bluefish run.'

She had smiled sweetly and was gone.

It wouldn't be beyond her to come back, Craig thought as the Chrysler whished off in a flurry of sand. He watched the car twisting out of sight. Then he went down to the beach and made false motions at fishing for another half hour, sharply indicating to Libby that she should stay hidden. At dusk, he went to the sand-dune and found Libby salty, sandy, and shivering. She had wept; her eyes were swollen and her lipstick eaten off.

'I had to wait a little bit,' he had said. 'I'm sorry, baby. I guess our little house isn't ours any more. I think she's gone for good, though. Come on back and let's have a drink. You're shivering like a half-drowned puppy.'

'I feel like a half-drowned puppy,' Libby said. 'I feel just awful. Oh, Craig, I don't like our house any more since she's been there. I don't like it.'

There had been no suggestion of love-making. They had a short drink and got into the Cadillac.

'We have to find a new place,' Craig said, as they drove towards the city. 'And a new car. Not a new car really. A very old, ramshackledy car. A battered, beat-up old Ford or Chev. Black. Something that even a nigger could own. Something nobody'll recognize. And a new house. There's one about two miles farther down the beach. I'll have a look at that.'

'Oh, Craig, I feel like a—I feel like a whore,' Libby said, 'changing places all the time.'

'Don't say it. Don't ever say it. But if we're going to see each other certain things are necessary. Such as . . .'

'Do you mean do I know how to take care of myself?' Libby's voice had been edged. 'Of course I know how to take care of myself. A girl in my position has to know how to take care of herself.'

'I don't quite like the way you said "a girl in my position",' Craig's voice had sharpened as well.

'Well, it *is* a position,' Libby said. 'A sort of strange position. I'm the boss's girl-friend. I go to bed with the boss. When we can fit it in. We go to bed in the office sometimes and sometimes in a fishing-shack and once in a while in the car and once in a while in the woods. I guess you could call me a girl in a strange position.'

Craig swerved the car to avoid hitting a dog.

'I know it, darling,' he said. 'But I'm in an awkward position, too.'

That is how they had come to rent another fishing-shack, almost the twin of the other. The other, which Craig never used now except when he really went fishing, usually with Red and occasionally with Libby and Red. The new shack had a slightly more functional stove. And the battered Chevrolet coupé which stood outside its door had been painted in a spatter-dash fashion, and was scabrous with rust. It looked exactly like what he used to call a nigger-dog, a small fice-dog with an up-curled tail and very few breed-distinguishing features. There was another building at the centre of the beach which Craig was able to rent as a garage. He and Libby would drive the Cadillac down to the building, take out the battered Chev, put the Cadillac inside, go to the new shack, and then return to replace the Cadillac with the Chev.

The entire operation rubbed some of the glister off their love-making. But, as Craig said, it was necessary. And as Libby said, she was a girl in an unusual position.

21

MY God I'm glad to be shut of both of them, Craig thought. Women. Love. I don't know which one is the most trouble. Actually I had less trouble out of Maybelle than I did out of Libby. He looked around the railroad club car, and fetched a relieved sigh. At least Libby didn't come to see me off. If I ever get elected to Congress I will pass a rule against people seeing other people off. I can't think of anything more gruesome unless it's a funeral. Or a wedding.

He sighed again.

He looked around and saw nobody of any interest whatsoever.

'Waiter,' he said. 'I'd like a drink.'

'We got kind of peculiar laws down South here,' the club car waiter said. 'I doesn't know myself just what applies here, as I has just been switched to this run from Chicago. May I be of service however?'

'You may,' Craig said. 'Would you bring me a glass and some ice-water and I will provide the hooch.' He reached into his capacious briefcase—he had bought a briefcase for the trip—and pulled out a brown paper-bag which contained a bottle.

'You drinks scotch, I see,' the waiter said. 'You doesn't see many folks drinkin' scotch down here.'

'I drink anything, but when I travel I drink scotch. Thank you.' He handed the Negro waiter a dollar.

'You doesn't see many dollar tips down here, either,' he said. 'You a Northerner, suh?'

'Not yet,' Craig grinned. 'But pretty soon. Pretty goddamned soon.'

The wheels clacked and occasionally the Pullman back-jumped on the uneven road-bed. Craig sat in the club car and read *Time* and *Life*, and drank. He had never felt so luxurious. He had taken a small compartment which he did not need and which was more expensive than a lower berth. He would have flown, he thought, but there was no air service out of Kensington. And trains were exciting, like ships were exciting. Trains and ships were constructed for adventure.

Dinner-time was coming up and he went to his compartment and washed at the little built-in zinc sink, used the little foot-stool-camouflaged toilet, and smiled at himself in the mirror. He wished there was a pretty girl on the train so he could possibly share with her the tremendous feeling of secret evil that just being shut into your own compartment gave a man. Maybe somebody interesting would get on in Rocky Mount . . . He rolled through the swaying coaches to the diner, and noted that although he was asked to write his order on a pad, the coloured waiter cleverly contrived to make him speak it. It was many years later that he discovered that a great many of the silver-woolled Uncle Tom types who served the Pullman dining-rooms could not read or write.

It was raining when he hit New York at four o'clock in the afternoon. It wasn't a proper rain, not a driving rain, but a dispirited grey rain that made the grey Sunday afternoon in the grey fur-trade district adjacent to the grey gloom of Pennsylvania Station an adventure in grey loneliness. Craig didn't know the names of many hotels in New York, except things like the Waldorf and the Ritz and the Plaza and the New Yorker. He thought that the first ones sounded too rich, too expensive, too uncertain in behaviour. So he chose the New Yorker, which had a commercial sound about it, and promised not to threaten him with too many head waiters or strange customs. He finally found the taxi-rank in the vast cave of Pennsylvania Station, and drove through the nearly deserted Sunday streets, seeing the grey closed shops, the grey soggy papers rolling in little grey tumble-weeds through the rain-wet filthy grey pavement. A few people walked, hunched against the rain, and some had sodden newspapers held scarfwise over their heads. Craig pressed his face to the rain-bleared taxi window, looking, trying to see what it was that made the town The Big Town. He saw signs saying: 'Curb Your Dog'. He saw a pizzeria here, a kosher delicatessen there. He saw ashcans and bars with neon signs. He saw people who walked, not only hunched against the rain, but people who walked as if they were hunched against the town, hunched against life itself. The people hurried in the rain as if they wished they were somewhere else, anywhere else but where they were. He hadn't known that the New Yorker was just across the street, and that he was being taken for a ride.

'Here we are,' the driver said, pulling up to the entrance of the New Yorker. Craig paid him, and received a surly thanks for a twenty-five cent tip. There did not seem to be a doorman or a porter on duty at the time, so Craig carried his bag and his briefcase into the lobby himself. The lobby was harsh with light, and looking swiftly round him, he thought: Why, these people look just like me. Strangers in the city.

They did, too. They looked clothes-rumpled, travel-stained, unused to the town. They looked like red-necked people from Mississippi, or Texans with voices too loud, or uneasy North Carolinians. They looked like unkissed wives and forgotten grandmothers and fat travelling salesmen and women with badly fitting girdles and too-sharp ferret-faced city slickers and former country louts embarrassingly self-conscious about a lack of straws to chew. They looked like hard-faced blonde women with too much false hair piled too high and they looked like women with shoe-heels too high and too thick, too-greasy lipstick scars for mouths, and much too much silver-fox. They looked like baseball players billeted in a city but unused to anything larger than the Alabama hamlet from which they sprang. They looked like querulous old women and men with snap-purse mouths and loud, hearty promoters with burst cheek-veins and incipent angina pectoris.

'Take your bag, mister?' A much-buttoned bellhop accosted him.

'Yes,' Craig had made up his mind in a moment. 'I've just checked out. I want a taxi.'

The bellhop accepted a quarter and handed Craig over t a doorman who had miraculously appeared.

'Where to, sir?' The doorman asked.

'The Ritz,' Craig said, and wondered if he had enough money to bail himself out. Well, he could always wire Uncle Charlie if he ran short of cash. It would have to be Uncle Charlie, because anybody else—Maybelle, Winken, Blinken and Nod—would throw a shoe if they thought Craig Price was staying at the Ritz.

Somehow at the Ritz it was all better, and Craig was surprised

448

to find that it didn't cost a fortune when he looked at the rates on the bathroom door. The people in the Ritz looked as though they belonged there. They did not look like transplanted strangers. They looked like people who would say: Meet me at the Ritz at five for a couple of drinks, and we'll finish that deal for the seven billion dollars' worth of moving picture or bauxite or new book. Craig felt as though he belonged there, too. Even the desk-clerk refused to show surprise when Craig said:

'I've just come into town in a hurry. I hope you're not full.'

'What would you be wanting, sir?' Like most desk-clerks, this one's hair seemed to be marcelled.

Craig's inclination was to say: The smallest, cheapest, room in the house. Instead he said:

'A small suite, if you have one. There's only me but I must do some business in the next few days and . . .' He let the rest of the sentence drift away.

'One bedroom, living-room and bath, then,' the clerk said, and looked at Craig's suit. Let him look, the pansy bastard, Craig thought. This ain't no Joe College suit. This is my banking suit, my best blue.

'Register here, please,' the clerk said, and snapped his fingers. A bellhop appeared.

'Take Mr. Price's bags to 516,' he said. 'You'll be with us how long, sir?'

'Only a very few days. Perhaps until Wednesday,' Craig said. I can always put it in the mill books on the expense account as administrative expense, he thought, as he followed the bellhop into the elevator. This was Sunday night, and the service lift was out of commission. I wonder what I'll give the 'hop, he thought, and decided that since he had only one bag fifty cents was more than enough.

Craig looked around the sitting-room. It was the first suite he had ever been in with the exception of John Grimes's rooms in the Inn of Chapel Hill, and you couldn't hardly call that a suite. It wasn't very big, but it had a sofa and two easy chairs and some small tables flanking the sofa. There were lamps instead of major lights, and there was a small panel in which three buttons proclaimed that you could summon a maid, a valet or a waiter even if you couldn't read. Over the buttons were illustrations of a hurrying maid, a hurrying butler, a hurrying waiter.

Craig looked at his watch. Where he came from it was damn' near supper-time. He punched a button. He had barely lifted his finger before a tail-coated waiter rang and then opened the door.

'Yes, sir?' he said, and almost succeeded in masking his surprise at Craig's youth. Craig gave him what he learned later to call the blasé bit.

'I'm tired,' he said to the waiter. 'I thought maybe I'd just have a bite in my room. I've come a long way on a very bumpy

449

train, and New York on Sunday in the rain . . .' Craig shrugged, a you-know-how-it-is shrug.

'Of course, sir. I'll bring the menu immediately. Would you like something to drink, first?'

'Yes,' Craig said. 'Suppose you bring me a double, very dry martini.'

'With Gordon's, sir?'

'Of course with Gordon's. And very, very dry.'

'Certainly, sir, I won't be a moment.'

Well, damn me, Craig thought. Me to the manner—or is it the manor—born. This red-nosed old boy in the claw-hammer coat thinks I'm a gentleman. That's more than Julie duFresne's old strawberry nose ever thought. He knew I was a bum, right from the start. Maybe I'm gaining on it. But you know, Craig, he said to himself, I think you like this. You ain't the commercial hotel type, my lad. You need a hotel with floor-service. You are also a complete and utter phony, you bastard, he said. You can't afford this joint but you've got to show off because when you talk to Nate Mannheim tomorrow he'll say: Where you staying, Price? and you will say, quote, I always stay at the Ritz. You get me at Suite 516-17, and that will tell him I ain't a one-room guy. I don't know why I ever considered the other joint in the first place. I'm a very Ritzy guy. A very, very Ritzy guy.

The waiter was back now. He carried a tray on which a large glass vase held what seemed to be a very cold potion, as it was sweat beaded. It was nestled in a dish which was filled with crushed ice. The waiter took the double-barrelled vase out of the crushed ice and poured the martini into a delicate goblet which also had been cradled in ice.

'Is that all right, sir?' he asked.

Craig tasted the drink.

'Perfect.' He nodded at the waiter. 'Lovely.' And made a properly appreciative face.

'Would you care to see the card, sir?'

'The what'—and then Craig saw that the waiter was extending a menu. 'Yes, of course. I'm not really very hungry. You know how trains are.' Help me, you bastard, he was thinking. Make it easy for me. This thing is all in French and I got no more French than Jazzbo. 'What would you say for a man who's tired of Pullman food?'

'Well, sir, the Vichyssoise is very nice, if you'd like to start with a soup.' That's a help, Craig thought. I don't know Vichyssoise from swamp water, but it's a help.

'I'll have the Vichyssoise.'

'And then,' the waiter said, 'if you'd like some fish, perhaps a little of the smoked salmon? It's very nice, sir. Very nice indeed. Will you have it with oil and vinegar? Or just with lemon and red pepper?'

450

'With the oil and vinegar,' Craig said. 'Now we have the soup and we have the fish. What else do we want?'

'Well, as long as everything is cold, perhaps we want something hot,' the waiter said. 'The rack of lamb is very nice. With mint sauce and perhaps a little tossed salad? Maybe with roquefort dressing? And some little potatoes, not many, but just a few little potatoes?'

'That sounds dandy,' Craig said, mentally computing the cost and figuring that since he had heard of the Automat he might just as well go eat in it tomorrow.

'And some wine, sir? You would be wanting some wine? There's a very nice white, and we have an excellent year of . . .'

'I think just a bottle of red,' Craig said. 'You choose it. If there's any Chambolle-Musigny around in a good year . . .'

The waiter's eyebrows flew upward.

'You know that one?'

'Of course I know that one.' Thank you, Julie duFresne. Thank you, Philip duFresne. Thank you for my education. I now have status in the Ritz-Carlton Hotel of New York City. I sound like a Frenchman from Charleston, he thought.

'If you don't have the Musigny, a Mouton-Rothschild would do nicely,' he said, and mentally applauded himself. Boy, how I do come on, he thought. Me and that Mouton-Rothschild. Double God-bless Julie duFresne and her pansy son. At least I know a fork from a knife. And I have managed to impress this bum in the tail-coat.

'Don't serve me, please, for half-an-hour,' Craig said. 'I want to wash and finish the other half of that Martini.'

'Of course, sir.' The waiter bowed himself out of the door. 'Very good, sir. I think, myself, we had better choose the Musigny.'

'As you wish,' Craig said curtly. And then to himself. Goddam. I feel like I been doin' this all my life. And man, I like it here so far. At least I got old claw-hammer stymied, me and my Musigny.

The waiter served him with grave dignity, and after the coffee, handed him the check to sign. Craig reached into his pocket for a tip, but the water stopped him.

'Much better if we have our little present all at once, when you leave,' he said. 'My partner and I will be looking after you, sir. Would I ring for the valet now, in case you want anything pressed?'

'How much time would it take?'

'Only a few minutes, sir.'

'In that case, suppose we press the dinner jacket now, and when I change you can let him press this blue suit I'm wearing in time for tomorrow morning. Also the grey flannel. I'm travelling very light.'

'Very good, sir.'

In a moment the stripe-jacketed valet was in the room.

'Shall I unpack you, sir?' The valet was fat, pasty-faced, and had stiff white hair. He was a man of more than sixty years. 'And Charles—your room-waiter—Charles said you might be wanting me to press your dinner jacket now?'

'That's right. I'd like to wear this blue suit tomorrow morning. There's no hurry on the grey.'

'It's been raining. Perhaps I'd better do your shoes now, as well.'

'That'll be all right for the morning, too. I've got some evening shoes in the bag. Just give them a little whisk.' Man, I like that, Craig said to himself. Just give them a little whisk. Classy all the way.

He dressed very carefully when the valet came back with his freshly pressed dinner clothes. His mind ran back, idly, to that time in Charleston when he had made the awful mistake of dressing for dinner that night in Julie duFresne's house in Charleston, remembered the embarrassment, remembered how beautifully Julie duFresne had recognized his horror at the mistake, and how wonderfully she had covered for him, taken him off the hook, by being unduly sharp with her son. I guess I'm not out of line tonight, he thought, expertly tying his tie. I'm in New York for the first time and it's Sunday night and I'm going out. I'm staying in a suite at the Ritz-Carlton Hotel and I'm going out and see this town. I think I'll start with the Stork Club.

Craig had only read about the Stork Club, how everybody went there, how anybody who was anybody went there, and about how rigidly selective it was. He had read about El Morocco, too, and how exclusive that was, and about Twenty-One, and how exclusive that was. And about the Colony and all the other places that were very very exclusive. He would go to Twenty-One tomorrow, maybe. Tonight he would go to the Stork Club.

He hailed a cab.

'The Stork,' he said.

'All right,' the driver answered. 'It's your funeral. But it's just around the corner.' He looked pityingly at Craig. 'Just come to town, Mister?'

'No, as a matter of fact, I have not just come to town. But it's a nasty night and my feet hurt and I just had my suit pressed. Do you mind?'

'Not if you don't. The meter don't care,' the driver said. 'Here we are. Sport.' He accepted a tip that amounted to the size of the fare and refrained from saying thank-you.

It's about cocktail-time here, even though I've eaten, Craig thought, as he walked into the Stork. I'll just have a couple of drinks and look around the place and maybe if I meet a girl I'll come back. He walked through the entrance, turned left,

452

and ran into the velvet rope. There was a smooth-haired young man behind the rope. Craig looked at the handsome, swarthy, tooth-gleaming, smooth-haired young man behind the rope, and suddenly his tuxedo was no longer a dinner jacket. It was just a tux.

'May I help you?' The smoothed-haired young man said, in a voice to match his hair and the flowing fit of his clothes. 'Were you meeting someone, perhaps?'

'No,' Craig said. 'I thought I'd just drop in for a drink.'

'I'm terribly sorry,' the smooth-haired young man said. 'But as you probably know, Sunday night is very busy here, and at the moment we're full.' Craig looked past him at the corner of the bar. It was devoid of people.

'I thought I'd have a drink at the bar,' he said, lamely.

'I'm sorry,' the young man said, and turned his back 'We're full. Perhaps some other time.' The hand had left the velvet rope, which was still hooked securely to its socket.

Craig was left standing alone outside the velvet rope that barred the door to the Stork Club. The exotic mystery of the harem gardens would be for ever lost to Craig Price.

'Maybe I'll buy it one day,' he grated as he walked back out to the sidewalk. 'But unless I buy it that's the last time I'll ever walk through that door.'

Even though he discovered, some years later, that the owner was a former bootlegger from Oklahoma, a country boy like himself, and probably still as frightened of the city as Craig Price was frightened of the city, he never walked up against the rope again.

22

THE city of New York on a rainy Sunday night, when you are dressed in your best and ripely ready for adventure, is a study in frustration. Most of the nightclubs, most of the restaurants, except the little ones downtown or uptown, are closed. Craig rode along Broadway, the great Broadway, and was obsessed with the number of shooting galleries and pineapple-juice stands. Illuminated advertisements winked and blinked, and the side-walks billowed with people. The picture-houses offered garish attractions involving the naked truth about sex. He had ridden down Fifty-Second Street and had seen the advertisements for the strip-tease shows and the jazz joints, but even in his youthful simplicity he figured it was too early in the evening.

Suddenly, on Broadway, a sign hit him.

'Stop here,' he said to the driver. He paid the hacker and went to the box-office to buy a ticket. The attraction was a double-feature. It was a re-run of 'Hell's Angels', starring Jean Harlow, and 'It Happened One Night', starring Claudette Colbert and Clark Gable. Once seated snugly inside, he forgot the rebuff at the Stork Club. It was almost as if Libby were sitting beside him, here in this great, wonderful, lonely city of New York. And Jean Harlow hadn't lost her looks with the years.

'How about Chinatown?' Craig asked the driver.

'Nothin'. No opium dens. Better chowmein off Broadway. We ain't had a tong war since Doctor Fu Manchu,' the driver said.

'Harlem, then?' Craig asked.

'Look, Mac, it's Sunday. You couldn't even get mugged in Harlem on Sunday. This town knocks off on Sunday. Why don't you be a good boy and buy some newspapers and go back to wherever you're stayin' and read yourself to sleep? You can start all over again tomorrow when the town wakes up with a hangover.'

'I guess you're right. But stop at the first news-stand we see and let me pick up the papers.'

'The papers we'll pick up are tomorrow's papers,' the driver said. 'Today's papers got sold out yesterday.'

I might just as well have stayed in Kensington, Craig said to himself. He had undressed and put on his pyjamas, and was sitting reading tomorrow's papers. He was reading Dan Parker's short-itemed 'Broadway Bugle', in the *Mirror*, and a name caught his eye. The item said: 'Moose Wilbur, mortal cinch to be named coach of the year, in town on a business holiday, was uncovered skulking at the Waldorf where he made a speech last night. Wilbur fears Communism in college. He says that there is a move afoot to make football players legitimately pass courses, which is in defiance to all tenets of the coaching faith. Wilbur says that there is an even dirtier Fascist move going to make reading necessary as a college requirement for athletes. Moose Wilbur shares a talent with Herman Hickman for not taking himself or the game at which he is so proficient very seriously, a most unusual trait in coaches, who generally appear to be deathly afraid of the alumni's shadow . . .'

By God, Craig said, old Jim. Good old Moose. Here in town in New York. And a big enough shot to have his name in the big town papers. I think I'll call up the Waldorf and leave a message. Maybe he hasn't forgotten the little fat boy he saved from the maniac. Maybe I shouldn't bother him. But hell . . . it's early yet. I can leave a message and if he doesn't call me I'll understand he's busy.

He reached for the phone.

'Give me the Waldorf-Astoria, please,' he said.

'The what?' A Sunday night voice answered.

'The Waldorf-Astoria,' he repeated. 'It's a hotel.'

'Oh,' the voice said. 'You mean the Waldorf-Astoria.'

'I thought that was what I said,' Craig said away from the receiver. 'I sure as hell don't talk all that Southern.'

The Waldorf answered.

'I'd like to leave a message for Mr. James Wilbur, the football coach,' Craig said.

'Just a minute,' the Waldorf operator answered. 'If you would like to speak with Mr. Wilbur he is in his room and is still taking calls. Shall I put you through?'

'Yes, please.' Craig heard the phone buzz.

'I already got them broads out of my room,' a well-remembered voice answered. 'Now who wants what? A man can't even smoke a little marijuana around here without every Tom, Dick, and Harry calling him up. What is it and who is it?'

'Why, it's only me from over the sea cried Barnacle Bill the Sailor,' Craig said. 'I got a maniac in my room and I need help. How are you, Jim?'

'It could not, it would not possibly be that little fat youth whom I saved from a fate worse than life when we were all so very much younger and I still had my pride,' Jimmy Wilbur said. 'How the hell are you, Craig, and where the hell are you? Come over here immediately. I'm about to die of the creeping New York Sunday Nightus.'

'Me too. I been looking for adventure and found nothin'. Until I saw your name in Dan Parker's column and he wrote you were staying at the Waldorf. You dressed?'

'Yeah. I'm dressed. I thought I'd go out and hurl myself under a taxi-cab. It would be at least something to do, and I wouldn't want to do it naked. Where are you?'

'I'm at the Ritz. I got undressed, so why don't you come over here? I bet my suite is prettier than your suite.'

'My boy Craig Price in a suite at the Ritz, yet. This is worth the trip. Ten minutes. What room, and have you got anything to drink? This sounds like it might work out to be a celebration.'

'I got something to drink. It's 516–517. Hurry, Moose. We got talking to do.'

'I'll hurry, little fat Craig Price, the lover of Jean Harlow, the maniac's delight, holed up in a suite in the Ritz. I will just be go to hell.'

Craig found himself grinning broadly. A rainy night in a dead, hostile town, and you have to go to an old movie to kill time, and there ain't any tong wars in Chinatown and you can't even get mugged in Harlem and you pick up a paper and read the sports news and there is your friend of ancient days in print, and he's at home in his hotel and just as bored as you. And he's famous, after two Rose Bowls in a row. Jimmy Wilbur. My God. Will I ever forget what that man did for me when I was a scared little kid at school. He rang for the waiter and ordered a bottle of scotch and one of bourbon.

'Plenty of ice,' he said to the waiter. 'And you better bring some soda, too.' Maybe all our tastes have changed from the corn licker and Dixie Cup days, he thought, and could barely wait for the ring at the door.

'So it's you. It's really you. Little old Craig Price, in a layout like this.' Both were grinning a little foolishly. As far as Craig could see, Jimmy Wilbur hadn't changed very much. No grey in the red hair yet. The grey eyes still steady. The nose still broken. Shoulders still bulky, hips exaggeratedly thin.

'I bet you could still run back a punt,' Craig said. 'Come on in and have a drink.'

'I could run one back better than some of these bums I'm trying to coach,' Wilbur said, scaling his hat at a chair. 'What a rat-race. A bunch of lousy specialists that can't do nothing but pass or kick. T-formations, all that crap. It was better the way we always used to play it. Get yourself a good strong body with no brains, and leave it in there until it dropped dead. And when in doubt, kick. Einstein couldn't figure out some of the new stuff, let alone me. How the hell are you anyhow, little man? Let me look at you.'

'I'm a big boy now, Papa,' Craig said. 'All growed up with a wife and the usual problems. Got a mill, too. Might have more.'

Wilbur nodded. He took in the broken nose, the scarred forehead, the prematurely aged eyes.

'I'll say you've growed up. You're even beginning to look like me. Before you pour me a drink, give me that ten dollars you owe me.'

'*What* ten dollars?'

'You know what ten dollars. The ten I bet you that you'd collect your room-mate's mother. You look just exactly like a man who would stop off in Charleston and collect his old room-mate's mother. How was it? Good?'

'Take your lousy ten dollars,' Craig said. 'I forget whether you owe it to me or I owe it to you. But it's worth it to see you. What'll it be? Scotch? Bourbon?'

'A little of both,' Jimmy Wilbur said. 'After some of the stuff I sold, I don't worry any more about mixing up my booze. I got to hear all about you. If you can read, you probably know about me. It's a lost cause. They're trying to make students out of athletes, and I am flipping my lid.'

'That's more or less what Dan Parker said in the paper.' Craig poured the drinks. 'But you've either been awful smart or awful lucky.'

Jimmy Wilbur took a gulp of his drink and snarled.

'The loyal alums have been sending me some very choice meat,' he said. 'I really got no complaint. But it's a lousy way to make a living. One bad season and *adiós, maraquita linda*. Move on to the next whistlestop that calls itself college.'

'How's it out there in Minnesota?'

'Cold as a polar bear's balls. I don't mind that so much. It's this off-season banquet circuit they make you do. Sometimes I think if I see another green pea or a creamed chicken pattie I'll kill myself. Well, skoal again. Damn, boy, you sure look prosperous. Tell me. Rob a bank? What?'

'Nunhuh. Married money.'

'Don't tell me. Not the daughter of that old gent who was going to send you to college, and dropped off at the wrong time? What was his name? Chimes? No, Grimes. That one?'

'That one. My wife's name is Maybelle. We almost had a baby. Had a car accident and . . .' Craig shrugged. 'No baby.'

'I suppose I say I'm sorry. But skip that. What hauls you into this lovely, lovely city? I know what the hell hauls me into this lovely, lovely city. The rich alumni. Maybe you don't know it, but I am supposed to be a very witty-type coach. I have read a book. I can make a speech. The alumni love it, especially when I kid the alumni. They think I'm fooling. Dear God. Sometimes I can barely not throw up at the banquet table, and believe me, Buster, the fault ain't all in the food. Well,' Jimmy Wilbur shrugged, 'a living is a living.'

'You still don't like it, being a tramp athlete? Playing it yourself or telling other people how to play doesn't make any difference? Still a tramp?'

'Still a tramp. Except that at least when I was playing I was an honest bum. Now I got to build character. I got to go to the trustees' cocktail parties. I got to pretend that these coal-mine morons are citizens who like to play ball. I got to pretend that I am making athletes out of students. No, I don't like it, but the last time U.S. Steel and General Motors asked me to be chairman of the board they couldn't meet my price. Yah.'

Jimmy Wilbur almost spat on the carpet.

'You haven't changed a bit, have you? Not a single solitary bit. You didn't like it then, and you don't like it now. I got a sudden idea. But tell me first, Jim. How come you never got married?'

'Me? Married? I never met anybody I wanted to marry. Did you?' The question was needle-pointed.

'Yes. Once. I did. But I didn't. The other, yes. I didn't. I did, though.'

Wilbur looked very long and appraisingly at Craig Price.

'Mary Frances was the did but didn't and Maybelle was the didn't but did? Or am I out of line?'

Craig shook his head.

'You ain't out of line, Coach. But there is this mill. Which is what I'm in town for. To see about. You know. Dough.'

'Pass the jug, Junior. Thanks. Let me see if I got this right.

457

You married a mill. You can afford a suite in the Ritz-Carlton. Now you are in town to see about dough. What do you want dough for?'

'I want another mill.'

'Now I got it. Craig Price, the boy tycoon in the dress-goods business. And what then, after the next mill?'

Craig sipped his drink and then raised his eyes coolly to meet Jimmy Wilbur's gaze.

'Everything,' he said.

23

'THAT's a large order,' Wilbur said, after a bit. '*Everything*. Everything is a large order. How do you intend to go about it?'

'I'll know more about how,' Craig laughed, 'this time to-morrow night. I'm seeing a man that knows about how to make everything work tomorrow. If he says yes to some questions I got in mind I would like to offer you a job. You offered me a job once. How'd you like to work for—to work *with*—me?'

'Nobody'll ever really work *with* you, friend,' Jimmy Wilbur said. 'But I wouldn't mind working *for* you You know,' he said, 'I had you nailed the day you hit school and that lunatic tried to kill you. What were you then, sixteen?'

'No. I was fifteen going on sixteen.'

'Well, I still had you tagged. You were born grown up. Now, saying that tomorrow brings forth its expected goodies, what do you have in mind that includes me? There can't be that many maniacs around in that home town of yours—what's it, Wilmington? No. Kensington—that need hitting over the head with flashlights. What would you want with me in this empire you haven't quite built yet?'

'Kind of a vice-me. Somebody I can trust to help me. Maybe,' Craig smiled, 'somebody to come get me when I'm in trouble because I'm stupid. I got a hunch, Jim. I'm on a big thing, I think. If you came along you wouldn't make as much money right now as you're making as a coach, but there would be some stock. And a title. Vice-president and general manager. And I think we'll be big, Jim. I think we'll be very big. Maybe I can tell you how big tomorrow afternoon if you've got time to meet me for a drink. But, my God, I think we'll be big.'

'I think so, too. I always thought you'd be big, one way or the other, if only you got electrocuted for murder. What does this splendid job pay for starters?'

'Not much. What I draw as salary. A hundred a week. And expenses. But as much stock as you want—if tomorrow turns out all right. And . . .' Craig grinned. 'There's this to think about. Kensington is not as cold as a polar bear's balls, and there won't be any alumni to consider.'

'How are the dames in that neck of the woods?'

'They ain't bad,' Craig said. 'I know one might have a friend, and if you don't mind husbands, I know a married one that's panting to be taught the double-wing-back shift.'

'I can barely wait for tomorrow afternoon. But this time, you come to my place. Now, having disposed of business, tell me. Was Missus duFresne really as good in the hay as she looked like she might be?'

24

CRAIG felt just as scared as the first day he went to college, just as scared as the first day he went to sea. Wall Street frightened him more than anything he had ever seen—the cold, cheerless canyons of the narrow streets between the forbidding buildings, the grit-laden wind that seemed ever to howl in these canyons. The buildings seemed to spell impossible wealth without possible pleasure. The people on the street seemed as grey and cheerless as the buildings, but without the implied wealth.

'If this is Monday,' Craig said aloud, 'I'm sure glad I didn't see it on Sunday.'

'What say?' the cab driver asked.

'Nothing. Here's the address. Let me out on the corner here.'

It was eleven o'clock of a Monday morning. Craig had phoned Nathan Mannheim at 9.30, and had been put through immediately. 'Yes,' Mannheim said, 'I'll be glad to see you. I'm free from eleven to twelve. Any friend of Uncle Charlie is a friend of mine.'

Craig got off the elevator, walked down a long marbled hall, opened the frosted-glass door and was confronted by a receptionist. She was young, blonde, and very pretty in her severely tailored grey sharkskin suit.

'Yes?' She smiled politely without enthusiasm.

'My name is Craig Price. I talked earlier with Mr. Mannheim. I have an appointment for eleven.'

'Oh yes. Please sit down, Mr. Price. You're a little early, and Mr. Mannheim has some people with him. There are some magazines. He won't be long.' She bent back to some papers on her desk. Craig picked up a *New Yorker* and looked at the advertisements, all of which seemed to be selling something far out of his price range. He looked at the cartoons and couldn't decide whether they were funny or not.

After what seemed an impossible length of time, and what was actually twelve minutes, the pretty blonde girl heeded a buzz-box.

'Mr. Mannheim will see you now. This way, please, Mr. Price.'

She led him to another frosted-glass door marked *Private*.

'In here,' she said.

Mr. Nathan Mannheim was standing behind a very large desk. He was small and plump—bald, hook-nosed, and foppishly tailored in a severe Savile Row fashion. He wore a white hard collar against a horizontally striped blue-and white shirt, and his suit was coal-black. He wore a grey satin tie with a large pearl for a stickpin. His eyes had a released look, as if they had been locked away for safekeeping in a vault the night before. He took an unlit, elegantly slim cigar out of his mouth, placed it on the rim of a large copper ashtray, and walked around the desk to extend his hand.

'So you're this Craig Price my Confederate uncle writes me? You shouldn't figure to be so young. Sit down, my boy, and tell me about Uncle Charlie. I haven't seen him in about forty years, but the family hangs together. It's one advantage of being either a Catholic or a Jew. The families hang together. No bum jokes about hanging separately. You like a cigar?'

'If you don't mind,' Craig said, 'I think I'll have a cigarette.' He sank back into a big red-leather chair studded with brass nail-heads. He had expected something special in the way of an office. This office was not as big, not as imaginatively furnished as his own. It had only one bookcase, and all the books were leather-bound in sets.

'So. And Uncle Charlie?'

'He's very old but very healthy,' Craig said. 'Also he and I are very good friends.'

'You must be. He never sent anybody else to me before. I suppose you need money? You must want money. That's why people come to see me. You are very young to need money. How much money do you need?' Nate Mannheim sank his head on his chest, and looked at Craig.

Craig took a deep breath, and looked Nate Mannheim straight in the eye.

'Half a million dollars,' he said. 'Sir.'

Nate Mannheim shot him a keen look.

'How old are you?'

'Nearly twenty-four. Twenty-three, sir.'

Nate Mannheim threw back his head and roared with laughter.

'Twenty-three years old and he comes asking Nate Mannheim for half a million fish! What'll he ask for when he's thirty?'

'Maybe five million,' Craig said. 'But right now what I need is fifty thousand in cash and some way to arrange to pay off another four hundred and fifty. I know how to run a mill. I'm president of one. But I don't understand big finance. That's why Uncle Charlie said I should talk to you. He said even if I didn't get the money from you you'd give advice. If you don't mind,' Craig grinned swiftly, 'if you don't mind I'd rather have the

460

advice than the money. Some way I'll get the money if I have the advice.'

Nate Mannheim cocked his head and looked even more keenly at Craig.

'Where you staying in town, son?'

'At the Ritz-Carlton. Suite 516-17.'

'The Ritz, huh? A suite, yet. Why? Why not the New Yorker or one of the commercial hotels that out-of-town people come to? Why the Ritz?'

Craig felt somehow that his future depended on his answer.

'I got a thing about going first-class,' he said. 'I travelled second-class long enough to know I didn't like it. They wouldn't let me in the Stork Club last night, and I didn't like that, either. I got a chance to go big, Mr. Mannheim. All I want to know is how.'

'Tell you what,' the factor said. 'I'm free for lunch. *I* can get into the Stork Club. You like to have lunch with me there?'

Craig thought swiftly. He gambled again.

'Thank you, sir,' he said. 'No sir. The next time I go there will be when I've bought it.'

'Good. Good.' Nate Mannheim clapped his hands. 'Very good indeed. In that case we'll go to Twenty-One. Now tell me. Do you know exactly what a factor is?'

'Uncle Charlie told me a little. I'm not entirely sure. He said— he said you were kind of a . . . kind of a pawnbroker, but on a bigger scale. That you didn't deal in unredeemed ukuleles.'

Nate Mannheim howled with laughter.

'By God,' he said, 'I must go down South and visit my Uncle Charlie. I never heard it put better. I sure as hell don't deal in un-redeemed ukuleles or banjoes either. But in case you don't fully understand, I'm a financier as well as a factor. I can generally borrow money for six per cent, sometimes less. And I can generally lend it for twelve per cent, sometimes as much as twenty. That's for people that need big money in a hurry. I take anything as securities—accounts receivable, chattels, other people's in-stalment financing, real estate, future production rights in Broad-way and, you should pardon the expression, Hollywood rights. I don't give a damn about the borrower's credit. What interests me is the borrower's present or future customer and *their* ability to pay off something I got a hook on. Understand?'

'I think so.'

'Well, we got nearly an hour before lunch time. Suppose you tell me all about Craig Price and the paying potential of his present and future customers. Don't leave anything out. I'll hear about it sooner or later, anyhow. Tell me everything. How you started. How you got where you are so fast. Everything.'

Craig gulped.

'Everything?'

461

'The whole *schmier*.'

'Well,' Craig said, 'the first thing I did was knock up the boss's daughter . . .'

25

'I HOPE you don't mind riding home in a Ford.' Red Forney grinned at his sister. 'I know you're used to Cadillacs, and all that. Maybe you're too proud to ride in a Ford.'

Libby Forney picked up her handbag, swept a last glance around the office, and locked the door.

'I'm not too proud. It was sweet of you to wait, Red, seeing you get off so much earlier than I do. With Craig away, I've been trying to catch up on some back work and clean out the files.'

'Don't worry. I had some after hours business to do.'

Red put his car in gear, and as they drove off, he said:

'When did the missus decide to go to New York and join the boss? Everybody in the shop asked me why. You know how things get around.'

'I don't know. She called this morning and said she was going to New York to join her—to join Craig. I suppose for a holiday, or something. He told me he was going alone. Business. I reckon something to do with another mill he's got his eye on.' Libby changed the subject swiftly. 'What *did* keep you so late, Red?'

'A meetin'. Office politics. That union business again. Now these—' he spat the words—'hamhanded, lintheaded no-good crackers want to join a union. They want to hold an election. They want to straighten out the seniority in the shop. They want to vote for who runs what shift and all like that. They . . .' Red took one freckled, white-haired fist off the wheel and shoved it under Libby's nose. It was swollen, bruised and blood-clotted across the knuckles.

'I had to reason with one of the boys,' he said. 'He said a couple nasty things and so I reasoned with him. When they picked him up I told him to turn in his his time-card and collect his pay.'

'Why did you have to hit him, Red? You shouldn't have hit him. That temper of yours . . .'

'Don't tell me who to hit, Sis. I know who I need to hit. I know who runs the spinning department of this mill and sure as hell it ain't Johnnie Faison. It's Red Forney. Until I meet somebody bigger'n me says I don't.'

'But what did he say? What did he say made you so mad you had to hit him?'

'Wasn't so much what he said. It was just the way he said it. All come out of this union business. Made some crack about

Craig's Cadillac bein' paid for in bed. Said the boss married himself into a job. Passed a remark about—oh, you know. Somethin' about the next step up for me, since I was such a boss-lover, was to quit bein' a foreman and go marry myself into a mill so the honest workin' folks could manage to work for one of their own people. Said a thing . . .'

'What thing? What thing?'

'I don't know as I ought to tell you.' Red spoke as if it physically hurt him. 'But I will, by God. Said I wouldn't be where I was today, I wouldn't be the foreman, if my sister wasn't workin' in the front office for the boss. Said old Marvin McCracken wouldn't have been fired if I didn't have a sister wanted to work in the front office. Way he said it sounded like, dirty, you know . . . Anyhow that's when I coal-cocked him. He got a chin like an anvil.' Red blew on his knuckles. 'These knuckles of mine are near about pushed up into my wrist-bone.'

He chuckled without mirth.

'Of course, you can split a anvil, you hit it jest right. I doubt he'll talk much for the next few weeks. Unless he can talk through that wire they wrap around busted jaws.'

'Oh, Red, Red, I'm sorry. I'm terribly sorry. We both know that I had nothing to do with you getting the job, or old Mc-Cracken getting fired, or Miss Mildred getting retired. Craig always said, when he first started coming to the house with you, that as soon as he was boss, you'd go to work as top spinner and I'd be his secretary. He even made me promise when I was just a kid that I'd switch my courses in high school and learn how to type and take shorthand. But I'm so sorry that they have to throw it back at you.'

'It's that lousy union business. They pick on anything to start a commotion, get the help unhappy. I reckon I'd have let him get away with it except for one thing.' Red's voice now was dully sombre.

'What one thing?'

'In a way the son of a bitch is right. Maybe it didn't start out that way but now the son of a bitch is right, even if he don't know it. I know it. You know it.'

'But Red, I . . .'

He took his bruised hand off the wheel and held it up.

'Don't say nothin'. Your business is your business. You're a woman grown, and you know your own way better than for me to tell you. One time I told you. I tried to tell you. But if you think you and Craig Price are a secret in this town, in this mill, you're crazy as a coot. They ain't a linthead in the mill don't know about your fishin' trips and how you switch cars and how much you pay for the garage at the beach. Okay. I ain't no angel, either. Forget it. I'm tired of listening to all that crap about workers of the world arise. I'm tired of bein' insulted. My hand hurts. Let's go home and have a drink and listen to the radio. At least we got home to go to.'

'Red, I don't know what to say. I don't, I don't!'

'Then don't say it. We got just about enough time to listen to Amos 'n' Andy after I wash this hand and put some more iodine on it. You can make my drink double.'

They turned into the street on which their house sat. It was still bright light of a late afternoon. The house still sat primly, like a nice little girl with her ankles crossed, and the shrubbery was exuberantly abloom. Flowers grew in the borders around the walk, and there were green leaves on the maples. Azaleas had sprung from the beds surrounding the house.

But the nice little girl in her party dress, with her ankles neatly crossed, had been playing with lipstick. She wasn't really a nice little girl in a party dress any more.

On one side of the green front door, with its almost-brass knocker, were the scawled words, still dripping, oozing red paint like blood: 'Company Pimp'. On the other side, in even larger, bloodier words was 'Company Whore'.

'Oh, no,' Libby said. 'Oh, no, Red, not us!'

'Yes,' Red said heavily, getting out of the car. 'Us. Maybe we'll have to get used to the idea. The paint's still wet. Maybe I can mop it off before too many people see it.'

'I'll always see it,' Libby said.

'So will I. Get the mop. There still might be time for Amos 'n' Andy.'

26

THE famous restaurant called Twenty One looked basically what it was, a good saloon. It had red-chequered tablecloths, dark oaken walls, and a low ceiling from which toy aircraft depended over the bar. A tall, saturnine, dark man and a smallish but stout, pugilistically-pleasant-looking man met them at the little reception table in the front.

'Welcome to your home, Mr. Mannheim.' the tall, saturnine, dark man said.

'Hello, Mr. Mannheim,' the smallish, stout, pugilistically-pleasant-looking man said. 'Haven't seen you in quite some time.'

'No, I've been out of town a lot. Monty—' to the tall one, and 'Jimmy'—to the smaller one. 'I want you to know my friend Craig Price from North Carolina. You'll be seeing more of him, I'm certain. Remember him, will you? I'll introduce him to all the brothers. He'll be wanting signing privileges here pretty soon, I'm sure.'

Both men shook Craig's hand.

'A pleasure, Mr. Price. Anything we can do at any time. Just call.'

'You'll meet the whole family,' Nate Mannheim said, as they walked into the downstairs room. 'This is a family, in a way. And the customers are part of it.'

Nate Mannheim was greeted at the entrance to the dining-room by a blond, balding man with a blond moustache. He was dressed almost exactly like Nate Mannheim.

'This is Jack Kriendler,' he said. 'Meet Craig Price. He runs a textile mill in Carolina. Jack's the head brother. What we'd like, Jack, is to go back to a little table so we can be quiet. You've got too many ladies in here today. But it's all right for Craig to sign. You'll have him on your hands for many a year.'

'Of course, Nate. Nice to meet you, Mr. Price. You're at home here.' Jack Kriendler bowed and went out into the lobby.

'Hello, Mr. Mannheim.' This was another blond, balding man, a head waiter.

'Craig, this is Vincent. He runs the room. We're going slumming in the back room today, Vincent. Business. But remember Mr. Price, please.'

'I certainly will.' Vincent bowed.

'In a minute,' Nate Mannheim said, as they were seated in a corner table and a boy brought a telephone and plugged it in, 'you will meet Charlie Berns, who is Jack's partner, and then you will meet the kids—Mack and Pete and Bob, and are Jack's brothers—and you will get to know the boys behind the bar, and very probably some day you'll consider this as home. For a great many people it is home. It's one of the five best restaurants in the world, and one of the reasons it's fine is that it started out as a speakeasy, and the boys got to know something about people. All kinds of people, good and bad. You don't find the gossip columnists here. There isn't any table-hopping. Watch this.'

He called a waiter.

'I want to send a note to that lady at the centre table over there. The blonde lady with the ostrich plume on her hat.'

'Yes, sir.' The waiter produced a pad. Nate Mannheim scribbled something on it, and handed it to the waiter.

'Watch,' he said. The waiter walked over and handed the note to a sunburned freckled young man who was sitting at the centre table in the first room, studying some papers. The sunburned young man read the note, nodded to the waiter, and then lifted his hand in a short salute to Nate Mannheim.

'That's another Kriendler,' Nate said. 'He just okayed the note. This thing that makes this joint work is that always there's somebody minding the store. Any check that's signed, any note that is passed. Somebody checks it. Don't forget that, ever, young Craig Price from Kensington. There's always got to be somebody around to mind the store. If you had just written that note and you were trying to pick up that lady, Jimmy and Monty would have you out of here before you could spit, and Red, the door-man, would have you in a cab before you knew it. Right now if you got up and walked over to another table, sixteen sets of eyes would watch you, and if the other person wasn't a friend, out you'd go. When you get banned here you really get banned. But once they know you, once they trust you, once you get to be a member of the family, you own the joint. I could stand on my head in my BVD's and somebody would say, poor Mr. Mann-heim, maybe we better get him home to bed, but that's all it would amount to. As far as I'm concerned there ain't but two good saloons in the world. This is one,' Nate Mannheim said. 'Now, what do we have for lunch?'

Craig looked at the deeply engraved letters on the furry bill of fare.

'I'd like some Vichyssoise,' he said. 'And could I have a little smoked salmon, with oil and vinegar?'

'Capers, sir?'

'Of course,' Craig said to the waiter. Craig had never heard of any caper except the kind that people cut when they were acting up, but he wasn't going to let Nate Mannheim know it.

'That's not much lunch for a growing boy,' Nate Mannheim said. 'You better have something else.'

'Well,' Craig said, frowning judiciously, 'that rack of lamb looks good. I'd like that with a few—a very few—new potatoes, and the mint sauce, of course.'

'I'll have the same,' Nate Mannheim said. 'How about a drink, first?'

'I won't, thank you,' Craig said. 'If you don't mind. I don't care much for drinking in the daytime.'

'Well, I do. Bring me a double Gibson, waiter. Sure, Craig?'

'Sure. Thanks very much.'

'I think you're a phony,' Nate Mannheim said. 'I think you'd love a drink. Come on. You haven't been a phony about every-thing else you've told me, including the boss's daughter. You making character with me? With a factor, yet? You ain't an account receivable.'

Craig laughed.

The waiter served Nate Mannheim his drink.

'If you can spot it that easy, I guess I am being a phony. I'd love a drink. A double Gibson. But as long as I'm being honest, what's a Gibson? It looks just like a martini to me, a martini with an onion in it.'

'That's exactly what it is—an onion surrounded by gin. I think I'll have another. They're so bad for my liver, the doctor says, that I generally always have two at lunch because I hate my doctor. He's got a lousy liver, too, and tries to take out his spite on the patients. Look, kid, you are strictly from country. Where did you learn about Vichyssoise and racks of lamb and

466

smoked salmon? They don't grow that kind of stuff down in your neck of the woods.'

'I learned it from the room waiter at the Ritz-Carlton last night. I'm not trying to fool you, Mr. Mannheim. On anything.'

'Well, all right. Good. Good. Old Charlie said if I didn't give you any money I would give you advice. You want the advice with the meat or with the coffee?'

Craig smiled.

'I'd rather have it with the coffee, please.'

'So okay. You know a thing I like about you, kid? I like that *yes sir* and that *please*. They are very short on good manners in this town, and it don't hurt to heave in a *please* or a *thank you* once in a while. Don't ever forget that. There are times when you want to make somebody real mad, and that's when you kick them in the nuts. But mostly it is very poor business to go around making people mad for free, gratis. If I can coin a parable,' Nate Mannheim said, 'a little horse-shit goes a lot farther than a lot of horse-radish.'

They ate, almost in silence, while Craig looked around him. Never, he thought, had he seen such handsome people, such gay and happy people. Never had he seen people extracting so much enjoyment out of the mere act of eating and laughing and talking. And the thing that struck him most strongly was the fact that the waiters and the captains and the bartenders all seemed to be *friends* of the customers. There was politeness, but no obsequiousness . . .

'I never knew a place like this existed,' he said, as they finished their meat. 'It's like a—like a happy houseparty, except everything gets done.'

'You answered it. I told you before. There's always somebody around to mind the store. There's an old Jewish joke about that. Papa is dying and all the kids are hanging around the bedside moaning and groaning and tearing their hair and the old man looks up to his wife, she's moaning and groaning and tearing her hair, too.

' "Becky," he said. "So tell, Becky. Who's looking after the store?" '

Craig laughed.

'I won't forget,' he said. 'I won't forget to mind the store.'

'You better not,' Nate Mannheim said, 'or you won't have no store to mind.'

The coffee came.

'That was a very good lunch,' Craig said. 'Thanks a lot, Mr. Mannheim. I don't know how to say anything else except thanks a lot for the time. And the lunch. I didn't expect it, really.'

'Don't expect and you won't be disappointed. Now, with the coffee, I know all your story, all the problems, all the everything. So now you get the fast hard answer.'

'All right,' Craig said. 'I had some fast hard answers before.'

'Okay. You're a young man, a smart man, and you come very far, very fast. You want to go farther, faster. You *yentz-ed* your way into a good spot. You can *yentz* your way out of it. I told you already how you can handle the financing, the big financing on that one new mill you need. Once you got that settled I can tell you a lot of other things and then maybe we do business. But there is a thing I want to see. I got a natural suspicion. I want to see how much inside moxie you got apart from just balls. You prove me this and I will help you any way I can. You want to be big? So be big.'

'How big?'

'Just go find the fifty grand down-payment you need on this new mill. You hustled a lot. You told me how you hustled the old lady. So go hustle fifty grand. Show me the fifty grand and I'll show four hundred fifty grand. But not until you show me the fifty. I got to see if you got some ki-yi in you before I produce. A kid smart enough he should hustle his mother-in-law and wind up practically owning a big mill at twenty-one years of age, he is smart enough to hustle fifty grand to make the down on another mill. Or else he ain't smart enough for Nate Mannheim to roll a half mil out into the street, the taxis should run over it, the dogs should wet on it. Find me fifty, I find you four fifty, and then we talk real expansion.'

'It would be easier if you lent me the original fifty,' Craig said. 'I got enough stuff receivable, enough real property, to cover.'

'You got the large nothing,' Nate Mannheim said. 'Your wife, she's got the large something. Right now you are an employee. When you start being somebody who has his own operation, when you quit being somebody who depends on whether he can get it up when Mama is yelling, get it up, you bum, when you are standing on your own feet, when you are Price Mills, almost, instead of some kid that screwed himself into a bargaining position, then you come to Uncle Nate and Uncle Nate will play. But right now, apart from this lunch check—which I will *sign*—it's deductible—Uncle Nate don't pay. Or play. You got my point, little *momser*?'

'I don't know what is a *momser*, Uncle Nate.' Craig grinned again. 'But I got your point. We'll play, and you'll pay.'

'This talk I like to hear. You give my forty-year-too-late regards to my Uncle Charlie, and tell him that Nate Mannheim thinks he picked a good horse for the Futurity. When do you suppose you'll be moving to New York to live?'

'When I've found the fifty thousand dollars and can do some business with you,' Craig said.

As they walked out, Jimmy and Monty bade them a fair good day, and said to Craig:

'Come back and see us as often as you can.'

468

'You can depend on it,' Craig said, and decided that he'd walk back to the Ritz. He wanted to stop in De Pinna's and buy a tie and he had always heard about Brooks Bros. and Abercrombie and Fitch.

They were eating in a place called Costello, on Third Avenue. The waiter brought a bouquet of young scallions, crisp celery, and chilled radishes.

Craig took a radish. 'I think we're in business, Moose,' he said. 'I know we're in business. And I want you in it with me. There's a technicality—fifty thousand dollars' worth—but I know how to beat it. And with Mannheim bankrolling me, boy, the sky's the limit.'

Jimmy Wilbur took an onion and dipped it into salt.

'Little man, you interest me strangely,' he said. 'Pray do tell me more.'

Over dinner, Craig outlined his plans, and described his talk with Nate Mannheim.

'Tell me one thing,' Jimmy Wilbur said. 'Where you going to get the big fifty? Tell me that, and I'm your boy. I guess I sound like Mannheim. If you get the fifty you'll start the empire, I'm certain of that, and I'd like to play. I'm as sick of this athlete wetnursing as I was of being an athlete myself. From where comes the large five-oh?'

'We got a house and quite a lot of property in Kensington. It's Maybelle's. It was all her old man left her except the mill. It's a big house, a good house, and it's got quite a lot of valuable land around it. It's worth a hundred thousand dollars right now, if you include the land. And it'll be worth a lot more in ten years or so. I can easy get fifty thousand for it. We've got quite a lot of new money around the town now, and this is really a rich man's house. God, you should have seen it when old man Grimes was alive. He had a Negro butler he called George Washington, on account of his powdered hair. He had him dressed up in red knee-breeches and silver-buckled shoes, to match the main living-room. I'll get the fifty, all right.'

'Well,' Jimmy Wilbur said, 'it sounds like we got quite a future. Except I still don't know quite what I do for you except wipe your nose and pull maniacs off your back.'

'I don't intend just to stop with mills,' Craig said. 'Nate Mannheim and I had a long talk about a thing he calls leverage. You pyramid one thing into something else, and you build that into something else, and that something else into something else. I'm going to be a very rich man, Moose, or kill myself trying. And I want somebody who's smart, whom I trust, who don't come running to me every ten minutes with a new problem. I think the man is you. I think we can go a far piece together. I'm keeping the operating dough down right now, but a hunk of stock in Price Mills, Inc. and Price Enterprises, Inc. and Price This-and-That Inc. is going to be worth a power of money in ten years. When I get rich you get rich with me. Deal?'

'I think a deal. When do you want me?'

'Say a month. Don't quit until I give you the word. You don't have to give much notice, do you?'

'I suppose not. It's off-season, and there's always more good coaches than there are good coaching jobs. The colleges hi-jack each other like the old bootleggers used to. I've had ten big offers since I won my first Rose Bowl game. No. I just quit, and they go raid somebody else's guy. The morals in this business haven't changed any, even if the playing technique has.'

'You've been bitter about this since about the first day I met you. You seem even more bitter now. Why? You're the hottest guy in the business, and awfully young to be so hot.'

'That's why I'm bitter. It doesn't have any feeling of even small sport any more. When I first started playing a man had some pride. You'd played four quarters, sixty minutes, and you were supposed to do everything well—block, run, pass, kick, tackle, catch a pass, and play just as dirty or a little dirtier than the guy who was giving you the knee or the knuckles in the eye. Maybe you don't remember, because you dropped out of school, but we had a guy, when I was backfield coach, named George Barclay. He was a guard, a linesman, it said in the programme. But Barclay scored more touchdowns than the whole backfield, just from intercepting passes and blocking kicks. That, apart from running interference, pulling out to back up the line, anything at all. He was the second All-American we had after me. We had one thing in common. We were pros, and we played sixty minutes. We were Pennsylvania boys from coal towns and we knew that what we were doing was easier than working in coal mines.

'Now what have you got? You got place-kicking specialists who can't do anything but kick. You got runners who can't do anything but run, and passers who can't do anything but pass. Whatever happened to guys like Cliff Battles and George Barclay and old Bronko Nagurski, who could make All-American playing either in the line or in the backfield? You don't see 'em in college any more. Outside runners and inside runners and scatbacks and T-formation ball-handlers. Balls to the ball-handlers. Let's have a brandy with the coffee and then go look at the town a little bit. I think we'll have a lot of fun working together, kid.'

Jimmy Wilbur called for the check.

'There isn't any,' the waiter said. 'Compliments of the boss.'

The boss waved at them as they left.

'Come back soon,' he said.

'Don't worry,' Craig replied, 'I will.'

27

'THAT'S a very funny fellow, that Danny Kaye,' Craig said as they left the nightclub. 'I haven't heard about him.'

'Neither have I. But I don't get around the clubs too much when I'm in town. I suppose there's a lot of new talent coming up that you don't really hear about until later when all of a sudden they're rich and famous. But this Kaye is never going to be any funnier than he was tonight. Look. Let's go back to Third Avenue and have a nightcap and then let's go to bed. I've got an early plane tomorrow.'

'This is a very peculiar kind of town,' Craig said. 'It seems to run in layers of snobbery. I've seen four or five examples of different kinds.'

He had just heard a bartender say to an evidently beloved customer: 'I'm not speakin' to yez. I heard yez was down to Clarke's last night. The next thing I'll hear is that yez are hangin' out in the El Morocco with the debbytantes.'

'With a few exceptions it's a good kind of snobbery. A snobbery of friendship. See those drawings on the wall. James Thurber, the artist, did those. Tim and Joe are jealous of their friends in the writing-drawing league, like the Twenty-One boys are jealous of their tried and trusties. It's a very small town, New York. Somebody will hear you are in town, in my case, when we've got a game here or something, and if I don't make the joint my first night I get read a riot act when I do come in. I suppose it's kind of nice. Look, I think I'll run. You coming?'

'I don't think so. I think I'll kind of wander around a little bit. I think maybe I'll go down to Greenwich- Village. I haven't seen that, yet. What's down there?'

'A lot of jazz joints, mostly, and a few girly shows. And a lot of Italian restaurants and lot of bars full of boys with long hair and girls with short hair. They all wear pants and are either painting or writing or learning how to act. None of them will ever sell a painting or a book or get a decent acting part, but they drink a lot of cheap vino and talk all night long and practise a lot of what they think is free expression in the hay. It don't necessarily matter which sex is doing what to whom. It's all in the name of art. The difference between the Village and Third Avenue is that the professionals—writers, actors, painters —come to Third Avenue. The longhairs go to the Village. And stay in the Village until they have to go home to Ohio to run the family feed-store. I'll expect to hear from you, Craig, as soon as you get squared away. It's been great seeing you, boy. Take care of him, Joe. Goodnight.'

''Tis a foine man he is, Mr. Wilbur,' Joe Costello said. 'Would you have a drink with me, what is it, Mr. Price?'

'I would indeed. Whisky and water, please. And the name is right. Price.'

He clinked glasses with Mr. Joe Costello.

'I went to college with Jimmy,' he said, suddenly feeling a need to justify his lonely presence. 'He was the first friend I made.' And then, with a sudden urge to braggadocio. He's coming to work for me soon.'

'Indeed, and that's very nice,' Joe Costello said. 'And at what, if I may ask?'

'I own a couple of mills,' Craig said. 'Running them is getting to be too big a job for me. Wilbur is going to quit coaching and come work for me. After we get things straightened out in North Carolina I'll be coming to New York to live.'

'Indeed now, and we'll hope to have the pleasure of your company often,' said Joe Costello. 'We run a plain saloon here, but the meat's good and the drinks honest and the customers first-class. They're a rare lot, especially Friday nights after payday, but there's divil a wicked man or woman among 'em. And say it meself as shouldn't, we seldom lose a customer. Except occasionally late of nights, through drink.'

Craig thanked Mr. Costello and went out into the night. He'd walk a bit, he thought, and perhaps not bother with the Village. What a very wonderful night and day, he thought, looking up at the bright-starred sky over Manhattan. Starting with Jimmy last night and Nate Mannheim this morning, and all the nice, kind people at Twenty-One and now this little Third Avenue bar-and-grill. That nice little Mr. Costello. I felt so damn' lonesome I could have cried last night. I felt like I felt that first scared day in college. Now I don't feel scared any more. But I wonder, I wonder, he thought, how a fellow would go about meeting a girl in this strange jungle? I suppose there are places where single girls go, where they are friendly with the management, and eventually if you drink a long enough time, somebody speaks to somebody else, and before long you're friends and going steady. And then I suppose there's always the odd pickup in the joints or the actual whore. I would certainly like to have a woman tonight, to just sort of round out the experience, but I wouldn't know where to start looking. And I'd be afraid of just anything, because it wouldn't be very good business for me to go home with a case of clap. Or even worrying about one. Maybelle is probably thinking, and so is Libby, that the first thing I'd do in New York is run down a woman, and I better get on my horse tomorrow and go back looking fresh and innocent. And, he thought, I better leave that house-selling idea alone until the right time to bring it up. And that ain't going to be the first minute I hang my hat.

But, he thought, I certainly would love to have met a pretty girl, a nice girl, so I could have asked her by my suite for a night-cap, and given her the choice of dinner tomorrow night. I'll bet that would have been half the battle.

He got into bed and his brain raced with plans. Fifty thousand dollars clicked over and over in his head until in desperation he got up, made himself a drink, and gazed out into the New York night. Suddenly he reached for the phone.

'Get me Kensington, North Carolina—six-six-four-two. That's right. I'll hang on.'

28

'WHAT on earth, Craig?' Maybelle's voice was thickly blurred with sleep. Is something the matter? It's three o'clock in the morning.'

'Nothing's the matter. I just couldn't sleep and wanted to talk to you. Look, you're always saying I never take you any place. How'd you like to come to New York?'

'Wha. . . Come to New York? *When?*'

'Now. Today. Get the afternoon train and come on up. I've finished up my business. This is a great town. We'll see some shows and ride in the Park and go to some nightclubs. You'll love this town. I've only been here two days and I think it's wonderful. Come on.'

'But Craig. I don't have anything to *wear*. I can't just get up and go to New York just like *that*.'

'Of course you can. Bring a couple of evening dresses and some light suits. And go to the bank and dip into your slush fund. You've got plenty of money. You can do a lot of shopping while you're here. You ought to see these shops, Maybelle. Bonwit's and Macy's and the rest. And bring an extra five hundred dollars for me. Let's burn up the town for a few days.'

'Craig, are you drunk? You sound crazy.'

'A little, maybe. But not so much drunk as happy. Look, I'll meet you at the train. But if we miss each other in the rush, and that's possible, grab a taxi and come straight to the Ritz-Carlton. I'll register you in, in the morning. Okay?'

'I don't know. I suppose so. It's so sudden. But it will be fun, won't it, darling?'

'It sure will,' Craig said. 'Goodnight, sweetie. And don't miss that train. Sweet dreams.'

He rang off.

He lit a cigarette and picked up his drink.

'Aaahh,' he said, and put his feet up on a chair. 'We'll have

473

fun, all right. Wait'll Maybelle sees how they treat me. It'll knock her eyes out. I'll take her to lunch at Twenty-One, and I'll get some theatre tickets and maybe ask one of those men at the desk in Twenty-One to call up some places like El Morocco and the Copacabana so I'll be sure to have reservations. And tomorrow I'll just sort of look around and investigate China-town and Harlem and Greenwich Village. But I better be sure to drop in at Twenty-One and see if they remember me. That nice little guy Jimmy at Twenty-One might have some ideas about what shows and where to take Maybelle.'

Craig put out his cigarette and this time his brain had stopped clicking over. Maybelle is going to love New York, he thought. Seeing as it's her future home, she'd better. And went dreamlessly off to sleep.

Maybelle was drunk when they came back to the hotel, but it was a pleasant drunkenness, far from the glass-throwing, name-calling category which usually distinguished the home-coming from the Saturday-night fiesta in Kensington. She had moved around Manhattan smoothly, armoured in alcohol, all evening, but had not performed a hula in her bare feet. She had not spilled a single drink, broken a single glass, or burned a single hole in her stockings.

'Oh, sugar, I feel so good,' she said. 'I feel just wonderful.' She pirouetted around the room, and stopped just short of a chair. 'Fix us the nightcap. I'm going to slip into something loose.'

When Craig came back with the drinks she was naked.

'I feel cute again,' she said. 'Don't you think I'm cute?'

'Yes,' Craig said. 'I think you're cute.'

'Well, goddammit, make me know I'm cute.'

'All right, sweetie. Let's go to bed.'

'That's right, let's go to bed. Bed's where I'm cutest. You know something?' She looked at him owlishly coy. 'When you're not always working and cross and tired, you're cute too. In New York you are awful cute.'

It was late May in New York. The waiter had come with whisky-sours, the Sunday papers, and breakfast. There was still a feeling of spring in the air, although the dogwood and most of the forsythia had gone from the Park, where they were going riding in a horse-drawn hack as soon as they felt up to it. Then they were going to have Sunday lunch at the Plaza. Somewhere in the last few days Craig had heard that Sunday lunch at the Plaza was where everybody went. Jimmy at Twenty-One said Craig wouldn't need a reservation.

'We've spent a mess of money,' Craig said to Maybelle. 'But it has been fun, hasn't it? I hate to leave and go back to that

474

hookworm paradise of ours in Kensington. I feel alive in this town.'

'People sure been nice to us,' she said. 'I never thought I'd be dancing on the same floor with all the movie stars at the El Morocco. Everybody I looked at, I sort of felt like I'd seen in the papers. I thought New York was supposed to be such a lonesome town.'

'Not if you know people,' Craig said, 'and have money. Here.'

Craig handed her a whisky-sour. The Sunday sun streamed into the suite, and the papers were as yet unscattered. Maybelle had a scarf around her head, and was wearing a Japanese kimono. She reached for the amber drink greedily.

'My God, I'm hung,' she said, draining half the glass. 'Ahhh.' She drank the other half, and handed him the glass automatically. 'Did I do anything bad last night?'

'Not in public.' Craig smiled and filled her glass again. 'When we got home . . .'

'Oh, God, did I take off my clothes again? I seem to remember . . . Yes, I do remember. Did I do anything about babies?'

'No, you didn't,' Craig said. 'You practically raped me. I didn't have time to go to the bathroom.'

'Mmmmmmm,' Maybelle smiled, as the whisky-sour took hold. 'I remember it all, now. It was wonderful. Different than it's been for a long time. I hope we have another baby. I *know* we'll have a baby. Maybe another boy . . .?' Her voice was tentative.

'I'd rather have a girl. Girls are lots nicer than boys. All little boys smell bad and always have dead frogs in their pockets. What'll we call her? Lizzie, or what? Wait. I've got matches.' Craig lit Maybelle's cigarette.

'It's your baby,' Maybelle said. 'You name it.'

'I had a grandmother named Caroline. I never liked her much, but I liked the name. How about Caroline? We could call her Carol. It's a nice name, Carol. Kind of Christmassy.'

'All this about a child we don't even know we're going to have. Is there anything more in that shaker?'

'Sure. Maybelle. Honey?'

'Uh-huh. What? I feel marvellous. Something real nice about this Sunday. I don't feel cute, but I feel real good. Would you mind very much if we insured the baby we started last night?' She stretched, and the kimono fell apart.

'I'm your man,' Craig said. 'Come on before the mood leaves you. What I had to say can wait.'

'Mood leave *me*?' Her voice was suddenly sharp. '*That* mood ain't ever going to leave me.'

Maybelle was in a beautifully mellow state. They had ridden with the Jehu around the Park, stopping at the Tavern-on-the-

Green, and then they had come back for a long lunch at the Plaza's Oak Room. The head waiter and the waiters had been most kind and attentive, and one or two of the people Craig had met at Twenty-One had come over to the table to say hello. Maybelle had giggled happily.

'Seems to me you know most everybody in this little old town,' she said. 'Who was that?'

'A writer. Fellow named Considine. A real nice fellow.'

'That looks just like Cary Grant over there,' Maybelle said.

'It *is* Cary Grant,' Craig said. 'He's in town for his new picture. I read they're having a première here.'

'I declare I never thought New York could be like this,' Maybelle said. 'Look out, here comes somebody else that looks familiar.'

'Hello, Craig,' a tall blond man with enormous shoulders said. 'Who's this pretty girl?'

'This is my wife. Maybelle, this is Mr. Wayne Morris. You saw him in that boxing picture, "Kid Galahad".' Craig stood up. 'Won't you join us?'

'Can't. Thanks. Just wanted to say hello. Nice to see you, Craig. Nice to meet you, Mrs. Craig. Excuse me. Mrs. Price.' The actor walked away.

'Where'd you meet *him*?' Maybelle asked.

'Oh, the same day you came. I had lunch here and one of the Kriendler boys introduced me.'

It had been a very successful Sunday.

Now they were back in the hotel. They were leaving tomorrow for Kensington.

'Sure,' Craig said. 'I wasn't fooling about living in New York. What we were talking about yesterday, and before I left Kensington to come up here. Here's where the money is. Here's where the big money is. And you've seen for yourself how nice the people can be. It's a good town, and we won't have to listen to any more gruesome details about Winnie Mae Maxon's last miscarriage. I want to make the move pretty soon. After I've bought that other mill, and have got it rolling.'

'But what would we do about Papa's house? We just can't leave it sittin' there and go tearin' off up North.'

'Papa's house figures in the plan. That property is worth at least a hundred thousand. We can easy get a mortgage on it for fifty, sixty, even from Winken, Blinken and Nod. The ground around it's worth more than that. And I need fifty thousand cash dollars real bad. We wouldn't have to sell it. We could rent it, if you wanted to, when we get ready to leave it.'

'I wouldn't mind sellin' it, I suppose,' Maybelle said. 'But if we mortgage it, can we sell it?'

'Sure,' Craig said. 'All we have to do really is keep up the interest payments on the mortgage. And if we want to sell it we just transfer the mortgage, to the new buyers. The bank'll handle all that. But I need the money now, or that mill is going to slip away, and it's too good a chance to miss, Your pa would like the idea of having more than one mill in the family again.'

'I guess he would, at that,' Maybelle said. 'All right, Craig, if you want to. You know more about these things than I do. All right.'

'It'll be awful good for the child, if we have another baby, to grow up with all the fine things here, the museums and the zoos and the good schools, and music and maybe art lessons. And all the shops and restaurants and nightclubs . . .'

Craig wheedled shamelessly. 'I won't be nearly so busy in New York, soon as I get the mill business straightened out and the labour business settled. We're on velvet, baby, velvet. I've hired a guy I used to know a long time ago to be my kind of general manager, and he'll do a lot of the things for me I used to have to do, and that'll give us a lot more time together.'

'Who's the man? That man you came to see?'

'No. This guy's name's Wilbur. Jim Wilbur. We were in school together. A real nice guy. He's older than I am, but he looked after me real good when I was a scared kid, first in school. Your daddy met him, and liked him a lot.'

'What's he going to do for you?'

'A lot of things,' Craig said.

'But what sort of things? What *sort* of things?'

'All kinds of things. Everything I need to do and don't want to do, all the things that eat up a lot of time. He'll make all the difference in the world. You'll like Jimmy a lot. We better hurry.'

'Craig,' she said. 'I know I'm awful, but I feel real cute again. Do you mind?'

'I don't mind a bit,' Craig said. 'I feel kind of cute myself.'

On Monday morning, just before they started packing, Craig picked up the telephone.

'Who you callin'?' Maybelle asked from the open bathroom door.

'Nate Mannheim,' Craig said. 'The man I came to see in the first place.' He gave his name into the phone, and waited.

'Mr. Mannheim,' he said. 'This is Craig Price. I just called to say I was going back to Kensington today to dispose of some property. And that I will be back to see you pretty soon. I think I got it made.'

29

'DID Maybelle have a good time in New York?' Libby said sweetly, when Craig picked her up on the first morning of returning to work. 'I suppose she did. It's been very busy here, all sorts of things happened since you left.'

All right, Craig thought. Let it hang. Let it hang right there until its neck drops off.

'Yes. I guess so. We didn't do much. After I got through with the main business there was a little bit of stuff stretching over, so I thought maybe I could kill two birds with one stone.' That's a great line, Price, he thought. Killing two birds with one stone.

'I thought it was going to be all business. What else did you do besides business? Where did you stay?'

Craig drove doggedly through the traffic.

'We stayed at the Ritz-Carlton. For business reasons.' I asked for it, he thought. I got it at home. Now I got it here. In the front seat. 'We saw a couple of shows. Went to a nightclub. Usual stuff two hicks do in New York. You know.' Don't third-degree me. Not in the morning. Don't ask me questions in the morning.

'I don't know. I was just asking. I'm a hick who's never even been to Washington.'

Libby's voice was all female, hurt-female.

'Well, I'm a hick who'd never been to New York before. It makes us nearly even. I never felt like such a hick in my life.' His voice was harsh. His voice was all male, protecting his flanks against the female intruder.

'Don't be mad at *me*, Craig. I'm sorry. I didn't do anything. It's just that Maybelle went and I didn't. I wanted to so and I couldn't and she did.'

'Look, Libby, it was necessary that Maybelle had to come to New York. I can't explain it to you now, but it was necessary. Believe me. Some things had to be straightened out and I needed ... Oh, Christ. I can't tell you now. It's not the time to tell you now. I got too many things on my mind. Anyway, I can't help it if I'm married to Maybelle.'

Libby made an obvious effort to placate, in a little-girl, I-know-my-place voice. It made Craig want to slap her.

'Did the business turn out well? Did you get a lot of things you wanted to do, done?'

You don't give a damn what got done. You're just sore because I sent for Maybelle.

'I suppose so.' I might as well tell her about the new deal now, he said to himself. Now's as good as any.

'I think we'll have a new mill, and you'll be having a new boss one of these days.' He held up a hand. 'Now don't blow your stack. Keep your hair on. It's just that I think we're expanding and I'm going to need some fresh help. We're going to have to have a vice-president around here when we get that other mill.'

'Oh, Craig! Not really! Not *Red*! That's wonderful!'

Oh Jesus, Craig thought. Certainly not Red. I hadn't even thought about Red that way.

'No, I'm afraid not Red. We both know he hasn't got the book-learnin' for it.'

Her face sagged. Then braced.

'I'm sorry. For a minute I . . . that would have been too good to be true. Of course he hasn't got the education. But what happens to Red then, if you're hiring a vice-president? And I reckon, general manager.'

'Come here.' Craig kissed his index finger and touched her cheek. 'Sit down like a good girl. Now look. On a ship, there's the captain. The skipper. That's me. Then there's the chief mate, the first officer. He really runs the ship, but the captain has to make the decisions. Then there's the bosun. That's the man who actually drives the ship, because he is the practical extension of the captain, through the first mate. The bosun runs the physical ship. In a way he's captain but without the responsibility of responsibility and paper work and customs clearances and all that damned nonsense that the captain and the mate have to fight through.

'So Red will be the bosun. Red will be the general manager on the technical side. He'll look after the men and machinery and the fact that we're supposed to make cheap drawers and shirts that don't shrink, with a maximum of production and a minimum of industrial accidents to either men or machines. We can call him anything he wants. Technical supervisor. Production manager. He'll have his own office. But he'll still spend most of his time in the shop, seeing that the spinners spin and the weavers weave, and that production stays up.'

'And what am I, then?'

Craig smiled and touched her cheek again.

'You're the admiral. You keep the whole thing together. You fly the flag. And when I'm in New York . . .'

'Oh, Craig, can I go, too? To be your secretary in New York? Can I? Can I?'

I'd better say yes, Craig thought, thinking of the cool, distant blonde receptionist in Nathan Mannheim's office. But I think I'd better have a Yankee girl for my secretary in New York, and not a very pretty one either. Lead us not into no more temptation.

'Sure, honey,' he said. 'When and if I go you can go, unless you'd rather be a vice-president too, and run the plants here.'

'I want to go anywhere you go, Craig,' Libby said. 'Anywhere. I guess I'll never be anything but your part-time girl, but that's better than nothing. Anyhow, welcome home, boss.' This on a note of false cheer. 'But I'm afraid I've got some news you won't like.' This almost happily. 'Red'll tell you more about it than I can. There's a man here named Kolinski who has been talking to a lot of the hands about unionizing the mill. He's got a strange-looking lot of people with him. They've come in trailers, some of them, and some of them are staying in motor-courts and some in hotels. Every day the buses bring more people. They say they're textile workers. Most of them look like foreigners to me. Not Yankees. Real foreigners. They're going to hold a big meeting Saturday. And Craig. All they talk about is you firing Marvin McCracken.'

'I didn't fire him. I retired him. You've been sending the cheques, haven't you?' Craig frowned.

'Yes, but he hasn't cashed any. You know that. The hands are saying now that you just kicked him out so you could hire Red because—well, because I'm a company whore! That's what they call me! That's what the organizers are saying. That you fired McCracken and hired Red just so you could get at me. The company whore.' Her voice ached. 'I've been getting awful letters. I didn't tell you before because I didn't . . . I didn't want to put bad thoughts in your head. I didn't tell Red, either.'

'My God, what a mess.' Craig ran his hand irritatedly through his hair. 'I can't afford a struck mill now, and I know about these goons. They strike me and I'm beat. I can't sweat out a strike. I got to have three shifts to keep alive . . . and it'll louse up this other mill deal. A strike'll kill me.'

Craig was speaking almost to himself. Then he spoke to Libby.

'Get Red in here.' Christ, he thought, I almost got it made, and now this. This. All I need is for Libby to get pregnant right now. That's all I need right now.

'Welcome back, boss,' Red came in and stuck out his hand. 'Hi, Craig. You didn't spend much time in New York. You must have got it wrapped up real good to get back so quick.' His voice was falsely hearty.

'Good enough,' Craig made an impatient movement with his hand, without shaking Red's hand. 'Hello, Red. Sit down. Now tell me what all this union stuff's about.'

'Well, you know, it's been building for quite a piece. But the people didn't start to move in until the other day. You know we don't pay all the money in the world here. We're still going pretty much on depression wages. About an average thirteen-fourteen dollars a week.'

'It's better 'n average for this business down South. You know that. Rome wasn't built in a day, for Christ sake. We ain't running the Ford plants.'

'Well,' Red drawled, 'these fellers that have been comin' in are talking twenty, thirty dollars a week, and time-and-a-half for overtime, and forty-hour weeks, and closed shop. And all like that.'

'Dammit,' Craig said, 'I just gave a five-cent an hour over-all raise without anybody asking me to. You know that. And you know about the recreational and welfare and sick benefit fund. I'm giving as good or better than anybody.'

'I know it. But these are old Gastonia hands, a lot of them. And the rest dam Yanks. Lot of foreigners probably never seen the inside of a cotton-mill. Lot of tough-lookin' dames, too. But they got one thing they talk a lot about. Seniority to prevail, they call it. That's where they've got old McCracken into the thing, and it seems like the old man is willin' to play along with them. He was mighty sore when you fired him. To make room for me.'

'Goddammit, I didn't fire him! If I hear it once or twice more you'll have me believing it myself.'

Craig felt his voice go shrill, and didn't like it.

'That's jest it, Craig. They's so much talk around that they got everybody believing you kicked him out on his tail. And you seein' so much of us, and you gettin' rid of Miss Mildred to put me and Libby to work. Well. Now that somebody helped them think it over, they takin' it nasty. Real nasty. People used to work hard for me, smilin' people I used to be real friendly with, look at me mean now like I was front-office folks and an enemy. And while I know it ain't true, they're sayin' lots of dirty things about you and Libby, you seein' so much of Libby and drivin' her to work and all. Look.' Red held up a right hand which was purple-swollen and red-scabbed across the knuckles. 'I had to teach another one of 'em some manners. Then I fired him cold out. This was yesterday. I guess Libby maybe ain't told you yet.'

'No.' Libby shook her head.

'We come home to our house, and nobody knows better'n you what store we set by that house. And somebody had got some red paint and wrote "Company Pimp—Company Whore" all across the front of it. And this morning when I got up to come to work all the tyres on my car had been cut and the windshield busted in. What are we gonna do, Craig? Sign up with this man Kolinski and his union, or fight 'em, or just wait until they find a way to strike us? Or what? You know about Gastonia as good as me.'

'A mess like that would wreck me,' Craig said. 'We're just beginning to make some decent money and we're about to buy a new mill. All that new machinery cut us way back in profits. This mill wasn't anything but spit-and-string when I took over, even though it was making some money. They hadn't replaced a loom in this place in ten years. I can't afford a strike, Red. Never mind. I'll think of something. Don't you think it's about time that Kolinski came to see me? I'm supposed to be the boss.'

'They don't work this way, Craig. These people don't work this way. They like to get the hired hands riled up first. They don't really want to make an easy deal. These people knock on the back door first.'

'How many guys you think might stick with me if this thing gets to be a little war?'

'Me. Most of the guys used to play baseball. Maybe the other shop foremen. Those guys we taught to box. Say fifty, sixty, maybe a hundred guys might play it rough with you if you asked them. We might get out one shift to keep workin'. Mostly single guys, though. The married men gonna herd the easiest way anybody push 'em, and the women they don't count. They just thinkin' about more meat, more beer on Saturday night, and a new pair of shoes for baby. And no trouble.'

'Apart from that dirty thing on your houses and the messed-up car, anything else rough yet?'

'No. But you can smell a slow-down. And a lot more talkin' time when they go to the can or open their dinner-pails. Kind of a mutter, like—like a squall that is just practisin' to break but hasn't made up its mind.'

'Well, I'll figure out something. Libby, will you call this number in Minnesota City, Minnesota, and get me a guy named Jimmy Wilbur on the phone? It's a college. Minnesota Tech. He's the head coach. See you this evenin', Red.' He dismissed him with a flip of the wrist.

Red Forney left. Libby spoke into the phone.

'They're looking for him,' she said after a minute. 'He's not in his office right now.'

'Well, tell them to try the field house or his apartment. Anywhere he might be. This is important.'

'They'll call back when they find him. Oh, Craig, what are you going to do?'

'I don't know what I'm going to do. That's why I'm talking to Jimmy Wilbur. It looks like I'll need him sooner than I thought. I've known this thing was building all along, but I didn't know what gimmick they'd use. They always got to have some kind of gimmick. I hadn't really thought they'd use you and Red and old Marvin McCracken to trigger it. But it does make sense. With these l—' he started to say *lintheads*, and checked himself. 'It makes sense with these people. Red was one of them and now they reckon he's got above them, being jumped up over older heads all on account of what they think about you and me. And you got to admit you are sort of pretty. If I was trying to organize a mill I'd look around for a weak spot I could build on, myself. You and me and Red seem to be the weak spot. I'll just . . .'

The phone rang.

'It's Mr. Wilbur on the line,' Libby said. 'You want me to leave?'

'No. Gimme.'

He stuck a cigarette in his mouth and motioned with his chin for a match. He picked up the phone. He nodded thanks as Libby lit his cigarette.

'Hello, Jim? It's me. Craig. I *know* we just left each other last

482

week in New York. But I think I need you faster than I thought. We got a real nasty situation building here. Union trouble. Maybe a strike. And I can't afford to be struck. It'll raise hell with all our plans. Do you think you could come down here for a couple of weeks and help me figure it out?'

Craig listened.

'No, you don't have to quit yet. You better hang on to your job, as a matter of fact. Unless this thing gets itself straightened out I'll be coming to work for *you*.'

Craig listened some more.

'Of course I knew I'd have to face it sooner or later. But these people are smart. They don't want to strike a sick plant. They've just been laying back waiting for me to get healthy. So they'll have new machinery to bust up, new trucks to upset. And it looks like they figure that now is the time, just as I'm on about a break-even and starting to show a profit. Could you come, then? Tomorrow? No, but you can fly as far as Raleigh. I'll hop in the car and meet you. It's faster and we can talk this thing out on the way down. It's only about a three-hour drive from Raleigh here. That's wonderful. I'll drive up tomorrow afternoon. Thanks, Papa. I can sure use you.'

Craig cradled the receiver and permitted himself a sigh.

'I feel better,' he said. 'Much better. The new vice-president-to-be, if there's ever going to be such a thing, is arriving. I'll leave in the morning and drive to Raleigh to pick him up.'

'Don't you want to talk to this Mr. Kolinski, the union agent?'

'Not yet I don't. I want to talk to him when I'm ready to talk to him. He hasn't really got himself organized yet. That filthy thing on your house was a first step. The next thing there'll be some busted windows. And like you said, there'll be a lot of speeches. Then come the hired pickets that never saw a mill. Then somebody will beat up somebody else. Then somebody will tip over some delivery trucks. Then somebody will sabotage some machinery. Then there'll be an explosion in the plant, or somebody's house—probably mine—will catch fire. I know how these people do it. Then, when everything's in an uproar, and every day we operate we lose another ten thousand dollars, then in will come Mr. Kolinski to talk business. Up to now they haven't even done anything we could call in the State Police on. That'd have to come from Raleigh and by the time we got enough cops around to keep order, there wouldn't be any order to keep. The hell with it. I'll think about it tomorrow when I drive up to Raleigh. It's still a nice morning. Let's drive down to the beach and look at the water.'

'All right,' Libby said. 'If you say so.'

Craig didn't particularly care for her tone, but he hadn't seen the other fishing-shack for quite some time.

30

'WHAT brings you home for lunch?' Maybelle said. 'You run out of food in the office? Your secretary quit?'

'I got to go to Raleigh and pick up that fellow I told you about. Jim Wilbur. I'm in trouble. Union trouble. It could wreck everything. I need some help.'

'I thought you had some help,' Maybelle said. 'I thought you had all the help you needed. You're gettin' to be a real gadabout. Now it's Raleigh. Last week it was New York. What next?'

'Nothing next. It looks like I may have a strike on my hands. The word's out that we're doing well and thinking of expanding. You know how these Communists work with stupid people. Now is the time, strike while the iron's hot, sort of thing. Economic royalists. Boss married the old boss's daughter. Look at his Cadillac. Look at his swimming-pool. Look at his wife's red car.'

'And look at the boss's red-headed secretary, and her red-headed brother,' Maybelle said. 'Look at that, too. I already heard about the little paint job they did on your girl friend's new house. Company *pimp*. Company *whore*. Could be they got a point, wouldn't you say?'

'I would *not* say,' Craig said savagely. 'And I'd advise you not to say, either. In any case I'm off to Raleigh to pick up Jim Wilbur. He knows how to play rough, and I think I'm going to need somebody who knows how to play rough. God damn these people. If they give me a little time I'd give them everything more than the unions promise, and they wouldn't have to pay me any dues, either.'

'Lintheads are lintheads,' Maybelle said, sweetly. 'You ought to know that. You've hung out with them long enough. I keep telling you that you can't treat them like people. They got no more gratitude than a nigger. And speakin' about niggers and gratitude, your precious little Jazzbo's run off.'

'And why has my precious little Jazzbo run off?' God, Craig thought, you can't turn your back a minute. Long as you're here everything runs along fine, and the second you leave town ... 'What made Jazzbo run off?'

'I took a stick to his hide,' Maybelle said. 'I tanned him real good.' Craig's face darkened.

'And why did you beat him?'

'For bein' uppity. I wore him out. I had him helpin' the cook wash dishes and he broke some of my best china. I blessed him out, and he run out his lip at me, and said he was Mistah Craig's boy, and Mistah Craig had told him so, and for him to tell everybody so. I cut myself a switch and tanned him real good. He was cryin' when he went out the back door.'

'When was this?'

'This morning.'

'And you didn't call me?'

'I didn't call you because I figured you'd have your hands full with this Company Pimp, Company Whore business that's already all over town. I figured one nigger more or less wouldn't concern you.'

Craig stood with his legs apart, his arms akimbo, his fists tightly clenched, his face red with wrath.

'I'm going to go find that little boy,' he said. 'And Maybelle, if you ever lay a hand on him again I'll lay one on you, and it'll hurt worse. He's right when he said I told him he was my boy. He is, by God, and if there's any punishing to be done, I'll do it. You just tell me when he needs it, and I'll do it. But there never was two people could train the same dog, and that goes for children, black or white. And it's a little harder on a kid when he's black.'

'If I'd of thought you'd get so worked up I wouldn't have done it.' Maybelle said. 'I'm sorry. I just thought he needed a tannin'.'

'All right. I'll go find him and bring him back. But he better be here when I get back from Raleigh with Wilbur. Have the girl make up your mother's old room. We might have a house guest for quite a spell. I'll go get the boy now.'

He found Jazzbo at his big brother's house. He was sitting sadly on the front steps. He began to cry when he saw Craig.

'Now hush, and be a big boy,' Craig said. 'We're goin' home now. Everything's gonna be all right.'

'Miss Maybelle done beat me,' the little boy snuffled. 'She hit me wid a stick jus' 'cause I say I'se yo' boy.'

'You *are* my boy, and Miss Maybelle's sorry. But she gets tempery once in a while. Maybe she might find a baby and then you got another sister or brother. And you ought to be more careful when you work in the kitchen. Then she won't be mad at you.'

'I doesn't likes to work in de kitchen. I likes to work in de yard, an' polish yo' car, an' run errands, an' fetch an' carry yo' stuff. I doesn't like workin' in no kitchen wid womans.'

'All right, all right,' Craig soothed. 'But right now I want you to go back home with me and tell Miss Maybelle you're sorry that you run off, then I'll tell her not to whip you any more. But you got to understand, Jazz, that if you're gonna be my butler when you grow up, you got to know about kitchens and how to serve careful so you won't break dishes. You got to learn all about the right kind of knives and forks and cups and saucers, and the only place to learn about this is in the kitchen and in the pantry. And there's always women in kitchens and pantries.

'The best way to learn about bein' careful with dishes is to start learnin' to be careful when you wash 'em. Then if you're real good about helpin' to wash and clean house, Miss Maybelle and the cook will teach you how to cook. Because any good

485

butler, any good valet, ought to know about cookin' and cleanin', because there's going to be a day, when we go North, when you might have to be my cook as well as my valet and chauffeur. Or at least you might have to tell the cook what to do, and to do that you'll have to know, or you can't tell her what's right and what's wrong. Understand?'

'I understands. I guess I don' think of it dat way befo'. I guess you has to start at de bottom befo' you earns up to de top.'

'Older men than you never said it better, my boy,' Craig said as the car pulled up. 'Now you just run in and tell Miss Maybelle you're sorry and you'll be very, very careful when you help in the kitchen after this, because I said that you wanted to learn how to do things *right*, not wrong.' There's enough of us doing things wrong in this family, Craig thought.

'Run along now. I've got to go to Raleigh.'

'I can't come wif' you, and maybe learn some more 'bout car-drivin'?'

'No,' Craig said gently. 'This is business. And before you learn about car drivin', you got to learn to not break things in the kitchen and how to be polite to Miss Maybelle.' The reproof went home.

'Yessuh. I be a better boy, now,' Jazzbo said. 'I try real hard. Good-bye, boss.'

'Good-bye,' Craig said. And on top of everything else, he thought, I got a race problem. Maybelle's pregnant, I'm certain. Let's hope to Christ Libby isn't. He put the car in gear and drove off to Raleigh to meet Jimmy Wilbur.

Craig met Jimmy Wilbur at the airport. He was travelling light—two small handbags. He looked as if he hadn't come to stay very long.

'It's not far to Chapel Hill,' Craig said. 'Should we drive over and have lunch at the Inn and see what the old place looks like?'

'I don't think so,' Jimmy Wilbur said. 'I think we better haul ass back to Kensington and get this mess of yours untangled.'

'All right. What did you tell the people at Tech?'

'Told 'em I heard of a couple of good sound mill-hands that looked like fullbacks, and thought I'd go have a word with their old man so we could buy 'em before somebody else did.'

'I sure hope we've got some mill-hands that look like full-backs,' Craig said. 'It may be we'll need 'em. We might as well get down to brass tacks, Moose. I'm about to be landed in a real lovely mess.'

'All right, I'm here to listen. Start at the beginning. This is a real nice car. You want me to drive it so you talk better?'

'No, thanks. I can talk better driving. It's like this. After you left New York, I had a brainwave. I thought that maybe if I had Maybelle come up to New York, and showed her around some, she might like it for an eventual new home. She loved it. Getting her to agree to mortgaging Papa's old homestead was taking candy from a baby. I'm seeing the bank tomorrow to arrange the mortgage. Then I've got to run back up to New York to straighten out the financing of the new mill with Nate Mannheim. It'll only be a short-term loan from Mannheim. With the new mill bought on Nate's financing, I can float enough stock to buy Grimes Mills outright from Maybelle *and* pay off Mannheim with the money. Maybelle'll give it to me in return for stock in both mills, which will now be Price Mills. Then . . .'

'Stop. You're making my head hurt. You sound like one of those football plays I keep trying to beat into my apes.'

'Okay. I'll stop. But there's going to be enough trouble, horse-trading in the next few weeks. You know how these things take time. I could handle this by myself. But I come home from New York and I find that the union boys have moved in on me. And from what I smell they don't want an easy settlement. They want a headline strike. Because we're getting fat at Grimes right now, and a big wildcat strike all over the headlines would be very good business for the Northern boys who want to con-solidate the South.'

'It figures. It figures.'

'Sure it figures,' Craig said. 'Light me a cigarette, will you please? Thanks. Well, anyhow, if I get myself into a strike right now, I'm done, while the delicate dickering is on. Maybe I can fight it when I'm set, but I ain't set. And somehow I feel they know I ain't set. God, I'm off balance, and I'm just be-ginning to move. And a strike right now—well, if I fight it, out of the window goes the other mill, out goes Nate Mannheim's "if" money, and we probably lose Grimes.'

'And you wind up organized anyhow, but broke, is that it? And with no new mill, and no Price Enterprises, Inc. Up the well-known creek with no paddle. Just as you're about to break loose in the open field, you trip and fall on your ass and the other side recovers the fumble.'

'That's about the size.'

'You talked with this union boy yet?'

'No. I was waiting for you. He sounds like a Polack. I thought he might be one of your cousins, or something, and we could go into a huddle and come out with something that wouldn't kill me. Like holding off until I got the other mill, with a promise to talk over-all business then. Except if we baited the trap with the other mill he'd know he had me. His name's Kolinski.'

'Kolinski, eh? Could be a cousin' Anybody with an *inski* on his name could be a cousin' Maybe we better have a talk with him. Maybe one Polack can talk better to another Polack than a little Southern boy. You ever think in terms of bribes? These union boys ain't above a little reason-money.'

'I could bribe him some. It would just be putting it off. But even putting it off would be worth money.'

'What they got to hang an organization on? You starving your people to death? Child labour? Sixty-hour week?'

'No. On the contrary. I just gave my shop an over-all five-cents an hour raise. They got a recreational programme and some sick benefits and a voluntary retirement fund, if they want it. Between that and the new machinery—the stuff I inherited was just about clapped out—we're breaking even, showing maybe a little profit. I practically had to rebuild this damned mill. I don't think the union could give them more than I'm giving them right now. But I've made some mistakes . . . mistakes a kid would make, I guess.'

'Now we're coming to it,' Jimmy Wilbur said. 'They have to have something to stir up the animals with. Remember, I'm a coal town kid. I knew about hardnosed unions and how they worked before you could spell. Suppose you tell all to your Uncle James.'

'The first mistake, I suppose, was me buying a Cadillac.'

'Bad business in a small town for a young upstart. Go on.'

'Maybelle wanted a car of her own—a red one.'

'Worse business. Waving a flag at a bull. Go on.'

'And she wanted a swimming-pool. She had quite a lot of money, Jim. Her money and her mother's. She paid for the car and the pool. And it *is* her house. A very big house, built when people with money built big houses.'

'I could beat you on this alone. Some more?'

'Well, yes. There's a guy and his sister.'

'And his sister is pretty and you hired her for your secretary.'

'I never told you that.'

'You didn't have to. Continue. Little boy with the short brain and the tight pants. The guy?'

'Named Red Forney. A guy with no education but a lot of sense and a lot of ambition. A guy with as much itch to get somewhere as me. A mill-hand that didn't want to be one all his life. We had a fight once, and I licked him, and then we got to be real good friends. I was just working in the office then as assistant to the general manager. A clerk, really. But we got to be friends, and we went fishing and talked a lot and drank some beer to-gether. He said he reckoned I was going places and he wanted to go with me. Then he took me home one day and I met his sister. Her name is Elizabeth—Libby. She was just a kid, then.'

'I can see this one, just as plain. I won't scout the play for you. Go on, sucker.'

'Well, one thing and another, and I said one day that by God when I got to be boss of this mill, I was going to fire a red-nosed old secretary we had and get me a pretty one. I was going to overhaul the mill and I was going to fire some more useless people, and the day that I was the boss I would fire one old guy in particular and Red Forney would be foreman of the spinning-room. And so I did. I actually didn't. I meant to, but I got soft-hearted and retired old Marvin McCracken and old Miss Mildred Mason. Old Marvin told me to take my mill and stick it up my ass, he didn't want no charity from me. The old girl got out real graceful, I must say.'

'So how long before you went soft-headed, as well as soft-hearted, and started banging your secretary? Don't tell me you didn't. I been going to the movies for years.'

Craig blushed.

'Nearly a year. I tried pretty hard not to, but when you see her . . .'

'All right. I'm a boy, too. Next time hire an ugly one who hasn't got a brother. Say on, my son.'

'Well, now it seems that the Bolsheviks have grabbed ahold of old McCraken as a kind of symbol. The old goat never has cashed any of his retirement cheques. They tell the hands that I fired old Marvin and made a foreman out of Red just so—just so I could screw his sister. That's not so. At least it wasn't so, then. Maybe it was somewhere in the back of my mind, but it wasn't meant to be. Red's done a hell of good job, and I was thinking that when we got really going, I might make him sort of technical general manager, because he knows the shop upside down and backwards, with Libby as kind of head of personnel through Red. All under you and me, of course. But now . . .'

'But now?'

'Well, the first thing they hit me with when I came back from New York is that a bunch of union goons are moving into town, and that the other day Red and Libby's nice little new house had been all slabbered up with "Company Pimp—Company Whore" in red letters across the front of it. And Red's got a new Ford. They hacked the tyres and broke the windows.'

'That's standard. So let me see. If I was trying to organize your joint, I'd hit these things. I'd say look at the president, he screwed himself into a mill. Look at his Cadillac, while we have to walk. Look at his wife, with a red car and a swimming-pool, when we walk to work and go to the toilet outside. Look at the boss, he belongs to the Country Club and wears a white tuxedo coat while we wear overalls. Look at the boss, he eats meat three times a day and we're lucky to get hamburg and onions once a week. Look at the boss . . .

'What sort of office you got?' Jimmy Wilbur asked suddenly. 'If I know you, it's fancy. Is it?'

'I'm afraid it is,' Craig said. 'I'm afraid it is. It's got a wood-burning fireplace and two bathrooms.'

'Jesus Christ. And I bet a divan?'

'Yes. It's got a divan.' Craig blushed again. 'One of the first things I did was give myself a nice place to work. I guess I made mistakes all the way.'

'So,' Jimmy Wilbur continued, 'you got two toilets in your office and they have to go out in the backyard. You got a divan to bang your secretary on. What colour hair?'

'Huh?'

'I said what colour hair?'

'Red. Dark red.'

Wilbur groaned.

'And he's got to hire a red-head, yet. Why not the chorus line from the Copa? Why not the Wampus Babies? Why not the showgirls from the Follies?'

' *You* got red hair,' Craig said, almost little-boy plaintively.

'Yes, but I ain't a girl, and I ain't your secretary, and I ain't your office lay, and I ain't got a brother that got raised up over other men's heads. I got a busted nose. I can afford red hair. I don't know. Times are still hard, no matter what they say in Washington, and look to get harder unless there's a war or something. All that paper prosperity hasn't percolated down here to the sticks yet. They're still eatin' sow-belly and cornpone and glad to get it.

'I tell you, boy, this union don't need much else to strike you to a standstill. Two cars, a swimming-pool, a company pimp out back with the boys and a red-headed company whore up front with the boss. I wouldn't even think they'd need the stink-bomb and window-busting boys. Word of mouth can walk 'em out on you.'

'I know it,' Craig said miserably. 'And that's why I sent out the hurry-call for you. I know it. A couple of months, three months of one-shift production, or no-shift no-production, and I'm gone. A mill that don't work and that still has some mortagge plastered on it ain't a mill. It's a skeleton, unless you got enough money to weather it out and starve the people back. And these people won't starve back too easy. We ain't a one-crop economy down here any more. I see the North movin' in all the time, because the labour's cheap, there's plenty of land, and plenty of cheap power and good roads and rails. That's why I want that other mill so bad. The hell with cotton. There's a new fibre a minute, and even this new stuff will be obsolete tomorrow. Rayon's already about as dated as cotton. Those DuPont labs can't work fast enough. I want to convert as fast as I can raise the capital. That's why I need Nate Mannheim and his fast money. What are we gonna do, Moose?'

'I got to think some. There ought to be something. What say I case this Kolinski for you, and see what he's got on his mind, exactly? And while I do that, why don't you just sort of dis-

490

appear? Put that Cadillac in the garage and tell your wife not to drive by the plant in the red car. Go do your deal with the bank for the mortgage on the property, and then run back to New York and sew up your business with Mannheim for the money. And then try to come back here and close the deal for the new mill while I delay the action a little bit. How do you feel about a closed shop contract, and the check-off dues collection, and all that?'

'I wouldn't mind a closed-shop contract—it's coming, anyhow—but about two thirds of the people I've got are old timers, most of them semi-pensioners from old man Grimes, and if I've got to carry that dead wood in a hundred per cent unionized shop I'm wrecked. Christ, I'll give them their increase, and overtime, and retirement fund and all the rest of it, but if I'm saddled with these doddering old . . . I'll be payroll-padded and retirement-benefited and overtimed right out of the textile business. Maybe . . .'

'Maybe what?'

'I don't suppose it would work. But if we could get this Kolinski to lay off a while longer, while I get rid of the dead wood—the old stagers that are just cluttering up the place—and jazz up the production with some new manpower replacing machines—sort of overhaul everything and clean house real good, I could live with a union shop. *And* make money.'

'You mean, just kick the old folks out? Like that? Lay off half your working force? You'd do that?'

Craig shrugged, and spread his hands. The car travelled for a second without guidance. Then he put his hands back on the wheel.

'It's one thing or the other. I'll have to close down if I fight a strike.'

'You'd kick 'em out. Just like that, you'd kick 'em out?'

'If it meant a good deal with the union I'd kick 'em out. The union don't give a damn about the people. All the union wants is the dues. The people don't know it, but I know it. Like I said, I'm giving as much right now as the union'll give 'em, and I'd like to give 'em more when we get consolidated. But look at it this way: if the silly bastards let themselves into a strike, they're all kicked out, anyhow, because there ain't going to be any more work. To save Maybelle's mill and to save this one I want for me, I'd kick 'em out. I'd kick my mother out if it meant saving the mills, if I had a mother to kick out.'

Wilbur looked at the bitterly grim young profile as Craig drove swiftly, carefully, eyes never turning from the road.

'I believe you would,' he said, softly. 'I really believe you would.'

Later, after a long silence, marked only by the humming of the tyres—

'And what would you hire to replace the old people that you're willing to kick out?'

'Younger people. Pay them more dough. But better machinery. Fewer people. Much fewer people. I could run a top-grade textile plant on half my payroll right now, with the right machines. Grimes Mills is just a kind of compromise between yesterday and tomorrow. It'll be obsolete in a year. After that, if you don't put in your own labs and keep up with everybody, you'll be obsolescent every month. Nylon's just a start. They'll have a thousand fibres to twist around those spindles. All different. Some made out of glass, milk, coal, humming-bird wings, everything.'

'You know this from where? Straight from Mr. and Mrs. DuPont?'

'No. I read a lot. A lot of stuff's still in the labs but you'll see it. You'll see people wearing it. And I want to be in on it. Right in the middle and on top of it.'

'One way or the other I expect you will be, Short Pants,' Jimmy Wilbur said. 'So it boils down to this: What do we want? Do we want to run a mill or wage a war?'

'I want to run a mill,' Craig said. 'If necessary I'll wage a war. But mainly I want to run a mill.'

'Okay,' Jimmy Wilbur said. 'I'm hungry. Let's stop off and have a barbecue and a Coke. In the meantime I will cite you the first principle of coaching a football team. When in doubt, kick, and hope for the breaks.'

'Will you stay with us for a bit? I told Maybelle to fix up the old lady's room. It's a nice house. A nice room.'

'I don't think so. Right now I don't want to be too closely associated with swimming-pools and Cadillacs and the boss. I am kind of a labour-relations counsel. I think I'll go hole up in the second-best hotel in town, and ride the streetcars for a little bit. Case the joint some, and accidentally get to meet Mr. Kolinski and some of his associates. Being a Polack, I keep telling you, has definite advantages, and while I blush as I say it, I ain't exactly unknown in Scranton, P.A., or some of the other Polack-producing communities. Having been an All-American football player will help. Having been a coalmine boy will help. My busted nose will help. And being Coach-of-the-Year, you should pardon the expression, for maybe two years running, will help. No. You go tend to your banking business, little man. Let your Uncle Jimmy sort of circulate and feel out matters. And I don't want to meet your Forney or his sister. I will have a mc-crack at old McCracken, though, if you'll excuse a bad gag. You just go somewhere and see if you can't clean up your banking while I prowl around and look for answers. Meanwhile, drop me off at the second-best hotel. What's its name?'

'The Kensington.'

'Bedbugs?'

'I don't know. I never stayed in it as a regular guest. When I first hit this town I stayed in boarding houses. It's got whores though, that you don't have to register if you slip the bellboy a buck. So it figures to have bedbugs. Or at least it used to. But that was a very long time ago. Before I got married.'

'And before you started banging your secretary?'

'Yes,' Craig said levelly. 'Before I started banging my secretary.' He pressed his foot harder on the accelerator.

31

JIMMY WILBUR was seated at the counter of the coffee-shop in the hotel. He looked at his coffee-cup as if he expected to find a salamander in it.

'What do you make this coffee in, or out of?' he growled. 'A rubber boot?'

The waitress gave him her best be-coy-to-the-travelling-salesman smile. She was a red-faced dumpling of a girl who would never lose her youthful double chin or the blackheads around her nose and on her forehead.

'You don't like it, Mister? It's the best we got in this town.' She simpered.

'No, I don't like it. Gimme another cup. I won't like that either, but since you got no bars in this gay metropolis . . . skip it. Give me the check.' The girl's fat neck disappeared in her shoulders as she shrugged. She sniffed. The sniff said: *Yankees.*

'The coffee not so good, eh?'

Jimmy Wilbur bestowed a gaze on the questioner—a gaze which was calculated to kill at fifty yards.

'The coffee is not so good, eh,' he said it flatly.

'Excuse me. I just make some polite talk. I know you. At least I know your face. You the coach. You Jimmy Wilbur. You the Pennsylvania boy who make All-American playing for University of North Carolina a few years back. I introduce myself. I am Anton Kolinski. Polish. Like you. I come from a town not so far from you.'

'Where, Warsaw?' Jimmy Wilbur was being intentionally rude. He looked at the speaker. The speaker was a heavyset man of about forty. He had almost invisible blond eyebrows and very light, but very sharp blue eyes. His lashes were white, pig-bristly, and his hair was almost a washed-out pink. But his face was meatily affable, and there was a large gap between his two front teeth.

'No. Not Warsaw. Irontown. I read about you a whole lot in the papers.'

'It's nice you got a nickel to buy the papers,' Jimmy Wilbur said. 'For a moment I would have sworn you were a cousin of mine. All my cousins look like you except the girls. They look like me. They all play football for Vassar. Broken-noses, you know. Big feet. Lop ears.'

'What?' Mr. Kolinski's voice was politely plaintive. 'I do not think I understand.'

Jimmy Wilbur's face became affable, in turn.

'Excuse me. I just had a Southern-cooking-type lunch, and a Southern-cooking-type cup of coffee. It gives me a bad temper. I got indigestion in a spread formation. Mental and physical. Can you tell me why they got to put grease even in the ice-cream?'

Mr. Kolinski spread his hands, and moved his shoulders upward. 'I still don't understand. If you mean the food stink, I agree. Pigs should not eat such food. In Poland . . .'

'Yes, I know. Mama tells me all the time about Poland. You can get tired of goulash, too. What brings you here, Comrade?'

'You call me Comrade. Are you a . . .'

'No, I ain't. No card. I call everybody Comrade. I'm just a football coach on a wild-goose chase. I come down here looking for some backfield material and all I wind up with is acute indigestion. Tell me, Comrade, are you a slivovitz man, or is vodka your only vice, or would you like to come up to my room and sample a bottle of scotch?'

'I like very much. You too kind. Thank you very much. I am very pleased to know you, Mr. Wilbur. What was your name before you changed it?'

'It's so long ago I forgot how to spell it,' Jimmy Wilbur said. 'It wouldn't fit the headlines. That's why I changed it. Come on, Comrade. Let's go up and knock a neck.'

'This is a terrible town,' Mr. Kolinski said. 'Nothing to do all day long except pamphlets and plans. And people. Such people you wouldn't believe it.'

'What business are you in, exactly, Mr. Kolinski?' Jimmy had summoned the bellhop, and he and Kolinski were drinking scotch out of thick bathroom glasses. Kolinski was in the only chair, and Jimmy Wilbur was sprawled on the bed. The room's motif was classic Southern-brindle, and it smelled strongly of mildew. There was only the single bed, the single rattan chair, the single table with the cloudy-splotched glass top, and some sort of a picture involving a dispirited rooster on the mud-brown wall, whose paper also seemed to suffer from crotch-rot.

'Such a business I myself wouldn't believe,' Kolinski said. 'Not even from Gdansk would I believe such a business. You know Gdansk?'

'No, I don't know Gdansk. But my people come from Lodz.

494

ing city?'

'A lousy mill. One more mill I got to organize. Believe me, I am a Leninist, I believe the doctrine, but sometimes these *schmucks* they give me to help organize . . . Foreigners. Dedicated people. Always talk doctrine. Always intense. Never letting down. Me, I like a little fun once in a while. You can find fun in North Caroline? I don't think so. You find any fun in North Caroline? You find any laughing?'

'I don't even find any halfbacks,' Jimmy Wilbur said. 'Have another drink.'

'Thanks,' Kolinski said. 'You are the first human being I meet since I been here. Women? Ptoo! Where to meet a woman in this single-horse town?'

'I don't know,' Jimmy Wilbur said. 'But I'll call the bellhop later on and ask him.'

A strange friendship had begun in the coffee-shop. There being few dining choices in the town of Kensington, Jimmy Wilbur and Kolinski, the union organizer, found themselves inevitably eating together.

They rose at about the same time, and either went to the cafeteria next door, or into the coffee-shop, or around the corner to the Greek's for breakfast.

'I swear to God, Tovarich,' Wilbur would say, jaundicedly looking at his hard ham-and-hominy, with red eye gravy, or baleful staring orb of the fried egg, whose lacy edges swam in grease, 'I know what licked the South in the Civil War, and it wasn't the Yankees. It was the cooking. How can you fight when you're dying with indigestion? And no Tums. At least today we got soda bicarb.'

'Yes, I agree. When the workers are organized in the mills I intend to start organizing the restaurants. But first, we have a blood-purge.' Kolinski's little pig eyes twinkled. 'That's a joke, *landsman*.'

'Joke, hell. If you want a strong right arm in the purge, just call me. I think we ought to shoot the Greek first. And that ain't no joke, *landsman*. Except really I don't think we ought to shoot him. Slow torture is my idea. Make him eat in his own joint, three meals a day.'

'Why they got to always fry chicken so it taste like wet feathers? Why they always got tomato soup with a skin of fat on it? Why nobody ever heard of borscht? Why never boiled beef? These people, they barbarians,' Kolinski would say. 'Pass the cornsticks.'

The first time they sat down for dinner together, Wilbur said: 'Now is when my heart and soul cries out for a good proletarian martini, Tovarich. It ain't civilized to drink martinis in a hotel room. Martinis should be drunk at the table while you wait for the right food.'

Kolinsky growled.

'In the old country we make a potato whisky, not vodka, worse than vodka, that the peasants drink so they do not mind a steady meal of potato soup. I would not waste potato whisky on this collard green, it say on the menu. What is a collard green? For cattle, maybe. For people, no. I learn a new language. What is hoppin' john? What is hushpuppy? Why these people don't learn to speak English?'

'Now don't you go knocking hoppin' john,' Jimmy Wilbur said. 'You are now knocking what is dearer to the South than the virtue of its womanhood, or its fine horses, or its noble cotton crop. Watch your tongue, Tovarich, or I will turn you in to the NKVD. You have just cast an aspersion on North Carolina caviar.'

'Caviar?' It was the only word that Kolinski caught. 'In North Carolina there is caviar?'

'I refer,' Jimmy Wilbur said, 'to the black-eyed pea. That is North Carolina caviar. And a *blini* is a hotcake.'

'Oh,' Kolinski's jowls sagged, 'for a minute I think you serious. Maybe they have sturgeon in North Carolina? If some day we organize the fisheries, perhaps . . . ?'

'Could be. But maybe we ought to think about organizing the farmers?'

'Not practical to organize farmers under democracy. Too scattered. Can't combine. Also, very bad business in Washington. All right for Russia but for here, no. Farmers got too strong lobby in Washington. Much stronger now than Labour.'

'I was kidding,' Wilbur said. 'Come on, Comrade. Let's go look at the nightlife.'

'Nightlife? Nightlife? In this town there is nightlife? They, how you say it, take the sidewalks to bed when the sun goes down.'

'That's not how you say it but I think you've said it better. A sidewalk is the only thing I've seen in this town worth taking to bed. Tell me something, Comrade. Ain't there any pretty female Communists?'

'It's a thing I wonder myself. I been in Party a long time. Never once do I see a pretty girl Communist.' Kolinski looked mock-furtively around him. 'I think there is something in doctrine which says it very bad not to have greasy hair with dandruff and long face. Very serious, always, these women. Even serious in bed. Like it was part of revolution. In bed is to laugh, is to have fun. Not revolution. No doctrine in bed but to laugh and slap and tickle. Me, I do not like doctrine in bed. The day is long enough for doctrine. Night is for men and women naked without doctrine.'

496

Wilbur looked shocked.

'Here, now, Comrade,' he said. 'That's heresy. People get shot in the old country for talking like that. And you know what the *Daily Worker* would have to say about Comrade Kolinski for suggesting that people should have fun. That ain't dedication, Comrade. That is bourgeois frivolity.'

'I don't understand frivolity. Ptoo to this kind dedication. I understand a good sweaty bed with laughing woman.'

'I think you're a phony,' Jimmy Wilbur said. 'I think you're as phony as me.'

'You're phony?'

'Sure, I'm phony. I'm as phony as you are. I'm in the organizing business myself. Come on up in the room and we'll have a few hundred drinks.'

'I said you're a phony,' Jimmy Wilbur said. 'So am I. I repeat it. Look at me for a real phony. What am I doing here? I am recruiting the mill towns. I am an organizer of athletes. We have a Central Committee. It is called the Alumni Association.'

'What exactly?'

'It is a kind of check-off system.'

'This I understand. A check-off system. How?'

'It is a thing called College Spirit. A doctrine. You go to school, and graduate, and then when you make some money the Alumni Association gets after you and threatens you until you pay some money. Perhaps it is a new stadium that the university wants. Perhaps a new library. But more often it is new football players who will play in the new stadium and pay off the mortgage and maybe even build a new library—and, impossible as it sounds—may even raise the salary of the professors, to where they make as much as a good amateur fullback.'

'This sounds a very good thing,' Kolinski said. 'To give the teachers more money. I never went college. I went steelmill instead. You learn many things in steelmill.'

'I know. I went coalmine before I went college. If you're still interested in why we're both phonies, I will tell you what a coach does. He wins game. A coach who loses games is not a coach. He is an ex-coach. He is unsuccessful Marxist. He gets purged. You understand purge, I expect.'

'I understand purge. Out. *Kaput*, *Todt*. Yes. I understand purge.'

'Well, they don't exactly shoot the coach, but they might as well, because nothing is as dead as an unemployed coach, unless it is an unsuccessful Communist.'

'Yes,' Kolinski said, seriously. 'This I understand.'

'Have another snort,' Jimmy Wilbur said, and poured Kolinski a stiff one. 'You know, *landsman*, I like you.'

'I like you too, *landsman*. If you are ever unsuccessful

coach, you come look me up. I find work. We think alike.'

'Thank you, Comrade,' Jimmy Wilbur said. 'I believe you mean it.'

'I mean it.'

'Now what I am doing down here is in conflict to your interests. I scout the mill towns, and my scouts scout the mill towns, to look for suitable material for my Party, which is represented by the football team for which the gallant alumni in the Central Committee pay big money to get them out of the mills. The reason we can get them out of the mills is that people in mills are generally so miserable and underpaid that a guy like me will do anything, even play college football, to get out of a mill. And so what do you do, Tovarich?'

'So what do I do, my friend?'

'You come down here and organize the mills and eventually, under your organization, with your strong Alumni Association collecting dues so you can organize better and better, mills will be so pleasant to work in that I will not be able to find any good raw material for my football team. I won't be able to get them out of the mills, they'll love the mills so much. My Central Committee will kick me into the snow and I will starve and it is all your fault for organizing the mills in the first place. You are my enemy, Comrade. I am a worker, too, and you will ride me down like a Cossack. You will be an economic royalist.'

'I do not want to be your enemy. I do not want to be an economic royalist. I am your friend. It is only a conflict of the systems. Your materialistic approach to education is Capitalist in the extreme. Through it you fatten off the misery of others. Not so?'

'You bet your Lenin-loving ass it's so,' Jimmy Wilbur said. 'Have another drink.'

'Thank you. It is a pleasure to drink in your company, Comrade Jimmy Wilbur. We think alike, you on your side, me on mine. It is a pity we cannot reconcile the ideology.'

'What does "reconcile the ideology" mean? I was a physical education major and didn't learn many big words.'

'You joke. You laugh. I like you because you laugh. You make me laugh. These people I work with they do not laugh. They do not like it when I laugh. They say Anton Kolinski is not serious. Anton Kolinski is serious, all right. It is because he is so serious he can laugh a little bit.

'I speak inside the walls. You are a dumb Polack like me. Why is it that they always say "dumb Polack", "dumb Swede"? Was Pilsudski dumb? Was Pulaski dumb? Was Tadeus Kosciusko a dumb Polack?'

'Was Knute Rockne a dumb Swede? I think not. You want to hear a funny story they tell? A football story?'

'If it's funny, sure.'

'The story goes that Knute Rockne—he's the Notre Dame coach that got killed in the air crash in 1931. Actually, he was a Norwegian, but everybody called him a Swede. He had a very famous backfield, back in the 'twenties, Jimmy Crowley, Harry Stuhldreyer, Don Miller and Elmer Layden. They called them the Four Horsemen.'

'I know. From the Apocalypse. Pure Communistic dogma, a Swede, an Irishman, a German, and what sounds like an American, all working together.'

'That's right,' Jimmy Wilbur said, 'pure Communistic dogma. Sure, plague, famine, war, death, all the necessary ingredients to wreck the world. Pure Communistic dogma. Skip it.

'Well, the story goes that Crowley, an Irishman, messed up a play real bad, and Rock ate him out.

' "Is there anything dumber than a dumb Irishman?" Rockne is supposed to have said, and Crowley answered:

' "Yeah. *A smart Swede.*" If it's true I would have liked to have seen Rock's face.'

'That's very funny. A dumb Irishman smarter than a smart Swede. In that case I got a lot of smart Swedes working for me. Stupids. Knives and bombs and busted heads. I don't like it. I do it, but I don't like it. I do it because I got a record to maintain.

'I still speak inside the walls,' Kolinski said. 'You are Polack like me. You come from a mill town. My people come from steel towns in Poland. I tell you, there is no difference between steel town in Poland and steel town in Pennsylvania. A steel town is a steel town. A tragedy. Dirty and cold. And a mill town in the South? A double tragedy. Dirty and hot. At least in Pennsylvania we can drink from bars like human beings. Not hiding in hotel rooms.'

'You're so right, pal,' Jimmy Wilbur said. 'Have another snort.

'I tell you it's a misery. I am good Communist. I got to be good Communist, because I got to say in public that I am Communist, and the Communists will save America from the economic determinists and from the capitalistic exploiters. I believe in this. I believe in this, believe me. I believe in this.'

'So you believe in it. I believe you believe it. All right.'

'I believe in the worker. I was worker as little boy in Poland. I was worker in Pennsylvania. Now I am big man with union. What am I with union?'

'Hold out your glass. What are you with union?'

'Tame monkey on a string, that is what I am with union. My English it's not so good, so I don't make long speeches. But the other people, they speak good English, they make me come on platform and speak about oppression in Poland and goddam old Czar and hooray Lenin, hooray Stalin, so forget Upper Silesia, the future of world is here, talk with bad accent, and then I sit down while some *nogoodniks*, they speak college English, talk Marxian doctrine, they talk Stalinist doctrine, they forget

Trotsky out loud, and they wind up, say: *chop off the boss head.*'

'That's right. Chop off the boss's head. What else?'

'Now you listen careful, Comrade Wilbur. I got nothing against the workers. But then I got nothing too much against the boss, either. What I got is union job. Union pay for working union job. But no union hours. Oh no. No union hours. Pamphlets, riots, what am I say, riots? Demonstrations. Orderly demonstrations of the people in favour of the people. All day long and half the night. No union hours.'

'Have another snort,' said Jimmy Wilbur.

'Thank you.' Comrade Kolinski drank half his drink in a gulp. 'So. I was saying?'

'Orderly demonstrations. Not riots. Orderly demonstrations.'

'I tell you, they don't want me to speak much, because when I get excited I speak Polish, but I suppose to run the operation. Me, immigrant, now citizen. I run the operation. So what I do all day long? I tell you, Mr. Footballer. I tell people go paint signs on people house, go talk to workers, and finally I have to say, go break heads, go bust up plant if boss don't see reason. To hire people bust up plant I got transportation bills, hotel bills, motel bills, you wouldn't believe it, these people I got to bring in they eat their heads off, you wouldn't believe it. Then I got to turn in expense account and the boss in New York say: "Chrissake, Kolinski, you running a night club, these charge so high?" I tell you, organizing is no fun.'

'Have another snort,' said Jimmy Wilbur. 'You'll have me crying in a minute. You sound like me when I talk about college football.'

'Then you got to get a bond against what you break,' Mr. Kolinski said bitterly. 'To find a man for a bond you got to find a fink. A fink, he's look to earn some *gelt* on his own, away from union, away from strike. A fink is a fink. Me, I don't like finks. But in this business is finks. In all business is finks. But you got to get bail-bonds to get people out of jail, they throw a bomb, they bust a window, they turn over truck, they damage a car of citizen. Accidentally. And the hospital bills. Terrible. You wouldn't believe it.'

'I'd believe it,' Jimmy Wilbur said. 'I'd believe anything. Have another snort.'

Mr. Kolinski extended his glass.

'I am man like any other man. I come down here organize mill. I like to walk in front door, stick out hand, say: "Hello, Mr. Millman. I come to organize your mill." That way everybody be happier. Everybody make more money.'

Mr. Kolinski shook his head gravely.

'Is not the way. Is to import bums from out of state. Is to create commotion. Is to look for nigger in woodpile. Is to make speech. Is to waste money. As good Marxist I don't like waste

500

money. Easier walk in front door and stick out hand. Oh no. Too easy. Dedicated people. Phoo. I got dedicated people got to make a hassel else papers don't write it. I think drunk, maybe, talk like this, but you Polack like me, you not dedicated people. I spit dedicated people! *Schmucks!*'

'Here, here, Comrade, don't overwork it,' Jimmy Wilbur said. 'You'll split a seam.'

'I got a problem. I talk too much. That is main complaint in Party. I talk too much. They say, Anton, he good fellow, knows work, but he talk too much. They don't let me talk much on platform. So I talk too much off platform.'

'I talk too much,' Jimmy Wilbur said. 'Everybody talks too much. A man's got to speak his mind once in a while or he'll go crazy. Speak up, Comrade. I will lend you my ears.'

They were a bit bleary-eyed when they met for breakfast in the cafeteria. Both men inspected each other's trays as they sat down.

'Tomato juice and coffee, nothing else, eh?' Jimmy Wilbur said.

'I look your tray. Tomato juice and coffee. Nothing else, eh?' Anton Kolinski said.

'I had a straight slug of whisky before I cleaned my teeth,' Jimmy Wilbur said.

'Me too. I think for a minute I don't get up. I think maybe I die. From the way my head feel, we make a lot of jokes last night, eh?'

'We make a lot of jokes. From the way my head feels. About two bottles' worth of jokes.'

'I categorically deny everything I said under liquor,' Kolinski said. 'All a dirty Capitalist plot to get me drunk and tell Communist secrets.' He smiled.

'I categorically deny everything I said about college football,' Jimmy Wilbur smiled, too. 'All a dirty Communist plot to get me fired.'

'Now we have made all the jokes and the categoric denial, which is what lawyers tell me to say, let us come to business, Wilbur. What you want of me? What you really do here? A big man, a man like you, don't come to a pisspot town to look for football players. He send somebody. What you do here, really?'

'Come on up to the room again and I'll tell you. No booze. Talk. Serious talk.'

'Okay. No booze. Serious talk. But we got to make it short. I got to see my people about some final arrangement.'

32

'I GOT a friend,' Jimmy Wilbur said. 'His name is Craig Price. He's a good kid. I've known him since he was fifteen years old.

He runs this Grimes Mills you want to organize. Some day he'll run some other mills which you'll want to organize. If you let him. You really do run this business down here, don't you, Kolinski?'

Kolinski's face was sober. So was his voice.

'I run it. I am responsible to New York. I got a lot of people, sure. But they nothing except people to do dirty work. Yeah. I run it. And I run it good. That is why they let me make jokes. Because I run it good.'

Jimmy Wilbur nodded.

'I wouldn't kid you. The reason I make jokes is because I run a football team pretty good. When I was a player I carried a football as good as the next man, and maybe a little better. You can't make jokes unless you do it pretty good, whether it's organizing a mill or coaching a team. Nobody lets a bum make jokes.'

'True.' Anton Kolinski nodded.

'You're in a peculiar position here, Kolinski. I've seen your imported "workers", your goons from the North. The South is a little different from the North. Down here they don't like Yankees first, and they don't like Yankee foreigners second. They don't even like up-country people. Anybody north of Raleigh is a Yankee. Anybody as far west as Asheville is a Yankee. I don't know if your bosses filled you in on this, my friend, but it's true.'

'The niggers, they like us.'

'Don't say "nigger", Comrade. A coastal Southerner can say "nigger" and maybe get away with it. A Yankee foreigner with an accent can't say "nigger". *Negro* is the word. Don't forget it. Somebody should have told you.'

'Thank you. I remember it.'

'In Carolina we have something called po' white trash. He isn't like anything you ever saw, Kolinski. Not in Poland or in Newark or in Irontown or Scranton. I know something about this. I went to college in this state for four years. Let me tell you about poor white trash. He hates himself, first. But he's Scotch and he's Irish, mainly, and he hates the bluebloods on top of him and he even hates his own class. And he loves the niggers, because down here a nigger is the only thing that he's allowed to kick. If you follow me, he hates the niggers, and he's the first one you'll find in a lynch mob, but underneath he loves the niggers, because he can elbow a nigger off the sidewalk and get away with it. In his mind, the nigger is the only thing lower than he is. To a nigger he's a white man. To any white man over him he ain't nothin' at all. "Lintheads", they call these comrades you're trying to organize in the sacred name of Communism and trade-unionism. "Clay-eaters", they call them.'

Jimmy stopped to light a cigarette.

502

'Go on, friend. I think I learn something maybe from you. You know, I think I like you sober, too, Wilbur.'

'All right. We'll go steady some day. But right now we ain't doing that old enough-of-this-love-talk act. Poor white trash, my well-indoctrinated, skull-busting, bomb-throwing, window-smashing friend, don't like each other, even. But mainly they don't like strangers. I can get you shot right easy up in the hills where they make the moonshine whisky. I can take you across the river and introduce you to a tobacco-chewing farmer with a squirrel rifle who will shoot your left eye out of your head just for trespassing on his land, and the local judge'll call it an accident.'

Kolinski held up a hand.

'Excuse me. You a Polack. You a Northern boy, too. Where you learn all this?'

'Some I learned by myself. Some of the rest of it Craig Price explained to me when I asked him some questions about his people. Craig was born and raised here. He knows his people. Right now you got his mill-hands all stirred up with a lot of labour agitation, but there's a hard hunk of his mill-hands that would rather go hungry than do what they call "mess around" with a goddamned Yankee foreigner. And there's some goons *we* got that can eat yours raw. Craig's coming back tomorrow. I'd like you to meet him in a friendly fashion, and I promise nobody'll shoot you when we go for a little ride in the country, across the river. We grow our own goons across the river. I would like for you to see these goons, Kolinski. From what Craig tells me, they're worth seein'. Oh, and one other thing. We got something down here called chain-gangs. You can rent the convicts cheap if you know the man that Craig calls the Cap'n. You interested in seeing some of these people?'

'I'm very interested. I'm always interested in the masses. I like to use your telephone, please?'

'Sure. I got a nickel,' Jimmy Wilbur drawled. 'Be my guest.'

Anton Kolinski picked up the phone and asked for a number.

'Hello, Mario?' he said. 'Yeah. Kolinski. Look, I am very busy this morning. Something new come up and now I am very busy. I see you later this afternoon. You take a morning off. Go fishing.' A pause. 'I said I'm busy. Drop dead if you don't want to go fishing.'

'They really don't educate you people very well, do they?' Jimmy Wilbur grinned. 'They teach you all the right words and the legal terms and things like ideological clashes but they leave people out of the course when they teach you, don't they?'

'No. People everywhere, high and low, is people. I believe what I do. Maybe sometimes I do not believe all that I say but I believe what I do.'

'Oh, balls,' Jimmy Wilbur said. 'We were drunk last night.

503

What you really mean is that you're a union man first and you're paid to organize mills. All the Communism business is a lot of crap with people like you. You don't give a good goddam about the worker and you wouldn't recognize Karl Marx if he came up and bit you on the behind. Here. Let's have a drink. Talking makes me thirsty. Everything makes me thirsty.'

'Okay, Wilbur. But today we have a sober drink. With no jokes, eh?'

'You want ice? I can send down for some.'

'Ice is for the bourgeois. Pour me some whisky in a glass, Comrade.'

'Okay, Comrade. But you better start buying pretty soon, don't you think? There must be some sort of expense account in your slush fund for labour relations.'

'Tomorrow I buy. Today you talk. They say talk is cheap. To talk with me is expensive. *Pros't.*'

'*Skoal,*' Jimmy Wilbur said.

They sat silently for a moment.

'You know,' Jimmy Wilbur said, almost to himself, 'you can lose this thing in the South if you strike that plant. It can hurt you plenty. All over the country it will hurt you plenty. It'll hurt your union, and it'll hurt your precious Party. I been around newspaper people ever since I made my first touchdown as a high school punk. They'll cover this story like they never covered a strike story. And you know what they'll cover it with.'

'Why you say that?'

'Because of what I just told you. Here is big union business with a loud Communist front moving in on a small Southern town that ain't bothering anybody. You read *Gone With the Wind*?'

'Yeah. I read some parts of it. Most I don't understand.'

'Well, friend, nothing much has changed down here in the Yankee-hating business. You raise a ruckus down here and it'll be just like General Sherman marching through Georgia to the sea. You can still get yourself a fat eye singing "Marching Through Georgia" in Atlanta today.

'These people down here got faces,' Jimmy Wilbur said. 'They ain't like those poor Bohunks you bulldoze in the factory towns up North. You know all the hell that is raised in the Gastonia strikes?'

'Yes. I know. I was in the Gastonia strikes. We made some mistakes there. In Gastonia I got some very valuable training.'

'Well, *landsman*, you'll get some more training down here. You're makin' a big thing out of an old guy named Marvin McCracken, ain't you?'

'We are not making a special big thing. McCracken is useful as, how you say it, a . . .'

'Symbol? A peg to hang the strike on if necessary?'

'Exactly. Listening to you makes me thirsty.' He held out his glass, and Jimmy poured it half full again. 'Yes. McCracken is very useful. He is fired without cause to make room for a fink, a company pimp, so that the rich owner can make bed-down with his sister, who was hired when a long-time faithful secretary was fired to make room for the whore. Yes. McCracken is very useful. So is this Forney and his sister who works for the boss. You might say that this strike in new territory is made to order.' Kolinski almost, but not quite, smacked his lips.

'You know then, of course, that since Craig Price retired'— Jimmy Wilbur emphasized the word *retired*—'*retired* Marvin McCracken, that he has been sending him half-pay. Will your union retire you on half-pay, Comrade?'

'I don't think so. But that is not the point when we are talking to the workers. McCracken has not accepted any money from the mill. He was thrown aside like an . . .'

'Old shoe. Cow-flops. Marvin McCracken is a man. When Craig Price offered him the retirement money he told Craig Price to take his mill and shove it up his ass. He didn't need no help from no union, or Craig Price, or anybody else. And he still has the cheques. I suppose you knew that?' Jimmy Wilbur shot the question at him.

'I did not know that he still has the cheques. No, my friend, I did not know that.'

'Well, in case you're interested, my naïve saviour of the world, there is a special account in the bank here labelled *McCracken*.' (I know there is, Jimmy Wilbur said to himself, because I opened it personally last week, and got those three nice old gentlemen to pre-date it.) 'Every week that has passed since Marvin McCracken *retired*'—he paused—'every week since Marvin McCracken retired, money has gone into that account. And will continue to go into that account. To pay the cheques Marvin McCracken still has. The lady—the secretary who was replaced by Red Forney's sister—got six months' severance on full pay, and is now happily retired on half-pay. Can this union of yours do that well?'

'No. Not in any particular case. But for the mass of the workers it will do better than you do for them.'

'With what? With recreation? With sick benefits? With a voluntary check-off for retirement funds?'

'Maybe not. But we get them a raise. We insure a solid inside so there will be no more of this company whore, company pimp business. Every man will know where he stands. The union will protect him.'

'And the raise will pay his union dues so you know where *you* stand. You don't give a country cuss about the worker, do you, Anton? Come on, confess it. You almost did last night. You just want a nice clean record with the union and with the Party on how many mills Anton Kolinski organized.'

'No.' There was dignity in the word. 'I told you, drunk, I believe in the doctrine. I believe in a man's right to hold up his head, to have a decent wage, to live a decent life. So it starts in Moscow and comes from there to New York and down here to Kensington, North Carolina, I don't care, me. I don't care how it comes, so long as it comes.

'I was poor and miserable and hungry and dirty a long time, Wilbur. I tell you, I don't like it. I like to laugh, you know that. I like the girls and the good food and a clean place to sleep. I want other people to have something like that, too. It make me feel better when I go to bed to think that maybe in a little way, Anton Kolinski help other people to laugh and have girls and be clean and full of food. Politics? Ptoo! Russia? Is for Russians!

'I don't care how all this come about. Believe me, Comrade, I don't care. So a head is broken. So a machine is smashed. So you use a McCracken or a red-headed whore or conversation or a speech or a riot, I don't care. You very right when you say I got a record to protect. You very wrong when you say I, me, Anton Kolinski, don't care about the worker. I care. I care plenty. I worked once and work now and will live to work again and I want to be clean and well fed and have a girl and laugh once in a while.'

'I think they're wrong to keep you off the speech-making platform,' Jimmy Wilbur said. 'For about half a minute you almost had me panting to ask you for a card in the Party.'

'You joke again. I speak honestly to you and you joke again. Okay.' Anton Kolinski's eyes closed briefly, and then looked straight at Jimmy Wilbur through their little pig's white lashes. 'I am professional, Wilbur, like you are professional. I do what I do, I use what I can, I compromise when I can, but always I am professional. I am proud of being professional from the first time I k—from the first time I had some trouble and had to leave the town I work in.

'A professional know when to say yes, when say no, when say maybe. I am a man with a long look. Maybe today I lose it but tomorrow I win it. They call us bargaining agents. So okay. I know how to bargain. All right?'

'You sound like a man with a lot of sense to me, chum,' Jimmy Wilbur said. 'Let's don't talk any more shop. Tomorrow you'll meet Craig Price and we'll do a guided tour around the countryside. Come on, Tovarich, let's go insult our insides with whatever the Greek's got for lunch. You make noises like a man about to talk business, and business is a thing I like to talk. In the meantime, no busted heads?'

'No busted heads.'

'And no more paint jobs on other people's houses?'

'No more paint jobs. Except, perhaps, Comrade Wilbur, just a

506

little paint job on the Greek's place. A paint job which says: *Poison*?'

'That I'll buy and help you paint it. Come on, Bolshevik. Let's go find out what new torture they can inflict on sidemeat and stringbeans.'

33

THE train was late, as usual. The terminal was dirty grey, as usual.

'Welcome to our city, little man,' Jimmy Wilbur said. 'I represent the Chamber of Commerce.'

'I am very happy to be aboard your city,' Craig said. 'I bring tidings of great joy. Price Mills, Inc. is off to a happy start—with only one small kicker. Nate won't give me any money if we have a strike. I hope, I certainly hope, that you have been working on that end. As Nate would say, so we shouldn't have a strike, yet. So we should have money, yet.'

'We ain't going to have no strike, as you uneducated peasants would say. I am practically a member of the Communist Party. I am the vice-commissar in charge of industrial indoctrination. Me and Mr. Anton Kolinski are just two happy Polacks together. With reservations. But if one of us was a girl I wouldn't be here. We'd be in the sack with each other. It's love. Plain passion with reservations.'

'So glad I could come to the wedding,' Craig said. 'When is it?' He beckoned a porter.

'It starts this afternoon. We are going for a ride in your lovely, undeveloped countryside. In your lovely, well-developed Cadillac.'

'Who is we?' Craig tipped the porter.

'We is you and me and Mr. Anton Kolinski, a Gdansk boy that made real good in the melting-pot. He'll melt the melting-pot some day, maybe, but right now I got him tamed. If he's melting, he's melting my way.'

'I feel better already,' Craig said. 'What say we stop off at your place and talk about this before I check in with the office or at home?'

'I was going to suggest that, myself. That hotel room has taken a power of clobbering since you went carpet-bagging up North. Me and Mr. Kolinski seem to have been solidly loaded ever since I let him pick me up a couple of days after you left. He reads sports-pages. I'm his hero. Also I am a Polack. I told you being a Polack was useful. Somehow one Hunkie makes sweeter music with another displaced Hunkie than you hundred per cent Aryans make with the local Indians. It must be the Magyar in my soul. Tell me all about Mr. Nathan Mannheim, the man with the fast money.'

'Not much. I showed him a cash credit of fifty thousand dollars, the option on the mill, some photographs and the annual treasurer's report. The report was just sick enough to please him. But somehow he knew more than I did about this organizing thing. Evidently our friend—your friend—Kolinski is the Babe Ruth of his business. He's got a record of don't lose, when his name is on the operation. Nate says that he's happy to play if there ain't a strike. In other words, if we make it with Kolinski, we make it with Wall Street.'

'That figures. Like you said, if there's a strike there won't even be any Grimes Mills, let alone Price Mills. So what we must not have, the teacher said, is a nasty old strike. On no account must we have a strike. Well, here we are at the hotel. I think I know some things we got to do. Remember, I said the first principle is kick, and then pray for the breaks. I have already kicked. Now we pray for the breaks. And if it's a tie score we can flip a coin to see who wins.'

They entered the creaky elevator.

'When I get to be a real big shot in the Party,' Jimmy Wilbur said, 'I aim to organize all Southern elevators as well as the restaurants. Soon as we get your mill business fixed up, me and Comrade Kolinski are going to start picketing nearly everything in this town, including the movies that run a whole week in the only three stinking theatres you got. Can you imagine the exquisite boredom of a union hoodlum, with no windows to break, and only three movies a week to see? These poor bastards really earn their money. Some day I may even organize the goons. Here we are. We talk, now.'

'Anton Kolinski, I want you to meet Craig Price. It's time somebody introduced you, seeing as it's Price's mill and you figure to organize it or strike it.'

'I am very pleased to meet you, Mr. Price,' Kolinski said, formally. His small bright blue eyes swept swiftly over Craig. He did not smile when he stuck out his hand.

'I am very pleased to meet you, Mr. Kolinski,' Craig said, remembering what Jimmy had said in the hotel room. (For Christ sake, play it straight, Craig. Play it corny-straight. Two business gentlemen doing business together.)

'Mr. Craig Price is an economic royalist.' Jimmy Wilbur said. 'Look at him. The clothes, the Cadillac. When you look at Craig Price you can smell swimming-pool all over him. A two-car man with a red-headed secretary, if I ever saw one.'

Kolinski cocked an eye at Wilbur.

'This one,' he said to Craig, 'make joke all the time. I never know if he is serious or not. You don't look like economic royalist, Mr. Price. Not with them scars and that broken nose. You look more like my friend Wilbur, or me, or one of my people.'

'If that's a compliment, I accept it,' Craig said. 'Most of these scars are not honourable. Some are. I was in a strike in Antwerp. I was an ordinary seaman. Also I was a scab. And I didn't have a card from the International Seamen's Union—which of course you know is no longer with us—when I got one of these scars for being a scab.'

Kolinski nodded at Wilbur.

'You know, maybe I convert him, too. This kid got possibilities. When we strike all the restaurants, maybe he can make the speeches.'

'The restaurants will have to wait,' Jimmy Wilbur said. 'Right now Craig and I want to take you for that little joy-ride in the country that I mentioned the other day. This country has got a lot of potential, Comrade.'

'I know it, Comrade. That's why I'm here. Comrade.' He winked. 'If it didn't have potential we wouldn't bother with it. Comrade.'

'You'll learn to love this bloody-handed Bolshevik,' Jimmy said to Craig. 'He grows on you. Like a cancer, maybe, but he grows on you. And he can drink more whisky than both of us, especially if somebody else is buying. Right, Tovarich?'

'I don't like that. I don't like it very much. Yesterday I bought. You drink one whole bottle all by yourself of what I buy. And not with expense account funds. For that whisky Kolinski paid out of his own pocket.'

'Don't believe him a minute, Craig,' Jimmy Wilbur said. 'This bum is getting rich on what he steals from the union. He's already going around asking quotations on swimming-pools.'

'Your friend is a very funny man, Mr. Price,' Kolinski said. 'He talk a lot, laugh a lot. But between you and me, I would not like to fight him. Somebody get hurt. Maybe even me. That's a compliment, Footballer,' he said to Jimmy Wilbur. 'I ain't so much for compliments.'

'I accept with gracious thanks and I kiss your foot, Madame,' Jimmy Wilbur said. 'Now, Mr. Kolinski, if you will enter the back seat. You too, Mr. Price. I have not as yet had a chance to conduct this superb vehicle, so I will drive and you will point out the sights to Mr. Kolinski as we explore the country of your birth across the river. Mr. Kolinski, as you have already heard, thinks this country has possibilities.'

They drove across the bridge and into the country, over the causeway on which Craig had had the accident. Craig pointed out the tree against which his car had finally come to rest.

'That is very bad, very bad indeed. I am so sorry,' Kolinski said. 'And the baby was born dead, not so?'

'Yes, the baby was born dead,' Craig said shortly.

'A pity. I always want to marry and have babies but I never seem to have time,' Kolinski said. 'This business of mine eats time.'

'I know. This business of mine eats time, too.'

'This a very pretty country,' Kolinski said. 'Plenty room here for more factory, more mill. Plenty water. Good roads. Cheap ground.'

Craig looked around him at the moss-hung oaks, the gnarled cypress knees, the deep bays of glossy green sparkleberry, the smaller pinoaks, the long-leaved pines and the towering gums and hickory. Plenty water. Good roads, Cheap ground. Room for more mills.

'Yes. Very pretty country,' he said.

'Not too much different from Eastern Europe—Poland, Hungary.'

'Not too much different from Pennsylvania,' Jimmy Wilbur said. 'What is a tree? Only a thing with branches. Christ, Kolinski, you got me talking like you do. A tree is only a thing with branches.'

'So is a mill,' Craig said.

'So is a union,' Kolinski said.

'So is a bank. This is awful heavy,' Jimmy Wilbur said. 'Can we lighten it up?'

'Sure,' Craig said. 'Why don't we stop around that next curve? There's a family there I'd like to talk to.'

Jimmy rolled the Cadillac round the curb and slowed down.

'That little road, there,' Craig said. 'To the right.'

Wilbur tortured the Cadillac into the narrow, sandy, rain-runnelled corduroy road.

'Here,' Craig said. 'Toot the horn.'

It was a dismal little shanty of a house, a sagging grey house of clap-boards warped out of shape. The clapboards were warped to show light through the gaps between the planking. The front-porch had drooped at one end and the steps were partially rotted away. The classically lean, mangy, washboard-ribbed hound-dog got up lazily, barked once, and then lay down again in the shade under the porch. Two chinaberry trees stood in the clean-swept white-sanded front yard. To one side was a smaller house. Beyond, on the fringe of the forest, was an upright coffin with a crescent cut in the door, an outhouse, called 'backhouse'. There was a pump-shelf at the back of the main house, and the handle of the pump was rusty. To one side of the house a garden lounged, its cabbage mostly infringed by jimsonweeds and rabbit-tobacco stalks.

Jimmy Wilbur tooted the horn again.

A woman came to the door of the house. She was sallow of complexion. Her hair was skinned back into a tight knot. She wore a shapeless dress of coarse cotton, with a grease-spotted apron hiding the lower part of the dress. The apron was of chequered calico. Her legs were bare, and she wore men's shoes with no laces. Her bleak eyes had retreated into guarded hostility when she saw the Cadillac. Then, when Craig Price stepped out of the car, the hostility vanished.

'Hello, Maria,' Craig said. He pronounced it Mar-eye-ah. 'Remember me? Been a long time.'

She permitted herself a small smile between lips in which snuff filled the lower half.

'As I live an' breathe, it's Craig Price. Little Craig Price. Come back to say hello after all these years.' Her face turned coldly hostile again as she raked the others with her eyes.

'They don't bite, Maria. And they ain't Federal men. Meet two friends of mine. Mr. Wilbur and Mr. Kolinski. Business people. I'm just showing them the county, and I wanted them to meet you. This is Mrs. Rivenbark.'

''Meetcha,' the woman said. Her eyes again had guarded themselves from the strangers. Her red-knotted-knuckled hands disappeared under her apron, where they writhed like live things.

'Where's Corbett? Where's Linwood?'

Her eyes slanted sideways at Jimmy Wilbur and Anton Kolinski. Her voice was very low when she answered.

'Corbett's workin' for the State. Linwood, he's off in the woods. Fishin', mayhap. You know Linwood, Craig. The weed can strangle the garden but when it comes huntin', comes fishin', Linwood he git hisself a sore back that nothin' but a shotgun or a fishin' rod or mayhap a rifle kin make to straighten itself out.'

'Maria, you don't mind me talkin' right out like home folks in front of these people? I can tell you they're friends of mine, even if they are Yankees.'

'Depends.' The voice harshened. 'We ain't much for talkin' around these parts, Craig. You-all like some coffee? I just put on a pot to bile.'

'Why, thank you, Maria. I'm sure the gentlemen would like some coffee. I'd like one thing, if you don't mind. Mr. Kolinski is a foreigner. He comes from Europe. He is very interested in how we live here. He never saw a smokehouse. Could maybe I show him your smokehouse?'

Her eyes darted now, from one to the other, like humming-birds.

'You sure, Craig?'

'I'm sure.'

Her eyes calmed.

'All right. All I need is your word.'

'In that case, tell me why Corbett's working for the State?'

'Cut a man. Cut him real bad.'

'How bad?'

'Died.'

'What did he cut him for, Maria?'

'Nosin'.'

'Around the business?'

'Yes. The still. You know Corbett. He always got a very bad

511

temper. A man got to do what a man got to do. This man too nosy, nosin' round Corbett's business. Corbett cut him.'

'And?'

'Less'n five years. Manslaughter, the judge say. Be good for Corbett. He kin use a rest. His back been devilin' him mightiful, too. He been workin' awful hard since Re-peal. They ain't the call for the good pure stuff like it was, not since these here ABC stores come.'

'That's a pure-T pity about Corbett,' Craig said. 'Now, if you don't mind, I'd like to show these gentlemen the smoke-house. It would be in the same place, wouldn't it, Maria?'

Maria took a hand out from under her apron and hit herself a lick on the leg.

'I declare to Jesus, Craig Price,' she said. 'If you ain't the one. It's still behind that keg of pickled pigsfeet, you know that as well as me. There ain't no call to move social whisky all over the county. That there stuff is for drinkin' with friends. Not for *sellin*'.'

'Thank you, Maria. I will just go show the gentlemen the smokehouse while you fix the coffee. We won't be long.'

'Maybe by that time Linwood will be back,' Maria said. 'Y'all have fun.'

'I do not understand, completely,' Kolinski said. 'Who is Corbett? What does she mean by working for the State? What is all this about the smokehouse?'

'I told you,' Jimmy Wilbur said. 'I told you to be careful in this country. It's got good roads and a lot of water and cheap building sites for factories, but it's got people with faces. I told you. Craig, what would have happened if we'd come here after dark without making some sort of signal so she'd know us?'

'Buckshot in the face. And ask questions later. Shall I satisfy Mr. Kolinski's curiosity?'

'Please,' Kolinski said.

'Well,' Craig said. 'Corbett is her brother-in-law. She's married to his brother, Linwood. Both are bootleggers, although Federal-stamped whisky is legal, Corbett still prefers to make his own. Some stranger came into the county and started prowling around Corbett's liquor distillery. Which would be over yonder about ten miles on a little creek I used to fish in. Far enough so you can't see the smoke from the highway.'

'So a man came interfering with this peasant's way of life?'

'A man came interfering with this peasant's way of life.'

'So?'

'So Corbett killed him. With a knife.'

'So he should hang, he should be electrocuted. There is capital punishment even here.'

'You don't understand. This man was an outsider. He came from outside the county. He worked indirectly for the Federal

512

Government. He was an informer, who gets so much for informing. He was a fink. He was a stranger. He was messin' around in other people's business. They don't like that in these parts. But you got to give the killer some sort of sentence. Manslaughter is the easiest. Out in three years, and in the meantime, Linwood is still making and selling whisky. And the word will be out that it ain't really intelligent to interfere in private enterprise. Not in this county.'

Kolinski's face was momentarily robbed of composure.

'This is barbarism!' he said. 'This is like . . .'

'The old days in the old country?' Jimmy Wilbur asked gently.

'Let's go see the smokehouse,' Craig Price said. 'A smokehouse is a very interesting thing. You can tell a man's life pretty accurately from what you see in a smokehouse.'

'In the horse-race business we call it a track-record,' Jimmy Wilbur said. 'Lead on, McPrice.'

The smokehouse was very cool and very dark. The sands of its floor were intergrained with the salt which had fallen from the carcasses which had been hung over the years. A chemically-minded man might have rendered down a sizeable supply of pure salt by just applying a simple rendering process to the earth which formed the floor. It took a moment for eyes to become accustomed to the gloom. But then certain objects could be seen hanging from steel hooks on the wall. There were sides of bacon. Sausages hung festooned from the ceiling. Kegs and kegs and kegs of things rimmed the walls. And on some hooks there were haunches of meat which were too big to come from sheep, too big to come from goats, too small to come from cattle. Most of the meat was cured.

Two haunches had been recently salted and hung.

Craig touched one gently.

'That's venison, gentlemen,' he said. 'Venison,' he said to Kolinski, 'is deer meat. That was shot not later than a week ago. And this is the month of May. It is against the law to shoot venison in the month of May. Over there'—he gestured—'over there is quite a lot of venison. In this State you are allowed two deer a year. I would guess that what you see represents at least ten deer, after allowing for what the family may have eaten.'

'But that too is against the law,' Kolinski said. 'How they get away with it? Why do not the police . . . ?'

'We don't take very kindly to police on this side of the river,' Craig said. 'Would you like to sample a little of the native culture?'

He walked over to one of the kegs. Behind it, buried in a nest of gunny-sacking, were several half-gallon glass jugs containing an amber liquor.

'Excuse me for drinking first,' Craig said. 'This is how you do it.'

He picked up the jug, unstoppered it, and stuck his thumb through the small handle at the long goose-neck. He balanced the jug across his upper forearm and elbow, and in a swift movement tilted it so that the base of the jug was higher than his raised elbow, while the opened throat of the jug met his mouth. The contents gurgled softly as he drank.

'Whew!' he said. 'Corbett must have put some iron filings in this batch. Here.' He handed the jug to Kolinski. 'Try it. It's home-made corn liquor.'

Kolinski awkwardly got the neck of the jug to his mouth, took a deep draught, and then coughed, spewing the liquid out in a fine spray.

'The idea's not to cough,' Craig said. 'What do you think of it?'

'I go back to old-country potato whisky,' Kolinski said. 'Or else I drink in hotel room with my friend Wilbur. This too much for me.'

'How about you, Jim?' Craig said.

'Oh, no. I been through this before. I go back to the hotel room and drink with my Tovarich, Kolinski.'

They walked out of the dim cool smokehouse into the bright sunny glare of the front yard. A rusty, rattly Model-A Ford came into the yard as they arrived at the porch, where Maria Rivenbark was setting out thick china coffee-cups and an old-fashioned iron-ware percolator.

'There's Linwood now,' she said. 'I best jest get another cup. And maybe fetch the jug from the smokehouse, Craig, if you'd favour me. Linwood do set a heap of store by his noggin offered fast when he come in tired.'

Craig went off to fetch the jug.

He came back to find Linwood Rivenbark staring hostilely at the Cadillac. His cold countryman's face lit briefly when he saw Craig coming with the jug.

'I didn't know whether to light out or not when I seen the car and these furriners,' he said. 'Howdy, Craig. Been a hell of a long time since we . . .' He paused. His face lost light.

'Since we jacklit that deer that night and the law just about caught us. Howdy, Linwood. Like you meet some friends. This here is Jim Wilbur. He's my new partner. This here is Mr. Kolinski. He's in the labour business. He organizes mills for a living.'

Linwood Rivenbark spat in the sand and carefully rubbed the spittle with his boot.

'Pleased to meetcha,' he said, and did not offer his hand. 'I see you remember where we keep the jug, Craig. Let's us have a snort. Maria! Bring some glasses.'

'I already got 'em,' his wife said. She came out on the porch with four jelly-glasses, held two to each hand.

'Here,' she said. 'You want me to pour?'

'Um,' Linwood said, and looked at Kolinski and Wilbur with

514

slitted eyes. They looked back, and saw a man in his late thirties, wearing the uniform of the country, blue denim overalls, blue denim shirt, and stout work boots from the Army and Navy store. He was hatless, and a lank lock of blond hair fell over his forehead. His face was burnt bright red, and little wrinkles cross-hatched his long turkey's neck. When he opened his mouth to spit it was apparent that what teeth he had left were bad. He had a long nose and bat-flanged ears. His hands were square, with stubby fingers and thick, ridged broken nails which would never be clean.

He drank a glass of the corn whisky straight, in a long, smooth gulp, and his Adam's apple worked up and down like a piston as he drank.

'Man, that were a good 'un,' he said. 'You fellers ain't drinkin'?' The question was an accusation.

'Sure,' Craig said. 'We're drinkin'. But not in quite so much a hurry. That stuff has really got a wallop, Linwood. You put some carbolic acid in the mash?'

'Naw.' Linwood permitted himself a small smile. 'But it seem like I remember I maybe did spill a can of lye in it. By accident. It do have considerable force.'

The other men drank in small gulps.

'Anything I can do to help you, Craig? You in any trouble, you come all the way out here to see me?'

'No. No trouble. Just passin' by, and I was tellin' my friends about how good you can shoot. By the way, I was sorry to hear about Corbett.'

'Don't you fret yourself none about Corbett. It ain't the first time he went to work for the State. A jailhouse to Corbett is like a vacation in town. He gits out of doin' any honest work. Anyhow, I guess Maria told you, or you wouldn't of said what you did. That feller didn't have no right to come messin' around, nosin' into what wasn't none of his business nohow.' Linwood spat again. 'Anything I do despise is any kind of people messin' around. They all a bunch of son-of-a-bitches and suck-egg dogs, and me, I'd shoot a suck-egg dog. Not you,' he said to the hound, who looked up. 'You too good a deer-hound to suck a egg.'

'Speakin' of deer,' Craig said. 'How'd you make out last season?'

'The law says I shot two,' Linwood said.

'I know the law says you shot two,' Craig laughed. 'But we already been out to the smokehouse, and my friends here ain't law. How many really?'

Linwood scratched his head.

'Lessee. Bought a whole box of ca'tridges. Got two left. Must be I shot twenty-three. No. I'm wrong. Had to shoot one twice. Twenty-two, I reckon.'

'All bucks?' Craig was teasing.

'Some were. Meat in the skittle don't wear no horns.'

Craig turned to Jimmy Wilbur and Anton Kolinski.

'I was telling how how well my friend Linwood can shoot. I wonder, Linwood, if we could waste one of those other bullets so I could prove my brag about you to my friends.'

'Well, I don't generally like to shoot close to the house.' Linwood paused and looked at Wilbur and Kolinski. 'Unless it's absolutely necessary.' He let the words hang. 'But seein' it's you, Craig, if you want me to shoot, why, I'll be jest obliged to shoot. The rifle's in the car. I'll just go get it.'

He came back from the ramshackle flivver with a long, ancient, single-shot .32 rifle, whose brown barrel had not known bluing for many a year.

'What you want me to shoot at?'

'How about that bird over there?' Craig pointed to a small bird sitting high against the sky in a tree top a hundred yards away.

'Why hell, Craig,' Linwood said. 'That's a oriole. A *songbird*. I wouldn't shoot no *songbird*. How 'bout that lizard on the same tree?'

'What lizard?'

'You mean to say you can't see that lizard? He's mighty nigh as big as a alligator.'

'Can you see a lizard?' Craig turned to Jimmy Wilbur and Anton Kolinski.

'No,' both men said together.

'Well, I can,' Linwood said. 'You want his head off or what?'

'Shoot his head off,' Craig said. 'Not too much neck.'

Linwood threw the gun to shoulder and seemingly, in the same motion, fired. They could hear the bullet *whunk* as it struck the tree-trunk.

'If y'all gentlemen want to walk a hundred yards or so you'll find a still-kickin' lizard with no head at the bottom of that there tree,' Linwood said. 'Me, I aim to sit down here on the porch and have another drink. I'm plumb wore out.'

The men walked across the broom-sedged ground, and Craig counted his steps. Exactly one hundred and thirty paces away, the tree, which was a black-gum, stood. At it's foot the headless body of a little four-inch-long blue lizard wriggled. There was a fresh, raw scar in the tree, where the bullet had hit, with a tiny frill of flesh around it.

Jimmy Wilbur looked first at Craig, and then at Anton Kolinski.

'I don't believe it,' Kolinski said.

'You see it,' Craig said. 'Seein's believin', in these parts.'

They walked back to the house, Craig carrying the headless lizard by the legs.

'You're slippin', Linwood,' he said. 'Look. You hit him a little low in the neck.'

'I guess I'm plain-out gettin' old and shaky in the hand,' Linwood grinned thinly. 'Too much of this here stuff. Have another drink, gents, and then I got to beg your pardon and run off. My business needs a little extra lookin'-after, since Corbett went to work for the State.'

'We'll just have a cup of coffee, thanks,' Craig said. 'We got to go 'long, too. Oh, one thing, Linwood. I know I got quite a few relations of yours workin' in the mill. How many, would you say?'

'Chrise, Craig, I don't hold no head-count on my kinry. Countin' second and third cousins I reckon maybe thirty, forty head. I don't know how they stand it, myself, with all that noise and the rules and hours and all. Drive me crazy, did I do it. But the fambly's pretty friendly. We goes our own ways, but we generally come a-runnin' do one of us holler hurt. You got anything' special in mind, Craig?'

'Well, one day I may have to holler hurt, and while I ain't one of the family, I pretty near feel like one.'

'All you need do is holler. We'll come a-runnin'. I am very glad to make you gentlemen's acquaintance,' Linwood said, very formally. 'Ordinarily we don't truck much with strangers, but seein' as how you come with Craig, why, me and Maria, our front door is always open and they's always somethin' in the jug. You come back more often, you hear, Craig? They's a big ol' buck deer I just been a-savin' for you. Good-bye, sirs.'

'Thank Maria for the coffee,' Craig said. 'Good-bye Linwood.'

They got in the car and drove away, after shaking hands all round.

34

'Hmmmm,' Anton Kolinski said. 'You friend, the bootleg, he shoot very good.'

'Yes, he does,' Craig said. 'They're a funny bunch of people, Mr. Kolinski. They fight inside the family, maybe, and now and then there's a cuttin'-shootin' scrape, but they stand united on one front: they don't like formal law, and they don't care much for strangers. They are very old stock in this county, and they view anything that's new with decided suspicion. I thought—Jimmy told me you were interested in the working people in the State—that you might like to meet Linwood and Corbett. It's a pity Corbett cut a man so bad he died, because Corbett is more fun than Linwood. He don't shoot quite as good, but almost. He cuts better. But in a way I suppose you might call them economic royalists. At least they're in business for themselves, and they don't like intrusion.'

'You got a smart friend,' Kolinski said to Jimmy Wilbur. 'He make a very plain point. What we do next, Mr. Price, you making points today?'

'Well, in a minute I thought we'd stop off at a little coloured farm. I have a personal interest in the family. As a matter of fact, I'm one of the family. That's to say'—Craig smiled—'that's to say I have kind of adopted a member of the family.'

'You got a nigger kid?'

'Careful, Tovarich,' Jimmy Wilbur said. 'Remember what I told you about calling Negroes niggers.'

'I'm sorry. Negro. How it happen you got a Negro child?'

'Because his father was a friend of mine, and a friend of my father. And his father's father was a friend of my grandfather. We're pretty close-knit in the South, at least part of it, Mr. Kolinski. Family's family, black or white.'

Kolinski shook his head.

'I think I do my organizing strictly in the North, from now on. You people down here—you like . . . you like a foreign country. Excuse me. Maybe it is the corn whisky. But I am confuse.'

'Relax, Tovarich,' Jimmy Wilbur said. 'We may even confuse you some more before we get back to civilization.'

A swarm of Negro children, one middle-aged Negro man, and a very old Negro man swarmed out of the clean, white-washed house under the inevitable grove of chinaberry and live-oak trees. The old Negro man had a knotted white beard, and was terribly stooped. He might have been a hundred years old. The eyes were rheumy but acutely intelligent. He hobbled across the white-sanded yard to the car. 'By de good Lawd name, Booker,' he said over his shoulder to the younger Negro man, 'I swears dis little Mistah Craig, done growed up to be a big man. How come you break you nose, scar you face?' he said sternly, as he shook Craig's hand. 'Ain't I raise you no better dan dat? What you grandpa think, he know you been fightin' and woman-runnin' and drinkin', get a face like dat?'

'Uncle Abe, I'm plain honest to God sorry,' Craig said. 'But I had a lot of accidents. Women-runnin' and whisky-drinkin' didn't have nothin' to do with this face.'

'You doesn't tell me no lies, little Mistah Craig Price. I smells whisky on yo' breath right now, jest as plain.'

'Excuse me, Uncle Abe. But I stopped off at the Rivenbark house to see Linwood and he . . .'

The old man's face expressed heavy disapproval.

'You got no call go messin' round wid po white trash like dem people. Dey make whisky, sell whisky. Dat Corbett, he in jail for cuttin' a man dead wif he knife. You's had better raisin' dan dat. You a little younger, I a little younger, I tan yo' hide myself, seein' yo' grandpa ain' there to make you mind yo' manners. Who dese other gentleman?'

'Uncle Abe, I want you to meet some friends. This is Mr. Kolinski, from New York, and Mr. Wilbur, who is going to be working with me from now on. Gentlemen, this is my Uncle Abraham Lincoln Newton, the father of Big Abner Newton, who was the father of my boy Herbert Hoover Lincoln Newton. And this, unless I am real wrong, is Booker T. Washington Newton, who would be—what is it, Book? The second or third son of Big Abner?'

'You wrong, Mistah Craig. I de firs' boy.' The enormous plum-black man smiled as he held out his hand. 'Den come Woodrow. Den come Hardin'. I gets mixed up myself, some time.'

'I should have known better but I kind of forget what order the Presidents come in. Pity Big Abner died without a Franklin D. to his credit.'

'Oh,' the enormous man smiled. 'I is already done fix dat. You, Frankie, you come here, meet Mistah Craig!'

A very black two-year-old with a very runny nose, wearing only a skimpy shirt, edged timidly forward.

'Dis here Franklin Delano Roosevelt Newton,' Booker T. Newton said. 'He de las' of de litter. So far. Makes yo' manners, Frankie.'

'Hi-do,' Franklin D. Roosevelt Newton said, and scuttled away.

'He still a little shy front of white folks,' his father explained. 'He ain't but only two. Just start talk. Don' pay Frankie no mind, gentlemen. Mistah Craig, can I offer you gentlemen a little pappy's best scuppernong wine, col' from de well?'

'You're making a drunkard out of me, Price. You and your friends.' Jimmy Wilbur grinned. 'I'd love a little scuppernong—whatever that is—wine, Mr. Booker T. Newton.'

'Supposin' you jest call me Book, lak Mistah Craig do. "Mistah" don't sit easy on coloured folk. Sound lak dey puttin' on airs, be called *mistah*.'

'Okay, Book,' Jimmy Wilbur said. 'My front name's Jimmy.'

'My first name Anton,' Kolinski said.

'I pleased to make yo' 'quaintance, Mistah Anton. I very glad to know you, Mistah Jimmy. Any friend of Mistah Craig and he family's friends of we's. We's practically raise Mistah Craig from when he ain't no bigger dan little Franklin D. Dat right, Mistah Craig?'

'That's sure right. You reckon Uncle Abe gonna let us have a snort of that scuppernong?'

The old man sniffed disdainfully.

'I never touches it, mahself,' he said. 'But de young folks . . .' He shrugged. 'I has a thing to say to you, Mistah Craig. It true you done took little Hoover to raise? It true you say he yo' boy, live in same house an' all, like Hardin' tell me las' time he come call? Dat true?'

'Yes, sir, Uncle Abe,' Craig said. 'True as I stand here. Little Herbert Hoover Newton is my boy. He's going to school, and he figures to amount to something. At least that's what he tells me.'

'You watch that young'un careful,' the old man said. 'He bad and need a switch. I don't mean he real bad inside, but he full of high sperrit, need a switch calm he down, yeddy? Spare de rod an' spile de chile, de Good Book say. Don' spare no rod on dat chile, Mistah Craig. It don't help no chillun spare de rod. I take a stick Big Abner, God rest he soul, when he twenty-one year old and three times big as Booker T. He whimper lak a chile when I lay on dat stick. He honour he father and he mother. I only wish he days been longer in de lan.' I guess I goes away now so you young people take a drink widout ol' man spoil yo' pleasure. I bids you good-day, Mistah Craig. And you, suh. You suh,' as he bowed to Jimmy Wilbur and Anton Kolinski. 'I is a little tired.'

Big Abner's Number One boy, Booker T., went to the open well and drew up a large jug containing the whitegrape scuppernong wine. He yelled at one of the children to fetch glasses from the kitchen, and the men stood around the well, in the shade of the chinaberry tree, and drank the cool, tart-sweetish wine.

'How old is your grandpa?' Craig asked Booker T.

'I doesn't rightly know, Mistah Craig. He be powerful old, though. Pappy sixty some when he die, and Pappy not Grandpa first youngun. Grandpa mus' is had thirty, forty youngun', countin' de woods colts. Grandpa talk powerful pious 'bout drinkin' and sich, because he ol' and reckon to die pretty soon. But I hear me some tales, some tall tales, 'bout Grandpa when he young feller. Dey say wasn't a black gal safe from here to Seaside, dis side de River, here to New Bern, t'other side de River. All I know is I got cousins, second, third, and fo'th, dat I never seen. Grandpa, he a old ram in he day.'

Craig looked at Kolinski for a moment, who seemed frankly fascinated at the wild-life around him, children tumbled together with dogs, cats, chickens and one goat.

'Tell me, Book,' Craig said. 'Offhand, just, how many brothers, half brothers, step brothers, cousins, uncles and newphews do you think you might have? Just a rough guess.'

Booker T. Washington Newton scratched his head for a moment.

'Pappy done wore out four wives wid chillun. I don' know how many Grandpa wore out, but I reckon five or six. I don' know how many woods colts Pappy an' Grandpa account for between 'em. But I reckon if I sen' out hurry-up call for big fish-fry in de Newton fam'ly, I might get many as three-four hundred close kin come say: "Where de fish? Where de watermelon? Where de corn whisky and scuppernong wine?" We's a powerful big tribe, Mistah Craig.'

'Yeah,' Craig said, looking at Kolinski. 'We're a big family, all right. Well thanks, Book, we better get moving. I got to go down to New Truro and I want to stop off at the turpentine camp. You take care of yourself, hear?'

'Yessuh, Mistah Craig,' Booker T. Washington Newton lowered his voice. 'I wants to tell you one thing. We all powerful proud of how good you do, and we powerful proud you take little Hoov come live wid you like he yo' real boy. Evvy nigger dis side de River know 'bout how you take little Hoov come live wid you. You wants anything dis side de River, all you's got to do is holler. A mess of niggers come a-runnin', do yo' bid.'

'Well,' Craig said, watching Kolinski. 'There might be a time when I'll need all the family folks.' He smiled 'But not right soon, I hope. Not all at once. Kensington ain't big enough to hold them. So long, Book. I'll look after Herbert Hoover Lincoln Newton, and you look after the scuppernong grape crop and also your grandpa. Thanks.'

'We thanks you, Mistah Craig. I bids you good-bye, gentlemens,' Booker T. Washington Newton said, and bowed formally with ancient savage grace.

35

'How do you like my country, Mr. Kolinski?' Craig asked as they drove through the low ground along the River Road, heading towards New Truro. They had stopped briefly at the old plantation, which was now open for public inspection at a small fee. Kolinski was usually able to keep his face impassive. But when he saw the stately, fluted columns of Eden, its white-pillared magnificence, the acres of fallow rice-land sweeping towards the river, the forests of blooming magnolia and acres of exuberant azalea, he was unable to repress an emotion foreign to his ordinary manner.

'Even the children's playhouse is bigger than a *dacha*,' Kolinski said. 'I never see nothing like this before. Maybe not even the Czars had places like this. What kind of people own a place like this? Who own a place like this?'

'A man like me, but possibly a hundred years earlier,' Craig said. 'They built it with cotton. Cotton and ships to carry the cotton all over the country—to take it North for the mills you organize. To take it to England. To sell it to me, or somebody like me, who would take the cotton crop and convert it into clothes.'

'But how you farm cotton on these many acre? Need anyhow a thousand people.'

'Slaves. That old gentleman you met, old Uncle Abe, his father was born in Africa. He's a Kru, from the West Coast of Africa. Pure Kru. With a conjure bag full of leopard floating-bones and a whole lot of charms I don't know about, still around his neck. Old Uncle Abe is still a wild African, in a way. So was my mammy.'

'Your who?'

'My mammy. She was born a slave. Who raised me. Except she wasn't Kru. She was an Ebo.'

'You pretty young, Mr. Price. How you can have a mammy who was born a slave?'

'My mammy was about eighty-five when I was born. Her husband was ninety. They had both been slaves. He was Swahili from Zanzibar—part Manyema, that's a Congo cannibal—and part Arab. He was very proud of his bloodlines. He said he fetched the biggest price ever recorded in a single slave deal. He was pretty proud of that, too.'

'How you know all this? About bloodlines with slave Negroes.'

'I know it because they told me,' Craig said simply.

Kolinski was silent a moment. Then he spoke softly as to himself.

'Is very wrong for one man, one family, to own a place this big. It wrong to make slaves do the work, so one man can be so rich. Is wrong. I don't like it. Is *wrong*.'

'Well, if it'll comfort you any, the people who used to own Eden are broke, have been broke ever since the Civil War. This place belongs to the State.'

'Oh, in that case, is a little different,' Kolinski said. Is all right for the State have a place like this. So long as everybody can share. Okay.'

'But,' Craig said maliciously, 'this place is maintained by convict labour. The chain-gangs, the criminals, keep the place up. Look after the flowers and all that.'

'You could call this a warm Siberia with azaleas and magnolias,' Jimmy Wilbur said to Craig. 'Kolinski's just sore because he wasn't around to organize the slaves. And not even as good an organizer as my Tovarich here can organize a chain-gang. They ain't got any union possibilities whatsoever. The State organizes them.'

'You make some more joke again,' Kolinski said. 'You always make joke.'

'I don't make joke at all,' Jimmy Wilbur said. 'You better be careful, Kolinski, in the deep South. In Georgia they'll put you on the gangs for just being a Yankee with no visible means of support. Am I kidding, Craig?'

'You ain't kidding, Moose. They slap you in the gang for just doing nothing in Georgia.'

'What a country,' Kolinski said. 'Here is a paradise. Its name is Eden. It got built off the whipped backs of slaves and now the State takes it and keeps the flowers growing with convict labour. This is economic royalism?'

'No,' Jimmy Wilbur replied. 'This is unionism.'

'I think I don't hear that last joke your friend make,' Kolinski said to Craig. 'This, for me, the maybe most interesting day, apart from pogroms and a few labour fights and, of course, seeing Statue of Liberty the first time, this the most interesting day I ever spend. What we see next, Mr. Millman?'

'Well, if the chauffeur will turn right at the next crossing, I thought we'd go into the higher country where the big pines grow and show you some more local culture. A turpentine camp.'

'And a turpentine camp is?' Anton Kolinski shook his head as if to clear it.

'A bunch of thugs, mostly, who can't get steady work anywhere else. You don't have to have any references to work in a turps camp. They don't care if you were in jail last week or not.'

'It's like running a union,' Jimmy Wilbur said cheerfully. 'They don't care if you were in jail last week or not. In a way it's a recommendation.'

'Shut up,' Craig said. 'You're very funny today, and I am trying to be serious with Mr. Kolinski.'

'You don't think you could maybe call me Anton? I am like the nig—the Negro. Mister in front of my name makes me nervous.' Kolinski hunched his shoulders and spread his hands quivering.

'All right, Anton. We're coming into the turpentine country now. Slow down, Jim. See that tree, Anton?'

It was an enormous pine, with its sap clotted in grape-sized clusters in a deep scar on the trunk, a scar which bled its waxy clotting into a tin receptacle.

'Yes. Somebody dig a hole in it.'

'That's right. You cut a hole in it and it very slowly bleeds its sap into the little bucket under the hole.'

'Like a rubber tree, eh?'

'That's exactly right. But you can't girdle it to bleed the sap out. If you cut the bark all around the tree will die.'

'I cannot repress this one,' Jimmy Wilbur said. 'Try as hard as I may. The case has too much in point if you are a union man like Kolinski and me. It's all right to steal the sap if you don't kill the tree. How do you like that one, Comrade? Steal its blood, but don't kill it.'

Kolinski laughed, shortly, harshly.

'I think I heard that, Comrade Wilbur. With that you make sense. No sense killing the tree if you can bleed it of its wealth and still let it live to produce more wealth.'

'All right, Price,' Kolinski said. 'What else you got to show me to complete my education?'

'I thought I might take you down to my old home town, New Truro, and let you see the shrimp-boats and the pogy-boats— pogy is menhaden, a fertilizer fish—come in. And I thought maybe you'd like to go to a convict camp and I could get the Cap'n there to put on a show for you. You know, happy niggers playing the banjo or maybe a bare-knuckled fist-fight. I thought you would be interested in the fishermen because they are all very big. You have to be very strong to haul a purse-seine. And the convicts are interesting because they can be leased for private projects. Also they are very happy if you feed 'em enough sowbelly and cornbread and greens. Swinging that sledge on the railroad line, or working on those roads makes a man mighty peckish—hungry, I mean. And they don't really have much fun on account of no women and no whisky. That's why they have the bare-knuckled fist-fights. To amuse themselves. And of course, the Cap'n don't mind too much if somebody gets hurt.'

Anton Kolinski sagged back into the Cadillac's soft upholstery.

'Okay,' he said. 'So okay. I get the message. You don't have to show me nothing else today. Not no fish-boats, not no turpentine camp, not no shrimp-boats, not no happy convicts dancing and singing and fighting for fun. I get the message. You fight, huh?'

'Why not? I got you outnumbered. I got you outnumbered with a kind of people you never ran into before. I got you outnumbered with people that aren't fighting for pay. You got a lot of your own people in town, all strangers, Kolinski. I got a lot of people out of town, and quite a few of my own in town and they ain't strangers. You break a head, I break five. You threaten one of my people, I'll have somebody pull the head off the threatener, and *eat it raw*. And throw up what he don't like in *your* face. Also the State police and the National Guard don't like you people, any more than I do.'

'The State Police. The National Guard. I heard that before.'

'But something you haven't heard before is a hundred Linwood Rivenbarks with single-shot rifles, four hundred big Negroes who are personal friends of my family, two or three hundred people like that Cap Goodman from the turps camp will send to work for me. You haven't run into the shrimp-boat fleet and the pogy-boat fleet yet. These boys know some things, and very few rules. I know you don't care about your goons. I care about mine and they care about me. And it's only fair to tell you, Kolinski, I can run a factory on a few guys I got stashed away who not only know how to run a factory, but know how to bust a head, as well. You want to talk some business now or you want to check with New York?'

'I know I ain't supposed to be listening, because I am only the chauffeur,' Jimmy Wilbur said from the front seat. 'But we got to talk about it sometimes, and now seems as good a time as any. Ain't neither one of you guys going to win if you fight. You might both win if you don't fight.'

Simultaneously, both Craig and Kolinski reached out and patted Jimmy Wilbur on his shoulders.

'Shucks,' Jimmy said. 'Next thing you know you'll be sending me flowers, and I never could go steady with *two* fellers at once.'

36

'YOUR mill ain't worth a war, Price,' Kolinski said.

'You're a liar, Kolinski,' Craig said, coldly. 'It's worth a war or you wouldn't be here.'

'Maybe I say it bad. Wrong. What I mean it ain't worth a war for us both to lose. You go out of business and me . . .' He shrugged. 'Maybe I go out of business too. Too many busted heads, they get in front of principles. My principle is to organize you. What is your principle?'

'To let you organize me without hurting me too much. Like a turpentine-bearing pine, I ain't no good to you dead. Right?'

'I agree. Dead you don't help me, the Party, or the union. Right. That we understand.'

Craig nodded.

'That we understand. Do we understand that, Vice-President?'

'I ain't listening,' Jimmy Wilbur said. 'I'm only the chauffeur. But if I was listening I would say I understand it. Right.'

'You want to talk now?' Craig asked Kolinski.

'No. You the mill boss, I just the union boss. You talk first. I tell you yes and no.'

'Right. You got your town filled up with so-called textile workers. I call them thugs. I call them goons. I call them phony workers. I call them a bunch of bastards who'll never work in this town once a deal is made with my mill. Mills, I should say.'

'You talk strong.'

'Please, for once, no crap.'

'Okay, so no crap. Not if you admit that you just show me a bunch of thugs, goons, phony workers. As a lesson in how to fight a strike. Or to conduct one. Okay?'

'Right. I admit that I can top you in spades, and it'll be a very interesting war. But it'll break me, because if we fight I don't quit. Not if I have to kill you personally with my own hands. Would you believe that, Kolinski?'

'You have the face for killing. I would believe it. Yes. I don't think you stop, once you start.'

'All right. We establish the fact that I can beat the strike and lose my mill while I beat the strike. What happens to you?'

'You want a frank opinion, I don't look so good back in New York and Michigan and Pennsylvania if some young country boy beat me here. That is a frank opinion. We talk frank in this car?'

'I'm glad I'm out of this,' Jimmy Wilbur muttered. 'I been an athlete so long I don't know how to talk frank. Even in a Cadillac.'

'Shut up, Footballer,' Kolinski said. 'We talk business now. No jokes.'

'Yes, boss,' Jimmy said. 'Who am I talking to that I call boss? You or Craig?'

'Shut up and we'll find out in a minute,' Craig said. 'Both of us are gaining on each other.' He turned to Kolinski, and offered a pack of cigarettes. 'Smoke?'

'Thank you.'

'Now,' Craig said, 'suppose you tell me exactly what you want, and then tell me what you'll settle for.'

'You talk very tough, you know, for a young man,' Kolinski said. 'You sound a little like me when I was a young man.'

'I raised him tough,' Jimmy Wilbur said from the front seat. 'He's a credit to his raisin'. God, how Southern I've got in just a couple weeks.'

'Shut up,' Craig and Kolinski said simultaneously, and then grinned at each other.

'I want the usual, Price,' Kolinski said. 'The usual points. You know them, but I count them off. One, I want more money. Two, I want closed shop. Three, I want a check-off for the dues. I want ten paid holidays. I want a lot of the usual crap about insurance and sick benefits. Forty-hour week, natural. Time and a half for overtime, natural. No fights with the union. A waste of time to fight with the union. Seniority, natural. All the usual.'

'I ain't going to collect your dues for you, that's damn sure,' Craig said. 'You can scratch that check-off clause right now. I might close the shop in the back, but I'll be good and goddamned if I'll close it in the front. I personally wouldn't be caught dead belonging to your union. Nor, I think, would our mutual friend, Mr. Wilbur—who, I must say, drives the car very well. Nor any of my personal people. Managerial staff, if you want to call it that.'

'He does drive well,' Kolinski grinned. 'If I ever organize chauffeurs Comrade Wilbur will be the head of the union.'

'We disagree on what, then?' Craig said. 'I won't give you any more money right now. I just gave the people a straight five-cents-an-hour-across-the-board raise. You can claim credit for it, if you want to. I've already got sick benefits and retirement plans and I don't mind Columbus Day or something like that as an extra holiday. I think they got five now. I'll give eight. Forty-hour week, I can't beat it. I don't mind time and a half for overtime, because the way I'm going to run my mills . . . well. Time and a half for overtime is good enough for me. You can take credit for all of that.'

'So what we argue? Check-off, and maintain good business friendship with the union? Why not check-off? Save everybody a lot of trouble.'

'I got a moral or so kicking around in my soul,' Craig said. 'I will *not* do your work for you. If these goddam workers want a union they can have one, but getting them to pay for the privilege is your business. It sure as hell ain't mine. And if they're stupid enough to want to run a closed shop out back, then that's their problem. But up front where the quality folks work, we don't even look at a union. You come in this plant, Kolinski, you come in the gate. Past the guard. You come in the back door, like the help you organize. Nothing in the front office. You stand in the back door with your hat in your hand.'

Kolinski held up a soothing palm.

'So. So. So don't get excited. I'll come in the back door, you're so proud your front door. I'll hold my hat in my hand. But look, Price, it occur to you that maybe if you have the check-off, collect the dues for us, you got less future union trouble when time come for renegotiate contract? This maybe sound like a bribe, or a threat, but it ain't. It's common sense. Once you organized and the dues come regular we say ourselves, Kolinski, don't worry about Local XYZ in Kensington. Let it ride. Go organize something else, somewhere else, another State, because this one all signed, sealed, delivered. That good business, because I know right now you going to ask me a big one which I supposed to say no to, but maybe won't if you see some reason on my side. Give me the big one, and I tell you.'

Craig drew a deep breath.

'Okay. Here's your big one. I want six months before I sign your contract. Once I sign that contract I'm saddled with everybody on the payroll, if we include seniority to prevail, retirement benefits, severance pay, the rest. Half of my people are products of the old days. Semi-skilled at best. Old cotton mill-hands, and tomorrow is a new day in the textile industry and you know it. You sign up all these bums and old people I got now and I'm crippled for life. I—the mill—can't stand that much of a deadwood load. Not unionized, with job security.'

'So?'

'I want six months. I want to unload the deadwood before I get unionized. I want new machines. Depending on you, I will buy another mill, and after that, other mills, all of which you will want to organize. So it boils down to this, Kolinski. Do you want an easy organization of all the Price Mills that will come, or do you want to fight a war we both lose? You ain't got but one answer.'

'I got an answer. But I also got a price, Price. What you ask me is against every decent principle any union ever fought for. You know that?'

'I know that. If we are speaking of decent unions. Not organized rackets, Communist-fronts, hired thugs. But you are a racketeer, Kolinski. Your union is a racket. I don't mind a racket.

527

I'm a racketeer myself. I'm talking like one thief to another. You understand that?'

'I understand it. So you want me to hold off signing until you can kick the old and the weak and the stupid out into the street, and put in younger, smarter people, and more and bigger and better machines? That is what you want me to agree to.' It was not a question.

'That is what I want you to agree to. If you don't, there'll be a dump-truck load of your imported so-called workers delivered daily in front of your hotel, and some of them might even be alive. And my mill will fold and your personal tit will be in a very tight crack.'

'You reduce your personnel. We are getting less dues from fewer people. It costs money to run a union. Money is from dues.'

'Ah, yes, Kolinski. But you are getting another mill right away, a mill you didn't even know I had up my sleeve. Two mills organized by Kolinski bring more dues than one mill organized by Kolinski. And if I have two, I will have ten. Ten mills organized by Kolinski, setting the pattern for unionization in this part of the South, is a big feather in the Kolinski cap. Twenty mills. Maybe a hundred mills, who knows?'

'You got a point. But now we come to my price.'

'Let's have your price.' Craig smiled. 'It's a nice word, price. I even took it for a name. I figured as a little kid that every man had one. Let's have yours.'

'I read in books how in the old days in this country not only the Indians brought home scalps. I got to go back with some scalps if I make this deal. One, I got to have more money for less people.'

'That's reasonable. So you get a two-cent-an-hour across-the-board raise. That'll make seven cents you can brag about. That's a good raise.'

'I agree,' Kolinski said. 'But you know something? I got some pride myself. I need some real scalps, not just some money scalps. If I am organizing your mill—mills—these people got to trust me. They got to know that Kolinski is a man of principle. They got to know that Kolinski looks after his workers, and that Kolinski is a hero, while the stinking boss is a bastard. You understand that?'

'I understand it. Yes. You got a point. If I wasn't the villain and you weren't the hero they wouldn't let you organize them. They wouldn't vote for a union. They'd actually be too smart to work in a mill.'

'You a smart young man to see it so clear, so black-white. Okay. We hang this strike on four words—"company pimp, company whore". Just four little words. We hang this strike on an old man named Marvin McCracken. We get the workers to thinking nobody got a safe job if the son-of-a-bitch-boss put his eye on a new woman. We say look, the boss, first he marry the mill. Now he got the mill. Then he want a new woman. So he fire an old man, a good man, to give job to woman's brother. This way he buy the woman. Keep in office. Make love in fancy new office. Who's next? Maybe the boss meet somebody else with pretty sister? Who can say who can be safe in non-union shop if the boss's eye hits on another pretty woman?'

'It's one way of looking at it,' Craig said. 'A cheap way of going about your life's work, the betterment of the worker.'

'Look, don't kid with me,' Kolinski said. 'Jokes our friend Wilbur makes. You and me don't make jokes. There ain't nothing any cheaper than people. You got to have a cheap angle. An old man fired, a young man hired, an old woman fired, a young woman hired, and all add up to one thing: You people need union. You been stepped on too long. So it's cheap. So is bread cheap. So is sex. It's free, sex, unless you buy it on the street or in a hotel room. Or marry it. Or hire it as a secretary.'

(Six gags I could make right now, Jimmy Wilbur thought as he drove the car. At least six good ones. But this is not the time for it. I am all alone in the wilds of North Carolina with two business men who see eye-to-eye on the nobility of mankind.)

'And so now that you got your so-called company pimp, so-called company whore, and your built-in martyr, what?' Craig kept his voice low, and very terse.

'You know what, young feller. You want me to lay off organization for six months until you ready to absorb it. You want me to lay off organization so you can kick out the bums and cut off the deadwood. You compromise my morals and yours, with that one. You know *what*, Mr. Millman. You sure do know *what*.'

'I think so,' Craig said. 'But I'm going to make you say it, Mr. Unionman. Say it.'

'I say it. So you fire a hundred, two hundred people. Okay. All I ask, to make me look good, is you fire a hundred and two, if it's a hundred, and two hundred and two, if it's two hundred. And hire one. You do that, you got your six months. You got your new mill. You got your new personnel and time to retool to cut down on people. All I ask now is the dues check-off, the closed shop, the other usual stuff, and that you fire two people and hire one.'

Craig sighed.

'All right,' he said. 'You got a deal. Red and Elizabeth Forney get fired, and Marvin McCracken gets re-hired.'

'You said it, kid. You said it exactly right. Red and Elizabeth Forney get fired, so long as you're conducting a purge anyhow. And old McCracken gets re-hired. And back in New York, Anton Kolinski looks good. And no strike. No war. And more mills to organize. Without the Forney man, without the Forney girl. That is my price, Price.'

'Okay,' Craig said. 'You got a deal. Step it on, Jimmy. I want to go home and take a shower. I don't like the smell in this car.'

'Were you referring to anyone in particular?' Jimmy Wilbur said, and the motor's hum rose to a roar as he took the next curve with a scream of tyres.

37

LIBBY had never been lovelier. It hurt Craig to look at her as she sat close by his side in the car on their way to the Forney house. She smelled like spring, and looked like a young Diana glowing with the secret wisdom of enjoyed love. Even with her clothes on, Craig saw her naked and abandoned to the afternoons they had spent making love together.

'It's so wonderful about the new mill, Craig,' she said. 'Red'll be as pleased as Punch. Not even to mention me, I think it's just wonderful. And I just love Jimmy Wilbur. He's so smart and so funny, too. He'll be grand to work with.'

'Uh-huh,' Craig said. He devoted undue attention to driving the car.

'And no more trouble with the union, they say out back in the shop. You're going to organize, and there won't be any more— there won't be any more *signs*—any more anything painted on our house.'

'Uh-huh.'

'You don't seem very happy, Craig. I'd think you'd be bubbling.'

'I got a lot of things on my mind. Money and contracts and banks and things on my mind. Let's don't talk until we get home and see Red, huh?'

'All right. If you don't want to.' Libby slid over to a far corner of the front seat.

I'll say I've got a lot of things on my mind, Craig thought. How do you go about firing people who love you? People who trust you? It was rough enough with Miss Mildred and Old Man McCracken. And I never really knew them. But this beautiful girl was in bed with me just a few days ago. This beautiful girl loves me. 'I love you, Craig,' she had said. 'I'll always love you, Craig,' she had said. 'I never thought that love was like this, Craig,' she had said. That's what she said. Beautiful and wholly loving, naked in a bed. That's what she said. I love you, Craig.

I didn't know about Miss Mildred or Old Man McCracken. But I know every inch of this girl's body, which she gave me so sweetly, so happily freely. I know her mind. I even know the calendar of her periods. I know the insides of her ice-box in her brother's house. Where she puts the butter, I know that. Where she keeps the breadknife, I know that. I am not firing a stranger

530

here. I am cutting off a part of me that I know as well as me. And I know me, too, he thought, almost with sobbing humour. What's the corny phrase? Moral leper. Lonesome Craig Price. Prominent young moral leper. That's me right down to the ground.

And her brother. That I fought with. That I fished with. That I drank home-brew with. Who trusted me. Who literally gave me his sister while he hated every aspect of the idea of giving me his sister. Big Red Forney, who finally made it all the way up top from a standing start from the overalls and the sidemeat. Foreman of the spinning room with his own house and his inside toilets and his own car. A house that got painted red with '*company pimp, company whore*'. I wonder what I'd paint on Maybelle's house? If I was describing me? Certainly pimp. Certainly whore And some other words as well. Craig shrugged.

Well. Corbett cut a man, and the man died. Maria said a man got to do what a man got to do. I got to do what I got to do.

'Well,' he said brightly, falsely. 'Here we are. I don't have much time. I want to talk to you and Red about a few things and then I got to run.'

'It's nice to get home. I never get tired of coming back here at the end of the day,' Libby said. 'It's a new thrill every time when I think it's actually ours. Ours and the Building-and-Loan, of course.' She smiled.

Red met them at the door.

'Congratulations,' he said. 'I suppose you know all the union guys have left town. You and Mr. Wilbur must have made a real good deal with that Kolinski. And look. I repainted the house and there ain't no sign of them . . . *Words*. Let's have a drink, Craig, to celebrate the new mill. I hear you signed the papers today on that. By God, boy, you come a far piece in a short time.' Red placed an affectionate freckled hand on Craig's shoulder.

'Thanks, Red. I don't think I want a drink.' Craig took a deep breath. Now, he thought, do it now, and get it over with, and if Red hits me in the chin I'll be very very happy. I won't hit back. Like Phil was when I smacked him that time in Charleston. I'll sit right down there on the floor and bleed.

'Red and Libby.' Craig was standing.

'I made a deal with the union. I got to fire a lot of people to live with the union. I can't afford to carry all the old personnel if we're going union, if we're getting the new mill, if we're going into big business with the new stuff. The deal was that they'd give me six months to get rid of the excess baggage before they stuck me with the usual terms.'

'You goin' to lay off a lot of people, old workin' people, then, before you sign up with the union?' Red's eyes narrowed.

'I'm going to lay off a lot of old working people before I sign up

531

with the union. It's either that or fight the strike and then every-body gets laid off. And no new mill.'

'It ain't right, Craig, you know it ain't right,' Red said. 'Not all them old hands dating way back to Mr. Grimes.'

'I know it ain't right. But I got to do it or lose a . . .' Craig started to say *fortune*, then changed it to *dream*, and finally said '*Chance*'.

'Chance for what?' Libby spoke now.

'To be big. On my own time.' Craig then spoke very swiftly. 'And there's another condition. The union organizer made it. He hung the whole strike idea around *your* necks. One of his conditions is that Marvin McCracken gets hired back and you . . .'

'You don't have to go no further, Price,' Red Forney said. 'I got it. Don't bother to explain it. It was nice knowin' you for while it lasted.'

'Believe me,' Craig said, pleadingly, 'I was in a corner. There wasn't anything else I could do. There'll be a job for you both a little later, when I expand some more, but right now, I . . . Look, I'll keep you both on my private payroll until . . .'

'Good-bye, Craig,' Libby said. She would weep later, but her eyes now were very cold.

'I ain't sayin' good-bye,' Red Forney said. 'You know where McCracken said you could shove your mill when you fired him? I ain't gonna repeat it, but I'm sayin' the same thing. You can take your private payroll and shove it. So long, Craig Price.' He nodded at the door. 'Don't ever bother to come back.'

'You heard what my brother said,' Libby Forney said. 'Don't come back. Ever.'

Brother and sister looked at each other, but not at Craig Price, as he left, alone.

'You can cry now, Sis, now the bastard's gone,' Red Forney said. 'I want you to know I was real proud of you. A lot of women would have made a big fuss. I was real proud the way you took it when he dumped us. Like a man.'

'I don't feel like a man,' Libby said. 'You took it like a man, I just feel like a left woman. Oh, Red. How could he, how could he . . .?' She went over and wept briefly on his shoulder. He patted her back awkwardly, soothing, and eventually the sobs that shook her body ceased.

'I'm sorry,' she said. 'I'm a real mess. Let me go fix my face in the bathroom.'

'I'll make us a drink while you're fixin' your face,' Red said. His voice rasped. 'We'll drink to Price Mills, Inc. and the new union contract.'

'Don't,' she said. 'Please don't I reckon he's hurt too, Red. Worse than us. I won't be a minute. But make mine stiff, please.'

'You know,' Red Forney said, 'we could both of us still hang on to his wagon. If you want to. If you love the bastard enough to want to, I might manage to strangle my feelin's and take that offer of another job in another State. If it would make you happy, I'll do it. But me, personal, I'd rather starve or beg.'

'You told him what old Mr. McCracken said, Red. You told him to take his mills and stick them up his ass. As far as I'm concerned, I'm telling him the same thing. And that goes for his love, too. If that's what it was. Love. It's a dirty word. It's a dirtier word than ass, that you didn't say but I did. I don't think I want to hear any more about love, or do any more about love, for a very long time. Here's to Price Mills, Inc.,' she said, and lifted her glass. Then she threw the glass against the wall and rushed off to her own room.

Red heard the door slam.

'I tried to tell her,' he said miserably aloud. 'I tried to tell her. I reckon it don't do no good to try to tell a woman nothin'. But nobody kin say I didn't try.'

Red Forney went back to the kitchen and got out the silver tea-and-coffee-set that Craig had given them as a house-warming present. He carried them to the little woodshed in back of the house. He took an axe off its bracket on the wall, and carefully, meticulously hammered the silver set into misshapen lumps, using the flat of the axe. Then he picked up the battered silver lumps and took them one by one, and cast them in the weed-grown side yard where the garbage can and the rubbish heap were. Then he went back into the house and poured himself another drink.

'They ain't no use me tryin' to ask her how she feels,' he said again aloud. 'They ain't no use me askin' her what she's gonna do or where she's gonna go. But I'll get work somewhere, and maybe she might go to college after all. She kin always work part-time as a secretary,' and when he said the word, *secretary*, he spat on the carpet.

I'm glad, I'm glad, I'm glad I didn't tell him when it happened, Libby thought as she wept into the pillow. I'm glad I went to Kinston and had it fixed. At least I didn't bother him with it when he was having all the other troubles. It wasn't very far along anyhow. I don't even suppose you could have called it a baby, except it was the first one I would have had. But at least he didn't have to fire the baby, too. Poor Craig. And most of it not his fault. Most of it mine and Red's and the world and just life. Poor Craig.

Libby got up and washed her face and put on a lot of lipstick. She went into the living-room where her brother was staring morosely into his drink.

She ran her hand over his bristly carrot thatch.

'I'll cook us some supper, now,' she said. 'And then we better sit down and have a real serious talk about what we're going to do. Maybe Greensboro, and I could go to school and work at the same time. Something like that.'

Red Forney looked up at his sister and took her by the hand.

'I thought I was tough,' he said, and his eyes moistened. 'I ain't tough. Yeah. We'll go to Greensboro or some place like that and we'll both get jobs and you go to school. Get away from here. And Sis?'

'Yes, Red?' Libby was moving off to the kitchen.

'If you don't mind, we won't have no coffee tonight.'

'I don't mind. I've kind of lost my taste for coffee lately. We'll settle for a glass of milk.'

She returned swiftly, bent down, and kissed the top of his head.

'Don't you worry about us, Brother Red,' she said. 'Us, we'll just be fine.'

That night Maybelle was very happy.

'It's not so much that you've settled the strike and got your new mill too,' she said. 'But I got a wonderful surprise. Unless the signs are all wrong we're goin' to have another baby.'

Craig poured himself a full glass of whisky and knocked it off neat, before he spoke. His face became a trifle less grey.

'Here's to the new mill and the new baby,' he said. 'We'll make a Yankee out of this one. Maybelle, pretty soon we're moving North to New York. I can come down here for one week a month, and Jimmy Wilbur will run it when I'm gone. He runs things real good, Jimmy does. Where's Jazzbo?'

'In the kitchen. Craig, this is awful sudden. You sure...?'

'I'm sure. Call Jazzbo.'

Maybelle got up and went to the kitchen and returned with the little boy.

'Jazz,' Craig said. 'You gonna be a Yankee. How'd you like to be a Yankee? Because we're movin' North.'

'Pappy say dat come to pass,' Jazzbo's eyes widened in delight. 'We goin' as far North as Richmond?'

Craig patted the little boy on the head.

'Yes,' he said gently. 'As far North as Richmond, and maybe a little further.'

Maybelle looked at him with a sudden pitying and rare understanding.

'I better fix you another toddy,' she said quietly. 'You look like you had a real hard day.'

'Yes, honey,' Craig said, closing his eyes as he sank into old John Grimes's favourite chair. 'Yes. I had a hard day. A real hard day.'

BOOK FOUR

1

CRAIG and Sue lay sweating in the sun, underneath the wind-creaking palms, snugged into the sugar-sand, while the opalescent waters murmured gently as they lipped the land. One of the sailor-suited waiters ran down from the central club, the Kawama, with a sheaf of letters.

'*Perdóneme, Señor Precio.*' This was joke, the translation of 'Price'. '*La correspondencia.*'

'*Gracias, Carlos.*' Craig turned over and stuck out a sandy hand. Oh yes. Excuse me, sweetie.'

'What have you got there?' Sue rolled over and sat up. 'Love letters in the sand, if I can make a terrible joke?'

'It's not such a bad joke at that. They're drilling reports. Let's see how we're doing—let's see if that oil-bearing sand is sending us any love letters . . . Hmmm. Hmmmm . . . hmmm.' He flicked the small pages. 'Mmmhmmh.'

'That's a wonderful one-way language you got there, boy. What does the message from Ghent to Aix really say?'

'Look at one.' He tossed her a page. 'Freely translated, that could mean either mink or sackcloth. Depending.'

She looked at the page, which seemed to be meaningless gibberish.

'What's "frac"?'

'Fracture hard-producing formation by hard-pumping pressure.'

'What's "perf"?'

'Perforate pipe to let oil and gas in.'

'NFDA?'

'New field discovery allowable.'

'And "nipple up"? Sounds dirty.'

'Prepare to complete.'

'Gimme a cigarette.' She put the drilling report on the sand, and wedged it against the wind with her sunglasses' case.

'Does this stuff always follow you wherever you go?' She spoke through the cigarette.

'Mostly. It's one way of keeping up with your business. These are pretty good reports. At least we ain't losing money. Only about one in sixty-six wells produces enough to buy the solid-gold Cadillac. Tricky business, oil, but I got real good people.'

'How'd you get mixed up in oil, may I ask? You seem to be mixed up in so many things . . . textiles, oil, banks, insurance . . .'

'I own a lot of things you don't know about. A small chain of hotels, a lot of motels, some supermarkets, a soft drink factory, a piece of an airline, real estate all around and about . . . I have a theory. You can't really go too far off the mark if you're mixed up in things that people not only want, but need. I've stood stiffly aloof from uranium, but I adore some manganese and wolfram mines I got a chunk of. All the world needs manganese. But what I like most are the simple things . . . things like Kotex and Kleenex. God Almighty, figuring the frailty of the human body, if you had all your money in sanitary napkins, toilet paper and stuff to blow your nose in, you'd never have to read a drilling report.'

'Do you actually own any of these things?'

'No, but I got kind of a talking interest in them. Hell, darling, I don't know what I own. One feeds off the other, and the accountants and the tax people balance one thing against the other, add here and deduct there, so I am either a billionaire or broke if you draw a final balance. In the meantime I live real good, and the whole rat-race is sort of fun. In a way I take after old John Grimes—or for that matter, people like Glenn Mc-Carthy. I like to *trade*. I like the excitement of doing business. I like deals. I'm a horse-trader at heart. For instance, I got me a bank here in Cuba. Now what the hell I need with a bank here in Cuba I couldn't say, but it seemed to be a nice place to have a bank because of the climate. I'm betting the current bunch of boys will stay. If they do, it'll be nice for little Joe the Rambler. If they don't . . .' Craig shrugged. 'Something else usually turns up. You can't go wrong lending the right people money to do the wrong things. That's what we call the twelve per cent doxology.'

'You still didn't answer me about the oil business and how you got in it. What precisely do you know about oil?'

'Not very much except that you run the world on it, and especially you run wars with it. Suez was oil spelt backwards. You could smell that elder-statesman war coming. I know, because in my early sea-going days you'd see the Japs loading scrap, and I knew what was being taken to the Germans, because in my tiny way, I was taking it.

'So anyhow we had the textile factories going pretty well, and I was in Dallas talking some cotton-futures with some folks, and a man I know from Memphis said he had a hunch that if there was enough money to pay off some people who owned a lot of leases around Houston, so you could get all the ground together in one big land-play, we could light up the world with the gas, and run all the machines in the world with the oil from this one area. But my God it needed money—big money, and it needed a kind of idiotic genius to buy up the various leases and titles without tipping the big mitt to all the greedy little participants. I was the idiotic genius, you should pardon the expression.

'About this time the Government did a very nice, a very decent thing. To encourage wild-cat searching for oil, the Government thoughtfully gave us a twenty-seven and a half per cent forgiveness on taxes, to speed the more adventurous buccaneers off on a search for that elusive elixir in the Never-Never orchards. This looked like a surprisingly intelligent move on the Government's part, and I decided I was born for the oil business. People who wear clothes got to move from here to there. Oil is what people travel on, and this big old dirty war was looming large and strong. Tanks don't drink water.

'So I got, simply, in the oil business. I went downtown to the sharks and reaped myself a mess of money—I hocked everything I had. I hocked some things I didn't have. But I had enough money to get a slew of people drunk enough to sell me their leases and their titled lands, and I put a field together. It was one hell of a big field. It stretched from Texas to Louisiana. We punched holes and if gas didn't jump out of the marshes, oil pleaded pitifully to be released from the ground. I won't say I was as much responsible as Hunt and Cullen and McCarthy for the fact that Neiman-Marcus is doing real good in Dallas, and Houson is not a cow-town any more, but I had a fair hand in it. At least I was responsible for a portion of Houston.

'Oil is a wonderful thing. When you got reserves, and you know you got reserves, you can borrow on the reserves. With what you can borrow you can buy other things, and once you've got the other things, you can borrow so much more on them to drill more wells to encounter more reserves. It is a kind of genteel beggar-thy-neighbour game. I really should have been a rug-pedlar,' Craig said. 'I would have made a wonderful Armenian.'

'I think you would have made a wonderful Armenian—a kind of reverse-English Saroyan type,' Sue said. 'Hate all people, and bend them to your wicked will. "C'monna My House" and get screwed, so to speak.'

'You see me with every flaw shining bright as a cleverly-cut piece of glass. Stick with me, babe, and I promise you'll wear rhinestones up to here.' He made a slashing sign across his throat with the hard edge of his hand.

'You would also have been a great hatchet man,' Sue said. 'I saw you with that murderous approach to an avocado. You know a thing about you, my boy? Everything you do is fierce. When you tie a tie, you jerk at it as if you hated it. Every move you make is violent. You act like a breeze which is trying to make its mind up to become a squall. I never in my life saw a man attack an egg before as if he hated the entire chicken tribe. What have you got against hens? And what did you do with all this violence in the late unpleasantness? If that's not too terribly rude, where are your medals?'

Craig smiled. It was a falsely sad smile, almost a pathetic smile, but it changed swiftly to become a bright toothpaste grin.

'I chickened out,' he said. 'Maybe that's why I attack eggs and avocados. Maybe I felt I had too much dignity to die in a stranger's jungle. My dear girl, I had been to sea, and had experienced violence. I didn't give the faintest fluffing fig for Mr. Hitler's villainy, the courage of the Russians, the crazy-mixed-up French, Mr. Churchill's bulldog stubbornness, or certainly the gallant spawn of our own brave nation, each GI Joe torn from his mother's teat with Ernie Pyle to write his requiem. We had a senile, overworked old man in the White House, and the Japs and Germans were really not worthy adversaries. Given time they will always contrive to defeat themselves, if only for the weakness of being so . . . so *eager*. The Russians, I grant you, are bores, but we had so many surplus millions of them that nobody really cared how many we lost. I felt, in face of all this rampant heroism, nobility, and sacrifice, that one Craig Price more or less wasn't needed to be *mort* in the *champs d'honneur*. After all, I said to myself, you've been to sea, boy, and you have fought side by side with the Russians in bar-room brawls, and you ain't lost nothing down that there long and lonesome road.'

'So?' Her eyes flicked him lightly as a lash.

'So? So I joined the working Navy.' Craig grinned deprecatingly. 'I didn't like it. So then I un-joined it. It was simple as that. Everything is simple as that.' He snapped his fingers.

'I was rather young to make lieutenant-commander in our glorious Navy,' Craig said. 'From a standing start of ordinary seaman in our glorious merchant service. I was like about twenty-six at the time, but old, y'unnerstan', for my age. But I had special skills, or so they said in Washington, where I was, by this time, not entirely unknown. I had borrowed a skill, a technique, from the late John Grimes. I wouldn't want to talk dirty to a lady, but baby-doll, I knew where so many bodies were buried you could have called me sexton and I would have tolled the bell. There is, you know, a certain amount of politics behind the politics, and it generally involves . . . well, money is as good a name for it as any. So,' he said briskly, 'I became overnight a lieutenant-commander. Even younger than the current admirals, I had the two-and-a-half-lemon-rinds on my sleeve.

'I gloried in my glory in a last drunken night in New York, where everybody saluted me, and then I climbed upon one of the worst trains in the world—a single-barrelled sort of train that eventually arrived some years later at White River Junction, Vermont, a dismal village, adjacent to which is a kind of male seminary named Dartmouth College, which I believe is regarded as very social in peacetime. Why, I cannot say, as it seems to snow there continuously and contiguously, especially on Sunday, but a certain snob appeal attaches and the Hanover Inn provides a very decent Sunday buffet. The lobster was not so terribly filthy, as I recall.

'This place was chosen to mould me into the kind of starched-collared Naval officer who would die in the service of his country, and whose final command, such as: "Where is my goddam collar-button?" would rank with all the better slogans of Dewey and Taussig and the other sea-going squares. I was assigned to a dormitory—they kicked out the poor civilian students—to a dormitory named Topliff Hall, rather a salty nautical name, I thought, for a land-bound college. Topliff had a big ditch in front, which figures in this narrative. I must say the sanitary facilities were inadequate, and indulging in hearty callisthenics in the snow at some extraordinary hour like six a.m. left me limply unenthusiastic.

'Also I was not entirely carried away with the idea of marching everywhere, to chow, which was dreadful, to classes, which were to say the least unedifying—you really don't need Bowditch when you've got radar—or the whole collegiate atmosphere which the Navy, grinding its teeth, managed flawlessly to maintain. I did not care for the Superintendent, an unsuccessful submariner who had been banished from active service as less likely to lose the war as chief of this particular boat, and I was less than charmed by the chief petty officers, and the Pearl Harbour rejects who claimed to be ring-bearers from Annapolis. But it was mainly the marching—the marching and the strength tests and the drills and the injections—which whipped me.'

Craig's grin was wolfish.

'Clean living will tell, I always say, and it will come as no shock when I tell you that I became leader of my platoon—as vast, I might say, an accumulation of professional civilian incompetents as ever got a pay-raise for volunteering as warriors —and our platoon won the Bible, the chocolate cake, and at least one free week-end in Montreal, a close suburb, in which I experienced a rather startling Saturday with the married sister of one of my platoon-mates.

'I mean to say, my military career was fraught with peril until I saw fit to dispose of it . . .'

2

CRAIG wouldn't forget the Navy. Because of his youth, he had settled for an ensign's commission.

'That one stripe seems awful lonesome,' he said over drinks with a friend—a member of the Naval Appropriations Committee—at the Willard's big green marble-pillared drinking room in Washington. 'Apart from that I like the suit. Blue always became me. Let's have another stinger. I hurt from last night.'

'Let's. Waiter, two more of the same. Now look here, boy, don't fret about your single solitary stripe. You'll have a couple more to add to them before you go to Dartmouth. It seemed

541

better to me to start you in the ordinary age-way, and then we get the spot-promotion after you're processed. Before you go off to indoctrination.'

'I suppose I really have to go through with this sea-scout business?' Craig sighed. 'I mean, couldn't we just hang the commission on me and put me to work in one of these offices like any other dollar-a-year boy, and relieve me of two months of seamanship? Learning to *hup-two-three-four-Harch*! and tying square-knots ain't going to improve my value to the country from an air-conditioned office in this awful town.'

'It'll look better, when we need you, if you did the ordinary course. Military bearing, and all that. Plus your graduation certificate. Who knows, we may even send you to sea for a while . . .'

'Naval officers go to *sea*? I thought they were all working for Procurement here in Washington. I thought it was only the Marines and dog-faces that went to sea. Look at this room. You're the only man in a civilian suit, and I can't spot a fleck of khaki in the house. Nothing but Alice-blue gone to war. Like Lucky Strikes' green.'

The Congressman finished his drink and summoned the waiter. 'Bear with us, Buster,' he said. 'I imagine you're fixed up for a place to live here.'

'Fortunately, yes,' Craig replied, reaching for his new hat with the white top and the pretty, untarnished gold chin-strap. 'I have an apartment on Wisconsin Avenue. A friend of mine was just called away to the serious wars and left me his place for the duration. I call it my quarterdeck, because from the penthouse wharf you can almost but not quite see the Potomac, but at least foreign shores of F.F.V., Virginia, come out loud and clear. I must remind myself to buy some binoculars and to soak my braid in salt-water, so I'll have that seagoing look which is so necessary to a successful career in the Washington Navy.'

'God, the horrors of war,' Craig said to Susan, as he gazed into the sun-shimmering turquoise of the sea, and wriggled his toes in the sand. 'The suffering. The grinding agony. The pure distilled hell of war.

'You don't mind if I talk about the war? My war? I got my extra two gold stripes, and being the only lieutenant-commander on what seemed to be a naval transport, but was hiding under the alias of the Pennsylvania Railroad, I was allowed to sit in a compartment and talk to some movie actress all the way from Washington to Manhattan. This later gave me great *chic*, not to mention cheek, at Dartmouth, because I was the rosy-faced boy with all the mysterious rank who had drinks with Miss X in her private room. I was a bigger hero than Colin Kelly when we disembarked at Dartmouth and a chief petty officer with delusions of momentary grandeur slapped a cigarette

542

out of my mouth and commanded me to remove my chin-strap from the hat and to address him as "Sir". I carried my own bags an interminable distance to Topliff, where an arrogant ass of an ensign informed me that for the moment, I was a boot. Me, Mysterious Craig Price, the man with the look of eagles, a lousy apprentice warrior . . . *dear*.'

'You must have been a beautiful baby,' Sue hummed, 'because baby, look at you now . . .'

'Rather wearily, for all my tender years, I submitted to all the juvenile indignities. People whom I had not met socially barked at me. I learned the silhouettes of aircraft and Japanese shipping from an Academy ensign whose incompetence had already achieved him sufficient recognition to relieve him of sea duty. I learned gunnery from a wise-cracking red-headed civilian who had never handled so much as a twenty-gauge shotgun. All I remember of that course is that there are several kinds of breech-blocks, one of which is nomenclatured—only the Navy could make anything but a noun out of "nomenclature"—was called a "French interrupted screw".'

'I imagine that would stick in your memory,' Sue muttered.

'Let me see. What else heroic did I do? Oh, I know, I sprained my ankle playing touch football, and so was excused from calisthenics in the snow. I managed a convenient faint at the first captain's inspection, Hollywood-produced in the blazing sun, in full uniform regalia including bridge coat. The inspection was held the day following multiple injections against all sorts of foreign menaces such as cholera, French civilians, dengue, the Black Death, and dysentery, not to mention smallpox and incipient syphilis. Everybody else was fainting. I didn't want to stand out from the crowd and so I fainted too. It was much more comfortable lying there on the meadow than standing stiffly at attention.'

'I suppose you graduated with honours? Top of the class, of course?'

'That I certainly did. I cheated shamelessly. They were trying to stuff us with four years of Annapolis in eight weeks, and I always cherished a deep disinterest in maths. The only part of a sextant that intrigues me is the first three letters. But by God I was a fine platoon leader. I was a marching fool. Apart from the first day, when, as senior officer present, I gave my first command, I was a demon.'

'What was the first command? Damn the torpedoes?'

'Almost.' Craig laughed. 'Actually it was "All Aboard!" I couldn't think of any other way to get twenty-five men moving. My cadence was rather amusing, too. I started off saying, "Hup, one, two, three, four," giving five beats to the measure, which created a certain amount of confusion as we bravely tackled the strange terrain in search of textbooks.

543

'Eventually came the day of orders for the sweet girl graduates. We had been allowed to apply for preferential duty. I toyed with the idea of something witty, such as supervision of Honolulu's red-light section, decided against it, and checked off a duty called "Armed Guard". I thought it had something to do with banks—armoured cars, you know, like that there. Then when the orders were issued, I found that some idiot in the Bureau of Personnel had actually believed me, and had granted me my heart's written desire.'

'What was Armed Guard?'

'That's what I asked the chief. The chief knew everything.

' "Jesus God,' he said, and drew his hand knife-wise across his throat. "Commander, that's what we call fish-food. You got too much rank for that duty. Generally, the Navy don't even waste jg's on that. Strictly an ensign's graveyard."

' "But what *is* it, what *kind* of duty is it?" I asked the chief.

' "Naval gunners on merchant ships," he said. "Right now it's all Murmansk duty. You can walk on the periscopes from here to the North Cape, and from there on the Focke-Wolfs and Junkers and Heinkels take over. I knew one guy made *one* run to Murmansk. I never knew no guy to make two, on a round-trip basis. You been a good Joe, Commander. It'll be a shame to lose you." '

Craig lit a cigarette and grinned, shamelessly.

'For a dreadful moment, I had the horrid idea that the Navy was serious, and that I actually was going to sea in a rusty hamper of high-explosives, with a court-house relic for the Number One gun. As I told you, my knowledge of gunnery was magnifecently less than sketchy. I had already called down the Jovian wrath of my red-headed ordnance instructor one day when he said:

' "Mister, suppose your Number One gun squatted?"

'I stood erect, proudly erect. "What, sir?" I said. "Come again?"

' "Squatted. Blew back out of battery after firing and refused to return to battery. What would you do, even though it's an unlikely possibility?"

' "I would tell somebody to fix it," I said innocently. "I am not really very mechanically minded, sir. Always getting fingers caught in doors and . . ."

'Jesus,' Craig said, 'when the laughter subsided, he really chewed me out. And poor simple me, I was being serious all the time.'

'I really wonder we won the war,' Sue said, making sand castles. 'What then, Captain Hornblower?'

'A triumph. A sheer triumph. It was late fall, and it had snowed copiously as if it had been impatient all summer. The ditch, at least five feet deep, in front of Topliff Hall was stuffed with that nasty white stuff to its high-water mark. On the last day, after the final meal, the last supper, I gave my ultimate command. As we approached the citadel of my military knowledge, I marched my brave buckos up to the front of the building. Instead of saying "Platoon, dismiss!" I barked, in the most approved military fashion, "By the right flank, *Harch*!" and marched them down into the ditch and across the ditch. All you could see was naval caps floating on a sea of snow, and in the incidence of the two end-men dwarfs, you couldn't even see the caps until they emerged from the crystallized deeps on the other side. Then I gave them the dismiss, and ended my adventure into patriotism.'

Sue couldn't help giggling at the mental picture.

'And how they must have loved you.'

Craig shrugged.

'I toyed briefly with the idea of pulling an act of bravado, and resigning my lieutenant-commandancy and joining the Marines as a buck-ass private, but I know about Carolina swamps and Southern mosquitoes, and that boot-camp bit left me strangely uneager. You know, the shaved skull, the night-marching, all that crap they use to convince civilians they're super-people. Battle-cries I needed not.

'I went to Washington, the orders got changed, and I settled down to a career of carpetbaggery. I was working as liaison to some subdued admiral who lost his row-boat and got sentenced to various stretches of penance, and I sat on a couple of boards for oil and textiles procurement. I don't suppose it was an accident that I manufactured a few million GI suntans, or that my keen and constant devotion to duty got me out of town often enough to keep an eye on personal production in my own mills—and on what had become, by then, a considerable selection of producing oil-wells.' He flickered his eyelids in mock modesty.

'You know us heroes don't like to talk about our decorations, but will you believe me when I say that I made full commander, with gold bird-stuff on my hat, and was awarded the Atlantic Defence ribbon for a flight to Guantánamo Bay, here in Cuba, and at some point they had me on view with drums ruffling and hung a Legion of Merit on my manly little chest?'

'I suppose you're proud of all this.' Sue was not even mildly sarcastic.

Craig's eyes veiled with an air of infinite boredom.

'Of course I'm not proud of it. What the hell is there to be proud of about being a civilian in uniform and making a fortune out of the nasty necessities of war—the khaki drawers the Wacs wore, the oil that drove the jeeps so the field-grade officers could date the nurses? It was part of the war effort, like that general moving his pianos and holding up Patton's columns—like that high society tea-party they ran in London, like that every-man-a-king operation they ran in Naples and Leghorn and Bella Roma after the Wops quit. At least I was *not* a doctor, selling GI penicillin to the Wop black market and raking in a fortune. I wasn't living it up at the taxpayers' expense in some distant but safe atoll. I was just a businessman playing sailor on the surface, and in the meantime we got some oil out of the ground for Patton's tanks as well as the General's mistress's command car, and we clad a lot of Wacs and Waves and Spars and Bams as well as GI's. I would prefer to say I was a spot-welder at Lockheed, but they didn't have any men's rooms so they voted me out. Christ.' Craig spat.

Sue said: 'At least I like your honesty. Your vocal approach to your past lacks a certain humbuggery, if that's a word. I met an awful lot of desk-borne commandos who made it sound important, a lot of chair-infantry . . .' Craig held up a hand protectively.

'I had a wife and a child, so I suppose I could have ducked it on those grounds—for a while, anyhow. But I also had some businesses to protect. I mentioned spotwelding. In a way I was just as valuable to the general effort as if I'd been pasting planes together. Soldiers got to have pants, and so do girls. War widows got to have stockings . . .' Craig smiled viciously. 'They used to last longer in those days, those nylons of mine. But then we were on austerity, and maybe you babes were a mite more careful of cigarette ash and general emotional stress.'

'Beast. You know I got through the entire war on six pairs of nylons, and now I ruin more than that many a month.'

'Therein the profit lieth, my sweet. Use 'em up fast and buy more, to keep woman's second or third best asset alluring. What, by the way, was your war record, Madame?'

'Too dreary, but too utterly dreary. I didn't do a damned thing. My husband was one of the eager ones, mad to whip off and die as painfully as possible, chewing the jugular out of the last Jap. He wound up in public—I used to think of it as pubic—relations when some of the reports came in. He fought the battle of the Mark Hopkins in San Francisco, and when the war really got so desperate it looked like we might actually win it, he deserted the Geary Street boondocks for Waikiki. San Francisco lost a good man to Oahu. I believe he did make it to Guam, after that was all settled, on a flying week-end. I just sort of hung around, when he was in the States.

'When the Big Push started—when they ordered him to Honolulu—I came on back to New York. No good works. I slept around, some, a little bit, like everybody else, but I got bored with the idea of being a professional war-widow, and quit. I read more dull books and went to the movies to watch Errol Flynn conquer the Japs. I rolled no bandages—like you, I figured they had enough bandage rollers. I yielded up a smidgen of alcohol-tainted blood once in a while, but not enough to dehydrate me. I drank some bad blends and got used to solitary beds. The nicer ginmills didn't want stag women, and if you went out with some returned hero he assumed you were already in the sack with him before he bought you a drink. I found that staying home wasn't too bad. It was all quite peaceful. There were a few 4-F's around who didn't grab me by the thigh before the first cigarette was stubbed out, and once in a while we'd have a Saturday night party where nobody got seriously wounded, or even a week-end in which the war wasn't mentioned except in a bored tone. I managed. I didn't like it, but I managed. Isn't it funny?' Sue said. 'Isn't it funny how unbelievably dull an international catastrophe can be to people who aren't directly involved?'

'Duller when you *are* involved, I'd imagine. It's a topic I've dwelt on,' Craig said, 'and generally encountered no favour in the process. Even the wives, the sweethearts, who were sweating out the letter-edged-in-black, were grimly bored. I wasn't actively bored, because I was too busy scuttling hither and yon, but there seemed to be a curious lack of adventure in reading war maps and looking at *Life*'s pictures. Seemed more like a long-distance, chess-game.

'You remember the New Guinea one, with the boys dead on the beach, or possibly it was Tarawa? I kept thinking what a great bore it would be to be dead on a beach in a place you had no need for in the first place. To kill some bloody monkey you didn't want to know, or to be killed by the same unintroduced monkey if he saw you first. Wars, to me, have always been something that old fat non-combatants thought up to alleviate their own personal boredom, and incidentally to make a little money. But to be starry-eyed about it . . . no, thank you very much.

'My grandpa was in the Civil War, and he said it was mainly a dismal matter of no decent food, over-cold nights, and a more or less constant dysentery. I think it's as good a description as any. He said that the only people he envied were blockade runners. They had a bit o' dash, and made some jack on the side. In my own fashion, I was a kind of blockade-runner in the last one, because believe me, kid, the priority business was a tricky thing, and it was all done with broads and booze. That social goose-grease was something. I had one friend whose swimming-pool leaked—it was enormous, about 360 by 200—and he needed steel to sheathe it. Steel priorities were real tough, so the gentleman borrowed—well, bought—a couple of Liberty ships and had them dismantled. He sheathed his leaking pool very well, and he said a marvellously cynical thing: "Hell, if they'd gone to sea, the Germans would probably have sunk them by now, and my pool would still be leaking.' In his own fashion he performed a patriotic act. America First stuff.'

3

THE waiter in the sailor-suit came with the breakfast. Craig and Susan were finishing a couple of vodka screwdrivers.

'It's the only way I can choke down orange juice,' Craig said. 'Somehow the vodka smothers the insidious health-building evil of a vastly overrated fruit. What have we here, *camarero*?'

'*Fruta bomba, Señor, con limón. Huevos de cuatro minutos. Un poco de jamón. Tostadas, naturalmente, y café.*'

'I love that *fruta bomba* bit. Any place else in the Spanish-speaking world it's *papaya*, but here *papaya* is a very bad word indeed. *No es verdad, hombre? No se puede decir papaya?*'

'*Señor!*' The waiter was shocked, and almost blushed under the swarthy heritage of an African grandmother.

'I won't ask you what the word means, but *fruta bomba* or *papaya*, it's wonderful,' she said, delving into the musky, ice-cold, black-seed-specked yellow fruit.

Craig picked up a knife and swung mightily at the end of a brown, freckled egg. The tiny end sheared sharply off.

'*Olé!*' Sue said. '*Qué matador!*'

'I'll stretch my luck and have another go at the second one. I've been watching the English decapitate eggs for years, but when I try it I usually lose a finger or strike oil directly in the yoke. Stand back, women and children!' He swung his knife again, crick! Another shell-skull tumbled. Craig clasped his hands over his head, like a victorious boxer.

'The winnah, and new champion,' he said. Then he picked up the hard, greasy fried ham, tore it into bits and dropped it into the eggs, which he had decanted into a coffee cup. He took a piece of toast, crumbled it, and stirred the whole mess—eggs, ham and toast—into a sort of impromptu stew. Then he carefully took the severed tops of the eggs and scraped the whites out with a spoon, adding them to the mess.

'You never throw anything away, do you?' Sue said, eyeing him narrowly.

'My great-grandmother saved string,' Craig said. 'And I have been hungry.'

She watched him as he ate, concentrating on the food.

'You know,' she said, 'you may have created a new vogue for the consumption of boiled eggs and fried ham. I never saw anybody do it that way before.'

Craig spoke through a full mouth.

'I do a lot of things in a lot of ways nobody ever did before. Hadn't you noticed?'

'I might say I have,' Sue said. 'Let's have one more swim in this divine water before we fly back to Havana.'

'I already had a bath,' Craig said. 'You have a swim in the divine water, and I'll dive into one of Juanito's divine daiquiris.'

'Cancel the swim,' Sue replied. 'I'll dive into the daiquiri with you. Whither thou goest . . .'

'Biblically speaking,' Craig said, 'I really should not like to see you turn into a pillar of salt.'

4

CRAIG woke first, in the cool hotel-room gloom of a late Havana afternoon, staring upward to the high frescoed white ceiling. Susan was curled like a puppy, with her head nearly buried under a pillow. She had tanned a warm biscuit gold, except for the skimpy area where the bikini had left two islands of white across her rear. It was dark, with the jalousies down, and her tan had darkened in the dimness to deep-tawny. Her trim buttocks looked, Craig thought, amusedly, as he crawled out of bed, like two jolly searchlights, peering outward from a dark-gold night. He touched the tips of her tousled hair gently, and noticed that the tendrils were sweat-curled on the back of her neck, which was as sweetly dewy as that of a sleeping baby. He kissed a fingertip and rested it gently on the incurving of her back, lightly touching the dimples on each side of her spine. Then he got up, to walk across the cool green-tiled floor to the bathroom, to close the door softly and start a shower. She stirred slightly as he left the rumpled, love-sweated bed, but didn't awake.

As the cool water streamed over his muscle-ridged body, and he soaped himself, he felt a surge of peaceful well-being he had never known before, a singing exaltation that was smoothed by the *siesta* and what had gone before. Every nerve had unknotted, but his perceptions had sharpened enormously. Everything seemed to have new shapes and textures, almost as if he had always been blind and had suddenly been granted sight, and was seeing now through his new eyes what he had only felt before with practised fingertips.

This was, he thought, all Sue. Nothing else but Sue. My God, he had slept in the same bed with her for a week, he who could never bear to sleep with anyone. He, Craig Price, who often woke himself by the harsh grinding of his own teeth, no longer gnashed his teeth. He, that Craig Price who could not stand physical contact unless he were either fighting or making love, slept snuggled in Sue's arms, or with her head on his shoulder and one arm flung carelessly across his stomach. He woke in the night, sometimes, woke drowsily smiling, knowing that she was still there, possibly with a lock of her hair in his mouth, savouring the moist warmth of her, the trusting helpless baby presence, and drew her even closer to protect her from all imagined harm in the night.

'Good God,' he said to himself as the shower sang. 'I must be going dotty. I never touched anybody in my life except in lust or anger, and now I seek and find excuses to pat her behind as she walks past me, or kiss an ear, or stroke her knee, or hold her hand. I never made sophomore in college, but I think I know how one feels. I wish she had some school-books for me to carry. Price, my boy, you're hooked. Really hooked.'

He turned off the tap, dripped over to the lavabo, and reached for his razor. The face reflected was brown and very clear-eyed. The hair had curled from salt air and the shower, and the harsh deep-cut lines seemed to have been planed away.

'I look a good ten years younger,' he said, noticing the mahogany of his upper face against the lather. 'And I feel about twenty. I feel silly, too. I want to laugh and shout and rattle a stick along a fence and pick daisies for my girl. For this to happen to me, at my age . . .'

He dried his face and walked naked except for a towel girded round his loins back into the other room, and leaning over the still sleeping Sue, kissed her steadily on the soft damp nape, under the moistened curls, until she woke, rolled over, yawned, and held out her arms. Her face was babyishly flushed with sleep. She pulled herself to sitting position with her arms linked behind his head, and snuggled into his arms, laying her cheek against his chest as he sat down beside her on the bed. She purred.

'Mmmmmmmmm,' she said. 'What a nice man. What a nice clean-smelling man.' She opened one eye and looked comically upward at him. He kissed her lightly on the forehead.

'What time is it?'

'Seven. Time to get up, you lazy slut. You going to spend the rest of your life on your back?'

She leaned her full weight backwards and pulled him down to her breast.

'That I am. I'm a nymphomaniac. Hadn't you heard? Given the right co-operation, that is. What's all this undue hurry about getting up?'

'We said we'd meet those people for a drink at La Rue's at eight . . .' Craig was mumbling, for his face was buried now in the hollow of her shoulder. Her arms seized him tightly, and her legs laced his.

'Damn the people. Come to Mama.' She swept her pillow to the floor. 'Come right back to where you slept last night.' And suddenly her body was printed on his—not *on*, *in*—and it all started over again, the slow ascent, step by careful step, the tiny spasms that rocked her as they achieved a fresh height, the spastic quivering that made her body one long, limpid tremolo, the head flung back, the eyes rolled back, a rising, rising moan,

550

then a soft wail of almost painful satisfaction, and finally the wrenching breathless shock as they reached the top of the long climb, paused, and then hurled themselves over the abyss, locked together into a violent death in the darkness below.

'This time you've really killed me,' Craig said, when the panting subsided. He reached for cigarettes and lit two. 'I thought my heart was going to quit on me for sure this time. Feel. It's still trying to fight its way back into my chest. God, woman, *what* you do to me. Nothing like it, truly, ever, ever before, and every time I feel we've hit the ultimate, something else I never suspected happens.'

'God, man, what you do to *me*. Feel.' She put his hand on her breast. 'I've heard all about it. I've read all about it. But nobody'll ever write this one in any language at any time. You're right. It's been sheer perfection all the way, and just when you feel that it can't possibly get better, a completely new set of . . . of *something* arrives. Do you suppose this could be the true love the poets sing? Are we unique amongst the billions who have practised the act over the centuries? Did we discover this all by ourselves, or do you suppose all other people, everywhere at this hour, in China and Greenland, are saying the same thing?'

Craig smiled and bent to kiss her cheek.

'I flatly refuse to believe it. There has not been perfection before'—the old sardonic grin replaced the tender smile—'unless you are old enough to remember Sonny Wisecarver.'

She slapped him lightly.

'Rat. Rat that I adore.'

'Apart from the precocious Master Wisecarver, who seemed to have a rather persuasive way with the ladies a decade back, I would say that nobody ever achieved this . . . this *bliss*.' Craig hesitated as if he were ashamed to form the word. 'But bliss is what it is, and I don't give a damn if I do sound silly. And may I, madame, pay you what might sound like a rather rude compliment, almost an insult to your unveiled charms and the rather reckless abandon which leads me to believe that you may not be a virgin?'

'Pay away, big boy, pay away. Long's Ah ain't gittin' no money outa these head callisthenics, Ah might as well take mah trade in sweet-talk.' The flip mood, in which they were both most at ease, was returning.

'All right. You are *not* the greatest technical lay in show business. Your practised tricks are nearly non-existent, apart from a certain eager response. You do not make a gymnastic virtuosity out of the simple act of love, which in any case is an undignified and generally rather sweaty business. You do not seem to be trying to impress the opponent, like a wrestler, with a new set of grapples. You do not shriek and talk aphrodisiacally dirty on purpose and chew my ears and carve me to ribbons with your nails.'

'I'd like to,' Sue muttered.' 'Maybe I will.'

'This is hard for me to put into words. Best I can do is this: in your giving you take, completely, but simultaneously insinuating with your body that I am giving, you accepting, with a deliciously flattering suggestion of rape, permanent virginity, and utter wantonness without any implication of harlotry or cold mechanical design to produce a spurious excitement.'

'God,' Sue said, 'maybe we better put me in for a patent. I'm too good for the po' folks.'

'Shut up. In my peculiar way, I am being sloppily sentimental. You have a pink-baby innocence I feel appallingly appealing, and complete mature honesty of body, utter lack of coquetry while conferring all of yourself shamelessly. I hate coquetry above all, as I hate blasé intimation of a favour conferred, as I hate proficiency which makes the partner acutely conscious of the mechanics involved in reaching a climax, and repeated spoken injunctions in a spurious passion shaped to rouse the gentleman to bestial heights of delight . . . and is mostly designed to get it over with and get the gentleman the hell out of bed so you can collect mental money off a figurative mantel and go buy an imaginary hat.'

Sue started to speak. Craig held up a hand.

'Quiet. I ain't finished yet. I've said some of this, in different ways, before, but I want it all in the same brief. For some reason, God knows why, since we're still practical strangers apart from bed and my loquacious renderings of my painful past, I think you are the *nicest* woman I have ever known. Don't balk at the word *nice*. It's a hell of a compliment, and not generally applicable to most people you meet these days.

'Nice is a deep-seated *inside* sweetness, a generosity, a simplicity, a kindness. Nice is outside also—ordered components of beauty and behaviour. Nice is spontaneity, honesty, lack of sham, a cleanliness of brain, humour and calm. Of all things, I believe I detest planned hysteria and voluntary pretending more than any of the serious sins. Nice is knowing when to talk, when to listen, when to read a book. And occasionally, without prodding, setting out the pipe and slippers or mixing a drink. Nice is laughter and picnics and sunshine of the soul and not dominating a place or an affair with a selfish mood. Nice is that outmoded quality—simple, honest, sweetness—which has largely been replaced by elaborate posturing and bottled glamour and semi-annual fashion menopauses and having yourself dyed blonde all *over*.'

Craig was very serious now. He held both Sue's hands in his, and stared at her intently, gravely.

'I've been roughed up pretty well by the world as I know it, and I was always looking for some secret something deep in the sea, behind those high plaster walls. I was looking for *me*, and when I found *you* I found *me*. I like the adult *me* I finally found. It is a *me* I remember. It is a young *me* I had almost forgotten. It is a *me* of tenderness, a wilful giver instead of a casual taker. I like this *me*, and I'm *not* going to lose it. I'm not going to lose it.' His fingers viced on her hand.

'You're hurting me, Craig.' He released the pressure on her hand.

'The reason we have been incomparable in bed is so simple it's silly. We have finally been able to transmute a latent niceness in me, and your readily discernible niceness, into a long-delayed bodily fusion, like two lost children finding comfort holding hands against the night noises.' He shook his head as if to clear it.

'Excuse me. I guess people don't talk about these things.'

Susan's snort was eloquent.

'Of course they do. Look. I love you, Craig Price. I never loved anybody before. I think I will love you all my life. Now let *me* talk for a change. I love the little boy inside the craggy man. I love you because you're scared, and when you talk about yourself it's like a . . . a harsh literature of sarcasm and self-hurting humour. I like all the protective fists you're raised against outside hurt. I like the way you don't play tycoon, and the deprecation of your efforts and successes. I like the little-boy preoccupation with food and fun. I imagine your temper is foul, but you always seem to keep it reined, like the other night at the casino with that drunk.

'I love you because you're a man in a world of boys—adult adolescent crew-cuts with pink shirts and large conversations about nothing. I love your broken nose and the scars on your face and body and your battered knuckles. The only regret I have about us is I wish you were all mine, for me to baby a little bit always and fight with once in a while . . . Oh, hell, kiss me and then I'll shower and get dressed.'

'We might as well shower together,' Craig said, releasing her. 'You got me all sweaty again. And I was so cool and clean, too.'

'That's another thing I like about you,' Sue said, as they stood together in the shower, with Craig soaping her back. 'You're the cleanest man I ever met in my life. How many baths *do* you take a day?'

'About six. Now, you scrub me. I keep thinking about bathing out of buckets, and I am suddenly constrained to shuck my clothes and remove the memory.'

As they dressed, Sue said, 'Let's not bother with those people we said we'd meet for drinks. I don't want to share this last night with anybody. Let's go back to that little place in Jaimanitas, the one on the water, and eat some beans and rice, and then let's go to the harbour and catch a ferry and go to Guanabacoa and watch the moon on the Morro. Let's *don't* go to any air-conditioned *nice* places. Let's sit and drink rum with the dirty peasants in that dreadful bar in Guanabacoa and listen to Cuban records

553

on the juke-box and you tell me how Miguelito Valdez sounded when he was with *La Orquesta de la Playa de la Habana*, before Cugat got hold of him, and then let's go late to the *Fritas* and mingle with the real rabble. And then let's come home and get drunk in bed.'

'That clinches it,' Craig said. 'I'll tell you about it on the plane tomorrow.'

'Tell me what?'

'Never mind. I don't want my judgment swayed by any Cuban moons on any Morro Castles, or any late night rumbas in the grisly caves of *Las Fritas*. Let's just go make us a Havana night as if I were still a sailor-lad and you were a rather attractive tart I picked up in Sloppy Joe's, and then after I've fed you and shown you the town, you find you love me for myself and won't accept any money for your favours. And I'll tell you all, tomorrow. I find airplanes wonderful for clear thinking . . .'

'You'll drive me mad, wretch. But all right. Deal. Here. Zip me.'

5

RANCHO BOYEROS faded, and they were headed north over the blue water.

Sue took Craig's hand.

'Thank you,' she said. 'For the most wonderful week of my life.'

'There'll be lots more. I'll tell you now. I'm divorcing Maybelle. And I'm marrying you.'

Sue's eyes widened as she turned to face him.

'Craig, you can't. Not after all these years. Darling, I don't *need* marriage to be happy with you. If I can just be with you once in a while . . . *Don't*, Craig. You owe Maybelle a lot. And then there's the child. Don't, please don't Craig. I'll be your mistress, or just your part-time girl, I'll be anything, but please don't wreck . . .'

Craig shook his head sharply, irritably. His nostrils flared, and his brows met over his nose.

'No, goddamit, *no*! It's not good enough—not good enough for me, not good enough for you, not good enough for Maybelle. Just not good enough. I don't want a part-time custody of my heart. I want a hundred per cent of it so I can give it all to you. I'm tired of sharing myself out, and of ducking responsibilities to myself. I've been lazy, and selfish, I know it, and willing to settle for half. Or a third. Or a drib or a drab. I'm tired of being a he-whore, landing in this bed, landing in that, all because I can't face the idea of home.'

'I'll do anything you say,' Sue said. 'Darling. But I would hate

554

to have your wife on my conscience. I don't want to be one of those bitches that . . .'

'Huh. She won't be on your conscience. She'll be on *mine*. This will be nothing new. She's always been on my conscience. Up to now it hasn't mattered, because I hadn't found anyone to make it matter. I was too damned busy with mills and oil and stocks and shares and debentures to pay much attention to anything but the great ego and the itch to grab it all. I had a taste of dough and power and all the things they could buy and I was what *Time* called me—a young man in a hurry. I wanted it all, right now, today, in a hunk. All of the everything. Some of it I wanted retroactively to yesterday, because I couldn't wait for today. For the best part of twenty years I rushed. I hurled myself at my own life as if it were an enemy. You see I got the scars to prove it. I fell into bed with everything I could catch. I drank all the liquor I could hold. I made every deal I could make. Because real early on, I was heavy-struck by a remark a Texas pal of mine made when I first got into the oil business—that I seemed vaguely to remember having heard before. From a man named Forney.

'This Texas pal had come up, on his own, from a lot less than nowhere. It took him eight years to get through college. He waited tables and had no fun at all. In the off-years, he rough-necked it in the oil-fields, saved every cent he made, and then went back to college for another year. After eight years of this ball-breaking peonage he was a geologist, the hardest way you can make it. He finally corralled enough hungry capital to drill some poor-boy wells, and one hit big. He leased some lands, and sold the leases, parlayed and re-parlayed, drilled and leased, leased and sold, merged and re-merged, until he was awful big. One day I was sitting in his office when somebody important called him and he got on the phone. He listened a while, rocking back and forth, nervous, waiting to say something when the buzz on the other end quit. If ever a man had made up his mind negatively, old Emmett was the man. Finally the voice on the other end buzzed off, and Emmet smacked the desk with his free hand. The gold pen-set leaped and scattered its wealth.

' "No, Goddammit, *NO!*" he roared into the phone. "If we do this one we'll wind up with thirty million dollars' worth of rusty machinery and no credit, and I ain't gonna be poor no more!"

'He slammed down the phone, and said, apologetically,

' "Excuse me. That was my partner. He's got a wild-haired deal he thinks he can make in Saudi Arabia, and another thing in South America, and I just don't want no part of it. I got more than enough to handle right here, and if I get to screwin' around with Arabs and South Americans I'm likely to wind up on my busted ass. I got enough stashed in the sock to keep me happy, and you can't drive more than one Cadillac at a time.

555

I got three ranches and an island off Galveston, and about 1,400 producing wells here and yonder. They'll keep me in tortillas and beans. Now let's go to the Petroleum Club and have us a snort." '

'He had a point,' Craig said. 'In a way, he and I were both cut out of the same cloth, as Maybelle's old man was of a similar pattern—except that old Grimes didn't know when to quit winners. I had made up my mind a long time before that I, too, was never going to be poor no more. We had enjoyed enough poverty in my family.

'I was drowning in work. I had experienced some of the fleshly exterior advantages of wealth, and found I liked them enormously —even such little things as head-waiters being nice to you, and your name in the papers. I horse-traded and gambled, mostly with a rigged deck. I worked a solid sixteen hours a day, butt-ressed by bourbon and youth. I had no time for my family. I hop-skipped-and-jumped the world. I bought this and sold that and borrowed from this to buy that to mortgage t'other to add to the original this and subtract from the original that. I bought some companies and milked them and threw them away. I met some women, attractive women, and repeated the process. I drained them dry and threw them away. And one day, in Africa . . .'

The stewardess came with drinks and a tray of canapés.

'Darling?' Craig nodded towards the stewardess.

'Martini, I think.'

'Two martinis, please,' Craig said. He snared a plate of anchovies, biscuits, and bits of cheese, pulled down the tray in front, and set the drinks and the hors d'oeuvres down on it. They drank and nibbled in silence for a bit, and then Craig signalled the stewardess for two new martinis.

'Every time I think of Africa I think of martinis—and other things. You haven't seen my office yet, sweetie, but it is loaded with exotic trophy. I was a mighty slayer of things like sparrows and quail and ducks when I was a kid, and one of my dreams, when I was heavily under the narcotic influence of Tarzan of the Apes, was that some day, if I ever got the money, I would go on safari to the Dark Continent and Beard the Lion. Observe the Elephant at Close Hand, and bring all the relics home to clutter up my life some more.' He made his capitalization stri-dently emphatic.

6

SAFARI had become very chic after the war. Everybody who was anybody chose up and produced a party. The professional hunter replaced the airline pilot, the racing driver, the movie star, as a popular idol. Rich gentlemen took their mistresses to Africa. Princes and marquises and millionaires and movie stars and society women of all nationalities went to Africa, on which fresh attention was currently being focused by the rising murder-cult of Mau Mau. Ultimate snobbery became invested in how long were your kudu horns, and in such unlikely places as the Stork Club and Twenty-One, bullet weights and muzzle velocities were being discussed learnedly. A man's financial status was not so much determined by Dun and Bradstreet as by his taxidermy bills at Jonas Brothers and Rowland Ward. Safari had replaced polo as a snob sport. Aly Khan and Rita Hayworth went on safari. So did Lauritz Melchior and the Prince Anybody, and all, but *all*, of the American industrialists, including Craig Price, who generally managed to write off the cost against taxes.

Craig went with some oil people, a retired general, and one automobile manufacturer. He shot, competently, all the trophies which now adorned his office—Maybelle wouldn't have them in the house, she said they made her nervous—and at night the men played high-stakes poker. The automobile manufacturer and one of the oil magnates refused to hunt at all. They sat in camp all day, drinking, playing gin rummy and talking business. They sent their professionals out to slay the animals which would later dominate the walls of their ranch-houses and shoot-ing-lodges. Craig never liked the second-hand heroes there-after, since he walked hard, crawled hard, and insisted on shoot-ing his own beasts. Gradually their company graduated from boredom into acute irritation, so Craig had taken his professional hunter, a pleasant, intelligent young chap named Mike, one lorry, one jeep, and Mike's string of blacks, and had gone off prowling.

'Where'll we go from here?' the hunter, Mike Townsend, asked, when Craig suggested that they split off. 'You've shot most of the stuff, all of it good. You want to improve on your elephant, or what? Maybe a forest rhino?'

'No,' Craig said. 'I don't want to shoot anything else except maybe a few birds and enough meat to feed us and the boys. I just want to look at the country. This Masai's pretty enough, God knows—almost too pretty. It looks like Switzerland in the spring. Let's go some place where it isn't so pretty.'

'Jolly good,' Mike said. 'I'm a Northern Frontier man, my-self. Let's totter down the dusty trail to Narok, maybe shoot one leopard at Oldonya Rash—it's stiff with them and you haven't got one and they *are* the loveliest trophy and most exciting to shoot—then we'll dash up to my private country and prowl the Abyssinian border. I think you'd like it up there, Mr. Price. It's a rough country, true, hot and dry and sort of beautifully ugly—fierce and crude and violent. Mountains slung all around, helter-skelter, in the midst of desert. I don't exactly know how to explain it, but you'll like it. Also we might spend just one night at the Mawingo Hotel outside of Nanyuki, on the off chance that the clouds won't be obscuring Mount Kenya when we get up for the morning tea. Quite a sight, that. I was brought up right under it, but I never fail to get a fresh thrill when I see old Kerinyagga, the home of God.'

Craig looked at his hunter with a fresh interest. Up to now he had regarded him as a pleasant companion, rather silent, terribly polite, a handsome young blond chap who spoke softly and briefly when he did speak, especially to the blacks—unlike some of the other pros who screamed at their boys. This lad was an intense, passionate hunter, and several times he had refused to allow Craig to shoot some animal which seemed as large or as long-horned as any other.

'Not good enough,' Mike would say, letting his thonged binoculars fall to his chest. 'Not nearly good enough, sir. Let's wait a bit, if you don't mind, and I'm sure we'll come upon something better. Actually,' he said with a shy smile, 'it's *my* reputation I'm trying to protect, more than yours.'

'About this Mount Kenya—this, what was the other name you called it? Kerin . . . ?'

'Kerinyagga, the Kikuyus call it. They believe God—*Ngai*—lives there, and looks down to survey the entire world, which belongs to His children, the Kikuyu. Rather a narrow view, I should say, but there it is. I believe that God has one clause in his contract saying that as long as the Masai don't leave this country, where we are now, they may inhabit this area without incurring His divine wrath. "I thy God am a jealous God" sort of thing. I believe that the Masai's *Ngai* entertains the same sort of feeling towards the Kyukes. Let them stay the hell away from the Loita and all goes well.' The boy smiled. 'Let's say our *kwaheris* and be off, shall us?'

They had made rather cold good-byes and driven, dust gritting in their teeth and drying their lips, to a favourite camp of Mike's a few miles to the side of the little town of Narok. It was a pleasant camp, pitched near a white-sanded, green-lichened-rock-studded river. It sat sweetly under tall, umbrella-topped fever trees, their trunks mottled as gold as the leopards which dwelt in them. Craig shot a wart-hog, which they placed in a tree a mile from camp, and was amazed at the knowledge which went into the exact selection of the tree, and all the skills devoted to luring the most elusive of beasts into that particular tree, in daytime, against all the beast's better judgement. The tree had to be located just so, in relation to the river. Its bole had to have a certain slant, and the bough on which the pig was slung had to be in correct relation to the one on which the haughty cat would be pleased to sit as he fed.

'It's really quite simple,' Mike said. 'We give the old *chui* a couple of days to become familiar with his pig, and when he's really stuck into it—and you can smell it a mile—we go off in the jeep one day, tumble out into the blind and shoot it. Leopards are really a matter of forestry and deceit. If you think like a leopard, you know exactly what sort of tree you'd most adore, and exactly what you'd like most to find in it. It's a strange thing. There is grand larceny in nearly all carnivorous animals. The leopard doesn't think it's strange at all to find a pig hoisted in the mizzen of a tree. He operates on the idea that the pig belongs to another leopard, and is delighted at the idea of stealing it.'

'Just like people,' Craig said. 'Especially people in my business. They'll steal anything, so long as they think it's somebody else's pig.'

'What a strange jungle you must live in, Mr. Price,' young Mike said, as they sat in the firelight, drinking gin-and-tonic that evening. The night sounds were comfortably close—a lion's irritable asthmatic cough a mile away, the steady sawing of a leopard prowling the river bed, the calliope virtuosity of the hyenas, and the mingled sounds of night-birds and the frightened barking of baboons.

They were sitting sprawled in camp chairs, feet to the towering, spark-exploding fire, waiting for dinner. The sky was a blue velvet bowl, silvered frostily with stars, and Craig had bathed in a brown canvas tub, and crawled into pyjamas and dressing-gown. He felt wonderful. Getting away from that African extension of Wall Street was enough to make anybody feel wonderful.

Once they had left his friends, he and Mike had enjoyed a blowsy, lazy day—shooting the poor old ugly pig, banging away at a few guinea-fowl and francolin for dinner, missing and laughing as they missed, preparing the leopard tree, and now talking in front of the snapping fire, with a hot meal sending delightful spicy smells from the cooking fires which glimmered fifty yards away, behind a patch of bush, where the boys had pitched their pup-tents. Strangely, as they had rid themselves of the other clients, Craig and the boy had swiftly become friends.

'Call me Craig,' he had said, when Mike continued to *mister* him. 'I don't have to be Mr. Price.'

'If you don't mind,' Mike said, 'I'd like to call you Mr. Craig, then, or Bwana Craig.' Craig barely suppressed a grin. His memory raced back to Julie duFresne and the whole intricate business of what he was supposed to call her.

'You'd have made a good Southern boy,' he said. 'All right. We settle for "Mr. Craig" until such time as you see fit to simplify

559

it to my first name. Carry on with that bit about the battler eagle, Mike.'

Mike got up and poured them both another gin.

'It's a simple commercial arrangement,' he said. 'The leopard and the eagle have a firm contract. The leopard's off, about his business, all day long, so the eagle sits in the tree and watches the kill. If some other leopard comes along, the eagle screams bloody murder, and old *Chui* gallops back on the double to defend his property. In return for this, the eagle is allowed a couple of pounds of flesh a day from the maggoty hog.'

'Commission,' Craig murmured. 'Just like in our jungle. The twelve per cent boys. They supply the pig. Once you've got your pig, you graduate to your battler eagle—the banks, who will exact two pounds of flesh daily to watch over your twelve-per-cent pig. Carry on, son.'

'Well,' Mike said, 'you find the same working agreement between the buffalo and the snowy egrets. In return for a free hand with the ticks and other vermin that afflict the old buff, the egrets ride his back, relieve him of a little annoyance, and serve as sentinels.'

'Brokers . . .' Craig murmured.

'Same again with rhino. Old *faro's* nearly blind, so he has a working agreement, too, with the tick-birds. In return for a free feed off his infestation of vermin, they serve as his eyes. They wa n him when danger is near, and they sit on his back until the la t minute. When the tick-birds jump, you can expect the rhino to charge.'

'More or less like lawyers, I would imagine,' Craig said. 'Keep you alerted and nervous and then jump off your back at the last minute and leave the rest up to you, blind or not. We have some more? This fascinates me.'

'Well, there's the honey-guide. He's the little bloke who is always squawking his head off, flying around, but if you follow him eventually you'll come to a bee-tree. I suppose he wants a cut of the profits, too, even when he thinks he's leading you away from it. Damned nuisance when you're trying to get up close to elephants.'

'Son, you are writing a history of New York. You have just touched on the beautiful blonde that you have met accidentally in El Morocco, who is supposed to lure you into a sugared trap, while allegedly steering you away from it, and then wants a reward from both ends of the arrangement, winner *and* loser. Let's cut this tonic nonsense and I will make us a martini.' Craig got up and went over to the drink table, pausing to stir a burning log with his toe.

'You like fire, don't you, Mr. Craig? And you're curious about animals. Pardon me, I'm not being rude, but most clients aren't interested in anything much out here except getting trophies—

560

and drunk. Fire is the life and death of this country. Did you know that when a native dies, they burn down the *shamba*, the farm, and move on? To get away from the ghosts, I mean?'

'I didn't know it,' Craig said, tipping a suspicion of vermouth into the pitcher. 'But I can believe it. I burnt a *shamba*, once, myself. To get rid of the ghosts. Too long a story to go into. Here. Try this. Extra hair on your chest.' He sat down. 'God, I love all this. Why didn't you bust me loose from those other guys earlier?'

Mike nodded his head in embarrassment.

'You know how it is—clients. We aim to please. We sign on for the trip. It's your whisky we're drinking. That's an old one. When you don't get along well on safari, but haven't had any outright clashes with the clients, and are a touch on the strained side, you say: "But we're still drinking their whisky." When it gets very bad, and sometimes it does, you retire to your tent and drink your own. I'd be proud to buy *you* several drinks in Nairobi, Mr. Craig.'

Craig bowed.

'I consider that a compliment, sir. Let's have some more jungle lore, if I'm not boring you. What other parallels to my kind of jungle can you offer?'

'Well, there's a bunch of damned fools around—wildbeeste and ostriches. Any time you've spotted a really good buff, for instance, you can bet your last quid that as you draw near, a herd of wildebeeste, snorting and running in circles, will spook you off the buff. The same for ostriches. They all have a way of getting in between you and what you're interested in and making so much noise and stupid confusion that everybody takes off in different directions and that's the last you'll see of that chosen animal. He went to Tanganyika to call on relatives.'

'In New York we call that public relations counsel,' Craig said. He quoted the old Navy one: ' "When in danger or in doubt, yell and scream and dash about." I have known intimately quite a few wildbeeste and ostriches and tick-birds and eagles in my time. Tell me, Mike, what finally happens?'

'Out here it's simple. When all the commotion is over, there are three winners. The hyenas, the vultures, and the ants. Everything dies, for one reason or another. I suppose you know the natives think the hyena is the angel of death, because they know that everybody winds up inside old *fisi*. He's a frightful beast, a stinking skulking coward, but he always gets you in the end. The vultures acquire the bloody shreds—the bits and pieces—and the ants finish off the job. I forgot to mention the jackal, a hanger-on, a stooge, you call it, but at least the lion will grant him a small portion of the kill, while the lion always fights off the vultures and the hyenas. But the lion knows, king or not, and the elephant knows, emperor or not, that they all have a

561

common finish: inside the dragging gut of stinking hyena, with the *ndege*—the birds—collecting the left-overs, and the ants as final winner. It's all as simple as that. I don't want to bore you. Tell me something about *your* jungle, please. Tell me about New York and business. I'd be frightened ill to go there.'

Craig looked at the fire, raised his eyes to the sky, and looked at the young hunter for a long moment before he spoke.

'So am I,' he said. 'Son, you have just given me the finest, most graphic description of commercial New York that I have ever heard in my life. I'd be embarrassed to attempt an improvement.'

They had a simple dinner: broiled francolin, the white-meated partridge, and Thomson's gazelle chops, with pickles and canned sauerkraut and a side dish of spaghetti. They had brought along a considerable assortment of drink: red wine and brandy, beer, whisky, gin. They drank Chianti with the meal, and were having a brandy with the coffee, as the fire flickered low, and the moon mounted in the sky, when Craig said abruptly:

'I've *been* here before.'

'I don't understand, Mr. Craig. Before? I thought this was your first safari.'

'No, I didn't mean physically actually. Some time before we pack it in I'll tell you. It's a long, and doubtless boring, story. I'm a little bit drunk, and full of food, and I think I'll hit the sack now, Mike. Thank you very much for a wonderful day.'

'Mr. Craig?'

'Yes, son?' Craig got up and yawned. 'What?'

'Please pardon me. But I'm . . . I'm awfully glad we split off from the rest. I hope I'm not being rude.'

Craig cuffed the young hunter on the shoulder.

'So am I, my boy. So bloody well am I. I think we'll have a lot of fun. G'night.'

That night he slept a sleep he had not slept in fifteen years. Perhaps the hyenas tripped over the tent-ropes, or a lion entered camp, but Craig Price would not have been aware if a bull mastodon had crept into bed with him. He had barely closed his eyes when his personal boy lifted the green mosquito netting and handed him his tea, as dawn crept rosily into life.

'*Chai, Bwana,*' the boy said. '*Bafu tiari.*'

7

'IT was quite something,' Craig told Susan on the plane. 'It was a long-repressed dream coming true. For the first time I could remember since I was a kid, I felt the kind of peace I get from you, and don't make any smart cracks. This kid and I got to be awfully good friends. He was full of curisoity about my jungle, and so was I about his, and for a month we talked each other into exhaustion. He was particularly impressed, I think, with the way I got along with the black boys. I read him quite a long narrative on my earlier days, of the complete interweaving of my life with coloured people, and something of my feeling for them. I think he liked me . . .'

After Craig shot the leopard, a very large tom who had come early on the fourth day of the bait-hanging, they piled into a Land Rover and drove towards the North.

'I was pretty proud of you, Mr. Craig . . . do you mind if I just call you Craig now?' Mike had asked that night, when they were having the celebration drinks. 'So many people who do the other stuff well completely funk it on leopard. There's something about that damned great spotted cat coming suddenly into a tree just at dusk, which causes people to throw their guns away or fire into the air.'

'Don't think *I'm* not proud of me too, my boy. It's a sight unlike anything I ever saw. I don't understand how they can move so damned fast. We sat there for two hours with the safari ants and the mosquitoes chewing on us, and nothing happened. Nothing except the baboons barking and that bloody dove—the one who sounds like he's saying "Merril Lynch, Pierce, Fenner and Beane"—mourning about his dividends, or whatever it is doves mourn about. And then that tree suddenly full of cat. He appeared as if somebody had just turned on a home movie. One minute, nothing but black bush. Next second, leopard. God, they look as big as a spotted horse. Heaven knows who pointed the rifle. It sure wasn't me.'

'*Shauri a mungu*,' Mike said. 'God's will.'

They drove through the choking lava dust for a while in silence, watching the silly little doves playing in the track, looping ahead to fly a few yards and settle again in a stupid game.

'The scenery's gone off, I must say,' Craig said. 'When we flew into your field in the Masai, I thought all of it looked that way . . . green and lush and the acacias all flowered out. This looks like the ass end of nowhere. Ever since we left Narok, I mean.'

'It's not much to see, I have to admit,' Mike said. 'Until we log another twenty miles or so. Then you get the big volcanoes, and when we stop for petrol and a Coke at Naivasha, before we head up to Thomson's Falls and Nanyuki—that's where it's all lovely and green, the Aberdare—when you look at old Longonot, red in the sunset . . . when you see how far the Rift stretches in the direction we're leaving. Then, as the Americans say, you really got something. And as I told you, the first sight of old Kerinyagga, close to . . .'

'On some belated honeymoon, my darling,' Craig said to

Sue, 'I should like to take you to Africa, blindfolded, and stow you in one of the better suites, late at night, in a hotel named Mawingo, outside Nanyuki, a pleasant green town in the high Aberdare mountains of Kenya, and I should like to waken you in front of a vast picture window, and without saying a word, lead you by the hand and confront you with Mount Kenya, God's home town.

'It should have only a jocular shred of cloud, about lip high, and then its snowy head should be proudly held against a sky of unbelievable blue. Beyond its shoulder would be the Northern Frontier, that angry desert land, with my other favourite mountain, Ololokwe, a gaudy bit of rock, all purple and red and white and black and square-headed, and then there would be some *lugas*—dry river beds which rage into torrents in the rainy season, when the area is closed to all but the nomads, the Rendille-Samburu and the other nice folk, like the Turkana and Somali, who live there, come rain or come shine.

'I would like you to meet some dry-river-bed friends of mine, with names like Kinya, Serarua, Seralippe, where the elephants and the Somal donkeys dig in blinding white sand for the water they know must be beneath it, or God's a liar, and where the big vulturine guineas with their high cockades of blue feathers race up and down, and the flocks of native goats and fat-tailed sheep come down to drink from wells that sometimes go so deeply into the sands that it needs six men, standing on earthen shelves, to pass the water upward so that the flocks may live.

'I would like to show you a rhino lumbering, heavy shouldered and surly, like a hung-over prizefighter, from one tight-clenched jungle of dwarf palm, wait-a-bit thorn and sansevieria bush to another, leaving his heavy hoof-prints in the sand. I would like to bathe naked with you in a sparkling pool at Buffalo Springs, under feathered palms, and I would like to show you a crossroads which has a signpost which bids you enter: Left, *Archer's Post*. Right, *Garba-Tulla-Shaffa Dikka*. You can't beat that for a signpost.

'I drove down, finally, hating to leave it, to Nairobi, and we stopped at Nyeri for a drink and a beautiful cold lunch at the White Rhino. As we came out, I felt I was losing my last identity with the old *me*. The North had got me, as it generally gets the lonely ones. Mount Kenya had me. I was not the first person to find God there. I thought of going back to New York. I thought of going back to Maybelle. I thought of the blazing scar of the Rift, stretching over a hundred miles, as seen from the high hill as you come down to Naivasha from Nairobi. I spoke aloud:

' "You poor, *poor* son-of-a-bitch," I said. Young Mike looked at me curiously.

' "What was that, Craig?"

' "I was referring to me, Mike," I said. "I am a poor miserable son-of-a-bitch. I've got to leave all this and go back to my own savage soil, where all the people are baboons, but without any humour, and the dry river beds are paved with concrete instead of dung—concrete so thick no elephant can dig himself a well, but has to sub-contract the job to Consolidated Edison. All the mountains have elevators, lifts, and the hyenas wear narrow-shouldered suits and undented hats with bows in the back. The vultures hover, ever waiting to pick the bones, and all about you are ants . . . ten million ants, each with a special problem and a hunger all of its own."

' "I'm afraid I don't quite follow you, Craig," young Mike said. He was so right. I didn't follow myself, but I knew, I knew then, terribly I knew, that up to that point I had wasted a life. Nothing had happened to me except motion until I saw you at that dreadful party. I was poverty-stricken while owning King Solomon's Mines. If you don't mind being confused with Mount Kenya and a few friendly hyena-noises in the night, I want to marry you to protect myself against poverty. As my Texas boy said, I do not want to be poor no more, and you're my only hope. It took Africa and you, to show me just how poor I've always been.'

Sue turned and kissed him swiftly on the cheek.

'You don't have to be poor any more, darling,' she said. Her voice sounded as if she were soothing a child. 'Mommy will kiss it and make it well. This is a hell of a strange place for a declaration of vows, but in sickness and in health, I will be your Mount Kenya if you'll just let me . . .' She squeezed his hand. 'Look, we're coming in to Idlewild now.'

'Back,' Craig said. 'To the jungle.'

One thing I didn't tell her, Craig thought, as they were landing, was the other bit about the hyenas and the wild dogs.

'The wild dogs,' young Mike said, 'are really rather not-nice types. They hunt in packs, and they run in relays, and they can pull down anything, eventually, hamstringing it, and eating it alive. And when one of them is wounded, his own brothers stop and eat *him* alive before they go on with their business. Definitely poor types. And the hyena, apart from his filthy scavenging, is worse. For one thing, one in about ten is a pure hermaphrodite. I dissected one out once, from curiosity, and it was equipped with complete sets of male and female reproductive organs. They can both impregnate and conceive.

'God crippled them so that they can't run very fast, so they must feed on the weak and the ill and the dead. They snap, with those enormous jaws, the udders off cows, and they wait in the breeding season for the ewes to drop their lambs, and they eat the weakened mother and the baby as well. And when they're wounded, with their guts dragging, they turn and eat themselves as well.'

565

'Eat *themselves*?'

'Yes, sir. I've gut shot a hyena on occasion, and have seen him sit down and eat his own intestines with more than relish. I've seen them chewing happily on their own legs. Dirty beast, that nobody loves.'

Craig looked again at the skyline as the plane circled the field in a planned landing-pattern.

'Yes,' he said softly to himself, 'back to the jungle, for sure. Me and all the other hyenas.'

8

CRAIG could see Jazzbo Newton waiting outside the customs, which would certainly be less than a brief formality. 'How was Havana, Mr. Price?' the customs man said. 'Anything declarable? No bird-of-paradise plumes?'

'No. Nothing. I travelled light this trip. Also I got enough rum in the office bottle-drawer.' He grinned, a grin which referred to Christmas presents for many years. 'The lady's a friend of mine. She's in the dope traffic, so you'd better search her bags closely. At least a hundred pounds of heroin.'

The clerk smiled and checked off the bags.

'We know you better than that, Mr. Price. As a gentleman, you'd be carrying it yourself.' He permitted himself the small familiarity.

'Thanks, Johns—no, Jensen, isn't it?'

'Jensen, that's right, sir. Will I have a porter take the stuff out to your chauffeur? Do you want the lady's bags in with yours?'

'Yes, thanks, I do indeed. If it's not violating regulations, I can see my chauffeur leaning on the door, and maybe he could just come get them and save everybody trouble?'

'Of course, Mr. Price. Charlie!' He raised his voice in the general direction of the customs guard. 'Tell the chauffeur to come get his boss's bags. That guy there, leaning on your neck.'

Jazzbo came into the customs sheds. He had his uniform cap in hand.

'Howdy, Boss. Everything all right with them Cubans?' Craig passed his hand automatically over Jazzbo's head and shook it gently. He smiled.

'Sho, man. Everything all right with them Puerto Rican gals in Harlem?'

'Yas-*suh*, I'm real straight in Harlem. Sho' is good to see you back. I been havin' trouble runnin' de firm. Seem lak it need yo' presence, although I does the best I can when you away.'

Jazzbo looked politely at Susan.

'This is a friend of mine, Jazz. Mrs. Strong. Jazzbo. She's hitching a ride with us into town. Her bags are over there with mine.'

Jazzbo beamed.

'I is sure pleased and proud to meet you, Miz' Strong,' he said, and bowed low. 'The car right outside, boss. I kind of reasoned wid a cop. You gon' know de car right off. It de only *Rolls*-Royce in dat cow-pasture. You jes' go to de car, I fetch de bags. Also, de bar open, ready for business.' He beamed again, and bustled off with the bags.

Craig handed Sue into the rear seat of the gleaming black Rolls, crawled in beside her, and reached for a silver handle. The back of the front seat collapsed into a small but adequate bar, with ice-bucket, glasses, soda, a water carafe, and bottles of gin, scotch, vermouth and bourbon.

'De bar open, Miz' Strong,' Craig said. 'This is Jazzbo's pride and joy, this little bar. I think he might even patronize it himself. What might your pleasure be, ma'am?'

'Y'all know what mah real pleasure is, sugah, but Ah thinks Ah fancies a little bourbon and branch, Beauregard, honey.' Sue said. 'How does it feel to have a slave, Cuhnel Massa Boss?'

'I dunno. Maybe you better ask Jazzbo. He's had me enslaved for years, with no hope of Abe Lincoln to loose me from bondage. I don't want to give away any trade secrets,' he said, pouring the drinks, 'but J. Edgar Hoover informs me that from time to time a black Rolls-Royce with a built-in bar has been observed in the vicinity of 125th Street, in the general area of Lenox Avenue, and further spies tell me that Sugar Ray is practically mauve with envy. After all, he's only got a pink Cadillac. Yessir, in the white-slave business, old Jazz has really cornered the market.'

'You really love that little black boy, don't you?'

'And why not? He's had me so long I'm an accessory. I told you, I reckon he'd die very cheerfully for me. Me and Jazz are two against this here rotten Yankee world. We is quality folks lost in a community of rich po' *Bokra*.'

'Do I know what is po' *Bokra*?'

'Possibly not, Scarlett. Po' *Bokra* means poor white trash. Up here in this cold north country dey be's jumped-up po' white trash. Jazz and me, we figure we's de aristocrats. We doesn't traffic much wid de trash.'

Jazzbo approached with a trundle bearing the luggage. He stowed the bags in the boot.

'Where us headed, boss?'

'First stop, we drop the lady. Then I'll look in at the office for an hour, and then I guess home.'

'*Home*, boss? In de middle of de week?'

'Shut up and let's move. I said home, ape. That Harlem jive is rattling what few brains you had to start with.'

Jazzbo shook his head, as he stowed the luggage.

567

'*Home*, in de *middle* of de *week*,' he said. 'Wid a pretty gal lak dat in de car. De boss mus' is losin' his mind.'

'This is going to take time, and quite a lot of doing,' Craig said. 'Maybe a year. There's the kid, and all the lawyer stuff. I hate to say it, darling, but maybe we better play it soft-shoe until all the papers are signed. I'm going to the country now and see what's up. Call you tomorrow?'

'I hope you're right, darling. I hope you're right. Call me tomorrow. I've got a strong intent to get up early and see if Monsieur Paul can do something about this Cuban sun-wrecked hair.'

'Let's have lunch then. Say two, at the Laurent?'

'Lovely.' Jazzbo had handed her bags to the doorman with stern injunctions for excessive care. 'See you at two. Thanks for, as daddy used to say, the buggy ride.'

Craig got into the front seat with Jazzbo. 'Let's skip the office,' he said. 'It can hang on without us until tomorrow. Let's get on out to Suffern.'

'Dat seem a real fine lady, boss. Where you meet her?'

'In Havana. At the hotel. She's a real nice lady, Jazz. We had a very pleasant trip on the plane together.'

Jazzbo slid a sly African eye at Craig, as he slipped into the Madison Avenue traffic.

'Boss . . .' tentatively. 'You knows me a long time. I *got* to say it. Things ain't good out home. Things *really* ain't good out home.'

Craig patted him on the shoulder.

'Thanks, pal. You know me a long time, too. Things ain't been real good out home for a long time. I don't want to talk, coon-jigger. Just see if you can jig your way through that traffic so we can get home and find out just how bad things are.'

Craig dozed on the long ride out to Suffern, and came fully awake as they pulled into the driveway leading to his house. It was dark, but the house was unlit except for the kitchen. The house loomed monstrous in the night, and Craig looked at it with sour distaste. It had a look of a blind man, of a long vacant castle. A chill travelled his spine. The goddamned thing was at least as big as the Taj, he thought, and not half so pretty.

'For Christ's sake,' he said. 'Ain't there nobody here but me?' Echoes answered.

Nobody had appeared to greet him. As Jazzbo came in with the bag, Craig said:

'Where's the bloody butler? Don't anybody do anything around here?'

'It probably de butler's night off, boss,' Jazzbo said. 'Wait a minute, I ring a bell. I don't know what become de Missus and Miss Carol. Dey was here yestiddy.'

Great, Craig thought. *Splendid*. I got a house with three

568

swimming pools and stables and a fowl-run and a kennel for a hundred dogs and a greenhouse as big as the White House and my own arrogant pheasants and the finest house a rich man's drunken son ever built and sold to me for no money. I got the social proximity of rich and famous neighbours and the nearness of Tuxedo, the old fancy Tuxedo, as an extra added attraction. There ain't no fire in the fireplaces, and nobody answers the door, and I suppose the tame pheasants are starving and the Weimaraners haven't been fed in the dog kennels and whatever happened to the cow and the sheep that were supposed to pull the grass up, or was it keep the grass down?

He walked back towards the kitchen, where Jazzbo was in heated conversation with a coloured maid.

Jazzbo spread his hands helplessly.

'Dis gal, boss, dis gal say everybody kinda done gone. De butler quit, and de cook quit, and de gardener down sick, and de plumbin' jammed up upstairs, and somepin' don' work wid de pumps on two swimming pools and de Missus, she say she cain' stan' it and shove off and Miss Carol gone some place wid somebody an' . . .'

Craig held up a hand.

'Spare me the rest of the grisly details.' To the maid: 'Do you know where Mrs. Price is staying?'

'She leave a note, anybody ask, say she go be stayin' de Plaza Hotel.'

'Thanks. Look after the place, will you, please, until Mrs. Price and I come back.'

'Nossuh. I'se quittin' too. I doesn't aims to stay by myself in dis big house. Too lonesome and full of spooky noise. I'se goin' back to Harlem.'

'All right, get your bags and we'll drive you to town.'

'Thank you, suh, Mistah Price. You *is* Mistah Price?' She walled her eyes. 'I'se kinda new here.'

'I'm Mr. Price. Yes. Hurry and get your things.'

'Yassuh. I'se already packed.'

Craig spread his hands, and looked gloomily around the depressingly functional kitchen, at the massive walk-in freeze-boxes, the long lines of metal-gleaming sinks, the humming refrigerators, the chromed garbage disposal units, the electric dish-washer . . .

He shrugged.

'You wants me to lock up, boss?' Jazzbo sounded anxious.

'Don't bother. There's nothing in this house anybody would want to steal.'

'Dat be all, boss?' It was late night and Craig was seated behind his desk in his Manhattan office, looking blindly at the foot-high stack of papers.

'That's all. Take the car if you want, and go have yourself a ball. Check in tomorrow morning about ten. Good night, Jazz.'

'Mistah Craig?' Tentatively, almost, Jazzbo put a comforting hand on his boss's shoulder, thought better of it, and withdrew the hand. 'I'se powerful sorry about de house and nobody bein' home. Seem a shame spen' all dat money and den nobody home...'

'Thanks, kid. Go have some fun. Get loaded. Find a gal. Good night.'

'Good night, boss.'

Jazzbo left and Craig dialled a number. The phone on the other end rang three times before a voice answered.

'Jimmy? Craig. Just got back. Problems. Reckon you could come over here? And do you know what the hell's going on with Maybelle? You do? Well, save it until you get here. Right. You can spend the night in the spare room like always. Thanks. 'Bye.'

He rang off, got up and walked to the bar. He poured himself a drink and leaned against an elephant tusk, resting his Cuban-sun-hot-face against the cool ivory, feeling mental relief, as always, from contact with the tusks. He raised his head and looked at the mounted heads on his walls. He smiled. Somehow, they soothed him. The sable, for instance. He could remember every single detail of that day, from the time he woke until all hands went to bed drunk and happy from celebration.

'My God, it's been a long time,' he said. 'And here am I, just like a short-pants kid in college, still calling on Jimmy Wilbur for help...'

9

ALL of a sudden, Carol has become seventeen. And Craig had never known her at all beyond the earliest baby days. He left home in a hurry, early, after a swift coffee, and when he got back during the week—if he got back at all during the week—she had been fed, bathed and put to sleep. Week-ends, the house was full of people—business people, mostly—and while the presence of a child was announced by the usual impedimenta—tricycles, dolls, bunny rabbits—a fast peep into the nursery was the formal extent of their acquaintance. Nanny skilfully shunted the baby out from under grown-up feet, away from grown-up cocktails by the pool, away from grown-up cocktails before the fire.

She was a pretty baby, and promised to be a beautiful girl. She was a silent, indrawn child, and resembled the young Craig in that respect as much as she resembled him physically. Un-scarred, un-nose broken, she was an almost ridiculous replica of her father. She had the same brown eyes, the same cowlick in the same hair, the same mouth and chin, the same impatient mannerisms. As a child she rarely cried except in sudden fury.

Her idol was Jimmy Wilbur. Craig had developed a habit of delegating parenthood to his old college friend, who had remained a bachelor.

'Jim,' he'd say, in the midst of a frenzy of business, 'for God's sake, I just remembered I promised the kid I'd take her to the zoo Saturday afternoon, and I forgot all about those people from Charlotte who're only in for the week-end. I've got to take them to lunch Saturday and then there's dinner and cocktails and the theatre Saturday night. Look, if I send Jazzbo out for the kid, will you be a good guy and take her to the zoo, and then see she gets back all right?'

'Sure, boss,' Jimmy Wilbur would grin. 'I baby-sat *you*. I guess I can carry on with the kid in the same frame. You ever wonder what would have become of you if it hadn't been for me?'

'Damned if I know.' Craig grinned. 'I guess I formed the Wilbur habit so early I never was able to kick it. And look. Sunday there's some sort of kid party that Maybelle has whomped up. You know, the neighbours' brats. I can't be there Sunday. Could you maybe spend the night at the house and make noises like a papa in front of the children? I got to be in Chicago Sunday, for a very rough Monday. Okay?'

'Okay, Craig,' Wilbur looked sarcastically thoughtful. 'Are you sure you'd recognize this kid if you saw her today? She's grown a lot, you know. She's a dish. The war's been over quite a spell. She's going off to school in September. Think you might make time to take her?'

'That I'll find time for.'

But when Carol Price went off to boarding school, Jimmy Wilbur took her. Craig had suddenly been called to Houston, and Maybelle was just a little, just a touch, under the weather.

'Where's Daddy?' Carol said, when Jimmy showed up in the car with Jazzbo. 'I thought he was going with us?'

'Sorry, sweetheart,' Wilbur said. 'Last-minute business thing. You know how hard he works. He sent his love and said he'd be up to school to see you soon.'

'I don't want him to be up to see me *soon*. I wanted him to come take me to school *today*. So the other kids could see him.'

'Cheer up, doll,' Jimmy said, and patted her shoulder. 'You always got your old Uncle James standing by . . .'

Somehow Old Uncle James was forced into a full-time job of standing by. When Maybelle really fell into the sauce and had to take a small retreat to a health farm, it was generally Jimmy who worked out the details and deposited Maybelle at the door.

If Maybelle went to Miami, and rockets were suddenly fired by distressed friends or nervous hotel managers, Jimmy caught the first plane to straighten out the troubles. Gradually, he had

571

become a sort of chief steward of Craig's private life and in the performance sacrificed much of his own.

'You know,' he said one day when some fresh crisis had arisen at home, 'I think I got a solution for all your troubles. You give me a million dollars. I'll allow you to adopt me legally, call me Craig Price, Junior, and I'll marry Maybelle. That'll give Carol the father she's used to—*me*—and Maybelle the husband she's used to—*me*—and you'll be relieved of even thinking about your family. Also you'll be gaining a son-in-law. For a million bucks it's dirt cheap. What the hell is wrong with you, anyhow, boy? I figured you to be a sucker for kids, and you don't even pay attention to your own. You got a wonderful house and you never see it. You got a wife . . .'

'Yeah, yeah. I know.' Craig held up a palm. 'Don't bother to tell me any more what kind of husband and father I am. I'm lousy: I stink. I ought to be shot. So shoot me. Tell me something, Moose.' Not very often did Craig call Wilber 'Moose' these days. 'This is a hard one. But did you ever go to a movie and feel so embarrassed for the actor when he was forced to make an utter ass out of himself, you cringed for him?'

'I feel that way every time I turn on the TV,' Wilbur said. 'So what?'

'Did you ever do anything bad, that you knew at the time was bad, for the sake of practicality?'

'I played college football while the other kids were playing pianos in whore-houses,' Jimmy's voice took on an ancient brutality. 'Yeah, bo. I did some bad things.'

'Right. Do you like to think about the old days—all the lying and cheating and stealing—yes, *stealing*, by God—that you *had* to do to eat so you could make All-America and help pay for a stadium and make the drunk alumni happy and keep the coach in his job and grab a lot of space in the papers? When you knew damned well you were more of a crook for playing college football than you were when you were bootlegging that time? *Do* you? Do you like to think about it now? Doesn't it make your flesh crawl a little?'

'Some. Some. But I had one thing going for me. I was never under any wild delusions of nobility. You think back to the first talks we had. I *knew* I was a whore. It's not so bad to be one if you know it at the time. What's all this leading to? Tell Papa Wilbur, like you used to, when you wore the short pants.'

'I still got the short pants. Look, I know I'm a lousy husband. I know I'm a lousy father. I know I never go home, and I wench around, and invent excuses to escape the normal penalties of parenthood and matrimony. I do it on purpose, and I can't help it, because every time I see Maybelle, every time I see Carol, I see me, and me I don't like. You want it straight, Max? I'm a coward, and an ego-maniac, and I can't stand to look in a

572

mirror that reflects me the way Maybelle and Carol reflect me. When I see Maybelle I see another man's cotton mill. When I see my child I don't see my child at all. I see a con man who literally held his nose, got his wife drunk, and seduced her into still another mill. Talk about your bitter aloes . . .' His voice trailed.

'What's an aloe?' Jimmy asked. 'Remember I was only a physical education major. No labs.'

'If I may make a small and bad pun,' Craig said bitterly. 'An aloe sure as hell ain't a halo. Not when I see this battered puss reflected through my wife and child. It's a dreadful thing, Mr. Wilbur, to saddle yourself with a late-blooming conscience, and at the same time know damned well you'd do it all over again. Just like every time you lay a broad, you wish you hadn't but know damn well you'll do it again. You ever read a book, or see a picture, called *The Portrait of Dorian Grey*?'

'Yeah. That British faggot wrote it. Didn't read the book but I saw the picture. Man sold his soul to the Devil, or something, and raised a lot of hell, and hurt everybody he touched, and one day his face fell off. The Old Joe finally got him. He looked terrible. Yeah. I saw the picture.'

'Okay. Every time I think about Maybelle, every time I think about Carol, what I see in my mirror makes Dorian Grey look like Tyrone Power.'

Jimmy Wilbur shook his head, and thumped his boss on the knee.

'You always were a strange kid,' he said. 'And now you're getting old I think you're getting stranger. Dorian Grey, yet. Play your cards right, boy, and you can work up to Frankenstein. You ain't been all that much of a heel, Junior, despite a few gross of girls here and there. Everybody runs around. But you seem to be trying to kill yourself in the process of making more money you can't spend, or at least don't have time to spend. When we going huntin' again? For God's sake, do you still want it *all*?'

'Not all. There's room here for everybody.' The mood lightened. Then darkened. 'But I want most of it. Yeah. I still want it all.'

'Well,' Jimmy said. 'Happy coronary. I got to go look after your family. Some time when you got a minute to waste I know a pretty young kid named Carol Price I'd like you to meet. She hasn't got many faults, except in some ways she takes after her old man. See you later, Short Pants.'

10

CRAIG smiled as he waited for Jimmy to come to the office. That was quite a boy, Jimmy. He was older, heavier, richer, better-dressed, but still didn't give much of a damn for anything or anybody—except, Craig thought suddenly—*me*. *Me*. Like that Chinaman who pulled the guy out of the water. The guy loves me and I kind of belong to him. He got me out of that mess with the nut and I been his boy ever since, even though he works for me.

'Hya, Moose,' he said, as Jimmy came into the office with his own pass-key. He got up, and Craig permitted himself a rare gesture of affection. As they shook hands, Craig let his left hand rest slightly on Wilbur's shoulder, much as he automatically passed his hand over Jazzbo's head.

'You look good, kid,' Jimmy said. 'That Cuban sunshine didn't do you any harm. You ought to figure on getting away oftener. Who was she this time, you were so busy with that gook bank?'

'Special. You drinking?'

'Am I never not drinking when it's free? I got a key to the cabinet, too, remember? Where do you think I spend my time when you're out of town? Orgies, every night orgies, right here in this zoo. What stories that buffalo could tell, what stories . . .' Jimmy Wilbur raised reverent eyes to the ceiling. 'I produced more sprained backs out of this room than . . .' He stopped suddenly. He took a vicious bite at his drink.

'You're in trouble, pal—several kinds, one of which is business. We skip that until later. Right now you got yourself a beautiful ripe family mess. The business we can fix, but I'm about to fire the coach on this family deal. Maybelle has really flipped, and I'm worried sick about Carol. Look, you bastard, I love that kid. Between having a crazy genius for a father and a lush for a mother, all the Uncle Jimmies and governesses in the world ain't going to make her into a normal woman. She . . .'

'Sit down and tell me about Maybelle first. What's she up to now that ain't usual?'

'Craig, *I* don't know. I just don't know. Jesus, I didn't sign on with you to play nursie to a grown woman who is drinking herself into insanity. This woman of yours has hit a point where she ain't washing very frequently, except on week-ends. Her face is swelled up like a basketball, you can't hardly see her eyes, boy, and she's never noisy-stinking any more, like she used to be. She's just kind of calm-drunk, like she'd wrapped herself in a fur coat and liked the way it felt. What are we going to *do* with her? She's never unloaded. She wakes up pissed and improves on it as the time goes by. It wasn't very nice for Carol—and not nice for me—when Carol used to say, "What's the matter with Mummy, she's so funny again? Is she sick, Uncle Jim?" And I had to say yes, baby, she's not feeling very well, just like I still say yes, baby, daddy's held up at the office again.

'Now it's different. Carol says: "The old girl's blind again, Jim. The old man doing something worse than usual? What do we expect to see in the papers now? Another actress or just some new babe he found on his doorstep?" She's a big girl, now, that Carol of yours—I should say *mine*. Christ, Craig, I was the one who had to tell her the bird-bee bit. You were in Venezuela . . .'

'All right, all *right*.' Craig's voice was desperately tired. 'I got a new problem I haven't even touched on yet. What is the status quo, exactly?'

'Maybelle got herself progressively loaded last week, each day a little stiffer, and then she fired everybody she could find. She said she always hated the goddamned house and everything in it, including you and me—I get this from the butler, who was on the pipe early about his severance pay—and she was going to the Plaza and then she was going home to North Carolina where people liked her for herself, and she was going to get a divorce, and kill herself, and set fire to the Price Building, and a few other side threats as well. Also, you haven't had time to notice it yet, but she cut off the trousers of all your pants at the knee. You're back in knickers now for true.

'I guess Carol couldn't stand too much of it—she took off to visit some friends, somewhere, I don't even know where. Nobody was sure about what anybody's done. Far as I know Carol is hopping cars in Hollywood, waiting to be a movie star as of yesterday. What we gonna do with this mess, boy? What do we do? You've ducked it long enough.'

'I'd like to sit here and cry,' Craig said, 'but instead I got news for you, friend. I'm going to get a divorce. Life is passing me by. For twenty years—yes, goddammit, I know it's all my fault, so shut up—I was willing to put up with it because I never loved anybody but me. But now, Moose . . .' His voice trailed and his lips relaxed into reflective pleasure. Then he fired a rapid salvo of words.

'Now, Moose, I'm in love. I'm in love with a woman I leaped into the sack with the first day I saw her. I'm in love like I thought I might be in love when we were in school, and I am to marry her, hear me, and be happy!' He grabbed Jimmy Wilbur by the shoulders and shook him. 'I want to be *happy*, goddammit! Happy!'

'Well,' Jimmy said, 'if happy means breaking my neck, you're half-way home.' He shrugged Craig's hands loose. 'You wouldn't want a sock in the puss to cement your happiness, would you? I could be tempted . . .'

'Sorry.' Craig quieted his voice. 'I guess you don't fall in love every day, not at my age. This girl . . . I banged her before I knew her. And then . . . and then I wished I could have gone back and pulled her pigtails and toted her books and taken her to the prom . . . You remember Mary Frances? You remember Libby Forney?'

'That was . . . sure. You had her up for some dances. She stayed at the Zete house. Sure. Her brother was a fraternity brother of mine. I sure remember Libby. We threw her away too. Yeah. And what?'

'This is the Mary Frances I threw away, that I found again when I was old enough to know what I was finding. I'm marrying this girl, Moose.'

Wilbur got up and poured himself another drink.

'You want a fresher?'

'No, I'm fine. Sit down and help me with this.'

'Well.' Wilbur's voice was elaborately precise. 'There is nothing standing in front of this great true love you've dug up except a business that's in trouble, a drunken wife, and a daughter who might be called mixed-up. I'll brush over the business, but you hit some dusters lately, you're hocked up to your ears. That airline you helped buy is going just a little bust, and the banks are throwing a shoe every time anybody says "Price". The market's off, too, and every time I pick up a paper and read about Europe I get an uneasy feeling that the next story I read will be about somebody hijacking Switzerland. So much for business, except that your tame insurance company has just been run out of another state. So much for business . . . but remember that McCarthy was able to lose the Shamrock. But you can always fix business. The point is Maybelle.'

Jimmy Wilbur narrowed his eyes against the smoke of his cigarette.

'What *about* Maybelle? She's got her name on a mess of paper, boy. You been eating a lot of her cake and having it too. She's just going to blow you a kiss and say, honey, be happy, get it all straightened out and send me a cheque every month? Not if I know Maybelle. She ain't Einstein, but she's got a kind of tough, if simple, brain. Face it, kid. You lose Maybelle, you really screw the works. You got in—and if you hit me I'll knock you cold—on Maybelle, and getting out is going to cost you. You parlayed your sexy personality, Buster, into an empire. But the sexy personality ain't enough. Half of what you got in textiles Maybelle's got paper on—enough to cripple you with the credit-boys, anyhow. You hocked a lot of stuff and you needed that signature. Your oil reserves are mostly escrowed against loans. Maybelle knows, pretty good, where enough bodies are planted to fix your clock good. And you know,' Jimmy said, 'she doesn't even have to be smart. You hit her with a

576

divorce and the first two-bit lawyer to come running will tell her where she's got you, and what her strength is. Pretty, ain't it?'

'Yeah, it's pretty. But pretty or not, I'm going to get rid of Maybelle. She can have what she wants. She can have anything liquid I got. The house is paid for. So's the thing in France we never use anyway except as a gimmick. She can take Villefranche and sell it to the Algerians, for all I care. But I'm getting out. Jimmy, would you . . . would you . . . *act* for me on this?'

Wilbur got up. He walked over and deliberately smacked Craig a hard blow across the face with the back of his hand.

'If you want me to close the fist, get up and tell me,' he said. 'You gutless bastard. *No*, I won't act for you. This is one snake you can kill for yourself. I'm tired of being your vice-president in charge of everything the boss hasn't got time or guts enough to handle. Get up and hit me, if you want, but consider I quit. I'm tired of pimping for a pimp.'

The imprint of Wilbur's hand was rosy against the tan of Craig's cheek, but he never moved from his chair. He put both hands, palm down, on his desk, and leaned back in his chair. All of a sudden, the day on the docks at Charleston came sharply back, Philip duFresne saying: 'No. Not this boy. I like it down here on the deck. I don't fight over whores.'

'I'm sorry, Jim,' Craig said. 'I was out of line. Way out.'

'All right.' Jimmy Wilbur sat down again. 'I'm sorry I smacked you. But this is one you got to play out yourself, friend. This ain't for substitute half-backs.'

'Jesus, what'll she do without me?'

Wilbur drawled:

'About the same as usual. She hasn't had any real part of you for years, since you got to be a big shot. She never had any part of you *before* you got to be a big shot. Look, friend. You got a busted nose and a bald spot. You want me to tell you that you look like Robert Taylor and got a full head of hair? You know your track record better than me. You think she likes reading in Winchell or Kilgallen that you're dancing around the Morocco with some new tramp, or when Hopper or Parsons track you down in Los Angeles with some other bum? This would be inclined to keep the girl sober? You didn't invent money, and other men have investigated women before your time. You ain't got a corner on loot and poon. There's eighty million Chinese broads you'll never even meet. You can't screw the world, Buster-boy. It's too big for you. There ain't time enough.'

'Do me one favour, then, Jim, please. She loves you. See if you can get her sober enough to talk business about the divorce. It's hopeless for me to try—it'll just wind up with her screaming and throwing things. When she's a little bit sober, then I'll talk to her.'

'I'll do *that*. In the meanwhile, what about your child? Send her to the Salvation Army, or what? She's there, you know. She exists. She may just represent a new mill to you, but to me she's a sweet kid with a drunk for a mother and a bastard for a father—a glamorous rich bastard who gets his picture on magazine covers and who never comes home nights. You ever think about taking her to the circus? I do. I've seen that circus so many times I could throw up, and the lions in the Bronx Zoo practically beg for my autograph. You ever hear about Hopalong Cassidy? I own him, just from practice, just from being a substitute father. Space Cadet is my godson. What, God damn you, Craig Price, are we going to do about your kid?'

Craig's tanned face was suddenly grey, and his voice greyer. He shrugged and spread his hands helplessly. He looked at Wilbur, who was suddenly moved to compassion by what he saw on Craig's face.

'Oh, hell, son, don't worry too much. It'll work out some way. What do you figger?'

'Hadn't thought too much. When we get married I'll buy another house, a new house, and the kid and Susan and I can all live together.'

'Maybelle's going to like Carol living with her new mama?' Wilbur's voice was elaborately sarcastic now. 'I don't want to burden you with trifles, tycoon, but such things as custody enter into divorces, as well as financial detail. And somebody gets the kid.'

'I can't leave Carol with her mother in the shape Maybelle's in . . .'

'Can't you now, my dear fellow? You've managed to leave her there for the last seventeen years or so, and her mother's been stiff most of the time. The only thing Maybelle's got out of you is Carol and a bad time. You going to pull this kid through a lot of headlines in a custody fight, as if she was some kind of proxy battle? You going to take advertisements in the *Times* and the *Wall Street Journal* explaining your point? The poor stockholders are getting screwed so you have decided to step in and unscrew 'em? Is that what you're going to do? This is a child, a girl, not an airline or a mail-order house or an oil lease. You can't bribe people to vote your way on shares in Carol.'

'Oh, God, Jim, why does it always have to be so complicated? Somewhere, sometime, someplace, there must be somebody who . . .'

Wilbur stood up, put his hands flat on the desk, and leaned across until he was speaking almost in Craig's face. His voice was harsh and flat and had almost regained its old Polish inflection.

'Don't make me cry, sonny. You were more of a grown-up when you were a kid. This big time has softened you up. You know damned well that you buy what you get, that you earn what you buy. Whether you earn it in bed or in the stock-market don't make a damned bit of difference. Don't gimme that wistful poet bit, or the next thing I know you'll be living in the Village and letting your hair grow. Sure it's complicated. Going to the can is complicated. Having a child is complicated. There ain't nothing simple. By now I thought you'd know that.'

'All right, all right, I know it. Don't beat me to death with it. One favour, Jim, and I ask it humbly. Tell some sort of elaborate structure of lies to Carol and hustle her off to Europe. Tell her I'll be there for absolute certain sure in a couple of weeks. Take her to Spain or France or England—any place, and cram her full of cathedrals while I get this thing with her mother finished. Skip that business of sobering up Maybelle. I'll do that myself. But get Carol away. Will you do that?'

'I'll do that. I won't like it, but I'll do it. And you're serious about meeting us over there? I don't want *your* kid to think *I'm* a bum, too.'

'I'm serious. You don't call 'em easy, do you, Moose?'

'You're a big boy now, Short Pants. You don't need any baby-sitting any more.'

'Don't I?' Craig's voice was very soft. 'I wonder . . . Good night, Jimmy. Bed's turned down.'

11

SOBERING up Maybelle was a chore slightly akin to the task Hercules faced with the Augean stables. She hadn't left her suite in the Plaza for days, and the management was frantic. The room was filthy, as only the rooms of drunks can become filthy. She was lying, snoring, half-in and half-out of a soiled nightgown, spraddled across the bed. Her lips were caked with dried spittle, and made little blubbering noises as she snored. A hand flung in her sleep had knocked a carafe to the floor, which was covered with broken glass. A quarter-full bottle of gin stood on the dressing-table. Ashtrays spilled cigarette butts on the bed, which had several holes burnt in its sheets. Her arms and one naked leg were covered with yellowing old bruises and fresh purple ones, where she had staggered and fallen. The spread fingers of one hand were blistered with cigarette burns. The reek of vomit and stale alcohol, old smoke and smouldering cigarettes filled the room, whose windows were tightly closed.

'See if you can clean her up, Nurse,' the doctor said, 'and get some clothes on her. I'll just give her a little shot to keep her quiet. Same place in Connecticut, Mr. Price?'

'Yes,' Craig said bitterly. 'The same old home-from-home. You'll go out with her in the ambulance, will you, Doctor . . . Nurse?'

'Of course, Mr. Price. She ought to be all right in a week or ten days. They know her history. Don't worry. There's nothing else you can do now. We'll handle everything.'

'Thank you, Doctor. Good night. Thank you, Nurse. Good night.'

Craig walked to the lift. He called by the manager's office.

'All settled now. Sorry if it caused you a lot of trouble, but I was out of town. Please send the bills for everything to my office. And see that everybody is well taken care of for their trouble.'

'Thank you, Mr. Price. No trouble at all, sir. Good night, sir.'

'Good night.'

Craig went into the Oak Room and ordered a double martini. He drank it at a gulp, threw down a five-dollar bill, and walked out into the night without waiting for his change. A week, ten days, the doctor said, would be a long week, a long ten days, the longest ten days he would ever spend. He'd call Susan and tell her that he couldn't see her until everything was straightened out. Somehow he didn't want to associate her with what was bound to be a mess.

The secretary, Connie, ushered Maybelle into the office. Her face was puffed, neck and chin now blurred into soft union. She was very pale, with an unhealthy lardish quality to the skin. Craig looked at her almost as at a stranger, as at a visitor sent by a hand-letter, as a . . . a . . . what? *Bug*? Somebody maybe to get theatre tickets for, and ring Twenty-One in advance for? He pecked tentatively at her cheek.

'Hello, sweetie,' he said. 'Sit yourself. Feeling better now?'

'No, just sober. I'll have a Coke. They're *so* good for me,' she said, her eyes sweeping the room. She sat primly on a chair, knees close together like a little girl.

'No rum in the Coke?'

'No rum in the Coke. You got a nice joint here, Mr. Price, although it took me a little time to get in. The bodyguards outside seemed to think I was somebody else. Maybe they just aren't accustomed to Mrs. Craig Price coming to call. Neither is Mrs. Craig Price. So this is where you keep all your animals, alive and dead?'

'This is where I keep the animals.' Craig's voice was level. He handed her the Coke. He thought she looked very chic in a neat Hattie black number, with not too many pearls and the diamond not too big. 'You look just fine, just dandy.' He poured himself a scotch on the rocks.

'So do you. That Cuban sun tan becomes you. What the hell kind of act are we going through?' Her voice roughened. 'Sell me the bill, charm-boy. What gets me up here into the inner sanctum? I been baptized in blood already.'

'Maybelle. Maybelle. Please. I got to play it straight. I want a divorce. Take what you want of what we have, but please give me a divorce. Please. There's no use kidding ourselves any longer. We don't go to bed any more. We're no good to each other. We're not even friends any longer.'

'That's not *my* fault,' sharply, swiftly.

'I know, I *know*,' Craig said. 'I keep learning about a lot of truths I ought to know. It isn't your fault. It's my fault. But I sort of can't stand it any longer.'

'You could come home more than once a year and try it out.'

'That's it. I *can't* come home. You know that. I *can't* come home.'

'What's she like?' Maybelle fitted a cigarette into a holder, and Craig extended a lighter to the cigarette. 'And don't say: "Who?" What's she like, this one that finally broke you out with the nobility measles? What makes her different from the other thousand tramps that kept you in town on business?' Maybelle made the word 'business' sound filthy.

Craig got up and began to pace the floor. He leaned, from habit, against the elephant tusk, for a brief moment. He spoke very slowly, making a distinct effort to keep his voice down.

'Let's don't go into that. She's a woman I met and want to marry. I love her.' His voice hoarsened. 'I love her, and I don't love you, Maybelle. I like you but I don't love you. I'm sorry but that way I just don't.'

'Make me a drink now you got the message across. Bourbon, straight.'

Craig walked to the bar and unstoppered a crystal decanter. As he poured the drink, Maybelle said:

'I got news for you too, Mac. I don't love you either.' She swept an angry hand. 'And you don't love anybody but yourself. The hell with it. You want a divorce. I drink too much, and you work too hard, and you don't like to sleep with me, and there's this Cinderella you want to marry, and I'm here so we can do something about it. That right?'

'More or less.'

'Well, bud, I got one thing to say.' She spoke tensely through closed teeth. 'Like they say in the Good Book or somewhere, naked you came into my world, and naked you're gonna leave it. I got a high price, Price, you should excuse my using my married name. You're a big shot with your picture in the paper, but you came into it on my time, in my bed, on my old man's money. You leave it, you're gonna leave it the way you come in. You gonna leave it broke, boy. You remember the night you got me drunk and screwed me into a new mill? On purpose, because you knew damn' well I'd do anything for you? Well, Bud, unscrew me.'

'What do you want exactly?'

'All of everything we—we, for Godsake—everything you

581

started with off me. Just what you got off me. *All.* I don't care about your other stuff. Make me another drink. You can take your oil and everything and wear it around your neck. You started off on Daddy's mill and you used me. You used me like a pimp uses a whore.'

(That's about the fifth time I've been called a pimp lately, Craig thought. Maybe there's something to it.)

Maybelle stood up. She took a sip of her drink, and then threw the rest of it in Craig's face.

'I more or less expected that,' Craig said, wiping his face with the back of his sleeve. 'There are some doors for slamming, too, and if you wish, the bar's open for glass breaking.'

'Goddamn you, goddamn you, goddamn you!' Maybelle had begun to sob. 'You never gave a good goddamn for me from the first day we met! You're worse than a pimp. And like any other whore I thought I loved you. Well, I've quit that as of right now.

'You want a divorce? Okay, I'll give you a divorce. On these terms. One million dollars. You work that one out, boy. And then consider that I want that terrible house in the country, and we have a child—a sort of by-product child—who will need about fifty thousand a year to keep her in her daddy's nylons until she's twenty-five. And a very expensive mother—say about another fifty thousand. I don't want to be greedy, but I don't want to cut into my capital. Until death do us part.' She spat. 'You like it?'

'I don't like it. But somehow I'll fix it. There's the thing about Carol. Who?'

'I never liked Carol very much,' her voice was deadly calm. 'I always remembered how I got her. A sort of business deal. On fifty thousand bucks a year she can make it, sugar-daddy. She's a big girl now. She started out in business and she can end up in business, like us. Meantime I suggest we could parole her into the custody of Mr. Wilbur. He's had a lot of practice playing father . . . Legally, I'll take her until she's of age.'

Craig clenched his fists, then flipped the fingers into a stiff spread.

'All right. You know it takes time to scrape up a million dollars. Would you start divorce on half of it, with all the papers right about the rest? Or would you just like to have the mills?'

'You're an *honourable* man, Craig Price,' Maybelle said. 'Sell the mills, get the money. I don't know anything about running mills, and I don't want to start now.'

Craig shrugged with exasperation.

'You know I can't raise any money on the mills. We've got an eight-million bond issue out, and money's tight, with the market off. I could maybe raise a million one way or the other, but you'd have to sign away your interests for me to make a move. You'd have to trust me—at least take my paper on the debt.'

582

Maybelle shrugged right back.

'I said you were an *honourable* man. Hand me the million, friend, and my first fifty thousand down, and the first down payment for Carol, and I'll sign anything you want signed. Why don't you float another bond issue—on *me*? That's how you big shot financiers do it, isn't it? When in doubt, float a bond issue.

'But you pay the expenses to Reno. That's customary, isn't it? Make over the house to me—and, oh, yes. I'll have the little villa in France, too. I aim to accumulate some culture. And a season abroad will be so nice for the child.' Her voice minced sarcastically.

Craig stood up.

'All right, Maybelle. Send your lawyer around and we'll straighten out the papers.'

'Send *your* lawyer around to mine.'

'Who is he?'

'I don't know. I haven't hired him yet. He'll probably call your man.'

'Maybelle.' Craig walked around the desk and touched her lightly on the shoulder. 'Believe me, I'm sorry about this, but it's all for the best. You're still an attractive woman . . . you . . . if you wouldn't . . . I mean if you'll take better care . . . you know what I mean.'

She stood up and smoothed her skirt.

'Yeah. I know what you mean. Lay off the booze, find the dream prince, and we'll all live happily ever after and play canasta together. Your wife and I can swap recipes. Look, ex-husband, life is lousy enough drunk. I can't bear to think about it sober. I'll drink as much as I goddam well please, and I'm going to Europe and live in that stinking villa in Villefranche, and I'm going to get myself a whole slew of young men who will love me for my money—which is what I've got used to—but who will at least come home and jump in the hay with me once in a while because if they don't I'll quit paying their bills. See? It's my money, not ours. And speaking of that money, get moving, because I'm bored with living by myself after twenty years. And I want to start making whoopee. I want to live it up. I want to be a gay divorcée. I'd rather be a merry widow, but you settle for . . .' Suddenly her face crumpled, and she put her hands over her eyes. Her shoulders shook. Craig put awkward hands on her shoulders, and she wrested free angrily.

'Don't touch me! I'm not crying because we're getting divorced. I'm crying because my life has been wasted, wasted on you. I wanted to have a husband, and I never had one. All I had was a business machine. I wanted to have fun, and I never had any. I'm forty and fat and . . . Oh, the hell with you. Where's your bathroom?'

Craig pointed. As she went through the bathroom door, he

thought: *It's as if we never were married at all. It's as if we never slept together, never lost a child, never had a child. I swear, I wonder if I'd recognize her on the street in five years.*

'Don't bother to see me out.' Maybelle's face had been repaired. 'Are you actually going to Europe to see Carol, or was that just another lie to get her out from underfoot while the divorce stories knock the world news off the front pages?'

'No. I'm going as soon as I can fix this business of your million dollars. That'll take a lot of doing, and for God's sake, Maybelle, please stay sober until we get all the paperwork out of the way.'

'I'll stay sober,' Maybelle said grimly, as she headed for the door. 'I suppose you know that no dame alive is worth a million dollars? It's no compliment to me, but I didn't know my nuisance value was that high. Good-bye, Mr. Price. I hope you'll be very, very happy.' She tilted her chin and closed the door exaggeratedly gently behind her.

12

'NATE,' Craig said. 'I make it fast and hard. I need a big one. Cash. And in a hurry.'

Nate Mannheim looked at him.

'A big one. That's a lot of money, my boy. You in Government trouble? What am I asking, trouble? You're not in trouble, you'd be at the bank, you're not sitting in my office asking the big one. A million cash bucks is *gelt*, son. What you lost, or what you buy? Tell your Uncle Nate.'

Craig wrestled mentally with himself, and a hundred past transactions with Nate Mannheim swept swiftly across his brain.

'So what is it now? You want another bum airline?' He shook his head sadly and waggled a cigar. 'You had an airline. Tell me the need for a big one.'

'All right,' Craig said wearily. 'I want to buy a divorce. The terms are one million dollars cash money. Tax free.'

Nate Mannheim was jarred out of his conventional calm.

'A whole mil to lose a broad? You out of your mind? With a mil you *buy* a million broads. To lose a dame you are asking me a million *dollars*? This broad has an inventory worth a million skins? This broad has a credit future worth a million rugs? Are you crazy? I'm a factor. I'm a loan shark. I'm good old Uncle Nate who'll help you buy a juke-box factory or a mail-order house, but I am not Santa Claus, I am not Rockefeller, I should be lending a million dollars to buy loose from a broad.' Indignation frosted his face.

'I'll tell you.' Craig spelled out the story slowly.

'So it's like that.' Nate rang for his secretary. She wiggled in.

'Shirley, bring me the Price file, please, doll.'

Shirley wiggled out and returned with a blue folder. Nate flicked the pages with a knowing finger.

'Hum-hah!' He paused to light a fresh cigar. He tapped the file with a highly polished fingernail.

'You're over-inventoried, son,' he said. 'You guys never learn, do you? A blind man can see we already passed peak buying, and every ex-GI and his brother has got all the cars, all the nylons, all the ice-boxes he needs and his dough is slipping, but you guys figure it'll go on for ever. You're gonna have to dump some inventory, son, or else ease it out real quiet and quit making commitments. You're sick, son. Also this wife you want to lose is hanging on to an awful mess of your operation.'

'She'll turn it loose,' Craig said. 'This is a peculiar one, Nate. All she wants is the million bucks. Cash. And to get rid of me.'

'A big one don't come easy in cash. I got 180 million out, right now, working for me, but I would have a hard time cashing for one spending big one. Paper, yes. *Gelt*, no.

'Let's look at some more of you. Oil? Reserves mostly hocked. Insurance company? Sick. Most of the common stock and cash assets in that investment trust of yours. Price Building? Mortgaged. Mills? Eight million bond issue, four paid back, interest met. That sounds healthier, especially if you get hold of your wife's stock. Looks to me, Craig, you got 51 per cent of more 51 per cents than anybody I ever met. But cash? You ain't got any, or you wouldn't be worrying Uncle Nate. Let's look at the building again. Hmmmm. All the floors rented, mostly twenty year leases. Now *that's* healthy. Those type people mostly don't figure to move. What do you propose that'll make me con a bank or a *reputable* insurance company?'

'Hock the mills,' Craig said. 'They're better than good for it. You know it. My stock and Maybelle's stock against your dough. the inventory's worth the price. You can always sell me out, Nate. But if you don't—you got the mills, you got the working treasury, you got the customers—if you don't, in a couple of years I can crawl off the hook. Or at least get a buyer for a decent price and pay you out of the action.'

Nate picked up the file again.

'That sounds very pretty, pal, except for the bond issue. I got everything you say except the eight million you raised on your issue. Remember who advised you to raise it? Uncle Nate. So actually the mills don't really belong to you and it's not nice to go around hocking what's already hocked, is it? Say I take the mills, you shouldn't be able to pay me, and who knows, two years, three years, we got another war, we got another slump, broads quit wearing stockings, people don't sleep on sheets— who knows? I wind up busted with beat-up machinery, bricks and mortar, can't meet the amortization or the interest, in comes the Government, out come the lawyers . . . No. Nothing with mills. Every day they invent a new fabric, you should have to retool to compete with. How about those all-way stretch stockings, look no bigger than a flashlight? How about them?'

'You ain't got such a sweet reputation, my friend. That sick insurance company don't look very pretty. You ain't been squeezing that oil out of the ground so good lately, and anyhow, people don't seem to want to buy so much oil as they used to.'

'But this is a ten-million-dollar property, Nate, for God's sake!'

'It's got some multi-million-dollar financing against it, too,' Nate answered. 'Until it's clean—until your bond issue's paid off and your wife's common stock and the institutional stuff is unhocked—it ain't a ten-million dollar deal. It's a hungry you looking for fast *gelt*. *And* with too much inventory. Who sent for you? Not me.'

'All right, all right.' Craig's voice was weary. 'That portfolio tells you more about me than I know. If I hock some oil reserves, if I pawn some of the other stuff, the Price Building? . . .'

'Now we talk sense. How much actual—now don't con me, Craig, you know I'll check—how much actual equity you got in the Price Building? Your own dough, not the insurance company's dough, not the investment trust's dough, your own dough?'

'About one million.' Craig sounded sheepish. 'But equity in the property, the usual. Fifty-one per cent. The rest is split between the insurance company and the trust. But seeing as how I own the insurance company and the trust, I . . .'

'Oh, balls. This ain't Shirley Temple. This is your Uncle Nate, that put you on to the racket. Look, money's tight. But Manhattan mid-town real estate with a steady classy bunch of tenants is one thing ain't going to fold. Too many crooks need working room. You got a good list of tenants. I'll get you a million now. It'll be tough *tocus*, but I can find a million. The rate is twenty per cent, and you got five years. For this you give me your fifty-one per cent of the Price Building as security—if your papers are clean. I trust the Price Building. People generally pay rent before they pay the butcher.'

'But for Christ's sake, Nate—'

'Don't but me. I ain't buying Price. I'm buying assets, receivables. I risk my dough on the credit of your customers.'

'But twenty per cent, for God's sake! Twenty per cent!'

'I don't need you. You need me. Any guy's nuts enough to go for a million skins to lay a new broad can afford the interest. Call it entertainment tax. What's this new one like, by the way? The greatest in the feathers, or does she see the buried nobility assets in you?'

Craig grinned weakly, defeated.

586

'None of your goddamned business, shark.'

Nate leaned forward. He tilted his head and his expression was brightly bird-like.

'A thing, tell me. Why do you have to get a million-dollar divorce to bang this other broad, when so easy you could keep the happy home going and knock off the broad week-ends and afternoons? This is a thing I don't understand. What are you, you should foul up your finances to lay another broad? What's with?'

'You wouldn't understand, Papa. Let's get back to business.'

'All right, so business. So I'm still curious. What's with this wife, she'll let loose her stock, when she could sell you out herself, when she could hang on and live good—when *she* could come here and hock her stuff herself with me? When she could let the stuff loose on the market? What is with this wife?'

'Too long a story. Let's just say she wants out, in a curious female manner—that she wants out from me, out from the mills, out from memories . . . out from me. Don't ask me any more, Nate. I'll clean up the paper, you get my building, but it'll take a hell of a lot of time. But if you'll get me the money—and get it now—my building stock is around ten million, and you know it—will be enough to hold you until I get the whole mess straightened out. Okay?'

'Kid, I think you're nuts. I think *I'm* nuts. But we've done a lot of business in the past, and you always come good on even the wildest-assed ones. So I get you your loot. Sure, I got a couple of bucks around. I take my commission monthly. But you better scramble a lot of common stocks and things, boy, because if this thing don't pay off, if there's any funny business about balloning things that ain't there . . . *if.* Your name is John the Baptist. No neck.'

'I love you, Nate. I really do. Some day I'd like to know you socially.'

'Why?' Nate smiled, and pointed at his own chest with the cigar. 'Me, *I* wouldn't want to know me socially. Get your shysters and what papers you can find and your wife collected, and meantime I'll go stick up a bank. Good luck, Craig. You goddamned fool.'

13

MAYBELLE was quite good about staying sober. She was quite good about signing over her shares. She was quite good about accepting a cheque on the Chase for a million dollars. She was quite good about accepting the first annual cheque for fifty thousand dollars, about accepting the deed to two houses. She was quite good about going to Reno. Everybody, in fact, was quite good. The lawyers, for once, were simply splendid about not infusing extra complications into the settlement. The fees were stout enough to preclude argument. Craig Price was quite good, too, for a man who had put himself in pawn for his future.

But quite good, as well, was Susan Strong, especially in face of what the papers said.

Not so equally good was Carol Price, off in Europe with her Uncle Jimmy, waiting for her father to show up, seeing all the sights, and reading about her father and mother in the Paris edition of the *Herald-Tribune*, plus the rather florid accounts in the British popular press.

She was lying by the pool at Gracie Fields' Club on the Piccola Marina. She was beautiful, Craig thought, her short curly brown hair burnt golden, like rippling wheat, by the Capri sun, her body golden-gleaming in a scrap of bikini. She was sprawled on her stomach, and a delicate-looking young man with greased duck-tailed hair was smoothing suntan-oil on her back. She didn't get up when her father said, tentatively: 'Carol?' She turned her head and drawled:

'What do you know? If it isn't dear Father come to call on his only chick. You still *are* my father, aren't you? I thought you'd be too busy to make the trip. I've been keeping up with you in the London *Mirror* and the *Express*. You've been awfully busy. Drag up a chair. Why aren't you in your swim-suit? You look awfully formal.'

Craig looked inquiringly at the young man, who had got to his feet. He was wearing trunks no larger than a jockstrap, and was tanned to a colour of fumed oak.

'Oh, excuse me.' Carol rolled over, sat up, and held out her hands to Craig. He pulled her erect. 'I suppose I'd better kiss you, or people will talk.' She offered an oily cheek. Craig pecked at it briefly. She caught Craig's glance towards the delicate young man. 'Oh, this one? What *is* your real name, honey?'

'Nash. Nash Whittaker, Carol. You know that as well's me.' He spoke with an exaggerated Southern accent.

'I'm sorry, I plumb forgot. You see,' she said, in a loud aside to Craig, 'here in Capri we call him the Memphis Belle. He's always flying a little bit, aren't you, Belle? This, as you may have judged, is my father. I *think*. I've seen so little of him lately it's hard to be sure.'

'How-de-do, Mistuh Price,' the Memphis Belle alias Whittaker said. 'Ah sho' am pleased to make yo' acquaintance, suh.' He held out a limp hand, which Craig took and dropped swiftly. 'We're mad about yo' daughter here in Capri. She's brilliant, but brilliant.'

Craig looked past the delicate young man.

'Can't we go back to the Quisisana and talk, Carol?'

'Why? I like it here in the sun. Why don't you go rent some trunks? We can talk here as well as any place, if there's anything to talk about. Where's my nannie, by the way? What did you do with Uncle Jimmy?'

'He stayed in Naples to do a couple of things for me—some business I hadn't time to . . .'

'Yeah, I know,' Carol said. She raised her voice. '*Cameriere*!' A waiter rushed over. '*Mi da due daiquiri.*' Then to her father: 'Drink, Mr. Price?' Craig nodded at the waiter. '*Tre daiquiri. Per me, doppio.*'

'Oh,' Carol said. 'The man speaks Italian. Is there no end to your talents, Papa? When did you ever have time to learn it?' Her voice was edged.

Craig flicked her with a smile.

'In my wasted youth. When I had time. When I was knocking around these parts. I was about your age, as a matter of fact.'

'Yes, I keep forgetting.' She turned to the delicate youth with the long greased locks. 'My father is what is known as a self-made man. A country boy from Wall Street. He made it The Hard Way. Rags to Riches.' Her capitalization of the words comprised a sneer. The delicate youth looked uneasy.

'Oh, here are the drinks,' he said brightly, as one who has discovered the secret of life. Craig downed his in a gulp. '*Un' altra*,' he said to the waiter.

'Dear me,' Carol said politely. 'I thought it was *Mother* who drank.'

'Please, Carol, could we talk . . . ?'

'Oh,' Carol answered, 'you mean without the Belle? Daddy wants to have a girl talk, Belle. Fly away like a good little bird, will you? I'll see you for coffee in the Piazza. Blow.'

The Memphis Belle mumbled something like gladdametcha and swished gently, with dignity, away. The waiter came again, with three more daiquiris. 'Leave the extra one,' Carol said. 'I'll deal with it.'

Craig jerked a head at the departing Memphis Belle.

'What is *that*?' he said. Carol shrugged.

'One of the local fags. Hell, there's nothing else here right now but fairies, and people getting off with other people's wives. I'm surprised you didn't bring your new woman, so we could all be comfy-cosy together on this romantic island in the beautiful blue Mediterranean.'

'Let's not have any of that, please. I didn't come here for that.'

'Why the hell not have some of *that*?' The girl's voice was bitter. 'The whole world has had plenty of *that*. I've had plenty of *that*. Every fanny-pinching Wop in Italy has proposed marriage or a convenient romance since the details of your divorce from Mummy hit the headlines. I'm rich, it appears. I got fifty thousand a year, it says in papers. It must be true because I read it in

Time and *Newsweek* and *Paris—Match* and *Corriere* and . . .'

She shrugged. 'Gimme a cigarette. How do I get my first
instalment? I'm tired of asking my baby-sitter for drinking
dough. I'm tired of my baby-sitter, too. I'm a big girl now, you
know. Or didn't you?'

Craig was silent as he lit her cigarette. She *was* a big girl now.
She was a ripely moulded woman, and already her conversation
had developed a brittleness, a conscious roughness, too far
beyond her seventeen years. If, Craig thought with a sudden
shock, she weren't my daughter and I was a little younger,
I'd make a play for her. There's not too much more difference
in our ages than when I went to bed with Julie duFresne . . .
but any minute she'll come off the continental sophistication and
say something with the word 'dig' in it. He wasn't disappointed.

Carol said abruptly: 'I don't dig this jive. You never used to be
able to make it home from New York. How come you let the
world run itself long enough to come over to Europe? What
is all this sudden father-daughter bit about? Come on, give.'

Craig kept silent. The sun was steaming, and sweat beaded his
forehead.

'For Christ's sake,' Carol said. 'Take off your coat. You look
like a commuter.' Craig shucked his coat and loosened his tie.
Fully dressed in the swarm of nearly naked brown bodies, he
felt as awkward as if he had stumbled, completely clothed, into
a nudist colony. His eyes swept the poolside, and a thought flashed
that so much naked flesh was as unattractive as so many sides
of beef. The girl to the right, in the almost transparent white
bikini, had just come wet from the pool, and her pubic hair was
frankly shadowed beneath her sketchy loin-cloth. He grimaced.
Carol caught the revulsion.

'What's the matter, Pop? You shocked or something? I
thought you knew all about girls. That's what I read, anyhow.
They're mostly the same, here or home. Don't let it throw you.'

'All right, Carol. Let's not fool around any more. I don't
like having to say it here, but I suppose one place is as good as
another. I came here for two reasons. One, I thought we might
have a little time together—perhaps have a little fun together,
and in some sort of way I might apologize for quite a lot of things.
I thought maybe you might even get to like me . . .' His voice
trailed.

'Like you? *Like* you? God Almighty, I don't even *know* you!
We haven't been introduced. I feel like a *pickup*! I feel like I
ought to ask you for an autograph! Look at these bastards
gawking over there, "The internationally famous financier,
Craig Price, united with his daughter at Gracie Fields' pool on
Capri after the largest divorce settlement since Bobo Rockefeller!"
I'd feel like a whore if I even travelled with you! *Like* you?
Jesus. All I know about you is what I read in *News of the World*.

Camariere!' Her voice rose to a shout, and the waiter ran to their table. 'Same thing, *doppio!*' she said. The waiter rushed away.

Craig felt suddenly old and helpless against his daughter's bitter logic. She's so bloody right, he thought, and spoke quietly, pleadingly. 'Look, sweetie, can't we go some place where it's more private and talk? All these people ... We're making a scene ...'

'What the hell do I care if we're making a scene! And don't call me sweetie!' Carol's voice shrilled. 'You've been making a scene all your life! You've been taking off your clothes in public since I was born! I might as well have a strip-teaser for a parent! Ah, look!' Cameramen had assembled and were shooting pictures. 'Headlines: "Father, daughter reunited in sunny Capri!" I'd like to throw up, and give them a picture of that! All we need is Mummy drunk and your girl friend holding both our heads to make it perfect!'

Craig shrugged, in a weary gesture that was becoming increasingly frequent.

'All right, Carol,' he said quietly. 'I admit what you say—all of it—is more or less true, certainly justified. But in a sort of sad way, I had some faint hope you might be willing to help me a little ... that you might give me another chance to pull us all together. I'd hoped—that was the second part—that I could get you to come back and live with Susan and me. You'd like her, I know ...' His voice had already lost enthusiasm.

His daughter looked at him in actual surprise. Her voice lowered almost to a pitying tone.

'My God, you don't know anything at all about women, do you, my gallant Romeo of a father? You really do surprise me. You're naive, pops, strictly a square, despite all the press notices. God knows the old lady's no gift, but I know what made her a mess, *you*. I probably *would* like this Susan woman—and what she sees in you I don't know—but can't you see it's *you* I don't like, it's *you* I want no part of? I never had any real part of you anyhow, and are you really stupid enough to think that you can come crawling around now to offer me a lollipop and say: "Darling, come sit on your dear old daddy's knee and he'll tell you about the Three Bears? And then come live with me and your nice new Mummy and you'll be real pals and go to the Colony for lunch together, and let's not think about that nasty old Mummy who's always drunk?"' Carol spat. 'This Susan woman must be real stupid. What *does* she see in you?'

Craig's voice was infinitely grey.

'I really wouldn't expect you to know,' he said. 'It wouldn't do me a lot of good to try to explain that maybe she sees something that I never saw in myself before—something that in my admittedly awkward fashion I'm trying to make a late start at discovering for myself, and hoping to have some help from my daughter ...' Again his voice wasted to a murmur.

'Daughter? *Daughter?*' Carol's voice angered again. '*I'm* not your *daughter*. Do you really think I don't know about how I got born? What do you think a drunk like Mummy yells about when she's loaded? I'm not a daughter, I'm a new cotton mill! I'm a by-product, like the newest nylon nightie when all along you've been making sheets! I'm a new entry in the inventory— "stockings, panties, shirts, sheets, towels, Carol Price"— *Daughter?* My aching ass!'

Craig had a momentary, untried paternal urge to tell her not to use language like that, and then almost grinned as he realized that she sounded exactly like this stranger, this interloper, this father. He looked at her again, and thought: *if we were strangers we might be lovers, certainly friends. The only bar to our friendship is the fact that I sired her, as impersonally as if I were the agent in an artificial insemination.*

'Okay, Carol,' he said. 'So I'm a failure as a father, right. So you want no part of my faint offer to reform. I knew this, of course, but I thought I'd at least make a stab at it. So now talk to me as if I were a referee at a bankruptcy hearing. What do you propose to do? What are your plans? I don't want you rattling all over Europe on your own, and Jimmy can't lug you around for ever. He's got work to do in New York. You're too young to be on the loose in Europe, on the loose anywhere.'

'Too young? Too young? This is the gay, debonair Craig Price, who keeps the cocktail parties in stitches with tall tales about his early days in the merchant marine—the pin-up boy of half the tough ports of Europe when he was seventeen? The bullyboy with the light brown hair? I'm as old as you were then, father dear, but with one difference. *I* got money. That mill I represent is finally paying me a dividend. You bought one factory with my actual body, so I figure that I got the money coming. At least the courts said so. On fifty thousand a year little Carol is going to have herself a ball. Mummy's still got custody of me—neither you nor she seemed interested enough to fight for my custody, which just filled me with wild enthusiasm for my parents, both of them, you know, honour thy father and thy mother kind of crap—so I'm going to do just exactly what I want to. Mummy dear couldn't care less, being loaded, and I wouldn't think there's much use in another court battle for the privilege of my company. I wouldn't live with either one of you on a bet. I may go to Paris and take up painting. I may follow in the footsteps of my famous father, and go on a safari. I may marry one of these busted Dago princes. I don't know just what I'll do, but it's a cinch I am not going to do it with either one of you. You both stink, with the difference that I'm sorry for Mummy and it would be putting it mildly to say that I hate your guts, Daddy, dear.'

At this moment, a photographer approached the table.

'Mr. Price,' he said, diffidently. 'I hate to butt in, but I represent Transworld Newsphotos. Would you mind posing for a kind of reunion picture with Miss Price, please?'

Craig started to speak, but Carol's cool voice cut him off.

'Of course not,' she said, silkily, and looked at her father out of the corner of an eye. 'How would you like it?'

'Would it be too much trouble for you to hug each other, and smile towards the camera? Just there, so I can get the rocks and the sea and a bit of the pool in the picture?'

'Certainly.'

Carol leaped to her feet, seized both of Craig's hands in hers, and pulled him to his feet. She hurled herself into his arms, and standing on tiptoes, snuggled against his chest.

'How's this?' She delivered a blinding smile.

'Perfect.' The Speed Graphic clicked, and the photographer swiftly changed plates. 'Now, if you'd stand apart with your arms stretched out, holding hands as if you'd just met. Fine,' as Carol took her father's hands and leaned backwards from him, pulling his arms to full length, rocking back on her heels, with her head tilted, chin thrust upward.

'Wonderful. Thank you so much, Mr. Price, Miss Price. Some people aren't so co-operative. Would you like some prints?'

'Sure,' Carol said. 'Send them around to me at the Quisisana.'

'Why did we have to do that?' Craig said tightly. 'I'd have—'

'Father, father, have you forgotten your reputation of always co-operating with the press? You can't go Garbo on them now. I just didn't want to let the old school team down. And,' she said, her eyes cold, her nostrils flared, 'I consider this interview ended. Please send the money to Barclays Bank.'

'All right.' Craig stood up, and put on his coat. 'All right. I'm sorry for all of it. There's no point in my staying any longer. You're a woman, even though you are a child, and there's no point in my trying to control you. I just hope you won't make too much of a damned fool of yourself. Try to take care of yourself.'

'I'll take care of myself,' Carol said. 'I've had a lifetime's practice at it. Bye-bye, father dear. Don't forget to send the money. I may develop expensive tastes.'

Suddenly she turned and ran for the ladies' room, and burst wildly into tears.

'I could have told you,' Jimmy Wilbur said as they sat over drinks at Zi' Teresa and looked out over the Castell' del Ovo, rearing its battered old head in the Bay of Naples. 'I could have saved you the trip on that bloody boat. This kid wanted to love you more than anybody else in the world, and you never gave her a nickel's worth of chance, not a penny's worth of your time. You think you're going to come back now and play Daddy

Longlegs? She's got too much of the old Craig Price in her for that.'

'So what do we do now?'

'Don't give me that "we" business, friend. Consider that I graduated from the nursemaid racket. If I'm still hired I'm going back to New York and go to work, for somebody. But I ain't, repeat ain't, going to run around Europe playing Auntie to a full-grown dame with full-grown tastes in guys and night-clubs and booze. Not no more, buddy. My tired old knuckles are scarred from beating guys off her. My feet are plumb wore down from tramping around cathedrals and *châteaux*. I know more about wine and culture than Lucius Beebe, and if I ever see another museum I'll kill myself. And worse than that, I did it mostly on my own, because every time I turned my back, our little Carol went over the hill. I also know a hell of a lot about the night-life of Europe, if only from running around town until all hours trying to drag your child out of some of the more unusual gin-mills. This is no kid. This is an epidemic.'

'So all right. But the question stands: what do we—what do I—do?'

'Nothing. Nothing at all. Not a goddam thing. Let her off the leash. Her mother can't handle her—hell, her mother can't handle herself—and she won't have even a little piece of you. You can't lock her in a convent. She's got dough. If you're worried about her virginity, don't. I never told you then, but I will now. I arranged a quiet abortion for her she was just over sixteen. It won't be her last one, either.'

'Why didn't you tell me? For Godsake, an abortion!'

Jimmy Wilbur shrugged, and waited until a singularly un-talented tenor, even by Zi' Teresa standards, moved his aria elsewhere.

'What good? Kid stuff, it was, but unlucky that she got caught. Very little point in letting her have this moonlight mistake, and what would you have done—shot the kid that knocked her up? Don't play father with me now, Craig Price. You're a little late for the party. I feel sorry for you, you stupid bastard.'

'It's all my fault that Maybelle's a drunk and my kid gets herself pregnant before she's seventeen, then?'

'It ain't mine, bud,' Jimmy Wilbur said. 'It's your wife and your kid. Not you or me or God Almighty can keep this girl from being a bum unless she might get lucky enough to meet some nice young guy and marry him before she gets so bedworn she has to take up booze or dope for her kicks. What are you going to do, commit her to an institution? You can't. Her mother's got the custody. That's about like giving a lush custody of a whisky store. Christ, if anything, Carol ought to have the custody of her mother . . . and maybe even you. She won't go back and live with you and this Susan of yours. And for damn' sure I have put in enough time playing Uncle. She don't need an Uncle. She needed a father who paid some attention to her, and a mother who wasn't loaded all the time—loaded because her father never paid any attention to her mother. You tell me one single thing we can do with Carol Price and I will do it gladly. Believe me, boy, Europe and New York and Blueballs, Montana, are full of Carol Prices. I didn't mean this to be a lecture. Only a practical approach. There is nothing, but absolutely nothing, that you can do for this kid now but leave her the hell alone until she's picked up enough battle scars to appreciate you a little bit.' Wilbur's voice softened. 'Like I do, Short Pants.'

'I guess there's not much we can do except what you say: leave her alone and hope for the best. But I wish . . . I wish she didn't hate me so much.' Craig's voice was ruefully low.

'You damned fool. Carol doesn't hate you. She's as crazy as you were—as you *are*. She loves you. But she loves you like a dame, not like a daughter, and like any dame, she's got to give you a hard time. Hell's afire, Craig, I'm no psychologist, but this sticks out a mile. She's had a kind of hero-worship of you as a *man*—not a father—but like a kid gets a crush on a movie star she's never seen. If you'd got Maybelle out of the way—if Maybelle had died, say, or been locked up like her old lady was —Carol would have been delighted. Then she'd have been your girl. She could have come and looked after her handsome daddy, been his hostess, gone with him on trips, and everybody would have said: "There goes Craig Price and that beautiful daughter of his, they look more like brother and sister than father and daughter. And isn't it wonderful how much fun they have together, always going to Africa and Europe and Mexico?" That kind of jazz.

'But what did you do? You murdered the long-distance crush. Losing Maybelle was fine with Carol, but to get rid of Maybelle in order to replace her with what Carol wanted to be, don't need a skull-feeler to diagnose. If I was in the couch business, I'd say that you killed the father image as dead as Kelsey's nuts when you latched on to this Susan dame you're going to marry. Now Carol not only hasn't got a father, but more important, she's lost her long-distance dream-boat. In a short word, boy, you are now, in Carol's mind, guilty of cheating on your own daughter.'

Craig sighed and poured some more Valpolicella in his glass, and looked at his *frutti di mare* with repugnance. This was not his day for shellfish—or for anything else, he thought.

'Boy, the head-shrinking business really lost a beaut when you took up football as a livelihood. "Father image" from Moose Wilbur, yet. What else, Dr. Jung?'

Wilbur grinned through a mouthful of spaghetti.

'All right, patient. You know damned well that every little

girl is in love with her old man, in various degrees, and generally hates her old lady. That's why the female kids are always crawling into bed with Papa in the morning, to cuddle up to Daddy, who is their first lover. That's why the boys generally get the best deal and the biggest piece of cake from the Mamas.'

'How the hell do you know all this stuff?'

'For one thing, I *did* learn to read in school. For another, I used to lay a broad who had a little girl, and the little girl thought I was her papa. And for a third, I have raised at least one girl-child. *Yours.* This kid, this Carol, has been having a mad love affair with her father since she was old enough to say "da", and it got worse when there generally wasn't any "da" there to say what does daddy's baby want, and tell her that she was the prettiest thing since God made rosebuds. And so what do you do? Just when Carol's figuring she'll finally get to know this mysterious lover-father, now she's a big girl, you hit her right smack in the kisser with a new broad. She handed you a beating in Capri today, didn't she? It was the same beating, pure and simple, that your Susan would hand you if you announced calmly that you were marrying somebody named Flo or Dottie and kindly invited her to come live with you and make it a happy threebie. For a guy that's been around with as many dames as you have, you're an idiot.'

'That's the second time today I've heard that one. It seems to me that between being a pimp and an idiot, I ain't very much of a hero. That moon's pretty, coming up over the Castell' del Ovo, isn't it?'

'Don't moon me no moons, Junior. I call you Short Pants, once in a while, when I'm remembering a scared kid in knickers who came to school and got mixed up with a maniac and got rescued by a tramp athlete. But speaking of other short pants, what do you think Maybelle was up to, that day, when she cut the legs off every suit you had in the house? Drunk she was, but in her head, in her heart, she was chopping off your balls. Every dame you had she ever heard about, every dame she ever imagined you had, went into that scissor bit. That's a different kind of short pants, Short Pants.'

'You know, Doctor Freud, I seem to take an awful lot of guff off you. Most of it I don't like. I guess because I know most of it's true. What the hell do you suppose is wrong with me?'

'It's simple enough, and lay back down on this Mediterranean couch. You wanted so many things so fast you forgot what you wanted them for. In the business of getting them you got lost. Your tools got dull from chopping trees you didn't need, when you had enough firewood already. About as simple as that. Blame it on your youth, maybe, blame it on your great-grandpa, blame it on the depression, blame it on Herbert Hoover, blame it on whatever you want to blame it on. You ever have jock-itch?'

'No. I wasn't an athlete. I was a lover. Remember Jean Harlow?' Craig grinned faintly.

'That I do. Even then I knew you had promise. But if you get jock-itch, and don't powder yourself enough, if you are in the jockstrap industry, you can eventually develop an ulcer where there was only itch before. I make myself clear?'

'I think so. My itch has hit the ulcer stage, huh?'

'Yeah. And if the ulcer gets bad enough everything drops off. That leaves you really in short pants. You know,' Jimmy said, and laughed, 'I'm in the wrong racket. I think I will get myself a job on TV or in the magazines telling people how to live their lives. Forgive me. Once in a while I run off at the mouth. Let's go look at this noble city, shall we? I hear these Neapolitan babes are something real fancy. That's what I hear. I haven't had a chance to investigate it yet because I've been so busy trying to keep your child from becoming a Principessa by way of one of these hungry, grease-jobbed bums.'

I love Sue enough to bet my bankroll, Craig said to himself, as he shaved. I love her enough to hock my future. I love her enough to have made a permanent enemy of my only child, and God knows what will happen to that one. God knows what will happen to Maybelle without me—I mean Jimmy—to look after her, loose with a million dollars in a villa in the South of France. God knows what will happen to Sue, whom I'm going to marry shortly. And God knows, Craig Price, what will happen to you. What kind of monster are you, anyhow, that you go out after losing your child and being read a riot by your best friend —what manner of man are you that can't even get married to the woman you hocked it all for until you find out whether or not you've got the clap? I sound like my old room-mate, Philip duFresne. Here am I in Naples, Italy, wondering the next morning with fuzz on my tongue whether or not little Marisa or Maria or Elena had a communicable disease? Nor do I remember where I met her, nor how we got here, nor where she went.

You are not a nice man, Craig Price, you're a louse, he said as he cut himself just on the right upper side of his moustache, and cursed. You are a louse, a jerk, a bum. Sixteen drinks down and you'd bang a boa constrictor. Simple reflex, the same simple reflex that's led you around by the gonads since you were a kid. She even had the hair under her arms, and smelled a little like cooking oil, with a suspicion of garlic. *Love Wops. Some of my best friends are Italians.* Jesus. I wonder if an Italian white spirochoete is kinder due to the sun, or stronger in an alien presence? But then there's always penicillin.

He shook his head in disgust. He walked over to the bedside table, looked distastefully at the rumpled bed, looked at the half-empty bottle of Vecchia Romagna that stood shamefacedly by the overflowing ash-tray. He took a drink neat from the neck, and shuddered. Then he picked up the phone and said: 'Signor Vilboor. *Due due sei.*'

'I'm alive, Jim,' he said into the phone. 'You ready to roll for Rome? Okay, call the car, and I'll see you in the lobby. I've changed my plans. I'm going to take a boat. There's one leaving here for New York in a couple of days. No, I don't really need you. And I don't want you, really. I just want some time to think. If anything comes up, cable me care of the American Export Lines. The boat's *Excalibur.*'

'What the hell got into you?' Jimmy Wilbur said, when they met in the lobby. 'You lost me. I went to the can and you were gone when I got back. Honest to God, trying to keep a hand on the Price family is like . . .'

'I don't know. I was just drunk enough to want to roam. I came down with the back-alley blues. I wound up in some joint, I couldn't tell you where. Some dame brought me home. I don't know. I was fractured. One of those couldn't-care-less jobs.'

'Son, you need a guardian. I'll hang on here and go back on the boat with you, if only in the best interests of the mermaids. In the meantime I suggest a bloody mary and then a slight jolt of penicillin. This Neapolitan clap likes to travel. Not to mention its older sister, a nasty disease, I'm told.'

'So you see,' Craig said to Susan, 'it wasn't a very successful voyage. You're a woman, you tell me what to do about this kid of mine.'

'Jimmy Wilbur told you better than I can. Nothing. Leave her alone. A few years and a few bumps and then we can play family, maybe. But right now there is not one single solitary thing you can do about Carol. But I see Carol's point. You haven't been much of a bargain in the father department, and certainly she isn't looking very eagerly for a new mama right now.' Sue got up and kissed him coolly on the forehead. 'Forget it, sweetie. Let's go back to Luigi's and eat some sturdy Wop food and pretend it's the first night we met.'

Craig winced.

14

THEY were married very quietly, after Maybelle's divorce went through, and Maybelle went to Europe to open the house in Ville-franche. The usual publicity attended the wedding, which was performed privately in judge's chambers—the judge being an old friend—with Jazzbo Newton standing as witness. Jazzbo drove them back to Susan's apartment.

'Where us goin' on our honeymoon, boss?' Jazzbo asked as he drove up. 'This jes' lak always. No change.'

'Us ain't going nowhere on our honeymoon, friend,' Craig said. 'Us gwuine stay right here in New York for a spell. But I tell you what. Suppose you take about two weeks off and go have a honeymoon for us. Take the car. I won't be needing it for a spell. I can always call a taxi, and Mr. Carey's Cadillacs still are for hire. Wait.' He reached for a cheque book. 'Here, have yourself a ball, and try to stay out of jail. Good night, Nubian.'

'Good night, boss. Good night, Miss Sue. I'm powerful tickled fo' you-all. Happy honeymoon.'

'Happy honeymoon, Jazzbo,' Sue said, and shook hands formally.

'Be happier did I have a bride,' Jazzbo said. 'But man, I'se been bit once or twice too often. I think I jus' go live off de country, lak de boss say. Good night.'

Jazzbo departed in the general direction of Chicago.

'Darling,' Craig said, when they had got out of the lift and he was mixing a drink in Sue's apartment, 'I don't feel like a terrific heel for us not romping away on a formal bride-groom deal, because Havana was honeymoon enough for me. And I think for you, too.'

'You can say that again, bud,' Sue said. 'Of course I understand. Darling, I know about the last few months. Craig...'

'Darling?' He finished pouring the drinks.

'I'm not a bartered bride. I am a very happy woman who knows her worth in love as well as price. And I know the kind of price you paid to make me a missus of the same name. No woman's worth it, but I'll try to give you some of your investment back, if love accrues at any sort of interest at all. I will *not* weep, although I want to, inside. And I will not play little-woman and be hurt because the next few months will find you up to your stickpin in commerce. See me when you can at night, as if we were courting, but get that big load of worry off your back. Then we'll have the proper honeymoon, and you can trundle me over the threshold. But don't fret, baby, don't worry about me right now. Get that business monkey off your back.'

Craig walked over and hugged her, nuzzling his cheek against her neck.

'This is a damned poor way to start a formal married life. But I have *got* to go to Houston tomorrow afternoon, and then to Dallas, and on the way back, to Memphis. You can come if you want, but I really would rather you didn't. It ain't nothing but sordid details, honey, and somehow I like to keep you in the sugar-spice department.'

'I wouldn't want to come, and I want to stay in the sugar-spice department. You go to the trade marts, and hurry home to Mama. Meanwhile, I will start thinking about bigger places for us to live, because it's too small here, and damned if I'll live in that office of yours.'

'Don't do anything drastic about housing until I get back,' Craig said. 'I have some ideas of my own. And now, Mrs. Craig Price, will you do the decent thing and prepare yourself for bed? I'm beat, but not that beat.'

'La, sir.' She swept him a curtsey. 'How you do go on. Last one in's a nigger baby,' she said, and dashed through the door.

15

'I HAVE an indecent proposition involving crossing state lines, and would like to include you in same,' Craig said. They had just come back from Mexico, on the delayed honeymoon, which had finally occurred after Craig unsnarled some of the tangled wires of his confused business. They had two weeks in Cuernavaca and Acapulco, fishing occasionally and lying in the sun on the little beach.

'Man, if I wasn't married, I'd slap you right in the face for even darin' to talk rough like that. But I'm game, George, I'm game. Where we off to now?'

'New Jersey, of all places. There's something out there I'd like you to see. Like your advice on. It's a piece of property.'

'What kind of property? Not another stinky mill?'

'No. A . . . wait. Let's talk about something else.'

'Yes, boss. How do you think the Dodgers will finish?'

The white brick and fieldstone house stood atop a high hill and was almost obscured from behind by a forest of pine, white birch and white and pink dogwood. Forsythia had just come in bloom and had gilded the fresh green of spring shrubs.

The house overlooked a ninety-foot slanting drop down to a blue jewel of a tiny lake which poured over a dam in a miniature waterfall, to make another smaller lake on the other side. A broad flagged patio leading to the lip of the rolling descent to the lake held a swimming pool in the shape of a clover leaf, for which the water was pumped from the lake and which constantly overflowed the far end of the pool, making another tiny waterfall whose steady drip was immensely soothing.

Flowers, daffodils, tulips, peonies, geraniums, filled the back courtyard and rimmed the circular drive, which led to a two-car garage almost obscured by the towering silver birches. On the steep slant from patio to lake was a solid bank of azaleas and gladioli, making a vast floral frieze.

They stood outside the house, on the flags beside the pool.
'Like it?'

'It is the most beautiful thing I have ever seen. Whose is it, exactly?'

'Yours. If you hadn't liked it I was going to pull a reprise and burn it down. Here are the deeds. At least, it's one thing I've got that is completely paid for.'

He handed her a sheaf of papers and the keys.

'Happy homecoming, Mrs. Price. Unlock the door. And would you mind if I finally carried you over a threshold? Been a long time a-coming.'

Sue held him tightly as they entered. He kissed her, plumped her to her feet, and swept his hand regally around the room. 'Your new home, madam.'

At least one quarter of the house was occupied by a living-room, and on two sides, one facing the lake and the other giving on to the patio and pool, was clear glass.

As they entered from the patio they faced a stone wall which was almost entirely a fireplace, of the old-fashioned Dutch walk-in type. The floor was flagged exactly on the same level as the patio, and one had the impression of still being outdoors. The view across the lake was staggering, as a forest of solid birch and fir reared steeply up a similar hill. As they looked across the lake a doe and twin fawns came down to drink.

To the right, two steps lifted to another floor level which contained a very old, scarred table top which had been converted into a bar and serving table. The door at the end of the bar led to the kitchen. Instead of bottles, the wall behind the bar comprised five shelves of bright-jacketed books. Craig peeped over the bar and shook his head approvingly.

'The booze is under the bar,' he said. 'When you are playing my personal bartender, I'd rather look past your face and see books instead of bottles, no matter what your grandfather said. Come on, let's see the rest of the joint because I want to show you where the proper folks sit when they come to call. We'll make it by easy stages.'

An enormous glass-topped iron-legged table stood in the centre of the room, was fronted by a modern couch and was surrounded casually by lazy sit-back Barcelona chairs. A few pouffes of white and yellow Moroccan leather were scattered around haphazardly. Beyond that the room contained nothing but a view: a flagged terrace to the left, a continuation of the floor, a short sward of grass and flowers, then the sheer drop and the glimmering lake against the black-green background of the far hills.

'I bought the land on the other side, too,' Craig said, 'it rests my eyes. This is where you and I live until death do us part.'

The interior living-room squeezed a gasp from Sue. It was an enormous room, not loftily ceiled, but giving the impression of height. It was carpeted completely in white Moorish wool. The off-centre black-marble fireplace was lifted a foot off the floor. One large green split-leaf philodendron raised itself all the way to the ceiling to the left of the fireplace, which was set into a wall of white brick. Balancing the plant to the right of the fireplace was a bright Haitian primitive painting.

White sofas, one high, one low, faced each other and were fronted by long coffee tables. Two of the walls were of deeply-grained cedar, stained almost, but not quite, black. The draperies against the large window overlooking the lake were of simple white silk, hanging in straight severe lines to the floor. Coral and green pillows were flung carelessly against the white divans.

In front of the low divan squatted a teak Japanese altar which had been converted into a coffee table, with a white woolly easy-chair at one end and a three-white-cushioned low bench at the far end. The same easy chairs faced each other across the room at either end of a long mottled-black-marble rectangular coffee table.

The lamps were ornately oriental with porcelain and deep green mosaic bases. One broad ottoman crouched to the left of the fireplace just beyond the towering plant. Also to the left of the fireplace was a fretted Moorish sliding screen of teak which admitted chequered light and led to the stairs.

'It's lovely, just lovely. It's too good for any people we know.'

'It's just right for the people we know. Upstairs is where it's too good for people. Upstairs is where we sit at night, before we hit the sack. That's where it's too good for people.' He took her hand. 'Don't worry about the dining-room. Let's whiz up the stairs and see the private country.'

'This is for the quality folks—us,' Craig said. 'Far as I'm concerned, it's off-limits to everybody, and I don't want us to ever wear anything more formal than a pair of pyjamas. See, it's just over the big outside room downstairs, and the same view, but with a balcony that stretches right round to our two bed-rooms. Then we cut the balcony with a partition, and commence it again, to go right on around the guest bedrooms on the other side.'

It was a big room. The wall overlooking the lake was a huge stretch of sliding-draped glass, adjoining a six-tiered bookcase which led in to a white-bricked wall containing a smallish fire-place, and topped by black panelling in sliding sections. The bookcases were filled with duplicates of the volumes in Sue's apartment. At night the vast window would draw the star-lit lake into the room.

'That's my secret weapon, just over the fireplace,' Craig said. 'In case we get marooned, there's a small refrigerator, a bar, and the hi-fi set behind those panels. That coffee table is big enough to put things, including ashtrays and feet, on, and I think that every young married couple should have at least a couple of big sofas to call their very own. Come the revolution, we can hold out here for years.'

'This carpet comes up to your ankles,' Susan said.

'I know it. I like to go barefoot in the winter-time, and I want to keep my feet warm. It's Indian chenille, I think.'

'If I didn't know you better, I'd think you were a frustrated interior decorator,' Sue said. 'What's next, through that door?'

'Your bedroom. All pink. Candy stripes on the wall, and a sack big enough to accommodate football, or other interesting games. Then your bath. Then my bedroom. All blue, for boys, you know. Then my bath. Then three guest rooms and three more baths. You'll have to prowl them on your own time. I left the dining-room alone, figuring we'd eat on the side patio until you made up your mind. What you don't like, you change. All right?'

'All right? All *right?* My darling Mr. Price, I have only one complaint. I have not yet tested the bed. Could we sort of christen it, shamelessly, before we go back to town? I never trust strange mattresses.'

'This way, modom,' Craig said. 'For the *Good Housekeeping* seal of approval.'

16

'DARLING,' Susan said, some months later, 'you're completely beat. You look, briefly, like hell. This last year has been a killer for you, and you're no good to me *or* to you if you get sick. Be my good boy and run down to Carolina with some of the fellows and shoot some birds and let your whiskers grow. You've got that wonderful lodge and you never use it. Go use it. There's a million things I can do about the new house, and what you need, my friend, is a little time away from New York and business and even me. Come on, scram. Go be hairy-chested for a week and get your muscles back.'

'I'll go if you go,' Craig said. 'Hell, I just got you. I don't want to run off and leave you to the wolves.'

'I wouldn't think of going. What you need to be is Lonesome Craig Price again, the Carolina Kid, and you don't need a woman along. Get yourself some stags—Jake, if he feels like it, or Don and Mac—and go murder a few quail.'

'I haven't got the time. I've got that deal with . . .'

'Damn the deal with whoever it is. Make the time. I've got a lot of future plans for you, boy, and they ain't going to come true if I'm a widow. Git out of town, before it's too late, my love, and leave me alone to change some curtains and do some other girl-stuff.'

'It would be nice . . . You know it's been two years since I touched a shotgun? I think maybe I will, sugar. Send Jazzbo down ahead with the car and I can fly to Kensington. He can round up the cook and the guides and the horses, and we'll be ready to hunt when we get there . . . Be fun.' Craig's eyes lit. 'Apart from you, I haven't had much fun lately. Been a rough year.'

Sue got up from her chair and came over to pat his head. She bent and kissed him.

'I know it hasn't been fun. It's been bloody awful for you. When I think . . . enough of that. You go murder some innocent birdies and get your vitamins back, huh?'

'Tired of me already.' Craig grinned. 'Okay, I go. Let the piney wind blow some of the stink of this town off me. Jake'll go, I guess, and Don and Mac. Back to the bush. Come home bronzed, as they always say, and clear-eyed. You're a pretty good kid, you know that?'

'Sure I know it.' Sue laughed. 'It takes two to know two, doesn't it?'

My God, Craig thought, the waste we make of our lives, the time we spend doing things we hate when there are so many wonderful things to do. All the lovely things we have to use and we never get around to using them. I've been here two days and already I feel about ten years younger.

The house, under the silver-mossed grove of live-oaks, was very small and unpretentious. It was made of raw-ended un-dovetailed logs, with the exception of one wall, which was rough field-stone, and which housed the enormous fireplace. In all, it contained three small bedrooms and one big double one, the kitchen and the living-room. It rested on thirty acres of North Carolina swampland, heavily forested with cypress and oak and towering pine. Craig had bought it more or less as a gesture to his youth, and had leased hunting rights on 30,000 acres of good quail ground around it. He had not wanted a grand show—not a baronial manse—and so the only servants were local Negroes. One family lived in a tiny cabin to the rear of the master's cabin, and was more or less supposed to keep the place from burning down. The bird-dogs, pointers mostly, and the horses on which Craig's guests hunted, were maintained on a separate farm by a proud and highly industrious Nego named Charlie Jonas. It was possible that Charlie Jonas had accumu-lated his hundred acres of pecan trees, peanuts, corn and cotton from an initial loan—you could describe it as gift—from Craig Price, but it was a paying farm, and gave Charlie a fine living and time enough to train the pointer puppies that Craig sent down from time to time. Charlie was a man of high purpose, with impeccable credit at the bank, and had the respect of the white community as well as the black.

They hunted from broad-backed, slow-shambling ponies, who stepped unerringly into pot-holes, generally losing jockeys, in a fragrant land of scrub pine, deep green bays of gallberry bush, pin oak, wild camellias, broom straw, cornfield and tender-grassed burned-over ground that always contained a lonely sawdust pile. It was pleasant, plentiful, easy hunting, because Charlie Jonas was a keen conservationist. He shot every tame cat gone wild that he saw, he was dedicatedly murderous on hawks and foxes, and he tenderly stole the fresh-laid quail eggs from the low ground and moved the nests to the high ground when the spring freshets threatened to drown the baby quail. In the late winter he religiously burnt off the long grasses, so that the spring chicks would not be trapped in the tangled yellow withes.

The men shot less than they talked and laughed and drank around the fire. They were not there to hunt so much as to relax and forget the various business details that made their lives a web of conferences and cocktails, stock-market preoccupation, advertising budgets and proxy raids. Jake Walker was editor-in-chief of a vast newspaper chain, a lean and rather quiet balding man who liked to drink whisky and listen to other people tell jokes. He had come out of Carolina, like Craig, and had clawed his way on cold ability to the summit of his profession, which he described generally as running an orderly cat-house for the American Saturday-night mentality.

Don was an Oklahoman, president of a major air-line, an aggressive country boy who had whipped the big city, and who used double negatives and 'ain't' much as Craig did, but who was, in his spare time, a secret poet. His name was Stevens, and he was short, red-faced and wore his white hair in a stiff crew-cut. He drank well when he was happy, but occasionally walked the walls when he had problems to preoccupy him. He fancied sour-mash bourbon and any brand of girl.

Mac was Malcom Reeves, publisher of a chain of magazines. They dealt mostly with such things as shooting, fishing, gardening and architecture, and the fact that all of this outdoor activity was conducted from a Swedish-modern, air-conditioned office on Madison Avenue did not prevent Mac's escape into the boy-scout life whenever the faintest excuse presented itself. He was a big man, hearty, had come originally from North Dakota, and still regarded the New York that nourished him as a hick town, less sophisticated than Fargo.

The men—reformed country boys all—comprised that strange product of New York saloon society which refuses to admit to city-slickerism. None had lived in their home states for at least twenty-five years, and none would have cared to dwell in Raleigh or Tulsa or Fargo or Kensington. (Actually they had all emigrated from farms or from tiny hamlets with Rural Free Delivery boxes in front of the sanded front yards.)

They all wore carefully tailored, very expensive clothes, made generally in London or Italy; hand-carven British boots, and Sulka shirts and ties. They all had chauffeur-driven limousines, spoke at least two languages with varying accents, and owned at least three residences—town apartment, country home and summer place. All maintained some sort of hunting or fishing lodge, generally in the vicinity of their birth, because of a dogged determination to cling to their origins. They all had second or third or even fourth wives, as the older models wore thin. Nearly all had children and some, grandchildren. They lunched at Toots Shor's or Nino's—in the upstairs wild game room, of course—at the Laurent and occasionally, with wives, at the Colony or Le Pavillon. They dined almost invariably in Twenty-One, and were such creatures of habit that their buttocks had worn individual impressions in the chairs, their elbows created private indentations on the bar. They had mistresses, subject to change and sudden whim, and when they went to Mexico or Bimini or Texas on an all-boy hunting or fishing binge, a casual bit o' fluff was not spurned as a bonus to the week-end.

They were harsh, keen-minded men of super-business sophistication—men who could merge an industry, raid a company, wreck an enemy, rig a stock, milk a company of its assets or fleece an insurance firm. They could drink all night, if necessary, and rise to jettison a magazine and fire its staff, fight a union or appear coolly confident before a Congressional investigation. They drank together—these Dons and Macs and Craigs and Jakes with cronies of similar stripe, and one end of the bar in Twenty-One and Toots' was called The Bandit Corner.

Yet they fondly perpetuated the delusion that they were still simple country lads, bewildered by a wicked big city, when they had actually toppled most of the giants of their trade. One—non-present at Craig's hunting trip—had three mistresses, all of whom strikingly resembled his wife. The mistresses' houses were replicas of the home which contained the wife, were similarly furnished, and the master's portrait, by the same artist, stood over the same fireplaces. Once, when somebody twitted the owner of these houses and women about his duplication of taste, he said simply:

'I'm a nervous man. I don't like to have to worry about where I am when I wake up in the morning.'

These men knew the difference between Astrakhan and Beluga caviar, the various years of the better vintages, and could order a meal at Maxim's with ease and confidence. They clad themselves in silk, and draped their women with mink and chinchilla. They had enormous expense accounts, and myriad excuses for investigation of a little action abroad, if it meant a safari on the side, and their yachts were basically for business entertainment.

Nearly all held foreign troves of securities and hard money in numbered accounts in Switzerland and Tangier.

Yet, on a hunting trip to the Carolinas or Texas or Mexico, a fishing trip to Acapulco or Cuba or the West Indies, they shed the glossy reptilian skin of their sophistication and played hearty-he-man, boisterous Boy Scout, with a Falstaffian corniness. They ate frijoles and beans and drank mescal. They ate cornpone and hard ham-and-hominy and hush-puppies, venison and quail, duck and wild turkey. They let their whiskers grow and attired themselves in plaid Pendleton shirts, moccasins and hunting boots, wore long red underwear and bathed infrequently. They told dirty jokes and played poker and gin for small stakes, gossiped eagerly, and laced themselves liberally with alcohol. Abercrombie and Fitch provided their rustic peasant costumery at Sulka prices, and the alcohol was apt to be twelve-year-old scotch or a sixteen-year-old sour-mash bourbon and the wine of the backwoods country could be traced to country stores such as Musigny or Beaune or Pommery, but they were all boys together again, seeking, rather pathetically, to walk backward down the years and find themselves once more poaching squirrels with a single-shot .22 rifle or lost, alone, in a boat in search of perch or catfish. Huckleberry Fin was once again united with Tom Sawyer and Joe Harper, and damned be he who mentioned merger or scheme except on the plane back, while the slaves tidied up the camp and New York loomed. Then the innermost deer-stand or quail-hunting thoughts emerged, and something rather peculiar generally happened to the market in the next few days.

As there were no factors, bankers, oilmen—save Craig—insurance-men—save Craig—no public utilities peoples, no manufacturers—save Craig—this party promised to be really relaxed, since nobody had anything at all to sell to each other at the moment.

Don, the air-line gentleman, was still brooding over three successive crashes which had been horrible for business, public-relationwise, and didn't wish to talk about it. Mac Reeves was losing heavy money on two magazines, and didn't wish to talk about it. Craig's private thoughts centred on the redemption of a trio of textile mills against a coming deadline, and Jake Walker was wondering if it wouldn't be smart to kill a couple of little papers and throw the operating costs into saving the lives of a couple more which seemed to have a slightly better chance of survival. All were concerned with the state of the market, the Russians, the French, the situation in North Africa, the strikes in Britain, and the President's bellyache, not to mention Nasser in Cairo and Makarios of Cyprus, the Arab League, and Suez. India and Saudi Arabia weighed heavily, together with cotton futures, steel, the CAA, the CAB, the Teamsters'

Union, the Newspaper Guild, and the impact of the coming jet transports on the old-fashioned piston-driven machine.

They were sitting in fleece-lined slippers, with Jazzbo Newton hovering in the background to keep the glasses brimming. It had been a good week, an excellent week. It was the time of year when you could shoot nearly anything. They had dined well. Don Stevens had slipped out one early morning to shoot a small, tender, spike-buck, and Craig had collected a couple of turkeys from a carefully (illegally) baited blind. There had been a couple of good mornings in the marshes with the ducks, some fat mallard and pintail and even a couple of canvasback, plus a slew of tender teal.

They shot quail in the warm sunny afternoons, the piney woods dappled yellow with the late light, the broom grass golden, the dogs frisking through the stands of fodder-stripped cornshocks and dried stiff cotton stalks. They were beautifully tired when they came back, kicked off boots, and sat before the roaring fire to start the serious drinking before dinner.

The last night they had delicate teal diapered in bacon, a sherry-rich terrapin stew, and broiled venison chops, with hot biscuits and apple pie with cheese. Don Stevens' private plane would be coming in to pick them up at eleven the next day.

They were drinking coffee and brandy, reviewing the week's shooting, and listening to the nine o'clock news, debating whether to start a poker game or just have another couple drinks and go to bed when Stevens said:

'Craig, you still do your old parlour trick? You know the one I mean, shooting the cigarette out of Jazzbo's mouth?'

'I haven't, not in a long time. Don't know if my hand's steady enough. It was a silly trick, anyhow.'

'Come on, let's see it,' Mac Reeves said. 'I heard about it, but I never saw it.'

'I don't mind. Jazzbo?'

'Yassuh, Mist' Craig?'

'The gentlemen want to see us play William Tell. You feel like getting shot at again tonight?'

'Sho. I ain't been a target in years. Where does I stand?'

'Other end of the room. There's good light there, and the bullet can go into the logs.'

'Same as befo', huh? I go get de gun.'

Jazzbo came back with a long-barrelled .22 target pistol mounted on a .45 frame. He handed it butt-first to Craig.

'Let's don't do it,' the editor, Jake Walker said. 'The boy might get hurt. Put the gun away and let's play a few hands of stud.'

'No, I want to see it,' Mac Reeves said.

'I've done it a thousand times,' Craig said. 'Go on down there, Jazz.'

608

Jazzbo lit a cigarette, walked to the end of the room, stuck the cigarette in his lips, and profiled in the light, with his chin up. Craig extended his arm stiffly, making a rifle of pistol and arm.

'Let her fly, boss.'

Perhaps the day's fatigue made Craig flinch, perhaps there had been too much to drink before dinner, or perhaps a sudden flicker of the open fire distorted his vision.

But when he squeezed the trigger, Craig would have given his own life to unsqueeze it, for something was suddenly, awfully, dreadfully wrong.

Jazzbo melted to the floor. Craig flung down the pistol and raced to his side. He dropped to his knees and lifted Jazzbo's head, holding him in his arms.

'Get a doctor—get somebody—do something!' His voice was cracked, frantic.

Jake Walker dropped to his knees, and touched Jazzbo's head with gentle fingers. A small round hole showing only a tiny trickle of blood appeared just under the lobe of Jazzbo's left ear.

'You won't need a doctor,' Walker said. 'The boy's dead.'

Craig Price sat on on the floor, cradling the boy's torso. Jazzbo's head had fallen forward on Craig's shoulder. Craig stared blindly over Jazzbo's head. After a long time he picked up the boy's body and laid it gently on his bed. Then he opened the door of the lodge and went out into the night. His friends looked silently at one another. There didn't seem to be anything to say.

17

There had been no trouble with the coroner's jury. Craig was local blood, he was respected, and his affection for his coloured servant-companion was widely known. A verdict of accidental death was brought, and Craig buried Jazzbo in the Price family plot in Kensington. Shooting accidents were always happening in hunting camps, somebody mistaking somebody else for a deer, or a gun suddenly going haywire in a duck blind. Everybody around Kensington said what a pity it was, 'because you know what a heap of store Craig Price set by that black boy. Wouldn't of been no worse if he'd killed his own child. But I hear he made a big settlement on all Jazzbo Newton's family—must have cost him a mint—and he give a big mess o' money to one of the coloured schools . . .'

'I know it was damned juvenile foolishness, a bunch of grown men shooting cigarettes out of human faces,' Craig said to Susan, when all the dreary business of funereal necessity had been settled, and the papers had stopped running headlines like: *'Millionaire Kills Servant in Joke'* and *'Modern William Tell Misses Apple, Kills Negro Chauffeur,'* and *Time* and *Newsweek* had wrenched the utmost in stylized triumphant tragedy from celebrity caught in tragic embarrassment. 'There would be no way to tell even you, Sue, how I feel about it. But I don't think they had to mix up airplane crashes and stockmarket sags and my divorce from Maybelle and a newspaper strike and my kid in Europe together with what we had for dinner that night and whether we fudged on the quail limit a little. From reading about it, you'd get the feeling that I shot Jazzbo on purpose, for fun, when the gag was as much his as mine. *Price Loses Rabbit's Foot, Kills Good-Luck Charm*—what kind of writing is that? Oh, Jesus.'

Sue got up, walked across the room, and knelt by his side. She took one knotted fist in both her hands, unclenched the fingers one by one and leaned her head against his thigh.

'If you could just try to think that Jazzbo wouldn't really mind the way he went, maybe it would be easier on you,' she said. 'He loved you. You loved him. It was an accident. Accidents happen all the time. Who's to say somebody wouldn't have stuck a knife in him in Harlem? Who's to say that he wouldn't get killed in an automobile accident? He's dead, Craig. Tearing yourself to pieces won't bring him back, and if I knew anything at all about Jazz, he wouldn't want you to fret. It was *his* parlour trick, too.'

'I know it, baby. I know it. But that headline *Kills Goodluck Charm* bothers me more than it should. I'm a superstitious bastard, basically, and what frets me is that *I* feel like I've killed my good-luck charm. It's like the leverage has started down . . .'

'Leverage?'

'Leverage. The only difference between a financier and a pan-handler is leverage . . .'

Craig was dissatisfied with his mills. They weren't bringing him enough keeping money. They netted a million a year, but out of the million the Government wound up with nine hundred thousand, after taking half in corporation taxes and another nearly four hundred thousand from dividends to stock-holders. There was a lousy hundred grand to play with.

It was a strange bastard economy, sired by taxes, dam-ed by deceit.

'You're a sucker,' Nate Mannheim said, when Craig had gone early to the factor for an inventory loan against the cost of new machinery and general expansion. 'A chump. You got ten million dollars tied up in bricks and mortar. Bricks and mortar ain't the answer, my boy. You can't shift them around to fit the times. You ought to invest in cash. You're literally starving yourself to death to feed a flock of machinery which keeps

610

wearing out. You're spending a fortune in advertising. What you make you can't keep. Wise up.'

'I'm just a baby in business,' Craig had said, grinning. 'Tell me all about it. What?'

'You're a baby, all right. It's so simple I'm surprised you haven't thought of it. A bond issue. Interest on bonds is deductible. For a ten million property you can place seven or eight in bonds. You still got the property and its earning power. You pay off the amortization and the interest out of earnings. But you got seven, eight million, to play with—plus your factory income.'

'What do I do with all this moo?' Craig played innocent amazement. 'Collect pictures? Buy a yacht? Run for Congress?'

Nate flirted an impatient hand.

'Leverage, boy, leverage. You wangle that eight million loose cash. I'll show you how to change the diaper. Buy yourself fifty-one per cent of an insurance company. You pick up a company with fifteen or twenty million in capital and surplus, but the gross ratio is ten to one so you'll have gross assets of a hundred million ...'

'But you can't monkey around with insurance companies. They put you in jail for it.'

'Balls. The insurance company's assets are only the middle step in leverage. The idea is to use the insurance company as a gimmick to buy yourself an open-ended investment trust, where you can do anything short of murder ...'

'I'll give it some thought, Nate. In the meantime, will you let me have half-a-million on my inventory?'

'Sure. But give it some thought and you won't need another half-million of mine. You'll have eight of your own. See you.'

It was all so pathetically easy. It only took a year. For half-a-dozen years, Craig had spent fantastically to advertise his products. He had cribbed shamelessly from the talented record of Elliott White Springs, whose occasionally outrageous Spring-maid ads had become almost a classic racy joke in the ad-business. Craig had used his surname to heavy advantage.

'*Price*,' Craig had said flatly to his agency men, 'is the most important word in the English language, next to *mother*. We got a natural gimmick here. Let's make Price Mills synonymous with *low price, short price, half-price*. Any gag that you can dream up which plays around with the word "Price", goes. Steal from Springs, he's a sport, he ain't going to mind. But let's see if we can't get Price in the language to where the Capital "Price" represents the lowercase "price", and all on the customer's side. Anything even as corny as "You're sure of the right price if you buy from the Right Price.' Anything at all. Sex it up.

'Springs has been selling sheets on sex—and imagination. He sells girl's pants on suggestion that what's inside the breeches is an important commodity. If we have to use a girl accepting money and the gent buttoning his Price drawers and saying that it was cheap at half the Price, let the son-of-a-bitch say it. Give me virtue in reverse. Have a rumpled doll say: "I just lost my pearl of great price, but I don't care so long as Price makes the best damn' stockings in the world." If Springs has his bust-buckets to keep him warm, let's us go hot and heavy on the leg department. Let's make legs so sexy the sock-buyers will forget what's upstairs. Let's have a dame crying in one panel, and smiling in another while she pulls on her stockings, showing plenty of meat. The caption is: "Virtue is cheap at any Price, but losing it is more fun if you wear Price pants." And finally, an obvious bunch of stuffy manufacturers fleeing from a department store, with a girl-driven bull-dozer, flying a stocking as a banner, hard on their heels. Caption: "Priced out of the market." Do I have to say any more, or can you guys go?'

'We can go, I expect,' the agency man said. 'But you must realize that some magazines won't handle the gamey stuff. Springs had a lot of trouble placing his copy.'

'Friend,' Craig said, 'if we can't place the copy it's a news story, and we get ten times the coverage for free. Consider that a female is compounded of tits, legs, and an orifice from which babies emerge, after a short, pleasant callisthenic and nine months of throwing up. We are catering to an unalterable necessity—woman—who bases the ultimate function of child production on whether she has pretty tits and sleek legs. If I have to draw you a plainer picture, maybe I switch agencies?'

'The picture is plain enough, Mr. Price. We'll get cracking on it right away.'

'Okay. But don't overlook any clichés. I'll be curious to see what you do with "The Price is Right". Good afternoon, gentlemen.'

The campaign was a sensation, and sales soared, but profits did not. Craig ploughed nearly all of his major increment back into machinery and advertising, fattening up the plant. He had been advertising heavily for years, and the leggy Price girls had become as much a part of the public consciousness as the Petty girls. He had honed his prices—that advertisement was "Price to the Hone"—and had used superior raw materials in his products. His mill profit-increases had stood to about one and a half per cent for five years. Then suddenly he knocked off his advertising budget at the end of the fourth year, and the increase jumped to two and a half and stayed steady for two years. Still riding a free publicity horse from his past splurge of advertising, he gimmicked up his mills and showed an earning increase to three per cent, as he shoddied his products and pruned his operation to the leanest essentials. The black in his books looked just beautiful.

The bond issue was a cinch. The brokers swarmed round him like starving trout, and the issue was fully subscribed. The plants were still earning a million dollars a year. He had eight million dollars in one hunk, to play with. The interest on the bonds was tax deductible. Four hundred thousand dollars interest annually paid on the bonds eased his tax structure to where his corporation taxes were predicated on only six hundred thousand. Of this he was able to keep at least two hundred thousand, and he still owned the eight million dollars from the bond issue. True, the mills were producing inferior goods, and the advertising had practically ceased in enormous volume, but nobody outside caught on and Craig Price himself now was becoming a walking advertisement for his wares. *Life* magazine covered the construction and the opening of the Price Building with the same florid eagerness it had devoted to the gala of Glenn McCarthy's Shamrock. The name of Price turned up almost daily in the columns, weekly in the news magazines.

It smashed in headlines when he bought the Formidable Life Insurance Co. of Ohio. For his eight million he acquired 51 per cent of Formidable, with a capital and surplus of $15,000,000 and a rough hundred million in reserves—future amortizations, investment loss reserves, future pay-offs-on-death reserves—distant obligations which held no immediate threat to solvency. Eight from fifteen leaves seven. Craig Price was now in control of seven million dollars' worth of somebody else's money, with borrowing potential on the side. And nobody to say him nay, since the minority stockholder's only inalienable right is to endorse the acts of the majority.

But the Government people are stuffy about insurance fund manipulation. They allow only a small per cent of total assets to be held in common stock in listed and seasonal commodities. Half the money must be in Government, State and municipal bonds. The rest ought to be cash and solid securities.

It is very difficult to fiddle an insurance company outright, because of the inspectors, but there is a way so easy that Craig wondered why he'd never thought of it before. While you could not, possibly, speculate with your gross reserves, there wasn't any law saying you couldn't have cash reserves deposited in various reputable banks. All you had to do was place your cash resources strategically. All of a sudden you were a very big man, with more than one hundred million of somebody else's money at your finger-control. Bond houses fawned like spaniels for your custom. Banks curtsied low. You accepted this pandering in a modest manner, and you put a million here—of somebody else's money—and a million there—of somebody else's money. Meanwhile, the mills' earnings are paying off the bond interest, and still showing a profit apart from their indebtedness, and you own a controlling interest in your private office building and an insurance

613

company, as well as a whole mess of oil—the reserves of which have been hocked because you are really going for the big kill.

Craig, like many another egocentric baron, disliked the fussy restrictions of investment which surround the insurance business. The limitation on common stocks precludes a big slaughter. But there are literally no restrictions on an investment trust, so long as you state your intent in advance. So Craig bought fifty-one per cent of Mastodon Investments, Inc., Ltd., S.A. He bought this with the cash and solid stock-bond reserves of the Formidable Insurance Co., plus ten million more that he raised because the banks and the bond houses loved him so pretty because he had the spending of a hundred million worth of somebody else's money. You can't really distrust a man who's got a million dollars on deposit on your bank, when he asks for a tiny little favour. All banks and bond houses adore life insurance tycoons, because they got so much lazy money to invest, and the banking business lives by interest on lazy money.

You return then to leverage. The investment trust business, apart from being flexible—you can buy a castle in Spain, a railroad, an airline, an island in the Pacific, controlling interest in a yo-yo firm or a jukebox factory—comes in very handy for privately knowing about a forthcoming bond issue, investing heavily in merging companies before they merge, and then doubling your money on common stock deals made before the merger, the bond issue is gently leaked to the suckers.

But you keep being offered bargains by the brokerage houses, and one day you run out of money because there are so many goodies around that you just can't resist. It looks so simple. You hock your mills and get eight million. You take the eight million and buy a fifteen million capital and a hundred million gross in the insurance company. You've got to fudge, you've got to borrow, but by using a part of the supposedly untouchable gross, hocking the insurance company's common stock, add it to the purloined parcel of gross, you buy fifty-one per cent of an investment trust. This brings you fifty million in capital and five hundred million in gross. And now you've got five hundred million to play with—buy a bus company, buy a kangaroo farm, buy a safari firm, buy building lots on the moon or in Miami. Anything the man's vanity chooses, buy it.

Because investment-trust money is funny money. A customer will pay, say, a thousand dollars down and a hundred a month, and the genius who controls the company will invest it for him. The only clinker in the investment trust business is that the client's supposed to be able to get his face-value money back at any time, on demand. In this respect the trust is like a bank. If you put it in, you're supposed to be able to get it out by asking for it. And the banker—the head of the trust—is supposed to have it handy on his hip.

614

Under the Investment Company Act of 1940, parcel to the Securities and Exchange Commission, you may have complete freedom of investment, but the Government's really got you by the short hair. Under the Act, when you are selling open-end investments, time-payment certificates, you must at all times have liquid resources sufficient to meet any contingencies. It doesn't make any difference if you can show a maximum withdrawal of a million a year for the past ten years from a fund of five hundred million dollars.

The door is almost laughably open for bureaucratic rule of thumb. A five-thousand-a-year titled clerk may decide, in his judgment, that you don't have sufficient cash reserves—that a depression is coming on, and that you better get up the entire amount of deposits, or else. If you can't lay hands on enough cash, the Government sends in what is called a 'conservator', to supervise what is called 'orderly liquidation', and the word spreads, and your credit flees, and the referees won't allow you what you spent on your ski resort or your castle in Spain or your yo-yo factory. They cite the instability of foreign governments and currency, the high incidence of accidents in skiing resorts, and the potential of yo-yo's to turn and rend you, and sell you out for a song. You must get rid of your bonds and shares at a haggler's price—and, unless you sign the papers they want you to sign, suit may be switched from civil action to fraud, which makes you liable for jail. And when you consider that you are operating five hundred million dollars with a ten per cent capital, and the market can drop ten points in a month, and you have to meet a rush, in no time at all your ten per cent equity is gone, lost in the financial fog. The extra dough you stole—borrowed—from your insurance takes a ten million dollar beating, plus the fat fifteen, and suddenly your insurance company has eaten its capital and ten million more of its gross, and you are out of the insurance business because the insurance inspectors don't like it when you have gross capital invested illegally. This is called fraud. Ten mil in the hole is bad enough for any business, but when you are dealing with the funds of widows and orphans, it is just plain crooked, like armed robbery, in the eyes of the law . . .

It was somewhere in the middle of this shaky balance of pyramided funds, of delicately undecided leverage, that Craig Price found himself at the time that Maybelle demanded a million tax-free cash dollars plus a hundred thousand a year for herself and her daughter, just at this time of his new marriage, just at this time of the unfortunate killing of Jazzbo Newton.

'You'll pardon me, sweetie,' Craig said to Susan, 'if at times I seem a little preoccupied.'

18

'*Craig*,' Jimmy Wilbur said.

'O my God,' Craig replied. 'I'm beginning to hate the sound of my own name. When you say "*Craig*" like that, something else has turned up. What is it now?'

Wilbur tossed a short nod towards Connie, the secretary.

'Blow, sweetie,' Craig said shortly. 'I'll ring when I need you.' Connie left the room. 'Fix us both a drink, Jim,' Craig said. 'I can stand trouble better that way. It is trouble, huh? More trouble, I mean?'

Jimmy was pouring two stiff shots over rocks. He watched his measuring intently. Then he raised his head, walked over to Craig's desk, handed him the drink, and fell into a chair. He looked at the buffalo over the fireplace as he talked.

'Yes, it's trouble. Large active trouble. Now it's the tax people. The Internal Revenue boys.'

'Hell, man, we can't be in any bind with the Revenue kids. I've moved around pretty frisky on some things, but we've always kept our personal income records as clean as a hound's tooth. We always declared everything, and I never stole any-thing—well, damn little—as a business expense. At least I did some business to justify what I said I spent, and attached the records. What's this all about?'

'I just heard from our eminent firm of Wagstaff and Blumberg, the legal eagles we've paid a million bucks to in the last few years. They have just had a tender message from Wash., D.C. The gentlemen down there wish to review you. They wish to review you all the way back to 1946.'

'They can't do that. I've been reviewed to current. This is 1957. You know as well's me that the statute of limitations on back taxes runs out over a three-year stretch. They can't...'

Jimmy Wilbur held up a hand.

'Oh, yes they can, and if you want to argue call Henry Wagstaff or Jules Blumberg. They can't review you on the civil side, but there *ain't* any statute of limitations on fraud, Short Pants. They can go back and review your dead grandpa if they want to. And they have got you in a beautiful little sling, asswise, at the moment, because your insurance company has been to the Government, as sidebar to this suit, and informed the taxeroos that the receivers are disallowing *all* your expenses incurred in the operation of Formidable until the suit is settled. That means every trip to Tangier for the board of directors, every suite in every hotel, every booze bill, your house in France ... all. And the tab is $198,756.22 until 1951. And when you've settled that, they are going to review through 1957. And you are going to pay, or else.'

'Else what?'

'Else this. Blumberg has been to Washington, and has talked fast. He gave me this form an hour ago. You're going to scratch up the dough for the johnnies in Washington, and sign this form saying you admit the review, even though limitations have expired, otherwise this lien will be predicated on fraud, and you'll go to jail, my son, just like Al Capone or Frank Costello went to jail. If you sign, they keep it civil. Don't sign, into the old courtroom, with the usual jail-house blues for wilful tax evasion. Sign, and you just been careless. Don't sign, and try to fight them, and you're a crook. If you don't beat it . . .'

'All right,' Craig's voice was softly defeated. 'Gimme. I'll sign. You suppose I can make some sort of deal to either reduce or else pay off in time payments?'

'You won't make much of a deal,' Jimmy said. 'Maybe if you could scrabble up say one-five-oh on this one, they'd hold still, and give you some time on the next one, which is going to be an easy double saw, in grands. You're hooked for half-a-million dollars, son, and you ain't really got half-a-million dollars, not in cash, inventory, reserves, or credit. Your corporate tit is well and truly in a crack.'

'Well, I'll get it somewhere. There's always Nate Mannheim.'

'I wonder. I wonder if we ain't run out of Nate Mannheim.'

'I don't think so. I've always levelled with Nate. I've always been at least legally honest with the Government. I've . . .'

'Quit singing your own praises. A lot of guys worked for you weren't level, which is why your corporate deductions begin to stink now. How many guys ain't working for you any more? Who screwed the bank deal in Cuba? You should have had better sense than to go for that deal.'

'It was a way to move money. You buy a bank, you bring in your foreign credits that you don't want looked at in the States, you make yourself a loan at one per cent and use the Cuban dough to purchase credits in the States—hell, I financed a million bucks' worth of action out of that bank at one per cent interest. So did the other guy I was in it with.'

'So can you go back to Cuba now? Those boys play rough. What you guys did was literally run off with the assets of that bank, just like you'd heisted it.'

'*I* didn't.'

'So *you* didn't. Torremolinos and Burke and Montoya did. They robbed it blind. The only more dishonest people in Cuba than your associates have been the presidents and their cabinets. And Cuba is a place where they don't set the Government on you. They shoot you. Remember Julio?'

'Yeah, I remember Julio. They never did figure who shot the top of his head off.'

'They didn't want to figure. Julio had been a bad, bad boy,

617

and had crossed somebody up something awful. So Julio comes out of the Casino and heads for his mistress's house and somebody road-blocks his Cadillac and somebody else on a roundtrip-one-day tour from Miami lets him have the hard wo.d right in the face with a tommy-gun. Don't go back to no Cuba, boy, not after what you lads did to that little old bank.'

19

CRAIG'S temper had shortened perceptibly. The daily fights in board-rooms, the endless unravelling of a seeming cavalcade of problems, resulted in an acute state of nerves. It was a strange feeling—a feeling that he was standing on a rug, but that hands yet unknown were flexing themselves to pull the rug out from under him. He noticed that he was peremptorily rude with the captains and waiters with whom he used to joke, asked himself why, and couldn't answer. 'Oh, for Christ's sake, can't anybody do anything right around here, have I got to think of it all?' became an increasingly frequent visitor in his home. Driving out to the house in New Jersey one day, he noted in the rear-view mirror that a permanent frown scarred his forehead, that the corners of his mouth were downdrawn, his nostrils extended, and his face was set in a snarl.

He pulled into a filling station and cursed unreasoningly because another car was ahead of him. Almost absentmindedly, he reached for the office bottle in the back seat of the Rolls, took a drink, lit a cigarette, wiped his moustache dry, and of a sudden realized that he had snarled into the mirror, reached for the bottle, lit a cigarette, and wiped his moustache dry as a simple reflex.

'Brother,' he said aloud, as he slid the car out of the service station, on to the road. 'Brother. You better watch it, son. This ain't the way you were raised.'

That night, over martinis, he asked Sue suddenly: 'You think I drink too much? Don't gimme no con. Do I drink too much?

Sue looked at him, and deliberately took a sip of her own drink before she answered.

'Yes,' she said. 'You drink too much. I drink too much. Every-bloody-body drinks too much. It's a cushion against whatever kind of times we're living in, I suppose. I know I smoke too much. What do you want me to say, that you don't drink too much? You get up on a screwdriver, my boy. I know vodka doesn't smell on your breath, but it's booze all the same. Tie the screwdriver into a martini lunch and the pre-coming-home cocktails and the home cocktails and the night caps and yes, my friend, you do drink too much. And frankly I don't blame you.'

Craig smiled a touch ruefully.

'You're a nice doll, you know that? I don't want to whine too much, but it seems to me that everything has been screwed up lately. I can't seem to unscrew it. For one thing I seem to take it all to bed with me. You notice I been grinding my teeth more than usual lately? I woke myself up last night, and I was having a horrible dream. Something about being eaten up by hyenas. My back was broken and they started to chew on me while I was still alive. I didn't tell you all about the hyenas.'

'Don't. And don't tell me about business, either. Tell me I'm pretty. Don't tell me anything except that I'm pretty and you love me.'

'You're real pretty. And I love you very much. And now I am in a good humour again. The reason I am in a good humour again is because you're pretty and we have the nicest house in the world and I love you. Also you're a good cook. How's that?'

'That's all right, Dad. How do I make out in bed?' Sue offered it as a joke.

'You make out just fine.' He parried the humour. Craig was grim. 'It's me that's the bum in the bed. I got to apologize for that. But sweetie, in this last few months, I know I've been a bum, but two people in bed is enough, and I seem to have been taking half the world to bed with me. All the chairmen of all the boards, and most of the proxy voters, and nearly 'bout all of Washington, D.C.'s, underpaid bureaucrats. I get tired of working, I get tired of thinking, I get tired of planning. God pity me, I was a better husband before we got married. I'll improve, I promise you, I'll improve. If I don't go to jail. I wish I hadn't hit that jerk.'

'What jerk do you wish you hadn't hit?'

'A jerk you'll never know, but he's got a brother, and they both have long memories. The unfortunate thing is that one of them works for the SEC. I believe that from time to time blood *is* thicker than water. Certainly in my case. You can put it down to temper. Call it my own fault. But if it wasn't for this bloody brother...'

It was in Memphis, Tennessee. Craig didn't know the name of his dinner companion, a grass-widow who had been supplied as the extra woman for a big dinner and a country club dance.

He had come down for the Cotton Festival, had made a speech, and now the local textile boys were showing him a big time. The grass-widow—what *was* her name?—was pretty enough, danced well enough and was no more than averagely stupid in her conversation. Craig had a lot to drink. There were some pleasant people—an editor of one of the papers, a cotton

broker and his pretty wife, and the dinner had been good.
They went then to the country club and danced and drank a bit
and had it all been quite fun with the exception of a sort of
fringe gentleman who, in a rustic way, fancied that he was
needling Craig. He was a big man, half-bald, and had some reputation as a local lawyer. Craig did not know at the time that he
was a disenchanted suitor—that the grass-widow, who had
stacks of money, had turned him down after a considerable
courtship. The disenchanted suitor-lawyer's conversation seemed
centred mostly on the theme of: 'So this is what it's like to be a
big shot from New York, down here giving us poor country
people a break.' This then progressed to: 'No Yankee-Jew
bastard can come down here and tell us how to run *our* business,
nigger-lovin'. . . .' The voice dwindled. Since he was talking
directly at Craig, some sort of gentle answer seemed indicated,
so Craig said, lightly embarrassed:

'Really, sir, you can't blame me too much. I'm a Southern
boy myself, and am only half-Jewish, on my mother's side. And
my father was a rather light-complected, poor but honest Negro.
After all, this is a democracy,' and turned away to talk to his
grass-widow dinner companion.

The party broke up early, and the grass-widow suggested that
Craig, the editor and the cotton merchant and their wives
stop off at her house for a nightcap.

A slim sickle of moon shone, a gentle breeze stirred the
fragrant flowers in the lady's garden, and sitting outside in her
patio in the dew-wet grass was very pleasant indeed. Conversation had become general, the scotch was sufficiently aged, and
the grass-widow's boy friend had disappeared when they left the
club. Someone was telling an only faintly dirty joke when tyres
screeched, lights flashed into the drive, and a large car nearly
bucked and reared a few feet away as the driver jammed on
his brakes. It was the disenchanted suitor again. He was weaving
drunk, and blindly angry. He said no word but lunged across
the patio, set himself violently, facing Craig in Craig's lap, and
slapped him hard, three times, right cheek, back of hand to left
cheek, forehand drive to right cheek.

'I swear to God, honey,' Craig said to Sue, 'I was so startled I
was stunned. I hadn't made any pass at his gal. I didn't even know
she *was* his gal. It's rather a rare thing to be sitting around with
half-a-dozen pleasant semi-strangers and have another stranger
come sit in your lap and slap you on the face three times. I
sometimes feel like I'm making it up when I tell this, but honest
to God, this is how it happened.'

'What did you do, then?'

'The first slap just stunned me. The second slap un-stunned
me. And the third one brought that well-known film of red rage
across my eyes. I wasn't Craig Price sitting in a garden any more.

I was Craig Price, Ordinary Seaman, back in Hamburg or Antwerp, where people fought serious. It was all a reflex, completely ungoverned.'

Craig had come out of his seat in a flash. His knee found the slapper's groin. The slapper went backward across a large round coffee-table, scattering bottles and glasses. Diving low, Craig ploughed across the table on his stomach. He regained his feet, and picked up the lawyer by the hair. Legs spraddled, body crouched, Craig brought the man's face forward to collide with repeated long swings of the flat of his clenched fist. The effect was much the same as a succession of perfectly co-ordinated tee-shots, all of the low gravity power of Craig's sweeping blows meeting the forced opposition of the man's face.

'His hair came out in my hand,' Craig said. 'There was very little hair left on his head, and not much face either. He seemed to have lost a nose and most of his front teeth. I am afraid I was kicking him in the stomach when the red mists cleared and I came back from Antwerp and Hamburg to the pleasant patio of a grass-widow in Memphis, Tennessee. I looked with horror at this mess on the ground and I looked inwardly with more horror at me. I said, suddenly:

' "For Christ's sake, I might have killed this man and gone to jail for twenty years for manslaughter, *and I don't even know his name.*" I apologized, of course, but the party was frosted. Somebody drove the battered boy friend to a hospital, everyone admitted I was within my angry rights, but they looked at me rather curiously, as if a pussy-cat had suddenly turned into a tiger. I've been trying to curb my temper ever since. These days I find it harder.'

Craig had been feeling generally lousy lately. Getting out of bed in the morning was a chore, and he spread his legs to keep his balance. His knees seemed unacquainted with his feet. It took him about four or five stiff drinks to get even with the day, and he was always very tired in the evening. When he lay down for a short siesta, he would find his pillow sodden with sweat, but sleep deserted him when he actually went to bed later at night. Until he'd downed half of a fifth of scotch or three or four double martinis, his hands shook badly. Specks occasionally blurred his vision, and once in a while his tongue thickened so that even the simplest dictation chore to his secretary caused her to ask him repeatedly just what he was saying.

Craig hated doctors, possibly because of his early indoctrination under his mother's semi-professional hands. And he maintained the idea that his really superbly constructed body was a fortress—impregnable against cancer, a bastion against heart disease, solidly sound against all ills. Other people would get sick, but not Craig Price. Perhaps other people would die—

he had stopped reading the New York *World-Telegram* sports page because the obituaries of so many of his acquantances were on the other side—but not Craig Price. His obituary was in type, he knew, with all the news services and newspapers and major magazines, but nobody would ever read it.

Then one day it hit him. Right over the head, it smacked him. He was very tired from a long, boring flight. He had felt a little queasy when he woke, but this was nothing new. He was standing in the lobby of the Savoy Hotel in London, talking to a business acquaintance, and was about to suggest a drink. He woke up in a London hospital, with a dent in his skull where his head had bulls-eyed a chair.

He looked vaguely around an accident ward.

'Nurse!' he said. 'Nurse!' A sister hurried to his bed.

'What happened?' he asked the nursing sister. 'Why am I here?'

'Shhhhh,' the sister said. 'You're all right now. The doctor will be around to see you shortly. He'll tell you anything you want to know.'

'What I want to do is get the hell out of here.' Craig said, looking round him at the grim drab ward into which he had been hustled.

'Get me my clothes, now!'

'That's for the doctor to say,' the nursing sister said. 'Shhh. You're disturbing the other patients. This is an emergency ward. Quiet, now, Mr. Price.'

They were sitting in Craig's suite in the Savoy, and Craig had mixed a gin-and-tonic for himself and the doctor. Craig still wore a bandage on his head.

'I want you to go and see Sir Archibald Fenston tomorrow. He's the best head-man we have here,' the doctor said. The doctor was a gaunt Welshman named Evans. 'What you had, I think, was an epileptoid seizure. The thing is to find out what caused it, unless you've a history of epilepsy in the family?'

'None,' Craig said. 'I never had a fit in my life. Neither did anybody else I ever knew in my family as far back as my grandfather. What exactly did happen, anyhow? I was talking to Goldsmith and all of a sudden I woke up in this charity hospital feeling like every muscle in my body had been stretched on a rack. With a hole in my head. One minute I was talking and then I woke up in the hospital with a hole in my head.' He grinned. 'As you can see, I already got enough scars. I don't need any extra adornments to enhance me manly beauty.'

'You had a simple short circuit in your brain which blacked you out and caused a convulsion. With those scars, you must have had one or more concussions,' the doctor said. 'Thanks.'

As Craig refilled his glass from the sideboard. 'How many would you say?'

'At least two. One from an automobile wreck, where I got this.' Craig pointed to the scar that went upwards through his eyebrow into his hair. 'And another from being hit over the head with a chair leg when I was a kid. When I was going to sea. But I never cut out before. It must have been very pretty.'

He grimaced.

'I shouldn't like to prognosticate, since I'm a simple general practitioner,' Dr. Evans said. 'But I strongly recommend that you go through the whole course of sprouts after you've talked to Sir Archibald. He's a dismal old blighter, frankly, and he won't tell you anything you want to hear. But he's the best. You'll need some X-rays, of course, and certainly a full physical by a good internist. I shall be delighted to arrange all these after I've heard what Archie has to say. In the meantime, Mr. Price, I would take it very slowly on the grog, and try to get myself a full night's sleep. I've sent for some pills. Good-day, sir, and I'll speak with you tomorrow after you've seen Sir Archibald. The appointment's for eleven tomorrow morning.'

Sir Archibald was a man of some seventy years, with a wintry visage. He had the long horse-face so common in specialists, and when Craig started to light a cigarette, he asked Craig sternly not to smoke as it proved disturbing to the other patients who might follow.

'Evans has told me the basic details,' he said. 'I should be interested to amplify them.' He uncapped a fountain pen and drew a scratch pad closer to him on his green leather-covered antique Italian desk.

'Were you very tired when this seizure occurred?' he asked.

'Yes. I had flown from New York after a very difficult week—actually months—of personal and business problems.'

'We'll ignore that for a moment,' Sir Archibald said. 'Did you eat on the plane?'

'No. I can't eat on planes.'

'Had you quite a lot to drink?'

'Yes, sir. All that week and on the plane as well. I find it less boring to fly if I'm a little drunk.'

'Hmmm.' Sir Archibald wrote rapidly. 'That might explain it. It is quite possible to induce a seizure of this sort merely by forcing an imbalance of liquids in the body. Had you drunk an abnormal amount in New York?'

'I'm afraid so. I had a little party for ninety or a hundred people the night before I left, and the party continued on until they poured me on the plane. Yes. I'm afraid I drank a lot.'

'I'm a neurologist, not an internist,' Sir Archibald said. 'The X-rays and EEG will tell me something, but I do not think that an X-ray and an electroencephalogram will tell me the whole story. There is a possibility that you may have a benign tumor which caused this seizure, in which case its removal is a matter of simple surgery. But I think your problem is more in your stomach, in the vicinity of the liver and spleen, than in your skull. If you don't mind taking off all your clothes except your underpants?'

Sir Archibald tapped Craig's knees and tested his foot reflexes to blunt needle pricks and his hand co-ordination with meeting fingertips, and delved deeply into his belly-hollow with a searching hand.

'You have a distinctly swollen and hardened liver.' he said. 'Your reflexes are reasonably good, with the exception of your right foot. That is possibly explicable by the operation you had for phlebitis. Judging from the scars on both legs, I would imagine they removed considerable vein. Certainly I think you should stop smoking. And very certainly—the internist will bear me out on this—you should stop drinking altogether for a minimum of six months. And, if possible, go on the water-wagon permanently.'

'What happens if I don't?' Craig asked, his soul hungering for a cigarette and a stiff shot of anything. His mouth was dry, and he was beginning to ache in strange locations.

'From what you've told me,' Sir Archibald said, 'and from what Evans told me, you have been a heavy drinker for most of your life, and judging from the nicotine stains on your fingers, you smoke sixty or eighty cigarettes a day. I would say that the combination of alcohol and nicotine has had a definitely deleterious effect on your nervous system. One of the more certain signs is that your left eye is decidedly larger than the other, and your foot response is definitely not good. I must say, though,' he permitted himself a smile, 'I wish I had your heart. If I can predict anything as a physician, you will never die of a coronary thrombosis.'

'What happens if I don't?' Craig repeated. 'Stop drinking, I mean?'

Sir Archibald placed his fingertips carefully together.

'Why, these attacks will become more frequent. Eventually they will make some imprint on your brain. You will become the kind of pathetic drunkard who causes people to refer to old So-and-So as "soft in the head". In the meantime, I should strongly advise against driving an automobile until you have given your tissues time enough to dry themselves of their alcoholic content.'

Craig got up.

'I would like to pay now, sir,' he said.

'That will be six guineas,' Sir Archibald said. 'You may pay my secretary on the way out. Good-day, Mr. Price. I shall need to see you again after I have had a chance to study the X-rays and the EEG. You have a good body. Mr. Price. What a shame to waste it entirely. The same also refers to your brain. Good-day.'

'Good-day,' Craig said. He lit a cigarette as soon as he entered the lift, inhaled greedily and then flagged a taxi from the footpath.

'Where to, sir?' the cabbie said, pushing down his flag.

'The nearest pub,' Craig said. 'And step on it.'

I am me, Craig Price, Craig thought, after all the indignities of the physical examination, the X-rays, the EEG, and the final talk with Sir Archibald had been concluded. So now I know who and what I am. Me, Craig Price. I have a small but rapidly growing cirrhosis of the liver and a propensity for fits. I have an angry spleen and something wrong with the lower end of my large intestine. But at least I have heart. Now, boy, have you got heart enough to quit being yourself and become a kind of male nun who doesn't smoke, doesn't drink, doesn't screw, and doesn't run around with the people who do? Or have you got heart enough to keep on being Craig Price, drunken bum, womanizer, nicotine fiend, so that you can eventually die with your identity intact? Or would you rather be Dick Stover at Yale, or Tom, the fun-loving Rover? Or would you rather be a fish?

'I'll settle for me, Craig Price,' he said aloud, and went to the telephone. He gave a number and waited until a cool English voice answered.

'It's Craig Price here,' he said. 'Just got in from New York. What are your plans for tonight, Diana? Apart from having dinner with me at the River Club? I have scored a succession of achievements and I feel like tying on a real one.'

The answering hum was of eager assent.

'Fine, then,' Craig said. 'Suppose you come over just a little early and we can have about nine martinis and find out what little boys and little girls are made of before we tire ourselves out dancing.'

He cradled the phone and lit a cigarette. Then he walked over to the sideboard and made himself a large pink gin in a water glass.

'Your very good health, Sir Archibald,' he said, and downed it in a single gulp.

'But I don't think I mention this to Sue. I'm tough enough to take without saddling her with my fits.'

It seemed to be the season for taxi drivers, or people connected with taxi drivers. Craig and Sue had been out on a mild Saturday evening with a business friend and his wife. They had been drawn, by whim, to Greenwich Village, and after eating at Nino and Nella's, they had stopped to catch the midnight show at one of the grimier clubs around the Minetta Street sector.

The whisky was bad and the show was worse, so they left early.

Craig hailed a taxi, which U-turned on Sixth Avenue, and came to a halt at a corner opposite a newspaper kiosk. As they crossed the street, Craig said: 'Hold the cab, girls, while George and I pick up a couple sets of Sunday papers. This ain't my night to howl. I want to go home and kick up the fire and play a little soft music and read the scandal columns. Come on, George, they're too heavy for one man to carry.'

The men crossed the street again, and the women stood on the sidewalk, leaning against the open door of the taxi, waiting for the men's return. Sue and Antoinette, George's wife, were talking idly of nothing more important than new hair-styles when an enormous blond man, young, wearing a camel's-hair coat, escorting a girl, approached the cab from the other side of the street, opened the opposite door, and said to the driver:

'Forty-second and Lex, and make it snappy.'

'The cab's taken, Mister,' the hacker said. 'These ladies . . .'

'I'm in the cab, Doc,' the burly blond man said. 'Drive, like I said.'

Susan and Antoinette set up a clamour in righteous anger.

'It's *our* cab! We're just waiting for our husbands!'

'You've got no right to steal our cab!'

The young man was just saying: 'If you goddam broads will just quit yelling, maybe I can make this driver understand where I want to go in *my* cab!' when Craig and George arrived.

'What's this all about?' Craig said. 'What's the trouble?'

'This man, he came in on the other side and . . .'

Craig looked coldly at the man.

'Out, Junior,' he said. 'Drag it.'

'Pipe down, Gramps,' the burly young man said, 'or I may have to hurt you. Now, driver, for the last time . . .' the driver shifted gears.

Craig picked up a concrete-based no-parking sign, which no one man is supposed to be able to lift, and in a swift surge of the old blind rage attacked the roof of the cab, deeply denting it. He cast away the mighty bludgeon and dived into the back seat, making mewing noises, his lips curled in a leopard snarl. He seized the front of the burly young man's coat, and yanked. The coat carried away, and Craig sprawled backward on the sidewalk, furious at the awkward turn. Still making little animal noises, he lunged back into the cab, and this time, when he returned to the sidewalk, he had the man's necktie and most of his shirt front in one hand, and had managed to bloody the man's nose with the other.

'For God's sake drive on!' Sue yelled to the cabbie. 'Take him away!' The bloated sneering arrogance of the young man's face had shrunken into fear, as Craig seized him by the leg and dragged him on to the sidewalk, across the lap of the terrified girl, and was going now for his throat with both hooked hands. Sue, Antoinette, and George rushed Craig simultaneously, and the combined weight of their bodies knocked him backwards from the now sickly terrified young man, who scrambled back into the cab, his face bloody, his front half naked.

'For God's sake, drive on!' Sue screamed.

'But my money's in that coat,' the man whimpered. 'All my money's in my coat!'

'The hell with your money! I'm worried about your life!' Craig had squirmed free from his friends, and was heading back into the cab. The man slammed the door, and Craig yanked it open.

'Drive, you fool!' Both girls screamed.

The cab surged away, leaving Craig holding the door in his hands. He looked at the door in a mildly curious fashion, and then hurled it into the street.

'I wish,' he said quietly to Susan, 'that in the future you would keep the hell out of my brawls. What happened to the Sunday papers?' All the way home he never referred to the incident.

20

SUSAN had sublet her apartment.

'We don't really need it, darling. When you have to stay in town you can always use your office-suites, and me, I got a hankering to be a country girl. I want to potter amongst my roses and concentrate on how much fertilizer to spread on the petunias. I'm sick of the city, anyhow. But it's not much of a drive—and it'll be much easier to drive it than try to cope with trains. You must hire yourself another chauffeur . . .' she stopped.

'I don't want another chauffeur. I'll either drive myself or take a Carey. I don't ever want another chauffeur.'

'I'm sorry, Craig. It just slipped out. But we've got some extra servants' space, and it would be simple enough to fix it nicely for the Carey man, or whoever drives you. You really need to be driven. Fighting that traffic after a rough day at the rope-walk isn't my idea of how a husband comes home relaxed. And I would like you to think of coming home as an exercise in relaxation.' She put a hand on his knee. 'The bass are biting like cannibals. If you could squeeze off from that office just a little earlier in the day there'd be time for some fishing and a swim and we could maybe do a steak out-of-doors and be really corny country-folk. Look, you silly man, I'm the woman as loves you, and I didn't contract to marry a corpse. Which is what you'll be if you don't ease up a notch.'

'I know, I know.' Craig shrugged irritably. 'But now this tax business on top of some of the other stuff. Seems to me if I ever see another lawyer I'll kill myself. They really got me over the hip right now, baby doll. I'm in a large, fat, stinking mess. The old thing about too many irons in the fire was never triter, never truer. That business with Maybelle's settlement jammed me pretty. For actual cash, I mean. And actual cash is real tight. And now that extra added wallop of the income tax people—I got enough trouble with SEC. I don't need the Revenue boys. The next thing you know it'll be FBI, and I'll have cornered the alphabet. Washington. Bunch of goddam penny-ante clerks pushing you around . . . Sorry. Honestly, sweetie, I haven't hit anybody this week.'

They were in the country, and the summer air was very soft. A pleasant croak of frog helped the cicadas in the night symphony. They had drawn deck-chairs out to the pool side, and were sitting in slacks and bush-shirts watching the lazy Morse-code of the lightning bugs. Sue had planted a small mint-bed, and so they were drinking juleps.

'Make me feel lak growin' me a goatee and wearin' a string-tie, like one of them four-colour-process Southern gentleman in the slick ads,' Craig said. '*You* take platinum. I'll just have that ol' pewter with the ice-beads on it, and a little Jack Daniel mashed up with a mess o' mint inside. Man, this is living. I'd like to quit the whole rat-race and just set here for a year.'

'Why don't you, Craig? Why don't you quit the whole rat-race and just set here for a year? You've got enough. You've proved it all. Why don't you settle it all up and take your profits and have some fun—some fun like the Havana fun, or go on another safari? I'm not afraid of snakes or night noises. I'd like to go on a safari with you. I'd be very brave and never complain about the bugs. Anybody who has withstood New Jersey mosquitoes wouldn't be afraid of *tsetse* flies . . .'

Craig made an irritable impatient gesture.

'I can't quit. I can't . . . Don't you know by now that half the bloody world is working for me? People I don't know work for me. People in countries I never saw work for me. I'm not a man. I'm a goddam institution. I'm a foundry. I'm a factory. I'm a way of life. I'm a . . .'

'You're a man I love who needs another julep. Sit back and relax, sweetie, and I'll fix it.'

'Relax? *Relax*?' Craig's voice sharpened. 'How in the name of God can I relax? Relax, with half the Government on my tail, with thirty appointments a day, with this little house of cards of mine fluttering in the wind? *Relax*? Jesus, woman, all the Miltowns they ever made wouldn't relax me. That little suit for six-and-a-half million bucks the insurance boys are hanging on my back . . . Nobody's got six-and-a-half million bucks in cash now. Being broke for that kind of dough is exactly the same as being broke for six bucks, or six cents, if you can't get up the dough. Say I'm wrong, and they're right. Still I don't know where to go for the dough if I have to pay it in cash.' He spaced the words deliberately. '*If I have to pay it in cash.* Cash Price, they used to call me. Man alive. These days I'm wondering what I could do to raise a buck off the men's room attendant in Twenty-One.'

'Where did it start and where does it end?' Susan had come back from the bar with a fresh julep.

'I told you where it started. Where it ends I can't say. I suppose everybody's trapped in what he does for a living. I got a tiger by the tail. And'—he grinned ruefully—'I'm afraid I wouldn't have it any other way. It's a kind of masochism, I suppose. See how much you can punish yourself. You want . . . you want . . . I don't know really what the hell you *do* want. Maybe some people are just capable of wanting more than other people. I always been a sucker for wanting it all.'

'Tell me, Mr. Price. You really like all this trouble, these investigations, these lawsuits, this Government tax business? Is that what gives you your kicks? Would you be happier if everything ran serene?'

Craig took a pull at his julep and lit two cigarettes. He handed one to Sue.

'Hard one to answer. I guess I thrive on strife. The challenge thing. To put together a deal, to make two-and-two come out nine, to know that everybody's hand's against you and still whip the bastards to their knees . . . Yeah.' His voice hardened. 'I like it. I wouldn't be without it. Take me away from the messes and the troubles and I'd wrinkle up and die like an old tomato.'

Sue changed her line of fire abruptly.

'Do you ever think of Maybelle? Do you ever think of your daughter? Come right down to it, do you ever think of anybody but yourself?'

Craig grinned a lazy wolf-smile.

'I think of you, honey-chile. You trying to start a fight, or what? I got enough fights outside to keep me gainfully employed. Is this known as the honeymoon wearing off, or exactly what?' His voice chilled. 'What exactly *are* you up to?'

'Girl stuff, I guess,' Sue said. 'I just wondered if I was going to wind up in the same ash-heap, the same dustbin, with Maybelle and Carol. I just wondered if what lost you to them might some day steal you from me.'

'Look, kid.' The voice was tensely fierce now. 'You married me because I got balls. You married the balls. If I didn't have them you never would have met me, for Christ's sake. That most indispensable masculine equipment carried me to where I could meet a Mrs. Susan Strong, whose husband I gather was not equipped overmuch with these male attributes. It took balls

629

to get me where I was, and balls to stay there, and balls to buy off Maybelle to marry you. A writin' man I know once wrote a very tough book which aroused a lot of criticism. He said a rather rudely cogent thing: "I am not J. M. Barrie," he said, "and I had no intention of writing *Peter Pan.*" Well, kid, I'm not writing *Peter Pan*. This ain't the world for Peter Pan. I am writing Craig Price, thug.' He sighed. 'I suppose this is a fight?'

'Not intended. But would you say that already you're regarding me as the price you had to pay Maybelle?' Her voice had deadened.

'I said not any such a damned thing. Getting rid of Maybelle would have been cheap'—he mimicked his advertisement—'at half the Price.'

'But in a way,' she persisted, 'you bought me with Maybelle's money, second-hand perhaps, but still Maybelle's money.'

Craig stood up, raging, and threw the julep mug down the side of the hill.

'It was goddam well not Maybelle's money, and I'm tired of being prosecuted in my own house, Madame District Attorney. It was my money, money *I* made, do you hear? Yes, if you want it rudely that way, I climbed into Maybelle's pants to get into her old man's mill. Yes, yes, Christ yes! And if anybody calls me a pimp one more time I'll bust things. But that was twenty years ago and what I bought I've paid for since! For Godsake, don't *you* start making me wonder if it was all worthwhile!'

'I think you're a little shook up,' Sue said. 'Sit down and I'll fix you another julep and then we'll go in and eat. These mosquitoes...'

'Women. *Women!*' Craig was still furious. 'They buy a man at his ball-bearing value, and then try to cut off what they bought! I had a bad time with my wife, I had a bad time with my daughter, now I'm getting the boots from you! What do you all want, for God's sake, perfection?'

'We want a man to love, and to be loved by,' Sue said calmly. 'We don't understand what makes a man the man we want to love and be loved by. Women know very little of men except to love them. And I suppose, being women, they can turn that love into persecution once the freshness has dried.'

'Well, Sis, if you think you can rouse a man to heights of true love by scourging him, by pointing the pistol of your love at him, by saying love me, damn you, or I'll stop your allowance, you're as mistaken as all the rest,' Craig said. 'I'm sick of this. You come home to escape from a lot of crap and then you get a lot more crap at home.'

'Temper, temper, Junior,' Sue said. 'Mama didn't mean no harm.'

'Mamas don't never mean no harm,' Craig said. 'They just play that Mama bit until Papa looks around for a new Mama.

And just try to remember the circumstances under which we met, my sweet. That was before you started playing Mama.'

'I remember, and I can't say I'm very proud,' Sue answered. 'I cannot in all truth say I'm very proud of my performance. You had me as easily as any whore, and I notice you still refer to Maybelle as your wife.'

Craig got up and raised his hand as if to strike her. Then he dropped it wearily.

'Consider yourself slapped,' he said. 'Say that to me just one more time and you won't have to consider it. I'm going to bed. In *my* room. I got a hard day in town tomorrow . . .'

'Craig, I'm . . .'

'Good night, Susan.' He walked through the door, stopped at the bar, and poured himself a long straight shot, which he knocked back in one gulp. He disappeared into the living-room. Susan looked after his disappearing back, seeing him in the inside light from the dark outside, and tears misted her eyes. He looked so . . . so *tired*, especially from the back.

His face has changed so much, she said to herself. In just this short year it's got a little grey, as his hair is getting greyer. It's got puffy under the eyes, which always seem just a little wearier. He drinks too much, he smokes too much, and he can't sit down for very long. Even when we go to bed together he's thinking of something else. Living with him these days is like having a flock of strangers in the house as guests and you wonder when, if ever, they're going to leave. And how much of it all is my fault, I wonder? If I hadn't met him, I mean? If it wasn't me, she thought, it would have been somebody else. And I *did* try to talk him out of divorcing Maybelle. I'd have been happy just to be his girl.

'I would like hell!' she said aloud. 'I would like hell! He was my boy when he first walked across that room, and I'd have stolen and killed to get him! In sickness and in health, it said. If this is sickness a lot of it's my fault.'

Susan got up and went upstairs. The doors between their rooms were slightly opened, and as she scrubbed her face in her bathroom, she could hear his teeth grinding. She went quietly into his room, and saw, in the moonlight, that he was sleeping with his fists tightly clenched. His head rolled on the pillow, and his grinding teeth made a frightful sound. Susan got quietly into bed with Craig, cuddled him closely as a mother would hold a child, and after a while the rigidity of his body slacked, the fists unclenched, and the teeth-gnashing ceased. Presently he snored, contentedly, and Sue got up to return to her own room. He wouldn't like it, she thought, if he woke up to find me in bed with him . . .

631

21

'CONNIE,' Craig said to his secretary. 'Call Mrs. Price and tell her I won't be home tonight, and get me a plane ticket for Washington. I have to go unravel some business. Call the Statler and book me a suite and another for my lawyers. And get me either Blumberg or Wagstaff now.'

'At least *he* could have called me,' Susan said, as she hung up from her talk with Connie. 'I wish we hadn't got into that hassel last evening.'

'I should have called her,' Craig thought, as he opened his brief-case on the plane. 'I'll call her from Washington.'

It was hot in Washington as only Washington can be hot. Steaming, sticky, collar-wilting, crease-melting hot.

Washington heat is something like a cross between the Sahara desert's *cafard*, the madness that comes from sun and sand and hot dry *khamsins*, the fifty-mile wind that turns the sky yellow and fills the air with a fine talcum of sand—and something like jungle heat, wet, green, fleshy heat, that perverts the air to water and makes breathing akin to drowning. Washington heat issues as much crotch-rot, as much armpit rash, as ever did Guadalcanal or Lae or Buna. It is an angry heat, a heavy heat, a sullen heat, and impregnates a midsummer madness as surely as the Sahara's *cafard* is born of the *khamsin*, as surely as the *tramontana* of Europe irritates people to desperation and sometimes drives them to insanity and even murder.

Washington heat also breeds a nervousness in the great halls of Government, as the heat smites concrete. The seersuckered behinds of the Government stenographers stick to the chairs, and leave great smears of dampness on the dresses of the hundred thousand pretty girls who have come all the way from Itching Palms, S.C., and Nowhere, Nevada, to accept a civil service rating and a faint beckon of matrimony.

Their carbons are smeared, their makeup wrecked, their arm-pits darkly damp and their hair clings streakingly, annoyingly to their powder-splotched faces. They go home, at the day's end, on verge of hysterical tears because the sweating boss has been unduly nasty about the smeared carbons. They go home on flatulent buses, filled with the odour of standing-up sweat-stale people, all tired, all angry, and mostly all hopeless of any future past an upgrade to GS-4, the women outnumbering the men, girls a solid glut on the matrimonial market, everyone teetering between shabby gentility and stark unemployment if the Senator or the Congressman doesn't get re-elected, or some distemper on the Hill cuts an appropriation. It is a town of constant economic fear.

Washington is a city where easy acquaintance is difficult outside an office, because Washington has incalculably stupid rules about drinking. One may not drink standing at a bar, but must be served at table. This precludes the easy, casual pickup which often turns into friendship, sometimes into a love affair, quite often into matrimony, in more congenial towns such as San Francisco, New Orleans or Denver. Somehow a girl alone at a Washington table offers herself cheaply if she responds to a wink, a direct frontal assault, and it wants thick-skinned masculine assurance in large doses to cross a room to proposition a woman formally. Two strikes are on the gentleman, and pos-possibly three on the lady, even when she realizes what the boy's doing out of loneliness and invites him to sit. Her guard is high, and the mental knees are tightly crossed even though he may do nothing more serious to affront her virtue than offer to buy her a drink and suggest a Chinese dinner.

Washington is a strange, gelded town, a city with no home of its own, no civic pride, a lousy ball club, and a strange, faceless transient population. It is one big bus station, with people coming and people leaving, passing, always passing each other without smiling. And it is the loneliest town in the world. Even its politics fail to make strange bedfellows, because the activity on the Hill does not apply to the political castration of the residents. The loudest wind ever heard from Capital Hill blows back to the Dakotas or the Carolinas or New York or Alaska, and no faint breeze of interest ever stirs the languid leaves of Washington's home-town trees.

Washington's better suburbs—mostly in Maryland, a civilized state of cracked crab, terrapin stew, slot machines, gambling joints, stand-up bars and crooked politicians—are as beautiful as anything in Kent or Surrey, with neat red barns, white rail fences, calico cows and mahogany horses . . . with blue wind-rumpled bays and quail softly calling . . . with field-stone houses and lush rolling manicured lawns and outdoor barbecues and snickering streams and heavy-leaved trees sighing dustily in August over the shaded lanes of Bethesda and Chevy Chase and all the lands north of the East-West Highway.

This is hated territory, hated by all the pious little clerks who run the nation, the little bureau boys who are living in thin-walled housing developments in Virginia, the petty sub-chiefs who will never own a field-stone house on Wilson Lane, who will never be invited to a columned estate on Bradley Boulevard, with its sweeping stretch of green lawn and sheltering trees and hints of rich-folks' merriment inside. Washington develops a tremendous inferiority complex in its hired hands—little lost folk from little foreign places, people who go through channels,

IBM punchcard people who always, quaking, look over shoulders to see if the boss is watching, and who in their dedication to the nation's business merely put in the time they have no wish to understand.

Washington's cherry trees were sent from Japan. Its streets, an incomprehensible labyrinth of circles and sectors, were laid down by a Frenchman, one l'Enfant, with a French Revolution concept of how to build a city as a barricade. Its traffic congeals on a mere suggestion of rain, and the farmers from the hinterlands make even ordinary driving an adventure into fear. All hands in Washington seem to have an unpaid-for two-toned car, which they drive in the raffish mood of the whistle stops in Georgia and Virginia and Dakota from which they stem.

Practically nobody in Washington has ever paid cash for anything, and there is a strong spring-night skunk-smell of nervous tension pending an administration change, a reverse of outside election, a world crisis, a scandal in Virginia or Maryland. Washington has a Supreme Court and disobeys it. Washington has a Congress and can't control it. Washington has its Georgetown, a formerly Negro-inhabited slum made popular by snobs, Foggy Bottom Irish, semi-permanent Communists in high places, politicians, pundits, the Georgetown University and journalists who always wear bow ties to explain to the world that they are journalists. A south-west or south-east address used to be a sign of social inacceptibility, but now the north-west is turning to the ragbag element and the shoddy Negro tenements close to the Capitol are being converted into frightfully chic houses, just as Georgetown's upjumped slum chicness made the senator or the minister neighbour to his washerwoman.

Washington, the men's-room-smelling bus-station town, peopled by the overnight politico, the visiting fireman, the frightened clerk, the impotent military, the current shaky administration, the uncertain newspapers, the lonely, frightened foreigners from the provinces, the people who will never have a permanency, either in home or office, whether it's a house in Rock Creek, an office in the White House or a furnished room and an office in a jerry-built paper-box extension of the Bureau of Overlooked Unnecessary Affairs. Washington, the sick-leave town, where you get thirty days sick-leave each year and you better be sure to take it, sugar, because it don't accumulate. Washington, the biggest hickory-shirted, blue-jeaned, tobacco-chewingest, corniest, country-storest hick town in the world. The cornball citadel, which calls itself the Capital of the World, a cockleburred town full of uniformed Zekes and Zebs and Jakes, all from the country, and all destined to return to the country. Corner-store kids who look lonesome without a pot-bellied stove to spit against, a biscuit-barrel to rob. All making policy, and deciding momentous issues, and all, all as transient as the stories that stem from the busy news services that gush daily into international consciousness. In Washington, Cotton Ed Smith and Huey Long were city slickers, and Marion Zioncheck was regarded as normal.

A floating town. Even the whore-houses have to float. The crap games float from shoddy address to shoddier address. The politicians float, the diplomats float, the investigations make a hell of a fuss and then everybody goes home and when you say McCarthy they think you're talking about the old manager of the New York Yankees. All the stinks, big and little, that hold the headlines day after dreary day, that dominate the TV, suddenly are buried in the circular file that the night-side charlady empties. Dear old Washington, the Washington like the fire the British made when they burnt it down. Except now it burns down every two years or so.

Craig was thinking, as he drove in from the airport, I used to be a part of it. How well, how frighteningly well, do I remember the old WPA headquarters down on New York Avenue—nobody knowing anything about what the accounting was about, how much Florida would get for snake-killing, but how rigid the caste system of salary. You were a big guy when you made it from $1220 a year to $1440 and when you hit $1620 you were really in the heavy chips. Then the Hecht Co. and D. J. Kaufman gave you credit, and you could even buy a car on time from Joe Cherner. And then they cut the budget and that job you had from some friend of a Senator's secretary disappeared into the mists. That's why you went back to sea, my boy.

'I guess I could still go to sea,' Craig said, without thinking, as the car drew up in front of the Statler. 'I guess I could always go back to sea.'

The air-conditioning of the Statler smote him across the face like an icy unseen ocean wave.

'I must remember to call Sue and get myself off the hook,' he said. 'I'm sorry about last night. She's a hell of a good kid, but I hope, I hope, I hope, she is not going to go wife on me. Brother. I don't *want* a wife. I want a friend. Why is it that soon as you get married you lose friends and gain wives? If you could only just keep it like it was in Cuba.'

He looked around the lobby after the bell boy had condescendingly accepted his bag. Nothing had changed. Merely a slight switch of costume would have taken the lobby-scene back to the war years. Military people, political people, and there was Dolly Madison, right over there, just waiting for somebody to light her cigarette. The toe-tapping call girl there, the businessman in from Pittsburgh there, the lobbygow there, the five-percenter there, the nice old lady come to see the sights there, all the people who infest Washington hotels there and there and there.

That one will be up the Washington Monument tomorrow if it kills her, Craig thought, as he crowded into the elevator and mentioned the number of his floor. Country people all. Rubes. Hicks. All on the make and all in town, whether it's for a gander at the Monument or to buy a Congressman or wheedle a little bit of extra leverage from that House with the big white front porch. Wonder whatever happened to Vaughan and Caudle and Maragon and the rest of that sorry lot?

But it was not so bad in the boarding house that Christmas Eve. It was not so bad. All the poor people, the worried people, the sad people clinging desperately to each other out of dirty loneliness. Maybe once, that Christmas Eve so long ago, I came close to touching a real brotherhood of miserable man. God knows we seem far enough away from it today. I thought Washington was a great big frightening city then, and didn't realize that it isn't the town, it's only the pathetic people.

He stripped off his sweat-ruined coat, and called for room-service. He ordered a battery of bottles—rum, Coke, scotch, gin, tonic, soda and a big barrel of ice cubes. Then he undressed and stood for at least ten minutes under the shower. He had pulled on his shorts when the bellboy came with the drinks. Craig mixed himself a long gin-and-tonic. He sat remembering, before he had to face the chore of calling his lawyers.

It was Christmas in Washington and Craig was back from the distant shores. The year was 1934, and nobody, much, wanted to hire anybody, much, to do anything, much.

He lived in a rooming house on Sixteenth Street. The landlady's name was Mrs. Finch, no kin to Miss Finch of the select school, and she had a son who played the oboe in a band that catered to the Fox Theatre. His name was Buzzy, and he looked like a man who might just possibly be nicknamed Buzzy.

Craig had read *Look Homeward, Angel,* and the people who lived in his rooming house might very well have peopled Mr. Wolfe's Eugene's mama's boarding house in Altamont.

There was a bleary, but whiskified-happy whore, past her professional prime, who really liked her work, when she could get it. Her name would have been Hazel, Iris, Ruby, Pearl, or Doris. There was a skeletal man, with tobacco-coloured pouches under his eyes, who was dying of tuberculosis. There were two drunken reporters, who had long since given up the idea of writing the great American novel. One was fat, with a vast untidy moustache. One was thin, with negligible chin, and a face as grey as an ancient sheet, but strawberried with the present pocks of long-forgotten boozings. There was a plump dark pouter pigeon of a Philadelphia Jewish girl named Ruth. There were other non-descripts, the sort of people who blend perfectly into a rooming house whose kitchen table is covered with yellow coffee-stained oilcloth, and where the bathroom is a little too far down the hall, and where somebody has always left curling souvenirs of pubic hairs in the tub. There would have been a perpetual odour of stale grease in the house, and the wall-papering would be mottled with moisture, and its colour best described as barnyard-brindle.

Rain accompanied Christmas. Not the kind of benevolent rain that forces you to a fire for snug comfort, but a negligent, nagging, grey-faced rain, as importuning as a shrewish uncosmeticked wife in a slatternly wrapper and sloven slippers. A grey rain, a soggy day, a dismal day, a perfect day for suicide or dope addiction, but not a day for old whores and broke youngsters and out-of-work oboe players and excommunicated Jewish girls from Philadelphia, to use as a Christmas Eve, when everybody in the house was busted flat and nobody had an invitation to drink outside eggnog tucked amongst the non-existent cards on the non-existent mantel.

'It was the best goddam Christmas I ever had in my life,' Craig had told Susan once. 'It was the first time I was ever able to put myself in Joseph's place, and realize that, with a housing shortage, a manger wasn't such a lousy place for a woman to drop a foal. Maybe I'm unclear, but I suddenly got myself a close-kinship with Jesus Christ on that horrible wet night in Washington, D.C.'

Craig had no friends whatsoever except the people in the rooming house. He had perhaps a dollar in cash money, and owed the rent. Everybody else outside was drinking eggnog in front of festive holly-decked fires, but not Craig and his friends. The little Jewish girl was not from Junior Hadassah. The oboe player had been canned out of his job. Missus Finch was behind in her own rent, and the press was out covering a fire in Northeast, where some drunken bum had staggered home fallen into a Christmas tree, and burnt down a tenement. The whore had acquired the curse and wasn't hustling, even if anybody needed her on Christmas Eve, which wasn't very likely.

Dickens couldn't have written the script any better. It needed only Scrooge and Fagin, got up as a sheriff, rapping on the door, and Bill Sykes lurking on the foot-blistered, habit-frayed and time-spotted hall carpets, and there were all the makings of a fine art movie, with a Russian director.

The first event was the arrival of the Three Wise Men disguised as a seedy old bum delivering packages from home for the Parcel Post people. Craig got one, and the little Jewish girl, Ruth, got one. Craig's had a jar of pickled artichokes, a half-fruit cake, some home-made cookies and candy, and a bottle of bourbon. Plus a cheque for five bucks. The cheque bounced, but not before it bought a rather wizened turkey. Ruth's parcel contained an assortment of exotic Semitic delicatessen.

Despite her Evish indisposition, the whore struggled into her draggle-tailed finery and went out on the streets. What she did to whom would be difficult to say, but she came back with a gallon bottle of muscatel and a carton of cigarettes. The newspaper boys rolled in, each bearing a jug of what is known as Christmas whisky—the bad blend with which grateful business men think they are bribing the press. The Bug—the TB gentleman—came down with an acute attack of candles. Why he had candles in his room, nobody knew, but they cheered up the kitchen considerably.

Missus Finch cooked the turkey, and Buzzy broke out his oboe, and while they were waiting for the badly-roasted bird they drank the whisky and wine and ate Craig's stuff and Ruth's stuff and got drunk as skunks and sang Christmas carols. Between coughs, the lunger had a pretty good bass on 'God Rest ye merry, gentlemen' and Craig confessed to a dubiously harmonizing baritone. The fat, drunkest newspaper guy succumbed to a sudden stroke of Dickens, and marched manfully through most of the dreary po' folks tale which winds up with 'And so, as Tiny Tim observed, God bless us all every one!' Craig produced a copy of O. Henry, and when sufficiently lubricated, was induced to render aloud a piece called the 'Gift of the Magi', in which everybody wound up with nothing, and which inspired everyone to waves of lachrymose applause, especially the whore, who then regaled the gathering with the story of her life, which further created vastly rolling salt seas.

Overcome by the emotional impact of Yule, Mrs. Finch forgave them all one week's rent, and then they ate the turkey. Some time before midnight it was decided in committee that the occasion demanded a Christmas tree. Mrs. Finch produced a rusty hatchet, and there was a convenient middle-class hotel near by. The hotel boasted brilliantly lit stunted fir trees in its scrofulous patio. The less drunk newspaper guy went out and, as they said in the recent unpleasantness, liberated one. He was able to disconnect the light cord, so all they had to do was plug it in to an outlet in the kitchen. They then proceeded to deck it with pathetic little gifts—a grease-spotted necktie, an old pair of ladies' rayon pants, a time-eroded bra, a souvenir programme from an Atlantic City orgy which the whore produced, as she had been photographed faintly, mistily, in the murky background of one of the scenes of revel.

Craig smiled as he recalled the evening and mixed himself another drink. He would call the lawyers in a minute, but this was fun. He hadn't thought of it for a long time. My God, but that was a night. When it got out of hand for Charles Dickens, Steinbeck took over. It developed into an approximation of Doc's surprise party in *Cannery Row*.

You mix enough muscatel with enough cooking whisky and the new-found brotherhood of men, stir in a little lost-soullery, add an unsuccessful whore and a banished Jew and two newspaper guys and a rough kid just off the ships, sprinkle with a touch of tubercular fatalism, and beat heavily into a late-blooming celebration of Christ's birthday, and you can produce anything, including the Wise Men's camels. At least one of the newspaper boys was certain there were camels in the kitchen. He followed a star to the toilet, fell down and broke a leg, which nobody seemed to care about at the time, including him. Mrs. Finch was sitting on the lunger's lap, and Buzzy bent his oboe, and the whore was weeping freely, swearing to give up her trade and become a nun. Craig was reciting Chaucer at one point, and then all went black. He woke up in bed with the Ruth girl— or rather across the foot of it. Neither she nor Craig was very clear about events leading up to this unlikely partnership. But she was a very nice girl, if a bit lush, and she later pursued the Holy Grail of all Jewish girls from Philadelphia and married a proper dentist. Whether the whore ever settled the get-thee-to-a-nunnery-go idea, nobody knows. The newspaper guy with the busted leg got fired, naturally, but this was no virginal experience for him. Craig became restless and went back to sea, shortly . . .

Craig sighed, and picked up the telephone.

'Give me Mr. Blumberg's room,' he said. 'Mr. Jules Blumberg, thank you.'

'Hello, Jules. Yes. All right. Sure. No, I don't need you,' he said. 'You got the appointment fixed for tomorrow? Good enough. Ten sharp in the lobby. Have yourself some fun, if you can find any in this town. No, Jules, there's nothing we can plan until we see how the feeling is. Make the Internal Revenue appointment for after lunch. I want to be back in New York by dinner time—one of you handle the reservations.'

Craig added another hooker of gin to his drink, cradling the phone between shoulder and ear.

'They got no leg at all. We're doing fine if they just don't rock the boat on me. I'll even out. We play it cool and keep it out of the papers if we can. The suit will take care of itself. All we got to worry about is these bastards in the SEC. They don't like me—*me* personally. All right, all right, I'm going over the stuff now. See you in the morning. Right.'

He hung up, opened his briefcase, and spread a bouquet of papers on the writing-table. Then he went back to the phone. He asked for his home number in New Jersey. The caretaker answered.

'Mrs. Price please. This is Mr. Price.'

'I'm afraid she's not in, sir,' came from the other end. 'She took the car and a small bag and said she was going to New

York for a day or so. Shopping, I believe, and wouldn't be home tonight. No, she didn't say where she'd be staying.'

'All right, Henry. If she calls back, ask her to ring me at the Statler in Washington. I'll be back sometime tomorrow, I hope.'

He hung up the phone, and went back to his papers. As he leafed through the stack he occasionally shook his head irritably. Finally he shuffled them all together like a pack of cards and replaced them in the briefcase. He dressed, took the briefcase, left it for the clerk to put in the safe, and strolled over to the news stand and bought the New York afternoon papers and a copy of *The Star* and the Washington *Daily News*. He walked to the men's bar and sat at a corner table, reading rapidly through one after the other. The *World-Telegram's* stock page induced a couple of whistling snorts, like a startled buck deer. He put it down distastefully and ordered another drink. Craig was bored, and the men's bar wasn't helping any. He called for his check. He went idly out into the lobby, wondering what he'd do with himself. It was too hot outside for a walk around the town. There was not one single solitary person in the village he wanted to call, except maybe one or two Congressmen who had done some business with him in the past, and this was no time to be doing business with Congressmen, not with that SEC bit coming up in the morning. There wouldn't be a guy on the Hill who'd be caught publicly dead in his company. The word spreads.

He went into the co-educational drinking-room where a stringed orchestra was playing dreary tea-time music, and all the housewives of upper-echelon Government seemed to be having martinis with each other. He flicked his eyes around the room, and past a potted plant there was one woman alone, sipping an iced vermouth. She turned her head, for some reason, possibly to call a waiter, and her face leaped out and clutched at him. The face was now surrounded by beautifully touched-up snowy hair, but it was still young, still beautiful, and still the same. It had to be the same. He almost ran across the room.

'If I'm wrong, madame, please excuse me. But you must be Julie duFresne from Charleston ...'

'My God, Craig Price! Sit down quick and tell me everything, but kiss your old Aunt Julie first! You always used to, you know, before you got so rich and famous.'

Craig kissed her briefly on both cheeks and slid into a chair. 'At least I did before you slung me out of the house.' He smiled. 'And that was never yesterday, was it, Miss Julie, ma'am? Tell me *every*thing, but before you do, let me say that I didn't know it was possible, but the hair makes you more beautiful than ever. You are a real dish, Miss Julie, ma'am.'

She was, too. In her latish fifties, she had maintained the same figure, and her enormous eyes and the bone-structure of her face would never change. Craig raked her boldly with his eyes.

'Same wonderful dress, same wonderful eyes, same wonderful room-mate's mama, and same wonderful ex-girl friend of Craig Price, boy delinquent.'

'Shush. Don't be rude. I'm a widow again. I *did* marry, you know, a delightful gentleman, and quite a change from Philip's father. He died two years ago.' Her voice sombred. 'Maurice was a fine fellow. But he was much older than me. His heart . . .'

'What about Philip? How about Phil?'

'Nothing of very much importance about Phil. There never was much of importance about Phil. He still lives in Europe, still hasn't done a lick of work, and looks quite distinguished in a left-bank sort of way. Hair still too long, but as white as mine. He's come out of the corduroy-suit and flowing-tie stage, and dresses rather beautifully now. He's pointed out as one of the chief sights of Paris—you know, Eiffel Tower, Place de la Concorde, the Louvre, the Dôme, the Crillon—then Philip. I suppose he was created to be exactly what he is—nothing. It ceased bothering me years ago. We exchange postcards at Christmas time, if either of us bothers to remember.'

'What so fortunately brings you to this awful hamlet?' Craig asked. 'And before you answer, will you have another drink, will you have dinner with me, will you spend a long evening with me so we can babble? If you're waiting for another man, I'll kill him first and you next and then commit suicide.'

'Yes, on all counts. Vermouth with ice. Yes, to dinner. Yes, to evening. And you won't have to kill us at all. I was passing through and decided to stay a few days and see some friends. I was supposed to go to dinner with them, but a phone call will fix that. I'm staying here, and I got tired of my quarters and came down to stare at the awful people.'

'Me, too. God, this is wonderful. I feel like a college boy again. I feel like I did the time I came back from Europe and stopped off in Charleston. That time . . .'

She shook a finger at him.

'No more hanky-panky, my boy. I was old enough to be your mother then, and now I'm old enough to be your grandmother, at the age you were then. Let me look at *you*.'

She leaned across the table and touched his cheeks gently after the waiter had set down the drinks.

'You've changed even more than me. You look rather sad, Craig. There's a lot of wear-and-tear on you. Of course, I've read everything that was ever written about you, and so I know most of the details of your fantastic success, but somehow I kept my image—my personal image—of a scared little, brave little boy, sort of snuggled to my heart. You have scars, my friend of the olden days, that were never put there by fists. The broken nose but goes to hide the broken heart sort of thing . . .'

'If you're polite you won't tell me that my eyes are bloodshot,

641

my face is puffy, my chin is rapidly doubling, and that all the hair which ain't receding is certainly grizzling. You might call me a monument to use. It's been a long tough twenty years, Julie. I been playing hard-ball in a hard-ball league, and the spike-scars are duty-bound to show. I suppose it's been worth it. Maybe so, maybe not. The stick floated that way, and I wouldn't change it. You know, soldiers get killed, newspapermen get drunk, financiers go broke, politicians get dis-elected, and he scoffs at scars who never felt a wound. But God, it seems like an eternity since that first day in your Charleston house, that first wonderful, frightening day, when I did everything wrong. You know, I never put on a dinner-jacket without thinking of my dreadful *gaffe* that night in your house, and how you covered for my youthful embarrassment so beautifully.'

'And I never forgot how you beat up my charming son for calling his mother a whore,' Julie said. 'I squeezed that out of him later. At least, I thought, there is some small manhood, if as yet unrealized, and a shred of chivalry left in the world.'

'I suppose I have to thank Philip for much of what's happened to me,' Craig said, lighting her cigarette and waving for the waiter. 'The same again,' he said to the waiter. 'If I hadn't socked Phil I wouldn't have had to leave your house. I wouldn't have met Mr. Grimes on the road when I was hitch-hiking, and if I hadn't met Mr. Grimes I wouldn't have married his daughter and acquired his mill, and if I hadn't acquired that bloody mill I suppose I wouldn't be in the mess I'm in now. Just suppose I hadn't socked Philip, what then? Messenger boy? Atomic scientist? Rich man, poor man, beggarman, thief, doctor, lawyer, merchant, chief? Who knows? I sure as hell don't.'

'You'd have been big at any one of the jobs,' Julie said, covering his hand with hers. 'I knew that when I first clapped eyes on you, that day in the hotel in Chapel Hill, when you were wearing Philip's clothes.'

'Well, it looks more like thief at the moment,' Craig said. 'The boys are after me. That's what I'm down here for: to see if I can tame a few Government lions before they claw me out. I been too big for my breeches in more ways than one. Over-extended a touch, you might say. It'll straighten out. It always does.

'What's it like, Craig? I don't mean business messes. I'm talking about the new wife. I think I'm still a little jealous. Never of the first one because I understand that. But the second one sounds faintly like she might have been me if I had been sixteen or seventeen years younger when you came along. I am definitely sure I'm jealous of this one.'

'There's a lot of you in her, Julie. Perhaps that's what first attracted me—a hungover heroine-worship from my early days. She's got you—and I told her this once—and something of the qualities of a very sweet girl named Mary Frances and something of a generous little Jewish girl and a nice whore I knew once—and between being a great lady and a sweet girl and fun and generous and kind—she is really a wonderful woman. But she's starting on a trait I don't like. She's picking up a little Maybelle wifeliness that I don't care for. I mean, too many loving hands around your throat. Too many conjugal blankets draped over your head.'

'You *are* still a silly young man, despite your wounds and your grey hair. Haven't you learned yet that any woman who loves you doesn't want to share you with anything? I said *anything*. She'll put up, perhaps, for a part-time distraction with another woman, or with other women, but she cannot abide competition with something she can't defeat. You have a mistress she can't conquer, Craig. It's your work, an insane obsession with doing more, making more and more, not to spend because you only deal in symbols. Work is a very demanding mistress, Craig. Tell me, you have a daughter, what of her?'

'Carol? I don't know. She's knocking herself out running around Europe. She never writes. Frankly, she hates my guts. I'm afraid I wasn't much of a father to her. I'm afraid I'm not much of anything to anybody. Susan and I seemed off to a fair start, but there has been practically nothing but trouble riding my neck since we met, and I don't know, Julie. I just don't know. You understand this business of coping, always coping, with so many things that you don't have time to cope with the one or two things you'd like to devote full time to? That's the trap I've worked myself into. I'm tired—tired of lawyers and contracts and finance and Government and . . . I'm tired.

'Look.' His face cleared. 'Indulge me a little bit, please. You can't know how wonderful it is seeing you again. Let's pretend I brought a dinner-jacket with me, which I didn't. Let's put on my imaginary dinner-jacket, worth at least $250 instead of £28.50, and let's go out like I would have loved to have taken you out twenty-five years ago. Let's not talk of me or the SEC or Carol or Maybelle or even Susan. Let's go out and drink and dance and jump around and pretend that this is Paris, France, and that the ersatz scallop cocktail is real caviar. There must be some place in this cultural desert where we can find a gypsy fiddle. Then, God willing, I'll be able to gird my loins and go see the nasty little men in the dreary little offices tomorrow. Be my girl, Miss Julie, please ma'am.'

'I'll be your girl. Just let me go and change, and I'll be your girl—if you want such an old lady to be your girl.'

'You know,' Craig said, as they were finishing coffee at Prince's, the new and almost uncanny restaurant in Georgetown, 'there is really only one thing I regret. I just wish to God that I could have been more people. I wish to God I could have been older

643

and abler to love Mary Frances. And I wish that I could have not been complicated when I met Sue. I wish I could have compartmented myself. And finally, I wish that I was capable of loving anybody, any time, completely.'

'I should think you might be,' Julie said.

'No. Not me. Not now. Look, Miss Julie, ma'am. In twenty years I have known at least a hundred women intimately. At one time, in one place, I might have been capable of marrying any or all of them. This tells me something of an essential shallowness of my character. How can you follow through with the basic idea that God created one man for one woman, when if you were free to marry you would have the shares of your heart split between a hundred? How can you be in love with a hundred women? Or even four or five?' Craig shook his head almost groggily. 'I don't know who I love. I'm a lousy sentimentalist and I expect I can love anybody. The only sure thing I got around to depend on is me—Craig Price. At least I know me—me and my limitations. I would not say I was a happy man, my dearest Julie.'

'Nor would I, Craig. But I should imagine that there are very few big, happy men. Bigness gives damned small time for happiness. Now I think it's time you took me home. I'm an old lady, and not used to prancing around with young men.'

'Julie?'

She looked at him with the old amusement, the amusement with which she had viewed him when he was a child.

'No, Craig. Absolutely *no*. Not even a nightcap. I'm an old lady now. Those things are past, little boy. Take me back to the hotel. It's been wonderful, seeing you again. But take me back to the hotel and see me to my door.'

God damn everything and everybody, Craig said, as he undressed and mixed a final lonely nightcap. I missed it all. I missed it all. I wanted it all and I missed it all. What was it Grandpa Sam said, that he was out of place in time and he should have been one of them fellers that went around playing the banjo to amuse the king? What a sad bastard I really am, he thought, and drained his drink. He would have a hard day tomorrow.

To say that Craig Price was hot under the collar after he had been more than a few moments in the presence of the SEC man would have been a violent understatement. The day was even hotter than yesterday, with a lowering hint of rain, and the very appearance of the SEC man raised itches on Craig's knuckles. Four-eyed little punk, to treat me as a convicted criminal even before I open my mouth. I'd like to run this joint for just a little bit. Just a little bit, my friend. And look at my lawyers. These are lawyers, Blumberg and Wagstaff, that charge me the earth. Bootblacks, more, in front of this nasty little clerk|who can wreck me.

'Tell me what you've got on your mind,' he said abruptly to the

SEC man. 'I haven't got much time. I must be back in New York this afternoon, and I have other appointments.'

The SEC man looked at him as if he had defiled a church. The SEC man was a pursy little fellow, bald, with the nasty air of self-righteousness so common to bank executives and tax collectors. Even his name—Smathers—fitted his dull brown tropic-weight suit and his general expression. When he talked, he touched his finger-ends primly together, and always spoke with the expression that his unlittered desk was a pulpit or, more likely, the sergeant's desk in a police station.

'Mr. Price,' he was saying, in a voice to match his suit, 'we here in the SEC don't very much like your general position. It is not a healthy one. Two things—the suit by your stockholders in Formidable for mismanagement with the disallowment of all company expenses and the consequent action by Internal Revenue for review. You run a public trust in Mastodon, Mr. Price, as sacred a trust as might be placed in a priest or a banker. We in SEC are wondering, Mr. Price, if you are in a position to discharge those trusts. You are entrusted with the investment of five hundred million dollars of other people's money, and we . . . Ah, we . . .' he coughed delicately, 'your divorce was rather colourful, and certainly expensive, Mr. Price.'

'Keep my divorce out of this,' Craig growled. 'It's got nothing to do with you.'

'But on the contrary, Mr. Price.' The voice caressed the words. 'On the contrary. How would *you* feel, as a policyholder in Formidable, as an investor in Mastodon, to read in the newspapers that the controlling interest in both companies had lost heavily in a airline venture before he paid a million *cash* for a divorce? Would that not disturb you as a policy-holder, would that not upset you as an investor, would not that cause you to wonder slightly as a bond-holder in Price Mills? It disturbs me as a member of the Securities and Exchange Commission. It disturbs us greatly, Mr. Price. We are not concerned with the Internal Revenue attitude, except as it reflects on the attitude of the insurance company, which again reflects on Mastodon Investments, with which we are very much, very much concerned.'

'I gather you're concerned,' Craig said. 'My lawyers and I are duly impressed with your concern. What else?'

'I am very much afraid that we must have a swift and accurate accounting of all your credits, debits, investments, and liabilities, your loans, surpluses, stocks, bonds and properties in order to determine your fluidity in Mastodon Investments. That money is a sacred trust, Mr. Price.'

'You already told me. As a matter of curiosity, how much money do *you* make a year?'

'Mr. Price!'

'I was just curious. I just wondered if the landlord and the butcher and the utilities people ever ganged you to determine the fluidity of your ability to pay rent, buy food, and keep the house lit and water running in it?'

Mr. Smathers sniffed, outraged.

'I fail to see that the point is germane. But at any and all times I should welcome an inspection of my accounts, Mr. Price.'

'I'll bet,' Craig grinned. 'Don't take it so hard. I ain't going to set the power-and-light boys baying on to your heels. But I was just curious as to whether a man of limited income such as Government service most unjustly provides for its *servants*'—he bit off the word—'I just wondered if a servant really understood the complexities of the business of his master, the man who buys the government's food and clothes and light and heat and law and order with his taxes, who keeps the land alive so there can be jobs for Government servants? I was only mildly curious. I think I'll be going. Work it out with my lawyers, please. It's hot and I'm tired. Good day, sir.' He did not offer his hand. He turned to his lawyers. 'I'll see you back at the Statler.' He picked up his briefcase and strode off, his heels clicking hard in the corridor.

Craig had been to see the tax boys. The tax boys had offered very little in the way of friendly tolerance.

'Mr. Price,' they said flatly. 'You are being sued by your own insurance company for spoliation of company funds. The referees are in the picture, the suit is in the hands of the courts. Your expenses have been disallowed—well, not disallowed, but denied pending the settlement of the suit—and we are only a collecting agency. We are also a reasonable agency. We are prepared to give you time to settle your differences with Formidable, and to discuss the right or wrong of your business expenses. But we must review you in light of the action. If your own company . . . well, I mean to say, Mr. Price . . .' They spread their hands and shrugged. 'You can see our position I'm sure.'

'Yes,' Craig said. 'I can see your position. You are only a public servant—an humble man, like Uriah Heep—and your business is to enforce the law. But before you start scattering liens around, further confusing my life, will you please give me six months to get you some money, and will you let me pay you in instalments of as much as I can muster at the time? And, if I can get my hands on a hunk of money, can we make some sort of settlement?'

'I'm sure you'll find us reasonable, Mr. Price,' they said. 'You have ninety days' grace. We will do all in our power to help you, and in the meantime, will you have your accountants produce your books through last year, for further review?'

'Yes, gentlemen,' Craig spoke through gritted teeth. 'Maybe we can arrive at a good round figure. Mr. Blumberg and Mr. Wagstaff will be at your service. Good afternoon. Jules, stay with the gentlemen and discuss any details. I'm going back to New York.'

Craig always thought well on aircraft. Thinking kept him from conversation with strangers, especially if he opened his brief-case and gazed unseeingly at a sheaf of papers.

I got to beat this tax rap before it hits the papers, he thought. I got to get out. If I don't get out, down she tumbles. Goddamn those stockholders in Formidable. So maybe I *was* stretched out a touch thin. I wonder who the friend was who started this little plot? No matter. I can whip that suit easy but I got to have some dough to get these tax boys off my back. Nate? No. I'm already into him too deep. Banks? Not now. Well, there's one thing. There's always the one thing. Price Mills. I got to find me a new pigeon.

22

WHEN he got to his office he called his broker before he called Susan.

'Henry,' he said, 'get over here. Now. I can't help if you've got a cocktail date. This is urgent.'

Then he called Susan.

'She hasn't come back yet, Mr. Price,' the butler said. 'I haven't heard from her.'

'Goddammitall,' Craig said, as he hung up. 'All I need right now is another whingding to cope with. Where the hell is she, and what's she up to? The fight wasn't that bad. Well, hell, no matter what the sawbones says, I'll have a drink.'

He mixed a drink and walked over to his penthouse terrace, and gazed down at the milling ants forty storeys below.

'Look at them,' he said aloud. 'Ten million poor little bugs crawling around, and every one with a problem, with an ego, with a worry, all his very own. Ten million people I will never know, who wonder whether they're a good lay, whether they can pay the rent, whether the old lady is mad at them, whether the kid's going to turn into a gangster, whether the dog's got distemper—all of them with problems which make them the centre of the universe. Just like'—and he grinned ruefully—'just like I think that the sun rises and falls in my own rear end. Me, Craig Price, centre of the universe, and I don't even know where my wife is. Well, if I got to do it, I got to do it. Henry's an accomplished thief. I'll cut him in and he'll cork his beak.'

He was mixing another drink as Connie announced that Mr. Henry Nelson was in the outer office.

'Run him in, sugar,' Craig said, 'and tell the switch I'm not taking any calls. And then go home. Go get your hair done, or something. I won't be needing you any more today.'

Henry Nelson was a big, grey-haired, oval man, impeccably dressed in financial charcoal flannel. He had a full English moustache, and it was immediately apparent that he would sit down and clip the end off a cigar with the gold cigar-clipper-offer which depended from a watchchain that stretched across his taut waistcoat. He would always wear a vest. The watch would be thin and platinum, a Patek, and you knew without seeing that it would be thin and platinum and a Patek, just as you knew Henry Nelson, in his sixtieth year, had never smoked a cigarette, as he had never been a prattling child, or a rambunctious pantie-raiding college student. Some people are born to be stockbrokers, as others are born to be safecrackers or shipowners or racetrack touts. Henry Nelson had been born with the express purpose of finding a permanent home in a brokerage office, which he would some day own as inevitably as he would space his children, boy, girl, boy, girl, as inevitably as he would buy a house in Westchester County and become a member of the Westchester Country Club and own a summer home in Southampton.

'Hello, Henry. What'll you drink?' Craig rapidly scribbled the answer in his head.

'I'll have a very light scotch with soda all the way up, thanks, Craig.'

(Won that bet again, Craig's head said. One day this bastard is going to say: Craig, hit me with a double shot of bourbon and dump in a slug of vodka and pernod and scotch and gin and two kinds of vermouth and don't put no ice in it at all, and I will drop dead on the spot.)

'Here you are, Henry. I won't keep you long. Cheers.'

'How was Washington, Craig?' He took a sip of his drink and clipped the end off a cigar with the tiny gold cigar-cutter which flopped arrogantly from the chain that leashed the wafer-thin platinum Patek watch.

'Bloody. Henry, I need some dough. I'm in a very narrow corner right now. The only thing I can see to do is sell my shares in Price Mills. Unload me, Henry. Dump me, but dump me gentle. You won't have any trouble at all. We've got what, four-five hundred thousand shares of common? Hang on to the preferred. But dump me gradually, over the next few weeks, and real quiet. It won't be any trouble, actually. The stock's up about as high as it can get, but I aim to run it up a little higher.'

'Do you know what you're doing?'

'I know what I'm doing. I got to get out of Price Mills. They'll keep on earning money. They'll keep on paying off the bonds. The mills won't change. But *Henry*. I'm going *short*. And that stock is going down. It's gonna jump off the cliff. As soon as we're out, get us as much as you can on the short side. I'm betting the *don't*-come line on this one. Lay the whole damned thing on the shorts.'

'Do you really know what you're doing? Because if you're in it I'm in it and I want to know where I'm standing. Your mills are doing very well, Craig. The stock's as sound as a dollar used to be. Short is a stupid position.'

'No, it isn't. Listen.' He picked up the phone.

'Public relations,' he said. 'Mr. Shaffer. Hear this,' he said to Nelson. 'Hello, Willie? Price. Listen, kid, I haven't had a talk with the newspaper boys in quite a spell. You know there's some talk around that we ain't as healthy as usual. Plant a question with your tame boy-friend on the *Banner*. Get him to grill me if necessary. Ask me all about the insurance suit. But tell him to ask me one specific question: *How healthy is the cornerstone, how healthy are Price Mills*, and have the books with you. We'll have the conference here in my office. The boys know my booze is good. Right. Five o'clock's dandy. See you.'

He rang off, and turned to his broker.

'Don't you bother to be here, Henry. Have a look at the *Times* and the *Journal* and the Telly day after tomorrow. Then check in.'

'I hope you know what you're doing,' Nelson said, and got up to go. 'I'm not going to ask you anything until the day after tomorrow. I don't want it on my conscience.'

'Right, Henry. Right. Talk to you Thursday. Good you came by. But start the selling apparatus. We leave the bears until later. So long, Henry.'

He called home again. The answer was the same. Craig decided to get drunk. No matter what the doctor said.

At eleven p.m. after a boring solitary dinner, he called home again. Mrs. Price had not returned. He played briefly with the idea of checking the major East side hotels, and then said the hell with it. If she'd run off she'd run off for a purpose, and damned if he was going to bird-dog her like a jealous adolescent. He went back to his office building, turned on the music-maker, and built himself a drink. He sat in semi-darkness and the luminous curve of the tusks, the lowering bulk of the buffalo, the delicate shadow-traced heads of the antelopes failed to give him their usual comfort. At midnight he called home once more. Nothing. Even the butler was out.

'The hell with it,' he said aloud. 'I can play funny, too.'

He went over to his desk and searched through a locked drawer and produced a red morocco address book. He dialled a number and waited.

'Laura?' he said. 'It's me. Mr. P. Yes, I know it's a long time. But I got divorced and married and business is lousy and things have been tough all over. You wouldn't feel like coming over

649

at this late hour, would you? I'm lonesome as hell and very sad and I want somebody to talk to and to listen to some music with. You would? You're a babydoll. Twenty minutes? Hell, sweetie, you don't have to put on any fancy face for me. Slide into anything and I'll grab a cab and come get you. These New York streets ain't safe for pretty girls. Ten minutes, front of your place. You're a real sweetie.'

Now why did I do that, Craig asked himself, as he went to the elevator. She's a nice kid but she *is* a kind of whore. What do I need with a kind of whore? You're a strange and crazy guy, Price. And a dumb bastard to boot. But there *are* nights when the thought of loneliness is terrifying, and this is one. I don't have to lay her. An hour's conversation and we're calmed down, maybe, and I'll take her home. She's not a bad kid, really.

She *wasn't* a bad kid, really. She was a very handsome redhead with green eyes and freckles and a flair for clothes, with fine bones in her face and a stylish walk and a good vocabulary. She had come from some tankola in the Middle West, and had gone through the usual New York apprenticeship—apartment store job first, to eat, then a stint over a checkroom counter, than a job in the line in a nightclub, then small part in a musical, then a brief fling at Hollywood's charming starlet system, where the lists were available for every visiting fireman, and finally she had come back to New York.

'To be a whore,' she had told Craig one time. 'I sort of searched my background for some reason against it, except I didn't like the sound of it, and I couldn't see any difference between what I'd been doing and what I'd proposed to do. It occurred to me that I didn't know how to do anything well enough not to pay the usual penalty for being fairly pretty in order to stay alive.'

'You could have tried marriage,' Craig said. 'A lot of girls seem to do rather well at it.'

'I had a shot at it back home when I was seventeen. All I got out of it was a hard time. He was one of the handsome ones who figured slick hair was good enough to get by on, and he had a way of getting himself tanked and beating hell out of me. I gave up marriage as the hardest way to make a living.'

'This isn't a hard way to make a living?' They were both in pyjamas and dressing-gowns. He got up walked to the bar, and Laura watched moody fire-faces of shifting shadow as the embers settled into a solidly comfortable rosy bed. The Hi-Fi was on, and it was 'Stormy Weather'.

'What's wrong with it? You're a nice guy. Most of my steady boy friends are nice guys. Look, Mr. P., my husband beat me up. When I was working in a store any date I had thought that a dollar-fifty dinner was a free ride to bed. The night-club guys wrote sleeping privileges into the contract, or I didn't dance, and the Hollywood little-shots, the producers' third cousins,

650

figured that any "starlet" was duty bound to practise elocution on her back.

'So I figured real steady: as long as I got to be working on a mattress to eat every day, why stand on my feet in a store or kick up my legs in a night-club until three a.m. or pose half-naked for still-pictures for movie magazines? Seeing as how I'm making my living basically on my back, why don't I just settle for that and save the wear and tear on my arches? Why settle for a lousy dinner and a taxi-cab grope when I can make a buck with a nice guy for the real moola? And you know Ethel. She doesn't let you in for many creeps, and when they get *too* creepy, I just don't play. The strange ones, I mean, the boys with the whips and chains and peculiar ideas of what's fun in the hay. You notice I never take the money until after.'

'I've noticed. I've known you to not take it at all.'

'That's when it's been a real social evening, and I've enjoyed it. I mean, enjoyed not being bought in the boy's mind. A friend-ship sort of thing, like something you'd do naturally for pleasure after a sunny day at the beach or a nice shore dinner or simple fun dancing. You know Craig, men have a strange idea about whores. You think they're a kind of different breed of cat. They aren't, really. There is absolutely no difference between a whore who takes a fee for giving her body to a man to use, or one of these wives that take food, clothes, housing, money and trans-portation from a man they don't like, a man they got to kind of hold their mental nose to go to bed with. Both of us are selling bodies—both of us earning our keep. And the little shop-girl, the stenographer, who pays for a dinner and a movie by opening her legs is still a whore. So is the milk-maid being nice to Hiram down on the farm. So are all these society bitches that make the papers every day, so is half the royalty you read about, the Palm Beach people, the actors—everybody in one way or another is a whore. I prefer to call myself one, and put a price tag on my product, just like you buy or sell the things you buy and sell. For a price. I got my price, too.'

'I must confess you make a point,' Craig said. 'You collect a hundred bucks out of the same social evening that other girls give away for free after playing a typewriter or standing on their feet all day. And generally get fed, too. We'll, I'll feed you. Come on into the kitchen. We'll knock us up some ham and eggs.'

That was Laura, the whore's whore, the honest perfectionist, who liked her basic work, and who loved to talk—seldom about other men, because the perfection of her presence was founded in the illusion that the man she was with was the only man she ever knew. Her business was the momentary lease of pleasure, of sympathy, of non-abrasive acquiescence in face of the fact that all men are really little bragging boys and want to be treated as heroes. As Laura said, she had dignity, too, as well as technique, and she would be as apt to slap you for getting out of line—her line—as the nearest virgin on the block.

'You look wonderful,' Craig said, when they got out of the elevator and went into the office. She did look wonderful. She was evenly tanned and her red hair had been lightened by sun. The green eyes were clear as pools.

'I've been out to the beach every week-end. I've got friends with a cottage at Montauk. Nice people. Something to do with television.'

'Spare me. I don't want to feel jealous right now. It's good to see you, Laurie-girl. What to drink?'

'This hour? Whisky and water. You look like hell, my friend. Is this marriage or what?' She sat down and crossed her legs. 'On a hot night like this the man's *still* got the fire going, yet. One day somebody better take away your matches before you set fire to the city. It's nice, though, especially when you're rich enough to turn up the cooling system. What you been doing, chum?'

'Up to my ass in escrows, as Polly Adler once said. I got more problems than the well-known pregnant fox in the well-known forest fire. Also my wife seems to have left me—temporarily, at least.'

'So that's the why for of the late phone call. Good old Laura to hold the sad man's hand. Well, come over here and I'll hold it. You know I always liked you a lot, Craig?'

'I always liked you a lot, Laurie-girl. Seems like we kind of had something in common. Excuse me, but all the nights we've spent —when you'd fly out to join me in Chicago or some place—I never felt we were on a business transaction. It never seemed like business. It always felt like a holiday.'

'It wasn't business.' She laughed. 'It was friendship with full compensation, plus fun on the side. But I don't like what I see. You look nervous. You look bewitched, bothered and bewildered. You want to tell me? You know Laura, the original girl who is all ears and no mouth.'

'No, baby, I don't want to bore you. I just want to sit here and play some music and have a couple of drinks and soothe me down by just letting me look at you. And to talk some. Funny. Last night I ran into an ol' gal I knew twenty-odd years ago, and . . .'

'She must have been—must be—a wonderful woman,'Laura said, after Craig had finished his recent experience with Julie duFresne. 'Not many like that around any more. Real sharp gals with a little tenderness and a lot of woman underneath. That dame could have wrecked you, Craig. A lot of women would have. Women have basically been pretty easy on you, Buster. Get me another drink. All this listening makes me thirsty.

'Level, now,' she said when he returned with the drink. 'How come the phone call? Evidently you got yourself a good girl. Whatever problems you got aren't really very strongly connected with your new wife—whatshername, Susan?—and you were never a man who really had to buy a dame. What brings old Auntie Laura into your life again?'

'Honey, I can't really say. I just got the woeful awfuls. Everything is all mixed up—business all screwed out of shape, wife gone, me just returned, saw Julie last night, boyhood comes back with crash, big deals in future, no place to go except maybe to jail. I don't know. I just wanted to see somebody honest who wasn't on the make for anything and I couldn't think of anybody but you. In some ways you're the only honest person I ever met. I needed somebody to talk to that I literally didn't *have* to screw, one way or the other. Maybe that's not a compliment. Maybe it is.'

'People go to strange places for strange comfort, don't they?' She smoothed his forehead. 'Now me, I go to the zoo when I got the nervous twitches. I look at the lions long enough, and all of a sudden I feel good again. I never look at the monkeys, especially the mandrills. They remind me of some clients I have known. But I love the tiger cubs and the outside animals—the seals and bears and the antelopes.'

'Funny, maybe not so funny at that. I get the same thing from these dead heads on these walls. And I go to the Museum of Natural History a lot, as well as the zoo. Animals, dead or alive, are a wonderful relief from people, now and again.'

'You have any fun, Craig? I mean real fun? Me, I have a lot of fun. I can lie on a beach with a book for hours in the sun, or go to the zoo, and forget that last night I was what the papers call a party girl. I got me a little log cabin in upstate New York, and I go up there in the winter time, alone, cook for myself, chop wood, and do any damned number of things you wouldn't expect a whore to be happy doing. I'm even learning to paint, and I'm spreading out my reading.'

Craig hunched his shoulders.

'I suppose I have fun. I hunt and fish a little and—this is one of the most unusual conversations ever recorded between a call girl and a client. Or could you call me a client?'

'I wouldn't say so. No. We have a friendly business transaction. Shall we transact it?'

'I am sort of tired, sweetie. Let's go fall on the bed for a little bit, and if I go to sleep, let me hang on to you. Hit me if I grind my teeth. But I don't want to be alone in bed tonight. I got my conscience with me, and I don't like it. It's ugly.'

Laura felt very smooth and warm and was fragrant next to him, and for a moment, maleness stood super-imposed over business, over Washington, over the future. But nothing very much came of the basic urge.

'I'm sorry, kid,' he said to Laura. 'My mind doesn't seem to be on this sort of business tonight. I guess my heart isn't in it, either. I just like to have you here, to hold you close so I won't be lonely in the night. Sort of spoon-fashion affection. D'you mind terribly?'

'Of course not. Go to bye-byes like a good boy, and when you're all comfy, I'll get dressed and take off. Don't worry about me going home. I'll get a cab from the night man downstairs. Try to take it easy, sweetie, I don't like my old boy-friend looking so tired. Now, go to sleep, and I'll kind of rub your back a little . . .'

'My wallet's in my inside coat pocket, baby,' Craig murmured, drifting off to sleep, as Laura stroked him lightly.

'Shush. This is known as friendship, friend.' And she crooned a lullaby Craig had not heard in forty years. 'Rockabye baby, in the tree top . . .'

When he woke next morning the scented print of her was on the bed, and there was a note on the night-table.

'Any time you need a baby-sitter,' the note said, 'call me. And don't bother to send me any presents. This one was on the house. Laura.'

'Jesus,' Craig said to his shaving mirror. 'And I know some ladies . . .'

It was while he was tying his tie that the awful suspicion smote him. Once a whore had given him his money back for performance above and beyond the call. Now one had refused to accept money because . . . because of the—*inadequacy* was not a nice word.

'Well,' he said grimly, anchoring the tie with a gold Twenty-One clip, 'as *Time* says, "as it must to all men".'

23

SUSAN was still not at home, and Craig resolved not to let it bother him. If she had been in an accident he would have heard. In the meantime, he had a press conference.

Craig and the press got along just peachy-dandy. He had spent enough time slinging hash, getting his nose busted, sailing the seven seas, and drinking likker to know that about the last thing you do with the newspaper boys was to address them as the 'newspaper boys'. The newspaper boys, adults with homes and bosses and problems of their own, definitely did not care to be patronized or cheaply bribed.

They came all of a cluster, and Craig was interested to see that in addition to the financial writers, there was also a syndicated Broadway writer and a cosmic columnist, a dyspeptic sort who wrote everything from cats-up-trees to a caustic condemnation of Washington or foreign policy.

By now Craig had hit a cynical peak of knowledge about press conferences. The idea was to take it right into the enemy camp before they laid it heavy on you, but first you slouched into it. You didn't press it. You sauntered.

'Hello, gents,' he said. 'I got a little thing might be worth a stick of type, possibly not. I think I know most of you—no, I don't know *you*' to a retiring gentleman with very little chin. 'You're new. I'm Price, as you possibly gathered.' He stuck out his hand. 'And who might you be?'

'I'm Joe Riley. New. Sort of stand-in for the A.P. financial man. He's got a sick wife, or something. I just came in from Kansas City, Mr. Price.'

'Nice to know you, Mr. Riley.' Craig never first-named the gentlemen of the press. 'Look, gents. I've had a rough day. Before we get into this thing, let's all sit down and booze it up a little. There's the bar over yonder. Fix what you want. And outside on the terrace, some of the incompetents who suck my blood have laid out some rat-cheese or something. They probably kept the better breed of caviar for themselves. When you've had a couple of drinks to cut the dust, there could be a question or so which I might, without help of legal counsel, be able to answer—some question which might—' and he stressed the *might*—'which might be a story. I don't know. The big boys been giving me the boots lately. I'm bruised from asshole to appetite. Meanwhile, if I turn on a small piece of Ella Fitzgerald, would it bother your tormented little ink-stained psyches?'

Damned good guy, Price, was the general feeling of the press. Doesn't patronize you. Got eighteen zillion dollars and makes you fix your own drinks. Makes a gag about rat-cheese and what is spread around here to eat would cost me a year's salary. Look at that fat greasy caviar. Look at that ham. But he makes you serve yourself, and he calls you Mister, and he lays it on the line, and he don't send you a cheap blend for a Christmas present. He knows you got dignity, same as he knows he's got dignity. You don't want to eat his caviar, so you don't eat it. But it's up to you. He ain't watching the till. Look at him with that hick A.P. stand-in, explaining the elephant. Right now, the A.P. guy thinks he's a combination of Ben McKelway and Paul Miller.

'I know damned good and well,' the financial gentleman from the *Times* said to the financial gentleman from the *Trib.*, 'that Uncle Craig is gimmicking something. But I am prepared to go along. This boy makes it so painless. When he starts to talk, we don't have to say: "What was that again, Mr. Price?" One time I covered Morgenthau trying to explain the devaluation of the dollar, and I never been the same since. Then I was set upon by Bretton Woods, and my morale dropped some more. Price generally hands it to you like a gangster explaining his plans to knock over a bank. Thank God for an honest *goniff* from time to time—at least a guy that's laying it out so even my feeble readership can understand it.'

After a certain amount of small talk, Craig got up and walked over to his elephant tusks, leaned on one, and rubbed his forehead reflectively on the cool ivory.

'You guys had enough whisky to support you through my terrible trials and tribulations? Why don't we fresh up the glasses and get the work over? We won't fiddle much with the facts and figures. The publicity gents have those all laid down nice and neat so even I can almost understand them. *Almost*. I been a stranger here myself too long.'

He grinned, and said to himself, you corny small-town bastard. You cheap ham actor. You posturing grinning bum, playing it sweet and homey with the gentlemen of the press. You stinking ham. Lay it on, boy, rub it in.

'Actually, men, I got my tit in a crack. Everybody's mad at me. I don't know who or why. The hell I don't know *why*. I bought myself an expensive divorce and expanded a couple of companies and there's somebody up there *don't* like me.' He rolled his eyes heavenwards. 'This young-lover bit don't go down so good in the Street. I won't make it long. My insurance company is suing me for some reason I haven't figured out yet, since I haven't stumbled over a single widow or orphan recently who is selling matches in the snow as a result of my—what do they call it, malfeasance in office?—but I wanted you guys to know one thing as a little private protection for me, when the rumours start playing the big-assed bird bit. The cornerstone of the Insurance Company, the Mastodon Investment Trust, the Price Building, and all the other junk I seem to have afflicted myself with—more in sorrow than in anger—' (and wait for the mild applause, Price, Smithfield J. Price)—'is a healthy baby, even if it does have more than a single head. You'll get the figures from Willie, but they ain't hard to check. Price Mills grossed a little more than twelve million large spendables this year, more than they earned last year.

'I'm kind of happy about Price Mills. Maybe we stole some business from the brassière market, but it seems to me that legs are up, and pants are down, and bed-sheets are up, but in any case we're making money due to a failing popularly common to boys and girls. We got a rather large bond issue, I'm sure you know, but if you care to check we haven't missed an annual interest or an amortization. The amount of dough we got spread around this happy city is considerable, and you can start with Chase, progress to Chemical Corn, and work your way down. And lastly, if I can find somebody stupid enough to lend me the money, I reckon I'm going to beard the devil and build myself a few more mills. This is known as hitting yourself over the head in the old joke.'

'What's the purpose of having us here, Mr. Price?' The planted pressman spoke up loud and clear.

'Not much. I just wanted somebody to ask me how full of vitamins is my basic daily bread. Me being a frustrated actor, I didn't wait to be asked. I came on without direction. I just know that pretty soon some people are going to claw me and I thought maybe I could buy myself a little friendship insurance if you guys had a drink with me. And I did want to give you the facts on the mills, because when these bastards get me into court on that insurance suit, a lot of people are going to be saying a lot of nasty things, and I want somebody that knows something in my corner. It's like wearing a jockstrap when you play football.'

Craig walked over to the bar and poured himself a drink.

'You got questions, ask. I'll try to level as best I can, but you guys know that a lot of other people run my racket—pardon'— he snickered behind his hand—'my business.' (Small applause, Price, but enough. *Ham.*)

Little dangerous man with a sort of intelligent face.

'Mr. Price, please tell me, what *is* this insurance squabble about? I don't really understand.'

Craig took a drink and lit a cigarette before he answered.

'Buster,' he said, very seriously. 'I'm with you. I don't know either. Anything you know makes you smarter than me. All I can tell you is that if you got a family with money to spend, you always got a quarrelsome cousin with a bone to pick. And I got a big family and a lot of cousins.' (That quote ought to hold the sons-a-bitches.)

'Yes, but what makes the cousin quarrel?' (Persistent little bastard.)

Craig shrugged. The world weighed on him heavily.

'Look, my friend. I try to make myself a living with oil wells and insurance companies and airlines. I play the piano in a cat house, and I'm kind of a financial doorman at all the worst kind of West Side hotels. I trade money, I owe money, I work in money. I'm a good cracker kid that should have stayed in North Carolina. As far as I know, the people in Formidable think I'm over-betting my hand in Mastodon. They could be right. Insurance companies are kind of like old-maid aunts. Show 'em a mouse and they think it's an elephant. That widow-orphan bit has really been overplayed.

'I flung this Irish picnic for just one reason. Somebody's apt to clobber me, and I just want you guys underneath the Donny-brook to know as much about me as I know. I got a tame Government auditor out in the other office—he don't drink—who will trot out the books on Price Mills. Twelve million in gross sales increase ain't ugly, and we paid a small but sincere dividend

657

this year. That was before us sharks had our bite, of course. And we did retire the loan a little piece, like a million, after we-all done got through with the interest on it. Take a look, and when that stuff hits the fan, remember old Honest Craig Price, the Baffled Boy Financier. I got nothing else to say, unless you want something said after you've had a gander at the private papers.'

'But Mr. Price, what . . .' the persistent little bastard started to say, when one of his colleagues shushed him.

'For God's sake leave it alone,' the colleague said. 'Let's have another drink and make it a good story that don't get lost with too much sidebar crap. Drop it and quit eager-beavering all over the place.'

Stock in Price Nills, Inc., went up a full point the day that the *Times*, the *Tribune*, the *World-Telegram*, the *News*, the *Mirror*, and the *Post* carried the stories of Craig's press conference. Price Mills had been steady at fifteen. It hit sixteen, and jumped another half-point to sixteen and a half the following day.

'Start dumping,' Craig said to his broker. 'But spread it around through some other houses. And lie low until we've got rid of most of it, and then take the short position. Take it for all it's worth.'

'If you say so,' Henry Nelson said. 'But as a company you look mighty firm. You could get hurt.'

'Don't worry about me, Dad. I'm on steady ground. Sell me out. Then borrow me back. Short.'

The thing with Susan hadn't been very serious.

Mr. Price, together with his beautiful wife, his rich and famous friends, was back in the gossip columns again. Price Mills firmed at seventeen. Everybody said how nice it was, with another Russian war scare on, that the market was showing remarkable steadiness.

'Craig Price, financier, oilman and textile zillionaire, was living it up to celebrate the new rise in his mill stocks last night, together with his beautiful new wife, the former Susan Strong, and half-a-dozen friends who might comprise an aristocracy of the business and banking world. In addition, there was Bruce Bainbridge, star of *Ring Down the Moon*, the fabulously successful play in which Mr. Price reputedly has invested . . .'

'I figured it was time I had to go get out of the house for a little bit,' Susan said. 'I love my house, and it still held a faint odour of quarrel. And I knew you'd be busy in Washington. Also I was mad. So I took off and spent a couple of days with Ruth in Oyster Bay. I was wrong not to leave a meassage. I'm sorry. I just took off.'

'It had me awful worried,' Craig said. 'But fortunately I was so damned busy, what with one thing and another, that I really didn't have time to find you and spank you and bring you home. Between Washington and the Market . . .'

'I've been reading all about you in the papers. What *are* you up to, exactly? Something. What?'

'Trying to shift a little heat. I got some Washington troubles that need some sudden sun to dry the mildew. It wasn't a very successful trip. The SEC don't love me, and neither do the income taxers. I'm going to need some money—a lot of money—and I thought that maybe some favourable press was indicated. At least we're very healthy at the source, and I wanted the world to know it. The stock's jumped. And speaking of jumping, would you climb into your best night-time armour and help me with a little more public relations? If you say so, we'll make some *bella figura* around the fair city. I thought Rex and Mary, Bob and Helen, Jerry and Jeannette, and maybe that ham, Bainbridge and his wife. Go around in a mad whirl, and be more than polite to Walter and Hy and Louie and Frank and Earl and Lennie.'

'You hate nightclubs,' Sue said. 'You're cooking something. And you don't like Rex and Mary, you've said so, and you like Helen but you hate Bob's guts, and you loathe Bainbridge, even if he is making you some money with *Moon*. And you don't pay any attention to the chit-chat columnists as a rule. I don't know what you're trying to do, but I promised to love, honour and obey—I'm old-fashioned—so I'll climb into my dancing drawers and smile steadily all evening. There just might be a cameraman in the house.'

'When is Jimmy getting back from Europe, Connie?' Craig asked his secretary. 'Any fresh word?'

'Some time next week, Mr. Price. He called when you were in Washington and said there were a few details that would take a little longer than he thought. That was from London.'

'All right. Get me public relations and tell Willie I want to see him.'

Craig bent back to his papers. His private phone rang.

'Yes,' he said, irritably.

'Darling,' Susan said, 'could you possibly make it a little earlier tonight? We've some people coming in for drinks and dinner, remember? The Barnes's and Ruth and Pop and Nancy and Jake.'

'I'll try. I may have to stay in town, though.'

'But sweetie, we've had this planned for a week. It was *your* idea . . .'

'I *know* it was my idea but I may have to stay in town, like I said. I've got to hang up now. Call you later. 'Bye.' He racked the phone and turned to his chief press agent, Willie Shaffer. Willie was fat, and had a red face which bore a spurious expression of honest sincerity. The face was Willie's most valuable asset. He rather resembled an English country vicar, and the deep-cored fact that he would, under duress, sell a sister into slavery or dust off his mother if she was crowding the plate of his project, was not visible to a casual glance.

Willie was an eminently practical press agent. He never thought of himself as a public relations counsel. At one time, when Willie was calling the horses wrong, he was taking his meals as payment for publicizing a Broadway restaurant. He was drinking on the cuff as a fee from a nightclub. He was driving a Buick convertible—on loan from a hire-car service he was publicizing. A nightclub singer, who was more professionally a call-girl, was paying him for his services to get her name in the columns at the rate of five free visits a week. Each visit was computed at $20.

The only problem—Willie was living like a king, and was getting a free apartment from the small hotel he publicized—was that he had no money. One day a cheque he had written to his bookmaker demonstrated a remarkable buoyancy and his bank manager called him to task on the overdraft.

'For God's sake, Willie,' the manager said. 'Why don't you publicize a bank so they'll pay you in *money*?'

The story got around, and when Craig heard it, he called Willie Shaffer and made him a sound fiscal proposition. They had proved a most excellent team, since both were dealers in gross realities, with little sentiment added. Now Willie paid $275 to Pat Caruso for his suits, but at heart he was still hustling nightclubs, driving borrowed cars, drinking on the cuff, eating on the arm, living for free, and collecting his dues from an ambitious broad on the side.

'Sit down, Willie,' Craig said. 'This is serious stuff, and's got to be handled cool. Want a drink?'

'Sure. The usual.' Craig walked over to the bar and poured four fingers of bourbon into an old-fashioned glass, and built a gin-and-tonic for himself. He handed Willie his drink and prowled the floor for a moment before he spoke.

Look,' he said. This one you got to handle tricky. What I need from you is a good sneaky leak. I want enough leak so that the press lads will be hot to see me, and I kind of won't be available for comment immediately. I want a gathering suspicion that the last press conference was a cover, a snow job, and that we're a sick duck at Price Mills.'

'Gimme a dirty detail or two so I can start to scatter the stuff.'

'The rumour is that I'm selling my stock in Price Mills. It's true enough. I'm sick of this mill business, and I'm going to play with something else for a while.' Craig didn't mention that he had spoken to his stockbroker, much earlier, and that he was sold out at the top almost completely.

'Hit the better bars and give 'em a lot of that this-is-strictly-confidential-but kind of crap, and when the questions start coming, be sort of shiftily embarrassed. When there've been enough questions and I've been unavailable for comment, break down and give the children a press statement. Here.' Craig tossed him a sheet of paper with a pencil-scarred paragraph on it. Willie read it aloud:

'Craig Price of (fill in) who (fill in) announced today that he was selling his controlling interest in Price Mills, Inc., in order to consolidate his holdings. Mr. Price is currently being sued for six million dollars-plus by the Formidable Life Insurance Co. of Ohio, in which he is a majority stockholder, as has appeared publicly in the newspapers.'

'Put that into your kind of words, Willie. And when you are spreading the stuff around, you might just hint that the old man isn't quite himself these days—drinking a little bit too much. Hasn't been the same, really, since he shot his chauffeur. Hasn't been the same, really, since that big divorce settlement. Hasn't been the same . . .'

'All right, Craig. I get the pitch,' Willie said. He finished his drink and got up. 'I'll tell you when your innermost secrets are in every blabber-mouth in every first-class saloon in mid-Manhattan.'

'Good enough. See you, Willie.' Craig returned to his desk again. He was studying the figures on the Price Building, which had cost twenty million to erect. It was a good racket, the building business. Good old depreciation, just like that lovely old depletion that forgave you twenty-seven and a half per cent on oil. You had the few hundred thousand bucks you needed, and your handfuls of twenty-five-year-leases from responsible people like the Du Ponts and Standard Oil and folks like that, and you had an option on some pretty good ground, where you only had to tear down a few houses—buy 'em out, of course—and the finance boys, the insurance companies, would lend you the rest.

If there wasn't an atomic war, there was no way they could lose. There was no way *you* could lose, so long as you kept your ratios straight. The rents roll in, you have the use of the building, the mortgage gets paid off, you pocket the surplus . . .

'My only problem,' Craig said to himself, 'is that I don't own my own share of this pile of rock and glass. I hocked it to Nate for my escape-hatch money. The building's doing fine, but it's doing fine for Nate Mannheim. But I'm okay here, I think, if my new gimmick works. You get a free ride for twenty years, and nine per cent ain't ugly money. All I got to do is pay off Nate.'

He picked up the phone.

'Honey,' he said to Susan, 'I'm sorry, real sorry. But I just can't make it tonight.'

'But Craig, *you* asked them. I didn't . . .'

661

'Sorry. Tell them it's business again, and so it is. I'll stay on in the office.'

'But Craig, I . . .'

'Sorry. I got to get some things unscrambled. Good-bye.' His voice chopped off curtly.

He bent over his papers again. After three hours he shook his head like a groggy prizefighter, and went to the bar to pour himself a drink. He stood, leaning, his cheek cool against the tusk.

'Man,' he said, 'when and if I get out of this mess I'm going to take about a year off, let Jimmy run the store, and go back to that Tanganyika bush and get lost. I suppose I *could* make it in time for dinner, but the hell with it. I'll just have to get up and come back before dawn.'

He went back to his desk and dialled a number.

'Laura? Mr. P. I got a feeling I don't want to eat alone tonight. Swell. Could you meet me at the bar in the Rex in half an hour or so? . . . You're an angel.'

He whistled tunelessly after he hung up.

24

WHEN the word spread that Craig Price was unloading—he had already unloaded—Price Mills dropped half-a-point in one day. When his press release was front-page news, Price Mills skidded another full point. This directed attention to his suit with Formidable, and Price Mills dropped another point. Craig had ploughed back his loose cash on the quiet bull-sale into a short position. He called his broker to come to the office.

'We'll buy at fourteen,' Craig said. 'I'm going to leak a little more to the press gentlemen. Then we buy it back, pay off the Government, and then I'll settle with the discontents at Formidable.'

'All right, Craig. But I don't like it. I've an uneasy feeling about it.'

'Forget it. Everybody does it. There's no crime about going short.'

'Not if you're just gambling. But to shout public confidence in your own company while you're dumping, while you're quietly selling a bit at a time, and then knocking the brains out of your own company with rumours and statements . . . The SEC doesn't care too much for it. You know it.'

'The SEC doesn't care too much for anything. Anyhow, when I publicly expressed confidence I *was* confident. It *is* a good company. It's still a good company. Can I help it if I'm bored with textiles and want to put my money somewhere else, to get off the hook with the Government boys, to settle my insurance suit? I just want to stay happy with Mastodon. We'll still be running Price Mills. When that stock hits fourteen we're back in business again. We have another press conference and the stock'll jump, because I will have decided, with proper rueful humility, that I am lonely for the sound of bobbins singing in the soft summer night. Up she goes again.'

'It's crooked, and you know it. I'm your broker and if you say sell, I sell. You say buy, I buy, as long as you put up the fifty per cent margin. I bet up, or I bet down. on the same fifty per cent. But I do *not* say I'm healthy when I'm selling out and going short, and then come back after I've unloaded and intimate that I'm sick so I can drive a market down on purpose. *You* do, but I'm just your broker. *I* don't.'

Craig grinned. He shook a friendly finger.

'Henry, Henry. This is Craig Price. This isn't little Lord Fauntleroy. You know as well as me that any sale of four hundred thousand, five hundred thousand shares of stock is going to depress a market. And at the same time you've been around long enough to know that three guys selling stocks back and forth to each other can drive up the price just through activity, and the suckers'll buy enough outside to keep it up high enough long enough for the inside boys to get out, and grab it short when it skids. Don't go moral on me, Henry. This is a thieves' market, as well you know, and you're all accessories after the fact, if not outright thieves yourself. Buy at fourteen. Good-bye.'

Henry Nelson walked out of the room, shaking his head. Henry Nelson was a dignified man, his wafer-thin watch was a Patek, he was a member of the Westchester Country Club and he was the father of two boys and two girls. Henry Nelson was a dignified man, and he did not wish to consider himself as a crook's accomplice.

Jimmy Wilbur walked in the door. He was lean, deeply tanned, and appeared at least ten years younger than Craig. He also looked grim as he shook hands.

'Nice to have you back in the lodge, Moose,' Craig said. 'Let me fix you a drink.'

'No, thanks. I want to talk. I want to talk seriously.' His voice was cold. He didn't seem overjoyed to be back.

'Good trip? Get the Tangier business settled all right?'

'The Tangier business was settled all right. So was London. So was Paris and so was Switzerland. But it was a lousy trip.'

'How, lousy?' Craig walked over to the bar. 'Sure you won't have a drink?'

'No. I don't want to think about drinking. I've seen a little too much of it, lately. It seems to me I've been looking after you all my life, Short Pants, but I'm fed up with it. I have seen a lot—a *lot*'—Jimmy Wilbur spoke tightly through his teeth—'a real

663

great, splendid lot of your wife and daughter on this trip, and I will have you know that it's a mess. Which one is the biggest mess I don't know . . .'

'Carol?'

'She's a young Maybelle. For a kid . . . Craig, you don't know that Capri-Rome-London-Torremolinos-Majorca-Cap Ferrat-Villefranche axis. Knocking around in that atmosphere would make a bum out of a saint. The same bums hit all the same places at the same time. And your daughter Carol is a bum, like her mother is a tramp. And I blame you.'

'Everybody blames me for everything,' Craig shrugged. 'There must have been at least one time when I did something right.'

'Yeah,' Jimmy Wilbur matched his shrug. 'But that was a long time, a very long time, ago.'

'Just what are my beloved ex-wife and the child who hates my guts doing that's new and unusual? Tell me all the gruesome details, and then I'll tell you some of my troubles. I'll top you.'

'I'll tell. I think I *will* have a drink. I need it when I think of them both.' Jimmy got up and poured himself a double slug of bourbon. 'We'll start with Maybelle . . .'

Carol and her mother saw each other briefly at the *feria* in Sevilla. They had met on several occasions before—at the *encierro* at Pamplona, at the film festivals at Cannes and Venice, at the Marqués de Cuevas' parties. This wasn't unusual, for everybody made the Marqués de Cuevas' parties. For a while they seemed to be hitting the same circuits. Then they had settled down in separate patterns.

Maybelle went to a little town in Spain's Costa Brava to visit friends. It was a tiny artsy-craftsy *bijou* of a town called Tossa, and its old Roman ruins were properly impressed by Maybelle's leopard-skin upholstered Bentley, and with Maybelle's chauffeur, a Monégasque with long sideburns. He was called Pierre, and was approximately twenty-five years old. He had a positive talent for doing what he was told, and always came home nights. The town enchanted Maybelle, and so she rented a villa. It was the same villa, perhaps, that she had rented in St. Raphael, at Tamariu, at Aigua Blava, at Torremolinos, at Positano—same umbrella-ed stretches of pines thrusting out of the rocks, sparsely furnished rooms, acres of mosaic flooring, roses growing profusely until you moved in, and then they died, of course. There would be a cook and a couple of maids laid on, and Pierre, among his other functions, was an acceptable butler, and made a very dry martini. For these villas Maybelle, who still kept up the big ragged unshorn-grass-one in Villefranche, was only charged five or six times the actual rental. The Mediterranean remained constant.

The chief reason Maybelle was enchanted with Tossa was that it reminded her of the beach in Carolina. It was like a little breath of home. The boys wore jeans, and their hair long, and the girls wore jeans, and their hair short. Everybody talked animatedly over cheap *anis* or rough red wine in the little bistros, speaking with many brave gestures about art and literature and using words like *gouache* and *démodé* and *avant-garde* and name-dropping Kafka and Rilke and Jean-Paul Sartre and Picasso and Casals. These cafés were located conveniently near the bay-front so that the boys and girls could watch the brawny fishermen come in from the sea—for separate reasons—and see the terribly picturesque old women either mending their nets or washing their clothes patiently in a little *riera*—a sweet-water stream—which ran between the Mediterranean and the cafés.

There is a saying on the Costa Brava of Spain that it is impossible to buy fish in the summer season because the fishermen are always under their boats with a *turista*—usually English—instead of in the boats with the nets. But culture abounds, although none of the self-acclaimed artists ever have sold, or ever will sell, anything they've written or painted, even if they took the time off from the handsome waiters and the bronzed fishermen to break out an easel, or shove a sheaf of paper into a typewriter. They feed on each other's conversation as incestuously as lobsters in a pot, and generally always have a small income from an ex-husband or a parent who is happy to pay for the privilege of having them out of the house.

Everybody spoke English, which Maybelle felt was wonderful, and they seemed ever eager to partake of a party. Maybelle had not made much of a mark on the Riviera, because it appeared everyone else had a villa and a Rolls or a Jag and a suite at the Carlton or Negresco. Or a yacht which regularly debouched passengers into other people's yachts. Despite her money, as a woman alone she was another wavelet in a sea of women alone —women with pale pink dyed hair, eyebrows pencilled straight up over faces which had been lifted so often they suggested the blankness of a boiled egg.

There were fat women and skinny women, women with dirty diamonds and obscenely fat hands; women whose lips cut purple gashes into the over-powdered flabby faces. They ringed their fingers to the knuckle, and talked incessantly of baccarat and roulette and always of the newest scandal. They all had little white poodles and generally, in hovering attendance, a Pierre or Juan or Rolande. These young men needed no corsets to buttress the slim line. They were usually in their twenties, were either French or Italian, occasionally Spanish, and they sang beautifully for their supper. Of course, after performing the callisthenics for which they were paid, they made a getaway down the stairs when sufficient brandy and *amour* had rendered the patroness unconscious, to meet in back-alley *rendezvous* with whichever peasant-girl had caught their fancy. Or even better, with some fresh *turista* who found Latins ever so fascinating. This group was referred to as *baksheesh*—the tip over and above the daily bed.

'Ramoncito is a shameless flirt,' a dirty-haired dowager would say of her reconditioned bus-boy. 'One must watch him every moment. He's so young, and so beautiful, I wonder what he actually sees in *me*.' Then the smirk. 'But always Ramon says that young women, like young wine, are only made to satisfy thirst, while the more mature types'—smirk—'have that delicate quality of a fine vintage wine or a rare brandy.' Pause. 'Ramon says that he couldn't live with one of those flighty young fribbets because I am his harbour, and he must have me to come home to.'

Ramon, at this very moment, has his hand halfway up the frock of some barmaid, or is dancing, hips glued to hips, with a fresh English lass greedy for sun and nocturnal exercise under a boat. He is saying: 'I'm sorry I was late, darleeng (or *cherie* or *guapa*), but the old girl's getting more demanding every day. Even since she took that cure—the Swiss one, with the sheep glands —she fancies herself a filly, and I swear her alcoholic capacity has doubled. *Ay*, what a way to make a living. But what use to the world is an impoverished count who must stand on his feet waiting at table all day long?'

'I wish I was rich,' the barmaid or *inglesa* says. 'Then I'd keep you all to myself.'

('Not bloody likely,' Ramon is saying to himself, holding the girl more closely. 'Fun's fun, but money's money, and if I can just keep on long enough without throwing up, the old trout will maybe settle some *peluco* on me. Lucky my family runs to strong stomachs.')

But it did not seem so snobbish in Tossa, and the other little towns—S'Agaro, Palamós. Tamariu—where everybody wore jeans and went barefoot and danced *sardanas* in the streets at night, and where a fisherman or a waiter was as socially acceptable as a duke. Maybelle had a lot of money, and she spent it. The imported gypsy *flamenco* dancers who flocked to her table had begun by ordering cheap sherry. They graduated to cognac, and finally progressed to scotch. She paid, and paid willingly, because for the first time she felt herself a queen with a tailor-made court. And the long-haired young men, the short-haired young ladies, the gypsies and singing fisherfolk cheerfully allowed her to pay. Life had indeed come to Mrs. Wentworth-Brewster.

She settled finally for one static site of her throne, a sea-front café called La Perla, which had beach chairs for the sun and awninged chairs for the shade, and also a very handsome waiter named Pepino. Pepino was tall and seemed distinguished even when he served. His moustache was clipped in the almost articulate perfection which only Latins are able to achieve, and his black hair was feathered as finely as any movie actor's. His teeth gleamed against the swart of his skin, his lips were rosy red, and he moved like a bullfighter. Every time he deposited a glass on the table, Maybelle could hear the trumpets blare and imagine the satin swirl of a *capote*.

One night she arrived at La Perla without Pierre, the chauffeur-companion, and she was in a frightful snit.

'Where is Monsieur Pierre?' Pepino asked. 'Why are you alone, Madame?'

'Double scotch, Pepino. I'll tell you when you come back.' It was early, and the café was nearly empty. He handed her the drink, and stood politely at attention.

'Oh, for Christ's sake, sit down,' Maybelle said. 'Have a drink.'

'I will sit for perhaps one cigarette.' Pepino slid cozily into a chair. 'You are very gracious, Madame.'

'Gracious-shmacious,' Maybelle replied. 'I have just kicked Pierre out of the villa. I'm through with that boy. After all the money I've . . . You don't know what's been going on with that little . . .'

'Yes. I know, and nearly everyone else knows. But we love you here, Madame, and we did not want to distress you. He was no good, an authentic *sin vergüenza*, that one. A worthless man. And it was not only with that little . . .'

'So it seems. But finding her in my own bed seemed a little too much, even for Pierre. My money's evidently made him careless. He used to do these things in *their* houses or in back alleys, not in my house. That I won't stand for. I had one husband that never came home, and now I got a'—she groped for a word—'a . . . servant that brings his other dames to my bed. Can you drive a car?'

'*Ciaro*. Surely. I was once a chauffeur before I became a waiter. I even know the Rolls and the Bentley well enough to make minor repairs. Not that one needs to make any minor repairs on either of those miraculous machineries.'

'Do you enjoy being a waiter?'

'Only when I am waiting on such a gracious person as you, Madame, a true lady. The rest of the time I hate it. There are so few gracious ladies who will invite you to sit, who never quarrel over the *cuenta*, who give such generous gratuities.'

'All right. Drive me home tonight and we'll see how well you can . . . how well you can *drive*.'

'I would be delighted, Madame. I'll close early here. Thank you for asking me to sit with you.'

'Don't mention it. Bring me another double scotch, will you?'

Service fell off considerably in La Perla, when Pepino gave immediate notice that he was replacing Pierre as the *señora's* chauffeur, due to the unfortunate circumstances which had necessitated Pierre's immediate presence in France, to arrange the financial affairs of his grandmother, who had died suddenly and had left things in a muddle. Pierre, sitting at that time in the sun in front of a café in Cannes, was saying to a small, brown-eyed blonde: 'Why don't we open a café, a little, *tres chic* one? I got plenty of money. You run the *caisse*, and I will be the *maître*. We can make a killing.'

'I would adore to,' the little brown-eyed blonde said. 'But there is a certain thing of respectability. One must have the *certificat* to place upon the wall, so that I am called *Madame* with respect. Did you mention marriage?'

'Why not? One marries. It is not a crime to marry. Let us marry, and open the small, but very *chic*, café.'

'*Je t'adore, mon cheri*,' and the girl kissed him wetly. Pierre made a small *moue* of distaste at the public display of affection.

'We will have none of that in the café, Suzette,' he said. 'Learn it now.'

'*Oui. Je comprends*. But what will we name our café?'

'I had thought to call it Chez Mabelle,' he said. '*Garcon, encore deux fines à l'eau*.'

'*Mais c'est merveilleux*, the name,' the girl said. 'Wherever did you find it?'

'Nowhere. I named it after an old aunt who was very, very kind to me, and who, indirectly, has made it possible for me to marry you. I have always been a man of much sentiment.'

25

CRAIG flirted a negating wrist. He shrugged irritably, his eyes squinted in a frown.

'What do you want me to do, for Christ's sake? She's a grown woman. She's got all the dough in the world. I can't make her be a good girl. We're not married any more, remember?'

'No, I agree,' Jimmy Wilbur said, and walked over to refill his glass. 'But there might be something you could do about Carol.'

'Oh, for God's sake, Moose. We've been through all that. You know what happened in Capri. She wants no part of me. She wouldn't listen to a word from me. She hates my guts. I *asked* her her to come and live with me and Susan. She'll be twenty-one soon.'

'That's if she doesn't drink herself to death,' Jimmy said. 'Look, mighty man. Your daughter, is the cheapest lay on the Riviera, because she buys the drinks. Your daughter is the drunkest lay on the Riviera, because she drinks. Your daughter is the noisiest drunken lay anywhere. Your daughter has tried being a lesbian, already. She runs around with a pack of fags, busted aristocrats, sailors, Arabs. Whatever's going, little Carol

is the life of the party. She's been thrown out of more joints than
. . . . when Carol gets her load she's apt to throw a glass or belt
the manager or jump into the bass-drum. She has a habit of
taking her clothes off in public . . .'

'In that respect she resembles her mother,' Craig said dryly. 'It
seems to run in the family. Continue with the sad song.'

'I'll continue. I finally caught up with her in Tangier. She was
in a bar called Can-Can when I first saw her, and she had
taken a house in the Medina. Tangier is a very interesting village.
You can buy hashish at the drugstore, and a few years back every
bum, thief, crook, confidence man . . .'

'Don't forget financiers,' Craig said. 'I've been to Tangier, remember? Spare me the geography.'

'She was sitting in the Can-Can. It was early. She was drinking
anis. It was ten o'clock in the morning, and already she was
bagged. Or better, still bagged from the night before . . .'

'Well, if it isn't Uncle Jimmy come to play nursie again.
Drag up a stool, Uncle James, and I will buy you a drink.
Joseph, this is my nannie. He disapproves of me.'

'So do I,' the bartender said. 'That shocking performance in
Parade last night.' The bartender was small, *café-au-lait* of
complexion, with a smile that embraced a close acquaintance
with all the evil of the past fifty years. As owner-bartender, he
lived apart from that world. He merely observed it, and drew
back his lips in a snarling smile of purest malicious interest. He
considered himself the superior of his daily flock, but he
knew all the gossip of the town, and owned not the slightest interest
in reforming any small particle of it. 'What would you have, sir?'

'I'll have a Coke,' Jimmy Wilbur growled. 'Carol, you look
like hell. What in God's name have you been doing to yourself?'

She *did* look like hell. Her eyes were milky, and just a touch
off focus. Her hands shook as she lifted her glass, and some of the
anis and water spilled. Her face was puffed, and her hair was
dirty. She was wearing a sweater, obviously with nothing under
it, over shorts. Her nails, Jimmy noticed, were bitten short and
untainted by polish. Her feet were poked into yellow Moroccan
slippers.

'I've been having fun,' she said. 'Living it up. Having a ball.
Enjoying myself. Free, white, and almost twenty-one. What do
you hear from my charming family? How is my dear, devoted
father? How is my loving mummy? I saw her for a minute in
Juan-les-Pins or Antibes or somewhere, but she was very interested in her handsome young man—I forget whether it was
the count or the waiter, Mummy's *so* adaptable, and in any
case I had a date. I went off with some people on a boat the
next day, and when I came back she was gone. Where, I don't
know. Somebody said Spain.'

669

'Let's go sit down in the back,' Jimmy said.

'All right. Achmet,' to the waiter, 'bring us another drink. Uncle Jimmy, don't you think you better get off that Coke kick and have something more nourishing?'

'No. And you don't need another drink right now.'

'Don't tell *me* what I need and don't need. Achmet, bring me a drink. Double!' She wavered slightly as she got up to go to the back room.

'All right,' she said. 'Start the lecture, Uncle Jimmy. I'm a naughty girl and I ought to be spanked but I'm my own girl and nobody's big enough to spank me. What have you got in mind, dearest Uncle?'

'Carol, I've loved you since you were a baby, you know that. Come on back to the States with me, honey, and get off this merry-go-round. Find yourself a nice guy and get married. Or go to work. There's plenty things you could do in our business —nearly anything you wanted. Or go to college . . .'

'College? Christ. What could I learn in college I couldn't teach better? Work for the old man? I'd kill myself first. *No.* Leave me alone. I got my own friends, my own life, and I don't want a chaperon. I got a nice little villa here and I'm happy here. Nobody ever goes to bed in Tangier except to . . .' Jimmy Wilbur winced as she used the terse verb. 'Everybody minds his own business in Tangier. Nobody cares what anybody else does. I like it.' She looked at him defiantly. Then she averted her eyes. 'I like it as well as I like anything.'

'Carol, baby, what's wrong with you kids? I hear a lot of stuff, I see a lot of stuff. What, who, are you mad at? You're young, you're lovely, you've got plenty of brains and plenty of money—too much money—what are you throwing it all away for? What are you looking for?'

'I'm damned if I know, Jimmy,' Carol said. 'Everything seems so . . . so useless. I haven't had a single love affair that hasn't turned out to be just so much douche-bag-and-mussy-sheets in my mind. Everybody I think I'm going to like turns out to be a bastard who is either after something I've got or just wants a quick lay for laughs . . . I don't know.' She shrugged, in a mannerism so like her father when Craig didn't want to think of something unpleasant. Carol yelled: 'I don't know Achmet! Another drink!'

A Moor, wearing short-coated European clothes and a red tarboosh, walked through the door and came into the back room. He dropped a hand familiarly on Carol's shoulder.

'Hallo, darleeng,' he said, in accented British-English. '*What* a jolly do at the Parade last night. Though I do think that throwing the glass at your boy friend was a bit much. Do you mind if I sit down?'

'Yes,' Jimmy Wilbur growled. 'I mind very much. This is a

private conversation.' He stood up, and the Arab measured him with insolently lidded eyes.

'Frightfully sorry, darleeng,' he said. 'It's got shockingly stuffy in here. Someday you can come weez me to de Casbah,' in ancient mimicry of Charles Boyer. 'Unteel den, *au'voir*.'

'Who was *that* coffee-coloured sport?' Jimmy said, sitting down again. 'He seemed to know you rather well.'

'I don't know *him* very well. I think I slept with him a couple of times, but his name escapes me.'

'You can't mean that seriously?'

'Why not? You meet a lot of people late at night, or early in the morning. I rather like Arabs, as a matter of fact. This one is a bit painful though, with that what-he-thinks-is-Oxford English. I like the peasants better. Anyhow, I don't find going to bed with a man very important if it's pleasant at the time and no emotions get tangled up in it. That's how you men feel about it, isn't it?' Carol looked at him nastily. 'The last five or six gentlemen with whom I was emotionally involved seemed to think that way about it. Most of them had very convenient wives to spring on you at the last moment. I *do* love men. Especially in the morning, when a certain lack of interest, plus stiff overnight whiskers, is plain for any fool to see.'

A woman strode in out of the bright Moroccan sunlight, stood momentarily at the door so her eyes could become accustomed to the gloom inside, and then walked rapidly towards Carol's table. Her iron-grey hair was cut nearly as short as a boy's. She wore a man's jacket with a severe skirt. She was wearing a man's shirt with a thin string tie. The shoes were common-sense, flatheeled, and she carried a slim ebony cane. As she approached she screwed a monocle into one eye.

'Darling—Carol,' she said. She sat down without invitation. 'You'd dashed off when I woke this morning. Oh, *what* a head. Who's *this*?' She fixed Jimmy Wilbur with her monocled stare, as if viewing a rather repulsive reptile.

'Mr. Wilbur, a friend of my father's, and mine,' Carol said. 'This is Monique St. Yves. We live together. We share the little house in the Medina. You must come to tea this evening, Uncle Jim. You'll love the house. It's got a wonderful patio and is completely surrounded by enormous walls, and you enter by a sort of slave-gate that has another gate inside. I got it from . . .'

Jimmy Wilbur got up. He raised an eyebrow at Miss Monique St. Yves. The glance was not friendly.

'I'm afraid I'm going to be busy.' Directly to Carol: 'What did you say *that* was? So long, Hank,' he said to Miss St. Yves, and stalked out. As he went through the door a lady walking five small Spanish waterdogs on a multiple leash nearly upset him, and she was followed by a mincing gentleman with delicately rouged cheeks. Jimmy could still smell the gentleman's perfume when he reached the street.

'*What* a rude man,' Miss St. Yves said as Jimmy Wilbur strode off. 'I'm sure I didn't . . .'

'Oh, shut up, Moe. Achmet!' Carol shouted. 'Bring me another double!'

'I'm afraid I kind of took things in my own hands,' Jimmy Wilbur said to Craig. 'I got a little bit drunked-up at El Minzah, and I got to thinking about our kid shacked up with a lesbian— a real comic-opera Liz, monocle and all—and sleeping around with Arabs and playing footie with the fags and throwing glasses and drinking pernod and smoking a little *kif* for her kicks, and living in the Casbah, and passing through one pair of hands after another, getting more and more dirty in the process. I got mad. I got real mad. I took another couple of slugs, which didn't make me any less sore, and I went out looking for trouble. I found it. Carol was in some dive back of the native section, I don't even remember its name, with the goddamndest collection of nothings I ever saw in my life.

'Old Monocle Moe had changed to evening dress, a dinner-jacket, of all things, and there seemed to be a collection of sweet young men, a few Arabs, one very black guy with a turban, a flock of assorted whores, a smuggler or two, and some people I don't know how to describe. Your daughter was high—and I mean high—and it wasn't off booze. You could smell the Mary-J in this joint so strong you almost got a charge just walking in. If you want to ask me how I located her, the bartender in Can-Can told me it was where Carol was hanging out mostly these days, and he was nice enough to send one of his waiters with me to find it. That's quite a thing, that Tangier native quarter. It stinks of every foul smell in the world—rotten meat, open sewage, piss-rotted plaster, but it didn't stink like that little box that Carol was living it up in stank.'

Jimmy Wilbur had walked into the room. Most of the people were smoking *kif* or eating the black tarry hashish candy so popular with the Moors. The *kif* fumes filled the room, which consisted of nothing much more than a few hammered brass *brazeros* serving as coffee tables, and some straw or leather pouffes. An Arab string orchestra was making cat-squalling sounds in one corner. Carol, stripped to the waist, and wearing baggy Arab pants, was performing a writhing parody of a harem dance, while the other guests clapped hands to the shrilling of the flute.

Jimmy walked into the middle of the floor and stopped Carol's belly-dance by simply grabbing her by one arm and pulling her off balance.

'Put your shirt on, Salome,' he growled. 'We're going home. Not yours, mine.'

'I will not!' Carol screeched. 'I'm having fun with my friends. How can you dare to—'

'Shut up,' Jimmy said, and smacked her hard across the side of the face. 'Where's your shirt? Put it on and come with me or so help me Christ I'll knock you stiff and carry you.'

Carol seemed suddenly subdued. She snatched a blouse off one of the pouffes and was shrugging into it when Monique St. Yves, she of the monocle, became a screeching fury, with both hands clawing at Jimmy's face. Wilbur was impolite. He hit her a short left hook to the jaw and she went down. He walked over and touched her with his toe.

'You're a man,' he said. 'You're a man,' and spat. 'So get up and fight like a man.'

'All in all it was a pretty gaudy evening,' Jimmy said to Craig. 'I ain't had so much fun in a coon's age. I'm kind of old, and a little soft, but by the time the white-helmet boys had arrived, there was very little left standing in this particular bistro. Everything dirty I learned in college football came in handy. I slung Carol over my shoulder—I had to tap her gently on the chin because she was playing on the other team—and took off while the whistles blew. I took her back to the Minzah and stared mean at the elevator boy as if there was nothin' real strange about me coming home with a doll draped around my neck, put her to bed, and called a doctor who gave her something to knock her out. Then . . .'

Carol regained consciousness with a mewing moan.

'Where . . . what . . .'

'Here. With me. Jimmy. I dragged you out of that notch-joint you were doing the shimmy in last night. And I'm dragging you out of this lousy town if I have to slug you again. I'm bigger than you are, little friend.'

Carol dug at her eyes with the backs of her hands.

'I feel awful. I feel just dreadful. I'm dying. I need a drink or a pill or something real bad. Anything, I feel awful. Please get me a drink, Uncle Jimmy. Please get me a drink. My skin's crawling. I itch. Where's the bathroom!' She closed her mouth with one hand and dashed in the direction of his pointed finger. Retching sounds came through the open bathroom door. Carol emerged, presently, her face greenish-white, her forehead dripping sweat. Jimmy handed her a glass of neat whisky with a Perrier chaser. She threw the whisky down in a gulp, took a sip of the water, and pleadingly extended her wavering glass again. Jimmy shook his head.

'Not for a little while, sweetie. Give that last hooker a chance to settle. Go take a hot bath. And a cold shower. Then we'll have another slug of painkiller and go collect your clothes.'

Carol was too weak to argue. She went meekly back into the bathroom and there was a sound of rushing water. After a time she came out wearing a towel bathrobe.

'Can I have the other one now?' she said. 'Please?'

Jimmy handed her another drink. She sipped it slowly, and some colour came back to her face. Her voice was belligerent, as the drink took hold.

'I'm not leaving here. You can't push me around. I don't belong to you. I don't belong to *any*body. I don't . . .'

'You belong to the United States Government as long as you travel on that little green book. If you don't believe me, listen.' Jimmy's voice was harshly cold. He picked up a phone.

'Give me the American Legation,' he said. In a moment, 'Mr. Wilbur calling Mr. Johnston. Yes, that's right, Wilbur. Thanks.'

To Carol. 'Pick up the extension in the bedroom and listen.'

'Hello, Tommy? Fine. Dandy. You? Swell. Look, Tommy, I may need some tax-paid help officially. One of your flock has been acting up and is a kind of bum advertisement for the U.S. in a town even as lousy as this one. Public nuisance kind of thing. Booze, dope consorting with the natives, fags, lesbians, orgies—you know. A complaint from the Mendoub to you would be enough to expel her, wouldn't it? No, I won't mention her name yet. She may decide to go of her own accord. Sure I can furnish the evidence.' Jimmy chuckled. 'If the cops in this town keep a blotter, it's on it.'

There was a drone of voice on the other end.

'Thanks, Tommy. Any time I can do you a favour Stateside, cable. Good-bye.'

He hung up. Carol came out of the bedroom.

'Satisfied?' Jimmy asked her. Her eyelids drooped, she hung her head, and her shoulders trembled.

'So that's what I sound like. Public nuisance.' She jerked her head up and her chin jutted. 'Public nuisance. All right, I'll go.'

'Not in those baggy pants. Wait a minute, and I'll send down for a *djellabab* and a *haik*. You can be a Fatima a little bit longer.'

'So we went and grabbed her things,' Jimmy told Craig. 'I talked her into going to Switzerland for a cure. I stayed with her for a couple of weeks while they sweated her dry. She's on the beam for the moment. But how long will that moment last? She's in London and London is a busy little village, friend. End of report.'

'I don't know, I just don't know,' Craig scrubbed a dispirited hand across pain-squinted eyes. 'Maybe she might get married to somebody and have a baby or so. Short of that I just don't know. In the meantime, it looks like I'm temporarily off the hook.'

'That's great,' Jimmy said. 'That's lovely. How are we off the hook?'

'I dumped Price Mills while you were gone, and went short.'

'I knew it dropped. It didn't have any right to drop. We grossed an extra twelve million bucks last year, and we're going better than ever. What dropped it? Don't tell me. I wish I didn't know already. You unloaded slow and made a strong speech to the press gents, and then after you unloaded and borrowed into a short position, you leaked it that you were going to sell out when you were *already* sold. That would be more than enough to depress it to where you could duck around the corner and pick it up double on the short side. That right?'

'That's right.' Craig did not look at Jimmy Wilbur. He stared at the elephant tusks.

Jimmy got up.

'You crooked son-of-a-bitch. You lousy thieving conniving bastard. I ain't even going to hit you. I got too much respect for my hands. You come a long way from the short pants, Craig Price, and a great deal of it wasn't strictly on the level. But you never were a thief, a lousy stinking thief, before. You're a thief, a lousy thief. Don't talk to me any more.'

Jimmy spun on his heel.

'I quit. This time I really quit.'

He turned back.

'I'm going to have a press conference myself. I'm a stockholder and officer in the company. I got a right to speak my mind. *I* know what shape the company's in, and I plan to emphasize it for the suckers to see. I hope you got enough dough to cover your shorts. Because when Wilbur's story hits the papers, that stock is going to *rise*.'

Craig watched him walk through the door. *There goes me*, he thought, and put his head on his forearms resting on the desk. *There goes me.*

26

JIMMY WILBUR'S press conference started out to be one of the shortest in the history of press conferences. No whisky was served, no canapés offered.

'I wish only to say that this conference is to confirm what Mr. Price announced some months ago. These audits will show that Price Mills showed a gross gain of twelve million dollars in the last fiscal year, and we expect, on present orders, to increase that another five million for this past quarter. I am holding on to my stock and to my position as executive vice-president. Thank you. Good day, gentlemen.'

'You can't just drop it like that, Mr. Wilbur,' the *Times* man said. 'Not if you're doing what I think you're doing. Are you?'

Wilbur whirled.

'Yes. I'm doing what you think I'm doing. I'm doing just what Craig Price did. I'm dumping. But I'm not dumping the mills at peak prices to go short. I'm dumping Craig Price. You can call him Short Price for real this time. And you can tell your readers that Mr. Price, my oldest friend and employer, is going to get stuck, left right outside in the snow, in his shorts.'

The *Herald Tribune* gentleman spoke.

'If I remember anything from the sports pages a long way back, you are Craig Price's best friend. You went to college together. You've worked together for nearly twenty years. You're almost a member of the family. How can you do what you're doing?'

'Because I don't like crooks,' Jimmy Wilbur said flatly. 'Price ran a rigged deck. Sharp business is one thing, but a crook is a crook. Craig Price is a crook. You can quote me. You must know in your business that it ain't real nice to talk up a company's stock while you're unloading, get yourself out, and then poor-mouth the stock down to where your carefully prepared short position lets you take the suckers two ways instead of one. Mr. Price is taking only one sucker, this trip. And that is Mr. Price. Because when that stock rises—and it will rise when this interview hits your papers and the wire services—Mr. Price is stuck. About two million dollars stuck with his short stock. And also, the SEC boys are not going to like it.'

The press gentlemen looked and saw a lean, red-haired man with a broken nose and hotly angry grey eyes. They saw a man who did not offer a drink to the press boys. They saw a man with heartbreak lines around his lips.

'How long have you known Mr. Price?' The Associated Press gentleman asked.

'Since he was fifteen. I pulled a maniac off his back his first night in college. We've been friends since, until now.'

The United Press had sent a sports writer as well as a straight newsman.

'That was the year you made All-American the first time?'

'No. It was the year I made All-American the second time. It was 1931.'

'Where is the ex-Mrs. Price?'

'In Europe.'

'And the daughter?' This was the gentleman from the *Mirror*.

'Also in Europe. Anything concerning Price's family I suggest you ask Price. It is none of my business. My business I consider I have already transacted. The figures I mentioned prove my point. I have no further comments. Just look at the books, gentlemen, inspect the record. Once more, good day.'

He disappeared into the washroom, and the press gentlemen scurried for their offices and their files. It had been a long time since a financial story had any juice in it, and this one was loaded. It had everything—including the daughter, which the wire services took immediate care to cable their European offices to 'UPDIG CAROL PRICE ALLCOSTS ETGET QUOTES UNCLE WILBUR DUMPING TYCOON FATHER IN STOCKRIG SCANDAL ALSO UPPICK EXMISSUS BELIEVE ROME OR RIVIERA SOONEST HOW.'

Sports-writers who had never been closer to a financial story than a sad accounting with their bookmakers suddenly were scourged into the files to exhume data on Wilbur the athlete, and all the *Times, Newsweeks* and *Fortunes* which had covered Craig Price were dragged from the morgue. It was a juicy story, all right, and would remain juicy for many a week.

'Jesus, I'm beat,' Craig said, ripping off his coat and hurling himself into a chair. 'It's nice to be home, darling. Would you make the old man a mint julep?' He heaved a long, gusty sigh. 'Baby, it's hot outside. *And* inside.'

He looked through the wide glass walls at the shimmering lake with its deep green drape of treees. He literally inhaled the view, and then exhaled as Susan brought him his pewter mug of julep. She was wearing pink corduroy matador slacks with a loose white silk blouse. She looked as lovely as the lake.

'I suppose you've been reading the papers.' No question implied. He loosened his necktie and unbuttoned his collar.

'I've been reading the papers.' Her voice was very low, very flat. 'Yes indeed, I've certainly been reading.'

'And?' He looked at her keenly.

'Is it true, Craig? What they say? What Jimmy said? Is it *true*. Craig?'

Craig attempted a feeble grin, and failed.

'I'm afraid so. Yes. I'm afraid Papa got caught this time with his bloomers at half-mast. Short Pants, Jimmy always called me.'

'Don't joke, because I'm not joking. If it's true, I'm leaving you, If it's true I want a divorce, Craig.'

'Oh for Christ's sake, stop talking foolishness.' Craig took a long pull at his drink. 'I got enough trouble already. You read the papers. You know I got enough trouble already. I'm ass-deep in trouble. I got nothing but trouble. I got trouble I never knew I had. Don't you give me any silly business about divorce right now, when I'm beating myself to death trying.'

Susan's face was very pale, her eyes very sad, and her voice very cold.

'I was wrong about you. I thought I was in love with an attractive pirate. I didn't know I was in love with a common thief. I'm still in love with the thief, but I won't live with a thief. I'm getting a divorce, Craig, before I get to be another

677

Maybelle. You don't come home often enough, Craig. You're too busy thinking up ways to steal.'

'That's rather a harsh thing to say to your ever-loving husband. After all, I . . .'

Susan held up her hand.

'I know. You're going to say it's all my fault. If you hadn't divorced Maybelle, if you hadn't jeopardized your financial position with that settlement . . . That's another reason I want a divorce, Craig. I do *not* intend to spend the rest of my life pre-digesting an I-told-you-so routine. Perhaps it *is* my fault. Maybe we started wrong. Certainly I'm as guilty as you. But I don't want that corrosion to make a long dreary tirade out of our marriage, when things go wrong in town and you can't get home *again*.' Her voice was very bitter. 'When you can't get home *again*. I'm no Maybelle, my love.'

'All right, I know you're no Maybelle. I know I'm a bum. But isn't there a clause in the contract which says for better and for worse? Isn't there an old saw about rats leaving sinking ships? I have just had the dagger in the back from my best friend. And now you, too?'

Susan dabbed briefly at her eyes. 'Ask Maybelle,' she said. 'You've had the dagger, as you say, from your best friend for the exact same reason that I am now the rat who is abandoning the sinking ship. Ask Maybelle how it feels to be abandoned. I'm not letting myself up even a little bit. If Jimmy left you, after all these years, how do you think a comparatively fresh acquaintance, a relative stranger, feels about sleeping with a thief? We started wrong, Craig, me grabbing you out of love at some other woman's expense. It never even looked like being right. I'm afraid I was a little love-blind, and possibly a little love-crazy, at the time. But I won't be another Maybelle, and I will not live with a thief. And you're a thief.'

'So I'm a thief. All right. I'm a thief.' Craig's voice was as dull as his eyes. 'Would you get the thief another drink, please? They don't serve juleps in jail.'

He looked at the lake. It didn't seem so pretty any more. It just seemed like a lot of water. The trees, which had appeared as an enormous green velvet curtain, suddenly looked just like trees. He pressed the heels of his palms to his eyes. His head hurt. His lips were very dry, and he felt a terrible constriction of his stomach muscles . . . *the very same*, he thought suddenly, *as at the moment after I killed Jazzbo*. He wrenched himself together and shook his head.

'You can't leave me,' he said, when Susan handed him his drink. 'You *can't*. You're all I've got now. You haven't even seen the start of my troubles. I can smell trouble. This ain't even the first nibble. I need you, Sue.'

'You don't need anybody. Nobody at all. Lonesome Craig

678

Price, the little boy you told me about, has really become the lonesome man. You didn't need Maybelle after you used her. You didn't need Carol, you didn't need Jimmy, and poor thing that I am you don't need me. You'll find another Susan with less scruples. I know how I got you. Another Susan will get you the same way.'

Craig sighed.

'Too much is happening to me. I can't seem to focus. I'm tired. Do you know how a man can go and go and go on his nervous energy, and then just suddenly be awfully, dreadfully, beat-out tired? I'm that man. Beat-up, and my head is solid concrete. There ain't but one me, and there are so many, so *many* other people . . . And now you.' He made his habitual shrug, the shrug which had now become almost a nervous tic. 'And now *you*.'

'Oh, God.' Susan walked over to the window. She whirled suddenly. Her voice shrilled.

'What's wrong with you, Craig Price? What's wrong with you? Why can't you be happy? Why have you got to stretch and strain and grasp and try to have it all? What the hell do you want, anyhow? How can a man with enough money to do anything he wants, keep on driving until you wind up as a common crook? What do you want, the world?'

Craig looked at her almost pleadingly. 'It ain't the money,' he said. 'It ain't money. And I don't know. I *really* don't. I don't know anything. Would you say I was a pathetic case? A sort of misguided egomaniac?'

Susan answered, very seriously, very softly:

'Yes.'

Craig nodded.

'I would too.' He straightened his shoulders and took another drink from his julep mug.

'Maniac, anyhow. You're not fooling about this divorce business? You really feel that strongly about my little caper with the suckers . . . about all this mess in the papers? You're really going off and leave me now?'

'Yes. Better now than later. And later is a certainty. I'm sorry. But later has got to be a cinch. We started wrong. It doesn't figure to get better.'

Craig lifted his scarred eyebrow.

'And now exactly how much money would you want? A million, like Maybelle? Two million? And how much a year?' His mouth curved downward, and his lower teeth showed. 'Two hundred thousand?'

Susan walked over and deliberately slapped him. The little knots of muscle bulged whitely at the corners of his mouth, but his eyes remained coldly impassive.

'I don't want a bloody cent out of you! I wouldn't touch a

stinking nickel of yours—not the way you make it! All I want is my clothes and just to go away. I want to go away and hide and cry and be sorry I . . .'

Craig got out of the chair and walked over to the fireplce. He picked up a heavy iron poker and looked at it curiously, abstractedly.

'I suppose,' he said, 'I ought to beat you up. I'd like to beat you up. I'd like to wrap this thing around your neck. But I keep remembering that other slap story, and tonight I find I'm not much in the mood for wrapping pokers around people's necks.'

His teeth set, and white showed over the top of his eyes. Suddenly, with one mighty surge of triceps and shoulder muscles, he bent the poker into a hoop. He cast the hoop on to the floor. He turned to face Sue.

'I should have stayed a roughneck. I always thought with my muscles. What you can't jump over, bust it or kick it or throw a chair at it. Except now I really got no target. All right. You can't say it wasn't fun at first. I still have Cuba to keep me warm. Am I allowed to stay the night, or must I dash off to my club, like they do in the books. After all, it *is* your house.'

'Oh, Craig, Craig, *Craig!*' Susan almost came into his arms, but held herself back. 'How did it get to be like this, how, why?'

Craig's eyelids dropped. His lips sagged into a weary sneer.

'I'm not a woman,' he said. 'I don't know how a woman thinks. You bought Price as a package. You bought Price, scars, drunk, wife, business and all. You bought bed. You bought fun. You buy, you sell. Buy the package, sell the package. Simple business. Trading. I think I will go into town, now after all. Sure you don't need any money?'

'Don't say money again!' Susan almost screamed. 'I hate the sound of the word!'

'It's a living,' Craig said dryly. 'Other people play pianos or write books. Perhaps I was unfortunately afflicted with a surname. Well, I'm off. I'll send for the clothes, as they do in the brisker Noel Coward comedies. You keep the house, of course. It's the one thing I have that's not likely to be entailed, since it's paid for and you have the deeds.'

'Take the house! Take the house! I don't love our house any more! Take it!' Suddenly tears flooded her face.

Craig walked slowly to the door that let on to the swimming-pool. His eyes swept slowly round the flowers, the trees, the lake, the . . . the house. He patted Sue on the shoulder, as one might console a troubled stranger.

'If you don't want it,' he said, 'you might try burning it down. I've had considerable success with arson.' He bowed, ironically.

'Let me know, my dear, if there's anything you need. I'll be either in New York or Washington. In any case I got lawyers who'll be in touch.'

And so this is how the good ones end, he said to himself as he climbed into the car. 'Let me know, my dear, if there's anything *you need.*' Jesus Christ Almighty, Craig Price, alone again in the uncharted sea, with no lights bright, sir.

Automatically he switched on the windshield wiper, and it was not until the dry wheesh-sheesh of the wiper attracted his attention that he noticed it wasn't raining. It had been a very long time since Craig Price had experienced the luxury of tears.

27

IT was all the so much of a sameness, Maybelle thought, unconsciously remaking her Carolina English into the stiffly translated words of her Pierres and Pepinos. What a boredom, what an *ennui, qué gran aburrimiento. What a pain in the ass,* all of it, she thought. *What a real pain in the ass.*

Of course Pepino had drained her of current money—not much, but a fortune in his limited waiter's mentality—and had gone away, as Pierre had gone away. And then there had been an Emilo and a Mauricio and a Jean-Paul and a Ricardo. There had been a third-category bull-fighter who could get no bookings, and a *flamenco* dancer who had the aspect of being just a touch *maricón*, and Maybelle was doubly annoyed to find him in her bed with a man instead of a girl. There had been the succession of vacation pick-ups; the piazza squatting in Capri usually yields some stout sailor for an evening's entertainment, or some American tourist short on travellers' cheques, some British tourist with only a limited number of spendable pounds abroad.

She had taken a suite in the Alfonso Trece in Sevilla for the *feria*, and had pitched a party every night after the bullfights. She paid for the whisky with enthusiasm, and noticed that the people who flooded the suite and crushed out cigarettes on the rug were the same people she had seen in the Parade in Tangier, the Villa Rosa in Madrid, the Masia in Barcelona, the Canne á Sucre in Paris, the Hostería dell'Orso in Rome, the Jungle Club in Cannes—late, that would be—and all the casinos where people gambled where gambling was allowed.

It was a terrible, horrible, awful world, she thought, for a woman alone—a world of concierges and taxis and ships and airports and taxis and always the same smile, as a benevolent shark might inspect a prospective supper.

'Ah, *oui*, Madame Price. But of course, Madame Price. Naturally, Madame Price. But certainly, Madame Price. So nice to have you back again, Madame Price.' The teeth bared, waiting for the entrée.

The politeness covered: Oh, so the old trout's back with a

new boyfriend. Wonder what this one is, waiter, chauffeur, or pansy? They seem to drift more to pansies when they hit that age. But I'll say one thing for this particular old misery. She pays well for what she gets.

'*Mais ou, Madame. Mais certainement, Madame.* We have placed M'sieu on the same floor, in case you should need him in an emergency. We have given you your favourite suite— 704-5-6, and M'sieu is just at the corner of the corridor.'

(With a door that opens in 704-5-and-6, in case you need him in the night, Madame. *Merci* for your filthy American money, you old bug, and I would rather be down here taking it than up there with you earning it in a more difficult fashion. At least all I have to do here is smile, and teeth are cheap. I really don't know how these young *maquereaux* have the courage to embark on such a distasteful livelihood. I'd rather scrub latrines. *Mais oui, certainement, Madame. Comme vous voulez.* We will adjust the furnishings immediately. Flowers have been sent by the manager, who is delighted to have you back with us again. The bidet'll be stopped up tomorrow no later than four p.m., but that's the business of the afternoon porter, not mine, thank God.)

Maybelle woke unwillingly. She had gone to bed naked, and the nightgown carefully laid across the turned-down bed was tucked under her chin. She had slept on top of the sheets, and her back complained of the crinkles. Her lips were dry, and although she tried going back to sleep with her head under the pillow, her legs spread and her arms trailing off the bed-edges, she found herself in the limbo between slumber and awakeness with the dreams half-formed, and the echo of last night's song running endlessly, like a squirrel on a treadle, through her head. Her eyes wept gratuitous tears, and felt grainy from last evening's cigarette smoke and too much booze after dinner, which had embraced too much wine, which came after too many martinis, which she had taken to repair the too many brandies after lunch, which had been preceded by too much wine with lunch, which had been foreshadowed by too many screwdrivers before lunch, which of course had been prefaced by too many getting-up shots before she could face the day.

She finally decided to get up, but her legs refused to co-operate, and she almost fell as she tottered into the bathroom and reached shaking fingers for a mighty draught of soda-bicarb and turned on the tub. She chased the bicarb with a neat shot of whisky, and rang down to the bar for her breakfast —vodka, ice and orange juice—and after the usual morning bowel function felt a little better, not much, but some. The ice-cold juice with the tasteless vodka moistened the parched lips and seemed to unswell her tongue to a point where her gums didn't hurt when she brushed her teeth. By now the bath was over-lapping into the drain.

It was a morning that might occur after the fifth waiter, the seventh chauffeur, the twentieth chic resort town, the ninetieth excuse about settling down somewhere and finding herself—I'll read, I'll write, I'll paint, as soon as I find my nest—Maybelle looked at herself with disgust. In a rare burst of morning honesty she said aloud as she towelled herself:

'I'm a cracker kid from a cracker town. Everything I got I buy. None of the Dagoes give a good goddam about anything but money. I ain't too bad to look at still, but every time I hit the hay I'm buying it like a reverse English whore. Not even a lousy waiter would lay me if there wasn't money in it for him. Not even a chauffeur, not even a pick-up in a bar, not even nobody. Take away Barclays Bank and I couldn't hustle a free cup of coffee from a stranger. If this is living it up in Europe I wish I was back home in Kensington.' The thought depressed her further.

She poured herself another stiff shot and lay naked back on a chaise longue, and gave herself up to morning alcoholic loneliness. She thought of all the women she knew in Rome and Paris and on the Riviera—fattish, forty-fiftyish, enough money, all with a boy friend, some even married to the boy friends, and all, in the end, cheated and lonely and miserable and pretending gaiety when mostly they would have preferred a blue-checked apron, a fat dull husband, and the eventful days when their grown children phoned to ask if Granny would come and baby-sit the kids so they could catch a night out. The thought of children forced her mind to Carol.

'My God,' she said, sitting suddenly upright. 'Carol and I are both in the same boat. Both thrown away, both bums. Difference is that I'm an old bum, and Carol is a young, pretty bum. But bums right on. Who would want to marry Carol except the kind of trash that she runs with—the busted-ass *principés* and the long-haired half-fags who'd do anything for a shot at Carol's dough?'

She got up and went to the bathroom to choose a couple of benzedrines, which she washed down with another straight shot of scotch. Pills. Pills to pep you up, pills to calm you down, pills to keep you awake, pills to put you to sleep, pills to wake you up, to pep you up, to calm you down, to wake you up, to pep you up, to calm you down, to wake you up, to put you to sleep . . .

And shots. Shots of B-1 in the behind to knock down the alcoholic fatigue. Shots to stir your whisky-bored liver into false enthusiasm. Shots against this, shots in favour of that, always with your girdle hiked up and some stranger plunging a spear into your can. I'll bet more strangers have seen my tail from a purely business aspect than ever looked at an old whore's anatomy. I got more needle wounds than a hophead, but thank God I haven't taken up the main charges yet. Whisky is good enough for Maybelle. Whisky and the pills and the shots in the All-American ass. What town am I in? Oh, *Rome*. I guess I'll drag myself together and go over to the Snakepit and see what else is cooking, what else is scandalous, and if there's anybody new in town . . .

Maybelle braced herself with an effort and made the first mighty move to climb into her clothes. She couldn't seem to put anything down. Morning catarrh racked her, and once she thought she would throw up, but concentrated against it and didn't. *She couldn't seem to put anything down.* She had lit a cigarette which fetched further coughs, and she roamed the room with a handkerchief in one hand, the cigarette package in the other, the lighter still clutched in the smoking hand, and looked desperately about her at a selection of clothes. *What would we wear today to go nowhere*?

Always the black, darling, she said, always the white gloves, darling, always the little silver-blue mink or the little grey mink or the little almost-black mink or the honey mink or the white mink for night, always the goddam picktoed shoes that had made the bunion popular again, the spike-heeled goddam shoes that got caught in cracks or gratings in the sidewalks and made you fall down when you least wanted to, and always the goddam girdles. There must be easier ways to keep your behind from wobbling. You haul up the butt-bracer by main force and take a deep breath and nail it home with the side zipper which don't zip all the way and wiggle until it snugs down and then you button on the detachable crotch—ugh—and then you draw on the stockings that run if you breathe on them and ease them, careful, girl, *ease* them up over your legs which you have had to shave because you forgot—face it, you were too stiff—to go and get the wax treatment and you cut yourself shaving, that's a laugh, ha-ha, cut yourself shaving, and then you cut yourself again shaving when you mowed the bristles in the armpit—the two nastiest words in the English language are armpit and de-tachable crotch—and you mustn't forget the Stink-O-No against body odour, any more than you must forget the bidet or the whirling douche so a girl can be sweet all *over*, inside and outside, or the chlorophyll pills—pills again—to make your breath as sweet as newmown garlic—pardon, to remove the stench of last night's garlicky dinner and replace it with the stench of newmown mouthwash—and now you grope blindly backward for the garter tabs and hope to hell you make it on the first try, because the stockings have seams and should be straight, but you don't put on the shoes yet, the goddam shoes because they hurt and that's the last thing you put on.

Might as well swish into the pettiskirt, and that's one more thing out of the way, and the bra as well, and you're reasonably armoured against the day, but now you really need another drink and those bennies aren't biting as fast as they used to, maybe better take another benzedrine because now it's the fingernails and the lips and the eyes and the pancake and the hair.

What first? Fingers, maybe, and while they dry I'll have another little bitsy drinkee and then maybe the bennies will have taken hold and I will have the courage to paint my eyelids blue and turn them up at the corners and get all that black crap on to my lashes and lay on six inches of pancake and then take the little brush in the now-oh-so-steady hands and make myself a new mouth, pink? Or was that last year? No. Deep red. I ain't got the face for pale lips. Red as a fox's you-know-what in choke-cherry time. Careful, now girl, very careful. A new upper lip. *There*. *Olé*. Hurrah for me. Slight fullness to the underlip. Mmmmhmmm. Done. Now the earrings. Where did I put the goddam earrings when I went to bed last night? Oh I know. I put the goddam earrings with the goddam watch and goddam bracelets and the goddam rings. But *where*? I knew I put them all together somewhere special so I wouldn't forget where I put them and . . . Hooray! I put them in the goddam soapdish and put the soap on the night table to remind me of why the goddam soap wasn't in the goddam soapdish so I would wonder about it and go look and there would be the goddam earrings and goddam bracelets and goddam watch and goddam rings and goddam all in the goddam soapdish. *What* a clever girl. Girl this clever deserves another drink because there is still perfume and hankie and hair—oh God, what a mess, six colours and all of them phony, I think I'll dye it purple and leave it alone, these streaks are driving me mad, and I haven't got the face for a severe one, I look like somebody's collie, or a spaniel, anyway.

Now what have I forgot. Perfume, yes. Think maybe this is a nice day for *Femme*. What, no *Femme*? I suppose I left it in Cannes. What does this say, in this bottle? Can't read the print. Where are the bloody glasses? Oh hell, slosh it on and hope for the best. Smell the wrist. Not bad. That's Balmain Vent Vert. Sprinkle a little around the ears and then the earrings, now, the big crusty ones, and clamp on the bracelet, it weighs a frigging ton, so that means no gloves, doesn't it, well that's one item less, no dammit better carry them anyhow, and now that great big vulgar brooch on the left tit—mustn't say tit, girl, not nice, ladies don't use words like that—Now, count off. Shoes, girdle, detachable crotch, stockings, brassière, pettiskirt, legs shaved, armpits shaved, pancake on, lipstick on, eye-shadow on, eye-brows on, eyelashes on, rings on, bracelets on, earrings on—there is nothing I can do with this hair, better wear a hat—what else? Oh, almost forgot.'

Dress, *Not* on yet.

Little black. Always the little black. Why is there never a *big* black? Or can't pin big vulgar brooch to left tit, mustn't say tit. Naughty. Breast horried word too. Better have 'nother little drinkee before pin brooch on dress haven't put on yet. *Why* put on dress? Dreamed I went to Snakepit in my Maidenform bra. Better put on dress. Rome very formal town. Pope and all. Take deep breath. Ooosh! Dress on Lipstick smears? No. Lucky. Now question how zip up back. Ring bell. Call maid, less trouble than breaking arm trying hook top hook. *Buon giorno*, maid. *Per favore*, hook dress, and swirl around. *Grazie molto*, maid. *Ragazza*.

Now. Pocketbook. Must check pocketbook. Lessee. Little black suede pocketbook go with the little black dress. Lessee. Two hankies. Little Kleenex, got slight cold, nose red? Look see nose red? No. Nose not red, but got hickey on chin. Better touch up.

What else? Tampax, check. Little late this month. Chequebook? Never know when might need money. Oh, money. Must have money, pay taxi, buy drinks, maybe take somebody lunch. Get money from nice man downstairs. *Remember: Get money* nice man downstairs. Spectacles? So that's where they were. Need them read newspapers after lunch unless have lunch nice accidental fellow. Then probably won't need read newspapers. Lipstick? *Si, signora.* Compact? *Si, bella donna.* Oh, address book. Almost forgot. And memo pad. Things do afternoon when shops open must go by bank Thomas Cook buy new gloves. Maybe new frock. Could do with little morale lifting. Definitely, new frock, *not* little black frock. Keys room. Where? Other pocketbook, maybe. Yes. Now keys. *Tsk.* Almost forgot lighter, cigarette case. Naturally empty. Fill. Oh. Pills. Where the hell is . . . Other pocketbook. Lessee. Dexedrine, dramamine, benzedrine, Miltown . . . Check.

What coat? Eenie-meenie-minie moe. Silver-blue stole. There. Hat, ass, and overcoat, as Pa used to say. Ready for the world. World is my oyster. *Must remember get money nice man downstairs.* Figure little slipping, face little tired, but got greatest credit. Little broke on the money comes in every year, but can always borrow against my mad money. Got more mad money anybody. Got million dollars mad money. No girl got walk home got million mad money. Good old Craig, like song say, Mummy and Daddy standing by. In pinch could always borrow from dutiful daughter. Carol. Always help old mother in trouble. Don't believe in being burden to children. Not nice mother be burden to children. Better have one little shot for road. Wow! All ready, Maybelle, pretty Maybelle, nice legs, good figure, nice little black dress, latest goddam picktoed wop shoes. Let's go meet the world.

'Good afternoon, Madame Price,' the frock-coated smiling gentleman at the cash desk said. 'May I serve you?'

'Yes, please,' Maybelle smiled. 'A hundred thousand lire will do nicely. See. I have a very small bag, so you'd better give them to me in big bills, but with enough change for the taxi. I'm only just going first to the Excelsior and then to Capriccio's. Thank you.'

She stuffed the bills into her pocketbook and stopped off to greet the concierge.

'Good afternoon, Madame,' he said. 'Permit me to say you look ravishing.'

'Thank you, Carlo,' she said. 'Any mail?'

'I'm sorry to say, no, Madame Price. If there is any while you are out I will send it to the suite.'

She walked into the upstairs bar of the hotel—sometimes called the Snakepit—and was met smilingly by a Giovanni and bowed to a table. Everyone in the room except a couple of bewildered tourists was wearing dark glasses. Nearly all the men had their jackets thrown round their shoulders, with the sleeves hanging free. The 'models' draped against the bar stood like models, their hips braced angularly, their tiny pointed shoes turned outward from one instep. Most of them still wore a very pale lipstick and a hair-do which appeared to have been ploughed up on purpose. The gentlemen were mostly lean, moustached, ravaged-faced, with very short coats rayed in broad stripes. Most wore sweaters under their jackets. Bella Roma can be the coldest city in the world, and its *bella figura* —show of good face—the phoniest.

One of the young gentlemen had recently been involved in a narcotics scandal, since the bored upper classes of the Holy City have not been unknown to leaven their boredom with an occasional shot of the real horse. Half of the 'models' on display were professional whores. Almost to a person the Italians were drinking Campari or Cinzano. Whisky and gin cost too much. The gabble resembled a congress of geese.

Maybelle looked around her. If it weren't such a dreary, grey, drizzling day, she would have preferred to go outside and sit on the Via Veneto, and watch the people. People-watching in front of Doney's was a feast of fun, because Maybelle had learned to stare frankly, rudely, as the Italians did, and a drama a moment was always happening on the Via Veneto.

The wicker chairs were comfortable, and if you sat long enough in front of Doney's you'd see everybody you knew in Rome. The pre-lunch promenade, the pre-cocktail stroll, was as much a part of the city's ritual as the clanging church bells.

After they finished the ogling walk, the tarts, the film people, the sort of undefined people, generally wound up in the Snakepit, the bar of the Excelsior. Odd scraps of conversation at the bar made provocative listening:

'And she said to this girl, come off it, darling, I was an old whore before you were born . . .'

'And when they got Filo at the border, and found him with about a kilo of cocaine, they asked: "What's this for?" And Filo said, proudly, he *is* a prince, you know: "*uso personale*." '

'And believe it or not, Lorenzo had Anna in one room, his wife in another, Gloria in another, and Maria in still another. *All on the same floor.*'

'You know the one with the little white dogs? My dear, the manager told me this. Every time she has a man she tears the sheets to shreds, but to shreds. And he told me this, too. He found out what the case of champagne they ordered every morning was for. And not for drinking. Give you one guess.'

'Italian men are really impossible. All they do is lie around in dirty shorts and talk about what great lovers they are, but in bed they're hopeless. I've let the last Dago up my stairs. Once they're up you can't get them out.'

'You know why he lost the job? He had three separate women pregnant at the same time, he had embezzled most of the firm's loose cash, and his wife was taking dope. But she was pregnant too.'

'It wasn't *my* baby, but I felt sorry for the poor girl. I paid her fare back to the States, and arranged to have the child adopted through a doctor I know. Everything was fixed, but damn me if at the last minute she didn't kidnap the child and catch a plane right back to Rome again. That's the last good turn I'll ever do.'

'I always thought that Betty was the lesbian, but she wasn't. It was the other one, whatshername, Olivia.'

'Ostia Antica has certainly gone off. Cheap people. So has Fregene. Cheaper people.'

'I think Ischia is so much more rugged these days than Capri.'

'Every time I go to Bricktop's I feel a hundred years old. You never see any kings there any more.'

'So the man said: "Shut up and let the poor kid sing", and when they didn't—they were English tourists and arguing about the high cost of Players, or something—he just picked up his table and slung it at them. They paid up and left. He was a very big man, and looked terribly fierce.'

'Dropped dead right in the lobby, my dear. Of course everybody knew that heart wasn't going to last forever. What *she'll* do, I haven't a clue. They hadn't a bean.'

'Has Tibby gone into retreat? I haven't seen her for ages.'

'No. She *says* she's painting. Actually she's got a new boy friend and is frightened to produce him in public. I believe she keeps him chained to the bedstead. You know Tibby. Once she's cottoned on to a good lurk . . .'

' "I don't drink at all, my deah," she says to me, and then she knocks off two fiascos of white wine. And then she wonders why her eyeballs are pale gold, and why she throws up every morning.'

'Do you think Roberto's serious about that Indian woman? They look so *sallow*.'

'No, but they say the world well lost for love is bloody well lost for nothing. He was always a bum, anyhow. Ask any of his women. Ask his cousin. Ask *me* . . .'

'There must be *some* men left somewhere. All the ones I seem to meet these days are in love with each other. The other night in Cannes, I swear, this French singer was swapping tongues with his boy friend on the dance floor.'

'You sure ain't kiddin', baby. In Paris the other night in some dive I made my chick go to the loo with me. I was afraid to go by myself.'

'Well, hell, one of these big lizzies made a pass at my dame, and I finally got tired of it and knocked her flat. Evidently she had a short word with the bartender later and I got fed the fastest, roughest mickey I ever heard about. I spent the next week in the bathroom, and my guts felt like they were entertaining a litter of wildcats.'

. . . Then the long pause, and conversation stops. Everybody gets up and goes to Capriccio's or George's for lunch. Nobody has ever explained satisfactorily why it all stops at the same time, but it is the moment of truth when the waiters arrive with the check.

She paused at the kiosk across the Veneto, noticing how lovely the violets were in the little plaza, and bought the papers to take to lunch. There was a quiet snug corner, just as you walked up the stairs, to the right, at Capriccio's, where you could lean back and people would slide past you in a heedless tide. A girl could put on her glasses there and read the papers without feeling so desperately conspicuous, as if she were seated in the middle of the big room. There had been nobody in the Snakepit— nobody at all—who looked worth lunching with.

She ploughed through the back page of the *Mail* to see what Tanfield had to say, and she whipped through William Hickey in the *Express*, to see what he had to say, and she read the America column on page two, and after she had finished Li'l Abner and Pogo on the back page of the Paris *Herald-Tribune*, she turned to the front pages. Same stuff. Atom. Eisenhower. Macmillan. Algeria. Russia. Nasser. Another cabinet losing its pants in France. Strikes, yes. A new look in clothes. The pansies are loose again. Goddam pansies like goddam spikeheeled, picktoed shoes.

'*Industrialist Divorced by Socialite.*'

Must be a big shot to make the front page, Maybelle thought. Mostly they keep it in the gossip columns.

'Waiter,' she called. 'Just bring me some antipasto and a bowl of soup. And a small bottle of Valpolicella. I'm not really hungry.' She smiled apologetically and reached for the paper again. Then it hit her.

'Craig Price, multimillionaire head of Mastodon Investments Inc., Ltd., banker, oilman, insurance mogul, was divorced today by Mrs. Susan Strong Price in Cuernavaca, Mexico, on ground of incompatibility. Mr. Price was formerly married to Maybelle Grimes, whose father owned a textile mill in Kensington, N.C. where Mr. Price first worked as a young man. The first Mrs. Price is living temporarily in Europe, where she has a villa in Villefranche. She has custody of their only child, Carol. It is reported that there was no financial settlement, although Mr. Price's last divorce from Mrs. Maybelle Grimes Price was regarded as the steepest divorce settlement since the parting of Mr. and Mrs. (Bobo) Winthrop Rockefeller. The first Mrs. Price received an outright payment of one million dollars, plus a reputed $100,000 a year in alimony.

'Cheap bastard,' Maybelle murmured. 'Didn't give this poor Strong dame a dime. But maybe'—she smiled slyly into her wineglass—'maybe he didn't have a dime left to give her. How do you like a guy like that? Don't love me and gives me a mess of money. Loves her and don't give her a damn dime. How do you like a guy like that?'

'Mr. Price was involved two years ago in a tragedy in which he accidentally shot and killed his chauffeur-companion, Herbert Hoover Lincoln (Jazzbo) Newton, aged ...'

'I would have liked to have shot a few of my chauffeur-companions,' Maybelle said, 'especially the last bastard, Ricardo.' She read on.

'Self-made man,' the *Trib* said.

'I'll say. Screwed himself into a fortune,' Maybelle said. 'Screwed himself out of one, too. Waiter! half-bottle of Valpo—valpoli—the same thing I've been drinking.'

'Decorated for distinguished service during the war,' the *Trib* said.

'And he should have been, too,' Maybelle said, 'he serviced every woman in Washington when he was earning his battle stars in the Pentagon. And me home alone as usual because of the housing shortage.'

'Mr. Price has recently attracted the attention of the Securities and Exchange Commission, concerning certain activities of his insurance company and the investment trust which he controls. He was also a heavy stockholder in the recent purchase of the ...'

Maybelle poured a fresh glass of wine and drained it in a gulp. 'Bastard's stretched out too thin,' she said to the bottle.

690

'Way too thin. Never knew man wanted so much everything. Why? Don't know. Only thing never wanted was his wife and daughter. Pretty wife, charming daughter. Dinwaneither.'

'Mr. Price was not available for comment,' the *Trib* concluded.

'They ought to come see me,' Maybelle said. '*I'd* be available for comment if they could only print it.'

She asked the waiter for a brandy and coffee. A woman she knew, an English divorcée, came from the other end of the café and paused at Maybelle's table.

'Hullo, sweetie. On your own, eh?' she said. She was a blonde, ten-pounds-overweight, formerly beautiful woman, of forty-five. 'Where's the last . . . what's his name, Ricardo, wasn't it, mind if I sit down and have a coffee?'

'Sure, Pam. Fall down. I just been sitting here reading about my husband. Ricardo? You tell me what happened to Eduardo and we can save ourselves an awful lot of time. Better yet let's *don't* talk about Eduardo or Ricardo. Brandy?' Pamela nodded.

As the waiter brought another coffee and another brandy, Maybelle said. 'Leave the bottle.'

'Well, sweetie, here's most enormous cheers,' Pamela said.

'You know, you ought to lose a little weight. Don't say it, I know it. Me too. Why don't we go to that place in Montecatini and take a cure? Hit the wagon and get pretty again. So the boys'll like us. The Ricardos and Eduardos . . .'

' . . . the Ricardos and Eduardos,' Pamela said. 'I am definitely off men, especially Italians. Also I'm having money trouble again. Eduardo bought a Ferrari when I was momentarily overcome with generosity, and now my funds haven't come through, something to do with getting the money out of Kenya, the trustees, bastards all, wrong address, possibly, but there's an overdraft and I was wondering if . . .'

'*No.* I'm broke myself. Ricardo . . .'

'But sweetie, I know about the enormous settlement your first gentleman landed you with. You *can't* be in trouble for cash.'

'No. Goddammit, no. I don't touch that money. I don't like that money enough to use it. It ain't money, it's . . . The hell with it. How much do you need?'

'A hundred quid would do me beautifully until my bank . . .'

'Okay. I got to go to Cook's later, Barclays is closed, and I'll get it for you. Credit I got, anyhow, because they read the papers, too.'

'I say, you are a darling. I'll pay it you back as soon as . . .'

'Yeah, I know. You'll pay it me back'—Maybelle exaggerated the English phrasing—'you'll pay it me back when I remarry this character in the papers. Mainly you'll duck me when I walk in here, honeychile, and you'll change your drinking habits until I move off to some place else.'

Basic business settled, Pamela was prepared to be interested.

'What's this about your ex?'

'He's ex-ed himself again. Evidently pretty smart girl, this girl. Evidently pretty nice girl. *She* left *him*. With me, other way around. Pretty dumb girl, too. Says here in paper didn't take him for a stinking nickel.'

'Silly bitch,' Pamela said. 'When I marched out on Roddy I . . .'

'I know, I know. Don't tell me again. You've told me. You were bored, and you couldn't stand him near you any more, and in any case you had this boy friend around the corner, but once he'd spent your money he . . . Christ. Let's have our faces lifted too, when we take the cure. I'll pay. I'll have more money then. Craig's very punctual about sending it, and obviously this girl didn't cost him a dime. Cheap bastard. What am I saying? Craig's a cheap bastard? Can't be. Gave me a million to get rid of me, always sends the fifty thousand on time, why didn't he give her some money, too? Poor girl. No money. Probably have to go work in a store some place. Feet hurting all day long, no money to buy clothes . . . Have 'nother brandy.'

'Of course, darling. But we mustn't get ourselves too jolly before we go to Cook's, must we?'

'Don't worry about your lousy hundred pounds. Worry about this poor girl. Divorced my husband and ain't got a cent. Kicked out into the snow. Turned out of house. And me sitting here Rome lending you money while this poor girl riding subways, living furnished room, all account that son-uv-a-bitch Price. This time when get hair dyed again going to get dyed all over, *and* face fixed. You getting flabby around the chin, kid.'

'They do it easily, I'm told. They make two little cuts behind your your ears, or someplace, and sort of draw your skin-muscles tight.'

'You know wellsme a skin ain't got any muscles,' Maybelle said. 'What they do is graft. They take skin off your ass and put it on your face, or take skin off your face and put it on your tits. Hell, I don't know, but let's do it, anyhow. 'Nother brandy?'

'No, thank you very much.' Pamela was nobly firm. 'Must get on to Cook's mustn't we? Also the head waiter is looking very sour. Most displeased. Two ladies overstaying leave.'

'Oh, all right. I got to go to the john. You need it?'

'No. I've been.'

'Okay. Giulio!'

'Yes, Madame?' The voice was suavely insulting.

'Check. *Il conto*. And don't take all day. I got to go to the . . .'

'But of course, Madame. The check will be here when you have . . .' His voice melted away.

'Christ, I hate Italians,' Maybelle said. 'All Italians. Pamela, go see if you can get the boy to find us a taxi. We mustn't be late for Thomas Cook's and your hundred pounds . . .'

God, what a long day, she thought. She had been to Cook's, she had been to the Hosteria dell' Orso, she had started in to drink with Pamela at the Blue, and they'd been joined by two ever-so-nice young Englishmen who hadn't any money, and in a flush of alcoholic exuberance, they had progressed upward to the eating room and then to the Cabila and then on to Brick-top's and finally to some cellar somewhere and now back home to . . . what? Damn Amadeo. Close the bar early again. But fine fellow, Amadeo. Wife, sixteen children, worked ninety hours a day, but damn fool closed bar. Lonesome, Maybelle said. What I am is lonesome, too. Like that poor girl Price kicked out of house. Like probably Carol lonesome. Like everybody, everywhere, lonesome. Must be some place people ain't lonesome. Where? Go there, take villa, me and this woman Strong be room-mates, have Carol come visit, all girls lonesome together. Poor girl, kicked out in snow by sonbitch Price. No fair give me all money kick poor girl out in snow starve.

She picked up the telephone.

'Want manager. Now. I know it's late. Still want manager. Very important. Look, you stupid Dago bastard, I don't care if he's in bed with Lizzie Borden, I want manager! Now!'

The manager, a Swiss, was not entirely unaccustomed to being routed from his bed at any hour. It was a hotel that catered to moving picture people, and semi-permanent transients. The manager was proud of that phrase 'semi-permanent transients'. The manager had once seen a minister from one of the darker colonies throw a night-lady through a plate glass door, and had remarked that he would not be surprised if somebody once complained because a dead giraffe failed to fit into the lift.

'Yes, Mrs. Price?' the manager said. 'Is there some trouble? Something I can do?' The manager's face was seamy with sleep. He was wearing trousers and a dressing-gown and rather seedy slippers.

'You betcha,' Maybelle said. 'Sit down have drink Junior, call boy send ice. Gonna make new will. Want witness. Comp' witness. Bellboy come ice, make him sign too.'

'Mrs. Price, Mrs. Price, this is no time to make a will. It's three-thirty in the morning and . . .'

'Don't tell me when time make will not make will. I pay bill every week. I know when want make will don't want make will. Want witness. Get night porter, want two witness. Want make will right goddam now after take off goddam picktoed wop shoes. Get night porter bring ice. What kind service we got this hotel where pay bill every week, tip everybody?'

The manager shrugged. He called the night porter for ice, and when the porter came, he mixed Mrs. Price a drink, and then decided he'd have one himself. Christ, he thought, the way you must earn a living. I have seen it all. I have seen the dopers and the crazies and the furniture smashers and the

693

commuters and the people with the rocks in their suitcases and nearly all of it, but I have made no wills at 3.45 a.m. before for drunken American ladies. I should have stayed in Bern.

'Yes,' he said soothingly, to Maybelle. 'Shall we make our will now and then go to sleep?'

'Absolutely. Pen ink in desk. No don't go night porter want two witnesses will. More legal that way. Know awful lot 'bout law. Had very smart husband, sonbitch. Write down.

' "I, Mrs. Maybelle Grimes Price, give all money I got Mrs. Susan Strong Price, until death do us part. I leave one dollar fifty-seven cents to my daughter Carol Price—" ' she leered at the manager—'don't think you can fox me on that one. "I leave one dollar fifty-seven cents my daughter Carol Price, and I leave one dollar fifty-*six* cents my ex-husband Craig Price. I now leave front competent witness one million dollars Mrs. Susan Strong Price, ex-wife ex-husband. Money Union Bank, Zurich, Switzerland." Write down, Mrs. ex-Price say this no joke, but all girls together, sisters under skin, want somebody get some good money, want other ex-Mrs. Price have some fun not work in department store. Write don't give damn daughter Carol she got plenty money anyhow. Write thing about sound mind. Mind sound enough know you need new pair of slippers, it's Tuesday morning, nearly four o'clock, and night porter stupid sonbitch. Write will.'

The manager scribbled away, and Maybelle had another drink.

'Read loud,' Maybelle said. The manager read an abridged version.

'Good 'nough. Sound and legal. I sign. You sign. Dumb sonbitch night porter sign. *Bene.* Now, here's passport. Put in passport. Put passport in office. Now get hell outamyroom.'

Maybelle went to sleep with most of her clothes on, but her mind was clear. She and Judy O'Grady were sisters under the skin, in any case poor girl not out in snow. Not like Maybelle was out in Roman snow working fingers bone.

Then Maybelle woke up. Brain said Maybelle out in snow too. Maybelle working fingers bone. Maybelle dry-mouthed parchlipped. Maybelle lonely all alone bed out in snow. She had a moment of peculiar luminous drunken clarity, then.

What was all that damfoolishness about making a will with manager and the night porter when I was drunk? What do I care about this dame of Craig's? Oh God, she thought, how would you get yourself on such a lonesome road that even drunk you'd make a will leaving your money to a dame that took your husband and that you don't even know? How far down that lonesome road, Maybelle, how far, where you are willing to lend an English slut a hundred pounds just so you can do something with your time? Drunk you were, drunk you've been, and

your body's accepted every waiter, chauffeur, tourist, pick-up . . .
Oh God. It's night and there's nobody in bed but me and I've
got the awful-awfuls and there's no place to go until one p.m.
tomorrow and nobody loves me and my feet are cold and I'm
getting older, getting fatter, and it'll probably rain again and
where, oh where, will I go next? Oh God, Maybelle. Maybe a
drink. Always that helps. Always got drink.

My God. Bottle empty. Forgot buy extra. Too late now.
Stupid night porter hasn't got keys to bar. Hopeless.

I wonder if I could have been happy with Craig? I wonder if I
would have loved Carol better if Craig hadn't put her in my
belly as part of his business? I wonder what it would be like if
I wasn't so stupid? I wonder what it would be like if Craig hadn't
left me in the first place? I wonder if Craig had any real fun
with this Strong woman I wrote the will in favour of? I wonder
if Craig ever had any fun with me? Answer: No. He married a
mill. I wonder if any time I ever got laid I was being laid because somebody was interested in screwing *me* and not in my
goddam money?

That's a joke. Of course it was always the goddam money. I
wonder if I'm really me? I wonder if I'm going on buying
Ricardos and Pierres and then wind up maybe taking dope and
being the top queen of all the busted pansies? I wonder if it's
going to rain tomorrow? I wonder if I'll have cancer? I wonder
if I'll get run over and my back will be busted or something will
happen to my eyes and I'll go blind? I wonder if the atom bomb
is poisoning us all? I wonder if I'm pregnant from Ricardo?
That would be *real* nice.

God, I don't know, I don't know I don't know I don't know. I
wish it was morning. I wish I could sleep. The only time I can
sleep is when I'm drunk or full of pills or when I used to get
laid long enough. Nobody in this bed. Nobody in this bed but
me and a nothing behind all of it. I wonder what made me make
that will to this Strong woman that married my guy and now
she's out in the snow on her ass, too? I wonder what I had in
mind, how do you get that drunk, was it that English bitch
Pamela sent me off, who, who, what, why?

I don't know.

She got out of bed and snapped on the light the manager had
very carefully turned off when he left with the will and passport.
She went to the desk and searched for the ink and pen and
paper they had used to write the drunken will. She sat down and
began to write:

'To whom it may concern: I Maybelle Grimes Price, divorced
wife of Craig Price, wish to say again that the last will and
testament I committed on this day at this hour three forty-five
a.m. of sound mind and in full possession of all my faculties.

I wish to restate that the will I made was signed by the manager of this hotel and the night porter, and that I wish all the worldly goods I own be given to Mrs. Susan Strong Price, former wife of my ex-husband, Craig Price, and that all terms of the witnessed will be carried out to the letter, including the bequests to my husband and daughter. I wish to say that I am 42, have a mole just beneath my left breast, and would like to leave an exact fifteen per cent in tips to the servants of this hotel. I would like the title to my house in Villefranche to pass to Mrs. Susan Strong Price.

Signed
Mrs. Maybelle Grimes Price.'

Then Maybelle went to the bathroom and counted out seventeen of the pills you took to put you to sleep.

28

JIMMY WILBUR'S story smote the front pages with a splash like a boulder suddenly toppled into a lake. After the first splash, the ripples spread. The headlines said: *'Multimillionaire Rigs Stock Coup.' 'Price Forbidden Stock Trading Pending Investigation.' 'SEC Smacks Price.' 'Price Signs Consent Decree Against Future Fraud.' 'SEC Banned From Insurance Business.' 'SEC Demands Accounting Mastodon Investment Trust.' 'Mastodon Crumbles as Price Unable to Meet Run.' 'Price Building Under Government Hammer.'*

Up she went, Craig thought. Down she goes.

'Yes, Mr. Smathers,' he said politely to the SEC gentleman.

'We have no alternative, Mr. Price. Your recent unpleasant publicity on the Price Mills stock transaction, and the necessary steps we have been forced to take—the injunction against bond-and-share trading, the consent degree you signed voluntarily, your problems with the Bureau of Internal Revenue—have created what might be called a run on your resources in the Mastodon Investment Corporation.

'Under the Act, as you very well know, you are bound to prove fluidity. Your entire deposits total four hundred and fifty million dollars. A sacred trust, Mr. Price. Can you prove yourself fluid in that amount?'

'No,' Craig said. 'Christ, no. Do you know anybody else in the world who can, including the United States Government?'

'That is well apart from the point. Under the Act, we have no choice but to order you to liquidate your physical assets under the direction of our conservators. You will be served with an order

696

to turn over your cash assets, and to dispose of your holdings under our direction.'

'My cash assets are not considerable,' Craig said. 'You may have read in the papers that I was able to cover very little of my short position before you enjoined me from stock trading. You may also have noticed that shares in Price Mills, Inc., have firmed at eighteen. I would not readily credit you people with being able to add and subtract, but even here in Washington the answer spells *mother*. I'm broke. I haven't got any money. I was able to cover less than 100,000 shares before you people lowered the boom on me.'

'What would you have in net assets—Government bonds and cash?'

'In Mastodon? A hundred million, more or less. I haven't counted lately.' Craig grinned. 'I haven't been well.'

'In your insurance company—in Formidable?'

'The market's been off, about ten points off. It still spells *mother*. I'm ten points overdrawn in Formidable. I owned fifteen million net. As you very damned well know, I am in a ten per cent capital equity in Mastodon. We will be meeting the run. My insurance company, which had fifteen million net capital and a hundred million in resources, is now ten million overdrawn. You might say, or let the watch-dogs tell you, that I am out of the insurance business. I believe that there may be some question of jail involved.'

'The mills?'

'The stockholders can tell you better than me.'

'Your oil reserves?'

'Hocked,' Craig lit a cigarette.

'Airline?'

'Losing money.'

'Price Building?'

'Second mortgage on my piece of it. Nathan Mannheim holds my paper. I would have some equity, I suppose, if Mr. Mannheim's mortgage were satisfied by a sale. The first mortgage is mine and is solidly secured by long-term rentals.'

Mr. Smathers spread his hands.

'You understand that we can take no other position?'

'I understand.' Craig smiled. 'Don't take it so hard, Smathers. Think of the Match King. Life will go on for you. But I suppose that now the Government owns me, you will be suing each other? I mean, who gets first grab? The tax boys? The stockholders in Mastodon? Will you or I settle the insurance suit? Do you liquidate up or liquidate down? Who gets custody of the child? Will John marry Mary?'

'I do not think that this is a time for flippancy, Mr. Price. Hundreds of millions of dollars and the lives of millions of people are involved.'

'You make me feel like a major war,' Craig said. 'Same sort of guilt thing. Millions of dollars and millions of people, and it's all my fault. Mercy me.'

'I hate to see a thing like this happen to a man like you, Mr. Price. A man of vision, a man of . . .'

Craig got up.

'Me too,' he said, amiably. 'I guess I overbid it a touch. It's happened before. Well, you and the lawyers carve me up at your leisure. I suppose I *can* go to jail?'

'You can go to jail, Mr. Price. I would think it very likely. Something like about four and a half years, maybe a little longer. We have several clients who are currently residing in Brazil and other interesting places until such time as extradition papers might be arranged. Not,' Mr. Smathers said, 'that it's very likely.'

'Not for me,' Craig said cheerfully. 'I can't speak Portuguese.' He paused in the doorway.

'Mr. Smathers?'

'Yes, Mr. Price?'

'I was rather wondering if you could let me have a dime for a cup of coffee?'

Craig walked out of the door. Mr. Smathers had actually, instinctively reached for his trouser pocket.

Well, that's leverage for you, Craig thought, as he boarded the plane for New York. You lever up, you lever down. Bad pun. I feel like one of the Lever Brothers. Awful pun. Sorry. But I will never really be able to forget what Maybelle said. 'You screwed yourself into a mill, and you'll screw yourself out.' Man, that poor kid was never righter. What do we do now, Price? he asked himself. Find a new pigeon? Difficult. By the time all these hearings and law-suits and the other charming aspects of this mess are wiped off the deck, I'll probably be too old to care. Funny I *don't* seem to care much. It was only money. Like betting with track money. You never had a chance to spend it, to buy anything with it. Symbols. The clashing of symbols. Boy, am I lousy with the poor puns tonight. I think I will go and get myself very plastered and remember to say, thank God, that there are such things as numbered accounts in Switzerland which are *not*, repeat *not*, open to Government audit.

The days ran on, days of injunctions, days of process service, days of liens, days of lawyers, days of conferences, days of headlines, days of televised Congressional hearings . . .

'Mr. Price, is it true that you deliberately shoddied your materials?'

'Not to my knowledge. You understand that the details were left to . . .'

'Mr. Price, is it true that you entertained lavishly in Las Vegas and Miami certain gentlemen—er-hum—gentlemen of this Congress—let me see, Mr. Rowden and Mr. Snowsby—in an effort to influence them to intercede for you on the charges that you...'

'I have always entertained my friends.'

'But Mr. Price, what would you care to say to the charge that you presented a false audit statement when you floated a bond issue on Price Mills?'

'The audit statement was not false. We had shown unduly healthy profits that year due to a cutback in advertising.'

'Might one assume that you reduced your advertising budget in order to show a . . . a hum-hah . . . false healthiness in the earnings of your company?'

'I had decided that the time had come for a reduction in general promotion of my products. I felt we had reached a saturation point in promotion.'

'Mr. Price, Mr. Price Mr. Price Mr. Price Mr. Price...'

'Categorically deny. Refuse to answer on the grounds that . . . Don't remember. Activities so widespread I . . . Fifth Amendment sixty-five times.'

Whew. Washington can get hotter than any other town in the world. For a short period of time.

Covering Craig Price became almost a full time job. The story had long since left the financial pages, and had usurped space formerly devoted to cats-up-trees, the Gabor sisterhood, and the latest playboy to enter the procurement business. But the coverage was almost tender, unlike the bitter reportage on Serge Rubinstein.

'He sold us a bill,' one press gentleman said to another press gentleman over drinks at a prominent Third Avenue bar-and-grill devoted to journalistic analysis. 'He dropped us a pretty. But somehow I can't hate him. He kind of represents American enterprise—maybe a little crooked, but is he any crookeder than the other big boys? The other big respectable ones that everybody's forgot what they did when they were on the muscle?'

'He served twelve-year-old Chivas Regal,' the other press gentleman said. 'And he poured with a free hand. You think those Government guys ain't on the take, too? They ought to put them all in jail, the whole damn' bunch. They're all a bunch of thieves, on both sides of the fence.'

'Who you knockin'?' the bartender asked.

'We aren't knocking. We were talking about Price.'

'Don't talk to me Price. I win a couple hundred on a horse once, horse named Priceless, and I put the money in Price common stock on a hunch. Don't talk to me Price. A crook.'

'You see?' The newspaper gentleman hunched his shoulders,

spread his hands. 'Poor old Craig is taking the bread out of the mouths of not only widows and orphans, but horseplayers as well. Gimme another bomb, James.'

29

CAROL PRICE woke late in the afternoon and looked blurrily around the room. She wondered briefly where she was. London? No. Rome? No, not Rome. Where was the bathroom? Always tell where you are by location of bathroom. The room was rocking. Possibly a boat? No, room still again, so couldn't be boat. Water outside window though. Got it. South of France. St. Raphaël.

What the hell am I doing in St. Raphaël? she thought. Last night I was in Monte Carlo. Or was it night before last? Or last week?

She looked desperately around the room, and saw a figure asleep on his face in a rumpled twin bed. She closed her eyes and shook her head.

Now who the hell would that be? she thought. She walked into the bathroom, stuck out her furred tongue, and grimaced as she brushed her teeth. She was just twenty-one, and she looked a dissipated thirty-five. Her eyes were puffed from alcoholic sleep and one side of her face was herring-boned with the red welting that comes from too-deep slumber in the same position. Her hair stood away from her head in ragged tufts. She blinked her eyes repeatedly and reached for an eyewash lotion to clear the burning. Her nose ran, and she sniffled as she turned on the tub taps. She went back into the bedroom, and ignoring the lightly snoring figure on the other bed, poured herself a stiff shot of scotch, downed it, shuddered, and then poured another. This she consumed in two gulps, and shuddered a trifle less. Then she went into the bathroom again and stepped uncertainly into the tub. Her knees felt very weak; her feet were strangers.

She soaped herself and thought: *My God, Carol, not again. I thought it was all under control in London, but here we go on a new one. I wonder where I collected that gentleman on the other bed, and what happened? We don't want any babies out of this one, if anything did happen.* She dried herself, ran a comb through her hair, slipped into a terry-cloth robe, and walked over to the bed which contained the sleeping figure. She shook him by the shoulder until he came blearily awake.

'Who are you?' she asked. 'What are you doing in my room?'

'Why, Carol,' the young man said, in only faintly accented English. 'I'm Angelino. *Angelino*. Lino. We met at Monte last

700

night and you wanted to go for a drive in the moonlight, and we got here and began to drink and sing with the fishermen and then . . .'

'All right, all *right*. I get the picture. Okay. Get dressed and get out of my room.'

'In point of fact,' the young man said, with considerable dignity, it's *not* your room. It's *my* room.'

Oh, God, Carol thought. *I've used somebody else's toothbrush.* Then she began to laugh hysterically. She laughed until she wept. She threw back her head and screamed with unhappy laughter. The young man looked startled at first, then annoyed, and finally frightened.

He seized her by both shoulders and shook her until the hysteria subsided. His accent by now was not so faint.

'I don't like thees,' he said. 'Why you laugh?'

'I think it's so funny, so very funny,' Carol panted, her chest heaving. 'You'll never know how funny. You do everything there is to do with a stranger and then you get in a turmoil because you used his toothbrush.' She started to laugh again, and the young man slapped her. She stopped laughing.

'I want my clothes,' she said. 'I want to get out of here.'

'But we were going to have lunch,' he said. 'We were going to send for your things tomorrow and spend the week-end. You said . . .'

'Never mind what I said. I want to go back to Monte Carlo. I want to go now.'

'All right,' the young man said. 'It's your motor-car. But you owe a certain amount of money . . .'

'I'll pay you,' Carol snapped. 'Exactly what you're worth. Now get dressed and take me back to Monte. I don't like the smell of this place.'

The young man shrugged. Crazy Americans. One night one thing, next day another. All crazy. But rich.

That afternoon Carol Price cabled James Wilbur in New York. The cable said: 'CAN YOU MEET ME LONDON EARLIEST POSSIBLE PLANE STOP LEAVING MONTE CARLO TODAY AND STAYING SAVOY STOP NEED YOU BADLY STOP LOVE CAROL.'

Then she asked the concierge about the earliest plane from Nice for London and went upstairs to have the maid pack her bags. She drove suicidally over the twisting Corniche towards the airport at Nice, as if pursued by her thoughts, and desperately hoping to leave them far behind.

Carol was pale but icily, shakingly sober when Jimmy Wilbur knocked at the door of her suite. He kissed her lightly on both checks.

'Hi, kid,' he said. 'I see you've registered me just down the hall. Thanks. You're looking a little under the weather. Why don't you get me a drink before we dive into what's eating you? Or I'll get it. Where is it?'

'There isn't any,' Carol said. 'You'll have to ring.'

Wilbur's eyebrows shot up in surprise. He punched the floor-waiter button and refrained from saying anything until the waiter arrived. He turned to Carol.

'What are you drinking these days?' He noticed the shaking hands, twisting, clenching and unclenching as they ripped a handkerchief to shreds.

'Coke. A million of them.'

'You can overdo anything. Waiter, a bottle of gin, a bottle of whisky, some ice and tonic and soda. And something to chew on. It was a lousy flight, and I'm both hungry and thirsty. But I'm thirsty first. Bring the drinks and then worry about the *hors d'oeuvres*.'

They made banal small talk until the waiter returned with the drink tray.

'How's that fancy red Lancia of yours?'

'I don't know. I left it at the airport in Nice and told somebody to put it into a garage. I don't care if they did or they didn't.'

'Shame to treat a beautiful machine so casually. How are things on the lovely Riviera, with all the beautiful bums? What's new in the boudoir set?'

'Lousy. As usual. Same people. And the bums bummier.' Carol tried to pluck a cigarette from a package, but her hands shook so that the packet flew out of her fingers. Jimmy picked it up off the floor. 'Here, let me.' He flipped out a cigarette, lit it and handed it to her as the waiter came with bottles. 'Open the whisky and the gin,' Jimmy said.

Then, as the waiter left: 'What'll you have that's not Coca-Cola?'

'A little gin-and-tonic maybe?' Carol smiled weakly, as a child asking for another tiny piece of cake.

'No. You need a solid slug of scotch to put a net on those butterflies. There's no point in overdoing nobility with a hang like yours, girl. Here. Throw it down and then I'll do you a scotch and soda, gentle-like, and then we can tend to what's biting you. Me, I'm going to have about six gins before I even start to be landborne again. My God, it was rough over that water.'

He sipped his drink for a moment without talking. Carol, holding her mixed drink in both hands, thought suddenly: *How young he looks, with the clear eyes and the red hair not very grey at all except over the ears. Somehow I never thought of him as anything but Uncle Jimmy, part of the household furnishings, who spoiled me rotten, who walloped me when I was naughty, and who has been Dutch-uncling me ever since.*

She's a wreck, Jimmy Wilbur thought, and lit two cigarettes, one of which he handed her. *She looks as bad or worse than she did in Tangier. She must have tied on a real one. But something special must have happened to inspire this hurry-call, unless she was just drunk and lonely. Wonder what? Wonder how come the wagon business, when she looked like a gal needed a drink worse than any gal ever needed a drink?*

'Better?'

Carol smiled unsteadily at him over the rim of her glass. She nodded.

'Mmmm. Much. Thank you. Yes. Much better. Maybe another little one?'

'Not just now. Suppose you start telling your Uncle Jimmy what's on your mind. Must be something tremendous.'

Suddenly Carol heaved herself out of the chair, went on her knees beside him, buried her face in his crossed knees, put her arms around his waist, and burst into a freshet of tears. Her shoulders shook as she sobbed. Jimmy set his drink carefully down, stroked her head, and let her bawl. Presently she sobbed, in hiccoughs, like a child, and then sniffed. He raised her head, put his handkerchief to her nose and said: 'Blow.' She blew. 'Now go wash your face.'

He handed her another drink as she came out of the bathroom, her eyes swollen with the weeping, her nose red. He handed her the drink without a word.

'I must look like a mess,' she said. 'And I am a mess. A real mess. I guess you know better than anybody what a mess I am.'

'You're not such a dreadful mess. I've seen worse,' Jimmy said. 'But it's nice you're beginning to think about it. What do you want from me, that had you hurry-cabling?'

'Oh, God, Jimmy, I don't know, I don't *know*. I suddenly got so very *tired*. I suddenly got so *frightened*. All at once I knew why my mother killed herself, and I was afraid that if I went on any longer this way, I'd be reaching for the pills myself. I woke up and saw a man sleeping in my room but it wasn't my room it was his room and I didn't know where I was and I used his toothbrush and then I had a fit of hysterics because it was so silly to think about it being his toothbrush when I didn't even know if I . . . if we . . . I think it must have been the toothbrush that did it. I don't want to be like my mother. I don't want to be a tramp any longer. I don't want to be a drunk any longer. But . . .' She sighed quiveringly.

'But I don't know how *not* to be. Everything's all been so mixed up and awful. Even when I thought I was having fun it was mixed up and awful. Then the fun starts going faster and faster and faster and wilder and wilder and dizzier and dizzier

703

and, and . . .' She stopped, gulped, and groped blindly for a cigarette. Jimmy lit one and handed it to her. He patted her knee.

'Easy, easy, baby. Slow down. Everybody races his motor a little too fast these days. You ought to see New York. Everybody's crazy there, too. Everybody's a little nuts everywhere. It's a symptom of the times. Get me. An ex-tramp-athlete talking about symptoms of the times. My, my. How things have changed since I just said "Ugh" and wound the eight-day clock for my bed and board. All right.' His voice stiffened, and his eyes narrowed. 'What?'

Carol spoke wildly.

'Is Daddy really going to jail? Is it all true that his last wife—Susan—is it true that she's really given him away? Is it true that you . . .' her voice shrank to a small whisper.

Jimmy Wilbur said tersely:

'Yes.'

'But why, why, why? How could you do it to him? How could this . . . this Susan . . . leave him when he was down? How could I . . . why was I . . . I'm sorrier for him than I was for my mother when she killed herself.'

'I'm glad you didn't say passed away. So many people do. Like so many people say your father was unlucky when as a matter of fact he was a crook. And knew he was a crook. Like I know about you. I love you but I know about you. You've been a tramp and a drunk and a lousy broad, so long as we're talking straight. Here. Your drink needs fixing.'

'Oh, my God, Jimmy, what is it all about? I'm sorrier about Daddy than I am about me, and right now I'm awful sorry about me. I wish I'd been nicer to him, because he tried, he honestly tried. I was a bitch in Capri when he came to actually try. I was a worse bitch when the newspapermen came to ask me questions.'

Jimmy's voice did not soften.

'You were a bitch. When he came to Capri. When he tried.'

Carol took a sip of her drink, and this time when she fished for a cigarette her fingers did not tremble.

'But you,' she said. '*You. You* turned loose the wolves on him. You. The only friend he ever had, maybe, except that poor little coloured boy . . .'

Jimmy Wilbur's eyes were deeply sad.

'I turned the wolves loose on him, for goddam sure,' he said. 'I smacked you in Tangier and blackmailed you out of town for the same reason. For Christ's sake, Carol, can't you see that I've done nothing but ride herd on this crazy family since your father spent his first night with a maniac when he was fifteen years old? You had to leave Tangier; Craig had to quit being a crook. There are degrees of crookedness but Craig had hit the end of the road. So did Maybelle. So have you. And don't you think I'm just maybe a little tired of looking after all the Prices, you included? You think I got a life of my own? All I am is a vice-Price, faithful James, the handy man.'

'You poor guy,' Carol said. 'All of a sudden I'm sorrier for you than I am for the old man, than I am for me, than I was for Maybelle. You poor, poor guy. To have us all on your back. All of us, and all of us no bloody good.'

'Spare your tears,' Jimmy Wilbur said. 'Maybe I like it. Maybe I'm a glutton for punishment. Maybe I'd be lonesome without it. Maybe . . . I got a regret. I did not actually enjoy lowering the boom on Craig Price, crook. And I won't give you the business about widows and orphans. I'll just say that one time I tried to get the kid into a mildly crooked operation and he had sense enough to say no. This time *I* had sense enough to say no, because this was big, and that was little, and it could only have got worse. I don't suppose he ever told you about a girl named Julie. Not girl. Woman.

'She would have made a wonderful wife for Craig, and a wonderful mother for you. But there was a little too much difference of time, like London and New York, mixed up in it. Maybe some day I'll tell you. But right now, you still haven't answered my question. What was the hurry call mainly about? Three times, now, I've asked you. You keep ducking. What?'

Carol spoke very carefully.

'You know about me. All about me. Everything about me. Booze, pills, men, women, everything there is to know about me. I've been a rotten girl and a worse woman.'

Jimmy Wilbur shook his head impatiently.

'This gets nobody nowhere. Also it makes me nervous. Quit showing me a technicolour picture of your past and get to the point.'

'I don't think I'm really competent to look after me,' Carol said, and her voice now was firm. 'I need a keeper, or a nurse, or something. But I can't look after myself. Would you . . . please, Jimmy would . . . please would you . . .'

'Would I what?' Jimmy's voice was harsher. 'Would I what?'

Carol's voice came hesitantly, softly as a child's pleading.

'Would you stay with me and look after me? Would you take me back home again and not let the awful people that come in the night . . . Would you?' The voice broke.

'I'm not a babysitter any more,' Jimmy said. 'You've outgrown Uncle Jimmy.' He shook his head. 'No.'

'I know I've outgrown Uncle Jimmy. But I haven't outgrown Jimmy. Would you—if I promised to be a good girl—would you maybe marry me, Jimmy? After all you know about me? Would you, please, please marry me, Jimmy, so I won't have to say Uncle any more?'

705

Jimmy Wilbur got up, hunched his shoulders, and let his arms drop in a gesture of resignation. He paced three times past the artificial grate, and turned in sudden fury.

'Do you know what the hell you're saying? What you're saying to a man older than your father? What you're asking? That you're asking a man to marry his daughter, which is certainly what you've been? God Almighty, Carol . . .' He smacked his forehead with his left hand. His right hand was shaking.

'You're all I've got to love,' Carol said. 'You're all I've got. Period. All I've got. In a way I'm all you've got, too. There wouldn't have to be any . . . there wouldn't have to be . . . unless you wanted to, there wouldn't have to be any . . . any. But I'd be a good wife, I think, if I had you with me. I never had a father and I'll never have a husband, if you don't . . . unless . . . you . . . Please?'

Jimmy Wilbur walked over to the chair in which Carol was sitting. He took her by the elbows and pulled to her her feet, still holding her firmly by the elbows at arms' length. He looked at her a long time before he spoke.

'I doubt very much,' he said, 'if I can get your father's permission, but would you marry me, Miss Price?'

'Yes yes yes yes,' Carol cried, and flung herself on him. She buried her head on his shoulder and held him closely. 'Yes yes yes,' she said again. 'Thank God.'

Jimmy Wilbur turned and kissed the top of her head. He spoke almost to himself.

'There were so many dormitories in Chapel Hill,' he murmured, against her hair. 'So many dormitories. And I had to pick *that* one.'

30

IT had taken some five months for the castle to tumble. Mastodon was finally in receivership, with a conservator on hand to proceed with the orderly liquidation. Formidable was in receivership, with a conservator on hand to proceed with orderly liquidation. Price Mills was in receivership, with a conservator on hand to proceed with orderly liquidation. Liens on all of Price's property had been served. The Price Building was entailed, pending settlement of all suits, but this was of no importance, really, to Craig. His interest in his personal pyramid, as *Time* had called it, was mortgaged to Nate Mannheim. Craig Price was no longer permitted to deal in insurance, or to buy and sell shares or securities. Craig Price's pants had truly been chopped off at the knees. Seldom had so spectacular a crash occupied so much violent public attention.

Maybelle was dead. Carol, thank God, was taken care of. Jimmy Wilbur would look after Carol. Good old Jimmy, who lowered the boom. And he was right, too, Craig thought. He was dead right. Susan divorced me. And she was right, too, Craig thought. A crook is a crook, and who wants to live with a convict? The Government's right, too, the SEC and the Insurance Board and the Bureau of Internal Revenue and the banks and everybody else is right. Everybody's right but me. What was his name? Wrong-Way Corrigan. That's me, Fixed Price. But they could have left me something. When they slapped a plaster on the Price Building . . .

He stood outside, looking at the noble pile of stone which he had caused to be erected. He looked at its slabs of green marble, its arrogant skyward reach, its frontispiece of sparkling glass. 'Price Building' the awning said. He shook his head.

'They really didn't *have* to keep me from moving out my heads and tusks and books,' he said. 'I must go see Nate some day and beg another favour—when I've found another place to hang them. Price Building—Price's Folly.' Suddenly he was almost amused. Craig remembered a little town south of New Truro in which a man named Lockwood once lived, long before Craig was born. It was a tiny town, with a twisting leaf-dyed creek which meandered aimless miles down to the river. Lockwood was a countryman, and a frustrated seaman. In his spare time he built a boat. It took him his major years and all his savings and all his spare time to build this boat. When the last nail had been hammered home, the final brasswork screwed to the planking, the port and starboard running lights wired, the engine installed, Lockwood set out to launch his boat. But the creek was neither wide enough nor deep enough to accommodate the boat. The boat sat there through the years, and the town which grew around that boat was called 'Lockwood's Folly'.

'Me and Mr. Lockwood,' Craig said. 'When we go bust we go bust real good.'

He felt a curious numbness, a cold detachment, as if all the hurried events of the last months had happened to somebody else—not to Lonesome Craig Price, the Captain-Admiral of the Ocean Sea. He had read about himself in all the papers. He had signed the necessary papers for the divorce. He had flown immediately to Europe to handle the dreary sad details of Maybelle's suicide. All of it left him chill and oddly unaffected.

The nightmare of his financial collapse still found him strangely unbothered. He had submitted to the indignities heaped high by conservators and referees, government officials and bankers, Congressmen and process servers.

It had been almost like the old days as a youngster at sea, when he passed the dreary hours standing watch on the fo'c'sle head by remembering something else, something pleasant—a duck hunt, a good dinner, a camp meeting or a fishing trip.

Now it seemed that he had never threaded through the devious complexities of oil and textiles, banking and insurance, investment and borrowing, lying, cheating, conniving, with final disgrace, bankruptcy, possible prison, death, divorce and disaster, all the things behind him. Those things couldn't happen to Captain Blood or Tarzan of the Apes or Cortez or Huck Finn or Drake, standing off the Spanish Armada. Nor to Lonesome Craig Price, the man nobody knew.

He gave the Price Building a last brooding look and strolled slowly up Fifth Avenue. Where could he go, he of the many mansions? Not Villefranche. Not the apartment in the Price Building. Not the big house in Suffern. Not the hunting lodge in Carolina. He exhaled a sigh almost of relief.

'It's almost like being that busted kid in Savannah again,' he muttered as he walked. 'It's almost fun, a new adventure. An adventure starting at zero. Maybe I never had all those things at all. Maybe I'm just starting out to make a life—a life full of travel and daring and beautiful women and whisky and good food—that I don't even know about yet. Do you suppose that could be? Or wouldn't you say I was a little old for it?'

He walked, dumbly, blindly, mind perfectly blank again, for blocks, and when he looked around consciously, he saw, suddenly, that he was in Harlem. He breathed again the smell of frying fish, savoured all the fetid odours he had loved in Havana, in New Orleans, in Africa. He turned abruptly into a neon-lit bar-and-grill.

The bartender was a big man, very black, with a broken nose plastered to the left side of his face. He put his hands flat on the bar and leaned across it, his face very close to Craig's. His eyeballs were lightly yellow, bloodshot, and decidedly unfriendly. They roved up and down Craig's richly tailored body.

'What you want here, Mister?' he asked.

'I thought a drink,' Craig said.

'I'm sorry, Mister. This place strictly for the coloured folks. We kind of old-fashioned. We ain't integrated here. Maybe you better shove off, go back your part of town.' Every black face in the bar was turned, every ear cocked. There was no friendship in their faces. Craig assayed the cold hostility. He shrugged slightly.

'All right,' he said, and turned to go. 'I'm sorry. I didn't mean to intrude.'

The bartender said, as Craig was going out the door, '*Mister.*' Craig turned his head. 'Yes?'

'Stay off them side streets. I suggests you take a cab.'

'Where to?' the hacker asked. 'Mister, I don't like this part of town. I been stuck up three times here. Where to?'

Craig thought: *What a hell of a question. Where do we go now? A hotel? I haven't had to think about that one for a long time. The simplest question in the world and I really can't answer.*

'Drive slow for a moment,' he said. 'While I think.'

Idly, he drew his key-ring from his pocket. Story of my life, he thought. All this meat and no potatoes. All these keys and no door of my own. Maybe I could go sleep in a numbered account in Zurich? Too far. Maybe I could go sleep in a safety deposit box in Tangier? Too far. He flipped the keys idly. One. Office Price Building. Two. House in Suffern. They call it burglary if you don't own it. Three. House in Villefranche. Too far. Four. Hunting lodge. Never again. Five. Susan's house in Jersey. Sue wouldn't mind. If there are any lights on I'll just turn around and drive back.

'Driver. You want a long haul?'

The driver, who was described on his licence as one Emmanuel Cohen, turned.

'I hack for a living. Anything this side of San Francisco is my business tonight. But I would like to see a little money before we take off.'

'I want to go to a place called Long Valley, near Chester, in Jersey. Would fifty bucks please you, in advance?' Craig reached for his wallet.

'Mister, you speak my language. Leave us roll.'

'Roll. No conversation, please. I'm a sad bird and I want to think. Maybe we could stop on the way and pick up a jug of something. Whisky feels like it needs me tonight.'

'Dames?'

'Dames. And other things. There's a liquor store over there. Get me a bottle of Jack Daniel. This acts like a bourbon night to me.'

31

THERE it sat, the house, her house, the lovely house, the house overlooking the lake where the deer came daintily to drink, where the hungry bass made smacking, plashing sounds as they leaped when the evening hatch tempted them from their deep cool beds, the lake of the friendly wild ducks and the mournful loons. There it sat, a house given in love—Susan's house, all the houses of my houses, *but not my house*, Craig thought. I'm still an intruder, but in a way it's kind of my house, although I burnt it down after my own fashion. The other one was easier. It's easier with matches, much easier, than with words.

'There's a spare bedroom, Mac,' he said to the driver. 'You want to spend the night and drive me back in the morning? I'm not queer or anything like that, if that's what you're thinking.'

'Sure. Be a pleasure. You're Mr. Price, ain't you? I seen your picture lots of times. Seems like I remember you were on *Time's* cover or something like that. You been in the papers a lot lately. Sure. I'll be glad to stay and drive you back. This your house?'

'No. As a matter of fact it's not. But it belongs to a friend of mine. A very old friend. I have a key.'

The driver leered. He had the face for leering.

'A broad?'

'Yep. A broad. A very nice broad. Come on in. I'll buy you a drink and then you push off for bed. I got some serious solitary thinking to do.'

The house was lonely as only unlived-in houses can be lonely. The memory of footfalls, the memory of love and laughter, the memory of food and drink and bed and even quarrels was gone. Craig shivered as they entered, and switched on the lights.

'My God, Mr. Price,' Emmanuel Cohen said, 'this is really a hell of a house. This dame's got money, huh? To build a joint like this?'

'Sure. She's loaded. Look, Mac, let's you go to the storeroom and get some wood. A fire might brighten the place up a touch. It's just over there'—he pointed—'past the bar and through the kitchen. The light switch is on the left as you go in. I'll get some ice and some sandwich stuff out while you fetch the wood.'

'Okay, Mr. Price. I like a fire myself. The one thing I hate about that housing-development apartment me and the old lady got is it's got no fireplace.'

Emmanuel Cohen came back with his arms stacked high with wood.

'This is the little stuff. There's some birch logs back there. You want I should bring a couple of logs?'

'Do that little thing,' Craig said, and knelt to make his tiny pyramid of kindling in the way he had known since he was six.

The fire leaped jauntily into life. When the kindling took firm hold of the fire, Craig placed two of the silver paper-scaling birch logs Emmanuel Cohen had brought, head-to-head Indian fashion.

'Why do you do that?' the cab driver asked. 'I never saw that before.'

'Old hunting trick' Craig said, going over to the bar. 'They burn in the middle and all you have to do is give them a kick once in a while, and they burn towards each other until they're completely consumed. What do you want to drink?'

'If you got one, I'd like a beer. That hard stuff is murder to me.'

'I reckon we got a beer. Sure.' He looked into the bar ice-box. 'Loads of beer. You like Heineken's?'

'I can't afford it but I love it. Yes, sir. Thank you.'

Craig opened the bottle and poured the beer into a tilted mug. He poured himself a large three fingers of bourbon. 'Cheers, Mr. Cohen,' he said.

Cohen smacked his lips.

'I never drunk out of one of these before,' he said. It makes it taste better. What are these here mugs made out of, silver?'

'No. Pewter. Makes anything taste better. Have a seat.' The fire now had caught the birch logs, and was roaring, leaping up the flue. Suddenly the room had brightened.

'I feel better already,' Craig said. 'Come on, son, I'll show you to your room. I got some private fire-watching to do. Let me get you another beer to take with you.'

While Craig was pouring the beer, the cab driver asked,

'If you don't mind me asking, Mr. Price, what's it like to be a man like you, have everything you want, go any place you want to go, do all the things you want to do? I mean me, I push a hack . . .'

'What's it like to be man like me, have everything I want, go any place I want to go, do anything I want to do?' Craig chuckled softly. 'Lonesome, son, lonesome. Come on, your room's up this way.'

Craig searched his record file. He wanted a lot of Sinatra. He wanted a lot of Ella. He wanted some very slow Bushkin. He wanted some sad Lee Wiley with Bushkin. He wanted some old Glen Grays and some Ray Noble. ('Thank God I had the old 78's taped,' he muttered.) 'Oh, Look at Me Now,' will do for a start he thought, the old Bushkin when he was playing for Dorsey when he was a kid, and Sinatra was still a bandstand singer. Bushkin's right hand rippled delicately and the old, young, fresh Sinatra voiced warmed the room. Craig kicked the logs into a sputter of sparks, turned off the lights, put his feet up on a hassock and sagged into a soft woolly contour chair.

He was playing the tape, and was unprepared for the old Hal Kemp 'Heart of Stone'. Nobody but Kemp ever played it, he thought, and Oh God, Mary Frances. Spring frolics and the Arboretum wantonly scattering its scents all over Chapel Hill, the air heavily drunk with jasmine and tuberose and blossoming peach and dewy grass. What would she look like now, he asked himself. Fat and grey and old enough to be a grandma? Two Cadillacs and a golf club membership, or a drab slattern of a housewife with a useless husband and too many kids who broke her body before she ever tasted any adult fun? My God, Mary Frances. All the sweet, the fresh, the young . . . Now why would I think of Mary Frances when I should be thinking of the great big mess I've made of everything? When I should be thinking of Maybelle and Jazzbo and Carol and Sue? I guess because Mary

Frances was the first big mess I ever made of anything. God damn my mother. I was twenty-five before I quit having the psychosomatic clap every time I went to bed with somebody. God bless Mary Frances, wherever she be. And I don't want to think of Libby Forney right now.

There were so many of them later, Craig thought. Most of their faces are blurred. Most of their names unremembered. A peggy a sheila a jane a nancy a helen a mercedes a francoise a gretchen a bianca a sonja a patricia a carmen a dorothy a rose a pearl a pamela an eskimo a zulu a masai a wop swede dutch russian irish english north south spick cuban australian new zealand frog south african new york boston san francisco new orleans sydney nairobi southport newport westport eastport port all . . . And I remember Mary Frances. And I remember Libby.

I remember a Susan, too, he thought. I remember a Susan very very well.

Funny she'd divorce me. Not really strange, come to think of it. She was that kind. She wouldn't have divorced me over another woman. She divorced me on high principle, like Jimmy quit me on hard principle. People with principles don't like, evidently, people without principles. I had a principle once. A pretty little principle. But like Jimmy says, that was a long, long time ago. What a sad bastard I am. What was it Philip Wiley called doctors? Oh yes. Sad bastards with big hands. That was in *Finnley Wren*. Kiss me pretty protoplasm. Really, Craig Price. The things you do recall. You and the well-known drowning man with all his life flashing before him. Only I can't seem to remember very much of importance except how the elephant looked busting out of the bush that day and that Christmas night in Washington and little things like the fire in New Orleans and how a horn can sound in the distance or dew-wet curls on the back of a neck or the sweet-scented hollow of a shoulder or the roar of quail underfoot or the sound and smell of a summer evening in a black-watered swamp with the bass just beginning to rise and the doves mourning. Or the lights of Liverpool, seen the first time through a boy's eyes, with all the promise of what turned out to be nothing. Nothing. That is what I got a lot of. Nothing. The Captain-Admiral of the Ocean Sea hit a reef. Brother, but what a reef.

Now it was 'Body and Soul'.

'Her name was Jane and she was just back from learning to play the fiddle in Paris or somewhere and I was fishing with the old gent that fall.' Craig spoke aloud, and thought: *Well at least I'm not nuts. I've got some sort of precise recall. 'Body and Soul'. That is what I would call a piece. It covers everything.* A cigarette fell from his fingers, and he picked it off the flags and threw it into the fireplace before he fell deeply asleep.

32

THE crunch of tyres on gravel woke him. The music was still going, and now it was 'Autumn in New York'. He shook his head, smacked himself sharply on both temples, and fully awake, went to the door just as a key was being inserted.

He stood limned, a dark figure silhouetted by the fire, in the doorway.

'Hi,' he said. 'You can call the cops, if you want. I suppose technically I'm a burglar.'

'Oh, Craig. Craig. I was in Mexico and didn't know about most of the awful everything until most of it was over. I didn't really know until my lawyers finally found me about . . . about Maybelle's will. Can I come in?'

She looked lovelier, even in the shadows, than he had remembered.

'*Mi casa es tu casa*,' he said, 'or for the moment, the other way around. I seem to have pre-empted your domicile. Come in and I'll fix us a drink. Of your whisky.' He snapped on a light.

'You look wonderful, with the tan,' he said, as he handed her a drink. 'Let's sit by the fire and knit, or something. Where were you?'

'Yucatan. Looking at ruins. It seemed a cheerful thing to do and at least there weren't any phones or newspapers. You remember what you said once about licking your wounds? I had wounds I wanted to lick. I needed a hole to crawl into. I got tired of Mexico City and Cuernavaca and Acapulco and went off jungling. The full impact of all your troubles didn't really hit me until the other day. I guess I had a closed head after the . . . the divorce.' She raised her head. She looked at him steadily.

'I was wrong. Dead wrong. It took me six months to realize it. And I'm sad about it. I tried to find you today in New York to tell you so. I couldn't find you. And then I had a sudden hunch I'd find you here. I would have called, but I stopped the phones, and . . .' her voice dwindled. 'I'll leave now if you want me to.'

'*I'll* leave now if *you* want me to,' Craig said. 'I got a cab driver staked out in the spare room. It *is* your house, you know.'

'It is *not* my house. It never was my house. It never was your house, either. It belonged to a small small boy that I loved.' Her voice, tender, harshened. 'Craig, I want to come to a point. I owe you some money. We might as well clear that one up now. It was a ridiculous thing, Maybelle, poor sad Maybelle, leaving me all that money. Ridiculous and wrong and a little vicious.'

'I don't know if it was *so* ridiculous or wrong and probably not vicious. She probably thought you'd earned it, living with me.'

Craig's voice was bitter now. 'Cheap at Half the Price,' he mimicked a television commercial. 'Half a Price is better than no Price at all.'

'*Stop* it. Her money's still in a Swiss bank. It's in my name. I didn't . . . I didn't want all these people to take that away from you, too. First, I tried to give it to Carol. She and Jimmy flatly refused. Said it wasn't theirs, any more than it was mine. Said it was yours, earned in sweat and tears. I gathered that Carol has mellowed a little. This was all correspondence, of course.'

'Keep the bloody money,' Craig said. 'You said once that you were sick of the sound of the word. So am I. Give it to the D.A.R. Give it to the W.C.T.U. If they put me in jail, I intend to learn a worthy trade and then go to work for Albert Schweitzer or somebody for ten dollars a month.' His voice had turned sardonic now. 'Everybody's going to work for Albert Schweitzer at ten dollars a month. It's the chic thing to do.'

'Will you stop it! Will you for God's sake stop playing man against the earth and listen to me? Mix me another drink.'

'You'll probably beat me if I don't,' Craig managed a grin, a very feeble grin. He poured a drink and came back, and stirred the fire with his toe. 'Yes, teacher?'

'God pity us both, I love you. I was wrong to leave you. I want to keep on loving you. I am proposing marriage, Mr. Price, this time with a few less complications.'

'That's if you don't consider a possible stretch in Lewisburg a complication,' Craig drawled. 'And I don't particularly fancy the idea of you coming down with a sudden attack of pity, or my being responsible for bringing out the mother in you. I *had* a mother once, and didn't like it.'

'Damn you damn you damn you!' Susan cried. 'I'm not coming back because your little sand castle fell down and I'm sorry for you! I'm not coming back because Maybelle killed herself and left me a lot of money that didn't belong to me! I'm not coming back out of nobility or motherhood or pity or any other such goddamned thing! I'm coming back because I love you because I can't help it, and I want to love you all my life, you miserable, stupid, arrogant, prideful, dishonest son-of-a-bitch!'

She got up in a rage and picked up the bent poker.

'I'd like to wrap this around your stupid neck!'

'Here, here, that's my material,' Craig said. 'This is the most untender proposal I ever received. I shall have to consider it, as long as I am marrying you for your money.'

'You're serious about prison? Really serious about going to Lewisburg?'

'Highly serious. There's a Contempt of Congress thing, which could draw me a year. But that'll take time—a couple of years or so before the laywers and accountants finish picking my bones. There's maybe a tax thing, but I think I can beat that. There's a stock-fraud action which could put me away for a spell, according to what they can actually prove. That'll take time, too. And I can't do any business with the stock market any more. The little men at the SEC have got me permanently enjoined from trading. All together I'm not a very pretty fellow.'

He grimaced. He lit two cigarettes absently and handed her one.

'And I don't seem to care, and that bothers me. I seem to have lost what I never really had anyhow and I wish it bothered me more. I was thinking that I would just kind of take off permanently, and go fishing or something until drink and a bad conscience done me in.' He smiled. 'Speaking of drink, I find it helps a bad conscience any amount. No matter |what the doctor says. Will you pour, or will I?'

Sue got up and took the glasses to the bar. She mixed the drinks and came back.

'Have you got any money left out of the wreck?' she asked.

'Some. A few bucks squirrelled away here and there—Tangier, Switzerland, London—enough to keep me from starving. There's always the export-import business, and opium-eating in Hong Kong. Or the French Foreign Legion. Or I could always go back to sea...'

The old joke wrenched a quick tear from Susan.

'Please. Listen to me. You said once when we were fighting that when I bought you, I bought the whole man, faults and all. I knew what I was doing, I thought. We started it wrong and it ended wrong. We're not either one of us very nice people. All right. I admit it. But as a woman in love I'm too weak to fight it.

'I want you back—and I want you back as you are, not as you might have been. We'll have plenty of money. There's a million left. Let's run away, Craig. I don't want you in jail and I don't want to see you as an object of scorn or pity. Let's go to South America, Mexico, China, Africa—let's go anywhere, and see if we can't start this all over again.'

'You hate yourself for this, don't you?' Craig's voice was very soft. 'So now I've come the full cycle. I've spoiled nearly everything I ever touched, and now I've even managed to ruin you.' He shook his head slowly, sadly.

'I think I'd better go now,' he said. 'I wouldn't want you on my conscience along with everything else. I wouldn't want to have you with me on the lam. If you don't actually want Maybelle's money, sure, I'll take it. Like you say, it was mine in the first place, and with it I can start something in some country where the Federal gentlemen won't be able to get at me. Mexico, I should imagine. I won't be the first man to build a hotel in Mexico to beat a rap. And the fishing's fine.' His eyelids drooped under the raised brow.

Susan's voice angered again.

'Do I really *have* to hit you with this poker to get anything through your thick skull? Maybe I don't *want* to love you but I *do*, and you're no good to me in jail. I want to be where you are, I want to be with you, and if I ever had a principle or a conscience it's not as big as my love for you. If you're on the lam, as you call it, I want to be on the lam with you. If you're bound and determined to go to jail, I'll wait, but I think it's stupid when you don't have to. I don't want to waste any more time. I want *you*, good, bad, honest or crooked.'

She paused for a breath. Her voice crumbled, pleading.

'I want *you*. All of you.'

Craig shook his head.

'No,' he said.

'*No*. You don't want me. And you sure don't need me. And more's the terrible pity, I don't want you or need you. I'm a well-poisoner, and you're too nice a well for me to poison any more. And I wouldn't want you with me on the lam. It's tough enough when you're by yourself. I'm going to be a real classy beach-comber, and I want to do it single-o. No. You don't want me. I ain't really worth the effort.'

'You *are* worth the effort! For Christ's sake, that's what I'm trying to say!'

Craig waved a weary hand.

'Skip it. *No vale la pena.* I'll go wake up the cab driver. I'm leaving now.'

'Of all the things they might have said about Craig Price, I never thought it would be lack of guts. That's what you're showing me now—no guts.'

'That's right,' Craig said. 'Why don't we leave it that way? Craig Price, the Gutless Wonder. I'm tired, sweetie. Very tired indeed. Enough accumulated mistakes make you tired. And I was wrong about loving you. What I thought I loved about you was an idea—a little boy's idea—I thought perhaps a reflection of all the people I should have loved, might have loved, and didn't. One time I said poor Jazzbo was my conscience. Well, so are you too my conscience. Retroactive. And I can't live with my conscience. It's as simple as that. I don't want to hit myself over the head every day with all my past mistakes. And you, my dear, are the lovely crystallization of all my mistakes. No. No more. I'm calling the cab driver now. Be brave, be happy, be full of cheer, and accept my apologies for mucking up your life. *Adiós.* What bank in Zurich did you say that money's in?'

She looked at him without tears.

'Union Bank. And you're right. You don't want me, and I don't want you. I'll write a letter transferring the money in your name. Good luck, Craig. You poor . . .' suddenly she fled, weeping.

'That was a good-looking dame passed me in the hall,' Emmanuel Cohen said. 'She the one that owns the house? She was crying like somebody stole all her money and bust her heart to boot.'

'Somebody did,' Craig said. 'Drive and don't talk. Take me to the Ritz Carlton.'

'But Mr. Price, there ain't any Ritz Carlton any more. They tore it down,' the driver said.

'That's right, so they did. They tear everything down. Take me to the New Yorker, then, if that's still there.'

'That's still there,' the driver said.

Let me see, Craig thought. We better make an audit. Let us inspect our position. Let us see where we stand as we speed through the night to the New Yorker Hotel. What has our young man accomplished in his time? He who loved houses owns no houses. His family is dead. His first wife killed herself. His daughter hates his guts. His best friend threw him over the side. Gave him the deep six. His business is wrecked, his credit gone, his reputation finished. His monument to himself, *Time* called it, is now another man's monument. A twelve per cent monument.

He took a long pull out of the bourbon bottle. He spoke to the cab driver.

'I am not supposed to drink,' he said. 'The doctor said not to drink or this advancing cirrhosis would kill me. I don't seem to be able to lay a dame any more. Even a whore wrote me a note about baby-sitting and refused to take my money. The graveyard of my life seems to be strewn with handsome stones—Mary Frances first, Maybelle, Libby, Red, Jimmy, Carol, Maybelle's mother, Maybelle's father, and finally Susan Strong.

'I suppose I loved her,' he said. 'But I don't know anything any more, and I don't know if I ever really had the capacity to love anybody. Certainly not me. Tonight, or this early morning, certainly not me.'

'You all right, Mr. Price?' the driver asked anxiously.

'I'm all right. Don't interrupt. Maybe I loved Jazzbo, but even he was a kind of toy, like a puppy. Maybe they left something out when they made me . . . a kind of capacity for caring. Well, I can't drink, I don't screw very well, and I haven't got any wives, children, friends or business. All I got is a million dollars, more or less, which comes from an ex-wife's charity over the dead body of another wife. You couldn't say a man with a million dollars was poor, and him not even forty-five years old, yet. A million dollars is a lot of money.'

'Mr. Price,' Emmanuel Cohen said. 'What you need is some sleep.'

717

'The hell with sleep,' Craig said. 'Take me to La Guardia Airport. I want to charter a plane.'

'You sure you're all right, Mr. Price?'

'I'm all right. Don't mind me. Just drive to the airport.'

Kensington looked much the same. Craig flashed his credit card and was able to acquire a white-and-blue Chevrolet from the hire-car people at the airport. It was just before noon when he arrived. Coming into town from the airport, it was necessary to pass Price Mills, Inc. They looked like damned prosperous mills, Craig thought, smoke rolling out of the chimneys, the grounds well kept, the paint fresh. He remembered a just-at-dawn morning when he had walked past the mill, hearing the soft whisper of the pines in the rosy light, as he came straight from Maybelle's bed. He'd been right, of course. He'd have that mill, and more mills, one day. And he'd had them, all right, that he had. You couldn't take them away. Maybe they weren't his any more but he'd had them. And they were damned good mills. Made good products.

He knew he was being silly, chartering a plane to fly to Kensington, on the off chance that there would be somebody living in the little white house which once had suffered the indignity of *Company Pimp—Company Whore*, written across its clean young face. He drove past, and sure enough, there was a woman in the yard, with two children and a dog. On impulse he drew the car to the curb and killed the motor. He got out, and dipped his head courteously to the woman, a blowsy blonde in too-tight denim slacks.

'Excuse me,' he said. 'I used to know some people who lived here. A family named Forney. They called the brother Red, and his sister's name was Elizabeth. I thought maybe you might know where . . .'

'Never heard of them,' the woman said, brushing the children behind her. 'Just moved here last year. And if you're selling something . . .' She glared.

Craig smiled.

'No. I'm not selling anything. I'm sorry I bothered you.'

'That's all right,' the woman said. 'You never know these days.' She released the children from the protective custody of her denimed behind. 'We just come down here from Shelby. My husband, he's one of the foremen in one of the big mills. Price Mills,' she said, with pride. 'I expect if you're a stranger you wouldn't know about Price Mills.'

Craig smiled again.

'I think I heard about them somewhere or other,' he said, and got back into the car. 'Thank you, and good-bye.'

He drove off, and the woman said to her young son and daughter: